THE IMMORTAL KNIGHT CHRONICLES

Vampire Crusader
Vampire Outlaw
Vampire Khan

Plus the Short Story:
Vampire Templar

DAN DAVIS

The Immortal Knight Chronicles Books 1-3

This book is a work of fiction. Names, characters, businesses, organizations, places, events and incidents either are the product of the author's imagination or are used fictitiously. Any resemblance to actual persons, living or dead, events, or locales is entirely coincidental.

For information contact:

dandaviswrites@outlook.com

ISBN: 9781703964073

First Edition: Dec 2019

VAMPIRE CRUSADER

The Immortal Knight Chronicles
Book 1

Richard of Ashbury
and the Third Crusade
June 1190 to November 1192

DAN DAVIS

1

The Oath

RIDERS GALLOPED AWAY from Ashbury manor house at dawn. I had slept in the wood again. The shadows were long but the first rays of the morning sun warmed my face as I walked to the house.

Though I was tired, I hurried. My brother's crossbow had to be returned before he woke, as I had promised never to touch it again.

It is impossible to sleep late when you sleep outside. You wake to the din of birdsong and light. Yet waking early has its rewards. The thought of fresh bread, hot from the ovens, made my mouth water.

But then hooves drummed against the earth and men jeered from beyond the hedgerows. The clamour shattered the morning and startled a pair of crows into flight overhead, cawing in protest.

I knew the sound of men with their blood up when I heard it. I ran forward, crashing through the mature barley.

The manor house was not a popular place. Visitors were rare, especially since my brother had turned even more sullen than he used to be. He had a handful of friends but none of those dour knights and lords would holler and whoop in such a way. Not at sunrise. Not for any reason.

My sword and mail I had stashed in a chest back at my woodland camp. The crossbow in my hands was useless because Martha had lost the last of the bolts in the undergrowth.

I tossed it and ran on. The only weapon I had was my dagger.

From the noise of the hooves and whinnying and the cries of the men, I guessed there were five or ten of them galloping off. By the time I pushed through the hedge onto the road they were almost away.

The last rider glanced back as he disappeared beyond the hill on the wooded road to Lichfield. He was a knight dressed in mail with a shield slung across his back. His surcoat was red. I could make out no further detail and yet something about him was familiar.

But he was in shadow and then he was gone.

I ran to the boundary of the manor house and leapt the drystone wall and ditch.

My brother's horses whinnied from the stables on the other side of the house. None of the dogs barked.

The hall door was open. A splintered hole had been hacked through the centre. The doorway was a black void.

I threw myself into the great hall.

The stench of warm blood and torn bowels was overwhelming. I retched.

The mutilated bodies of the servants lay all over. The old, the young, the men and the women had all been dragged into the hall and slaughtered.

I knelt by a few, hoping that some would yet live. Most were still warm to the touch but their wounds were terrible. Throats gouged out. Bellies slit open. Daggers punched through the eyes. There were no survivors.

The fire was unlit and the windows shuttered so I could not see clearly but none of the dead appeared to be my brother, his wife or their children.

A noise. From the floor above. No more than a faint scraping upon the boards.

I gripped my dagger and ran through the great hall through to the rooms beyond, crying out for Henry and for Isabella.

There were more bodies lying in the passage to the pantry and buttery but I went the other way, into the parlour. Streaks of blood led through the door out to the stable and more stained the stairway up to the solar. I leapt up the stairs, ran through the solar and barged through the open door to their bedchamber.

I froze.

"Isabella," I cried.

She lay on her back by the bed in a pool of blood. It soaked her dress and her eyes had rolled up, the lids half closed. A jagged gash had ripped through one shoulder and half her neck was in tatters. The splintered edge of her collarbone jutted from the wet, sucking wound.

I knelt in her blood and lifted the back of her head with one hand. Only the fact that blood flowed and bubbled from the lacerations suggested she had not yet died. But there was no chance that she would live.

"Henry?" Isabella mumbled, her eyes flickering open.

"It is Richard." I clutched her hand in mine. Her skin as cold and white as marble.

"Richard." Her voice a whisper. Her eyes unfocused.

"What happened? Who were those men?"

Her eyes stared through me, unseeing. Or perhaps she saw Death.

Blood had been flung about the room; sprays of it reaching the painted ceiling above us. I could taste it in the air. Yet there was no other body.

"Where is Henry, my lady? Where is your husband?"

"Gone," she whispered. "Slain."

"The children?" I said, though I did not want to ask.

She squeezed her eyes shut. "He killed them." She sobbed and blood streamed from her mouth. "Oh God, he killed my babies."

I struggled for breath. "Who?"

"Satan himself." There was blood in her voice and she coughed, struggling for breath.

Perhaps I should have told her that she would soon see her sweet children in Heaven.

I could have told her that I loved her, that I would do anything for her. But in that moment the weeks and months of my romantic infatuation were insignificant. Absurd, even.

I should certainly have told her to lay still and held her as she drew her last breath.

Instead of compassion, I was full of outrage and wrath.

All I wanted was to destroy.

"Who do you name as Satan?" I demanded, lifting her head up further. "Isabella. Who were those men?"

Her head rolled back and I grasped it and held it up to mine.

My voice rose. "Isabella."

Her eyes flickered open and she breathed, shuddering then coughed a spray of blood.

"Richard?" Her voice was weak, confused. She had always been so slight, so delicate but she clung on to the last moments of her life.

"I am here." I squeezed her cold hand, blinking away tears.

"Richard." Her voice was so quiet I stilled my breath to hear it. "Richard, it was William." She coughed more blood, fighting for breath.

I struggled to understand. I had assumed that war had come to Derbyshire. That the Welsh had attacked across the border or the Scots had somehow raided this far south.

"William? Earl William de Ferrers did this?"

I should not have been quite so surprised.

"Richard," she said, grasping my arm with desperate strength. She opened her beautiful eyes wide to look deep into mine. "Richard, you must avenge your brother's death. Avenge the death of his children."

"I will, my lady."

"Swear it."

"I shall not rest, I shall not live, I shall not die until William lies dead by my sword. This I swear to you and to Almighty God with all my heart."

Her mouth twitched. "Amen."

She died. Her last breath a sigh that was stoppered with blood. I held her as she choked and drowned on what little blood remained in her body.

It was 1190. In the eight hundred years since that day, I have travelled the world in pursuit of my enemy, William de Ferrers. Many times, over many centuries and in many lands I fought him.

William left a trail of horror in his wake. I did my duty to avenge all those that he and his followers slaughtered. I spent centuries hunting and destroying the monsters that he made. Always he made more.

Wherever there was great death and evil in the world, William was never far. I fought him in the New World, the Far East and in Napoleon's Europe. I tracked him through the horrors of the Black Death and the overwhelming destruction on the Eastern Front.

He was crusader, outlaw, khan. He was a count, a cavalier and a cardinal.

William was a murderer, a devil.

A vampire.

* * *

My brother Henry lay eviscerated, beheaded and dismembered in the courtyard between house and stables. I gathered the pieces of his body together.

His strong face, in life so often twisted in anger, was now blank. One eyelid was open and full of blood. As though it was staring at me in silent accusation.

"I slept in the wood again, Henry," I told his head, holding it in my hands. "I only just missed them."

It was a scorching summer morning. Yellowhammers chirped and warbled in the trees above as I dug graves for my family. I lined them up next to the recent grave of our father and the much older grave of our mother.

The ground was baked hard but I was young and strong and hacked through into the softer soil beneath.

I laid Henry's limbs in the grave beside his torso. His guts I had pushed back in as much as I could. Luckily, I had not eaten for a day or so, otherwise I would certainly have vomited.

I stopped and eased off Henry's rings from his pale, stubby fingers. One was the signet ring that had belonged to our father. The ash tree emblem was worn almost flat. I ran my finger over it and I felt an echo of the anger that had flared up between my brother and me over that ring. I had argued that it should have been buried along with the old man. In truth, I had wanted it for myself. After all, Henry had inherited every other object, title and land. But Henry had flown into a blind rage at my suggestion and had remained sullen until I acquiesced. By then he had already taken to wearing it.

I scooped out a handful of dirt from my father's grave and pushed the ring into it.

I found few remains of the children. The baby Henry had been barely out of swaddling and Joanna was still often falling when she tried to run. There was not much of them to find.

I gathered those parts together in a blanket and wrapped them up into a bundle. I placed them in their grave together even though I was unsure whether such a thing was allowed. But those sweet children had been inseparable in life and I wanted them to share their resting place.

I knew I should summon the prior from Tutbury to speak the necessary prayers. But I was numb. And there was much work to do that day.

The servants I dragged into a single long grave along the edge of the consecrated area. I hoped they would not mind sharing their burial. I was sure to dig it north to south and laid the bodies side by side so that everyone would wake, on the day of judgement, facing the rising sun. Ashbury was a small estate by any standard but still we had two dozen servants and labourers to see to the house and to the land.

Many of the bodies had their throat and neck hacked out, just as Isabella had suffered.

Almost all slain in such a manner were women.

I found Barbary, Isabella's wet nurse, strung up by her ankles from a beam in the kitchen. There were pails under her that had the residue of fresh blood coating the inside. A funnel, still dribbling blood, had been tossed into a corner. Barbary's skin was as white as chalk and she seemed to have been drained from slashes through her neck.

It reminded me of the time I had watched a pig slaughtered at Duffield Castle. The creature's blood was drained and saved for sausages and blood cakes. I watched that pig screaming and bucking as it died, flinging itself around in mindless terror.

Barbary must have gone the same way but there were also teeth marks gouged into her breasts and belly. I cut the poor woman down and covered her up with sacking before carrying her to the grave.

Most knights favoured the sword for its versatility and prestige. Others used mace or falchion or axe. I wondered what form of weapon the murderers had used to tear and shred the necks of my family and servants. Likely a dagger, worried back and forth. I was training to be a knight from the age of seven and we learned the quickest, simplest ways to kill a man. That the murderers had used such elaborate, unnecessary methods was alarming.

In the cellar were three more bodies in a heap. Their blood pooled along with the cider and ale leaking from barrels hacked open and thrown over. I kicked the rats away from the bodies and carried them one at a time up the long grave.

My mind was shattered. I'd never seen much death and blood and it seemed the horrors would never end. I felt the world turn under me, somehow. When I had awoken that morning, the world had been one way. Then, after I stepped through the door to the hall, everything had changed, forever.

The last of the bodies in the cellar was that of Mabel. She was a simple old woman with a twisted back who cleaned in the kitchen and scrubbed the floors. Her neck was slashed almost clean through. When I lifted the body the last vestiges of her decrepit skin ripped off and the head thudded to the floor and rolled over once.

Someone gasped and whimpered in the darkness.

I lay old Mabel's body down by her head, grabbed the lamp and explored behind the remaining barrels in the corner where the noise was coming from.

The girl hunched in the corner, her hands over her hair. She was the daughter of Osbert, the man who tended the gardens and brewed sour ale. I had already dragged his body to the grave.

"Rose," I said, my voice so loud and sudden that she jumped out of her skin. I tried again in a soft whisper. "Rose. It is Richard."

She kept up the whimpering to herself. The girl could manage no more than fragments of words. No amount of coaxing could elicit any further response so I scooped her up as gently as I could. She flinched but then clung to me. Rose was an ugly child, with prominent teeth and no chin. She had pissed herself and was shivering in a thin dress that stuck to her legs.

"The bad men have gone," I whispered as I held her to me. "No one can hurt you now."

She buried her face into my chest and I held it there as I stepped over Mabel's remains.

"Keep your eyes closed, child," I whispered.

Not all the servants were killed. Walt and Marge had hid in the orchard and when the killers had left they ran through the wood all the way to the priory for help.

I stepped out of the house carrying Rose and found Prior Theobald riding his pony toward the manor house with a group of brothers scurrying behind on foot.

They were almost up to the door and when they saw me they froze. The monks turned to the prior and the prior's face drained of what little colour it had.

I glanced down. There was blood all over me.

Poor Rose. Blood covered the girl, too, where I had carried her against my sodden clothes. I must have looked like a creature from a nightmare and still she had allowed me to carry her away from that cellar. To the prior we must have appeared as the risen dead.

"Help us," I cried.

Prior Theobald spurred into action and rode up. Even mounted he seemed small.

"By God, Richard," the old man's voice shook and his eyes betrayed the horror they saw. "What have you done?"

I did not understand at first so I merely stared in response.

But, thank God, he took control. He took control of me, of the girl and the surviving servants.

"Ride hard for the sheriff," the prior said to a young monk and handed over the reins of his pony. The prior kept his eyes on me.

"I did not do this thing," I mumbled. "There were riders on the road."

The prior looked disturbed. He nodded.

"For the love of God, someone take this child away from him," Prior Theobald said.

Our servant Marge came hurrying after the prior. She took Rose away toward the village. The girl seemed to be staring back at me from over Marge's shoulder. But her eyes looked through me, into the past. Into Hell itself.

"It is a miracle that the girl survived this," the prior said, reaching for something holy to say. "We should all be thankful for that small mercy."

I wanted to smash his teeth down his throat for uttering such nonsense. There was nothing to be thankful for. But the good prior was kind enough to have his monks and lay brothers help. They took over the burials while I sat in dumb shock upon the wall outside.

"You are the lord of Ashbury now, Richard," the prior said, perched next to me.

The new sheriff, Roger de Lacy arrived with his men in a thunder of hooves late that afternoon. He had me escorted to the Priory. His men even watched while I scrubbed the blood from myself and dressed in clothes the prior provided. The prior insisted I be allowed to wash before being questioned.

The Bishop of Coventry had been visiting the sheriff. He came along to Tutbury Priory to question me, too. The bishop was one of the most powerful men in the kingdom. Not merely a bishop, he was also Sheriff of Warwickshire, Leicestershire and Staffordshire.

It was dark when the sheriff and the bishop sat me down at Prior Theobald's sturdy table. It was one of the few private places in the priory. As I walked in, I heard the bishop arguing that I be taken to the nearest castle or anywhere that had a dungeon or with a sturdy door.

They were sitting to discover my guilt.

The bishop stared across the table with ill-concealed hostility. Bishop Hugh de Nonant was a big man, almost as tall as me and heavily muscled. I had always thought he looked like an ox herder rather than a man of God. But men so filled with ambition have little room in their souls for holiness. And the bishop was about as holy as a turnip.

The sheriff sat to my right, scratching words onto parchment every now and then while we spoke. The prior sat at my left side and said little but I welcomed his familiar presence. Before me was a jug of wine and while we sat I drank my way down the road toward oblivion.

"Where were you when this happened, Richard?" Roger de Lacy was not much older than I was. The sheriff had inherited vast estates across central England. He was Sheriff of Derbyshire and Nottinghamshire. I had come into my brother's blood-soaked manor.

"The sheriff asked you a question, boy," the bishop said, his voice a deep rumble. "Why do you claim you were not at home?"

I sighed and drank.

"Perhaps we should let the man sleep," the sheriff suggested. He was short but with big bones and a lumpy head. Scabbed pimples and a wispy beard covered his face. His eyes were soft and brown and seemed kind.

"He will speak first," the bishop said, overruling the sheriff. "Then he may rest."

"I was in the wood," I said, which was true. "Shooting Henry's crossbow."

"We are informed you often meet with a girl from the village," the sheriff said, glancing at the prior.

"Martha," the prior said quietly.

I nodded. How often our secrets turn out to be common knowledge.

I drank down my cup of wine. It roiled in my empty belly. My hands were shaking and the cup rattled on the table as I set it down.

"You have told us it was Earl William de Ferrers who did this... this evil thing. But did you see him do it, Richard? Did you see the murders happen? If so, how did you survive?"

"If your story is true," the bishop said. "It means you hid like a coward. And if you are lying, well..." He sneered at me. He was trying to scare me but I had looked through the gates of Hell that morning. Still, I had no desire to be executed.

"I saw the merest glimpse of a group of men galloping away," I said to the sheriff. "I did not see who they were."

"Ha." The bishop slapped the table with his meaty hand. "What did I tell you?"

The sheriff ignored him. "Then why say it was Earl William?"

He poured me more wine and I drank before answering. Chucking that dark, sour stuff into my stomach made me sick but I needed it.

"Isabella told me," I said. "Before she died."

"A likely story," the bishop said. "Very convenient, indeed."

"Convenient?" My voice rose and the bishop's jowls grew red. I bit back my anger. "Walt and Marge saw the murderers, surely? They came to tell you, prior. What did they see?"

Prior Theobald opened his mouth to answer but the bishop jabbed his finger at him.

"Say not a word," the bishop said. "This man may be a murderer. Until we decide he is not then he does not get to make demands of us."

I could not believe they could be so dense. "Why do you not ask Earl William where he and his monsters were last night instead of gathering about me? I swore to bring him to justice. If you lords will not provide it then, by God, I shall take it for myself."

"A shame you did not take justice this morning," the bishop said, sneering.

I lurched to my feet, bumping into the table, my chair scraping upon the floor and intending to shout. But my voice cracked as I spoke. "I could not have known what they had done," I said.

The bishop held my gaze for but a moment before he looked away.

The sheriff stood too and placed a hand on my arm. "William has gone," the sheriff said. "It is certain that he rode out from Duffield Castle last night. He rode with his six knights, armoured as if for war, so the servants say. He has not returned."

I felt the anger leech out of me and I sat again. The sheriff poured more wine into my cup.

"He could have gone anywhere," the bishop said, sulking. "It proves nothing."

"You were a friend of Earl Robert," I said to the bishop. "You visited many times. You know what William is like."

The bishop pursed his lips for a moment. "I do not see what my friendship with the late Earl has to do with this. And I am surprised to hear you of all men speak ill of—"

"I admired Earl Robert," I said, hearing the wine in my voice. "I was ever grateful that he had taken me away from Ashbury."

In truth, he scared me from the first day until the day he died. Robert was huge and stern and he beat me with his own hand. Which I suppose was an honour, of sorts.

"I know William," I said to the sheriff. "I knew him from when I was a child up until he went away to the Holy Land. And the first thing I learned at Duffield Castle was to stay away from William de Ferrers. My first night, in the hall, he coaxed over a cat using some meat. He stroked it. Then he speared it through the chest with a long dagger and tossed it still living into the fire. He did it just to frighten me, I think." I drank down my cup. My hands would not stop shaking.

"William killed a cat?" the bishop said and scoffed. "Good. Cats are evil. Anyway, boys have been the same since time out of mind."

"He must have been fifteen or sixteen and almost a man. Old enough to know better."

"And William went to the Holy Land years ago," the sheriff said. "And came back because his father was dying?" Despite owning so much land nearby, the sheriff did not yet know our shire.

"No," the bishop said, shaking his massive head.

"He was in fine health," I said. "He stuffed himself senseless with a whole mushroom pie in the evening and the next day he was dead."

"Never a heartier man in all Christendom." The bishop nodded. "Strong as bull. But you can never trust a mushroom."

"That was when you returned to Ashbury," the sheriff said, scratching away on his parchment. "Your brother was lord by then."

"Me and the other lads were told to leave in the same breath William used to tell us Earl Robert was dead."

"What other lads got thrown out?" the bishop asked.

"Curzon, Baskerville, Levett," I said, tallying them on my fingers. "Vipont, Barduff. And the rest."

The bishop grunted. "Good families."

"What did you all do to warrant expulsion from William's service?" the sheriff asked.

"William brought his own knights back from the Holy Land. Proper fighters, he said, not whelps like us. He said he could not afford to keep us as well as them."

The bishop shrugged. "You boys were his father's men. Makes sense that a lord would want loyal followers."

"When I left he said that he would make everything up to me," I said, taking another drink.

They all exchanged a look that I was too tired to interpret.

"What did you think he meant by it?" the sheriff said.

"I was the strongest knight," I said. "I believed he intended to take me back into his service once the others were too far away to take it as a slight. I was wrong."

The bishop shifted his huge bulk forward to peer at me. "Perhaps it was you he was hoping to kill last night?"

I had not considered that. "If that were the case, what reason would he have for slaying every living soul in the house?"

"There is no reason here," the prior said, his throat dry and raspy with emotion. "Only madness. Madness and evil. Those men are devils, perhaps, or even Satan himself."

After a pause, the sheriff continued with his questions. "You returned to Ashbury and yet you sleep in the woods?"

I shifted in my seat and took a drink. "It is a fine summer," I said. "I made a camp down by the stream. I practice with sword and crossbow by day."

"And by night you practice with young Martha," the bishop said, smirking. The prior scowled at him which made the bishop laugh. "Tell me, son. Does her father know you are ruining his daughter?"

The bishop liked to take local girls into his service. Especially the poor ones with no family to protest when he started feeling them up. And worse.

"Martha is a decent girl," I said. "All she wants is to learn to shoot the crossbow." We kissed often and fumbled at each other through our clothing. But Martha was too bright to give up her virginity to me.

"Shooting your crossbow right up her, morning, noon and night, I wager." The bishop chuckled to himself.

The sheriff coughed. "A crossbow is hardly a knight's weapon."

"The crossbow intrigues me, is all. After his time in the Holy Land, Henry brought the weapon back from Aragon."

"Along with his wife," the bishop added and smirked as if he'd been clever.

"Forgive me," the sheriff said. "But I hear that you often quarrel with your brother?"

I understood that they believed William and I had committed the crime together. Or at least that I was involved in the massacre in some way.

Everyone had heard that I quarrel often with Henry.

I remembered my father's voice. *You take after your damned mother.* Before I had gone to Duffield Castle my father would often shout and batter me about the head. *You clumsy oaf. You useless goat turd. Why could you have not been like Henry?*

And then there was Isabella.

Isabella was far above his station. She had an astonishing, delicate beauty. She seemed utterly out of place in dusty old Ashbury manor but her family in Aragon had fallen upon hard times. It was enough of a disgrace that she was willing to stoop as low as a poor English knight.

Henry wanted me gone. Wanted me to offer my service to someone, anyone who would take me.

Go to the Holy Land, Richard. By God, there is nothing for you here.

He would fly into a rage at the smallest thing. The servants I was friendly with had told me he had become that way since I returned from Duffield. It was my presence that had made him so volatile.

I did not know what I had done to anger him so and had no desire to stay with him. But I could not bear the thought of being apart from Isabella. So I stayed in the wood all that summer, fretting on an inevitable future apart from her. And yet doing nothing.

"I had no quarrel with Henry," I said.

They looked at each other, knowing I was lying.

The bishop stared. "Yet your father had a falling out with your brother, many years ago, if I recall?"

My eyes ached. Their pointless questions and prying into my life was more than I could bear. And, after swallowing cup after cup of wine along with my anger, I was drunk and my guts were churning.

"William and his knights did this," I said to the bishop, the sheriff and the prior. "Those men. You know his men? If you knew them, my lords, you would not be asking me so many questions."

"Please name and describe them to me. My bailiffs must know exactly who they are looking for," the sheriff said, ready to write on his parchment. "William is dark of hair and tall, is that correct?"

"Tall as me, if not taller. But he is much older, close to thirty, I think."

"Thirty and unmarried?" the sheriff asked. "Are all his men unmarried? Are they perhaps sodomites?"

"How dare you," the bishop growled. "Robert's son is no sodomite. He has been at war with the heathens for many years, I am sure he will take a wife when he is ready."

"I meant no offence, my lord." The sheriff smiled to himself while he scratched away. "Tell me about these knights."

"Hugh of Havering is William's closest man," I said. "He is of an age with William. Fair haired. Men listen when he speaks. Then there is Roger of Tyre. Older but still quick with a blade. Quick of mind and tongue, too. Dark."

"These men have holdings of their own in Outremer," the bishop said, muttering. "Odd that they would follow William de Ferrers back here. Unless they have reason to flee."

"One of the worst is Rollo the Norman" I said, suppressing a shudder. "A vile man who delights in torment. The call him the Beast."

"I have heard much talk of this one," the sheriff said, scratching at his parchment. "The Beast Rollo. He is said to look like a bear."

"A fat bear," the bishop said, smirking. "But hairier."

"And there is Ralph the Reaper who I heard boast of murders he had done in Outremer," I said. "He is supposed to be from some great Saxon family but Hugh of Havering told me he is a tanner's son. And he has Walter who is a little dark Welshman who is quite mad. He rants always that dead men walk the earth. Men who have risen too early for the Last Judgement. Ugly as sin, has wens on his face and your men could not miss him. And of course Hugo the Giant, you must know of him?"

"The giant, yes," the sheriff said. "So he's taller than you?"

I snorted. "Tallest man I have ever seen. Strong, too."

"It is true," the bishop said, shaking his head. "I have seen this man."

"There was never men like them in all Derbyshire until William returned," I said, my voice growing louder. "And they ride away unpunished. If you know of them then you know it was they and not I who did this thing."

The sheriff raised his hands. "We have spoken to the surviving servants. I am sure that it was Earl William and his men."

“His men, yes,” the bishop muttered and allowed himself a single tight nod. “Yet I find it hard to believe that Robert’s boy could stoop to such a thing. The real question is if there was some purpose anyone might have had in committing these acts.”

“We have not been sitting idly.” The sheriff leaned forward. “My men ride in all directions as we speak,” he said. “If Earl William is hiding in Derbyshire I shall lead my bailiffs there and we shall take him. Justice shall be done, I swear.”

“I will go with you,” I said and drained my cup, thinking how much I did not want to face William and his knights. But I had sworn an oath.

The sheriff thought for a moment and nodded. “You are welcome to join us.”

I felt all the aches in my muscles from digging the graves that morning and lifting and carrying body after body. I had worked beyond the limits of my endurance. I could not recall eating. Peering at the dirt and blood under my fingernails I had to close one eye to focus my vision. My head spun and the most important thing I had to do was to get away from all their questions and judgements and simply close my eyes.

“My lords,” I mumbled, heaving myself upright. “I am afraid that I must retire to my wood.”

I watched with interest as the floor lurched up to smash me in the face.

Someone slapped me. I was on a low pallet in a small, bare room. It was light outside the high window.

“I’m awake,” I mumbled.

The prior slapped me again.

“I said I’m awake, for the love of God,” I said, grabbing his wrist.

“You purged yourself upon my floor, young man,” Prior Theobald said, yanking his hand back from my grip. He seemed to be considering slapping me a third time.

“Oh, God,” I said and covered my face, remembering all that had happened the day before.

The prior’s tone softened and he placed his hand upon my shoulder. “The sheriff has returned to see you, Richard.” He hesitated. “This is a terrible thing that has happened. All you can do is trust in God. All of us here shall pray for you.”

I lay upon my back, hungover and bereft. “Thank you, prior.”

When I was young my father had tried to force me to become a monk. My family supported Tutbury Priory so they would take me, unruly as I was. As the second son I may have one day diluted Henry’s inheritance. I ran away, then fought and screamed when they brought me back. Earl Robert somehow found out about this and took me into his service instead. Me being a monk would have been like forcing a fox to become a chicken. But our father granted everything to Henry anyway. And Henry gave me nothing.

"It breaks my heart to bring this up so soon," he said. "But your brother had confirmed the Priory's grants when he became the lord of the manor. Sadly, we are yet to receive any of the promised—"

I sat up and pushed past him. "You shall get your grants, Theobald," I said, just to shut him up.

"Thank you, Richard," he said. "My Lord."

I splashed water over myself. One of the brothers led me to the cloister where the sheriff sat reading upon a bench in the centre of the square. Swifts chirped and swooped above and the sun was painfully bright. Two men attended the sheriff. They took the parchments from him and retired to the shadow of the cloister when I approached.

"Where is the bishop this morning, my lord sheriff?" I asked. My mouth tasted like vomit and my head pounded. Nothing I was not used to, of course. At least it was another fine day.

"Call me Roger," the sheriff said, smiling. He looked as fresh as a daisy, the bastard. "The bishop has more responsibilities than a mortal man can undertake, he tells me. And he rode away last night claiming to be returning to Coventry. Imagine my surprise when I discovered this morning that the bishop instead rode to Duffield Castle. More of his men have ridden up from the south to join him."

"Surely he cannot seize the Earl's castle for himself? Should William be stripped of his lands and title, they are for the king to distribute."

"The king is sailing for the Holy Land. He may even have already left. It seems as though most men of quality are sailing with him." The sheriff sighed. "I have half a mind to take the cross myself. Although I wonder if I would have land and position to return to if men like the bishop are staying to carve up England in the king's absence."

The politics of the realm was of little interest to me. I kept seeing bodies, graves and blood. I had an oath to fulfil. "What of William?"

The sheriff sighed. "I am afraid that William and his men have ridden south for Dartmouth. One of my bailiffs rode back to me through the night. William and his men were seen on the road, dressed for travel. Armed and armoured. That disgusting beast Rollo was heard by my man bragging about getting away with murder and heading for Dartmouth and there to catch a ship."

I had never travelled beyond Derbyshire.

"Surely that is a ruse? Why would he say such things? Perhaps they will take another road?"

The sheriff nodded. "My bailiff said Hugh of Havering battered Rollo about the head for speaking where they could be overheard. My man is trustworthy and I believe him."

"Why did your bailiff not stop them?" I demanded.

The sheriff looked at me but did me the favour of not pointing out the foolishness of my question.

"I must go after them myself," I said.

"I mean no offence when I say this," the sheriff said. "But you will be killed. I doubt you have a chance of besting a single one of any of those men. And together they are seven."

"I was unbeaten in practice," I said. "And I won a melee last summer."

The sheriff held up a hand against my protests. "Of course, of course. But William fought the Saracens in the Holy Land. He was one of the few to survive the massacre of Hattin. And his men sound like the vilest brutes in Christendom. Tell me that I am wrong when I say you will die, Richard."

I did not want to admit it. "Come with me," I asked the sheriff. "You have men."

"I have no authority beyond this shire," the sheriff said. "What about your friends? The others fostered by Earl Robert before he died. The Levetts have a reputation. Can they ride with you?"

Unsure of how to say it, I hesitated. "I was not well liked," I admitted.

The sheriff frowned. "Ah," he said. "The bishop is convinced that you are a great one for chasing girls. That will make you unpopular."

"I never chased a girl in my life," I said, shrugging. "I don't know why they like me."

"Oh dear. That makes it worse, in my experience," he said, chuckling.

"I always won in practice bouts. Even though I was almost the youngest," I said. "They said it wasn't fair because I was bigger."

"You should have gone easier on them," he said. "That would be the political thing to do. You need allies, Richard. Look at me. I never won a fight in my life and here I am a beloved sheriff."

I laughed. "I should have gone easier, yes. But I enjoyed humiliating them, the bloody bastards. They will never help me with anything."

The sheriff sighed. "In that case, I suggest you do not throw your life away on a quest that cannot possibly succeed," he said. "That enormous and disgusting man who now goes by the name the Beast Rollo? One of my bailiffs suspects he is from Caen. He escaped a hanging a few years ago by killing the hangman, hacking his way through the crowd and running to Outremer. He truly is a beast. A devil. He should have been killed years ago and many men have tried. I beg you not to go up against men like him. You are a lord now. Stay here and see to your lands."

"I swore an oath to God to avenge them," I said, seeing Isabella's blood welling from her mouth and the pleading in her eyes. "I have no choice but to bring William and those six knights to justice. Rollo included. Hugo the Giant included. If God is just he will lend strength to my arm that I might slay the murderers."

The sheriff shrugged. As well he might. The killers had fled his shire and were unlikely to return. And if I threw my life away chasing after William and his men, well, who was I to the sheriff? He had done his moral duty in attempting to dissuade me but he made another attempt.

We stood. "Go home, Richard," the sheriff said, extending his hand to me in friendship. "Keep swyving Martha in the woods. Take a wife, have some children. Men like William always die by the sword."

"There are no men like William," I said. "But he will die by my sword."

The truth, of course, was that the sheriff was right. Those men terrified me.

No surviving servant could be induced to stay at Ashbury Manor. It was cursed. I paid some serfs from the village to scrub the blood stains from the floors and walls. I stayed to oversee the work. I was the lord of the manor. The proper incomes from the land would be mine but I could find no steward to manage the work of my own land or gather the rents from my tenants. My standards were low; anyone who said yes would do. But everyone knew that the manor house and my family was cursed by God and to take up with me would curse them as well.

I slept in the wood.

The night before I set out, I rode to Duffield Castle. The bishop was giving a feast with William's meat and bread, in William's hall. The sheriff was there also and I spoke to him at the top table.

"I need a man to look after my land," I said to the sheriff, leaning over to him.

"I will do what I can," the sheriff said.

I knew that when I rode away from Ashbury that I would be riding into penury.

I looked around at the great hall I knew so well. The servants had dutifully served Earl Robert and then served Earl William. They now served Hugh de Nonant, sitting in the Earl's great dark chair and I suspected they would serve him for a long time. William had left no instructions for the care of Duffield and no man knew when he might return. Indeed, there was no indication that he ever would.

"Richard of Ashbury," the bishop slurred. His mouth dribbled William's good wine and flecks of meat. "Why in God's name are you still in Derbyshire? I thought you were charging off like a bull at a gate."

"I am almost ready to leave, my lord," I said, fighting to keep the anger from my voice.

"I shall pray for your success in hunting down those murderous dogs." He staggered over to me and dumped a heavy purse onto the table.

"My lord?"

"Hire yourself a couple of good fighters," he said, kneading my shoulder and breathing wine into my face. "Or a band of mediocre ones. Give yourself half a chance to be rid of him. If you succeed, I shall give you more."

"Thank you, my lord bishop," I said. He waved a hand over my head and muttered something about God that I suppose was a blessing.

The sheriff laughed at my expression. "Those men deserve the Lord's justice, delivered here on earth by your righteous hand." He held up his wine. "An eye for an eye, a tooth for a tooth and all the rest of it."

I drank heartily to that and then paused. "To apply that principle to William I should have to burst into his home one night and slaughter him, his family and his servants."

"That does sound like rather a lot of work," the sheriff said. "You had better get to it."

I packed everything I needed onto my brother's palfrey – my palfrey now – and went to sleep one last time in the woods.

Almost everyone in the village had ignored me and it was clear they believed my family cursed. But I got one of the lads to ask Martha to meet me in the woods by the stream. That place was ours. It was where we practised the crossbow. And where we practised pleasuring one another.

She came at sunrise. The dawn was clear and hot and the light fell upon her face. Martha had a strong face and clear skin and my heart flew when I saw her picking her way through the trees toward me. I took her hands in mine.

"I have to go away," I said.

"Go then," she said without looking at me.

"I may never return."

That made Martha at least look up. "Who will be lord of Ashbury then?"

"Some other lord, I suppose," I said. Strange to think of some other family taking what had been ours for over a hundred years.

She looked intrigued and then sighed as if she begrudged even speaking to me. "It were right bad what happened to your family, Richard, weren't it."

"I am sorry about running off like this," I said. I assumed she was going to be heartbroken because I was abandoning her. "But you always knew that you and I could never have married. This had to end eventually. You will find a good man from Ashbury to marry. Or from Scropton or even Yeaveley."

Martha laughed, bitterly, twirling her hair. She looked up at me with her huge green eyes. "What you doing with that crossbow?"

I nodded, wondering why I had bothered to say farewell to her. It was not that she was simple and ignorant that put me off her. She lacked even a rudimentary capacity for affection.

"Crossbow? I have no idea what I did with it. If you can find it in the barley near the manor, you are welcome to it, I suppose."

"You suppose? Suppose?" She was angry. "After all I done for you under the oak tree. The least you can do is give me that weapon. And you don't have to be so mean-spirited about giving me what's owed. My dad reckons that a crossbow will fetch a fine price in Chesterfield on market day and I don't doubt he's right."

She was just a girl. Just an ignorant girl and I had been an idiot boy up until William de Ferrers had massacred everyone at Ashbury. But Martha had remained Martha.

"If it's money you are looking for then you should know that the Bishop of Coventry pays his servants well," I said. "You should go see him at Duffield Castle."

I rode south for Dartmouth. If I caught up with William and his knights, I knew not what I would do.

2

The Chase

IT WAS A FAIR FEW DAYS OF RIDING south and west to get to Dartmouth. I saw more of England in those days that I had in all my previous twenty-one years. The weather turned and once I got drenched, I remained either sodden or damp for a week. At least it was not cold.

The folk at the roadside inns whispered about the group of men who had ridden through before me. A rich man was the leader. Some knew him for an earl.

"Fine-looking man, he was," a stocky old woman said as she slammed a bowl of stew on my table. I was at an inn outside Cirencester and it seemed like she owned the place. "Just like you, my lord." She winked at me. "Taking the cross, God bless him. But those other men were an evil looking bunch. I have thanked God every night since they passed through that they caused no harm while they were here."

"Didn't you know Edith's little lad's gone missing?" a young serving woman said to her, overhearing.

"That's not got nothing to do with those men, though," the older woman said, scoffing. "What would a band of grown men want with a little boy?"

Others remembered the group passing through at the beginning of spring, heading north. Everyone remembered the giant, Hugo.

"Tallest man in all the world, he was, my lord."

I followed the old road south through hills and across rivers. England was bigger than I had imagined. And everyone was talking about the Crusade. King Richard had spent three years robbing the country to pay for it and he had finally embarked with thousands of knights, mercenaries and most of the great lords of the realm.

That was why asking drunk men in taverns and inns for tales of knights passing by became tiresome.

"Bit late, ain't you, lord?" I was asked about a hundred times. "They left last month."

"The King's in France now, lord. You better hurry or Saladin's head will be on Jerusalem's wall before you ever get there."

Such is what passes for wit amongst English country folk.

Still, men remembered William passing and when I was closer to the south coast, I knew his destination port for certain.

"And you are sure you heard them say they were heading for Dartmouth."

"They did. But then, he was a liar," an old ditcher with gnarled hands said, sitting behind the great cup of beer that I bought for him outside Shepton Mallet. "They was all liars."

"How so?" I asked.

"There's no Earl in his right mind who would ride in the company of men such as them lot."

"I agree with you," I said. "But he truly is an Earl."

The old man scoffed. "Probably a bloody Scotchman." He knocked back the beer.

I had never ridden so far or for so long and I was saddle sore and weary when I rode along that lovely valley and looked down into that sweet port. My lungs were filled with the salt spray tossed into the wind by the rocky coast.

Dartmouth nestled against a wide river, surrounded by hills green with trees and grazed grass right down to the water's edge. The sea beyond the far mouth of the river was slate-grey to one side and blood red from the setting sun to the other. Between the clusters of ships in the river the water was a glassy silver and black. There was a forest of masts and rigging and furled sails. Wharfs dotted with buildings and men carrying things to and from the docked boats and ships. The men there called out to each other and across the still waters to the ships. It smelled of fish and smoke and life.

I took a room at an inn near the old wooden castle that overlooked the town. After stabling my horse, I descended to the waterside just as the sun fell below the distant horizon. Heart clamouring in my ears I sought out Earl William.

At the inns and taverns, I met indifference, mistrust and downright hostility. I had left my hauberk, helmet and shield at the inn. Perhaps I was making people nervous with the sword at my hip but I saw other men so armed. Perhaps it was because I was an outsider but then I was in a busy port filled with boatloads of strangers.

"We know what you did," one man who was already drunk breathed into my ear in a particularly filthy tavern.

"I have no idea what you mean," I said.

His friends pulled him away from me but their dark looks persuaded me to leave for the next establishment along the dockside, where the welcome was hardly friendlier.

In the last tavern I finally found a merchant with one eye and a hacking cough. After draining the sixth cup of wine that I bought him he told me that William and his men had taken one of his ships just the day before. I sighed, feeling a profound relief flood through me. A relief that I had the decency to feel ashamed of.

"Awful gentlemen, so they were," the merchant said, swaying in his seat. "One of them were a giant. Tall as this room, so help me, God. Threatened me into letting them onto the ship. There weren't the room for them and all their belongings, I told them. Just weren't the room and I begged them but they said they knew where my wife lived. I had to unload twenty four barrels of good salt herring to get them on board, the dirty bastards."

"To where be the ship bound?"

"Going all the way to Marseilles and that's right where your friends wanted to be." He spat on the floor. "The devil take them."

I had heard of the place. "Why would they want to go there?" I asked, almost to myself.

"You can get anything you could ever want there, if you can pay the price," he said, licking his lips and squinting at the jug of wine with his eye. "Pilgrims and the crusaders leave off from Marseilles for the Holy Land. That's where you knights are always heading, ain't it. Any chance of another cup, my lord? I'm right parched, I am. Right parched, by God."

That night I took a room at the inn by the castle. Lying in bed with the stench of the rotten straw mattress filling my nose, I squirmed and itched at the fleabites. As I began finally to drift away, a sobbing came through the walls from somewhere else in the quiet tavern. It betrayed a desperate, inconsolable soul. Instead of sleeping, I listened to that mournful weeping. I resisted shouting for silence.

In the morning, I went to check on the care of my horse. I knew I would have to sell her soon and after a sleepless night, I was in a foul mood.

"Someone in the inn was crying all night," I said to the stable boy, a stocky lad with a dirty face and the stink of horse shit about him.

"If you got something wrong with the rooms you got to tell Old Bert," the lad said, staring at the floor. "My lord."

"I am merely curious," I said. "It sounded like a recent hurt."

He looked confused. "That's just Mags. Joan's mother. Weeping like a spring tide, she is."

"Ah," I said. "And something happened to Joan, I take it?"

"What, you ain't never heard about Joan the Maiden?" the boy said, his face suddenly full of joy.

"I have not."

"She was a girl who works in the inn kitchens. She got found on the banks of the Dart a couple days ago," the stable boy said, full to bursting with importance. "Up at the castle they saying she got her throat savaged by a dog or a bear or something. But that ain't what truly happened."

I saw Isabella, her blood soaking my clothes.

My throat was dry. "What truly happened?"

The boy stopped brushing my horse and lowered his voice. "Folk seen her go off with some rich man that night, lord. But then I heard she went off with a whole group of men. Strangers."

"Why would a maiden go off with a group of strangers?"

"Oh," the boy said, taken aback. "She weren't really a maiden, lord. They just call her that. It's a jest. Because really Joan would lift her skirts for any old—"

"I understand," I said. "So you know who did this terrible thing?"

"No one recognised them," the boy said in a hushed tone. "Which means only one thing, lord."

I assumed he was going to claim they were shape shifters or some form of man-beast because children love such stories. He stared at me so I forced myself to ask. "What does it mean?"

"Jews," the stable boy said and lowered his voice to a whisper. "It was the Jews what done it, lord. They can make themselves look like other men. So me and my brothers are going to set a fire under the Jews" houses tonight. Send them all to hell, right and proper."

"The men responsible have sailed for the Holy Land," I told the stable boy. "A group of men led by a great lord from the north and many here noticed them. One of the knights was a giant. You have no cause to burn the homes of the innocent."

He scoffed at my ignorance, all deference forgotten. "The Jews ain't innocent," he said. "Even if they didn't do Joan, they did our Lord, didn't they?"

I smacked him in the ear hard enough to knock him to the straw.

"I'll get my brothers on you," the sobbing boy said from the ground, his hand over his ear. "You ain't nothing round here, big man."

"Please do direct your brothers to me," I told him. "I will knock them on their arse too, then I will drag them to the town reeve for planning murder and fire setting. Any fires get started in Dartmouth tonight then we shall know whom to hang, won't we. Now, brush down my horse properly or I'll cut your balls off and feed them to the Jews."

That day I watched the ships bobbing in the port and asked for passage from traders and masters. It seemed to me that the town was a mistrustful place full of muttering and unkind looks that turned away whenever I glanced in their direction. But still I spoke to everyone who would hear me.

"Don't take crusaders," one said from his gangplank after looking me up and down. "Sling your hook."

There was one large vessel with high sides, teeming with men. "You cannot afford the cost of a place on my ship," the master said, leering at me as the ship was loaded behind him.

"I am sure that I can," I said, thinking of the silver the Bishop had given me. It seemed a shame to spend it all on a single passage but I was willing to do so. "I will pay whatever it takes."

The master took my elbow and led me to one side, lowering his voice. "The cost is for you to allow me to lay with you, every night, as a man lays with a woman."

I looked at him to see if he was in jest. "I am unwilling to pay that cost."

He scowled, spat at me feet and shoved me aside on his way back to his ship.

Disheartened, I went back to the inn and drank wine until my head span. Across the room from me a group of impoverished young men muttered and stared at me. I grew certain they were intending to run me outside and beat me bloody. I knew not what I had done but I would have welcomed a fight. So I staggered over to them and loomed over their table. One of them leapt to his feet and I shoved him back so hard he fell on his arse and sat there stunned.

"What is it with this place?" I slurred as I spoke. "Are you lads looking for a fight? Because if you are then you have chosen the correct inn for I am rather keen to pummel a man's face into offal." I doubted that the individual words were uttered with any clarity but I trusted that the general thrust would be clear enough.

They were afraid of me even though they were many and I was swimming in wine. "We know it was you what did that to Joan," one of them said.

"Joan?" I spluttered. "What in God's name are you talking about?"

"You was seen," one said, with tears in his eyes. "It was you, clear as day."

"That girl was dead before I even arrived in this goat turd of a port," I said, placing my hand on the hilt of my sword. "Are we fighting or not?"

They declined.

I lay on my mattress that night with the room spinning around me listening to the sobs of the dead girl's mother through the wall. I was certain that William and his men had carried out other murders before Ashbury. They had continued to kill again and again on their way to Dartmouth.

I stuffed my fingers in my ears, prayed to God to give me strength and swore to take any outward bound ship the next day.

***

I woke late, mouth dry and head pounding and went to the docks and to ask everyone I could about getting passage onward. Dartmouth was heaving with ships. I forced my way through shouting gangs of men and the rising stench of fish as the hot morning got hotter throughout the day. Finally, I heard of a French ship that was ready to leave that night. I was to speak to the sailing master.

That man was Oberto and when I finally tracked him down I discovered that there was no way that he could have been more helpful. For Oberto was an experienced sailor and he knew a young fool with a fat purse when he saw one.

"I hear you are heading for the Mediterranean," I shouted to him after I climbed the gangplank to a deck full of barrels and men. The ship was *La Bon Marie* and it was a slab-sided cog with a huge mast, crisp square sails. She was manned with Frisians, had a French name and owner, was commanded by a Genoese sailing master, but she flew an English flag.

"No more room for merchandise," Oberto the master said, scowling. "Can you not see we are full?" He indicated the barrels and boxes stacked everywhere upon the deck and tied in place. "I cannot stow so much as one more rat."

He was well dressed, dark and reeked of wine. He swayed on his feet though the ship was not moving.

"I am no merchant," I said, full of my own importance. "I must get to Marseilles."

His ruddy face lit up. "A passenger. How wonderful. I am bound for Genoa which is so close to Marseilles they are almost touching." He held up a dirty thumb and forefinger by way of demonstration. "I have a luxurious cabin currently unoccupied and just waiting for you, young man. You are eager to become a warrior of God. You wish to raise your shield in defence of the Holy Land and win back Jerusalem. Well, God has blessed you, my friend, but we must leave this day, on the evening tide."

Because I was looking for one, I saw the destination of the ship as a sign from God. I was eager to make up for my earlier delays and I wished to show the Lord I was eager and willing to pay for my sins. I could not wait to get away from the unkindness of the town and the sobbing of the woman at the inn. So instead of waiting for another ship, striking a hard bargain or inspecting the cabin I ran off. I sold my very fine palfrey for pennies to the innkeeper. He protested that there had been a glut of fine horses sold just a day or two ago and he could pay no more. I then paid half a fortune for what Oberto said was a cabin. I was so ignorant of the world I did not even know to buy my own supplies for the long, appalling journey.

We bobbed out of the harbour that evening as the sun sank on the distant horizon. We headed south into the English Channel, toward Brittany. And once again I was in pursuit of William and his murderers.

"But this is no cabin," I protested.

The cabin in question was no more than a filthy curtain slung across an alcove in the airless belly of the ship. It stank, it was dark as boiling pitch and full of rats. They scratched and scrabbled along the beams. Water dripped everywhere.

"How dare you deceive me, so? I demand a better cabin. A real cabin." The motion of the ship was unnatural and made my head spin and my guts roil.

"It's the best cabin in the whole ship," Oberto lied, grinning. "Even my own cabin is nothing but a hole compared to such luxury as this."

"You swindler," I growled. "You no good Italian cheat."

"I shall be happy to drop you at the next port along the coast," Oberto said. His smile faltered at my clumsy insults. No doubt he sensed the violent thoughts bubbling up. "Of course, I shall have to retain your payment."

"How dare you, you swindling little swine." I was a whole head and shoulders taller than him and I leaned over him, feeling the anger building within me. "Find me somewhere suitable to bunk or I shall take back my payment and more besides."

He swallowed. "I am afraid there truly is no other place, my lord. The men sleep in hammocks below deck with no more than eighteen inches between them."

"What about your own cabin? Perhaps I shall take that from you?" My threatening tone was immediately undermined by a violent gagging that gripped my guts.

"Please," he said, lowering his voice. "My men would not tolerate such a loss of face for the ship's master. They are a proud crew. They would kill me."

"Then they would be doing me a favour."

"I am the lone man aboard who can navigate. They would put into the nearest port and find a new ship. You, they would have to kill also."

"They can try," I said. I was angry with myself.

"The best I can do, my lord," Oberto said looking down and backing away from me. "Is when we land in Brittany, I will buy a ship's cat to deal with the rats."

I was already ashamed of delaying my pursuit of Earl William. More to the point, I was already suffering from the sea sickness and I clutched the low beam above as my stomach turned over.

I gave in.

There followed many days of vomiting in the dark. I purged myself inside out and after I was as empty as a man could be my limbs and mind were hollow. Despite laying in rotten filth with the stench of ancient bilge filling my nose day and night, I felt cleansed. As if I had left the past behind me when I had departed England.

Of course, I was wrong about that. I had not yet learned that we carry our histories with us wherever we go.

It took weeks of sailing down the coast. We hopped from port to port waiting out storms. Sometimes we were caught in the most astonishingly vast waves. I stayed out of the crew's way and clung to my bunk and every single time I thought that the ship would be sunk. The final storm came as we were closing on Marseilles and we were forced to run before it. Or so Oberto claimed. But we found ourselves in Genoa, many weeks after setting off. By then it was beyond the end of sailing season.

Oberto claimed he was yet willing to sail back to Marseilles but the crew rebelled. The swirling sky above was the same for days on end; a dark smear of roiling cloud, full of storm. To sail out now would be risking their deaths.

"They do whatever you tell them to do," I said.

His eyes twinkled. "Not in this."

"But it is so close," I said. "If we had not met that storm we would have made port there days ago."

"Hmmm," Oberto said, shrugging.

So I bade farewell to the fat little drunkard on the deck of his rotten bucket of a ship. The sailors ignored me and most ran off into the bustling madness of the port of Genoa, no doubt to the brothels and taverns.

"I am so very sorry to see you go," he said, grinning.

"I bet you bloody are, you swindling Italian cheat," I said.

Still, he had been my only company on the ship and I was about to be alone again.

I reached the bottom of the gang plank and dumped my heavy pack and other belongings onto the dockside. Oberto called my name and stood for a moment looking down. Then he yanked the gangplank back halfway where it quivered in the air over the strip of water between the sides and the wharf. He stood at the rail.

"I told you before that Marseilles was this close to Genoa." He held up his hand with finger and thumb pushed together. "But I did not know you, then."

"What are you saying?"

"Marseilles and Genoa? More like this far away." He held both hands out at shoulder width apart.

"You bastard."

I appraised the distance to the rail. The dark water below was full of debris and a film of slime.

"You are a good man, Richard," Oberto said. "You will not hurt me."

In fact it was something like two-hundred and fifty miles to Marseilles, through storm and rain and appalling weather. Few boats risked those conditions and none would take me.

I cursed Oberto's name with every step.

All the while the enormity of my task weighed on me. Finding William somewhere out in the world, which was larger and more terrifying than I had imagined, seemed impossible. Surely, he would not have remained in Marseilles.

But I finally trudged into that grand old city.

And there I found the Beast.

3

The Beast

I BLUNDERED INTO MARSEILLES before sundown, bone tired and ravenous and looking for a hot meal and a dry bed.

It had taken me ten days to walk from Genoa along the road that ran roughly west with the coast. Sometimes the coast turned north, other times south. But always it felt as though I was going back on myself toward England and away from William.

The landscape of that Mediterranean coast was one of astonishing beauty. I had seen nowhere along the outer edge of Europe to match it. There was coastal plain, mudflats and sand dunes but mostly it was mile after mile of field and forest, dotted with villages and towns. Inland were great hills. The other side, often out of sight, was the storm-wracked Mediterranean. The folk living along that coast were decent enough, though getting them to understand me was sometimes difficult.

Many travellers welcomed me as a companion. Without a horse to carry it, I wore my mail hauberk. I slung my helmet from my pack and wore my shield across my back as I walked so I was sought out as a deterrent to robbers and bandits on the road. Little groups would walk together between the towns. Oftentimes the grateful travellers provided food and wine for me and the other knights and soldiers.

A couple of days out from Marseilles I fell in with an Italian master mason who was heading to the city with his family to build a church. He was in fine mood for, starting in the spring, he would have work for years to come. The eldest daughter was rather lovely and she seemed quite taken with me also. Yet we could not converse and the mason watched us like a hawk when we sat together, smiling at each other and miming.

I reached Marseilles at sundown. It was a dry evening, for once, though everything was soaked and glistening in the sunset. It was a magnificent and ancient place with a vast stone wall and a gateway carved with shapes it. Inside were more stone buildings, some two or even three stories high. Masses of people hurrying about here and there but I was too exhausted to be much aware of it. The air was all smoke, salt, fish and orange sunlight.

Bidding fond farewell to the mason and his family inside the gate - especially his eldest daughter, who winked as she was dragged away - I asked locals politely for directions to somewhere I could sleep and be fed. Some ignored me, hurrying off. Others scowled and cursed me for a foreign devil. I spoke the language of northern France and the city folk spoke the language of the south. I was able to understand them but they treated me as if I was a Saracen.

Oberto had told me that Marseilles was a port city that favoured and welcomed travellers but I supposed that he had lied to me once again. Assuming I would be likely to find a room near the docks I walked toward the water. Some filthy children found me and pestered me for coin until I roared at them waving my arms and they ran away screaming and laughing.

Finally, one man who was fixing nets with his boy directed me down a narrow street.

"Tavern down there," he said, glancing around. "Cheap. Good wine."

I thanked him earnestly.

But it was a trap.

I thought I was imagining that I was followed down that street because when I turned I saw nobody. The street lead to a small square with stone buildings on four sides. It stank of faeces and rotten fish and I could see no obvious way out.

I turned to leave. First six and then a dozen and more men stalked out of the street into the square. They spread out around me. They were ordinary townsfolk but grim and muttering.

I backed away and backed away until I was cornered against the walls of two houses. They stretched up above us and there was nowhere to climb out to.

"Can I help you good fellows with something?" I said, smiling.

They close in on me, still muttering to each other. I saw a wine skin passed around. They stood staring at me. More men walked into the square from the alley which seemed a long way away.

"I can assure you," I said. "That if this is about a woman then I never touched her. I just arrived."

They surrounded me further, swearing and cursing. Some seemed full of wine's bravery and there were many of them. But I wore my hauberk and had a sword at my hip and shield on my back. I was taller than any of them and they would know that a knight is trained from youth in fighting. But I was exhausted and hungry and their numbers and unexplained anger concerned me.

My instinct told me to draw my sword but I knew that there would be no turning back from such an act.

"Where are you from?" a man demanded, pushing his way to the front to stand before me. He was old, about forty and he had the neck and shoulders of a bullock and a red, angry face.

"Genoa," I said, angry at the shaking in my voice. I was a lord, armed and armoured and I would not be afraid of a gang of fisherman.

"He lies. He's not a Genoese."

Others took up the cry. "Liar! Liar!"

"I never said I was born there, I said I just came from there." I looked over the sea of heads. The exit to the square was a long way away.

"He's English," another man said. "He's an Englishman if ever I saw one. His skin's as white as a fish belly."

"Tell the truth or we'll gut you like a fish," the bull-necked leader said. He mimed what I assumed was a gutting motion in front of my face with his meaty fists.

"I am a Norman," I lied. "I arrived in your city mere—"

But my words drowned in the braying of the mob.

"He's a Norman. Another Norman. We found another one."

"Another what?" I shouted, terrified. "Another bloody what?"

The mob leader shuffled near, his face red and shaking with rage. "You killed my wife." He shoved a meaty finger in my face. "You cut out her throat and God forgive me I shall cut out yours in return." And yet he stood and shook rather than attack me.

"I did nothing of the sort," I cried. "I arrived in your city tonight. You can see the dirt of the road upon me. Just now tonight, by God."

No one heard my words. No one wanted to hear them. They were yelling about women killed, about children torn apart.

They prodded and pushed and they had murder in their eyes. But murder is a hard thing for most men and they had not killed me outright, I wondered if there was a way out.

"It was Earl William," I screamed. "William and his men. I am hunting those men myself."

A stout stick hurtled at me and I ducked and it clattered off the wall behind me. And then a jug smashed, splashing dark wine against the wall. They surged forward.

They were going to kill me.

My guts churned. My heart hammered against my ribs pounding in my ears like the sea against black rocks. I struggled to breathe as the hands clawed at me and teeth were bared.

I sent a final prayer to God and drew my sword, intending to slay as many as I could before I was born down.

Different shouts intruded. Barked orders from the rear. The mob before me was drawn back by unseen hands.

Soldiers of Marseilles had arrived.

They yelled and beat at the men attacking me. They forced their way through and stood in front of me making a protective screen and ordered the mob to return to their homes. It took a while and a few of the city folk staggered off with head wounds but they dispersed.

Falling to my knees I thanked God for delivering me from death. I knew then that He was guiding me on my quest.

As I finished my prayers, my saviours gathered me up and beat me into a bloody pulp.

***

When I woke I was in a gaol. Some frozen black dungeon with no light. At first I was afraid I had been blinded.

Feeling around my body I found that my sword, pack, purse and hauberk were all gone. I lay on a damp stone floor in nothing more than my underclothes. The floor reeked of sweat, mould and the acrid, throat-burning sourness of old piss and human shit. I was already shivering when I woke. My face was stiff with dried blood and my beating by the soldiers came flooding back.

"Awake, are you, boy?" The voice spoke softly but in the close blackness the sound made me jump out of my skin.

"Where am I?" I asked, but it came out as a moan.

"God loves me. Bringing you to me." The voice chuckled. "I saw you. When they opened the door." He spoke English with a strong accent. "I knows you, boy."

The voice was familiar. "Who are you?" I tried to sit up.

Laughter again. Low, deep laughter.

"The Earl was heartbroken that you was not at home. He had plans for you, boy."

Before I got higher than one elbow he scrambled over to me in the dark and pinned me down.

I am a big man and strong. Even then when I was so young but this was a man who had grown into his strength over many years. A man who had filled out with flesh over his muscle and dense bone. I felt his weight pressing down, his giant belly and smelt his stench and I knew who it was.

"Rollo," I said.

One of Earl William's men. That stupid, huge great Norman beast who had murdered his way out of his own hanging.

He laughed again, a low rumbling I felt inside my body.

His breath was rancid as he leaned his face close to mine. "We gutted your brother real nice, didn't we, boy. Oh yes, we gutted him like a trout and he wept when he died. Sobbing like a baby for his poor bit of cunny getting savaged by the Earl right in front of him."

The Beast Rollo thrust his hips and belly down onto my body and I felt a soft-hard rod pushing against my stomach. It could only have been Rollo's enormous, tumescent phallus.

To throw him off I heaved myself up, the muscles in my back and legs straining. But I had no hope. He was twice my weight and he had me pinned on the bare stone floor.

"I cut off your brother's head myself," Rollo said. His lips sounded wet, like he was salivating. "It weren't a quick one, neither. It was a shame but the Earl wanted her ladyship all to his self so he dragged her off to her bed. I would have liked to have seen what he did to her. But I can imagine it pretty well enough, oh yes indeed." There was a wet slithering sound as he licked his lips right over my face.

"Coward," I growled and writhed and twisted. He fell to one side and I got a hand free and punched the darkness where I thought he would be. My fist punched his skull and I nearly broke my hand. I punched his face and neck and shoulder but as I was on my back my blows had no weight behind them. Rollo was a monstrous, fleshy oaf and he felt nothing, grabbed my wrist and pinned me again.

"I been hungry," Rollo said, almost whining. "Please lord, I know he is yours. But I been so hungry. Oh dear me, Christ, I been ever so hungry down here. Ever so hungry. And thirsty." Warm spittle dribbled down onto my chin, neck and lips.

The world turned. And I knew.

I saw Isabella's ripped and torn neck.

The woman in Dartmouth. The wives and children of the mob in Marseilles. The teeth marks on the wet nurse's skin. Their wounds caused not by saws or knives but with teeth.

William and his men were tearing into their victim's living flesh with their teeth. And drinking the blood.

I slammed my head forward, his nose smashing under my forehead.

Rollo grunted. Lifted his head away a fraction.

I butted him again, hard. I felt his grip loosen so I crashed my head forward a third time and Rollo growled, stood and picked me up like a rag doll, dragging me to my feet in the dark.

His fist hit me in the guts so hard I thought I was going to die.

That a blow could hurt so much was astonishing. Unable to draw breath, the panic rose inside me, certain I would suffocate from the paralysis his blow had dealt me. Even as it wore off and I could sense a breath on the horizon, I was certain that my insides had been minced. My guts ruptured. The humours would leak into my body rot me inside out.

I curled upon the floor and as soon as I gasped he kicked me in the face. The darkness burst with silver fire. Some instinct made me roll over and I avoided the next blow. It rushed by my head and I jumped to my feet and limped away as far as I could, trying to control my heaving lungs. I crouched against a damp wall.

Rollo was panting in the dark.

"Where you think you're going to go, boy? He chuckled that deep, low sound. "You're my lovely little feast, you are. You're my lovely little lamb." His feet scraped on the floor as he circled. "Come here, little lamb. Let me taste you."

I slid sideways along the wall, feeling my way with a hand on the crumbly wet stones. If I could just get behind him, I thought, I could knock him senseless. A blow to the back of the knee to bring him crashing down, followed by kicks to the temple until he was dead.

My foot whacked into something solid under foot and a bucket clunked over, spilling a pile of stinking, liquid shit over my feet.

His triumphant growl alerted me to his charge and I tried to jump to the side.

Instead I slipped in the shit.

He caught me with a glancing blow powerful enough to send me staggering into the wall just as Rollo thudded into it where I had been standing. He snarled in pain and I smashed my elbow toward the sound, connecting with something hard. As he backed away I stalked forward swinging my fists and elbows into his face, his neck, his hands. He grabbed my forearm with a meaty hand and squeezed, bringing me to him.

Instead of pulling away I grabbed his wrist, stepped forward and threw him with my hip. Earl Robert always said the bigger your enemy is the easier he is to overbalance. But Earl Robert, as far as I know, never fought in a black dungeon with his feet covered in slimy shit.

My feet slid midway through the throw and I collapsed with Rollo half on top of me.

We were both stunned. Exhausted by the fight and the fall. His weight had crushed the air from my body. He himself was old and corpulent and he could not catch his stinking breath fast enough. I recovered my breath after a moment but he lay across me, his throat dry and rasping, breathing ragged and hot in my ear. I tried to wriggle out from under him but he pushed my face down and leaned his massive weight on top of me while he got his breath. My head was being crushed, the skin on my face grinding against grit on the slimy stone floor. There was no chance I could lift myself up against his immense force. He may as well have been a mountain atop me for all the use my shaking arms were pushing against it.

So I slid my face along the floor. The skin under my eye scraped into shreds and the flesh of my cheek tore.

"No you don't, boy," Rollo growled above me and heaved down harder. "Where you going?"

It may have been my imagination but I was sure I could hear my skull cracking.

I squirmed my legs up like a frog and shoved myself away further, ripping and gouging my face down to my lips. I got far enough away that his weight was not right above me. It gave me enough space to twist out from under his hand and I lashed out, catching his locked-out elbow with my own. It cracked and Rollo cried out, lifting his body from mine but staying on his knees. I jumped up, ignoring the pain of my bleeding face and grabbed out toward the sound of his panting.

My fingers snaked into his greasy hair and gripped his massive head. He grabbed my wrists but I used my knee to smash him in the face.

It hurt me but it hurt him more. I smashed him again, bringing his face down onto my knee each time. His grip weakened until I was kneeing a wet, crunching mess and his hands dropped.

Still, he stayed upright.

Moving behind him, I got my arm around his throat and another behind his huge neck and squeezed for all I was worth. I ignored the pain in my face and knee.

Rollo reached behind his head and punched me in the face and he slapped and scratched my arms and hands but I held on. He writhed and bucked but I squeezed harder. He coughed out a spray of blood from his smashed face.

He went limp. I squeezed more until I was sure he was not pretending then let him drop. His body hit the stone floor with a thud. I backed away and sat, heaving down air until my heart slowed.

Rollo was not dead. A flicker of life remained inside his vast lump of a body and after a short while he stirred.

"Tough lad," Rollo mumbled, wheezing. "But a week ago I'd have killed you."

I kicked him in the face and stamped on his hands with a shit-covered heel until I felt fingers break and Rollo was hissing in agony. It hurt my foot but it was a satisfying trade.

"Where is William?" I asked Rollo, feeling the tatters of my cheek.

"Gone." Rollo found it difficult to speak with so many teeth broken. His skull must have cracked, too.

"Do not try me," I warned him.

"Gone," Rollo muttered. "To find God."

"Where in the Holy Land has he gone?"

"Back to Acre," Rollo said. "From there to Jerusalem. Where he died and where he was reborn, as the Christ was before him." He chuckled and then coughed blood.

Acre. Earl William was heading for Acre. I let out a great shuddering sigh.

I had a destination.

"He left you here alone?" I asked.

Rollo wailed. "I couldn't stop. He ordered me to flee. She tasted so sweet. The Gift. I wanted it to last. I am so weak." He wailed again. "Forgive me, lord."

"Why, Rollo?" I asked to the darkness, picking pieces of grit from my face. "You are drinking blood? What is this madness that has possessed you all?"

"Madness?" Rollo spat. The sound was wet and thick, like a slap. I thought I heard the hard tinkle of teeth mixed in with the blood. "We are angels, boy. Earl William died and God Himself rose William up. Turned him into the Angel of the Lord. He is the Destroyer. William chose us to share in his gift. We taste of him and we gain his strength. To keep it we must drink. Drink from the Destroyer on God's day. So we each of us drink to stay strong, Sabbath to Sabbath. And we share. We share his sacrament and we become strong. Once we prepare the way he will ascend. Ascend on a pillar of flame to sit in judgement beside the Lord. From now until the end of days."

I kicked him in his huge belly to silence him. He groaned and I kicked him again. I felt him swing at me in the dark so I kicked and stamped down on him once more. Kicking his head with bared feet was like kicking against a rock. But he fell mute again. Other than his laboured and wheezing breath. The foulness of that breath was greater than that of the shit bucket.

If there had been some way to restrain him then I would have done it. I had more questions. But soon he would become dangerous again and I could not share that black cell with him. And I knew that if I allowed myself to sleep even for a moment while Rollo lived then I would never wake.

Instead I prayed that God would see justice in my actions and forgive me if he did not. Anyway, the man was convicted before his hanging. I would be merely carrying out the sentence he had escaped from.

"None but God Himself can sit in judgement, Rollo," I said, standing and stretching my aching limbs. "Which you are about to discover."

"No. Murder. Murder." Rollo cried as I crossed to him once more. "Murder," he roared. My ears rang.

I beat him unconscious and sat across Rollo's back. I got my arm around his neck and pulled upward.

And that was how the guards found me when they threw open the heavy door and blinded me with lamp light.

The guards lifted me from him and took me away. A grizzled old sergeant cleaned my wounds, allowed me to wash, bandaged my face, fed me and gave me a bed. All the while there was a local dignitary and a couple of priests apologising for locking an innocent knight on crusade in with such a monster.

Witnesses including a stone mason had sworn that I had been on the road when the murders had taken place. They said I had entered the city no earlier than the night I was attacked.

"The killings of the women and children lasted for many weeks," they told me. "Soon after the English left."

"The English were here?"

"King Richard the Lionheart and thousands of Englishmen gathered here. They camped to the north. The French, too, led by Philip. The French army was bigger, of course. They left two months ago and then the murders started. A shipwright's wife was taken. Her body found mutilated. More women followed, always taken in the night. Children too. Every man went armed in his own home. Then that one was found asleep in an alley clutching a dead woman and her child to him. They had been cut about the neck. We believed we had our man. But there was another killing the next night while we had this one locked away. No more followed yet everyone thinks another is still out there."

"The other men have fled for the Holy Land," I said. "You can cease fretting."

You are following King Richard the Lionheart, yes?" they said.

"Certainly," I lied.

"When you see him," they said. "Tell him that Marseilles treats Englishmen within the law."

The very idea that I would ever speak to Richard the Lionheart was laughable. "Of course I shall tell him," I said. "It will be the first thing I say."

I gave thanks to God that the good fathers of Marseilles thought enough of justice to let me go, despite what the mob wanted.

The next morning, Rollo hanged.

They let me watch from afar, up on a balcony away from anyone who might attack me.

Rollo was still raving about serving the Angel of God while he dangled. With the noose tight about his neck, still he wailed in despair and wept and cried out for William. The hangman had to climb up and clutch onto Rollo's legs and jerk up and down to hasten his end.

The first of my prey brought to justice.

Six more to go.

4

The Lionheart

THOSE MEN OF MARSEILLES even returned my sword, helmet, shield and mail hauberk and most of my remaining coin.

"We pray to God that you will forgive us for throwing you in with that devil," they said on the docks. "Take that great cog at the wharf and join your fellow Englishmen, Richard of Ashbury. Never come to Marseilles again."

It was good advice. William headed for Acre. The city of Acre was in Outremer, as us Franks called the Christian parts of the Holy Land, much reduced since the rise of the Saracen king, Saladin. The English were heading for the Holy Land so I resolved to join them.

I took that Italian ship toward the city of Messina on the island of Sicily. Messina was where King Richard had finally gathered his forces for the crusade. That ship crept down the Italian coast spending days and even weeks in some of the ports while wind and storm kept ships from sailing out again. My face, thank God, healed and there was no scar.

Always I asked after William and his pack of murderers. If I found them I had no way of fighting them all but still I asked. But whichever route they had taken to Acre they had not come my way.

Battling through the last of the bad weather, I arrived in Messina before the Christmas of 1190.

The city of Messina nestled against the isle of Sicily at the far eastern end, opposite the toe of Italy. It was another ancient place, unlike anywhere outside the Mediterranean. A hundred years before I was born the city was conquered by Normans as the first step in the eventual reconquest of the island from the Moors.

Even in winter the sky over that city could be so blue that I would find myself staring up, open mouthed. There were statues everywhere; the marble tarnished and speckled with salt and age but no less impressive for all that. The buildings that surrounded the perfect arc of the bay were of a golden sandstone. The waters were well protected from the elements by a magnificent hook of land that curved out and around so far that it almost closed off the entrance to the harbour.

Philip the King of France was also overwintering in Sicily with his vast army. The two kings had fallen out but they had committed to winning back Jerusalem from the Saracens.

I paid little attention to those high above me. There were two or three thousand English soldiers and knights at Messina. After so long a time in the company of hostile foreigners I was happy at finding so many Englishmen that far from home.

Ragged and filthy and bordering on penniless I was no different from many other knights there. We were second sons and adventurers seeking glory or escape from boredom or from a woman. My father had not been rich nor a very good soldier. Yet a handful of knights remembered Henry of Ashbury as a solid, dependable man and I was acknowledged as the new lord of Ashbury.

Rumour of the nature of the massacre at Ashbury had flown before me and some treated me warily, for a curse is infectious.

No one had seen Earl William. If it had been him alone I was seeking I would have assumed he was disguised, travelling incognito. But his companion was the giant Hugo who could no more hide among men than a castle could hide among houses. So William and his knights had taken another route toward Acre.

Perhaps I should have hurried on ahead before William could get further beyond my grasp. Instead I convinced myself that crossing paths with the English crusader army was a sign from God that I should travel with my countrymen.

And my fight with Rollo had reinforced the impossibility of my sworn task. Against one of his men, a man much weakened by hunger and age, I had barely survived. With the rest, I stood no chance. I would break out in a cold sweat at the thought of facing the terrible power of Hugo the Giant or the lunatic fury of Roger the Reaper.

But the true reason for staying in Sicily was that, within my first week, I saw Alice.

"In the name of God," I said to my new friend Reginald outside our favoured tavern in Messina. "Tell me who is that woman." Many men sat around us, eating and laughing.

The day was once again dry with no more than the slightest chill in the air. We had a good view of the main road through the city. I was content to sit and watch the lords and ladies and servants walking to and fro. We sat between the waterside, the castle, the market and the countryside beyond where some of the richest lords had taken over houses. Children ran everywhere. The English, French and local Normans mixing together as friends and falling out as enemies just as their parents did.

The woman walking down the street with her companions stood out from the world around her like a sunbeam piercing a black cloud. She wore a dark green gown that was demure and respectable and yet it seemed to emphasise every line of her full body beneath. I do believe I gasped when I saw her. I was never before struck in such a way.

"What woman would that be?" Reginald asked, airily.

"You know what one," I said unable to drag my eyes from her.

I watched the way her hips lifted up and down as she walked. She went over to a small group of women in the open courtyard of a large house off the side of the road. Children ran squealing around them. Stray hair fell from all around the front of the woman's cap. Those wisps of hair were as golden and as bright as the dusty Sicilian sunlight. She looked happy. And yet, from the restrained way she smiled at the others who were talking and the way she kept herself apart from the group, I sensed that there was also a sadness about her. A sadness that felt familiar.

In that moment, I wanted more than anything to be able to take her sadness away. Her smile was wide and her lips full. Her face was white but flushed from walking. When she glanced round to light-heartedly curse a child that had bumped into her, I saw her eyes flashing with sudden joy. I wanted to feel the happiness that she felt and I wanted to make her laugh so.

"Do not even think about it," Reginald said wagging a finger at me across the table. "That is Alice de Frenenterre. She comes from Poitou. Her husband was Roger de Sherbourne. He died of a summer fever and he has no surviving relative. She has family in Outremer. Jaffa or somewhere close to Jerusalem, so she's not going back to Poitou."

"Well if her husband is dead, why should I not think about it?"

"The king was swyving her," Reginald said, leering. "Before his betrothed arrived, of course. Wouldn't want the future Queen of England finding out you are a bedswerver. But I tell you King Richard was ploughing her furrow ten times a day."

Reginald was from a wealthy enough family somewhere boggy in Norfolk but he had gone on Crusade as penance for some unspecified disgrace. Over the few days I kept his company I became convinced it had been a crime against a woman. At least one.

"I'd wager that's an exaggeration," I said. I watched her full lips twist together at some joke that had her noble companions suddenly laughing themselves silly. I watched the way she seemed to be the centre of those women's attention and yet a woman with her own mind. Strong enough to not fake a laugh simply because it is expected of you.

Though I had listened to stories of chivalric romance at Duffield. In the few moments I had observed her I awarded to her every virtuous trait in the world.

"She's better than you," Reginald said, intruding into my fantasies. "That is all there is to it. She is several places above you. She's a well-bred lady, from a proper family."

I stared Reginald down. "I am of good stock," I said. The group began to walk through the courtyard toward the door to the house.

"No doubt you top it the lord where you come from," Reginald said, nodding. "But you are piss poor and from some tumbledown shit hole no one outside of Derbyshire ever heard of. But that lady there has royal blood. Or an Austrian cousin married into the Holy Roman Emperor's family. I do not recall." He looked annoyed and drank down his drink, cuffing his mouth.

"It's not her Austrian cousin I want." I could not drag my eyes from her as she swayed away, her body shifting under her gown, drawing the cloth tight across her hips and arse and chest.

"She's got two children," Reginald pointed out. "A boy called Jocelyn and a girl barely out of swaddling. You wouldn't want to burden yourself like that."

"That's true," I said, staring at her as she finally disappeared from my sight. It was like a light going out. "But it would be worth it."

"But she's ancient," Reginald spluttered. "She must be at least twenty-three years old, Richard. You want to find yourself a nice fresh girl, thirteen or fourteen at the most. Fifteen would do, I suppose, if she's lovely and plump and has good teeth."

"All good advice," I said, turning to him. "You know an awful lot about this lady, Reginald. So tell me, how many times has she turned you down so far?"

"She has never so much as agreed to see me," Reginald wailed. "Whenever I call on her she sends word through some damned servant that she is engaged or out riding in the country. The lying bitch." Reginald turned and spat on the floor. "And if she never saw me then she will never see the likes of you, not never."

Reginald was correct that I had nothing to offer Alice. My land was inconsequential, my inherited manor cursed and my wealth so meagre I could not even afford a proper war horse.

I resolved on the spot to become rich.

"Dear God," I prayed. "I will fight the Saracens in your name. Please grant me glory in battle and riches and let me know that woman's love."

God heard me.

After a few weeks of waiting around, drinking and getting fat, word got about that the storms were lessening. Our winter in Messina would be over just as soon as the weather turned. In preparation for the fighting that was to come I went to get my hauberk properly repaired and the rust scrubbed away with sand and my sword and daggers sharpened. My coin had dwindled in Messina but every penny paid to an armourer was a penny toward the defence of your life. For soon I would be making a name for myself. A name I could use to find William.

I strolled back to my tiny room in the city through the crowded streets dressed as if for war. I had not bothered to purchase a horse I would only have to sell before setting off. There was no way I could have paid for the passage of a horse which could be ten times the cost of carrying me to Outremer. Messina was a lovely city, with wide streets lined here and there with decorative olive and lemon trees. Even under Norman rule and packed with stinking knights from the north, it retained an air of exotic luxury.

A young boy ran hard into my leg and fell down on his backside.

The boy looked to be about five or six years old and he looked up in fear until I winked at him. The boy grinned.

He had been playing Knights and Saracens with a much bigger boy. A boy who proceeded to stomp over and yank the little one up by his ear and clout him about the head.

"You stupid oaf," the big boy said. He had the idiot fat face of a noble. He was carrying a real sword, forged small enough to fit his hand. I hated the child on sight. "If you go running into a man during a real fight and you will die upon the battlefield. You die puking your innards out into the dust. You will be crying for your whore mother while you bleed all the blood out of your body and shit yourself to death."

The little one looked furious and close to tears in equal measure, gripping his little wooden sword to his chest as if it were a doll.

"Don't listen to him," I said to the younger lad. "He's never been on a battlefield in his life. He's talking out of his arse. Why don't you try fighting me, then, you horrible little twerp?"

The younger boy grinned up at me again.

"How dare you," the fat one shrieked, his face turning a sickly scarlet. "How dare you speak thus, you ignorant peasant. Do you know who I am? Do you? I shall have you executed for this."

"And do you know who I am?" I asked him.

The boy stuck out one of his chins. The top one. "Tell me your name," he commanded.

"Get out of here before I rip your guts out," I said and knocked his sword down, spun him around and kicked his arse hard enough to pitch him onto his belly. Men walking around us laughed and he ran away in tears to the sound of jeering.

"Bohemund will be angry," the little boy said as we stood watching him go.

"Well, I had better teach you how to fight properly then, hadn't I," I said.

He nodded solemnly, his eyes huge and round.

I ripped a spindly dry stick from an olive tree and we fought a few mock battles until he had killed me two or three times and was smiling from ear to ear. "Right, be off with you, lad," I said. "And stay away from fat Bohemund. I know his type. Get some better friends."

"He's not my friend," the little lad said, with a viciousness quite startling in one so young. "I hate him. Mother says I have to play with him so that I have proper acquaintance when he inherits."

"What's that fat shit going to inherit?"

"Sicily."

"I see." My guts churned over. "And what's your name, lad?" I asked.

"I am Jocelyn de Sherbourne," he said.

"So," I said, the name catching me off guard. "Your mother is... Alice?"

"That's her up there," Jocelyn said and pointed to a figure in a high window above the street looking down at us. She was bareheaded and those golden hairs blown by the wind caught the sunlight like sparks from a flame. I locked eyes with her and I saw the corner of her mouth twitch upward.

She invited me inside for refreshments. There were other ladies in the room, of course, and we conversed of topics that held no interest for me. Just being near to her made my heart race and I could not meet her eye for more than a moment at a time. I mumbled and stumbled my way through and I was certain that she thought me an utter fool.

"It would please me if you were to return tomorrow evening," she said as I left. "But perhaps wearing something more suitable." She laughed at me. I felt a true horror when I looked down and realised that my hauberk was not appropriate dress.

"My lady," I said, ready to offer a thousand apologies.

She laughed again and pushed me out. "See you tomorrow, Richard."

We met a few times and each time I grew more comfortable in her presence until I could hold her gaze. My heart still raced to be near her.

Soon enough, one day as I left she placed her fingers gently upon my arm to delay me at the door. She whispered up at my ear as I bent down, her breath upon my face.

"Return after dark."

The sweetest words that ever were spoke.

There was a strange feeling among the army and the followers while on Crusade. It reminded me of the high excitement of the shire fair or a celebratory holy day, when all of the normal rules are suspended for the duration. It was as though we existed outside of the true world. Love affairs bloomed and died many times over between men and women who would never have conversed in England. But we slept in strange houses in strange cities in strange countries. It mattered nothing if the servants or local people saw goings on. We would be gone from those places before the whispers could do damage. Coitus outside of marriage was against the law, against God and against common decency and it was so ingrained that most couples ensured they were discrete.

"People will talk," I whispered to Alice in the night.

"Not if we are careful," Alice replied. Even when she whispered, her voice sounded as though it came from deep inside of her.

"The men look on me with loathing," I said proud beyond words that they suspected where I had been spending my nights.

I heard the smile in her voice. "Think what the women say of me. Taking a lover in my widowhood. They say I am mad with lust." She pinched my chest. "And they speak truth."

Neither of us were breaking any vows spoken in the sacrament of marriage but it might blacken her good name.

"Should we not marry?" I asked.

Alice sighed. "And what happens to me when you are killed by the Saracens? Twice widowed in my youth. No man shall want me for fear of death."

It was a strange answer. "I know that I am very much beneath you," I started to say.

"You are beneath me," she whispered in my ear and slid her leg over me and sat up across my loins. "Right where I want you."

It was April 1191. We had spent the coldest nights of winter in each other's arms and every day of spring we knew our time together was coming to an end.

When the fleet set off from Sicily I saw her no more.

I swore to her on our last night together that I would think of her every day and every night.

"I know you will, Richard," she said.

The fleet spread out over hundreds of sea miles, calling at the ports of Italy and Greece on different days. Being apart from her felt like a blade through the guts. I could not wait until we reached Acre. I was going to win back the Holy Land single handed and become a lord and marry Alice and we would raise some fine boys. Boys who would become knights and make us proud with fine deeds. And I would ride down William and his men from the back of my horse. I pictured a huge grassland and two dozen knights in service to me riding with me. We would dispatch William and Hugh of Havering and Ralph the Reaper and Hugo the Giant and the all rest to Hell with a lance to the spine. Such are the fantasies of a lonely young man.

Alice was in the fine, seaworthy ship that carried the future queen whereas I was slung inside a rotting sponge that had once been a galley. The only reason it floated at all was because woodworm are buoyant.

And yet when the great storm hit, the royal ship that Alice and her children were in ran aground upon Cyprus whereas ours survived to limp on to Rhodes. I thought the ship from Dartmouth had been through bad weather but it was nothing like that storm. The wind seemed to come from every direction, one direction after the other and the waves were a chaos of choppy great peaks. When it passed our galley was so low in the water that should a single man on board have sneezed we would have immediately rolled over and sunk.

The Byzantine ruler of Cyprus had treated King Richard's shipwrecked family discourteously. There was a rumour that Richard's sister and his betrothed were kidnapped, or threatened or imprisoned then released. Whatever had happened, it was a serious affront to his authority. Richard the Lionheart dealt with challenges by charging at them headlong and battering them into submission.

He decided to conquer Cyprus.

I feared that Alice was hurt also and I threw myself into the conquest.

"Don't get all worked up about this stuff, son." A knight said to me while we crouched behind a field boundary wall. We were awaiting the horns sounding the attack. We were going to capture the city of Limassol on the south coast of the island. The walls of the city bristled with defenders and we were close enough to smell them.

Cyprus was hot; hotter even than Sicily had been and it grew hotter every day. When the sky was not full of storm it was blowing up dry dust and scorching heat. I shared the last of my water with the knight beside me so he felt as though he offered me something in return. Sadly, all he had was advice.

"The king's wife was never in any danger. That was an excuse. Richard has planned to take Cyprus for years. Ever since he took the cross back, three years ago. Or is it four now?"

"How do you know what the king planned?" I asked him.

"Everyone knows," he said.

"I did not know," I replied.

"And who are you, son?" the knight asked, scoffing. He was old, forty or so, but he looked tough. And he had a good point.

We picked up the long ladder along with half a dozen other men and ran forward under a hail of crossbow bolts. Limassol's ancient walls stood defended by thousands of men and we were hundreds. But our leader was Richard the Lionheart.

I was fighting for a chance of a life with Alice. I was fighting for riches enough to fulfil my oath.

So I was one of the first to scale the wall. Stones and arrows pelted my shield. It is difficult to scale a long, unsound ladder under such conditions. But I reached the top, threw myself over the crumbling wall and drew my sword.

The first man I ever killed died by the thrusting point of my sword entering his throat. His blood gushed out onto the dusty wall and mixed with the blood of the men dying around him as my fellows reached the tops of the ladders all along the wall. He was very slim, with a short and trimmed beard and I watched as the man died, his eyes wide and confused, as if he was shocked that this could happen.

I did not know those men. If I had never arrived on their island they would have never done me harm. If I had held back in the rear ranks as many knights do then I would not have had to kill them. And yet I was screaming with a mindless hate as I hacked down the defenders on the walls.

They fell back. Into the edges of the city, between the walls of houses, we found walls of men arrayed against us.

I had been training for war since I was seven years old. Day after day of grappling, riding, sword, shield, footwork. Thirteen years of practice and it finally became useful. My sword was like lightning flashing in a cloudless sky. I hacked up and down on shields and hammered at men and clashed against their raised weapons. I watched myself ducking and swerving around blows, as if every other man was blind and I alone could see.

But all the rage I had saved up over that time came pouring out. All my grief and fear and I lost myself in the fighting.

It is a strange to experience the part of you that is your reason, your goodness and your soul sit to one side. You watch the animal rage take control of your body.

Somehow, I cut my way through a line of Byzantine soldiers. I found myself far from my companions, cut off and surrounded by the enemy. I had no choice but to keep moving through the city. If I stopped moving I would die. I kept laying about me, cutting and snarling at anyone who came close. At some point, I lost my shield.

I was finally trapped down a narrow street. The faces around me twisted in anger and fear but they hesitated. My sword dripped with blood onto the dusty street. Blood and chunks of flesh drenched my hauberk and surcoat.

I had time to wonder whether my own men had abandoned me intentionally. I had been lost in my rage and could not remember what had happened. I waited, sweating and attracting flies. They were afraid to attack me. And no wonder. Soaked in the blood of their friends, I must have looked like Satan himself.

Shouting filled the street behind them and the Byzantines ran. There were Englishmen everywhere, slapping me on the back and laughing. Soon, cheering started.

The old knight from before the battle found me afterwards. He threw his arm about my neck as we walked through the streets of Limassol.

"What was your name again, lad?" he asked.

Later that day the king himself approached me.

I sat on a low wall with my head in my hands before the administrative building near the highest point in the city. The man sitting beside me jabbed my ribs with his elbow and dropped down to his knees. When I looked round I saw that everyone else nearby was kneeling.

King Richard stood over me, smiling down with regal condescension. Dust and red sunlight filled his fair hair. His face was sunburned red but otherwise it was fine and full of heartiness. I remembered that he was said to have lain with my Alice and I felt a moment's desire to run him through.

Instead, I knelt.

"Get up, lads," the king said. His voice was loud, friendly and clear as a summer sky. "Richard of Ashbury? Stand up, son."

He called me son, even though I was over twenty years old and he was barely into his thirties. I stood. Few men were of a height with me back in those centuries but Richard was able to look me straight in the eye.

"I heard you charged right through their lines," he said, chuckling. "And you kept going and they chased after you, leaving the way open for the rest of us." He laughed a full-throated laugh. "And you went running all the way to the palace and the bloody idiots chased you all the way."

"I didn't know what else to do," I said.

The king threw back his head and roared with laughter. His men, some of the greatest men in Christendom, laughed with him.

The king raised up my hand my hand before our tired army and called out to everyone around.

"Listen up, boys. This is Richard of Ashbury," the king yelled. "The knight who won us Cyprus."

Everyone laughed and cheered. The truth was I had gone charging off like the arrogant, idiot boy I was. If the enemy had been of quality I would have been hacked to pieces in moments.

But at least my blundering had caught the attention of the king. That was the start I needed to speed me on my way to a fortune.

For soon we would make the short voyage from Cyprus to the city of Acre on the coast of Outremer, long besieged by the Saracens.

And it was beneath the walls of Acre that I would find William.

* * *

Alice sent for me. Later, we lay in her bed in her new apartments in Limassol.

She stroked the tips of her fingers down my face and whispered into my ear. "If you continue to win such favour from the king then you won't be beneath me much longer."

"Then you would marry me?" I asked, as subtle as a kick to the face.

She sighed and stretched out like a cat. "The Holy Land presents great opportunity for a man who can fight."

"I shall fight well," I promised. "I shall win renown. When I have enough men I shall find William and bring him to justice."

Alice scoffed at my quest for vengeance. "William de Ferrers is a great lord," she said. "He could have dozens of men, perhaps a hundred."

She was quite right, of course but I had no wish to hear reason. "I have no quarrel with any men other than those who massacred my brother's family."

Alice sighed. "You think those other men will stand idly by while you kill their lord? Or that the other great lords who are his friends will allow you to get away with murder?"

"It would not be murder," I started to protest.

"Yes, yes," she said, running her finger over my bottom lip. "But justice to you will seem a crime all its own to those bound to de Ferrers."

"I care not," I mumbled, petulant and irritated by her good sense.

"If you were my husband," she said, making my heart race. "Would you not care that your crime would destroy my reputation also? And darken that of my son?"

In truth, I cared little for Jocelyn then, who was nothing but a reminder that Alice had loved and lived with a man well before I had slunk into her bed.

"Well, what am I to do, then?" I snarled, sitting up away from her.

"Precisely as you are doing," she said and drew me back down.

We landed at Acre in June 1191; almost two years after the struggle for the city had begun. King Guy of Jerusalem had surrounded the city entirely. Saladin and his vast armies were in turn besieging the Franks for all of those two years, cutting the Christians off from the rest of Outremer. The sea there was the bluest thing I had ever seen and sun was hotter and whiter even than in Cyprus. But it stank. It stank of the sewage from thousands of men who had encamped and been trapped for such a long time.

King Philip had arrived weeks before us but his thousands of Frenchmen had no impact on the struggle. It was a mighty tough city; well protected. Acre sat on the coast at the end of a short peninsular. The landward side blocked by two great defensive walls dotted with towers.

Only when King Richard and the English landed did the Franks mount any serious assault on the city.

I did not find William.

There was little chance to move about amongst the besieging armies. The English were on one side of the peninsular, the French on the other. Between were the forces of Jerusalem and the barons of Outremer. I asked after William and his knights but I could find no word of them. It was a huge disappointment as well as a relief.

The Holy Land presents great opportunity for a man who can fight.

So I put myself in the thickest of the fighting. For a month I fought for the walls. I climbed ladders and manned siege towers while under desperate attack from the garrison. There were thousands of Saracen knights inside the city but they were still merely a tenth our number. Still, they fought with the knowledge that losing the city might mean their slaughter. Many of the Saracens had their wives and children with them. I have no doubt that without those families to protect the garrison would have surrendered years before.

We also came under attack from outside where Saladin redoubled efforts to crush us before we could retake the city. I fought there, too, manning the palisades with my shield held high to block the endless shower of arrows.

Outremer was nothing like Messina or Cyprus. The feeling of a country fair was long gone. The social rules were not suspended. If anything, they became amplified in the cramped, hungry camps and ships. Jealousies raged and petty scores settled between men and women who were sick of the sight of one another. I could not see Alice. I knew that nobles and wealthy knights were wooing her with promises of security and a bright future for her son.

Often, I thought of my brother Henry. He never spoke of his time in the Holy Land, not in the whole time between his returning home and his death at William's hand. But I imagined him here, fighting and wondered if he had fought well, or even fought at all.

I killed many Saracens at Acre. But there were thousands of other mad, prideful and ambitious Englishmen and I did not stand out from the crowd.

A month after the English landed, terms were agreed and Acre was handed over to the Franks. We took the brave Saracen garrison and their families as prisoners. Saladin was to pay a vast sum of gold in exchange for their freedom. But Saladin delayed his end of the bargain. Payment was promised by a certain date and then he would beg for more time when that day arrived. Saladin was gaining time to build up his forces while the Franks ground to a halt at Acre, unable to take advantage of our victory.

All Saladin's previous Frankish opponents had been weak. But Richard was not like those other men. Common decency, fairness and charity were as nothing when compared to King Richard's lust for greatness. Since his youth he was known as the Lionheart and he had a lion's instinct for violence.

Richard ordered that the three thousand Saracen prisoners - all of the men, many of their women and even some children - be taken to a hill in full sight of Saladin's camp.

And there be executed.

We knights imagined that it was a gesture to force Saladin to pay up so I made sure I volunteered to carry out the act. It was a confusing jumble of shouting and angry Christians and Saracens who gathered outside the walls of the city. Everyone poured out to watch, unable to believe that Richard was truly going to do it. It was a scorching day and the sun burned my skin.

We marched the three thousand prisoners to a low hill just a little way from Acre across the stony plain.

And there, in full view of the Saracen armies and with Saladin's distant banner fluttering above them all, we cut off three thousand heads.

The prisoners lined up in columns, stepping forward to the row where they had to kneel and have their heads struck from their bodies. The screams came down the line as hundreds of us began hacking into the kneeling prisoners. The first few hundred bodies were dragged away but then those men gave up because there were so many. And the bodies piled up. The dusty ground became saturated with blood.

The Saracens accepted their fate. Some stood silent, many prayed under their breath as they shuffled forward. Just a few wept and sobbed. I saw none at all trying to fight or escape and although to do so would have been useless, it struck me as strange that thousands could be so utterly resigned to their terrible fate.

Sergeants walked up and down behind us, shouting. "The king wants every head cut right off. So do it properly. When did you last sharpen that blade? Go get an axe, son."

A young man, emaciated from captivity, knelt before me. He was mumbling a prayer and his brothers were cut down either side of him but he did not shake. I sent my own silent prayer to God and hacked down. My blow broke his spine and he died immediately. But King Richard had ordered three thousand heads be cut from three thousand bodies so I hacked it clean off.

By my third I could no longer see through the tears and my hands shook too much to continue. Men willing and able to take my place jostled me aside, sloshing through the blood and laughing at the madness of it all. To work up the will to do such things many men had drunk themselves halfway senseless. It felt like something between the joyous anarchy of a village fair, a battlefield and the fervour of a special mass. It was as though we had allowed ourselves to lose our minds

The horror of that day was like nothing I had ever seen and have rarely seen since. Three thousand necks pumped blood out from their bodies in arcing spurts. If each Saracen lost as little as three or four pints of blood then we had shed well over a thousand gallons of the stuff. I watched it pouring over that hillside, running in rivers down the sides into gullies, pooling in hollows and soaking into the dry earth.

I staggered away shaking and covered in blood, stepping over the dead and dying, the screams ringing in my ears.

And there was William.

Earl William, as bloody as I and standing there clear as day.

Through the press of soldiers and prisoners he was staring at me as if he had been waiting for me to notice him. He was grinning. His teeth red with blood.

William wiped chunks of flesh from his face. And then he sucked them all up into his mouth, chewing and swallowing them down.

Roger of Tyre, one of his most loyal men, brought William a cup and he threw it back. Blood poured down his cheeks and neck. He cuffed his mouth and smacked his lips, tossing the cup back to Roger who laughed and went to get more.

I looked around but no one else seemed to notice the knight gulping down the blood of the enemy like it was wine. But then, who could possibly have noticed such a thing? The only Franks upon that hill were drunk madmen intent on hacking even women and children in two.

Around the hill were groups of mounted knights and ranks of crossbowmen who stood ready to defend us should the Saracens decide to break the truce and attack. The distant armies of Saladin seemed to be working themselves into a fury of vengeance and it seemed as though they would soon attack. No doubt our knights would share my disgust that an English Earl was drinking human blood and even eating raw human flesh. But none of them would have helped me take him.

William saw me looking all around and he laughed.

"We do God's work, my dear Richard," William shouted, his voice powerful and clear through the screams of those dying and the prayers of those waiting to die. William sucked more blood from his fingers and licked his hands.

His knights were with him. They were nudging each other and jeering me. Hugo the Giant towered over them all, his face as blank as it ever was.

"I killed the Beast Rollo," I shouted.

They were surprised. William, I thought, was impressed. The others were angry.

I readied myself, loosening my sword arm. Surely they would not attack a fellow knight where all could see?

Men fell all around us and the blood flowed underfoot.

William smiled and spoke to his men, who laughed.

"Who's looking after your whore, Richard?" Hugh of Havering shouted.

"Should not leave a lady undefended, my lord," Roger of Tyre cried. "I hear there are bad men about."

I turned and ran through the blood back to Acre, their laughter ringing in my ears.

Their threats were nothing more than mockery. Alice was alive and well inside the walls of Acre.

But they knew about her. She could pay no knights to stand guard over her and so I raged at her to flee to somewhere that she could be safe.

"I will not run," Alice said, scorning my fears. "What could he possibly do to me here? I am under the protection of King Richard."

We were in her living quarters. She had ordered the servants from the room when I burst in straight from the massacre. It was a fine, compact home that she had found. The city and a smear of sea was out the window over her shoulder.

She was under the protection of King Richard. "And everyone knows exactly what you had to do to gain his protection."

She pierced my heart with a look of contempt. "I shall not defend my actions to you."

Running to her chambers to find her alive and her children playing had given me such relief that it took me a while to understand why she was angry. As far as the nobility was concerned, she and I could have no reason for being together whatsoever. Charging into her home crying her name was idiotic. It was dangerous to her position and her continued good name. If that name was ruined, if she was known to be having intimate relations with a penniless knight, a powerful lord could never marry her without himself becoming tainted. Rumours could denied but common knowledge would be a disaster.

We had not lain together since Limassol and I knew that she may never lay with me again. But I was willing to risk my own happiness and her future position if it meant she would understand that William was dangerous.

"I am so sorry that I said that," I said, although I wasn't. "But even the King may not be able to protect you."

"And you can?" She looked at me with such pity that my soul withered. "I never realised what a child you were until this moment."

"You do not understand." I strode across the room and loomed over her. "William is evil."

"Evil? I know what is happening outside the city. Is that not evil?" she said, backing away from me. "I know that you demanded a place for yourself. Tell me, how many women did you kill before you came running to me? How many children?"

"I killed merely a few soldiers," I said, wincing. "Saracen soldiers. Killing them is no sin, the Pope has said so. And anyway, I did it for you." I told her proudly, like a cat who brings home a dying rat for its owner.

"For me?" She recoiled further toward her window. "How dare you associate such an act with me? Do not sully me so. What you did, you did for yourself. You love killing, I have seen your eyes shining when you speak of battle."

I was shocked. "We decided that our one chance of being together was to win favour with the king. It is my only hope of bringing William to justice. But my victories in battle come to nothing," I said, pleading. "I needed to prove to King Richard that I was willing to do anything for his crusade. That way he will remember me when it is time to hand out estates when the Kingdom of Jerusalem is restored."

She shook her head. "No, Richard. No, he will put this massacre out of his mind and it will be as if it had never happened. And any man who reminds him of this will never be close to him again. Did you see any great lords out there upon that hill? No, of course not. They are all with the king, feasting and pretending this is not happening. No, I am afraid that you have quite ruined your prospects."

I was about to demand how she could know the inner workings of a king's mind but then I imagined her and him in Messina before the king's betrothed arrived. Alice and Richard, entwined in a vast bed, him whispering whatever it was that kings whisper. It was like a knife to the chest.

I thought of all the nights Alice and I had spent laying in her bed whispering to each other. I'd had my share of frenzied humping in the woods or castle storerooms but those moments with Alice were my first experience of intimacy. Yet she had shared countless quiet, special moments with both her husband and the King of England before me. Perhaps with others.

A young man's heart and his sense of worth are the most fragile, pathetic and useless things on earth and mine shrivelled up like a worm on a drystone wall.

"Please, Alice, promise me you shall protect yourself from William," I said, lowering my face to hers. "No matter how you feel about me. Promise me you shall never be alone with him or allow his men to approach you. Never be alone anywhere. And keep your children close."

"Richard, get away from me," she said, her nose wrinkling.

I saw myself in her wide, shining eyes. I had washed the worst of the blood from me and had put on fresh clothes. But my hair stuck out wildly from the blood that I had not washed away. I could see my own drawn and wild face staring back at me.

"I am sorry." I held up my hands and backed away from her. "I am sorry for everything. Alice, I beg you, do not go near that monster nor any of his men. If you do nothing else—"

"Leave," she said, pointing at her door.

On my way out, Jocelyn stared up at me with a hurt and fearful expression. I should have ruffled his hair or bid him a good day. But I stormed right by him without a second look.

William had been with the French forces at Acre all along, keeping his men quiet and well out of the fighting. But they could not resist that massacre.

I did not know what to do about William. And there was no time to think about it. Immediately after the massacre the entire Frankish army along with our women and children were marched south along the coast.

We were marching for the port of Jaffa. Once that fell we would retake the Holy City of Jerusalem.

William and his knights marched with us.

5

Renown

JAFFA WAS SEVENTY MILES AWAY south along the coast. The huge Saracen army that had surrounded us while we won back Acre matched our course further inland. They mirrored our advance and harassed us with attacks by their light cavalry.

Our infantry marched on the inland side of the road in tight formation. Outside of them were our crossbowmen who warded off the Saracen cavalry. Safe inside near the coast was the baggage train.

I rode with the mounted knights between the baggage and the infantry. I spent the last of my silver on a steady black mare before leaving Acre. Good horses were hard to find in Outremer and the prices were enormous. Most knights rode a destrier, a war horse trained in the forward charge and the richer knights had two or three held in reserve. I had no chance of buying a destrier so my mare was merely a rouncey that had once belonged to a squire. She was too old for war but she was all I had. Because she was black I called her Morel and I took care of her and prayed she would survive the march.

Off the coast, our fleet matched us and shipped food and supplies and took off the wounded and sick.

The Knights Templar lead the way as our vanguard and the Knights Hospitaller guarded the rear; the two most vulnerable positions.

King Richard was lord of vast and diverse lands and it was the Poitevins, the Bretons and the Angevins who marched behind the Templars. The English and the Normans and the forces of the Kingdom of Jerusalem marched behind them. The king rode his golden horse up and down the lines often with his huge retinue of lords and bodyguards. He was keeping an eye on us all, ensuring that we stayed together. But also he shouted encouragement, told us what was happening and reminded us that we were led by a man who knew how to lead.

Behind the English were King Philip's French and the local barons of Outremer, as well as all the Germans and Austrians and all the other Christians who were with us.

William, as a lord of Outremer holding land in the County of Tripoli, rode among them with his men.

I did not know what to do about William. No king or great lord or bishop would have paid me any heed had I made accusations about William and his crimes in England and elsewhere.

For many nights I imagined creeping through the darkness to where he camped and slitting his throat. I would have to move silently and to do that would require ridding myself of hauberk and helmet. Even leather creaked so I would need to go unarmoured. I would take no more than a short sword or even a dagger. I would blacken my face and my blade with ground charcoal mixed with oil and slip through sleeping forms until I found him. I pictured sawing my blade back and forth across his throat, the blood bubbling out with his screams.

His men would wake, of course. They would cut me down in moments. But at least my duty would be done.

I was too much of a coward to do it. It was easy to convince myself that I would likely fail before ever reaching William. I would be discovered before reaching William. Even if I could find him in the dark amongst so many thousands of others. And if I failed there would be no one to stop William from killing Alice out of spite or whatever madness it was that possessed him. I told myself that I was willing to die for my oath, for justice and vengeance but I did not want my death to be certain.

We marched and rode for many days through the intense heat and Saladin's cavalry harassed us without fail on every one of them. We marched in full armour and the roaring heat claimed many of us, fainting away into shaking madness and death.

But still we did not hurry.

At the Battle of Hattin five years before, the Frankish knights had marched right into a land with no water. Their true battle had been fought against the heat of the desert. Saladin had lured them that way and the fools had fallen for it. And that was why the combined Christian forces were slaughtered almost to a man. Without thousands of knights to protect the Holy City, Jerusalem was ultimately lost and thousands of good Christian people sold into slavery by Saladin. And so King Richard had us march only in the cooler mornings, rising before dawn to march from water source to water source. I thanked God every day that we were led by a king with common sense rather than by the fools who had blundered out to Hattin.

The women rode in carriages and covered wagons by the coast in the safest part of our army. Alice was one of them, along with her children. I could not see Alice but my thoughts were with her. I had soured her feelings toward me and any distant hope I had of marriage was dashed. And yet again and again I heard William's man shouting to me across that hill of blood.

How's your whore?

The thought of Alice being rent asunder as Isabella had been drove me mad on that march, more even than the baking sun did. William could attack during the march and I would be too far away to do anything. We had to stay in our formations. If men were allowed to move up and down the column then our entire strategy could fall to pieces. I was bound to stay where I was but would William would not consider himself bound by such orders.

At least the baggage train and precious supplies - including the women - were guarded by sober and vigilant men. And William must know that to commit such a crime, even if he escaped, would ruin his name throughout Outremer. But then he had thrown away an entire Earldom in England so he was utterly mad and perhaps cared little for self-preservation.

And so we marched. In ten days we came to a vast woodland; a precious rarity in the low coastal regions Holy Land.

The Wood of Arsuf was not the familiar lush, bright green woods of England. It was an astonishing mix of dark green pines and cedars with black bark. There were wild, gnarled olives, whole groves of scented bay and strange local oaks, like the English kind but different. Unknown and familiar birds chirped and flitted about above. After so long exposed to the scorching sun that wood was sweet relief.

But feelings of peace never last.

Whispers of the coming ambush sped up and down the lines. Always on the march the Saracens had ridden along our landward flank. But once we reached the woodland they now lurked in front and behind, tightening the noose about us. We were cut off in front and cut off behind. The single thing protecting us from slaughter was that we kept tight together.

"They are forming to attack. No matter what they attack with," Richard told us as we approached the southern end of the woodland. "We must all hold until they have exhausted themselves. And keep moving, always together."

At Hattin, the Saracens had weakened the Franks with endless storms of arrows and javelins, goading them into the knight's charge. But once the Franks had expended their devastating charge they were cut down and destroyed. Earl William had been at that battle and had been one of the few to survive and escape. I prayed for William's death in the coming battle.

"We hold until they exhaust themselves," Richard shouted as he trotted past us. "Wait until six blasts of the trumpets. We hold and hold until with God's will we will destroy them in one glorious charge. We hold and then charge on six blasts. Remember Hattin."

The Saracens burst from the trees with a cacophony so daunting it was as if the doors of hell were opening before us. They pounded vast drums and clashed mighty cymbals and gongs. They blasted hundreds of trumpets and the wide swathe of horsemen and infantry screamed and bellowed their war cries.

I had never been in a true battle. I had fought in sieges, stormed walls and taken towns and I had killed so many men that I had lost count. So I thought I knew all there was to know about war. But I was mounted, behind ranks of heavily armoured infantry and still I shook. Already sweating freely I was hit with a sudden chill and the need to evacuate my bowels.

The Saracens charged forward on foot and on horseback and the first of them launched thousands of javelins and darts into our men.

The javelin men on foot threw their missiles and pulled back. The mounted forces launched theirs and they too retreated back into the edge of the wood where more horsemen streamed forward.

Our infantry held up their shields and those missiles thudded into the heavy wood like thunder. Some found their way through the shields and the hauberks and helmets and the first cries of the wounded and dying began.

We moved forward a few dozen paces and formed up again as the dreaded horse archers thrummed a thousand arrows into us every few seconds. Our crossbows clicked and thronged, their bolts felling the man or horse whenever they found a target.

The Saracens had more men and they had more arrows. But their arrows were smaller, lighter and lacked the power needed to penetrate our men's mail hauberks and thick doublets beneath. Soon I saw many of our men marching with one or even half a dozen arrows sticking out from their backs or shoulders. There was no time to stop and remove them from the armour. But any arrow can find the gaps in armour. If a shield is not raised in time an arrow will smash through a man's face like a knife through a boiled turnip. Many of our men had rents in their hauberks from previous battles and arrows found their way through. Our wounded were helped inward away from the fighting.

Swords are as light as air but holding up a shield is tiring. Even for men trained to it and as the day wore on we lost more and more men to the relentless arrow storm.

We knights were itching to charge out and take the fight to the Saracens. We were close behind our infantry. Should Saladin send his heavy cavalry then we had to be ready to counter it. Instead we walked our horses or held them steady as the arrows rained down upon us, too. The mounted knights were as well protected as the infantry and usually more so. But we lost many horses. Some got hit in the rumps and led away toward the coast and baggage train with hopes for recovery. If a knight did not have a spare mount he went forward to join the ranks of the infantry.

King Richard was everywhere, riding up and down with his loyal knights surrounding him. "Hold, men, hold. Stay together. They shall not break us. God is with us, God is with us." His throat rasped and no wonder for he had been bellowing encouragement for hours and thousands of feet and hoofs had kicked up clouds of fine dust.

My horse, my precious, sweet black Morel, took an arrow in the neck. It went through one of the big veins. The poor beast reared only a little and stood bravely while I dismounted. Then she bent her legs and went down slowly, blood pouring from her muscled neck. I thought of Isabella.

I held her head and looked into her huge dark eye. "I am sorry, girl," I whispered in her ear as I drove my sword up into her skull.

I grabbed my shield and pushed forward through the crossbowmen towards the infantry. I had no wish to fight on foot but I was too poor to have a spare mount or a squire to look after it.

"For the love of God, Richard," I heard Henry of Champagne cry out. "Let us run them down."

"You will hold," King Richard roared, yanking his reins close behind me. "Remember Hattin." The king was attended by dozens of knights and lords and I scurried out of their way.

I wondered if I should run back to the baggage train to guard Alice. The madness of a battle was just the kind of situation that Earl William could use to get to her and her children. Holding my shield up high over my head against arrows raining down, I peered back through the thronging mounted knights behind me. I wondered how I could get away from the front line without being accused of cowardice.

The man next to me was laughing with his friend when an arrow struck him through the cheek, slamming down through his mouth into the back of his head. He was down and thrashing like a fish on a hook and hot blood gushed out to drench the man. Mouth wounds bleed profusely and the ground beneath him was soaked. But he did not die right away. His friends dragged him to his feet and walked him back through the massed horsemen. They went toward the coast where the wounded were thrown onto wagons to die or, if they were wealthy, be cared for.

I looked down at myself. Horse blood soaked me. If discovered, I would be ridiculed and perhaps condemned and ostracised but still I decided I would feign injury for long enough to get to the baggage train and then check on Alice. Once I knew she was well I would return to fight. It was worth the risk to my reputation.

"Richard of Ashbury." The king bellowed my name and I jumped from my thoughts, terrified he had known my intent. "Where is your mount?" He was pointing his sword right at me and shouting over the heads of crossbowmen and through milling horsemen.

"Dead," I called back. "Arrow."

The king knew I was nothing but a poor knight. But he knew I could fight like the devil and he needed warriors that day.

"Give this man a horse," King Richard shouted at one of his men and turned back to me. "You ride with me."

Men around me looked on me with admiration, jealousy and hatred. I crawled upon my new horse's back. He was a very fine destrier, one of Henry of Champagne's spare mounts, no less. I rode after the King and his retinue back down the line to where fighting was even fiercer. I rode among kings and princes and famous knights and was out of place with my cheap armour and faded, battered shield. But I would never have a better chance of making a future for myself.

The rear of our forces was suffering an all-out attack. Saladin was throwing his entire right wing at the Knights Hospitaller. And as fine soldiers as they were they were being slowly crushed. It was madness. Arrows darkened the sky and men shoved and pushed and screams filled the air. Banners of all colours and designs danced back and forth above it all. The Saracen army was endless and stretched over a mile or more from our lines to the trees and more came to join the press of men and horse. The Hospitallers were being surrounded and pressed back.

And then there he was.

William rode toward me through the madness. He was wore black-painted mail under a black surcoat with a white cross and a black helmet with a black shield and white cross. I shook my head to clear my vision, as surely William would not be riding to speak to the king of England.

But he was riding alongside a black-helmeted lord who I knew was the Master of the Order of the Hospitallers. It was the Master who rode back to address Richard. And William rode with him.

As they reined in, I was surprised to see King Richard glance between me and William. I had not known that Richard was aware of William's crime but of course rumour had reached him. The other nobles looked to me, too.

"We are being destroyed," the Master shouted as his horse slewed to a stop. "My knights, my men are being cut to pieces and you do nothing."

William yanked his horse's reins, jerking the poor beast's head so hard I thought its neck would break. My enemy caught my eye and his lips spread outward into a reptilian grin.

"You will hold," Richard shouted back at the Master. "Or I will pray that God damn you, my lord. Stay together and hold until all their forces are close and committed. We have but one chance to catch them all."

"They are not committed now," the Master said, waving at the scene. "If we do not charge immediately we shall be lost."

William laughed. "Perhaps that your desire?" He spoke to King Richard. "Perhaps you wish to be rid of the good Hospitallers? You want no challenge to your own control of Outremer, is that not true?" William laughed again and glanced at the Master of the Hospitallers who simply scowled at him in return.

Richard's men cried protests but the king silenced them with a look.

"William de Ferrers," the King of England said, his face twisted as I had never seen before. The king was angry. "You are a murderer."

"Aren't we all?" William said grinning and indicating the battle around us. The nobles around me cursed him again.

"He is my man," the Master interjected. "He is convicted of no crime."

"I am his liege lord," King Richard said. "But no longer."

I could not believe what I was hearing, it was as though God had begun answering my prayers.

William spat. "I shall never return to England." He had found a new protector and new brothers in arms by joining the Order of the Hospitallers.

"This is irrelevant," the Master said, in something approaching a wail. "My men are dying. The best knights in Christendom are dying and it is your fault." He thrust an accusing finger at my king.

"Saladin's horses are lighter and faster than ours," Richard explained, with astonishing patience considering the Master's disrespect.

While he spoke, William and I stared at each other. His eyes were burning with intensity. Arrows and screams fell all about us.

Richard continued explaining to the Master as if we were on a training ground not a battlefield. "If we charge too soon they shall pull back from us until our horses tire. They shall turn and slaughter us while we are separated from our soldiers. We must suffer and die until they have exhausted themselves. Then we shall catch them." Richard rode close to the Master who put his hand warily to his sword. "My lord, if we catch them when they are close we will crush them all. We can recover Jerusalem for Christendom if only we hold. Until the signal. Six blasts of the trumpets, then you may charge and win back the city of Christ in a single stroke."

The Master looked almost convinced but still desperate. William, his eyes flickering between me and the king, walked his horse sideways a step and leaned in toward the Master, speaking quietly. The Master nodded once, he wheeled his horse about and charged back to his dying men.

William gave me a final grin before scything his reigns hard and rode off after the Master of the Hospitallers.

"Saladin's banner," a knight shouted. "Saladin himself is there."

"Is he correct?" King Richard shouted to his men.

"It may be his, sire," one of the barons said. "Or his brother's."

"If it is Saladin," the king said to one of his barons. "Then he means to break us here."

"Perhaps we should charge after all," Henry of Champagne said from next to the king.

"Not yet," the king said, irritated. "We are in no true danger."

"Yet we have lost so many horses I wonder if we will have enough to make a deadly charge," the mercenary lord Mercadier said. "We have to flatten the bastards."

A huge cry went up on our left.

The Hospitallers were surging forward and bellowing a battle cry. "Saint George!"

They roared it over and over and hundreds of horsemen were galloping from the ranks of infantry into the Saracen forces.

"Damn him," King Richard shouted. "Damn that man."

The Master of the Hospitallers was leading the charge into the Saracen horses, who were indeed pulling back away from the charge.

It was William who made that charge happen. But even I admit that the Hospitaller charge was glorious to behold. They formed ragged lines as they rode, drawing close to charge knee to knee forming a wall of man and horse and armour, lances couched and deadly. When they reached forces who could not ride away the crash of arms on armour and flesh was loud enough to wake the dead. Unmounted Saracen archers and javelin men, lightly armoured and packed tightly together. Pinned by the thousands behind them were crushed. When their lances stuck fast into men or shields they were dropped and swords and maces seized. The

Knights Hospitaller, released finally from hours of suffering, began to pay back what they had received.

"Shall we call them to retreat, sire?" Richard's men asked.

The king stared at the horsemen. They would soon be surrounded and cut off and I thought the king was going to sacrifice them. If they could not obey orders then let them die, I thought. It's what I would have done.

"Sound the attack," Richard cried. "Our whole line, every man, all-out attack. Destroy them!"

The trumpets sounded six times, the signal repeated again and again all along our line.

The Hospitaller foot soldiers had begun their charge even before the king had ordered the trumpets to sound. They were the first to reach their mounted knights and they ran right into the Saracen counter attack.

The French knights and the barons of Outremer charged by us through their infantry into the Saracen centre and the men ran after them to support. The ground shook and drummed louder than a thunderstorm. The trumpets sounded and cymbals crashed and men bellowed the names of their lords and favoured saints.

Saladin's banner fluttered at the rear. King Richard stared at it across the thousands of men and horse. Saladin had committed heavily but not yet completely. The Saracens were restricted by the weight of their own men at the back who did not know to flee but here and there gaps began to open in their lines and their mounted archers began to slip away.

King Richard had no need to fight. Our counter attack had stunned the Saracens and we were carving our way into them. But he loved to fight and he believed a king should fight and lead by example. He was raised in a chivalric court and so he grinned at us over his shoulder, raked his heels back and charged into the battle for the centre.

We rode hard with him. I was in grand company.

"For the Lionheart!" Henry of Champagne cried on my left, his lance tight under his arm.

"God wills it!" the Duke of Burgundy shouted.

I had no lance but I extended my sword and charged into the massed ranks of Saracens. The press of men was terrifying and arrows cracked into helmet and mail. Dust kicked up everywhere and the sweat ran into my eyes, half blinding me. I hacked down again and again. I found myself with enemy on all sides. Swords stabbed up toward me and hands grabbed at my legs and feet, trying to heave me from my saddle. I stabbed and hacked. My horse was trained well in the ways of war and he snapped his teeth at the men about him and kicked his feet back and raked the air in front as I tried to clear a path and keep moving.

A gap opened on my left and I was fighting toward that gap when King Richard charged into it, away from his men and thrusting deep into the Saracen lines.

His barons, his bodyguard, his household troops were cut off from him and shouting and pleading for him to come back. Those men laid about them trying to reach him. They were the finest warriors in Christendom and they loved their king dearly but the mass of men and horse was so dense that even when horses were killed there was no room for them to fall over.

Mercadier, Richard's beloved chief mercenary roared and battered friend and foe alike to force his way through.

"Save him," Henry of Champagne shouted at me with tears in his eyes.

For I was the man closest to the king.

Other lords and knights took up the cry and shouted at me to bring him back. They begged and in their voices were the tears they were shedding at the thought of his death.

I fought harder and urged my horse on toward the king. My sword arm was numb from use and there was little strength left in my blows. Earlier I had been crashing my blade into helmets so hard that the men beneath fell from a single blow but it was all I could do to keep my arm rising and falling.

The king was so close I could hear the juddering of his breath. The sound of a man close to collapse from exhaustion. A huge, armoured Saracen knight on a heavy war horse forced his way between me and the king. He had a magnificent great beard and a face like an eagle that showed no fear. Whether he recognised the king's lion shield and coat or just knew he was a lord worthy of a fine prize, it was clear he wanted to take the king. Yet he knew he had to deal with me first so he swung his curved blade into what remained of my shield. The man's blows were powerful and swift and he hacked it into splinters in moments while I held off attacks from behind me. I gripped hard with my knees while my horse kicked and bucked.

The last of my shield was smashed away and I stabbed my sword through into the armoured Saracen, catching him by surprise and piercing his head under the ear. I sawed my blade back out and blood gushed everywhere and he slumped over still trying to fight.

I looked up in time to see king pulled slowly from his saddle down onto the ground.

Pulling my feet from the stirrups I got my feet underneath me on the saddle. As I crouched, my horse had his guts torn out. A spear was stabbed up into his belly and dragged back and forth and the destrier screamed and tried to rear up in the cramped space.

I leapt from the saddle across the dying Saracen knight and fell down where the king had fallen.

The fall stunned me.

Beneath the press of men and horse it was dark and airless. The ground drenched with blood. Richard was dazed and two Saracen bowmen pulled him away by the feet. Another furiously yanked at the king's helmet.

They wanted to capture and not kill the king. Some men shoved each other trying to get at him. Others stared up, no doubt at the king's bodyguard cutting their way toward him. Those Saracens hesitated, edged back into the throng while those behind could not push through to reach him.

Stabbing up with my sword, I cut into the man trying to steal Richard's crowned helmet. It was easy to push the blade into his kidney as he wore no armour. Crawling over the king I pushed him down into the drenched ground and bullied the other two away from him. On my knees, slashing wildly above I flung the king onto his back to check how badly he was wounded.

The blood made it impossible to tell at a glance but his eyes were open, though unfocused. He may have been stunned or dying.

Above me, the Saracens were closing in again, blades and bows being used as clubs smashed into my back. I felt ribs break and catching a single breath was hard. A powerful blow rang my head and I staggered upright, swinging my sword all around and driving away the crowd to make a space about us.

I never saw the spear. The Saracen who thrust it into me must have been strong. It pierced the mail outside my left forearm, tore through the muscle and then the mail on the other side of my arm, rent the hauberk again and lodged deep into the bone at my hip.

What a shock that blow was. Incredible, pinning me against the king's horse who snapped his teeth at me. The Saracens roared victory and charged forward for the king who was gaining his feet. Blinded by the agony I staggered forward, scything my sword back and forth. I clove a man's hand in half down the middle. I bashed an archer's jaw from his face. I narrowly missed striking the king's head from his body. They attacked me, someone grabbed the spear in my side and twisted. The agony brought me to my knees. My lips snarled back into a grimace so tight I felt them split.

Hooves drummed on the earth and I knew we were dead. The Saracen knights had reached us. I threw myself across the king and blindly batted away the hands that reached down.

A voice and hot breath in my ear. "They are friends, Richard. They are friends. You have done your duty."

I was flat on my back. Shapes moved above.

"Have him healed," the voice said. "Mercadier, bring me your surgeon. I want this brave man treated as if it were me under the saw."

"Do not take my arm," I begged but the noise I made was a moan and no one answered.

6

Loss

TIME PASSED. THERE WERE MOMENTS when I thought I must be in Heaven but then I would feel agony lancing through me and I knew I was not dead. There were flashes of faces and sensations. I was burning hot and another time I was washed with cool water. A woman sang to me. A great lord stood over me asking questions of someone I could not see.

Please do not take my arm.

"Is he awake again?" A woman's voice said. It sounded familiar. "He's mumbling."

"His wound has not festered," the physician as I came to. He was prodding my hip through stiff bandages that reeked of vinegar. "The fever has passed." He did not seem happy about my recovery. I could tell he was a proper physician because he was old and arrogant and he seemed offended by the very existence of my body.

I reached up with two arms and looked at both my hands. One was bandaged all around the forearm. They had not removed my arm. A great sigh poured out of me.

"Where am I?" It was daylight but I lay in shadow. A hot breeze fluttered the yellow walls of tent. There was blue sky beyond the flapping canvas.

"Do not attempt to speak," the physician said, peering down at me. There were other men behind and about him. On a long table I saw glass jars, bowls of piss and blood and leeches.

It was Alice who then spoke. "Surely his swift recovery is a miracle?"

The physician scoffed. "Ha." Which I believe was intended to convey what he thought of God's intervention on earth compared to his own medical abilities.

"Alice?" I looked for her.

"I am here, Richard." Her face appeared over me, smiling. Behind her were two of her ladies that I recognised from Messina.

I knew that time had passed since the battle but the last clear thing I remembered was being skewered with a spear. "What happened, Alice, with the battle? Does the king live?"

She laughed softly and patted my arm. "You ask that every time. You were gravely wounded, many times over, saving the life of the king. He is extremely grateful. But your wounds healed, miraculously."

"It was no miracle," the physician said, intruding. "In all likelihood it was simply a matter of receiving a superior standard of medical attention. In all likelihood."

"What happened?" I asked. "How did I get here?"

"Leave us," she commanded the physician and he bowed to her and backed away, waving his hovering attendants with him. They huddled in the corner of the tent throwing irritated glances back at me.

"How are you?" I asked her. "Your children?"

Her face lit up brighter than the sun outside. "We are all well," she said. "You are sweet to ask."

"Did we destroy the Saracens?" I said. "What has happened?"

She laughed. "The battle was won, my darling. We could have destroyed the Saracens army if only those stupid Hospitallers had not charged too early. But it was a great victory. They were beaten badly and have pulled back to Damascus or wherever to lick their wounds. And so we took back Jaffa really quite easily. So everyone says, I did not see anything of it, thanks be to God."

"It was William," I mumbled. "Earl William started that Hospitaller charge. Where is he? Why in God's name was he riding with the Order? Did he survive the battle? Has he been seen?"

Her face clouded over at the mention of his name and I thought I had erred in bringing him up. "Since the battle everyone has been talking about him. He was with the Hospitallers because he lost his lands in the County of Tripoli for some dark crime. He swore his service and the service of his men to the Order. I suppose they did not realise what they were accepting. After the battle he did another great murder. He slaughtered a group of Saracen nobles. They were valuable prisoners and he did it in some bloody fashion that grows with the retelling. People are saying that he drained their blood into barrels so that he could drink it like wine. Isn't that absurd? Anyway, Earl William has taken flight once more. The king declared his lands in England forfeit. The Hospitallers have disowned him also and even sent men to hunt him down but he eludes capture. It seems you were right about him. And everyone of note agrees." She smiled again, a sudden brightness. "But he is gone, do not concern yourself."

"He is gone," I repeated. "Praise God."

"They told me you would die," Alice said, her mouth drawing tight. "Then they said they would have to take your arm before infection set in but I commanded them to wait. Then that it would take you months to heal. They know nothing."

"How long have I been here?"

"A week? Yes, seven days, or eight. So much has happened."

"Where is here?"

"We are in Jaffa, in the grounds of my house. The servants are clearing all the Saracen nonsense from inside. And the doctors said you required air that is fresh."

"Your house?" I did not understand how we could have moved from such disagreement and bad feeling to me being welcomed, I assumed openly, into her household. She was chaperoned by her ladies but still it was strange. I lowered my voice. "I had assumed we would not see each other any longer. Not like this, at least."

"Like this?"

"Me laying under you so."

She smiled but I saw pain in her eyes. "I thought I had lost you," she whispered. "When I heard that you had fallen I thought that I would never see you again." She looked away for a long moment and sighed before continuing. "You are a fool, Richard. An uncouth, ignorant blustering great fool with no clue how to speak to a lady."

"I am."

"But I cannot imagine spending my life with anyone else." She smiled again and took my hand. Her fair skin had been darkened by the sun since I last saw her and her hair was even fairer. She was so beautiful that it took my breath away.

"What do you mean?" I said.

"You sweet fool, Richard. The king has granted you an estate here in Palestine, not far from Jaffa," Alice said, her huge eyes shining over me, her face ringed with golden locks lit from behind by the glare of the sun. "Now we can be married."

***

The king did not attend our wedding. In truth, it was a rather modest ceremony. But a few nobles from across Christendom were there in the small, beautiful church of Saint Michael near Jaffa's harbour.

They wanted to have my acquaintance. For I had saved the life of the King of England by defending him from uncounted enemies and an otherwise-certain death. And I had done so alone and done it so successfully that the king was hardly wounded.

Over wine and at table the king had sung my praises ever since, for it was a good story and he told it well. He had me granted land. A home that had belonged to a lord who had gone mad with homesickness and returned to Burgundy. My liege lord in Outremer was the King of Jerusalem. King of a city held by the Saracens but the kingdom included Jaffa and Acre and so I was a man of standing. And my dear, brilliant wife Alice was content. Her children had protection and stability and she had me.

The war was not over. Saladin was beaten but far from broken. The lords and kings pressured the sole remaining leader of the crusade, King Richard, to push on from Jaffa toward Jerusalem. The Knights Templar and the Knights Hospitaller told the rest of the

Franks that we would never hold Jerusalem. We would be unable to protect the supply line from Jaffa if we took it. But the Hospitallers remained out of favour for their brash charge, even though they had denounced and run out the instigator. And the great lords and the archbishops needled Richard into attacking anyway, convinced that God would give them victory.

Twice we got so close that we could smell the Holy City. It stank to high Heaven. But we were driven back. First by appalling weather that winter of 1191 and then, when the deluge had ceased, by the squabbles between the lords of Outremer. They despised each other far more than any of them despised the Saracens.

By the second attempt on the Holy City both sides in the war were exhausted. After so many years of constant warfare, even the most battle-hardened and war-mad knight had begun to lose his will to fight.

Saladin and Richard loved war at least as much as they feared God. But by 1192 both men seemed to lose their famed energies. Both seemed willing to accept that though neither had won, neither had lost, either. Both men were also pulled away from the war by internal political problems back in their homelands. Richard was hearing whispers that his brother John was plotting to steal his throne back in England.

The King and Saladin negotiated over the winter and well into the spring but still the war dragged on without resolution.

My wife and her children moved with me to my new estate. In truth it was a somewhat sad little place, much abused by the war but Alice set the servants to work in that way of hers and in a few weeks it was repaired and cleaned and comfortable enough. With my new estate I had income enough to keep four men of my own to fight for me. They would ride with me in battle and guard us while we slept. Franks who had fought in battle and were said to be trustworthy, sober men. Four tough men were enough to protect against petty thieves and perhaps even a middling level of banditry. More importantly, I finally had men to scrub my mail, oil my leather and carry my shield.

It was strange to find myself with a complete family. But I enjoyed it immensely. Emma was a joy because she was full of life and devoid of fear. She was always bringing us every horrific, giant thing that crept or slithered or crawled that she could find for half a mile of our house. I was terrified that she would be killed by some venomous foreign evil thing that she presented to me as though she had discovered the greatest jewel in Christendom.

"Stop worrying," Alice would say and laugh at me. "She knows which are the dangerous ones."

I was astonished that a three-year-old child could have such knowledge. "Which are the dangerous ones?"

"Whichever do not run away, of course."

When I looked at Jocelyn charging about with his wooden sword, his stocky body and fair hair were a vision of my brother Henry from when I was young. Thoughts of Henry lead immediately to the memory of holding his severed head. And fearless little Emma was a vision of Isabella's little girl Joanna who last I saw as tattered skin and bloody bone. My thoughts ran always to William, intruding upon my happiness. I hated him for that more than anything

So I could not rest. I could not be happy, not ever, until I fulfilled my oath.

I looked for him. I went to Jaffa and asked after him. Many knew of his treachery and everyone told the same story; that he and his men had slaughtered a dozen Saracen nobles held in the chapel of Saint George. The prisoners had belonged to Henry of Champagne and he was furious. And then William and his knights had slipped away after the incident.

William was lord of an estate up in the County of Tripoli, granted to him after some service long forgotten before Hattin. I looked for him there.

The steward was bitter and ancient. "He ain't here," he said, his voice creaking like dried leather. "My lord ain't been here for years and years."

I got the impression that the steward was not unhappy about his masterless existence.

"Where else might your lord be?"

The steward shrugged. "In Hell, I hope."

"My liege lord is Earl William's uncle, back in England," I lied. "I have been sent to bring the Earl home for he has inherited a magnificent castle. There will be coin for the man who united me with William and your lord will be thankful to you for telling me."

The steward never told me anymore, pleading ignorance. I was unsure whether to believe him but knew not what more I could do to get the truth out of the old man.

Still, I used the same lie or variations of it all over Outremer in the hope that someone, somewhere would reveal the truth of William's location. That whiff of reward meant I heard many stories from men who would say anything for a dream of silver. The truth was I had exhausted my ideas and pitiful gambits and I had no idea where to look next.

"You are wasting your life and your strength on an old promise made to a dead Aragon whore half the world away," Alice accused me after I returned from a long foray to the north with Otto, the oldest and steadiest of my men.

"And you are jealous of a dead woman," I said, angry at her because what she said was true. "My brother's wife, who I never so much as touched."

"You love her more than you love me or else why are you out there all the time instead of at home with your wife?" Alice said, her eyes filled with her fire.

"You know why," I said. "I owe it to my brother."

"Oh, your oath. Your famous oath," she said. "You do not even have affection for your brother. What about your oath to me, sworn before God? What about what you owe to us?"

What could I say?

"And," she said, knowing that she had me on the run. "What if you are called upon to fight while you are away in the north? And also you do not leave enough guards to protect us when you are gone."

I could no more resist Alice than the sea could resist the moon. She did not have to compel me for I wanted to give up. I never forgot my oath; I simply ceased to act upon it.

And so we had a year of something approaching bliss. We delighted in each other. I belonged to a place and together we were a family. A home of my own and one that had no connection to my father. A home I had won through my own efforts.

A beautiful woman who shaped me with her love and wisdom and discourse. I recognised that my infatuation with Isabella had been a childish fantasy based on nothing more than her exotic mystery. Isabella had been an idea for me, a metaphor for the promise of the great and strange world out there beyond the close horizons of Derbyshire. The lady had shown me kindness and courtesy that was so unlike the simple coarseness of the other girls I had known. Isabella had been a bright bird flying into my drab hall and I was a puppy staring at it, wanting it but not knowing what I would do if I ever caught it.

Marriage to Alice was real. As real as the earth beneath my feet and the sun upon my face. My wife opened my eyes to what sharing your life with another person could be like. She saw me feeling happy and sad and she saw me raging and reflective and still she looked at me with tenderness in her eyes and a smile upon her lips.

"Do not stare at me so," she said as she dressed one morning, smiling and covering her heavy breasts. "I have the body of an old woman. Your lust is unseemly."

I grabbed her, then, and pull her back into bed. Her body was full and round and strong and it made me lightheaded just to stroke her pale skin or to grab a handful of her warm flesh and breathe her in.

"Be gentle," she said and then hesitated. "I may be with child."

I whooped and leapt up and span her round and round.

"Be gentle," she shrieked, laughing.

All I had ever been good for was fighting. I had no idea how to assess my income or dispense justice. Alice tried to teach me but I am afraid I was never a good student and she took care of most of the estate management day by day while I did my best to keep up with her and learn by watching the adeptness with which she handled our tenants" disputes and our neighbours" scheming over dinner.

Her children would never truly be mine but I felt I was becoming an adequate father. Whenever he wanted, I instructed Jocelyn in the rudiments of armed and unarmed combat and taught him English words that for some reason he found hilarious. Some of those occasions where our serious training dissolved into laughter are among the happiest and most blissful moments of my long life.

The girl, Emma, was as full of joy as it is possible to be. She delighted in stories and would happily listen to anyone willing to tell her tales. Although she remained somewhat afraid of me, she began climbing into my lap in the evenings and sleeping there because she knew I would never allow her to be sent to bed once she did so.

It was its own reward but was also good practice. For soon, I would be a father to a baby who would be truly mine.

Of all the hundreds of years I have lived, 1192 was one of the best.

Often since then I have asked myself how I could have continued to underestimate William. I had seen the depths of the evil that he was capable of. I suppose it was just so much easier to pretend otherwise.

They came in the night.

They always do.

* * *

Something woke me. I sat up in bed listening but there was nothing but the wind against the half-open shutters and Alice's soft, steady breathing. Disturbed by my movement, she mumbled and rolled over next to me, her body under the sheets a series of waves edged in moonlight.

One of my dogs barked once and then fell silent. Sometimes they would bark themselves into a frenzy at the hyenas in the night. My huntsman swore it was because lions roamed about us in the dark, though I had never seen one. But a single bark was unheard of and the fact that neither my huntsman nor his son was shouting at the dog to be silent sent shivers down my spine.

I slipped from the bed and went to the window. The moon was bright and the sky clear and I could see out across my land. I had no significant defences, merely thorn hedges and stone walls to keep wild animals out and my own animals in. The wall of the stables was picked out clearly but I could hear nothing. A horse snorted and whinnied and then I knew that thieves had come. I took down my sword from the wall, silently cursing my useless bloody men for failing to post a proper guard.

The hills of Palestine could be cold at night but I was naked and looking for something to pull on when the screaming started.

It was a throat-shattering scream of agony. Whether of man or woman was hard to tell.

The scream, undoubtedly, had come from within our house.

"Stay here," I said to Alice. But she leapt from the bed and ran naked by me toward the children's rooms down the corridor, her feet slapping on the tiles.

Planting my feet in the corridor I stood guard while she gathered the confused children into her arms.

"Take them back to our chamber," I commanded her and she trotted back with Jocelyn on her hip and little Emma held to her shoulder.

"Where are your clothes, mother?" Jocelyn asked as she dumped him on the bed. Emma was rubbing her eyes.

"What is happening?" Alice asked me.

"Thieves," I said. "Perhaps raiders."

"Let us flee through the window," Alice said to me. "Take the horses and ride for Jaffa."

"They are already in the stables," I said, looking out. "I shall discover what is happening. Get dressed and wait here for me to return."

Fateful words but I believed them to be for the best.

Another scream pierced the night.

"They are in the hall," I said, guessing but sure I was right.

The children looked terrified, clinging to their mother.

"Let the men earn their keep," Alice said. "Stay with us."

"What kind of lord would I be if I allow thieves and robbers to attack us at will?" I said.

She hugged her children to her and nodded.

I ran back down the corridor. In my haste I had still not dressed.

A man in a black surcoat rounded the corridor. He carried a torch in one hand and a mace in the other.

It was Walter the Welshman. I knew him as a nasty piece of shit who terrorised the women and girls of Ashbury after William had brought him back from the Holy Land. As ugly as a man could be, with wens on his face and eyes as black as sin. His face was in shadow and flickering light from the torch that multiplied his hideousness. But I had seen him practice combat back in the yard at Duffield Castle before William had thrown us out and I recalled his speed and viciousness.

The mace in Walter's other hand glistened and had pieces of skin and hair stuck to the flanges.

Shouts echoed and the screaming began again but this time it did not stop. It did come from the hall, beyond Walter. There was the clashing and ringing of weapons now. My men fighting the attackers.

If Walter was in my house then that meant William was too.

"That's right, boy," Walter laughed at the expression on my face. "He has come for you." Walter stood his ground blocking my way to the hall. "Fall to your knees now and welcome your fate. Come, Richard, come and feed the Angel of the Lord. Offer up your blood. Offer up the blood of your wife and children."

I leapt forward in a headlong charge but he was expecting to provoke me so I checked my forward motion and ducked under his mace. Fighting had always been easy for me but Walter was faster than any man I had faced. Only by the grace of God did the weapon skim through my hair to smash through the wall plaster above my head.

My sword flicked up into his face but he was so fast. He weaved sideways, dropped his mace and stepped forward while drawing a knife that he slashed low toward my guts and balls. But I was fast, too. And I was unencumbered, young and filled with hatred and vengeance. I twisted from his lunge, stepping sideways to smash my blade into his forearm shattering his bones through the mail. His weight carried him forward while I stepped beyond him. I reversed my sword and ran him through at the base of the spine. I forced my blade through his mail coat so hard the point ran deep into the plaster and pinned him face forward to the wall.

Swooping up his dagger I held the point against his neck under the ear.

"How many are you?" I said, breathing hard. "Are my horses guarded?"

From the cries coming through the walls, my fighting men sounded desperate. I had merely four and one was a boy and one an old man and I knew that they could do nothing more than delay William's men who were brutal, experienced warriors.

"He has come for you," Walter said. "Earl William will feast upon your flesh. You are the cup and he shall drink of you."

"My horses," I said, hissing in his ear. "How many men guard my stable?"

Walter laughed. "We shall cover the earth with our numbers. You will become one of us or you shall feed us. And you shall eat the flesh of your sons and the flesh of your daughters. And all shall eat the flesh of their neighbours. For he is the Destroyer, the Angel of the—"

I punched the dagger into the base of his skull – a quicker death than he deserved – and pulled my sword out. Walter collapsed, his dead eyes staring at the Hell that awaited him.

William had come. No doubt there were men in my stable. Unless William had left such a menial task for Hugo the Giant or a gifted swordsman like Roger of Tyre then I would be able to take our horses.

But would I have time to saddle two of them and would Alice and I be able to outrun William's men all the way back to Jaffa? We would have a child each on our horse and it was a long ride. Our horses would tire or die if we rode hard all the way. And galloping through the moonlight could cause a horse to trip and even a single fall would mean death. I imagined sending Alice with Emma and Jocelyn on his pony off while I kept William's men fighting but they could have run her down easily while keeping me from leaving.

Perhaps I should have gone back to our room to say farewell to Alice and the children. We could have spent our last few moments together instead of leaving them alone and waiting for a man who would never come.

There seemed to be only one course of action. So I went toward the sound of the screaming with my sword at the ready, fantasising that I might finally have my vengeance.

My hall was where we ate, as a household, and where some of the servants slept. It was where I spoke to my tenants and it was rather finely decorated, though Alice assured me it was terribly old-fashioned. It was the beating heart of our home and our estate and it was an almost sacred space.

I found it full of blood and death. Because of the clashing weapons and shouts and screams I expected to find my four men valiantly facing off against William's knights.

Instead, the fighting was over. Two of my men had been cut into bloody pieces and scattered about the floor, blood soaking into the rushes. The other two men were panting and bleeding from head wounds surrounded by half a dozen of William's armoured men who were prodding and jeering at them. I did not recognise William's new men. They were all were in hauberks or the shorter haubergeons and carrying swords, daggers, falchions and axes and a spear.

It was like watching bear baiting. My men were barely defending themselves, resigned to their fate. They were already bleeding to death so they had every right to be. The clanging of weapons was no doubt to encourage me to come running.

Eight of my servants lay bound and beaten on the floor at the centre of the hall by the cold hearth. Ralph the Reaper was torturing them by slashing the soles of their feet into bloody ribbons. The cook and his girl had been murdered. The others were groaning and screaming in pain and terror.

And there was William.

Standing at the head of my hall as if he owned it, leaning against my table. He was in a half-rusted hauberk and helmet. The surcoat covering his mail was of fine cloth dyed red though it was filthy and stained all over with the brown mottled pattern of old blood. His face lit up with a smile when he saw me.

"I told you he would come," William cried, clapping his hands together. "What a fine knight you are, Richard, to come save these worthless peasants rather than finish swyving your whore." He laughed heartily, looking down at my nakedness. His men, too, laughed and stood staring at me, no longer tormenting my own.

All together there were eight of William's men. Ralph the Reaper standing over my servants, the six armed and armoured men tormenting my men and William himself standing tall and terrible at the far end beyond his men.

My two men leaned upon each other breathing heavily. Neither could provide me with help in a fight. The servants would be worse than useless. Those that were not tied up in the hall were probably already dead.

I regretted not riding hard for Jaffa with Alice. Perhaps there was yet time, I thought, and edged backward toward the corridor.

"You cannot run," William said, as if he was disappointed in me. He stalked forward with his sword still sheathed at his hip. "My men have your horses. They are praying for you to make an attempt for them."

I wanted to scream in frustration. "There is no need for you to do this," I said.

William stopped, his face a mask of pretended shock. "No need? Need? What need have you to ask after me through all the towns and cities of Outremer? Well, seek me no longer for here I am." He flung his arms wide. "So, you want to kill me, Richard?"

"I seek you no longer," I said and he scoffed. Some of his men chuckled. "You murdered my brother and his family. And so many others. I swore to bring you to justice. But I gave up my search. I would never have bothered you again."

"Truly?" William asked, as if he was surprised. "But why would you give up your duty to your dear brother?" He spat out the last word as if the taste of it were repulsive.

I did not want to speak to William of my happiness. "I gave up," I said.

"Ah," William said, nodding to his men as if everything made sense now. "So you are suggesting that I allow you to live because you are incompetent? Or because you are lazy?" His men laughed. Ralph the Reaper cackled like a madman.

"Leave us in peace," I hefted the war sword in my right hand and Walter's dagger in my left. "Save yourself the trouble."

"But trouble is what we are here for, brother," William said and laughed. Again, his men laughed with him. He sighed. "I hoped for a long time that you and I could become friends."

William nodded at his six men. They hacked my men down with brutal efficiency. Neither men had time to utter a sound before they were dead. William's new soldiers spread out away from the bodies. They encircled me to cut me off from the corridor behind.

I recalled Henry's body, beheaded, dismembered. His torso laying upon a jumble of shit-stinking guts trailing from a great black wound slashed from hip to hip.

The men were grim. Their eyes had the dead gaze of those that who have seen too much of war.

Doing the unexpected in a fight can often keep you alive. Nevertheless, when I darted forward, stark naked, into the centre of those six battle-hardened, armoured men I knew I was charging to my death.

Speed was the single advantage I had. Or so I thought.

William bellowed a warning but by then I was already upon the two men in the centre of the curving line of six. The one on the right held a spear that I could get inside the reach of. He had time enough to raise it and step back once before I was beyond the head of it and I stabbed the point of my sword through the bridge of his nose. He fell back, screaming and dying, his spear flung away clattering on the floor and my blade was already out and moving, my feet carrying me away from the attack I sensed coming.

The man next to the spearman swung his mace back handed, round in an arc and upwards to smash the side of my jaw but I leaned down so it whooshed over my ear and I stabbed my long blade through his unarmoured knee. Crunching through the joint, my blade scraped on the edges of the bones. I moved forward to finish him but the others were closing so I danced back out of the way.

From nowhere, Ralph the Reaper was there at my elbow and he slashed overarm with a wicked curved dagger. By God, he was fast. Too fast for me to even flinch and it sliced deep into my skin along my bare upper arm before I could pull away. I snarled and lunged at him. For I was fast, too, and in his panic to retreat he tripped over the bound servants underfoot. Ralph fell amongst them and I kicked the knife over in desperate hope any servant could free themselves and skipped away across the room from the other knights moving up behind me.

Too late I realised how they had herded me away from the hall entrance. I watched aghast as William slipped into the corridor that lead to my bed chamber.

He was going for Alice.

I moved to chase him but those men moved like cats pouncing and they cut me off, weapons up.

"Alice!" I bellowed. "Alice, run!"

The one chance I had was to cut through them but when I charged forward they backed away leaving two men covering the corridor doorway, where William had gone. There was no way through. When I advanced on them I exposed my back to the others and spun to deflect the blows aimed at my back. Every man there was faster than they had a right to be. I barely got back into the hall without being gutted.

Ralph the Reaper regained his feet and joined them so there were five around me plus the man wounded in the knee who stayed down, groaning and bleeding near the servants who were crawling back out of the way leaving trails of blood from their slashed feet.

I had to save Alice.

I barrelled toward the one with an axe and as he scurried back he stumbled on the severed arm of one of my men and fell. I was on him and slashed down on his helmet so hard it bent the steel and I stomped my heel down on his face hard, hoping he would choke on his teeth. The bones of his face cut my foot open but I hardly felt it as I ducked away from the others and swung my blade at one who came too close. I was surprised to feel the edge of my blade crush that man's throat and he went down without uttering a noise and suffocated, his heels drumming upon the floor.

Three, now. Three men who waited calmly for me to come to them. Two stood between me and Alice and they knew all they had to do was keep me in the hall rather than fight me. Ralph the Reaper stood to one side, grinning.

Alice screamed. It was a cry of anguish and anger and it was the worst sound I ever heard.

I charged forward for the doorway. The two in front closed in on me and I checked my dash, meaning to duck to one side and force one man into the other to get around them.

But the blood welling from my wounded heel caused my foot to slip and my leading leg slid forward. A deep-down reflex caused me to throw my arms out wide to keep my balance and I watched in surprise as one of the men ran me through with his sword.

It was like being punched in the stomach but I watched the point of the sword snick through the skin of my stomach and I could not stop myself from moving forward and down and it kept on pushing through until the cross guard slammed into my body.

Even back then when I was young, I had seen a great number of men killed. They often wore the same expression. One of shock and disbelief. As though every man was thinking the same thought in the moment he received a mortal wound. *This cannot be happening to me*. The fact that I was naked and could see precisely how the blade pushed the skin deep into the wound made the fact of my death inescapable. Yet I have no doubt I was wearing that very same expression when the man who had run his sword through my belly butted his helm into my face and the blow crushed my nose and knocked me out.

A wound of such severity as impalement by a thirty-inch sword is a significant shock for the body. But was nothing to what I felt when I was slapped awake.

Two of William's men held me upright, while Ralph the Reaper stood to one side held a dagger to my throat. My blood was flowing from my wound to soak my stomach, loins and legs in shining dark blood.

Before me, both facing me; William stood behind Alice, towering over her. He held her upright with mailed fists digging tight into the bare flesh of her upper arms.

The children lay sobbing on the floor next to her, both had been struck and Jocelyn had been beaten bloody. Both were scarcely conscious. The boy, especially seemed badly hurt.

Alice's eyes were filled with tears and hatred. Hatred for William and the men in her hall. And, I am sure, hatred for me for bringing them down upon her and her children.

"You cannot die yet, Richard," William cried as I blinked away tears. "You must witness me feast upon your wife. For the Lord God has commanded me to eat the flesh of a thousand women. And He has commanded me to eat the flesh of their sons and the flesh of their daughters. And when the time is come, all men shall eat the flesh of their neighbours and devote to destruction all that they have. Do not spare them, He has commanded, but kill both man and woman, child and infant, ox and sheep, camel and donkey. You mortals shall present your bodies to me as living sacrifice. The old has passed away. Behold, the new has come. I am the resurrection and the life. Whomsoever feeds me with their flesh, though he die, yet shall he live in me, and everyone who lives and feeds me shall never die but help me grow stronger with every feast of living flesh from this day until the coming end of days."

He bared his teeth like a rabid dog and threw down his jaws upon Alice's neck. She screamed and writhed but William's fingers dug into her and blood welled from her throat and flowed down her shift. Emma screamed and buried her face against her brother's chest.

The men holding me had the kind of strength that only seasoned warriors can ever obtain. An iron steadiness that comes after years of holding up a shield and swinging a sword every day while wearing heavy armour. I had lost pints of blood and more pumped steadily from my guts. My face was mangled so much I struggled to draw breath.

But rage filled my arms with strength.

I roared and grabbed the men who held me and heaved backwards and down, leaning back from Ralph's dagger and rowing backward with my arms to drag them down off their feet with me. Their animal instinct took over and they released my arms to brace their fall. The pain of hitting the floor took my breath away but they were caught off guard and were wearing armour so fell heavier than I did.

The man on my right twisted away and fell out of reach but the one of the left was laying half under me. I reached across his body and drew the sword from his scabbard. In the same motion I swung it back hand over and down into the other man's face so the edge cracked through his skull across the eye sockets, crushing his eyes and face into pulp. I dropped the sword, rolled over and pulled that man's dagger from his waist and rolled back to thrust it into the other man's temple. It ground against bone and my hands were too weak and slippery with blood to free the blade.

As I struggled, Ralph the Reaper leapt on top of me, straddling my hips, laughing like a maniac. He stabbed me once, twice and a third time in the chest before I could grab the back of his head with one hand and punch my thumb into his eyeball, bursting it.

He screamed and dropped his dagger to hold his destroyed eye socket. I grabbed his dagger and hacked into the veins of his neck, drenching me with hot blood as he flopped onto me in panic, not realising that he was already dead. The blood gushing from his neck spewed into my face and into my mouth and I could not avoid swallowing many mouthfuls of his blood before I pushed his body off me. I felt the hot liquid sliding down my throat and the warmth of it churned in my stomach. I wiped it from my eyes.

It was not until later that I discovered that ingesting human blood heals my body. Perhaps it was Ralph's blood that gave me the strength to stand after being stabbed repeatedly in the lungs. But all I knew was that instead of dying I was able to climb to my feet.

Alice still held upright by William but was drenched with her own blood and her head was flopped forward. Her hair hung wet with blood in ribbons over her face. She seemed dead.

William looked up, his face dripping with my wife's blood. His eyes were wide and he dropped Alice to the ground. She fell heavily and her head cracked into the floor by her children. She lay still.

William backed away from her, drawing his sword.

"How is it that you yet stand?" William's voice sounded far away. He gestured at my chest, my guts. "You should be dead."

I took a step toward him. "Not until..." I started to say until blood welled up from my lungs and choked me. I could not take a breath. My head swam and I fell to one knee but I forced myself to my feet.

William lowered the point of his sword, his head tilted to one side as he regarded me.

I lunged forward, waving my dagger at him.

William scoffed and backed away to the door.

"I think that you will die," William said to me, hesitantly.

My vision blurred and I dropped to one knee, leaning on it. My head dropped and I could see the state of my chest and gut, with blood weeping from my body. The chest wounds bubbled and sucked with air. It was not possible that I lived.

Two men came into the hall from outside and William spoke to them but I was dying and my sight and hearing were failing. One of the men I am sure was Hugo the Giant. They stooped to the floor and carried things away with them.

I hauled myself upright and opened my mouth to curse him but blood ran from my lips and I coughed and fought for breath. It was as though my chest had iron bands around it.

William laughed and stepped backwards into the doorway that lead outside into the night. Was he afraid of me?

I sank to one knee again. William was just a streak of colour in my blurring vision. The darkness crept inward from the outside.

"I will not desecrate your corpse," William's shape said to me before he vanished. "I will leave some of your servants to bury you. I owe you that much."

I inched across the floor to my wife. Alice was dead. Her eyes stared up, empty of life yet filled with accusation.

Jocelyn and Emma were gone. William had taken her children.

I drowned in blood.

7

Rebirth

I AWOKE TO SCREAMS AND CONFUSED FACES. Then I slept and woke and slept.

Light speared through the shuttered windows across my bed and onto the blankets that covered me. Alice was not next to me and then I remembered and I despaired.

Servants clattered and banged in the house and out in the stables. Someone was sawing wood. There was the regular thwack of a pick digging into the hard earth.

I slid from my bed and stood. Someone had dressed me in a clean, long loose shirt. I pulled it off to inspect my wounds.

My body was healed. There was not a scratch upon the skin of my chest or my stomach. Not even a scar.

In fact, I felt strong, fast, and more alert than I ever had before.

Opening the shutters, the sun bathed me in heat. It felt glorious. My skin was alive with the light and the warm wind blew upon my face.

It was all so strange that I held on to a faint hope that it had all been a nightmare. Pulling on my shirt I walked to my hall.

In the corridor there was the damage to the wall from my duel with Walter and a huge blood stain. When I walked into the hall itself my servants stopped washing the floor and came toward me and fell to their knees.

It had not been a nightmare.

For a time I kept to my bed and drank wine. Someone sent a physician from Jaffa and I had to growl and threaten to stop him from examining my body. Because he did not know what else to do he looked closely at my urine. I would not let him bleed me.

A few days later the King himself came to visit me.

"The physician tells me that you died," Richard of England said, standing over my bed, his fair hair filled with golden light from the window.

"That tells you everything you need to know about physicians."

That made him laugh. "God save us from the pissprophets. They will be the death of us all. Still, you were pierced through the chest many times. Your servants were actually burying you when you took a breath. Scared the life right out of the poor bastards." He laughed again. He was nervous.

"So I heard," I said.

The survivors of the attack had told me and everyone else what a miracle my survival was. The ones who had been tied up in the hall had seen me kill most of the enemy. In their eyes I had driven William and the rest away.

My grave had already been dug, set apart from the graves of my servants as was proper, when I sat up.

"God must have plans for you on earth," King Richard said, with the confidence of a man who had been so honoured since the moment that his father's seed had quickened in his mother's womb.

"Perhaps He did not want me in Heaven," I said, morose and unappreciative that the most lauded king of Christendom had taken the time to travel to my estate and was being kind and generous to me. His guards lurked in the background and I could feel their silent displeasure radiating across the room.

"Come with me to England," Richard said, sitting upon the bed next to my legs. "My dear little brother is being rather troublesome and I need good men with me to put things right." His eyes took on a faraway look. "In truth, there is trouble in many of my lands. Plenty of work for a man of your abilities. And evident gifts."

"Why would you want me?" I said, ungraciously.

Richard was not a man to be trifled with and for a moment I saw his face cloud with anger. But then he smiled.

"There is no man I would rather have by my side in battle," Richard the Lionheart said to me. This remains one of the finest compliments I ever had.

"And besides," he leaned over and punched a fist into my shoulder as if making a joke. "You recover from wounds that would kill a bull. Perhaps you can teach me your secret." He coughed to cover his embarrassment at his clumsy joke but of course he was intrigued by my recovery.

"I have a task, my lord," I said, embarrassed by his affection. "One I should have completed long ago."

He shrugged. "I have left instructions for Henry. I am certain that you heard how my nephew Henry has married the queen of Jerusalem. That means he is now the king and the most powerful Christian in the Holy Land. Once I am gone. Henry will provide you with guides and men. After all, it is in their interest to round up such a villain. You shall finally bring William de Ferrers to justice. I simply regret I shall not be able to witness his punishment."

"I am honoured by your confidence in me, my lord." The king still did not understand the depths of William's evil.

When you are done, you will join me in England then I shall find you a new... a suitable estate. You could hold William's lands. It should probably be yours anyway, I am sure and perhaps I could make it official. What would you say to that, Richard? Duffield Castle and all the rest."

I had an inkling that Richard was one of those men who would promise things he did not mean, especially to strong young men he held in high esteem. There were always rumours that he was a secret sodomite. And perhaps he was but he seemed to me to simply be full of passion, not lust. His enthusiasm consumed him and he esteemed soldiers very highly indeed, so long as they were useful.

Perhaps he truly did believe I knew how to cheat death. Either way, there was no chance he would pass over greater lords to grant the likes of me such a vast estate.

"Thank you, my lord," I said. "That is very generous of you."

"With the invincible Richard of Ashbury at my side, I shall conquer all who stand against me, shall I not?" Everything that man said was spoken with such absolute confidence that I could never be sure when he was speaking with sincerity or in jest.

"You shall, lord." I muttered.

He left for England the next day.

I never saw him again.

While I was lying dead myself I had missed Alice's burial. She had been taken to a family crypt in Jaffa. Her cousins told my servants in no uncertain terms that my body could be tossed down a well in the desert for all they cared. And thank God her family were ungenerous bastards or I might have woken in a coffin, inside a lead box locked in a crypt. Her family in Jaffa shut their doors to me. As well as losing Alice they had lost Jocelyn, who could have become a lord. And they had lost sweet little Emma who would have made a good marriage to further the family's wealth and renown.

After setting my house in order, I rode to Acre to meet with Henry de Champagne. A king by marriage only, he never referred to himself as King of Jerusalem in part because we had lost the city after Hattin.

The king, Richard had told me, would help me hunt William. He would put all the power of Outremer at my disposal. I knew I would need gold and silver for bribes to discover where he was hiding and guides to take me there. And I would need at least a dozen good knights with horses and remounts, fully equipped and supplied.

"I cannot provide you with men," Henry of Champagne said over his shoulder while his armourer measured his limbs with string.

We were at his palace in Acre. It was still a new home for him so his knights and attendants were everywhere on hand to ensure he made it his own. The palace was beautiful but I had been shown through up to the top of it where the king had his apartments. The queen was nowhere to be seen and she was rarely spoken of. Once, she had been powerful and beautiful. But I am sure that for Henry she was nothing more than a tool to make him king.

Henry stood in the good light pouring in from the huge open sides of the room, most of which opened onto balconies and so the sea wind could flow in from three sides of the room and keep the royal person cool while in the city below the people roasted and gasped in the airless streets. Beyond the windows the sea was so blue it hurt my eyes.

A long table ran the length of the wall, covered in the armourer's measuring tools and many examples of his fine work. Next to me lay rows of helmets polished to such a gleam that I could see my distorted reflection in them.

It was an informal audience. That meant I had been forced to wait for days in the city before Henry allowed me inside, then made me wait all morning on a bench outside his chambers and then when I was hurried inside he hardly acknowledged my existence.

No doubt he felt duty bound to see me, as his uncle had insisted. Henry owed his kingly position entirely to Richard's political manoeuvring and, so rumour said, a paid assassination. But our joint benefactor had sailed for Europe and Henry was too busy picking out his new royal armour to bother overly much with me.

"I understand, my lord," I said. What else could I say? He was my liege lord.

"Well, I'm not giving you money, either," he muttered. He was not much older than me but he was a big, burly man and filled with royal authority. "How much longer will this take?" This was directed at the arthritic armourer who was mumbling measurements to his assistants.

"Almost done, my lord king, but perfection takes time, you understand. Your armour will be impenetrable only so long as the fit is perfection itself. No weapon shall harm you, I swear it. You shall be invulnerable upon the battlefield, impervious to blade or—"

"Yes, yes, just get on with it," Henry said, then glanced over his shoulder at me again. "So if you do not want men or money, what in God's name do you want?"

In fact, I did want men and money and had fully expected plenty of both. I resisted the urge to shove King Henry out of his God damned window.

"Information, my lord," I said, resigning myself to lower expectations. "Introduction to men who know lands where William is rumoured to be hiding. Having spoken to many people while I awaited this audience, I suspect he is hiding beyond Outremer. Possibly in an abandoned fortress somewhere in the desert. If that is in fact where he is I shall also need to approach the Saracens who control the land near there. You, my lord king, could perhaps request peaceful passage through those lands."

"Yes, yes, of course he is. It sounds like a lot of bother to go through, does it not?" Henry said, without looking me in the eye. "I think we should let the Saracens kill him. We know that he's gone to ground half way to Damascus. He won't last long up there with those heathens roaming about. He will be dead before the year is out, mark my words. Probably best to forget about William and be on your way."

I fought down my urge to grab one of the helmets from the table and smash his idiot face in. I kept my voice level. "Are you saying that you know that is where William is?"

He hesitated then wafted away my question. "I am saying that you need take no action for William to be killed. He shall not live to see Christmas, I have no doubt."

"I must perform the task with my own hand," I said, stiffly. "I swore an oath, my lord. It must be fulfilled."

"Yes, yes, your famous oath. Is there anyone in Outremer who has not heard of it? Dear me, what a chivalrous man you are."

I ground my teeth, lest I sink them into his face.

At least he had the good grace to appear embarrassed when he turned around and saw the look in my eyes. Embarrassed or fearful, perhaps. "That is to say, I heard what he did to your wife, of course. A terrible thing. An unholy thing. I had the honour of meeting her merely twice but she struck me as a remarkable lady."

"She was, my lord."

"Still, she's in a better place now, I don't doubt," Henry muttered.

I looked out to sea while the armourer finished his measuring and bowed and made further promises that Henry waved away.

A servant brought Henry wine and the king walked to the open window that looked out to that brilliant blue sea beyond. Wine was not offered to me.

"I wish I could help you," Henry said without looking at me. "But if I send my knights into Saladin's lands so soon after the peace treaty is signed then I could start another war."

"I have no quarrel with any Saracen," I said.

Henry glanced over at me and chuckled. "Do not let God hear you say such a thing."

"I fought to regain the Kingdom of Jerusalem, sire," I said. I was willing to act humble if it meant getting what I needed. "I would never do anything to endanger the peace. But the treaty does allow travel by pilgrims and traders, does it not? I would pretend to be a merchant looking to buy spices, perhaps."

He turned and leaned on the railing that ran across the window. It creaked under his weight.

"You do not have the disposition required for deceit," he said. "And you could never pass for a merchant."

I did not know whether to be offended or feel complimented so I said nothing.

"So," the king said. "Tell me truthfully. If I tell you that I will not only provide you with no support but that I expressly forbid you to travel into Saracen land, what would you do?"

I took a deep breath and said nothing.

"You would go anyway," Henry said. "You would disobey your king for the sake of your oath."

It was pointless to object.

"So you leave me with a decision to make, Richard," Henry said, talking down to me as if he had gained wisdom along with his kingdom, though he and I were of an age. "Should I throw you in gaol now, before you can start a war?"

He watched my face carefully for a reaction. "I would pray that you not do so, my lord," I managed to say.

"If I took such an action against most of my knights then his family and friends would pressure me to release him. After all, you have committed no crime. But you, I am sad to say, have no friends or family."

He was goading me but I did not know why. "I have friends," I said.

Henry sighed. "You are a difficult man to know, Richard. I think most men are afraid of you."

"Of me?" I was shocked.

"Many of us have seen you fight," Henry said. "And some men are afraid that you will be like William."

"What in God's name do you mean? Why would any man think that?"

Henry looked alarmed and held up his hands. "Of course I know you are a decent man. But you make others nervous."

"What is your point?" I said. "My lord."

Henry let out a breath and leaned on the window railing again. "If I was a ruthless king then I would lock you up until William gets himself killed." He left the words hanging between us before continuing. "I wonder what dear Uncle Richard would do in my position."

I reckoned that if he thought it would serve his interests Richard would have me quietly killed. "He would give me men and pray God grant strength to my arm, my lord."

Henry looked uncomfortable and he hesitated for a long while. "The Archbishop of Tyre has an Egyptian priest. This Egyptian has been in the city for some days now. He claims to know where William is hiding."

It took a moment for me to respond. "Why not tell me this immediately?" I said, my irritation no doubt apparent for he threw me a warning look. "My lord." I was ready to walk out and find the priest myself.

But Henry smiled and turned back to the view. Ships bobbed in the harbour, bringing wealth from everywhere in the world into Henry's kingdom. No wonder he could not stop looking at it.

"I have no way of knowing this Egyptian's true intent," he said. "Perhaps he is telling the truth and William is preying upon locals and travellers but if that is so, why do the Saracens not clear William out of his refuge?"

"What does this Egyptian priest say to that?"

"He says that Saladin wants the Franks to deal with the Frankish demon," Henry scoffed. "The Archbishop tells me he pressed the old man and he admitted that the Saracens are wary of him. Can you credit such a thing, Richard? Saladin afraid of William de Ferrers and a handful of outlawed knights and bandits? Absurd."

I could well believe it so I said nothing.

Henry held out his cup for more wine. "But what if Saladin is baiting a trap for us? Perhaps, Saladin has been waiting for King Richard to sail home and now he wishes to provoke me into sending my knights into Saracen lands and so breach the peace."

"But if you send me out there with just a man or two then you could always deny you had knowledge of my actions," I said.

Henry drank his wine. "If you are captured by the enemy in such circumstances I would be unable to pay your ransom."

I actually laughed, surprising everyone in the room including myself. "I do not expect I will be held for ransom, my lord."

"I suppose not," he allowed. "Draw up a letter for the Archbishop," Henry said to one of his servants. "Hand the Egyptian priest over to Richard of Ashbury and send them on their way into Palestine. Have the Archbishop pay for their supplies and horses and so on. And draw up a letter from me instructing Richard here to escort the priest back to Damascus. Make it very short and have the Latin translated into Arabic and added underneath. That way, Richard, if you are captured it looks better for me and for the kingdom."

"I understand. And thank you, my lord," I said and I meant it.

"I pray God gives strength to your arm," Henry the King of Jerusalem said. "Truly, Richard. I will pray for you."

"An unholy mess," the Archbishop of Tyre said to me as he led me through his palace in Acre. One of his men escorted us. "Your Earl William has put us in rather a difficult situation."

The Archbishop had the Coptic priest locked away in a room on the third floor of the tower of the Archbishop's Palace and I walked through those cool corridors and up the stairs. There were old, cracked pictures painted upon many of the walls that showed many figures frozen in action that must have once been brightly coloured but had now faded.

"Yes, Archbishop," I replied, not sure what he wanted me to say.

"Preying upon honest pilgrims and travellers," the Archbishop said. "Something must be done."

He was an old man and he was not tall or broad and yet he possessed a great moral authority and he walked briskly. He had been the Archbishop for a long time. I knew his name was Joscius but no one would have ever called him anything other than Archbishop.

"Yes, Archbishop."

"I would rather not be involved in this," he said to me, conspiratorially. "But I feel a certain responsibility for the situation."

I could not imagine why he would feel such a thing. "Yes, Archbishop."

"So it would be a welcome relief if you could help us. I would be rid of this priest," the

Archbishop explained. "And you can take him off my hands."

"I will take him as my guide with a glad heart," I said. "But if you have wanted to rid of him, my lord Archbishop, why have you kept him locked up?"

"I told you why," the Archbishop said, his voice flailing me. "Something must done about Earl William."

"William must die," I said, nodding.

The Archbishop sighed. "I wish it were not so." He stopped outside a heavy door. "But I fear you are correct," he said, peering up at me. "In here."

He invited me to peer through the viewing slot. It was not a gaol cell but a comfortable room. There was a bed and a table and a high, slit window showing a streak of brilliant blue. The priest lay upon the bed, evidently sleeping and shrouded in a sheet.

"You tortured him?" I asked the Archbishop before we went in.

He frowned. "Of course not. We simply asked him some questions."

"You trust his answers?"

The Archbishop sighed. "My men have made enquiries. He is known in these parts. They tell me that for a long time he was a hermit in the Sinai and a few years ago he left the desert and travelled through Outremer, administering to the local Christians. His touch was said to be holy and he lived on charity. He tells me he has been in Damascus, living happily enough under the Saracens and seeing to the poor Christian souls there. Did you know there are thousands of them there? My men found someone who knew him and brought the fellow here. He confirmed this was Antonius of the Sinai."

"So, forgive me, Archbishop but why lock him up?"

The Archbishop gave me a long look. "Perhaps the desert addled his brains. He certainly looks as shrivelled as a dried date. But he argues with himself when alone."

I shrugged. "Just because he is mad, does not mean he is a liar."

"Indeed not. But I am uncertain of his trustworthiness. And you should be too. Shall we go in?"

It was fairly clean. Even the nightsoil bucket was empty.

"My Lord Archbishop," the little old man said as he sat up. He had very dark skin, wrinkled and tough and shiny like the bark of an ancient tree. When his startlingly blue eyes flicked over my face I saw a glint of surprise in them.

"Antonius, this is Richard of Ashbury," the Archbishop said. "He has come to ask you some questions."

"More questions? Why do you Franks always have so many questions?" Antonius asked, his French heavily accented but otherwise faultless.

"Where is William?" I asked.

"I told the Archbishop's men," he said, looking to the Archbishop. The Archbishop said nothing and shuffled away toward the narrow window. "But I would very much enjoy telling you all over again."

"So where is he?"

"The hills of Golan," the priest said. "North of the Sea of Galilee."

"Where exactly?" I said.

He looked surprised. "I do not know where they are hiding. No one knows. The Saracens know simply the rough area where men disappear."

"Why do the Saracens not hunt him down? Their access to Jaffa from Damascus is almost cut off by William's raids on the merchants. Surely they want to end him? They certainly have the means."

Antonius shrugged his little sparrow shoulders. "They sent men. But the demons melt into the hills and cannot be found. And also, Lord William is a Christian baron of Tripoli. Perhaps if the Saracens were to kill him, your king Henry would see this as a betrayal of the treaty and use it as an excuse to start a war? Perhaps, some in Damascus say, the Baron William is there with the support of the king?"

The Archbishop spun around. "That is a lie. We do not condone this monster's actions. We want peace. We want trade and we want pilgrimage to Jerusalem. William is an outlaw."

The little priest spread his hands. "It is not I that says this. I tell you merely why perhaps Saladin does not wish to solve the Frank's problem."

"You are willing to lead me to the area?" I asked him.

Antonius shrugged. "Very well. Perhaps I shall take you to where they were last seen. But then I shall continue home upon the Damascus road."

"I will let you go when I find William," I said to Antonius. "If we do not find him then I shall bring you back here."

The priest opened his mouth to argue, looked between me and the Archbishop and closed his mouth. It was curious that he did not object further to such unreasonable treatment.

The Archbishop looked at me.

"He'll do," I said.

"Come," the Archbishop said and we left the priest's cell, leaving him sitting on the bed with his skinny legs dangling off the edge like some ancient child. "You shall be released into this man's custody soon. I suggest you spend the time praying."

The Archbishop's man slammed and locked the door behind us.

"What do you think?" the Archbishop asked me in the corridor.

"I do not know," I said.

The Archbishop nodded. "Good."

I do not trust you either, I thought. "If he can bring me near to William then that will do well enough," I said. "King Henry said you would give me men," I said to the Archbishop.

"He did, did he?" The Archbishop said. "Well, I suppose you can take Adelard, here." He gestured to his man, who looked surprised and then silently furious, his face colouring and his jaw tensing.

"Thank you, my lord Archbishop. The king said I could take four men," I lied.

The Archbishop scowled. "Adelard, who is your best man?"

Adelard, an older man who looked sturdy and steady but angry, cleared his throat.

"Young Elias."

The Archbishop nodded. "You can have my two best men and you will be grateful for that much."

"I am, my lord Archbishop," I said, thinking about some of the taverns where I could hire more men.

I thought I would be escorted out yet the Archbishop hesitated. "You may wonder why I take such an interest in this situation," he said.

"Because God wants peace?" I said.

A flicker of irritation passed over his face and he walked back the way we had arrived, his heels echoing down corridor. Me and his man Adelard hurried to catch up and he continued. "After the Battle of Hattin, Earl William came to see me. He felt he had experienced a profound revelation."

"You knew William?" I was shocked.

He ignored me as he stepped into the spiral tower steps and instead of going down the way we had come, he went up and I followed, wondering what in God's name the Archbishop had to tell me about William.

"Let us converse in here," he gestured me into a lavish room near the top of the tower. The room opened to a balcony on one side with views out across the compact city and the sea beyond. There was a silver cross on the wall and a large golden cross with jewels embedded upon a table by one wall and decorated in an ornate, almost Saracen style with colourful and richly patterned carpets and cushions. I took the seat he invited me to take; a delicate chair carved with curving olive leaves near the balcony and watched him ease his old bones into a huge, gold leafed thing like a throne opposite me. He let out a huge sigh, wincing a little and when he was settled he closed his eyes for a moment and I wondered if he was going to fall asleep.

"So you knew William, my lord?" I asked.

His eyes snapped open and he sighed again. "Speaking about these things brings me no joy. But there are things you must know."

A servant brought a jug of cold, sweet lemon water that he poured into silver cups. The Archbishop took a long drink and smacked his thin lips.

"Five years ago the largest Christian army ever assembled in this kingdom rode out from Jerusalem to meet Saladin. Foolish. Impetuous. I knew it would end in disaster but what warrior listens to an ancient, decrepit priest like me? Thousands of knights rode out from all over Outremer, with tens of thousands of soldiers in their wake, so certain that they would smash the Saracens. They were impressive as they marched off. Well, they all died. Thousands upon thousands of them slaughtered in the dust and the fools left Jerusalem emptied of men able to protect the Holy City. Those poor souls who could not escape Jerusalem, thousands of them, sold into slavery."

He shook his head. He had tears welling in his eyes. I stifled a sigh and settled into my seat.

"Then Jaffa and Acre fell and everything collapsed. We fell back from city after city. Those idiots threw away the Holy Land. Only thanks to King Richard of England have we regained some of what was lost."

"Yes, Archbishop," I said. "All Christendom has been awash with the tales."

His head snapped up. "The young are ever impatient. You rush toward death, never taking the time to appreciate where you are." He indicated the room around us and then the sea beyond the balcony.

I leaned forward. "I swore an oath to God to kill William. You want me to take that priest from you and kill William. If you have something to tell me about William that will help me do my duty to God, please do so, my lord Archbishop."

The servant poured the old man another cup of the lemon water while he regarded me with a look I could not read. "Did you know William's wife and son were killed?"

"William was married?" It took a moment for my mind to adjust. "I never knew he took a wife. And he had a son?"

"A babe in arms. They were murdered, in the madness that followed after Hattin." He looked at me strangely, carefully, judging my reaction.

"But I thought Saladin enslaved the Christians of Jerusalem. Not killed them."

The Archbishop nodded. "It was not the Saracens but Frankish knights who murdered them." He sighed. "It was a very bad time. There was no law. The survivors of the battle fled in front of the Saracens as fast as their stolen horses could carry them. Homes were looted and people were killed."

"William survived the attack?"

"William was laying among the dead at Hattin when it happened. He knew nothing of the murder when he came to me, back from the dead, filthy and stinking but filled with the light of the Lord."

"I have suspected that his madness began at Hattin."

The Archbishop shook his head. "He was struck down in the battle and thrown into a mound of Christian dead. William lay in that mountain of death for two days, dying. He told me he had a vision of God. There was a bright light, warm and peaceful but instead of welcoming William into Heaven God told him to drink. God told him to become the cup of Christ. So William drank the foul blood that was leaking down onto him from the men above and around him. And that blood gave him strength enough to push his way out and rise up to fight his way clear, killing forty Saracens and stealing a horse and returning to me ahead of Saladin's forces."

"Forty Saracens? I wonder that you did not lock him in a dungeon for such ravings."

"It was a miracle. I told him as much." The Archbishop looked up at the ceiling. "You must understand that he seemed far from mad. He was filled with God, I tell you. Any man could have seen he was filled with joy, not madness. There was such vitality to him, such vigour and clarity. In the face of that terrible defeat I took it as a sign from God that there was yet hope. That the Christian kingdoms in the Holy Land would likewise return from the dead to take back what we lost."

"He has used that vigour to murder uncounted innocents."

"It was when he returned home to find his wife violated and murdered and infant son slain that he lost his mind. Can you imagine it? What would you think of God's plan, then? What man would not descend into madness?"

I stared at the Archbishop.

His face flushed and he looked horrified.

"Please accept my apologies," he said. "That was utterly thoughtless of me."

"Of course," I said, wiping my eyes. I looked out at the sky. "How was it that Christians killed his wife? Why?"

He coughed and looked up at the ceiling for a moment. "Perhaps they were stopping to steal horses or simply looking for coin to pay for passage home before Saladin came. When it feels as though the rule of law is ending, men can forget God and instead look to earthly things for their salvation. They gather to them jewels and trinkets. The base instinct overwhelms their fear of God, their reason and their trust in the law. Or perhaps there was another reason. William seemed certain there was. Only God knows."

"Who were they?"

"The leader was noble. The others were common soldiers and when William had recovered from the first shock of his grief he hunted them down. As I recall, the leader ran to hide in Aragon. William stayed to hunt down all the others one by one. His madness was growing and he gathered those other monsters to him. I am ashamed to say that I thanked God when they left Outremer, even though I knew they were just taking their evil elsewhere. I have few contacts back in France any longer so that was the last I heard of him until William returned and started this bloody madness again."

A coldness had tight hold of my heart but I forced myself to ask the question. "The name. The name of the leader of the men who murdered William's wife."

"Yes," the Archbishop said, grim and nodding. "I see that you now know."

"The name," I said through gritted teeth, my hands gripping the arms of the chair.

"The man who killed William's family was Henry of Ashbury."

On the second day from Acre we crossed into a great valley with high, rolling hills studded with dark green bushes and Antonius told us happily that we were on Saracen land. Most knights would have found such news to be disconcerting but we rode to find and kill William and his remaining men so the presence of a few thousand Saracens within a day's ride was of little concern.

"William drinks their blood, they say. He drinks it up and cuts their limbs from their bodies to better collect every drop." In the full light of the burning sun, Antonius the little

Egyptian priest was as shrivelled as a date. Riding beside me on the road, he looked at me and grinned as he spoke, revelling in the horror of our expressions.

"Stop speaking," Adelard said, riding behind us with Elias, who was the other of the Archbishop's men.

We rode through a land as hot and dry as an oven. The road from Acre to Damascus had until recently been well travelled and yet we were the only people anywhere within sight or sound. It was hot and there had been drought for months so we went easy on our horses. Even though we feared ambush, my two men and I rode without wearing our hauberks or helmets because of the heat. My shield was slung across my back and at least it shaded me a little.

The road wound down along the side of the valley, crossed the dry river and wound back and forth through the distant hills to disappear over the horizon. Antonius, the priest, claimed William was hiding out beyond those hills so my intention had been to make camp there. We rested in the shade of a cliff through the middle of the day and we would push deep into them during the night. The moon would be almost full so travelling should be easier and it would be cool enough to comfortably wear our armour.

I hoped to catch William unawares in the darkness.

"William is no man," Antonius said. "He may have been a man once but he has been transformed. I think he is some other kind of being, perhaps."

"You think he is a demon?" I asked. "Surely you do not think he is Satan."

Antonius scratched his face and sighed. "No. I certainly do not say that William is Satan. But Satan was once an angel, hurled down from Heaven. The fallen angel is said to have taken other angels with him and these are the demons. Some are bound in darkness in everlasting chains but others walk the earth doing Satan's bidding. They delight in torment and pain and seek to undo God's will on earth."

"My lord," Adelard said. "Do we have to listen to this nonsense?"

Antonius grinned at me and turned back to smile at Adelard, which was inviting a severe beating.

"My whole life I have paid little attention to the priests," I said to Adelard. "But recently I have become interested in some of the stories."

Adelard said nothing and I glanced back in time to catch him rolling his eyes at Elias.

"Tell me about the Destroyer," I said to Antonius who looked startled. "William's men have referred to their master as such. But I do not understand."

Antonius shifted in his saddle and hesitated. "The Destroyer is called Exterminans. In Greek he is Abaddon. The angel of the abyss."

"Another demon?"

"No," Antonius cried. "No. He is the Angel that does the Lord's divine will. The Destroyer was sent by God to bring the plagues to Egypt. Some say the Destroyer is God's most loyal, most powerful aspect. They say that the Christ was the Destroyer sent to earth to bring destruction to the heathens, to the unjust and the unworthy."

Adelard grunted. "I never heard nothing like it before."

I had to agree with him.

"We follow the true way," Antonius snapped. "In Egypt."

Adelard looked offended and contemptuous. Elias looked disturbed.

"Be quiet now, priest," I said to him. "I have heard more than enough of your nonsense."

I glanced back and my men were smiling again. It was important I keep them happy for they were the only help I would have out there in the hills.

I had intended to hire as many men as I could. But the Archbishop and King Henry put a stop to that.

The two men I did have were burly enough. Adelard was older, Elias was his wife's nephew. Both were experienced and though Adelard was painfully slow his timing was faultless. Elias was fast as a snake but forever forgetting to raise his shield and both I and Adelard easily rapped him upon the head when we had fought mock duels while our preparations were made.

Neither man was happy. They had survived the crusade and until I had come along both had faced a future of easy work. I wondered if they would stand with me.

I was lost inside my grief and thoughts of my brother Henry. Charming Henry, the apple of our father's eye, who had travelled to the Holy Land on a pilgrimage and there committed the murder of a woman and a child. At first I could hardly credit what the Archbishop had revealed but the more I considered it, the less it surprised me.

Memories of Henry bubbled to the surface. Powerful, hateful Henry punching me to the ground as children, standing over me and cursing me until he was red in the face. I could not remember his words but I could quite clearly recall the look of mad savagery in his eyes. What had I done, I wondered, to deserve such spite?

There had always been some sort of feud between Henry and William. Henry was destined to swear fealty to William, just as our fathers had sworn to the de Ferrers back to the Conquest when my grandfather's grandfather was raised up and granted the Saxon hall at Ashbury. Perhaps it had started because they were close in age and both were proud and prickly boys.

Both had gone to the Holy Land but that was not unusual, even outside of a crusade. I always knew something had happened between my father and my brother for Henry to have suddenly run off. Whatever it was, Henry had murdered Earl William's family halfway across the world.

Perhaps it had been mere chance. Henry was fleeing the Saracen army, looking for loot and it happened to be William's undefended home. Desperate men can do evil things.

Still, there seemed to be a secret just out of reach. A secret that I could solve if I remembered hard enough, thought clearly enough.

Something in the present had been nagging at my thoughts as we crossed the dry river bed by way of the ancient stone bridge. Only after we had begun climbing out of the valley to the east was it that I noticed how Antonius kept glancing off up the hill. There was nothing there but jumbles of rocks and spiky bushes, with the clear sky above.

"Something catching your eye, Antonius?" I asked him.

"Oh, no, my lord," he said, smoothly. "Merely enjoying my freedom once again. Being a guest of your Archbishop for such long time has made me appreciate God's creation even more."

"Adelard," I said to him over my shoulder as we rode slowly, our horses" heads lowered. "Do you think we are being watched?"

Adelard snorted. "What, you just realised, lord?" he said.

"What makes you so sure?" I asked. His scorn, absurdly, had wounded me.

Elias swivelled his head, wide-eyed at the hills about us.

"The people are gone," Adelard said. "Empty homes mile after mile. If they'd ran off when they saw us coming we'd see cooking fires smoking and smell food. There's no livestock, either. We'd hear the goats if there were any for miles. And we have seen no travellers upon this road for many a mile."

"I believe you," I said. "But why does that mean we are being watched?"

"Lord, if the locals are gone then who is kicking up the dust in front and to the south?"

I peered at the sky in those directions. Perhaps there was a touch more dust there than elsewhere but I would have to trust on Adelard's experience.

"You know these lands, Antonius," I said, watching him closely. "Are we in any danger?"

He rubbed a skeletal finger along his nose. "Perhaps we are," he said, as if he had no cares either way. "Perhaps William's men are waiting for us. The road is notorious for surprise attacks." He coughed. "Perhaps we could ride down into the valley and along the valley floor. There is a way out up there across the pass at the end."

I nodded and looked up the length of the winding valley. Far away at the head of the valley it rose up into an outcrop like the prow of a great ship, a flat deck at the top covered in rocks and scrub. Behind the flat area, the hill rose to a peak behind. It looked like a long, heavy climb.

"Perhaps," I said but the world had shifted again and I knew that the priest would have to be dealt with.

I kept us moving slowly with the rocky hills stretching above us on the right as it cut back and forth up the valley side. After a short while we rounded a cluster of huge boulders on the side of the road. My heart was racing at the thought of ambush waiting there but I had to deal with the priest. I pulled my horse up in the shade, shielded from view from anyone above. Antonius stopped further ahead and looked back.

"My horse is favouring a leg," I said, dismounting." I pulled my dagger and bent over, pulling a random hoof up. "A spine of some plant. In deep." I looked up at Adelard. "May as well dismount and rest, lads. Have a swig of Adam's Ale. I shall have to draw this slowly or I shall lame her."

Adelard and Elias were happy enough to stop but Antonius looked miserable. When a hot and thirsty man begrudges a few moments shade and a drink of water then something is very wrong indeed.

"Come soothe her while I draw it," I commanded the priest. He knew something was wrong but he came anyway.

I grabbed his scrawny shoulder, threw him against the wall of the boulder and put my dagger to his throat.

"What is waiting for us out there?" I said to him.

"How dare you?" Antonius said, as if he were baffled. "Take your filthy Frankish hands from me."

Adelard and Elias jumped to their feet. "Hold on to the horses," I told them. "Stay out of sight but watch both approaches."

They drew their swords and stood ready without a word.

I turned back to Antonius. "I will not ask again."

"The sun has baked your humours dry, lord," Antonius said, trying to grin. "Richard. My lord. I am a good Christian. I am helping you, yes?"

Perhaps my humours were dry but I knew he was lying. Was he in the pay of Saladin? Luring us into a trap to spark a war?

Whatever the truth, if I was ambushed and killed then William would go free and Alice, Isabella and their children and all the other innocents' deaths would go unpunished. Surely God would forgive anything I did in pursuit of my aim. He forgave Christians who killed Saracens for Christ so I was certain he would forgive me.

I slashed my dagger through his filthy, long robes. He flinched and chewed on his dry lips but held remarkably still while I cut and ripped a ragged strip of cloth from his sleeve and stuffed the lot into his mouth. He gagged repeatedly until I slapped him, hard.

His eyes were white all the way round and they swam out of focus from the blow to his head so I waited until they fixed upon me once more.

"I am afraid that I must cut into your flesh now, Antonius. I shall do this in the hope that you understand how much the success of this quest means to me," I explained. "And after I have cut into your flesh I shall remove this cloth from your mouth and then you shall explain to me what is waiting for us up in the hills here."

He began moaning, speaking with rapid hums from his throat.

"It's no good trying to talk now," I said, shaking my head as if I was heartbroken. "You had your chance. You can tell me all about it when I am done. I promise you that I take no joy in this and I regret its necessity immensely."

Taking my dagger, I sliced a deep cut along the outside of his forearm. He whimpered and shuddered as the sun-baked skin split aside to let the gloriously red blood well up and pour out along it. His eyes were wide as he stared at it dripping into the pale dust.

Next I cut into his left shoulder. There was no fat there. I cut through just skin and bone in a line from his collarbone right around to his shoulder blade. Blood gushed out. Antonius's breath was whistling in and out of his nostrils.

The third cut I sliced deep into the skin on his face under his left eye, opening it down to the cheekbone. He whimpered and shuddered as the blood welled and ran down in a steady stream.

I pulled the cloth from his mouth and he vomited thick bile and then gagged repeatedly until I shoved him upright, cracking his head against the rock.

"Now you get to tell me the truth," I said, smiling.

The hatred that filled his eyes was startling. "You are doing the bidding of the Angel of the Lord. He has called and you have come. And he will drink the blood of your—"

"Not this again." I kicked him in the balls and he fell to the ground, winded and writhing. That, at least, shut him up.

"Let us put on our mail," I said to my men who were both staring at me with a look somewhere between horror and newfound respect. "The priest is William's man after all and we should expect his bastards to attack us on the road."

We helped each other into our doublets and hauberks.

"We are a mere two days from Acre, lord," Adelard said once we stood ready. His tone was humbler than it had been before. "A day if we ride through the night."

"You may go where you think is best," I said to them. "But I swore an oath and there can be no turning back for me."

They stared.

"We are here because of a ruse, lord," Adelard said slowly. "Surely you know it would be madness to continue?"

"We know they are waiting for us," Elias explained, as if I was simple-minded.

I nodded. "And I shall fight my way through and on to William's hiding place. There, with God's will, I shall cut off his head with this sword."

A deranged chuckling coughed its way out from the curled-up priest. "He cannot be killed. He will never die. For he is God's final prophet and God shall bring about the—"

I kicked him in the stomach so hard he stopped breathing. After a long moment, he juddered into movement again, wheezing like a broken bellows.

My men whispered and gestured to each other while I waited.

Whether it was honour, a sense of duty to the Archbishop, the Kingdom of Jerusalem or that they believed their chances were better beside me than riding back by themselves, they elected to head on with me and Antonius.

The priest I gagged, lest he cry out and give us away and I tied it in place around his head. I tied the rest of him up tight, too, with wrists tied together and then tied hard against his belly. Then I sat him back on his horse and left a few yards of rope to hold on to, lest he attempt to ride away.

I left his wounds open and bleeding. I had no doubt his cuts would become infected but then as soon as I found William I was going to kill the priest anyway. His poor horse was disturbed by the blood but she calmed after some reassurance.

"How many?" I asked him again before we moved off. "Nod your head once for each man waiting to ambush us."

He shook his head.

"If you do not tell me how many of them there are then when the fighting begins yours shall be the first throat that gets cut," I ventured.

He shook his head again, mad eyes shining.

My men shrugged and I had to agree with them. When slicing a man open does not cause him to talk then there is not much more one can do without a range of sharp implements, a lot of time and a special kind of creativity.

"Let us try a different route," I said. "Along the floor of the valley by the river." I pointed.

"That is the way he wanted us to go," Adelard said.

"Quite right," I said, looking at the huge promontory high up at the head of the valley.

I wanted to ride into William's trap. I longed for his men to attack us. I wanted to kill those men and I wanted them to lead me to William.

As long as I found success, I did not care if I lived to see the coming dawn.

But I did not say such things to my own two men. Having no true idea of what I rode toward, I thanked God for their company.

"Come on," I said.

We rode down into the valley.

8

Valley of Death

WE AMBLED ALONG THE VALLEY as the sun fell lower and lower toward the hills to the west.

I expected to get an arrow through the neck at any moment. I imaged what it would be like to look down and see an arrowhead poking through my chest, glinting with shiny blood.

Below us the riverbed was dry but for patches of mud and isolated pools with areas of tall plants growing. Despite the drought, the land all around us was green and good for some crops and goats. Adelard said the water for the valley came from springs. Far behind us out of sight beyond the hills to the South was the Sea of Galilee. It was likewise forever filled by the springs even when the river ran dry and the rains did not fall. And there were trees. Spindly things with pale bark and small dark leaves but there were plenty of copses all over the valley. Copses dense enough to hide a group of horsemen.

It was ancient land. Here and there stood stubs of walls or stones with remnants of ancient carving upon their faces. Long ago there had been wealth in the hills. Now it was a land of scattered houses, sometimes gathered in clusters. It had been much ravaged by war. The sight of Frankish knights would have been enough to cause them to flee but it seemed that everyone had been gone for quite some time.

Damascus was merely sixty or seventy miles to the north-east. Although we were off the main road there should have been people moving around within and along the valley. There was no-one.

The heat of the day finally faded. The road climbed up the eastern side, away from the relative lushness below. We came closer to that high rocky promontory that jutted out above the riverbed and hills below. A single man up there could keep watch over miles of country. Our road lead there.

The surface of the road showed heavy use. Dusty hoof and cart tracks had kicked and rolled through the dried, cracked earth.

"What's this?" I asked.

The dust had been greatly disturbed and there was a scatter of bark and tiny twigs.

Adelard peered at it. "Nothing, lord. A load of logs fell off a wagon, that's all."

It was quiet even in the scattered villages on the other side of the valley. The sun fell behind the hills to our left. The sky was yet bright but we rode through shadow. Other than the warm wind it was deathly quiet and I saw no movement and heard no sound of pursuit.

I prayed that William was close.

We came to a spring that bubbled from a stone-lined crevice. Water ran trickling down the hill in a narrow ditch toward the huge riverbed below us. A little brown bird like a sparrow fluttered about in it, ducking its head under and shaking itself.

"We should make camp here," Adelard said and Elias nodded. Their heads swivelled back and forth up and down the hill and both repeatedly looked behind us.

"Water the horses. We camp there," I said, pointing to the high outcrop looming above us.

They were deeply unhappy at the prospect of the climb. I hoped that they would not be too tired to fight when we reached the top.

Antonius was drifting in and out of wakefulness. The blood from his wounds had mostly dried hard. Sometimes he was jostled by his horse over uneven ground and he would jerk his wounds open and they wept afresh. The flies could not believe their luck and swarmed him. I wondered if he would live to reach the top.

Night proper fell. The sky fading into black.

It was a long climb in the dark and we had little strength left for discussion. We trusted the horses to feel their way up. It was unkind and foolhardy to push them further but I wanted time to set up a proper defence. My men also needed rest. Adelard was puffing and blowing as much as his mare.

The moon rose and cast a beautiful silver light brighter than a midwinter noon back in Ashbury.

Our horses were breathing hard when we wound our way out to a flat shelf near to the top of the hill. Crisscrossing stone walls had been left to crumble into ruin. To the rear of the shelf of land the hill rose abruptly to a scrubby peak fifty or a hundred feet further up. There was a foul smell in the air, like a goat had fallen into a cave and rotted.

I assumed the ruins had once been a watch tower with a few outer walls. It was a perfect place for one. Even in moonlight the view was magnificent.

My men were ready to drop but without rest or complaint began unburdening the horses. The poor creatures were all shaking so Elias said he would walk them about before allowing them to drink.

"Keep watch," I commanded Adelard and he went to lean on one of the ruined walls, peering out at the valley. His battered old shield slung across his back.

I dragged Antonius the deceiver from his horse with the rope around his waist and he fell, hard. He whimpered. I tied the trailing end of it tight around his ankles. Then yanked them tight so that his ankles were bent up to his backside. I bound them to his waist. He was a scrawny streak of piss but that did not mean he was not dangerous. I could not afford to take chances. When he was secure I pulled the strip of cloth from out of his mouth.

"Please," he said, his throat sounded dry as wind-blown sand. Even though it was night, black flies buzzed on his scabrous wounds.

I left him bound upon the dusty rock, pulled the cork from my precious skin of water and held it near to his face. Sticking out his tongue he gasped for a drop.

"When you tell me what I want to know," I said. "I will allow you to drink this whole skin of water."

His eyes told me he did not believe me which was fair of him because I was lying.

"He will come for all of you and he will eat your children," Antonius mumbled past cracked lips.

I sighed and looked out down the valley through which we had ascended. The moonlight edged every rock and bush in silver and cast moon shadow ribbons between the dotted lines of trees. It was bright enough to see fields and houses. Far off was a jagged black band under the silver black sky.

"Where are all the people?" I asked Antonius.

He smiled, cracking his lips and wincing as the blood seeped from the cracks. "Serving a higher cause," he said, throat rasping.

"Horsemen," Adelard said from the edge. "Riding slow, following our way."

Elias immediately ran by me to join Adelard.

"How many?" I asked.

"Five," Adelard said.

"Seven?" Elias said.

"What in God's name's wrong with you, boy?" Adelard said and clouted the back of his head before turning round to me. "Perhaps as few as four, lord."

"Not much of an ambush, is it," I said.

"Our horses will never survive a pursuit, lord," Elias said.

"Four is nothing," I boasted. "This is a good place. We shall stand here. How long do we have?"

"They're a fair way off yet," Adelard said.

"We could keep on by walking our horses out of the valley northwards," Elias said, pointing. "Theirs will be blown by the climb, too, we can stay ahead of them."

I crouched down with Antonius. He eyed the dagger at my waist and licked his lips, tongue rasping over the sores. Clearly the trap was being sprung so I held the mouth of the skin to his mouth and squirted in the tepid spring water. He sucked it down like a babe on the breast until I took it away. I wanted him able to speak but not sated. The bastard could suffer. And I needed every advantage, no matter how small.

"William sent you to Acre to lead men to him?" I said.

Antonius savoured the water for a moment, sighing. "He sent me to the Archbishop, yes. My lord wished me to get soldiers," he shrugged. "Or priests."

"But why? We could have brought a hundred men down upon him, had the Archbishop chosen to do so. Why would William risk his destruction by sending you?"

The men were listening but kept keeping watch over the edge.

"He swore to us that they would not send many," Antonius said, eyes shining. "And he spoke the truth, did he not? My lord sees things mortal men cannot see. He is the light of the world and his blood is the light of the life."

"Yes, yes," I said. "But why lure anyone at all?"

"My lord seeks new brothers to join us," Antonius said. "Our numbers must grow, my lord says, if we are to bring his revelations to all the people of God's land. You shall see, all of you shall see and then you shall follow him as faithfully as I have and you will be rewarded with everlasting life on earth."

Adelard laughed from over by the edge. "Why in God's name would we join with William?"

"Once you received his Eucharist," Antonius said, mad eyes shining in the moonlight. "Then you will know the truth. I was like you. I doubted. I was on my knees looking up with contempt and pity for his evil. But once I tasted it, I became filled with the strength and the power of God made flesh."

"His Eucharist?" I asked.

"His holy blood is fire in your veins," Antonius said, his voice rising in passion. "I was old and weak and then I was strong." The priest coughed and winced and his voice fell to a whisper. "But the Gift fades, day by day. Every Sabbath we share the sacrament. It has been so very long since I drank from him. I am so hungry. So very hungry."

Adelard and Elias looked as confused and disturbed as I felt.

The wind was full of dust and the smell of juniper. Our horses whinnied and stamped their feet, nervous. They snorted. Perhaps it was the smell of the priest; that old and new blood and the beginnings of rotting flesh.

There was a sound. Faint enough to almost be the wind but not quite. It reminded me of a millstone in use. I stood and looked across the intersecting ruin of walls for the source but saw nothing in the deep shadows. After just a moment the sound was no more.

"Adelard, Elias. Listen to me," I said, speaking softly and they turned around. "This was always the place of ambush. Those men in the valley are but one part of it. Others will be coming from the north. Elias, get my shield and your own."

But both men jumped in surprise and drew their swords, staring behind me. At the same time I heard footsteps approaching and I leapt to my feet and spun round, drawing my own blade.

Five men approached in the darkness spread in a wide row, stepping carefully across the ruins. They took up position, arrayed before us.

In the centre was Hugo the Giant.

He stood flanked by two Saracen knights. They held their curved swords already drawn and at the ready. To either side of those Saracens were two crossbowmen of the Italian style, with their weapons loaded and aimed us.

All the men were filthy. The stench of stale blood and rotten meat was so bad I could not believe I had failed to smell them on the wind as they had approached.

A slow chuckle emerged from Hugo's belly, deep as a rumble of thunder.

"It is too late to flee, Richard of Ashbury," the voice said. "You belong to the Destroyer now. Come with me."

"Hugo the Giant," I said, my heart hammering in my chest at the thought of fighting such a monster. "I have come to bring justice to Earl William de Ferrers. I shall slay you also. As I will Hugh of Havering, Roger of Tyre and any man that stands against me."

He stood grim faced and unmoved by my words. The Saracens and crossbowmen also stood and stared. The crossbows did not waver. One pointed at me, the other at Adelard or Elias over my shoulder.

I knew crossbows. A man can learn to shoot one in very little time. They are simple to point and squeeze and at close range a bolt will punch through mail and bury deep into flesh. Even a boy could use one with ease and the men with Hugo were experienced specialists.

Hugo the Giant spoke French with a strange accent and I recalled that he was from Antioch. "Come," he said, his voice a landslide. "I swear you will be safe if you come with me. My lord loves you and wishes that you join with him. If you do not you shall be sacrificed to him and your blood will feed him and he will feed us with his Blessed Sacrament."

One weakness of the crossbow was that you could pull too hard to release the bolt and then miss the target. This tended to happen when a man was panicking. The other weakness was the length of time they took to reload.

"He loves us?" I asked, picking a single drop from the torrent of madness simply to keep Hugo talking while my men shuffled behind me. I prayed that they would fight.

Hugo shook his giant head. "The Angel of the Lord has sent for you and you have come to him as—"

I threw myself forward at the crossbowman on the farthest left. By moving outward I hoped to stay away from Hugo long enough to kill his men. I looped around then changed direction and charged right at the man pointing a sharp steel headed bolt at me.

I roared a wordless battle cry and wheeled my sword over my head like a maniac. He panicked and squeezed the mechanism too early. I danced further left as he pulled. The weapon clacked and the bolt ripped through the air by my head. The crossbowman hesitated, reached for another bolt, thought better of it and raised his crossbow ready to block my attack. But anything other than immediate flight had been his final mistake. For I ran by him and swung the edge of my blade into his throat, crushing it into pulp. He fell, dying.

The other crossbow clanked too but the bolt shot toward Adelard or Elias. Both charged the other side of the enemy line.

I kept moving. The nearest Saracen knight closed in on me with Hugo looming behind him, striding around to the other side of me. I had to kill the knight before facing Hugo. Or I knew I was dead.

Heart slamming in my chest I closed on the Saracen, thrusting with the point of my sword to push him back away from Hugo. I had to isolate him, drive him from the others. Hugo was behind me and my fear of that giant threatened to overwhelm me. Still I pushed the attack. The Saracen gave ground.

Hugo the Giant charged in like a bullock. The giant's arms were long, his sword was longer than mine own and it was twice as wide. So I had to duck and dance away from his powerful swings without ever being close enough to harm him. And so the Saracen closed on me again. Changing my direction I swung my blade toward Hugo. He checked his attack and blocked my sword with the edge of his. It was like hitting a boulder. The shock of it rang through my bones into my skull. I was afraid my blade would break and shatter but it remained whole. I retreated backward, my teeth aching from the impact. Hugo's face was expressionless as he stalked after me, poking his blade at my face. I fended him off. The Saracen came at me full charge and I deflected and countered with a flurry of blows. He blocked or dodged them, blades clashing in the night. My sword was being dented and blunted and I cursed myself for not having a shield.

The Saracen was so fast. The unnatural speed of his sword arm and footwork was just as it had been when William's men killed me in my hall. As full of fire as he was, there was not much skill in the man and I would have bested him but for Hugo. The giant pushed forward and kept me from getting away. He was so slow but skilful and possessed an inhuman strength. So I kept my distance. I was faster than he was, faster even than the Saracen and I kept them both away. My point jabbed into the Saracen's shoulder, hard, and he reeled away with a shout. The Saracen looked to Hugo, confused and clutching the point I had struck.

Hugo stopped. He looked at his Saracen. He looked at me. He had the tiniest fraction of expression on his face, something like curiosity or confusion. "You move like he does," Hugo said, his voice like an iron door slamming in Hell. "How is that possible?"

I stamped my foot forward to feign an attack and drive him away so I could finish the Saracen. But just then one of my men cried out. I glanced toward Adelard and Elias. I did it so briefly that I could see nothing other than figures fighting across the far side of the rock platform. We were too far to help or hinder each other.

A glance was all it took. I was distracted enough for Hugo to decide to come at me, bellowing like thunder. It was immediately clear that Hugo's relative slowness had been a trick. He was actually just as fast as his Saracen was. In fright I swiped his huge sword away, the impact jarring me to the teeth again. I stepped back into the path of the Saracen's blade. That sneaking Saracen swept a glancing blow into my back, slicing his curved edge down the mail.

Such a blow could not cut me for my mail protected against cuts. But the force of the impact was enough to snap ribs and knock the breath from my body. And it threw me off balance. I ducked and swayed away from their blades in something close to panic, certain that

I was going to die and stepped backwards as fast as I could, my heartbeat hammering in my ears and my breathing rattling my ribs.

I never saw the wall behind me. A little stub as high as my calves that sent me flying backwards. The hard earth slammed into my broken ribs and cracking into the back of my helm.

The Saracen leapt the wall and his blade sang toward my face. I swung my sword wildly, knocking his aside and kicked out at his knee as he landed on that leg. There was a loud pop as the bones there snapped and his knee crunched as the shards ground against each other. He fell on top of me, his helmeted head crashing into mine. My sword was gone and he was so close I could feel his hot breath on my face. Grabbing his head with both hands to hold him to me I sunk my teeth into his cheek and bit down as hard as I could. I was astonished that my teeth bit through his beard and muscle right through to his cheekbone. He screamed in my ear and jerked up away from me, pulling a strip of flesh off his cheek and spilling hot blood into my mouth. I held his head, biting down harder and he thrashed his head about trying to get away which simply served to tear his cheek right off his face. I had a glimpse of shining, bloody teeth and skull inside and I had to swallow the blood and drool that gushed into my mouth, lest I drown in it.

Hugo yanked the screaming Saracen away as if he were a child, tossed him down beside me still screaming and thrust down at my chest with his sword. I twisted my body sideways, rolling from the blow so that it sprang against the stones that had been under me. Immediately I rolled back onto the blade, trapping it against my mailed back and kept rolling until I was flat on my back. The blade bent but it could only flex so far and the sword was levered from Hugo's grasp and flung out to the side.

I reached for my own blade laying just out of reach but Hugo yanked a dagger from his belt and sank toward me. He was monstrously heavy but he had about seven feet to descend and I was fast and filled with fury so I grasped his wrist, which was as wide as a ham and held the blade away from me. The rest of his body smashed into me and I felt more ribs popping in my chest as his knee landed, the breath squeezed out of me and I thought my heart would burst.

But I held on. More than held on, I forced his wrist and the blade it held away from me to the side. Hugo finally allowed his face to show something; astonishment.

I used his own momentum to throw him over with my hips and rolled him over and down onto the Saracen who was shrieking and cupping the hole where that half of his face had been. I twisted the dagger from Hugo's massive hands and smashed his face with my armoured forehead. Again and again I struck him until he stopped moving and then I stopped. His head was like a horse's; the bone of his skull as thick as stone and I wondered if I had smashed my own brains out.

Underneath his body the Saracen squirmed, trying to get out so I snatched up Hugo's dagger and stabbed it into the Saracen's throat to silence him.

Hugo's face and skull was partly caved in but he was not dead. His massive hands groped blindly up towards my head. I stabbed the blade through the smashed cracks around Hugo's eyes and into his brain over and over again. His hands fell away.

Only when I ran out of breath was it I realised I had been screaming.

I rolled from Hugo and fell down next to the bodies, my chest heaving, not sure what damage I had received. The Saracen knight and Hugo lay next to me one atop the other.

There were two others I had not killed. Another Saracen and a crossbowman had been fighting my men. Cursing and wincing I looked for my sword.

Footsteps scraped toward me in the dark from the other side of the low wall that I had fallen over and I scrambled to my sword and swung it up toward Adelard's face. He blocked it with his shield. There was a crossbow bolt sticking into it. I let out the breath I was holding.

"You are alive," I said, stupidly.

There was blood all over his head and hands. But it was not his.

"Elias is dead," he said.

Together they had killed the other Saracen knight and the crossbowman but not before Elias had been pierced through the chest with the bolt. He had drowned and suffocated after killing the man who had shot him.

"Fast pair of bastards, they were," Adelard said, shaking his head.

Antonius still lay tied up on his side, head craned up looking at me with fear in his eyes. That, at least, made me feel happy.

"There's still those other men on horseback heading up here for us," Adelard said. There was a black rage in him and he wanted more men to kill.

I was hurt from the fight and limped over to him. The monstrous weight of Hugo falling upon me had crushed my ribs and my back ached and I knew I would be massively bruised. But the thought of another fight to come made the pain melt away. My mouth still tasted of the Saracen's blood. I felt it all roiling in my otherwise-empty belly and somehow I began to feel better. Strength returned to my limbs and my breathing slowed.

"How skilled are you with a crossbow?" I asked Adelard as he stood looking down at the bloody corpse that was once Elias.

"Held one a few years ago," Adelard said. He was breathing hard. There's nothing in all the world so tiring as battle and it was remarkable I was not more exhausted.

"Then I shall take both weapons," I said and we gathered them, along with a half-dozen bolts and I stood at the point where the road reached the top of the plateau. The point where our pursuers would emerge. "You take your shield and wait behind that corner of wall. Ensure that they see you after they reach the top."

I gagged Antonius again, dragged him squirming into deep shadow. I hid behind the walls beside the top of the path and glanced over the edge. The horsemen were climbing slowly but the scraping of their horse's hoofs and clashing of their armour grew ever closer.

We did not have long to wait.

I was certain that they would have heard the fighting from atop our rock outcrop, the sounds travelling easily in the still night air. They would have heard it and then heard the silence that followed.

There were merely four of them after all. So certain their friends would have defeated us that they called out for them in the foreign tongue of the Saracens. No doubt they were imagining rest and sustenance awaiting them at the top and that was good for if men are unprepared for a fight then they make easy prey. They trudged up, making a huge noise and at the top of the hill they tied up their blowing horses near to our own.

I was in shadow but they came so close that if anyone turned in my direction they would see the gleam of the bolt upon my loaded bow, as well as the other loaded one sat ready upon the wall before me. I could smell the sweat and the stench of horse from the men in the warm night wind but I held my shot until they had stumbled closer into our trap.

They called out, becoming nervous that their friends were not responding to their hails.

One of them saw Adelard duck his head down behind the ruined wall and cried out a warning. I jumped up and shot a bolt into his lower back. He grunted and went down with his sword half out of his scabbard.

The other three were frozen in indecision when Adelard ran around the wall then charged toward them with his shield up and growling some guttural war cry. I shot another of them in the centre of the spine and he fell straight down like when you drop a rope. I tossed that second bow away and leapt over the wall.

A small part of me felt sympathy for the way the two remaining men turned to run from Adelard just to come face to face with me bearing down on them.

It was small part of me only. The rest of me was filled with a cool rage and I cut one down without hesitation. He hardly had time to scream when I smashed his head in with my sword. The idiot was not wearing a helmet.

I allowed Adelard to cut the other man down. The Saracen was staring up at me in confusion and terror when Adelard smashed him in the side of the head. I stood and watched as Adelard stabbed all four men in the throat with the point of his sword, just to be sure.

"Got to bury Elias now, lord," Adelard said. "Can't leave him for the vultures."

"Fine," I said, stretching my back. The Christian thing to do was bury him, I supposed but I was not going to waste my strength on it. "Pile up stones to cover him. You will never get through this ground." Adelard should not have wasted his strength either and if I'd been a harder man, as hard a man as I later became, then I would have forced him to abandon his friend's internment.

As it was, while he grunted and clanked rocks about I searched the ruins for the place where Hugo and his Saracens had crept out from. I had been distracted talking to Antonius when they appeared but there was no chance those five men had snuck up from any great distance and I knew there must be a way into the hill under our feet. There were too many shadows for me to find it without knowing where to look.

"Dear God," Adelard said, standing at the head of the cairn he had built against one wall over the young man's body. I went to join him. "Elias was just a lad. He never wanted much from life. To tell the truth he was half simple. But he was a good fighter. He never did nothing bad. He's the sort of man you want up there, Lord. Amen."

"Amen," I said and tried to remember that this man's death was on William's hands, not my own.

"Don't know how I'm going to tell my wife about this," Adelard said in a whisper. "Promised I'd take care of him."

"Go drink and eat, if you can," I said.

"Good advice," Adelard said. "You should take it yourself, lord."

The blood in my belly seemed sustenance enough so I patted him on his shoulder and then stood over Antonius. "I swore that I was going to kill you should we be ambushed."

He looked up, eyes shining.

"You will lead me to where William is. If you tell me the truth and help me then I swear I shall not harm you. If you lie or lead me astray I shall bury a blade in your heart. Do you understand?"

He nodded and I took the gag from his mouth.

"We should kill him now, lord," Adelard said, chewing bread. "He's no priest."

"But I am," Antonius said. "Saladin's men sent me to Acre to tell your people that the attacks on the caravans and pilgrims were not of his doing. I spoke French, I was a Christian, and they said I would be trusted. But I was taken on the road, brought before William. And then I saw."

I shrugged. "William has Saracens fighting for him?"

"Saracens," Antonius scoffed. "An idiotic word. Our lord's followers were once Franks, Kurds, Turks, Arabs, Egyptians. Any man who drinks from him, no matter what he was before, sees the truth once they taste his blood."

"How many followers?" I asked. "How many are knights?"

Antonius screwed his face up. "Twenty? Thirty? I never counted."

Adelard groaned. "Lord, we must return with more men."

I ignored him.

"You said before that you take William's Eucharist," I said, prompting Antonius.

"He saw in me that I was ready to receive the sacraments. The blood of Christ straight from William's veins. It filled my arms with such power, such strength. My mind was sharpened like a sabre. My body was fast as a striking snake and strong as a lion. My wounds were healed in an instant. My eyes saw through this world to the edge of the next one. And I knew. I understood. Before me stood the cup of Christ in the form of a man."

"You all drink the blood from William's veins on the Sabbath?" I said. "Thirty of you?"

Antonius sneered. "Of course it is on the Sabbath. Unless the men are sent out to raid," he said, bitterly. "Then they get it before they depart."

"What day is it today?" I asked Adelard.

"Saturday, lord," he said then looked at the sky. "Sunday, now, I suppose."

I looked through the darkness to where the bodies of Hugo and the other men lay waiting for the sun to bring thousands of flies to feast and lay eggs in their flesh.

"Drinking his blood makes a man faster?" I asked Antonius. "Stronger?"

Antonius grinned. "Strong with the power of God."

"And William's knights also drink the blood of the innocent? Why?"

He shrugged. "It prolongs and increases the effects of the sacrament."

"Can it really be?" I asked, almost to myself.

"You shall see," Antonius said, giggling. "Oh yes, you shall see when you drink from him that the Christ has come again in the form of William, the Angel of the Lord, the Destroyer."

Adelard cleared his throat. "Should he not be slain for such blasphemy?" He could barely contain himself. "Calling this evil the Eucharist, lord? It offends God."

"You swore you would not harm me if I spoke truth," Antonius said, squirming away, full of fear.

"He should be slain," I said to Adelard. "But not by us. I swore an oath."

Adelard spat to show what he thought of that. And he was quite right but still I cut the ropes about Antonius" waist and ankles and, with Adelard's sword at his back, he led us to a square cut into the bedrock in the corner of some ruined walls. It was the same size and shape as a grave. There was a slab beside it that Hugo must have pushed out of the way before climbing up to ambush us.

The black rectangle had rock-cut steps at the nearest edge leading down into darkness.

"It stinks," Adelard said.

The air coming up from the hole reeked of death. I recognised the smell in the air, now, the smell I had detected as I had reached the head of the valley. It was the wet foulness of fresh blood, mixed with wood smoke. Fresh blood and the corruption of old death, too.

"What is waiting for us down there?" I asked Antonius while Adelard lit a torch.

"Death."

Adelard stared at me, his eyes pits of inky blackness flickering with reflected yellow torch light. I felt as though I should tell him everything would be well and to trust in God but in truth I agreed with the priest. The stench of death was pouring out of from the entire hill. It stank of butchery and battlefields. My stomach churned again.

"There may be death down there," I said, drawing that withered old creature so close to me I could smell the dried blood and stale piss on him. "But I shall bring even more."

He grinned.

The three of us descended the steps into the depths of the mountain.

9

Cavern of Blood

DARKNESS. OUR STEPS ECHOED on the stone underfoot through the long, narrow tunnel that led down into the hill.

Adelard's torch gave off a hot light behind. He held it up close to the natural stone ceiling but still I trod into blackness with my shield raised and the point of my sword before me.

The air was smoky. That foul wind blew through the passageway, guttering the torch and carrying with it that stench of dank corruption.

My eyes played tricks with the darkness. I could see swirling shapes ahead that vanished. There were distant voices like whispers on the wind. Antonius' breath was loud behind me. Adelard's laboured panting threatened to overwhelm any noise I might hear ahead. It was as though I could smell his fear and hear his heart clangouring against his ribs.

With every step, I feared falling into a spike pit or stumbling into an ambush from the walls either side. Surely, I reasoned, they would have heard the fighting atop their lair? Surely, they would send men looking for Hugo and the others?

But William was up ahead. He had to be. And nothing was going to stop me. I was so close and all the hesitant shuffling forward seemed absurd.

I stopped and sheathed my sword.

"What is it?" Adelard hissed.

"Antonius goes first," I whispered. "And if you know of anything waiting for us ahead, speak before we reach it or you shall die before I do."

"I told you," Antonius said, his voice echoing. "Only death waits for—"

I slapped the words from his mouth, span him round and pushed him before me down the tunnel. Adelard ran to catch up behind me. I hurried forward, pushing Antonius at close to a running pace, ready to drop to a knee and raise my shield at the first sign of danger.

It seemed that the tunnel went deeper, downhill, but I could not be certain. Every so often there was a whiff of cool night air from cracks in the rock or from other tunnels and shafts. We rounded bends and corners until I was utterly disoriented. I knew not what direction we walked. Nor how far we had gone. When we got further in I thought I saw doorways cut every so often passing beside me; black, cold yawning maws with no life down them.

Soon there were voices, growing louder. The smell of smoke and death was stronger and Antonius slowed.

Light ahead. Flickering lamp light on the wall of the tunnel.

I suppose I should have waited. I should have crept forward, taken my time to assess and devised a plan with Adelard. But I was certain William was close. And I was so filled with rage that I shoved Antonius onward toward it ever faster.

The tunnel ended in a sharp turn to the left and there was an arched entranceway hewn into the bedrock. Beyond was a huge cavern where the lamp light spilled from. I dragged Antonius to a halt and peeked a little way in.

The cavern was lined with ancient wooden beams and planks around the edges, presumably for holding back rock falls. The ceiling above was lost in darkness. I stepped forward toward the opening and saw deeper inside. It was as long as the nave of Acre's cathedral church.

"Lord," Adelard said behind me, caution in his voice.

"Watch the priest," I said to him.

Hefting my shield and readying my sword, I strode into the huge space. And froze.

The stench hit me first. A thick, cloying taste of blood on the air; like a battlefield. Like Ashbury manor house, like my own hall, after William.

The far end of the cavern was lit up by a roaring fire in a brazier. The bonfire was at waist height, blazing upon a vast iron bowl, supported by three legs.

Men moved down there at the far end of the cavern before the fire. Many stripped to the waist or naked. Some carried fuel for the fire, others heaved bodies around a large stone cistern in the centre of the floor. More stood and watched. Chains hung down from the ceiling, clicking against each other. One of the chains ended in a terribly long hook of the sort used to hang meat or a cauldron over a fire. The floor shone with fresh blood.

The light threw everyone into half silhouette. The long space between me and them was in shadow.

A man stirred to one side down by my feet.

He had been laying by the door in the shadow. There was a lamp on an alcove above him and from the corner of my eye I saw him jump into wakefulness. As a cry of warning began in his chest I ran him through, pushing the point through his ribs and into his heart. He stared at me, astonished and offended and in utter disbelief. A poor excuse for a guard.

"Sweet suffering Christ," Adelard muttered at my shoulder, staring down the cavern.

I turned back. My feet rooted as one man dragged a struggling figure from somewhere behind the brazier. He dragged them toward the big cistern.

They came into the light from the fire. The man was Hugh of Havering. The struggling figure was a woman. She was naked, old, begging and sobbing.

Hugh fought her, struck her senseless, got his hands on her hips and heaved her up onto the hooked chain. She writhed and groaned and tried to pry his hands from her. The huge hook pierced her back. She screamed once but the weight of her body bore her down and punched the spike through to burst from her chest and she was silent.

Another man pulled the other end of the chain from by the wall and she lifted higher up, her feet raised above head height. Blood welled out of her, ran down her skin and gushed from her toes into the cistern below her, spattering all around it. The fountain of blood was lit from behind by the fire. The woman jerked around like a fish on a line and the man who had hung her upon it reached up and tugged her down, hard. The hook sunk deeper inside her chest cavity with an audible crunch and she stopped moving again. The blood kept coming.

"Bring another one." The familiar, dreaded voice echoed around the cavern. "One of the children, I think. I can wait no longer."

William.

I had heard him but could not see him down there. But knowing he was there was enough for the rage to fill me.

Before I had left Jaffa for Acre I had stopped at Alice's tomb. I had begged her forgiveness and promised her justice for her and for her sweet children. Another oath that was no more than meaningless words unless it was fulfilled. I remembered her eyes fixed upon mine as William had sunk his teeth into her neck.

It was only when I was halfway across the cavern that I realised I was charging the men.

I had my sword in hand, my shield up before me. My own breathing in my ears, my hauberk jangling and my footsteps slapping on the ground.

God be with me, I prayed.

There were warning cries as I burst into the fire light by the cistern. A filthy man beside me leapt up in panic and tried to run away but I speared my sword through his neck and bore him down under me.

William's men, the murderers in that cavern of blood were not armoured and most held no weapon. And yet many of them came right at me, full of mad fury and seemed ready and willing to tear me apart with their bare hands.

My sword slashed left and right and I kept moving and slamming men with my shield and stabbing them. Few were killing strokes but their naked skin split to the bone from strokes that mail would have turned away. My sword was like lightning, leaping from the flesh of one man into another. One or two men ducked through a doorway but I knew not where they went.

They were not fast. They were not lightning quick as the men up top had been. And I was faster than I had ever been and filled with a mad fury of my own.

Men collapsed, screaming, all around me and survivors laying upon the blood-soaked floor would not be long for the world. I edged through them, moving deeper in, heading towards the fire.

When I reached the cistern I stopped. The woman's body swung back and forth above, blood still trickling down her skin from the hook wound to drip and run from her toes.

I saw William.

There, finally. Standing to one side and behind the raised brazier where he was hidden in its glare. He was smiling.

More of his men came toward me. These ones had grabbed their weapons from that that side room and were coming to kill me. A couple of them had banged a helmet onto their head but otherwise were also unarmoured. Swords, maces and spears swung and stabbed at me. Blows struck me in the shoulder and the leg and they were powerful but I kept moving around the cistern, back and forth. A man tried to trip me with his spear but I trod on it and stabbed through his loins in the same movement. A crossbow clanked and the bolt bounced from my shield to my helmet and then I killed the man who had shot from one knee.

I killed them all until just a handful remained. Those men did not rush in. There were six of them and they spread out slowly around me.

One was Hugh of Havering, William's right hand man. Another was Roger of Tyre. These were men I wanted to kill. But not as much as I wanted to eviscerate their lord.

"Fight me yourself," I shouted at William.

He smiled and shook his head, as if I had invited him to share a cup of ale at the village fair.

"Coward," I shouted.

William laughed. "I feared you would never come."

His men kept circling; two of them moving behind me. One of them, a great bearded lump of a Saracen hefted a huge two handed axe. Hugh and Roger stayed between me and William.

"Nothing could keep me from killing you," I said.

He tilted his head. "Not even your own death, Richard?"

He nodded to his men and they charged in all together.

There is no way to defend yourself against six skilled, armed men. It is impossible.

So I attacked.

I twisted from William, from Hugh and Roger and ran at the axeman behind me. His blade crashed through my shield from the top, sending a great chunk flying and chopping down to my forearm. The impact almost broke my arm but I threw my shield wide which yanked the axe from his hands and I smashed my blade into his face as I ran by him.

The edge of my blade was dented and bent by the earlier fighting. But even a blunt sword can smash a man's brains out if you swing it hard enough.

The next man, another Saracen, retreated from me, sensibly drawing toward the tunnel so that I would have my back to the other men.

But then Adelard was there. He cut down across the back of the Saracen. Then he impaled through the kidney the other man on that side of the cistern. The man jerked away, tearing Adelard's sword from his grasp. Adelard threw himself back from the mace that came at him. He ducked and dodged away.

Three of them left, not counting William.

I glanced over at William. He had his eyes closed and his head tilted back as if in prayer. The brazier fire blazed next to him so his face was flickering yellow and deep shadow. I had killed almost every one of his men and yet still William did not fight me.

There was movement a little way behind him against the far wall and for a moment I feared dozens of more men were waiting to attack. But then I saw that behind the fire was not the wall but a stockade. Arms stuck through upright wooden beams, joined by crosswise planks. Hands grasped. In the gaps between I saw faces.

It was full of people.

The people of the valley along with the survivors of William's raids.

Hugh of Havering came at me, with Roger of Tyre approaching and ready to fight with him. I felt the rage boil over and I hacked down into them one after the other, driving them down. I slipped in the blood and a sword point nicked my cheek.

I recovered but fell back. Blows rained onto my shield from both men. They moved with the same speed and ferocity as the Saracen and Hugo had upon the watchtower ruin. Their blows splintered my shield into tatters so I shook off the strap and flung it away

I blocked with my sword, trying to squirm and back off. It was hard to breathe and I was shaking. An unseen blow from Hugh or Roger got through and clanged against my helmet so hard I was sure my skull was caved in. But the good steel saved me and when my vision cleared I struck out with my foot and felt it connect with a knee or ankle. Roger fell and Hugh covered him until he got up and both backed away from the scything of my sword.

Adelard was retreating from the attack of the third man, a great bear of a fellow, and I staggered toward him.

William finally drew his sword. His face twisted in rage as he came for me. He positioned himself to cut me off from Adelard. My man got knocked from his feet, smashed down by a brutal blow from the bear knight. The bear knight raised up his mace for a blow that would crush Adelard's dazzled brain. The cistern was between me and Adelard. Hugh and Roger blocked one way around it. William walked forward, blocking the other.

In the centre of the room the dead woman spun on the chain, suspended over the wide cistern of blood. I ran toward it, slipping but I jumped up, got a foot on the edge of the cistern and leapt for the woman. I grabbed her ankle with my shield hand. It was slippery with blood. I held on and swung myself over the cistern and landed with a crash against the man with the raised mace. We both fell. But I was on top. I got the edge of my blade across his throat and sawed back and forth, leaning into it with both hands and his blood frothed and spurted under the edge of the blade.

My breath rattled as I stood. Adelard hauled himself up beside me. We faced William and his two remaining men, Roger of Tyre and Hugh of Havering. The three of them standing together. But Adelard was puffing, exhausted and outclassed. I was at the limit of my endurance.

The three of them looked strong. They were fresh. I thought I understood why William had held himself back from the fighting. Around us came the groans of the dying.

"Why?" I asked William, hoping for a few moments with which to catch my breath. I looked at the lumpy, congealed blood in the cistern. It splashed underfoot across the floor. There were piles of fresh bodies against the far wall. The cistern held gallons of it. How many innocents had his men drained to make so much?

"At least tell me why this? What did these people do to you?"

"Why? Why, Richard? Blood is life," William sheathed his blade. He strode to the cistern, grabbed the edge. He plunged his face into that congealing mass. He gulped down mouthfuls and straightened again, swiping away lumpy strings of blood clots. William grinned a red smile.

"By this blood do I live. And by my blood my men gain a glimmer of my strength, my invulnerability. The Christ himself told us that unless you eat the flesh of the Christ and drink his blood, you do not have life within you. Whoever eats my body and drinks my blood remains in me and I in him. Are his words unclear, Richard?"

William slashed a tiny blade across the inside of his wrist and blood flowed and William offered out the wound. Hugh of Havering bent over and sunk his mouth onto the wound and drank it down, suckling the blood. I could hear the fevered gulping. He stopped and smacked his lips, grinning.

A smile spread across William's face. "And thus do we carry out God's divine will. What is the life of some peasant compared to taking this Blessed Sacrament?" Roger of Tyre bent to William's wrist and drank too.

"Sacrament?" I felt the rage returning. I glanced at the stockade beyond the fire where the prisoners were whimpering. "You are mad. And you have spread your madness to these other men." Bodies still writhed and groaned all across the floor. Men I had slain in pursuit of my personal justice.

"Madness?" William laughed, echoing from the walls. "Was it madness that brought me back from the dead at Hattin? Was it madness that made me drink the blood from the bodies piled upon me? It was a sign from God, there can be no doubt. I died but I was reborn."

I scoffed, even though I was almost convinced. "You were injured and you survived. The same has happened to me. Because of you, I died and they were going to bury me but I awoke and here I stand, ready to strike you down. I drank no blood to make it so. God gave you nothing. Your blood is not special."

William's smile faltered for a moment. He gestured to Hugh of Havering. "All men who take my Eucharist grow strong. If a man is injured a few drops heal his wounds. I take in the blood of women and children and within this holy vessel it is transformed into the blood of Christ. I do God's work."

"You killed my brother Henry because it was he who murdered your wife, I know that now. And if he truly did kill her? Then he deserved death."

William stared, unmoving. His men glanced at him and back to me.

"But you killed Alice. And you killed Isabella. And you killed their children. And that was not God's work. It is for those crimes and for all the other innocent blood you have shed that I take my revenge."

"I killed them because they offended God," William said. "Why should Henry have happiness when he took mine? No, what I did to him was justice. What I did to our father was justice. I killed him for you, Richard. For you and for your mother."

I felt a terrible sinking feeling in my guts. "What is this madness that you speak now?"

William's mouth gaped. "You cannot mean that you do not know? You cannot be so dim witted if we are of the same blood? We are brothers, my dear Richard."

I shook my head, denying his words. Resisting the dawning realisation of their truth.

He grimaced. "Our father forced himself upon your mother, one Christmas if I recall. You are sprung from Robert de Ferrer's loins just as I am. Henry, that useless bastard you call brother, shared your mother but he despised you. You know that he hated you, surely? That hate was for what our father did to your mother. Did you know your mother slashed her wrists when you were a baby? Everyone pretended she had not but we all knew. Our father was the cause of it all." William's face twisted further into bitterness. "Perhaps it was that which drove Henry to kill my darling Katherine and my son Richard."

I felt the world turning under me once more. As hard as it was to believe, many things that had once seemed strange began to make sense.

The men in Dartmouth believed it was I that murdered the local girl. They thought I looked like William. I rarely saw my own reflection but I was of a height with him. We had the same dark hair, same build. And, I supposed, a similar face.

King Richard had said something about me inheriting some of the de Ferrers lands. *By rights it should be yours anyway.* My father's hatred for me. His attempts at making me a monk so that, even if Henry had died, I would never have inherited Ashbury. King Henry said that men were afraid I would be like William.

Such things only made sense if those kings had known or at least suspected the truth. How many men had known?

Had the Bishop of Coventry back in Derbyshire moved so quickly to take Duffield from fear that I would claim an inheritance and beat him to it? He gave me a full purse to encourage me to ride after William. But it was not to help me. I was delaying setting off and he must have wanted me to confront William. For even with a hired man or two I would have been killed had I found him.

I felt certain Alice had not known. Had not suspected. Had she?

But William was still speaking.

"Henry never would have done such a thing if our father had not caused such violence to his mother. A violence that put a bastard in her belly. A violence that shamed her into self-murder. But I put things right. I did justice to all. I poisoned our father when I returned home. Poisoned him so thoroughly he was dead and cold in a single night." William laughed. It echoed from the walls. "But the old bastard woke up. Can you believe it? A day later, he lay on the table ready for burial and he sat up. He was very angry and I had to cut him down and bury him before the servants found out. It took rather a lot of work to kill him the second time. Practically had to cut his heart out. Tough old sod. We take after him, do we not? But know that he paid for his crime, though it was twenty years too late. I did it for you, Richard. Dearest Ricard, I take pride in telling you that your poor mother, God rest her soul, is avenged. As was my own mother, who died from the shame of her husband's ways. As was my wife, when I killed that evil little shit Henry of Ashbury."

I found I had little breath but William was looking at me. Waiting for me to speak.

"We are brothers," I managed to say.

William's eyes flashed sideways beyond me, changing focus for the briefest of moments. His smile twitched.

A tiny movement in the corner of my eye.

"Adelard," I cried out, wheeling around.

But I was too late.

Antonius. The dark priest had crept after Adelard. He had freed himself from whatever bonds Adelard had left him in back in the tunnel. I watched as he rose up from behind us and sunk a dagger into Adelard's throat. He sawed it back and forth, blood welling out as Adelard screamed.

I smashed the priest's head so hard with my blade that his skull was almost cloven in two. Bone and pink brain sprayed out as I yanked back my sword.

William's men were on me. They were fast. I fell back under their assault, deflecting blows with my battered sword.

But I had tired. I was more exhausted than I had ever felt. I was hurting all over and both Hugh and Roger were full of renewed strength and speed. Where I had to block with the blade, their attacks jarred my sword arm hard.

There were bodies everywhere underfoot and they were hard to avoid.

I never even saw the sword that ran me through. The pain, though, was like fire and ice tearing through me. It had happened again. I was stabbed, run through the ribs.

My face was slapped, hard. I woke, knowing that it had been mere moments. Hugh and Roger held me by the shoulders suspended before William. The fire on the brazier felt hot and the metal sizzled.

"Does this feel familiar?" William asked. He was close.

I had failed.

"I told you this was God's will," William said, his breath reeking of blood.

"Yes," I said, a jolt of agony speared through me. "I see now."

William's face flowed before me. It was lit on one side by the fire that was finally dying now no one was there to feed it from the vast pile of desert brushwood. The wet blood on his face reflecting the flames like a thousand flecks of gold.

"So you see?" William asked. "You see I was given a gift by God?"

My head bobbed. "But I have it too," I said.

"No." William frowned. "You were not chosen," he said.

"We were born this way," I said. "Or perhaps we are born so and yet still we must die to become as we are. You killed me before but I was brought back. Just as you were at Hattin."

I coughed blood and darkness at the edges of my vision closed in.

William's face swam, a red and gold beacon in the darkness. "I have the Gift. I am the Angel of the Lord. I have the Christ's holy blood in my veins. Not you. Me."

"But Lord Robert, our father. You poisoned him and he died. But he, too, awoke."

"No!" He screamed in my face. "No, I was chosen, not you. Not father. Do you understand? Will you drink my blood and become my man or shall I drink you dry, brother?"

The stench of his breath made me gag and the convulsion wracked through me.

"Please, Lord," I mumbled. "Allow me to share your sacrament. Brother."

"You will serve me?" William asked. "Swear with God as your witness."

I was running out time and the world turned under me again. I saw then that oaths are worthless. Meaningless. Actions alone are important.

"I swear it,"

My eyes closed or I was losing consciousness. I heard but did not see William order his men to hold me steady. He warned them of my strength.

I felt skin pushed against my mouth. William intoned some twisted version of the ceremony as blood welled into my mouth.

My lips made a seal around his skin and I sucked in the hot blood that pumped and spurted into my mouth and swallowed it down. It was liquid gold. It was quicksilver. It was nectar and ambrosia.

In my travels I had felt the hunger of many days. I had felt the emptiness, weariness and weakness transformed after eating a piece of bread or meat. Felt the sustenance flow through my body and out into my limbs and into my mind, filling me up with strength once more.

Drinking William's blood was like filling up with lightning. It was wildfire in my heart. The hurricane in my lungs. The wound in my belly knitted together. My bones became iron. My muscles ached to be free, to throw down mountains and lay waste to cities.

Someone was growling. A low, threatening, evil cry that grew and rose to an animal cry like a wolf or a bear.

"What is happening?" I heard William cry. "Hold him, God damn you. Hold him still."

I stood. Neither man could resist my strength. I thrust my hands up and grabbed the throats of the two men beside me. Roger stabbed his dagger through my forearm up to the hilt but I felt nothing.

I crushed their throats to pulp, lifted them both from their feet by the neck and I tossed one after the other at William. He leapt aside from them both, their heads cracking on the floor and clattering against the piles of bodies in a loose-limbed jumble.

I stalked toward him. William snatched up a mace and swung it. It crunched into my arm and staggered me and he stepped in, sweeping it down on my head. I yanked it from him and swung it hard into his chest, ribs cracking like twigs. The force of the blow threw him back into the vast brazier. He thumped against it with his back and his head. It clanged and tossed up a shower of sparks.

"You are like me after all, brother," he said from under the brazier, eyes wild. "God has chosen us both." His voice pinched, his chest half crushed and struggling to breathe.

"No," I said, stalking forward, an animal growl coming from my chest.

"Come with me," William said, his eyes in shadow. "It is God's will that we be together."

"You will die by my hand," I said, stalking forward to finish him off. The strength his blood had provided was already dying away. Fading with every moment. But I had enough rage left to slaughter him a hundred times over.

He scowled. "We shall see," he said and he stood up, fast and heaved his back against the underside of the bowl of the brazier. He braced himself. William's back hissed as it pushed against the metal underside. He screamed and pushed harder, lifting it. Tilting it.

The brazier fell backward, the tripod legs lifting until finally it tipped and fell with a metallic crash. It flung the contents of the bowl into the stockade and against the huge pile of brushwood. Half a hundredweight of glowing charcoal and flame tossed into a tinderbox.

Screams came from inside the stockade as the straw underfoot ignited and spread. I watched, mouth agape, at the speed with which the ancient timbers sparked into flame.

I turned back for William. To finish him. But already he was up and scuttling round behind me, back to the blood cistern in the centre of the room. His chest was smashed and he bent double. Yet he grinned and ducked his head into the cistern, gulping down more of the glistening, thick liquid.

The Saracens in the stockade screamed and rattled the wooden bars. They were shut in behind a sturdy door that was already on fire. The wooden beams that kept them in were too thick for them to break.

William backed away from me, snatching up a sword. "Fight me and they burn. All those women and children." He stood straight again. His voice was strong and his breathing steady.

"I will kill you," I said but made no move toward him.

"You forget I know you like a brother." He laughed, pointing at the fire. At the stockade. "Your wife's children are within."

William turned and strode away toward the tunnel, his laughter echoing from the walls of the cavern as he disappeared into the darkness.

I ignored his escape, scooped up a huge axe and ran to the wall of flame. Between the bars, I could see the movement of the people screaming in terror. Flame leapt and crackled along the floor. The straw underfoot had caught and none of their frantic stamping helped to stem the blaze.

The huge axe was a whirlwind as I chopped through the beams farthest from the flames. Chips of wood flew. Flames crept closer until I was hacking into burning wood and the heat singed my hair and scolded my skin. I was sure I was too late, too weak, too slow but then the wood cracked and I kicked it through.

Hands and arms appeared and I pulled them through. I yanked out one after the other while the fire spread and the smoke choked us. Women and children, mostly. My eyes filled with smoke. The flames grew until the fire engulfed the hole and the people I dragged through were burned.

I used my body to shield them as best I could. I pushed my back against the flames until they were all through. The pain lashed me, spasms wracked my body. My helmet and armour were roasting me alive.

I had not seen Alice's children. William had lied to me. Romantic fool that I was I had allowed myself to be tricked. William did know me. And yet for all that I was burning, I forced my head through the gap and squinted through the pain and the choking fumes.

Shapes moved in the corner against the back wall. I clambered through. Two children clasping each other.

Jocelyn and little Emma.

I was passing out from the smoke and burns on my skin so I grabbed the children, kicked out more of the burning wood and hurled them through the gap.

On the other side I carried them away to the other side of the cavern where it was lit by a tiny lamp.

My seared skin cracked and oozed as I set the children down beyond the blood. Black smoke billowed in a layer above our heads, getting thicker and lower. The other prisoners were panicking at the far end of the cavern, shrieking and wailing, trying to get out. It was dark and they could not find the entranceway.

Jocelyn clung to my arm, his strong fingers digging into my burned skin.

Emma was not moving.

My hands and eyes were shaking and I could not tell whether she was breathing. If only I had some of William's blood.

William's blood.

I seized my dagger, stabbed my wrist and held it over Emma's mouth. Blood dropped onto her lips.

"No," Jocelyn wailed. "Do not make her one of them."

"She will not be," I said, my voice a raw whisper from the smoke. "And if I do not, she may die."

He nodded once, giving me permission. His trust moved me deeply. It was not merely the smoke that made my eyes run with tears.

I worried about drowning Emma with my blood but still I held my wrist to her mouth. Her lips stirred and her throat bobbed. Her eyes sprang open. She gulped down life and her fingers dug into my arm like claws. When her eyes were alight with astonishment I gave her to her brother, who held her to his strong little body. She had recovered enough to walk and I knew she would live.

But I was dying. I could feel black poison from the burns seeping into my flesh. I knew what I needed.

The vat of blood had been warmed by the fire. I climbed up and in and submerged myself, the thick substance covering my head and I lapped it up, drinking down that filth, that life. Gulping down chunks of clotted blood, I came up for air, vomited black blood and drank more until my belly was bulging.

And the strength of it flowed through me. My burns were soothed and my skin became whole and soft again.

I climbed out, blood slewing off of my helm, my hauberk in sheets. The prisoners gathered, stood staring at me in fear, pleading for help. They were coughing, suffocating and terrified of the blood-drenched Frankish knight before them. Poor souls lost in the darkness and had come back to the light of the raging flame, looking to me to help them once again.

Carrying Jocelyn and Emma in my arms, I lead the peasants out through the tunnel. I groped my way through darkness and smoke until a prick of light appeared ahead. I staggered up from the black hole gasping for air and life.

Dawn was breaking over the hills. It was astonishing that I had been underground for so little time. A pale pink light growing and the promised warmth of the day already in the wind. Smoke drifted from holes all over the hill until the underground blaze burnt itself out. I looked from every vantage and not a soul moved anywhere down in the valleys or across the hills. From somewhere, a single goat bleated.

William was long gone.

The local Saracens helped each other away down into the valley. Those folk I had saved kept as far away from me as possible. Many glanced back at me, their faces masks of despair.

I found and collected our horses and fed the children with what food and water remained in the packs.

We rode for Acre.

"So dozens of men and women died but you let William escape," Henry of Champagne, King of Jerusalem said to me, some months later in Acre. "In fact, everyone died but you and William, is that correct?"

It was not correct but I was in no mood for rising to his bait and I said nothing. It was another informal audience in the cool room at the top of his palace. Such was the desire to keep my actions as quiet as possible. I stood before him while he lounged ungraciously with the Archbishop sat next to him.

"Richard is to be congratulated," the Archbishop said, smiling and inviting the king to share in his praise of me. "He put an end to William's raids and trade is now flowing once again. He stopped the abductions of the locals and returned many innocents to their homes. Surely Saladin will be grateful to you for the fact it was a Frank that saved them."

"I doubt that," Henry said and drank more of his wine. "And William is free to start again at any moment."

"Not in your kingdom, sire," I said. "He fled north, I am certain of it. Near Tiberius two weeks later there was a woman with her throat savaged. A few weeks after that I heard of two children wounded about the neck at Antioch. They were buried by the time I arrived but I am certain it was William. There were other tales that may have been him but his trail went cold not far into Anatolia. I was most unwelcome there, as you might expect. Then I spoke to merchants who told me of more sudden deaths in Antioch so I returned, thinking William had also doubled back on me. But it was just a bloody flux and I could find no further trace of him."

"So, you failed," the King of Jerusalem said. "I think that perhaps it is convenient that William walks away from this unharmed. I do not say that you were in collusion with the man but this is all too convenient, too convenient by far."

I was thinking that it was convenient for the king that his guards had taken my sword at the palace gates. But still I imagined dragging him from his chair and beating him senseless. Perhaps the Archbishop could read my thoughts.

"William is gone from your kingdom, sire," the Archbishop said, quickly. "Certainly gone and likely gone for good. And if ever he dares show his face once more, then Richard will most certainly slay him, will you not, Richard?"

"William shall die by my sword," I said, picturing that very thing.

The king looked like he had a bad taste in his mouth. "I suppose I must present you with land and a title," he said. "As a reward for scouring out and destroying William's raiding camp and preserving our fragile peace. It is good land, I stayed there once, I think. It will bring you a better income than that accursed pile of dirt outside Jaffa. Income to buy men and men's tales of William. Your search will go better with it, will it not?"

And, of course, he wanted me as an ally to help protect his fragile kingdom. There was no denying now that I was a great knight.

"I am grateful, my lord," I said.

I shall not live, I shall not die until William lies dead by my sword. I would take the land but if Henry called upon me to fight I would have to deny him. William would have to come first. But not because of any oath. My duty was to the dead.

"Good, then. Speak to my chamberlain, he will see to everything. Now, go. Go and find a wife and when the Saracens stir themselves again, you shall help me win the war."

I took my leave from the king, my liege lord, and he waved me away while sinking another cup of wine.

The Archbishop rose and accompanied me out of the room and into the corridor where he placed a hand upon my arm. He still gripped his cup of wine in his other gnarled hand.

"You are deeply troubled, Richard," he said as the door was closed behind us.

"William lives," I said.

The Archbishop sighed and sat upon the bench that ran along the wall. "Sit," he said and patted the bench next to his backside. "My old bones ache. I find I need rest more often every month. Every day, some times. It shall not be long before I finally join God in Heaven." He leaned over to me and lowered his voice conspiratorially. "I find that wine, the very best wine, you understand, is the one thing that helps with the pain."

I sat. It was quiet. Through the door to the king's chamber I could hear muffled voices as the king's men got on with the business of governing and the king got on with drinking. I was burdened by what I knew and I wanted the old man to believe me. But how could I convince him?

"What of the children?" the Archbishop asked, softly.

"The boy Jocelyn and his sister I took to Alice's mother's sister in Jaffa," I said.

"Do you have no love for the children?" He asked it softly but it was a cruel question and he twisted it further into my guts. "You are now the lone other soul in the world who they know. Can you truly abandon them to distant relatives?"

"Leaving them with a family they do not know may be the greatest sin I have committed, my lord Archbishop," I said. "I am aware of the agony those children are in. But leave them I must. With William roaming free, my presence may bring death down upon them once more."

And seeing them reminded me of Alice.

"Who better to protect them?" he asked.

"I tell you I am dangerous," I said.

I would confuse them and upset them if I went to see them, I told myself. It was cowardice, of course. I could not face the loss of my wife. Thinking of those children made me think of her. When I thought of her I felt like dying. The horror of it was that her death was my own fault. I had fought to become a knight worthy of her but I had thought that meant having wealth and social standing. If she had never met me, if she had rejected me, then she would have been alive to be mother to those children. The only way I could cope with such thoughts was to pretend I did not have them.

"And how are they, Richard?" he asked, again, gently.

"Jocelyn is angry at everything," I said. "When he is older he will come into some of his father's land in Poitou. He is seven, now, I think. I told him to train hard and to become a good knight before then and if he ever needed my help I would fight alongside him. He's a good lad. The girl, Emma. She does not speak. Perhaps, in time. She is yet very young and has time to mend."

"Well, quite," the Archbishop said, nodding. "I shall pray for them."

"Would you look in on them, my lord?" I asked, my throat tight. "From time to time?" It was an absurd request for he was just a couple of steps down from God Himself.

"I shall keep an eye on them," the Archbishop said. "I suppose I owe them that much, for my part."

I thanked him sincerely.

"I shall pray for you too, Richard. I shall pray for your soul."

"Pray for William's soul," I said, ungratefully. "For he shall be facing judgement soon enough."

Such words come as easily as breathing. But words mean nothing and the Archbishop knew I was full of bile and nonsense.

"I do pray for William's soul," he said. "Anger and bitterness, if he holds on to such things, fill up a man's soul until there is nothing left that is good and decent." He peered up at me.

"I do not wish to be like William," I said, irritated. "Perhaps it truly was the death of his wife and son that turned him so completely to evil. It is likely that it sent him mad. But he was vindictive and cruel from birth."

The Archbishop nodded. "I see now what is troubling you."

"My wife is dead. Her death was my doing and I have failed even to bring justice to her murderer. It is years now since I swore an oath, to Isabella, to slay William and every day is another day of failure. Of course I am troubled. My lord."

"You have slain all of Williams's followers. Six of whom were the vilest, deadliest creatures who walked or crawled upon the earth. You have scoured him from the Holy Land. If I were you I should call such victories a success." The Archbishop shifted his buttocks on the hard bench. "But you fear that you are as William is, do you not?"

"Does every man in Christendom know that he and I are brothers?" The shame of my ignorance made my face burn.

I felt him shrug beside me, his robes rustling softly. "Perhaps only to those few of us who have known you both. You are so very similar to each other. In stature and features. Your manner of speech is almost identical. It would not be the first time an overlord has forced himself upon his vassal's wife. I am sorry to hear that the old Earl died unpunished."

"William returned to Derbyshire to kill his father. Our father."

"Good God."

I found I had a burning need to tell the Archbishop everything. "William said he killed our father with poison. Earl Robert was dead and cold but then he woke up and William had to kill him again."

"Terrible. A terrible sin."

"Do you not see, my lord?" I said. "Does the tale not sound familiar to you? William was cut down and tossed into a pile of corpses at Hattin. He was truly dead. Do you think the Saracens are so incompetent that they cannot ensure we are dead? They stab us before they strip our bodies. William died. Then he was reborn and reborn fully healed with strength enough to fight his way clear. Perhaps he truly did kill forty Saracens in his escape."

"Once I thought it was a miracle. Now I doubt it happened at all."

"I tell you it may well be the truth. I know that when I was reborn I found myself with greater strength that I ever had before."

He looked up at me. "When you were reborn."

"William's men killed me. At my estate, when Alice was killed, I was stabbed many times, deeply, in the chest."

"Your robustness is well known, Richard."

"I was always remarkably quick to heal, yes. Which in itself is very strange, is it not? But these wounds were different. I have seen more men killed than I can count and I know for certain that no man could have suffered so and lived."

"And yet you did. A flaw in your reasoning."

"I died. My servants said I was cold and lifeless for a day before I woke up. And when I did, I found that I was stronger, faster. And a good thing, too, because William's men possessed their master's own strength."

"William's men were the risen dead, also? Come, Richard, you go too far. You were out in the hills too long."

"They were not dead but had drunk William's blood. His blood has power. Power to heal wounds. Power to grant strength and speed."

He looked gravely concerned. "I am beginning to fear you have become as mad as William."

"There is more," I said. "My own blood holds the same power."

"Because you are brothers?"

"We were both grown from our father's seed. Why would it not? When I pulled the children from the smoke, Emma was dying. I gave her a few drops of my blood and she woke. Fully healed and full of life."

"Are you saying you imbued her with the strength of a knight?"

I smiled at the thought. "The strength of a strong girl, perhaps. The powers last no longer than a week, and they fade over that time. Emma is returned to her old self."

"I must say, I struggle to believe what you are telling me. You have always seemed a sober, reasoned young man."

I plucked the cup from his hands, stood and tossed the wine from the window.

"That was a particularly fine Burgundy."

I took my dagger and pierced my thumb where the large vein is and squeezed my blood into his cup.

"If you think I am going to drink that then you truly have lost your mind," the Archbishop said.

"My mind is perfectly clear," I said, taking my seat by him again while my blood spurted into the cup. "It has grown clearer and stronger ever since I died. Whatever it was that happened to me, the change in me was for the better. My whole life I was amongst the fastest and strongest. But since I woke from death it is as though all other normal men are wading through mud." There was enough blood in the cup for a mouthful. I pinched my thumb, stopping the flow. The smell of it was strong and good and it glistened, dark and shiny in the shadow of the cup. I looked at the Archbishop, seeing disgust and wariness in his eyes. But also curiosity. He wanted to believe me.

"If you taste this," I said. "I am certain that the aches in your bones will ease. For no more than a week or so but you might feel young again."

"What makes you think I want to feel young again? I am perfectly happy being old. God wills it. And the only blood I will drink is the blood of the Christ. This smacks of blasphemy."

His protestations were so weak that I was sure he needed no more than a nudge.

"I swear it is true and if it does not work then I shall do whatever penance you instruct of me."

He paused and I knew I had him.

"Richard, I would not make a man do penance for madness. I may have you thrown into a dungeon until you stop this raving."

"Here," I said and gave him the cup.

"God forgive me," he said. He looked down the corridor to be sure no other man was there and drank, grimacing. Good on the old man; he knocked it right back and handed me the cup.

"How do you feel?" I asked as he wiped his mouth.

"I must say that was the vilest–" he froze. His eyes widened until I could see the whites all around and his pupils grew until they were enormous black pits. He sprang to his feet, knocking the wine cup clattering into the corner. He bent his knees, bouncing up and down. The Archbishop stretched his hands up above his head and then squeezed his knees and shoulders and he laughed.

"The pain is gone," he said, his voice breathy and excited. "I feel as though I could leap from this window and fly."

I laughed. "Please do not try that."

"You feel like this all the time?" he said, flexing his hands and peering at the knuckles.

"Perhaps even more so," I said. "William gave his blood to his men and they became more than they were. But still I was quicker than they were. Mostly. But when I tasted William's blood myself it was as though the power was many times stronger still. I remember William's astonishment at the ease with which I killed his men. My body could scarcely contain it. Thankfully, it lasted but a few moments."

"By God," he said, full of wonder. "I am sorry I ever doubted you."

The chamber door opened beside us and one of the king's men came bustling out carrying a bundle of scrolls, begged our pardon and walked by.

"Let us take some air, Richard," the Archbishop said and before I could reply he had hitched up his robes and charged off toward the stairs. He barged the king's attendant out of the way, sending scrolls bouncing all over the place. I heard him laughing as he ran.

Following the trail of startled servants, I caught up with the Archbishop in the palace gardens. He had his legs planted wide, hands on his hips looking up at the sky. It was a cool day but the air was crisp and clear.

"You have a gift, Richard," he said as I drew near to him.

"I wonder," I said. "Perhaps it is a curse? For William and I are the same. And William is evil."

The Archbishop turned to me and his face was full of joy. "I do not believe that this could be an evil thing."

"And yet," I said. "If William and I drink human blood, we become even stronger than we are." I explained what had happened in the cavern. My burns and how I healed them.

He shook his head in wonder. "God is so very mysterious."

"You asked how I could abandon the children," I said. "The truth is that I wonder if I am a danger to them."

"But you would not harm children, Richard. You saved them. You are a good man."

I said nothing.

"Perhaps William is cursed," the Archbishop said. "But perhaps God has given you this gift so that you may stop him. So that you may be a perfect counter to his evil."

"I am not that good, Archbishop," I said. "His evil knows no bounds and I myself am full of sin."

"Then be as good as you can," he said. "We are all sinners but it was you who was given this gift. Whatever God's reasons take comfort in knowing that he has a plan for you."

I suppose I felt comforted. I thanked him.

"You say this shall last less than one week?" he asked.

"It will fade until you are just as you were before," I said.

"Do you know," the Archbishop said. "I have not run like I just did since... I do not know that I ever ran before in all my life. Even when I was a boy. Do you know what else I have never done? Swam in the sea. Care to join me?"

In those days no one swam. I laughed. "They will call us madmen," I said, grinning. "And I do not know how."

"I am the Archbishop and soon I shall be dead. I care only what God thinks of me. And we shall learn how. Come on, you coward. Race you there."

He lived almost two more years. The last time I saw him he was wasted away into nothing, laying in his bed. I offered him more blood and I saw he was tempted but he refused. I mourned him.

After I had climbed from that cavern of blood, I stayed in Outremer, Cyprus and the lands of Byzantium for seven more years. Always I was moving from place to place, living in cities for months or even years, listening for tales of blood. God knows, there enough of those but none led to William.

King Henry of Jerusalem died, tumbling from a window like an idiot. There were whispers of assassination but drunks often come to foolish ends. The new king, my liege lord, did not know me and was irritated by my existence. A steady stream of knights and other madmen arrived in Outremer, my few acquaintances died or returned to Europe and I saw new faces everywhere.

I was tired. Tired of the Holy Land. Tired of hiding from the world and of watching it go by without having any real part of it or having any significant connection with anyone. Tired of loneliness. I had grown sick of the heat, of the dust and the memories but still I waited for

William to show himself again. Certainly, he could not have gone to any of the vast Plantagenet lands for King Richard would have had him arrested.

Then, in the summer of 1199, news reached Acre that Richard the Lionheart was dead.

The greatest soldier of the age had been killed by a child shooting a crossbow bolt into his neck in a petty squabble in Poitou. Richard had survived countless battles since childhood and recovered from many terrible illnesses and still no man could equal his vitality. Perhaps that was why he stood before the walls of that worthless castle with no armour. Then a boy, orphaned in the conflict, chanced a lucky shot. The boy was brought before the king. Richard commanded that the terrified lad be awarded a hundred shillings for dutifully protecting his lord and avenging his father. That part had enough of Richard's saintly bravado about it for me to believe it. It was a shame, then, that as soon as the king died the boy was flayed alive.

Of course, Richard's death presented an opportunity for William. Without the Lionheart's fury directed against him, William could make a case to the crown to be reinstated lord of the de Ferrers lands.

So I returned to England. It was my yearning for a home more than my duty to the dead. But I convinced myself that William would be unable to resist the lure of his Earldom.

I was half right.

William was being worshipped as a Green Knight and lord of Eden by a band of outlaws deep in the ancient forest of Sherwood near Nottingham. He was in disguise, using his father's name Robert. And he was going about cloaked and hooded, robbing coin and drinking blood from rich and poor alike.

But that is a tale for another time.

VAMPIRE OUTLAW

The Immortal Knight Chronicles
Book 2

Richard of Ashbury
and the invasion of England
May 1216 to September 1217

DAN DAVIS

1

Archer Hunt

WHEN YOU WANT TO ATTACK A HALL and kill those inside, it is best to do it in the hours before dawn. Your victims will be sleeping at their deepest and will be easy prey. I have carried out such attacks myself on many a dark night over the centuries.

One late spring night in 1216 it was my own hall that was attacked. It was I that slept inside when William's blood drinking monsters came to burn my home to the ground. My home was the manor house of Ashbury in Derbyshire, England. I was still the lord there but I would not be for very much longer.

"Richard," Jocelyn said. He shook me awake. "Richard, wake up, you drunken sod."

"Get off me," I said to the man-shaped shadow above me. My head pounded. My throat was full of wine-flavoured bile. I had been sleeping heavily, dead to the world.

"We are attacked," Jocelyn cried. "Arm yourself before they force their way inside."

It was dark but for Jocelyn's lamp, held high by his head. The shadows it cast on his face made him look older than his thirty-one years.

I rolled from my bed and pulled myself upright on his arm. "Out of my way."

Usually, I slept naked but I had fallen into bed without fully undressing the night before so I wore a long shirt and hose. I staggered to my swords. Always, I have kept at least one near me when I slept. Keep your weapons within reach at all times, or else why even keep them? I grabbed the best blade from the stand in the corner and the familiar feel of a hilt against my palm brought me to my senses.

A man was shouting outside. A sharp thud echoed through the building. Then another. It was coming from the ground floor, just below my bedchamber.

"What is happening?" I growled at Jocelyn as I pushed my bare feet into a pair of shoes. "What is that fellow yelling about?"

"Sounds as though he is urging us to wake up," Jocelyn said. "And the banging noise, I assume, means they are attempting to break down the hall door."

I grunted. I had made sure that the main door into my hall was reinforced with iron bands and heavy timbers. "They are welcome to try. What of Emma?" I asked him.

"I checked on her. She said her door is barred and she had armed herself behind it." Jocelyn shrugged. "What she is armed with, I can only imagine. A stern word, perhaps."

"Where is Anselm?" I asked as I pushed by Jocelyn. He was not tall but he was as broad at the shoulder as an ox.

He stomped after me out of my chamber and through what was called the solar, or the day room, that led to the stairs down into the hall below. Two other doors led off the solar, Jocelyn's bedchamber and his sister Emma's bedchamber. Both very small rooms but I could never have afforded to build anything larger.

"Stay in your chamber, Emma," I shouted as we stomped through.

She shouted something I did not hear but no doubt it was very witty.

Jocelyn answered my earlier question. "Anselm is carrying our shields to the hall." He spoke French, as we did when talking amongst ourselves.

"Good man," I said, meaning his squire.

Two more thuds in quick succession resounded on the timbers downstairs.

The shouting man outside the hall fell silent. Yet the massive thudding continued as I clattered down the stairway into the rear of the hall. A dozen of my servants waited down there in the parlour, gathered together like frightened geese. All but two were men. Some faces were young, most were old. They smelled of stale smoke and the shivering-sweat stink of fresh fear.

"Do not be concerned," I said to the servants in English as I descended the stairs. "It sounds as though we have a few drunken robbers attempting a raid." I looked at each face in turn. "We must suppose that they do not know who is the lord here. If they know this is the manor house of Sir Richard of Ashbury then they are desperate outlaws indeed, are they not?"

I was never particularly gifted when it came to levity. A few of them chuckled but they were nervous. Everyone in Ashbury remembered the attack on the manor house twenty-five years earlier when the lord, his family and almost all the servants had been slaughtered in the night by William de Ferrers and his knights. The lord back then had been my brother Henry. My half-brother, as I had discovered, although no one in Ashbury knew I was a bastard. So they feared the Ashbury family curse had returned. A few of the people before me had lost family of their own in that same attack.

A huge blow from the fellows pounding and hacking on the door shook the timbers again. A couple of servants jumped, startled at the sound. They had been woken from where they slept in the hall, were shivering in thin shifts and undergarments under their cloaks or blankets. Most were ashen-faced in the candlelight.

Yet, Old Cuthbert, my faithful, sour-faced steward, clutched a splitting axe to his chest and had his ancient iron helm jammed down upon his narrow head. Others had grabbed their spears. Those without true weapons had their daggers in their hands, even the women who clutched tight to their husbands.

"Look at you all," I said. "You brave souls would strike terror into any man who broke in here. I could almost pity them. Perhaps we should pray for them, what do you say?"

The pounding continued. There was a crack as one of the door timbers split.

Jocelyn pushed past me and through the servants and strode into the hall, calling to his squire, Anselm.

"They must be hungry indeed to attempt such an attack as this," I said to my servants, speaking lightly. "We must ensure we give them a proper welcome. Cuthbert, see that the hearth fire is started. Light plenty of lamps and candles and have them placed throughout the hall, especially by the door. Do so as quickly as you can and then wait together at the back of the hall where I can see you all."

"Yes, my lord," Old Cuthbert said and turned to the others, his weasel face pinched with concern. "Right then, you heard the lord. Let's prepare for visitors." He snapped out orders like a veteran commander so I left him to it and followed Jocelyn into the darkness of my hall.

At the far end was Jocelyn's squire, Anselm, who was sixteen years' old and full to the brim with a powerful sense of duty. Anselm held a lamp aloft, casting a faint ring of yellow light about him and Jocelyn.

"Your shield," Jocelyn said and generously held it for me while I threaded my arm into the strap. It was kite-shaped, with a flat top. Jocelyn favoured the old fashioned sort with the longer, tapered shape, like a beech leaf to better protect his left leg when on horseback.

"Shall I bring your hauberks, my lords?" Anselm asked, his eyes wide in the torchlight. The lad was, strictly speaking, Sir Jocelyn's squire alone but the boy was performing double duty. I decided I had to hurry up and accept a new squire. It was not fair on Anselm to look after two knights.

The door thudded and cracked again. There were angry voices outside, beyond the door. Likely, it was no more than two or three men, I thought. I could hear no other voices through the timber walls to either side of the hall.

The axe blade on the other side squeaked as it was wiggled from the cleft it had gouged into my door.

"We have plenty of time to put on our hauberks, Richard," Jocelyn said, seeing my hesitation. "They would need an army with a battering ram to break down that ridiculous door."

My servants busied themselves behind me, whispering to each other as they lit lamps and tallow candles. Few of them understood French well enough to know what Jocelyn was saying.

"No need for us to be armoured," I said, loudly and in English for my servant's benefit. "It is no more than a handful of desperate peasants. We could deal with them in our underwear."

Jocelyn looked unconvinced. Of course, he was quite right. I was being an arrogant fool, as usual.

The door shuddered again. The reinforced frame shook.

"He's strong," I said, appreciatively.

Jocelyn grunted. "Still take them forever to get through it. What are we going to do with ourselves until then?"

It was light enough in the hall to see by. My servants gathered at the back of the hall by the top table, as far from the door as possible.

"Do not be absurd, man," I said to Jocelyn. "I am not allowing them to damage that door any more than they already have. Do you know how much that timber cost me? I had to send Cuthbert all the way to Nottingham to buy the iron for the hinges. We shall open it and let them in."

"I understand your reasoning with regards to preserving the door," Jocelyn said. "But you have no knowledge of what is on the other side of it. You yourself have said to me that knowledge of your enemy should be the first place that you strike."

"I have never uttered anything as absurd as that. Go on, Jocelyn, stand by the door and be ready to lift the bar," I said and drew my sword. I swung it in arcs to loosen my arm. "I should have taken a piss," I said.

Jocelyn shook his head. "I have not seen you this happy since Normandy."

"Men are breaking into my home," I said. "I am not happy."

He snorted and went to the door, leaving his squire standing by my side.

"What should I do, my lord?" Jocelyn's squire Anselm asked.

"You know your duty," Jocelyn said from the shaking door.

I glanced at the boy. His eyes shone in the candlelight. He was brave and strong but I remembered well what it was like to be young. "Stand by Jocelyn's side, with your sword and shield held ready. Remember your training. Anselm, have I ever told you that you are as fine a squire as I have ever known?"

There was just enough light to see his face flush. "No, sir."

"You'll do well. "

"Yes, sir."

The door cracked again, shaking under the power of the blow.

"He is not tiring, is he," Jocelyn said and he spat on his hands and rubbed them on his tunic. His sword was sheathed and hanging from his belt and he slung his shield on his back by the shoulder strap.

"If it goes against us and we fall," I added to Anselm. "You run to the Lady Emma's bedchamber and defend her door against intruders. Understand?"

"I shall defend her with my life, my lord," Anselm said, swallowing hard.

"Good lad."

I nodded to Jocelyn. He waited until the centre of the door resounded once more from a blow and he lifted the locking beam out of its iron hooks. It was a heavy thing, thick enough for a castle keep, but Jocelyn was strong and he pulled it up and tossed it aside, it bouncing and rolling to a stop.

Jocelyn yanked the door open wide.

When that door opened, I expected to find two or three starving peasants, shivering in the night air. I expected the largest of them to be holding a woodman's axe. I would see them cast in the lamplight from my hall and hopefully they would be blinded by it. My intention was to charge into the men there and knock them senseless. I was hoping that they would not give up without, at least, having a go at me. Depending on how well they fought, I would either knock them senseless or spill their guts onto my doorstep.

So I was not afraid.

And despite all that, I lifted up my shield.

It was a reflex. It was the most natural thing in the world. I had trained for years to hold my shield high and head low at the beginning of combat. It was as natural as taking a deep breath before plunging into a cold lake.

And a lucky thing it was, too.

An arrow shot through the door before it was halfway open. It thudded into the top of my shield, sheering off to the side but hitting with power enough to knock the rim back to strike me upon the forehead.

It hurt.

I kicked myself for not taking the time to dress for war. Why would I not take the time to put on a helmet or a mail coif or even an arming doublet? Sheer arrogance. My anger boiled up and I stepped forward to murder that bastard bloody peasant archer.

A man charged through the door, two-handed axe raised over his head. He came right at me, screaming a wordless challenge. His hair and beard were wild, matted and filthy. The fellow was soaked, his dark green clothes heavy with rain.

For a big, heavy man he was faster than he had any right to be.

I let him come to me. He swung the axe at an angle, down and round at my head in a wide arc. Instead of taking such a wild, log-splitting blow upon my shield, I stepped back. His axe whooshed past my face leaving him overbalanced, his mouth snarled up behind his beard. I braced and smashed the side of his body with my shield.

With my incredible strength, a thump like that would knock most men down, sprawling, dazed, and weeping. Instead, with that huge hairy madman, it was like bashing a stone wall. He rocked back, shook his head like a bull and swung again.

His hand speed was fast. But he was swinging for power, not for swiftness. His strike came from down low, up toward my balls but he assumed that I would stand and wait for the blow to fall, as if I were a tree trunk or a hall door.

I stepped forward and drove the point of my sword through his chest, punching through his clothes, skin and flesh up the crosspiece, which I punched into him and bore him down. My blade was as sharp as the devil's tongue and I yanked the steel out of his body without catching on ribs or cloth, before the point touched the floor. Blood gushed and bubbled out of his chest, front and back. I had managed to run him through the heart, or close enough. The smell of that fresh blood was delicious. I wanted to bury my face in the body, to close my mouth about the frothing wound and drink it down. Instead, I resisted and came to my senses.

To shouting and the clash of arms.

A second man drove Jocelyn back away from the doorway, snarling and smacking against his shield with a huge blade. Jocelyn was trying to turn the attacker, stepping sideways as he retreated.

Anselm shuffled away in a guard position to give his master room to fight. My servants shouted encouragement and screamed in terror behind me.

Another arrow flashed from the darkness beyond the open doorway.

I raised my shield and the thing thudded hard through the layered wood and leather. The whole arrowhead, barbs and all, punched through. The wicked point on it stopped an inch from my eyeball.

I peered over the rim.

Two bowmen lurked outside in the dark, ten yards beyond the doorway on the path. Little more than shadows in the shade.

"I'll gut you bastards," I roared, shaking my sword and shield like a madman. I strode toward them.

The archers fled. They flitted like black-grey birds and ran. I reached the doorway in time to see them swarming up and over the ten-foot high gateway like rats. Then they were gone.

They moved with a speed and manner the like of which I had not seen for more than twenty years and a thousand miles.

Full with the blood lust, I ran back inside to the remaining attacker. That man hacked at Jocelyn's shield with the widest falchion I had ever seen. It was a cross between a sword and a meat cleaver.

"Out of the way, Anselm," I shouted at the squire, who should have been running the attacker through instead of standing back from him.

Despite his attempts at clever footwork, Jocelyn had cornered himself. His shield was being chopped to pieces by the huge blade that the man smashed down over and over with an animal ferocity. His shield all but gone, Jocelyn was parrying with his blade.

"Now you die," I said to the man as I came within range of a strike.

He spun like a whip and his blade slashed at me, roaring in anger with his reeking, rotten mouth. I was expecting it, wanted it, but he was faster than any man I had fought in years. Faster even than the axemen I had felled. The blade cut the air over my head but he was hugely overextended and before he could recover, I straightened to smash the pommel of my sword into the top of his head. It cracked his skull in and his legs buckled.

Still, he fell no further than to one knee, resting his weight upon his falchion. It was a blow that would have felled a horse and yet the fellow struggled to his feet.

William de Ferrers' men, those he had fed with his own blood, had been able to resist such a strike.

Jocelyn pushed forward and bashed what was left of the shield into the man's back. He staggered forward, slammed into the wall beside the doorway, breaking off a whole section of the painted plaster I had done a couple of years before. The man slumped and dropped his falchion by his side. His eyes glazed over and a trickle of shining dark blood ran down his cheek from the crack I had made in his skull.

Jocelyn, his face twisted in anger, stalked forward to finish the stranger off.

"Wait," I commanded.

Jocelyn half-turned to me. "He is mine to kill."

"Yes but I wish to know who he is," I said, fighting the urge to crack Jocelyn on the skull for speaking to me with such disrespect.

"He's a bloody madman, is who he is," Jocelyn said, his eyes wide. "Do you see what he has done to my shield, Richard?"

I was laughing when the man leapt to his feet and charged me, screaming like a demon.

"Christ!" Jocelyn shouted and jumped back out of the way.

I checked the man's rush, the arrow stuck in my shield snapping against his body. He rebounded from me and I pushed him back down against the wall in a shower of plaster. The damage to the wall was particularly infuriating because I had spent money I did not have in order to brighten up my hall in an effort to keep Emma happy.

So I stamped on his knee, hard and all he did was growl at me so I smashed his nose with my fist, crunching the bone and splitting the skin apart. His head rocked back and he settled down, finally, clutching his destroyed face and whimpering.

He was younger than I had first thought. His green clothes were dirty but not ragged and had barely been mended, suggesting they were new. He wore a cap dyed the same shade of green. Like his friend, he was sopping wet from the night's rain.

"You are a keen fellow," I said. "Who are you?"

He snarled and started to rise so I stabbed my sword through his knee and ground the point against the bones inside. He screamed like an animal. And he smelled like one, too.

"He moves as quickly as you do," Jocelyn said, sounding offended. "Or almost."

The man thrashed around and cursed, his voice hoarse from screaming. He was smearing his blood all over my wall and floor.

"Go and see to the door," I said to Jocelyn. "There was a third and fourth man. Archers, both. They ran."

"I am sure they did," Jocelyn said and ran to the door. His squire followed and together they shut it and came back to me.

"Watch him closely," I said to Jocelyn and turned to my servants. "It is over for now. The sun will be up soon enough. There are at least two more of these fellows but I doubt they will return. Cuthbert, I shall ride out for those archers this morning. Have the horses readied. My grey courser. Bert the Bone, wake up your bloody useless dogs. We shall all need food. God bless your brave souls. Worry not about this man here, nor the filthy fellow over there. I shall deal with them both. Now, be about your day."

They busied themselves with excited whispers and I turned my attention to my prisoner.

The man was jammed up against the wall, half propped up and half lying to one side. He leaned on one elbow and his other hand clutched his ruined knee. I had no doubt he would walk with a limp for the rest of his life. His head was bleeding and his nose smashed. A stream of blood welled from his head and ran down his face and neck onto his chest. The blood from his leg leaked onto the floor. It smelled wonderful, almost masking the foulness of his skin and hair.

"I am Sir Richard of Ashbury," I said to the man speaking English. "I am lord of the manor. I should take you to the sheriff, I suppose but I think that instead I shall kill you."

In truth, I had no intention to kill him. My blood lust was fading. His speed and power intrigued me, as it reminded me of the men I had fought many years before, in Palestine. Instead, I was attempting to unsettle him.

He laughed. A gurgling, hacking laugh that shook his body.

"I cannot die," the man said, his manner of speech that of a commoner. His voice was a growl like gravel grinding on steel. "I will live forever in Eden. By the power of the Green Lord's blood in this life. I die and I live again. I cannot die. You can do nothing to me, nothing."

Jocelyn bristled. "He is truly a madman," he said and stopped when he turned to me. "What is it?"

His words were echoes of the mad ravings of the followers of William de Ferrers twenty-five years before, in the Holy Land. The talk of a Green Lord was new but it was the same madness.

"Richard?" Jocelyn said, prompting me. I shook my head.

Could it be, I wondered, that William had returned to England? It was the sort of attack he liked to make. If so, why send merely a few men to attack me? I was almost offended that he would send so few, and those few barely competent. If it was indeed William, surely he would have known they would fail.

Jocelyn sighed at my prolonged silence and sank to his knees before the man. The hall behind me grew lighter as the hearth fire grew to flame and the servants busied themselves lighting more tallow candles.

"Did you not hear?" Jocelyn said. "Are your ears stoppered with mud? A lord has commanded you to speak your name. From where have you come? Why did you attack us so? You know that we are knights, do you not? You could never have defeated us."

The man stared at Jocelyn. His eyes ran, behind his smashed nose, a small smile on his bloody lips. He chuckled, like a saw catching on a knot of wood.

"Do not think feigning madness will save you," Jocelyn said. "Madness or not, you shall be tried and the court will certainly condemn you to death. Do you understand that? Do you? But perhaps you can do right by God. Perhaps the court will treat you with sympathy if you were merely doing as commanded. Did your lord send you here? Who is he? Is he one of the rebels? Which of the rebel barons is your master?"

The man's eyes were wild and full of joy. His bloody smile spread slowly wider across his face. The man licked his lips.

"Jocelyn," I said, starting a warning.

Jocelyn half turned to me and the man darted forward, quick as a cat and yanked Jocelyn's dagger from his belt.

Startled, Jocelyn fell back and scrambled away. I moved forward, ready to stop the man in green from stabbing Jocelyn.

Instead, the man plunged the dagger into his own eye, up to the hilt.

He was laughing as he died.

We all fell silent as the body slumped sideways to the floor. It lay still, but for a jerking foot.

"What in the name of God?" Jocelyn cried.

The hall crackled with the sound of the growing hearth fire. My servants froze in the middle of whatever task they were doing. Anselm's face, behind me, was white.

"He murdered himself," Jocelyn said.

"I saw."

Anselm cleared his throat. "Why would he do such a thing, lord?"

I looked back at the body of the other attacker. It may have been my imagination or the flickering of the firelight but I thought perhaps the dead man's body moved. A leg jigging. Bodies did that sometimes and yet I wanted to be certain.

Jocelyn spoke to Anselm. "He was a madman," he said. "Moon touched."

"We will carry both men into the yard," I said to Jocelyn and Anselm. "We three. We shall take their heads and toss the corpses into a pit by the pig sty." They both stared at me as if I was mad. I cuffed at my mouth. The smell of the blood was making me salivate. "And then we shall eat while our horses are prepared. We have a pair of archers to catch."

With those archers, I had two more chances to discover if my old enemy had truly returned to England.

If so, I would torture from them the truth of what William de Ferrers' intentions were.

And where, precisely, I could find him.

"But why did we take off their heads?" Jocelyn asked as we mounted our horses in the courtyard in front of the house.

It was an unpleasant business and I had taken their heads by lamplight out beyond the workshops by the middens. I did not truly expect them to rise up from their deaths but I could not be sure. If they were William's men, and I thought it likely, then they would have a bellyful of his blood. His blood made them strong, fast and quick to heal. I doubted the blood could heal them from such terrible wounds but it was not worth the risk.

So, to be safe, I hacked their heads from their bodies before tumbling them into a shallow grave. After that, we three men-at-arms had dressed in our mail hauberks and carried our helms and undamaged shields. It was light enough to see by, the sun brightening the damp world from over the wooded horizon.

"Sometimes a man can seem dead but get to his feet again," I said. "I did not wish to take any chances while we pursue these archers."

"Surely they were dead," Jocelyn said. "Did you think they were witches?"

"Perhaps," I said, not meeting his eye.

Jocelyn looked at me suspiciously. He might not have said it but he must already have suspected what they were. When he was a little lad, William and his followers took him. I had saved Jocelyn and his sister Emma before William could drain the children of their blood. Even then, I had barely rescued them from a terrible inferno that had engulfed their wooden cage, started by William so that he could escape while I saved the prisoners.

We never spoke of what happened in that cavern, what the siblings had seen. Emma was far too young at the time to remember anything of it at all. I was sure, though, that Jocelyn must have remembered me bathing in a bath of blood, drinking it down and curing myself of terrible burns in mere moments.

But it had happened twenty-five years before and Jocelyn was a man in the prime of his life so if he wanted to pretend ignorance then I was willing to let him.

We rode through the gate and out into the dawn, scattering chickens. The air was damp, but spring-damp, a smell of succulent young leaves and the whiff of blossom here and there in the grey-purple light. The manor house and outbuildings at Ashbury were surrounded by a timber wall and deep ditch but they were meant to deter petty thieves, keep animals from crossing the boundary either way. Properly manned, it could also have formed a sturdy barrier against an armed attack.

Mostly, I had built it as a way of announcing my return to the ancestral home after ten years in the Holy Land. My intention was to bring the villagers and servants together in a sort of festival of digging and log splitting. That had been fifteen years ago and the wall was sagging in places. I did not have the money to rebuild yet it remained an adequate defence.

But without a guard posted, a ten-foot timber wall would never keep out a determined man.

There were footprints in the mud that Anselm claimed to be able to interpret as the tracks left by two men running. It seemed as though the archers had run east along the track toward the smaller of my woods near to the village. That track and the wood came out on the roads toward Derby and, beyond, Nottingham.

I wished I had more men with which to cover more ground but times were hard and all I had was the ancient hunting dogs and their more ancient kennel master riding one of my sway-backed old nags.

Though it was not raining, the world was sodden. Water dropped from every leaf and the grass drenched with fresh rainwater. The sun struggled to shine through the wet blanket clouds hanging over us. But it was light enough to hunt.

We rode along the track toward the wood. It was a lane, really, with dense hazel hedgerows both sides and the hedge on the northern side growing thicker until it became the Ashbury high wood. The air was clear, refreshed. Even wet, an early summer morning in England was a lovely thing. I felt good to have killed a man again. I looked forward to catching the archers. I looked forward to them telling me where their master hid.

"They could be miles away," Jocelyn protested again. "In any direction."

"Not according to your squire," I pointed out.

Jocelyn scoffed at Anselm's tracking and hunting abilities. The lad was ranging ahead so could not take offence. The dogs bounded ahead of us, excited to be outside but useless at tracking the archers. It was simply too wet for them to sniff the men out.

"You should have those dogs killed," Jocelyn said. "They're far too old. Half of them are mad and the other half are blind. All of them are as stupid as Bert the Bone."

Bert was the kennel master and nothing Jocelyn said was entirely incorrect.

"We shall find them," I said, loudly, because a lord must appear confident even when he is not.

Anselm rode back along the track. He rode very well for a lad of sixteen, nothing flashy about his style at all.

"A smear of mud, my lords," he said, grinning. "Up ahead where the wood begins beside the lane."

Off the side of the track, he showed us where the ground had been disturbed by something. Perhaps a man slipping, dragging a swathe of long grass up leaving the wet earth bared below. It was right by a gap in the hazel and alder, leading into the blackness of the wood proper. A mixed wood of hazel, ash and oak with elder everywhere in the understorey. A couple of great elms poked above the canopy in the centre. The leaves were heavy, dripping and subdued. The air felt dense and close. Even the birds were keeping close counsel.

"We cannot ride through there," Jocelyn said. He loved sitting atop his horse, a fine bay courser that I had bought for him, and fairly detested walking.

The dogs were so far up ahead they were almost out of sight and playing with each other and the kennel master Bert berated them.

"If you find a scent," I shouted to Bert the Bone. "Blow the horn."

He raised a skeletal hand in acknowledgement and I dismounted.

"How did those dogs miss this?" Jocelyn said, nodding down at the disturbed ground. "I told you they are useless. You should invest in a new pack. I heard Ralph's brother Walter has a pregnant bitch. Good dogs, his lot, you should see them track a deer."

"That would break old Bert's heart," I pointed out.

"He's even more useless than his dogs," Jocelyn said.

"Says you who won't even get off his horse," I said. "Come now."

We tethered our horses and went forward into the darkness on foot with our shields raised, me, Jocelyn and Anselm. A bowman was worth little without his bow, whether he used a crossbow or a war bow. But a single arrow could fell a knight, no matter how brave and skilled he was. Something that King Richard found to his cost so many years before when he blundered into the range of the crossbow that killed him. I intended to keep my shield up.

Anselm went first and we followed. The morning wind rustled the leaves in the canopy above, shedding a steady pattering of rain down on us. My shield, helm and everything else caught on branches and budding twigs and the drenched leaves soaked my mail hauberk. Anselm and my servants would be busy scouring the rust off everything. I decided again that I needed to find a new squire.

"The branches are broken here," Anselm said, over his shoulder. "Someone pushed through this bush, not long ago."

"You fancy yourself a tracker, Anselm?" I asked, keeping my voice low. "I know that hunting appeals to you."

"Yes, my lord," he said, whispering. "My father loves to take deer."

"Surprised he has leisure time," I said.

"How can you even see anything?" Jocelyn muttered behind me in the darkness.

"Spread out," I said to them both. "Leave space between us. Together we make too tempting a target."

It was yet black as night under the dripping trees and I imagined an archer taking aim at me from the shadows. It smelled powerfully of mushroom and mould under the canopy. We pushed on through the woodland toward the fields beyond, my shoes sinking into the soft woodland floor with each step. I was slowly realising we had no chance of finding men, creeping through at a careful walking pace.

Ahead, a group of rooks chattered in their high nests. They began cawing wildly, jostling and flapping in the branches. A few swooped through the trunks before us, like apparitions. Their cawing set off more birds, the noise spreading through the wood in every direction.

"Our archers have scared them," I said, meaning the rooks. "They sound rather far ahead, would you not say? We must hurry."

"They will be running for their lives," Jocelyn said. "And they will be unarmoured. We will never catch them like this. We should get back on our horses and ride around. We could get in front of them by midday."

"You are probably right," I admitted. While I knew I could out-pace and out-distance any mortal man even in my armour, I also knew my men could not. "Anselm, what do you think?"

"Me?" The lad spluttered, looking down. "I do not know, my lord."

"Ah," I said. "So you disagree? Come on, speak up, boy. And keep going. That way."

We kept moving forward and Anselm spoke without looking round at us. "It is simply that following a trail is the best way to find a man who does not want to be found. My father says a man can go to ground in an acre of woodland and it would take a dozen men a week to find him."

"He does, does he?" Jocelyn said. "I take it that your father likes to exaggerate. Or perhaps you do."

"No, sir," Anselm said, ducking the water-laden leaves of a wild stand of hawthorn. "He also says you can flush a man out if you frighten him enough. You and your men can thrash the bushes, curse his name and list the things you will do to his family if he does not give himself up."

"Your father is the most honourable knight in Christendom," Jocelyn whispered, snapping branches aside with his shield. "He would never say such a thing."

"But he did," Anselm blurted. "He won his fortune taking hundreds of knights in tournaments. Many of them fled the field and had to be hunted down."

"Keep your voices down," I hissed at them.

Jocelyn grumbled. "These robbers are hardly tournament knights."

"Nevertheless," I said. "I agree with Anselm. Or, rather, I trust his father's advice in this, as in all things. We should push on a while, follow this trail. Follow our frightened little birds."

The trees got larger in the centre of the wood. Many were still coppiced but more were single trunk oaks, scraggly-topped elms and a few beech that spread their leaves so well that little grew beneath them. The under layer thinned out and the going became easier. Still, we were all soaked from brushing against sodden leaves and branches and the dripping from the trees above.

"If these bowmen are fleeing," Jocelyn said, stomping through the wet litter behind me. "Surely catching them matters not? Their friends have received their earthly justice and will no doubt be suffering their eternal one today. Why not let these men go?"

"It is a lord's duty to protect those sworn to him," I said over my shoulder to Jocelyn. "If we do not capture these men, the folk of Ashbury will be nervous for weeks. And what if they raid the village? Or the Priory? This is our duty. Remember that when you have your own lands."

Jocelyn scoffed. "The chance of such a thing would be very fine indeed."

Anselm stopped by a small clearing and peered at the trampled grass.

I lifted my shield up higher. "What is it?" I asked, standing behind him.

"Deer, perhaps," the squire said. "Or men."

"Watch for arrows," I said. "Keep your shields high."

Anselm walked around the edges of the clearing, poking at the ground with his toes, looking out for what supposed trackers like Bert called sign. There were a couple of badger or deer tracks leading out of the clearing but I would not have known a man's trail if I had laid eyes on it. That sort of thing was beyond me so I left Anselm to it.

"Did you not wonder why those men were so fast?" I asked Jocelyn. "So strong?"

Jocelyn stared at me. "You are imagining things."

"You were very young," I said to him. "Perhaps you do not remember how William's blood drinking monsters were in Palestine but—"

"I remember everything." Jocelyn stared at me, his eyes wild.

"Of course," I said, as gently as I could. "Yet when was the last time you were bested by a single man?"

Anselm, across the clearing, glanced back at us. He knew little about our past. I gestured at him to keep looking.

"I was not bested," Jocelyn said. "I defended, knowing that he would tire."

I said nothing.

"Perhaps we should return?" Jocelyn said. "We have no hope of finding the peasant bastards."

"It may be best if you go to the manor house," I said and a thought struck me. Had we been lured away intentionally? I should have left one good man at home. "Yes. Yes, go. Guard your sister while Anselm and I push on for a while. That is if you do not mind lending me your squire?"

Jocelyn agreed and turned to head back when Anselm hissed a warning from up ahead.

We all dropped lower, crouching behind our shields.

"What is it?" I whispered as I crept up beside him.

"Ahead," Anselm said, peering low through the trees. "Man lying in wait for us."

I followed his outstretched finger. Water patted down all around, dripping and dripping.

A dark mass lay in the shadows beneath a cluster of young oak.

The scent of blood was in the air.

"He lays in wait," I said. "But not for us."

I stood, drew my sword and approached the dead body, listening for movement. The others stalked behind me.

"Keep your shields raised high," I said as we came near.

One of the bowmen lay upon his back. He wore the same kind of dyed green tunic, cloak and green hood as the attackers who had died in my hall. A bow lay nearby, his arrow bag squashed under him, the arrow shafts poking out into the mud. The dead fellow in green staring up at the branches with one open eye.

The other eye had been obliterated by an arrow. The shaft stuck straight out of the socket. The goose feather fletching shone white in the gloom.

"I suppose they had a disagreement," Jocelyn observed.

"Perhaps the killer did not want his fellow caught and questioned," I said. "Protecting his master, as your beast with the falchion did in the hall."

"Why did they go for the eyes?" Jocelyn asked, pointing at the man's lack of armour. "Surely that is a needlessly difficult shot to make?"

"It is a sure way into the head," I said. "When a man has a belly full of William's blood then he can recover from blows that would fell a mortal man. But I found that a blade to the brain is a reliable way to kill them."

Jocelyn shook his head. His doubts were understandable. "At least there is one archer left for us to take. I suppose there is no need for me to return to the manor."

"Indeed," I said, looking through the trees. "Stay vigilant. He could be watching us now."

"Forgive me, my lord," Anselm said. He had gone further ahead and stood looking down at his feet. I was about to berate him for lowering his shield but he kept speaking. "There are tracks of two men leading away from here."

"You cannot possibly know that from tracks in the leaf litter." Jocelyn sighed and stomped over to his squire. "It is too dark beneath these trees to make out anything."

"Here, right here," Anselm said. "One footprint here, with another laid over it, distorting it."

"It belongs to the same man," Jocelyn said. "Retracing his steps. Or it belongs to the dead one and he was dragged back here after he was shot. Yes, that is it."

Anselm opened his mouth to protest and I was about to say that it did not matter either way when the uproar started.

Through the trees, up ahead. Men yelling.

I ran, pushing past them both with a clatter of shields. They followed on my heels.

At the edge of the woodland, the coppiced trees ended abruptly. Beyond, strips of fields ran away uphill, a sea of bright green shoots, wet and shining in the morning light. We had come out in the upper village field.

Halfway up it, two men fought in the furrows.

One was on his back, scrabbling away from the man standing over him. The one on his back in the dirt was gangly, young, and skinny limbed, like a spider. He wore a dark brown tunic, covered with mud, his hood pulled off to reveal his blonde hair.

The man over him was stocky, older, dressed all in green and held a long dagger high over his head. He was wavering, swaying and shaking his head as if to clear it.

He also had three arrows driven deep into his chest. Blood soaked his green tunic.

Any remaining doubt that I was dealing with William's men was immediately gone.

I ran up the hill, shaking my arm from the strap and tossing my shield aside. Though I wore a thick gambeson under a heavy hauberk, I ran as if I was naked. My sword in my right hand, I pumped my legs to close as much of the distance as I could before they noticed me. I was faster than I remembered and immediately outpaced Jocelyn, even though he was fifteen years younger.

I shot up that hillside like an arrow from a bow, the damp earth flying out beneath my heels, trampling the shoots of wheat and rye.

The stocky man turned as I was almost upon him and his mouth gaped open just in time for my fist, closed around the hilt of my sword, to crash into his jaw. The impact jarred my hand up to the elbow. It shattered his teeth and knocked him into the furrows.

He groaned and rolled over, trying to get away but by so doing he bent, snapped and pushed the arrow shafts further through his flesh.

I stalked after him.

I heard Jocelyn and Anselm behind me seizing the youth.

The man I had struck coughed out a few teeth and spat them out with a mass of blood and sputum onto the new shoots of spring. He fumbled next to himself for his dropped dagger but I stabbed my sword point through his wrist and placed my foot on the back of his neck.

"You do not get to murder yourself," I growled. "You will tell me about William."

I reached down and rolled him over, thrilled to be able to discover where my enemy was hiding.

Unfortunately, however, the man in green died. His breath bubbled as his mouth worked, opening and closing, forming words with no breath. His eyes rolled back. I slapped his face but there was no life there. The man was drenched in blood. Tunic through to surcoat and down to his stockings. The earth was pooling here and there with it. The delicious aroma filled my nose, my head. It was dizzying. The arrows, I supposed, had finally finished him. Drained him of blood.

I turned about in time to see Jocelyn strike the side of the young man's hooded head with the back of his mailed hand, the skull resounding with a sickening thud. The lad fell, senseless and Jocelyn stepped forward to finish him.

"Do not kill him," I shouted.

"He struck me," Jocelyn objected. "This peasant struck me."

Jocelyn's jaw was bright red.

Anselm stood staring at the scene. His eyes wide but I was pleased to see that they were unwavering. The squire started hunting around again, looking at the tracks and he moved away, looking for something.

"These are no ordinary peasants. We take that one back to Ashbury," I said, sheathing my blade and staring at Jocelyn and Anselm, both breathing heavily from the short chase and fight. "We shall bind him tightly. And you shall treat him gently, the both of you, no matter what he does. He is the last one alive. This lad could lead me to William. Jocelyn, watch him while I deal with this skewered one."

"Here is a bow, my lord," Anselm said, trudging a few paces back to us through the furrows with a huge bow held aloft in one hand, with a quiver and a few arrows over his shoulder. All were muddy.

As I took the head off the dead man, a horn sounded nearby, from the wood at the bottom of the hill.

My dogs howled from the trees and came bounding from the shadows, through the brush and up the hill toward us, mud kicking up in a shower of soil.

Bert the Bone, the kennel master, rode behind on his nag. Soaking wet, covered with leaves from following his dogs through the wood and a huge grin on his scrawny old face.

"They found a scent, my lord," he shouted, as his dogs sniffed and howled at the body, their tales wagging. "There is a body in the woods. He's got an arrow right through his eye, he has."

"Keep them away from the blood. Do not let them drink the stuff or who knows what they will become," I roared, startling Bert from his idiotic joy. He had no idea why I was afraid. Perhaps the blood of William's men would have no effect on animals but it was not worth taking the risk. "And keep them away from the prisoner. We ride for Ashbury. I have questions for this boy."

2

AMBUSHED

"WHO ARE YOU?" I asked as the young man opened his eyes. I spoke English, as the lad was clearly a commoner.

Jocelyn had not cracked the side of his skull apart but the lad had a lump above his temple the size of a goose egg. The young fellow's eyes were unfocused and he blinked and peered about.

When I pulled off his dirty, brown hood, the blonde hair beneath was long, tangled and filthy. He reeked of old sweat and mushrooms.

I had ordered him sat upon a high stool and bound to a thick post in the scutching workshop. It was late morning and plenty of light came from the open door and open window. Poultry scratched and clucked in the yard beyond the door.

I would not have one of William's beasts in my house. Not least because I planned to bleed him dry. Nor did I want to frighten the servants with what I was going to do to the boy. Though no doubt they would hear his screams from across the yard and inside the house. I could not bleed a man in the stables and frighten the horses. Thus, I decided that the workshops were the best place to flay this man.

"Where am I?" he asked, blinking and mumbling.

"Look at me," I said to him and slapped his face.

His blue eyes flashed with anger as they focused on mine.

"Yes, here I am," I said. "You are mine now, boy. You will tell me what I want to know."

The eyes flicked to Jocelyn and Anselm standing behind me. I slapped his cheek again.

"Look to me," I said. "No man here will save you."

There was murder in his eyes.

"Must Anselm be here for this?" Jocelyn asked.

I kept my eyes on the boy as I answered. "Yes," I said. "Anselm, you do not mind seeing a murderer's blood spilled, do you?"

"No, my lord," said Anselm.

I saw the flicker of fear I wanted to see. "Of course, if this scrawny streak of piss answers my questions then no one will see any more blood this day. Murderer or not."

"I am no murderer," the young man said, speaking with passion.

His voice betrayed his status. A commoner, of course, though he spoke clearly and with confidence. Often, I found that a villager I had treated kindly for ten years would still mumble and stare at the floor when he addresses me.

"Not a murderer?" I said. "Are you claiming that you did you not kill your two friends back there?"

He looked confused for a moment. "They were no friends of mine."

"Yet you did shoot your arrows into them, did you not?"

He stuck out his chin. "Is it murder when the men you kill are murderers themselves?" he asked.

"Yes," Jocelyn said. "Of course, you fool."

The lad shot him an angry look. "Then it should not be so."

Jocelyn scoffed. "The arrogance of this serf."

"I am no serf," the boy said, straining at his bonds. "And it is you who is arrogant."

I thumped him hard with the back of my hand.

"Do not speak thus to a knight," I said. He glared at me, both cheeks now bright red, and I was certain he would have tried to kill me were he not restrained. "What is your name?"

He looked at me and said nothing.

I drew my dagger, slowly and I held it front of his face. "Do you see how sharp the blade is? I do not use this one for eating or for common tasks. I keep it honed so that it slips through flesh like butter. What is your name, lad?"

His eyes fixed on the point of the blade as I twisted and turned it for him so that it caught the light.

"Is it worth losing your finger," I said. "To keep your name?"

"Swein," he blurted. "My name's Swein."

"What is your real name, boy?" Jocelyn said. He had been raised in the Holy Land and had come to England as a grown man so he spoke English somewhat awkwardly.

"It's Swein," he said, gritting his teeth, still looking at the blade.

"You lie," Jocelyn said.

"It matters not what his real name is," I said. "Swein, then. Tell me, where is your master, William?"

"Who?" he asked, as if genuinely confused.

I flipped the dagger over in my hand, holding the blade and rapped the hilt against his nose.

Swein jerked back, crying out, coughing as his eyes ran and blood streamed from his nostrils and down his throat. He leaned forward as far as his bindings would allow, blood dripping onto the earth floor, drip dripping and spattering amongst the dusty remains of last year's chaff. It was bright and shining upon his lips.

I wanted to drink it from his face and found myself leaning forward, breathing in the hot metallic scent of it.

I denied the desire, pushed it away. It was unworthy of me. Base, corrupt.

"Do you see, Anselm," I said over my shoulder, "how a small blow to the nose can be so terribly disorienting? Such little damage caused and yet the distress it affects is remarkable."

"Yes, my lord." Anselm was a dutiful squire.

"Now, Swein," I said. "I shall ask you again and this time, please ensure you answer truthfully."

"No," Swein coughed. "I have no master. I know no William."

"If that is true then who do you truly serve?" Jocelyn said.

"I am a free man," Swein said, sitting up straight as he could with his arms tied behind his back. "As was my father."

"But you have a lord," I said. "Who is he? What village are you from? Where in England were you born?"

Swein spat blood on the floor. Jocelyn bristled but I waited. "Yorkshire," Swein admitted. "I was born in Yorkshire. We lived just north of Sherwood. Me and my dad."

"How did you come to leave your shire?" I asked.

"Is it not obvious?" Jocelyn said. "The boy is an outlaw."

I examined Swein's face and knew it to be true. The youth looked back at me, steadily, defiant. I should have slapped him again or, at least, threatened him but my heart was no longer on the road I had set it upon.

"Yes," I said. "You were outlawed. You fled Yorkshire and went to another county. In some way, you came to serve a new lord. A powerful man. A man who can bestow great gifts upon those that follow him. He may not go by the name William but you know the man I mean."

"No. You are wrong. I do not serve him," Swein said, straining at his bonds. "I would never serve such evil."

My heart raced. Whether he served William or not, he knew of him.

The lad could lead me to him.

"Why were you with those others?" I asked. "The ones who attacked my home, who you fought in the village field?"

"I was not with them," Swein said, watching me closely. "I followed them."

"Why?" I asked.

"To kill them," he said.

"A murderer," Jocelyn said. "He admits it before witnesses."

"Quiet, Jocelyn," I snapped. "Go on, Swein. Why did you think you could kill four men, alone?"

Swein nodded at me and took a deep breath.

"They were six when they set out," he said, smiling. "After I shot the first one, they got careful. And they were quick, quicker than any man has a right to be. But they were all six of them from towns. Me, though? I'm from the wood."

"I knew it," Jocelyn said. "An outlaw."

I ignored him and Swein continued.

"They hunted me but they never found me. I followed their trail in the day, stalked them and watched from afar when they rested. Like the first, I waited until he come away from the others. Arrow through his head just in front of his ear. Went in one side and poked right out the other. So I reckon, anyway. Don't rightly know what they thought had happened. They just drank his blood and moved on.

"But when I took the second of them, they knew then that I was hunting them. They kept watch. They were ready to chase me, baiting me, so I waited. Then last night, it was raining, so I crept up close, waiting for one to go piss so I could send a shaft right through his eye. The rain weren't too loud and I got close enough to hear them talking, arguing."

He hesitated, aware no doubt he was talking too much himself.

"Tell it all, Swein, tell all and tell it right now," I urged him on. "No point to holding on to anything. Only the whole truth will help you now."

"This were just outside your house," Swein said. "Outside your wooden walls, in a meadow."

"Why did they argue?" I asked.

"Two of them were saying they were supposed to burn your house down in the night and burn all the other buildings. They were supposed to start fires outside the doors and throw brands into the thatch but it was raining so those two they wanted to wait. The other two said their strength was wearing off every day and they should attack anyway, burn down the house from the inside after they killed everyone who mattered."

"No need to ask who won the argument," Jocelyn quipped.

"They got over the walls like they were nothing. Almost jumped right over the gateway. And what could I do about it by then? A wall between me and them and my bowstrings, even my spares, were wet through because I slipped when crossing the river down by the crossroads. I did not know what to do. So I thought I should warn you. I climbed the wall myself and while they were trying to find a way in, I tossed stones at your house and cried out warnings."

"That was you shouting," I said. "In the night. I remember. I thought it was them, jeering and mocking us, meaning to frighten us."

"I did shout. Then I ran and waited. I hoped you would finish them all off. They were afraid of you, even the ones who said they were not. When the two outside ran, I followed until it dried and I got one of them. The other man chased me. He was moving too fast for me to hit his head so I shot into his torso while he charged me. Three arrows in the chest and he did not even slow. He would have killed me for certain if you had not arrived and killed him for me."

"Your arrows killed him eventually," I said, shaking my head. "Not I. I wanted him alive."

A smile grew under his bloody nose.

"So you killed four out of six men," I said. "Six of William's monsters. Men filled with the power of William's blood. Men who were stronger and faster than most knights."

"If what he says is the truth," Jocelyn said.

"Indeed."

"It is the truth," Swein shot back, his blue eyes reflecting the bright sunlight of the doorway behind me.

"But why?" I asked. "Why would you do this?"

Swein opened his mouth and thought better of whatever it was he had been about to say. "Because they deserved it."

"Do you know where their leader is?" I asked. "The man of evil you mentioned."

Swein nodded. "I followed them to here from there."

"Well, where is it?" I grabbed his shoulder. "Out with it, for the love of God."

"Sherwood," Swein said. "The man of great evil is in Sherwood."

"Anselm," I said and stood up. "Untie this man."

Jocelyn started behind me. "Surely, you do not believe this pack of lies?"

"I do."

"His story is preposterous," Jocelyn said.

"We shall clean him up and bring him to dinner. I shall have Cuthbert find him an old shirt and tunic of mine. They will hang slack upon him but he is almost of a height with me, do you not think?"

"Richard," Jocelyn said, his tone grave. "You cannot invite this man into the hall to eat with us."

I considered Jocelyn to be a dear friend and he was, along with his sister, the closest thing to a real family that I had in the world. But I was also his lord.

"It is my hall," I said, fixing him with my best stare. "And I say who dines within."

Swein looked between Jocelyn and me with wonder, fear and amusement in his eyes. Anselm untied the many knots securing Swein to the post.

"What are you smirking at?" I said to Swein and leaned in once more. Close enough to breathe in the scent of blood drying on his nose and lips. I held the point of the dagger to his face. "If you do anything to make me suspicious of you, if you make any sudden movements or touch anything that I have not given you leave to touch, then you will be the next man who gets a dagger to the eye. Do you understand?"

He paused for a moment and nodded.

"Good," I said. "Because I am famished."

"Emma, may I introduce Swein," I said as I escorted the freshly scrubbed young man into my hall and to the top table. The servants had the hall trestle tables set up and ale and food were being served. Dinner, held at midday, was both the first and the main meal of the day. So it was hearty and could take up much of the day itself. I had known many a dinner to become daylong drinking sessions, depending on the company.

Emma broke off speaking to my steward Old Cuthbert, turned and smiled at Swein as if he was an old friend.

"A pleasure to meet you, Swein," she said, "I am told that we have you to thank for saving our lives last night."

"Lady Emma is Jocelyn's sister," I said to the skinny young fellow.

Like most men, Swein was flustered by her beauty and stood to gape at her like the commoner he was. Emma wore a simple but long, pale green tunic with unfashionably short sleeves. Her hair was styled simply but it shone golden, even in the dimness of the hall.

I nudged Swein with my elbow. "Speak a greeting, you simple-minded young fool," I said.

Swein, I guessed, had lived as a farmer or worked in the woods his whole life, even before fleeing justice and living as an outlaw. His life had no doubt been rough, green, and small. No doubt, he knew every soul in every village for ten miles around and not a single thing about the world beyond.

Emma was a creature from another world. She and Jocelyn had grown up in the Holy Land in a wealthy, noble family after both their parents died. I had abandoned them there, truth be told, when they were very young. But they had received an upbringing that was proper to their station. Emma had been married and widowed by the time she and Jocelyn found me again in Derbyshire. She was around ten years older than Swein, perhaps pushing twice as old, but it seemed to me that the years had only enhanced her beauty.

"Morning, my lady," Swein mumbled and bobbed his head.

"Sheer poetry," I said.

Emma laughed. "Come and sit with us," she said.

Jocelyn stomped by and took his customary seat next to my empty chair. Anselm moved to sit beside him. Emma sat in the chair to my left and invited a stunned Swein to the stool next to hers. The lad had murdered two men, almost been killed himself, was then captured, bound and threatened with flaying just that morning. Yet now we treated him like an honoured guest. He kept looking about at the servants laying food and drink before us as if fearing it was all a trick.

In truth, I was not especially afraid of him. He could shoot a bow, no doubt about it but he was barely into his manhood, I guessed, and willowy as a girl. And I mostly believed his story. I wanted more of it but he was too nervous. I wanted him to feel safe and to begin to trust me.

And if he attempted to flee or to harm anyone in my house then I would take off his hands and torture the whole tale out of him.

"What do you intend to do now, Richard?" Emma asked, pouring ale into Swein's cup. While my servants made Swein presentable, Jocelyn had told his sister everything that had occurred that morning.

Jocelyn spoke up before I could answer. "Turn the lad over to the sheriff and be done with him." He took a slurp of his ale.

Swein's head shot up. "I ain't done nothing, my lord," he said. "Nothing that weren't their due."

Jocelyn paused with his cup half to his lips and stared at the lad in shock.

"Speak like that again," I said to Swein, "and I shall cut out your tongue."

"Richard," Emma said, offended. "Cut out your own instead. This is not a tavern."

I caught Jocelyn smirking. "And you can wipe that idiot smile from your face," I said to him, feeling like a disrespected father to bickering children. "Do not leap down the man's throat every time that he opens it and do not disagree with me. I know your feelings. You have made yourself perfectly clear on this matter. Stuff your mouth up with bread, won't you? Why, in God's name, can I not have peace in my hall?"

"A lord himself sets the example for his household to follow," Emma said, cutting bread for Swein.

I rubbed my face.

Jocelyn and Emma had never respected me. I was their last resort, their last port of call in their travels from the Holy Land to their ancestral seat. I knew they were with me because they had nowhere else to go in the whole world. That was fine by me. I loved them both and without them, I would have no one. So I put up with their disrespect. And they knew it well.

"Those who attacked us were certainly William de Ferrer's men," I said to Emma, as gently as I could, for William had murdered her mother. "It was in their manner."

She nodded. "By that you mean they fought with that ferocity particular to William's devils?"

"Indeed, and there is more. William sent them. Swein here says he followed the attackers from the Forest of Sherwood," I said, looking beyond her at the young man shoving cheese into his mouth straight from the platter, not offering any to Emma's plate. "And that is where their master lies. I shall have the full tale from Swein on the way."

"On the way?" Jocelyn said, coughing out his ale. "You do not mean to travel to Sherwood?"

"William is there."

"That monster is most likely long dead," Jocelyn said. "Those men were strong, I grant you but enough ale can drive a man into a killing frenzy, we have both seen it on the battlefield. You desire William to be so close because you want to kill him yourself. And that has you seeing things that are not true and trusting the word of a peasant outlaw and confessed murderer. William is dead, I tell you. Leave it. You cannot know different."

"Dead he most certainly is," I said. "But that has not stopped him from sending men to burn us in our sleep. I am sure. It must be William. It was in the way they moved. Although he is not using his own name, I am certain it is him. The way those men spoke. They were filled with his madness, with the way William twists men's minds. He has come home. Come home to England, bringing murder and madness with him. I know, yes, I know."

"This is not suitable talk for the table," Emma said, her face pale.

The servants were listening very closely. It was so quiet in my hall that I could hear a blackbird trilling in the courtyard.

"You are quite right," I said to her. "Let us eat. We have preparations to make. I will leave in the morning. And Jocelyn, Anselm and Swein will accompany me."

"In God's name, you do not mean to ride us into Sherwood looking for a dead man?" Jocelyn said.

"Firstly, we will ride for Nottingham," I said. "To see the sheriff."

"Please, lord," Swein said quietly. "Do not take me to the sheriff."

We stood in the stable yard, in the murk before dawn the next day. My grooms preparing our horses and my servants organising our supplies and equipment. Jocelyn and Anselm were with us, seeing to their own horses. Anselm was across the yard whispering sweet words to his sorrel rouncey, a well-tempered beast with good stamina and a charge that would embarrass no one.

I wondered what I could do to bind Swein to me. Whether I should attempt to frighten and bully him into compliance or to be kind and welcoming.

"I am not taking you to the sheriff," I said. "I am going to see the sheriff, a man who is my friend. You are merely coming with me so that you may help me find William. Your great evil in Sherwood."

Swein looked me in the eye and lowered his voice. "You cannot hold me captive," he said. "I am free to leave. I am not wanted in this shire."

My instinct was to punch his teeth down his throat and choke him but I controlled myself. Perhaps he saw my thoughts reflected in my eyes, as he took a step back.

I grabbed his upper arm. He twisted away. For such a skinny young fellow, he was immensely strong. But my grip was iron.

"You go nowhere but where I say," I said. Swein looked about for help but my men paid us no mind. "You are outlawed in at least one county. You appear to be friendless. And no man who is not mine knows you ever were here. What is to stop me from burying you with the men you killed, out beyond the rubbish heap?"

"The king's justice?" Swein said, holding my gaze. "Or God's?"

I laughed at that. "I have seen little of either. Listen to me. Does the sheriff know your face?" I released his arm.

"One of his bailiffs does." Swein rubbed his arm. "A great giant of a man, a nasty piece of work."

"So, a single man. I doubt we shall see him and if we do, I shall swear that you have served me for years. And Swein is not your true name?"

He looked sullen.

"Well, Swein you shall be from now on," I said. "Tell me, for what crime were you summoned?"

He scuffed his boot on the ground. "A crime far outweighed by the punishment."

"Do you want me to beat it out of you?" I asked. "I would rather not do so. If you tell me true, no matter the answer, I shall not take you to justice nor allow you to be taken while you serve me. Not even if it were murder or homicide."

He plainly did not believe me. But what choice had I allowed him? "I took a deer."

"Ah," I said. "In Sherwood?"

"My father were outlawed in Yorkshire when I was a boy. Few years back. We went to Nottinghamshire, my dad's brother died, left his land to us. Sherwood was a good place. But the foresters are proper bastards. My dad bought a few pigs and herded them back to our little wood. But to get there he had to go through Sherwood, he had to. No other way. The forester found him, said he was feeding his pigs on the king's acorns. Then they said our land was in the king's forest and that we hadn't permission to dig a ditch around the boundary. They charged him and fined him so much that we lost everything. Then, last winter I took a deer. We were starving. They caught me. Said that as I were sixteen years old I would be tried as a man. I ran into the wood."

I understood why he had run instead of face a trial. A friendless man had no chance against the warden, verderers and foresters.

The penalty for taking a deer in the king's forest was death.

In 1216, nearly a third of the land in England was under the law of the forest. When people say forest today, they mean to say a large wood. But back then, a forest was an area of land where the king himself had legal control over the management and distribution of all resources within the borders of the afforested land. Mainly, the kings claimed land for themselves as a means of generating wealth for themselves and also to create lands for hunting. A forest could be wooded but also had heathland, farmland and villages within. Sherwood had all of the above but was one of the few forests in England that remained almost entirely dense woodland. That wood was some of the finest hunting land in the country and contained thousands of deer and boar, the hunting of which was the exclusive right of the king and his foresters. The shire wood of Nottingham contained a half dozen deer parks and a couple of remote hunting lodges maintained by lords that existed for the king to hunt in.

"So that was where you found William?"

"He ain't called William," Swein said, shaking his head. "They call him the Green Knight. They call him the Lord of Eden. Some folk say his name is Sir Robert. I never saw him. Saw his men, though. They're stronger than you would believe. Faster than you can see. They rounded everyone up. My father fought them. They killed him and I ran. Some of the men who attacked your hall? They was there. The rest are back in Sherwood. I'll go back and kill as many as I can before they catch me."

I looked closely at him. If he was telling the truth, it meant he was a remarkable young man.

"Your arrows took William's men in the eyes," I said. "You must be a fine archer."

"Finest in all England, lord," Swein said, his eyes shining.

Jocelyn snorted. "So says every other peasant in England."

"It is the truth," Swein said to me without even glancing at Jocelyn, who mounted, eager to be off. There was little he loved more than riding.

"What other weapons can you use?" I asked.

"My fists?"

I made a decision.

"Swear service to me," I said.

"You what?" Swein said, looking left and right. "Lord."

"I need a squire."

"Richard," Jocelyn said from atop his sleek courser. "You cannot mean to take this peasant as a squire."

"A page, then," I said. "Does it matter what we call him?"

"He is a man grown," Jocelyn almost wailed. "He is as common as the dirt under his nails. You would make a mockery of the position, whatever you call it.

"It is not as though I mean to make him a knight," I said. "Someone needs to replace Geoffrey. I was happy enough without while we were at home. We can look for more men in Nottingham but with the country the way it is, I may need someone to help me."

"It takes years to train a squire," Jocelyn said.

"We will not teach him to fight," I pointed out. "I do not want him as a cup-bearer at my table. I do not want him to recite poetry and play the harp. All he needs to do is carry a spare shield, clean my armour and pass me a waterskin when I ask. Hardly a task beyond a man such as this one."

"May I carry my bow, lord?" Swein asked.

"A bow is not a typical squire's weapon," I said, wondering how it would look. "Yet you shall be no typical squire. But let no man in Nottingham see you with it or there will be questions to answer. We wish to be asking them, not answering. Do you understand?"

"Do you have it, lord?"

"It will be brought with us, yes," I said. "I even had the bow cords dried out because I have seen the power of your bow and your remarkable ability with it. Yet, I cannot hand you a weapon unless I know that I may trust you with it. If you swear to be my squire, then you shall have my trust and you shall have your bow."

"What if I do not want to be your squire, lord?" Swein asked.

"How dare you," Jocelyn cried. "It is the greatest honour you should ever have, you rotten little turd."

"Jocelyn," I said. He turned his courser away, mumbling about having nothing to do with it. "If you do not swear to be my man, Swein, then I will never be able to trust you. If I cannot trust you then I have no use for you. I will have to hand you over to the sheriff."

"If you do that you may as well kill me yourself," he said, shaking with the injustice of it. "My lord."

"You have no family, now. And you have no friends."

"I did have," he said.

"But now you are alone."

"What if I do not want a master?" Swein looked down. "What if I like living in the wood, answering to no one?"

I was pleased that he was reluctant to swear to me. It showed that he would take his oath seriously, not swear one day and run the next. Although, anything was possible.

"Every man has a master," I said. "All that living outside the law means is that any man who is not can have power over you. Can kill you on sight. But when you serve me, you shall have food in your belly and usually a roof over your head. You will learn much that you could not learn any other way."

He scraped at the ground with his shoe. "How long would I be bound by this oath?"

"Until I release you from it," I said. "And I will do so when I find and kill William. Or if I am myself killed."

"What must I do?" Swein said, sighing. "There is a ceremony?"

"There is," I said. "But we must make haste."

And, I did not add, you are too low born to warrant it.

"Kneel. Hold out your hands to me as if in prayer. I will take them, you will repeat my words back to me and mean them in your heart. For the men here will bear witness and God will know the truth in you. Now, speak thusly. I promise on my faith that I will in the future be faithful to my lord Sir Richard of Ashbury, never cause him harm and will observe my homage to him completely against all persons in good faith and without deceit."

The lad did so swear, I clapped him on the back and saw to my horse.

"My lord," Swein said. "May you grant to me my bow now?"

"Gladly."

A servant brought the unstrung bow stave, quiver and arrows, all of which Swein snatched.

The lad caressed the thing like a lover, checking it all over for damage. He licked his thumb to wipe off some stain or other.

When all was ready, I gave the servants my final commands and told Anselm to ride out. Jocelyn was by then through the gate and ranging away, gloomy and irate.

"Lord," Swein said, looking anxiously at the packhorses and remounts as Anselm swung onto his fine young rouncey. "I know not how to ride." Swein's cheeks coloured.

I laughed at his ignorance. "Nor shall you learn," I said. "You will walk. As befits your station. We will not ride quickly, merely fifteen or twenty miles a day or so. Now, follow Anselm. Carry these bags."

Swein was relieved and angry at the same time.

When all was ready, I kissed Emma at the gate.

"We shall not be far," I said. "I shall miss you."

"I will not miss you," she said, smiling. "I may finally get your house in order with you out of it."

"It is your house as much as it is mine," I said. "More so. I would have been ruined many times over without you, as you well know. Bar the gate and the doors each night long before dark. The men know their duty and someone or other will be on watch every night. Every labourer able to fight will sleep in the hall and take turns upon the walls. The door is repaired so thoroughly that it is stronger than ever. I would not leave if I thought I left you unsafe."

"Do not go hard on that boy Swein," Emma said. "He is a bright young man. I know why you took him into your service but with the right kind of guidance, he could serve you well."

"He'll never be tamed, that one," I said. "It is only a matter of when he breaks his oath and whether he commits a grave crime or simply flees. Oh, do not glare at me so, I know his station is not of his making but he is an outlaw, I will not have him."

"At least, promise me that you will look after Jocelyn," Emma said. "He is in one of his black moods again."

"And do I not know it," I said. "He needs a battle."

"He needs a wife," she said. "As do you."

"As you need a husband, girl," I shot back, for the hundredth time.

She hesitated. "I know that you do not wish to hear it," she said. "But I will pray that you let God back into your life. You stop yourself from feeling anything that has hurt you but you are also denying yourself any joy from life or from God's love. It is not God's will that you continue to deny your soul his love."

I ground my teeth and took a breath before answering. "I will feel joy again when I bring justice to William de Ferrers."

"God be with you, Richard," Emma said, disappointed in me, somehow. "I hope you find that which you seek."

"I shall find it," I said, swinging into my saddle. "Find it, and then stick its head upon a spike."

It was a day's slow ride from Ashbury to Derby. From there it was one road straight to Nottingham. A simple, two-day journey. But before we reached our destination, we were ambushed.

That first day, Swein was battling within himself, wondering if he had made a mistake when he had sworn himself to me. He trudged silently, bent under the loads he carried and the decision he had made.

I wanted to question him about William but I let him be, walking beside the horses, his bow stave resting upon his shoulder.

Jocelyn ranged ahead, watching for trouble.

In 1216, England was at war with itself. King John, the youngest and favourite son of old King Henry had ruled the country for the seventeen years since Richard the Lionheart had died. John had faced enormous problems from the start of his reign, losing his family's vast possessions in France one after the other. He had spent years mounting unsuccessful campaigns to regain those lands, beggaring the country with taxes and fines.

Tired of being divested of their money for over a decade, the rebel barons had finally taken up arms against King John. England was a country up in arms. One lord after another had declared for one side or the other and everywhere there were armed knights, men-at-arms, their squires, mercenaries and locally levied commoners assembling here and there to defend or attack one castle or another. Men-at-arms were what we called anyone who fought in full armour, usually on horseback. All knights were men-at-arms but not all men-at-arms were knights. They could be squires or mercenaries or freemen and burgesses who could afford the equipment to so arm themselves.

In fact, every man in England would be armed and armoured in the appropriate fashion unless he had good reason to do otherwise. Arming yourself to the fullest extent allowable by your station was not just desirable, or honourable, it was carefully prescribed in law.

But the road to Derby was familiar and well travelled and I felt safe. Anselm stayed beside me, leading the packhorses with his well-behaved rouncey.

"I do not wish to add to your burdens," I said to Anselm as we rode. The day was cold and blustery but winter felt over and it was dry. "Since Geoffrey left us you have been squiring for two knights. You are already overworked. Even squiring for Jocelyn without the help of a page or two is too much for one squire."

"No, my lord," Anselm said, his cheeks flushed pink with the cold.

"I grew up with many knights and many squires," I said. "It was hard work, I remember it well. I wish I could afford to keep more men. With things the way they are in England, I do not know when this will change."

"I understand, my lord," Anselm said.

"I know you do," I said. "And that is why I will ask even more of you. You must show Swein how to pass for a squire."

Anselm and Swein shot looks at each other, one looking down and one looking up.

"I know this task is not possible, even with a year of work," I said and held up a hand to forestall Swein's protests. "I say this not as a slight to you but because it is true for any man. It takes years to make a knight. Any knight. I was seven when I started my training. How old are you, Swein?"

He did not want to tell me but he did. "Sixteen years old, my lord."

"The same age as Anselm," I said. "How long have you been learning to squire, Anselm?"

"Nine years."

"How long from now before you can become a knight?"

"Another five years."

"You will never be a knight," I said to Swein. "I do not try to make you one. But you will listen to Anselm. He knows everything that you must learn. You must keep rust from my armour and weapons. You must carry them and prepare them for me, should I need them. You will fetch me food and water, on the road, at inns, in battle. You will stand watch at night. You will rise early to build a fire. You will do all that is asked of you, without complaint."

"A servant, then," Swein said, his voice full of bitterness.

"Yes," I said. "That is what a squire is. You think these tasks beneath you?"

He looked away.

"I did these things. Jocelyn did these things. I also served as a cupbearer and server at banquets, bringing drunken lords their wine. I emptied nightsoil buckets and dug pits for my lords to shit in. Anselm scrubs our armour with vinegar and sand, scouring his hands raw. You never get the stench off your hands, I know. You think service is beneath you? Anselm, who is your noble father?"

"William Marshal, the Earl of Pembroke."

Swein's mouth dropped open and his step faltered. He looked upon Anselm with amazement. "I have heard of that man."

I laughed aloud. "Have you, indeed?"

"I am merely a fifth son," Anselm said, undermining my point.

"Nevertheless," I said. "His father is the most famous, most celebrated knight in Christendom. Anselm, would you dig me a pit to shit into, if I asked it."

"You have asked it," Anselm said, smiling. "I do it gladly."

"So," I said to Swein. "You will learn everything Anselm teaches you."

"I already know how to shit in a hole," Swein said.

Overnight we stayed at Darley Abbey, sleeping upon the floor of the hospital. Darley Abbey had been one of the many houses partly founded by Robert de Ferrers, the great lord who had sired me. William de Ferrers was his son and heir, whereas I had not known about my true parentage until I had confronted William in Palestine. Our special blood came from our father but if the old man had known any secrets of our bloodline, it had died with him. William had poisoned our father and then cut off his head when he later rose from the dead.

Darley Abbey had many benefactors in the years since but it was no great religious house. The hospital was small but it was ours alone. There were so few travellers at that time. Most folks stayed in their parish and went no further than the nearest market but there were always travelling folk, tradesmen and ambitious men going from place to place. But not in 1216.

It suited me. I had not travelled without servants for many years. Doing many simple things for myself on that journey was almost refreshing. It would have reminded me of the lonely travels of my youth were it not for the constant bickering between my sworn men, who were all children whether grown men or not.

From the Abbey outside Derby, we had one more day's ride to Nottingham Castle. The road was quiet. We saw hardly a man walking and none riding. The war had frightened many into staying at home or, at least, staying away from the main routes. The brothers in the abbey had warned us about folk preying upon travellers outside of the towns.

"It is sad that England is such a dangerous place that her people go about in fear," Jocelyn said. He spoke in French, as we usually did but I knew he was purposely excluding Swein.

"Jocelyn grew to knighthood in the Holy Land," I said to Swein in English. "He claims that the roads there are so safe that a woman can travel without an escort, with gold in both hands, from Antioch to Acre and remain unmolested."

"I said no such thing," Jocelyn said.

"Not sober, anyway," I said to Swein, who grinned. "Listen, all of you. Monks are terrified of the world. They shut themselves away because they are cowards. Monks impart nothing but fear because that is all they have to give. Never was there a monk in all the world who did not warn travellers of the dangers of the roads. They seek to frighten you into giving alms. Monks and priests are peddlers of fear. A war in the land is good fortune for every religious house, order, monk, deacon and bishop."

"Do not listen to this man, Anselm," Jocelyn said. "He is making a jest."

Perhaps Jocelyn was warning me not to say anything that may get back to Anselm's mighty father. If so, it was probably good advice.

"Sherwood stretches north many miles from Nottingham, does it not?" I said to Swein, wondering how I would search so large a place.

"It's a right big place, alright."

"Then you had better lead me to where William hides."

We rode for a while up and down the hills. The land was coming into full bloom. White blossom lining the hedgerows.

"Are there outlaws in these parts?" I asked, looking at a dark band of trees on the horizon.

"There are outlaws everywhere, lord."

Ten miles from Derby, the road passed through a sizable wood, at least, a couple of miles long. It looked to be full of sturdy oak and uncounted coppiced ash beneath.

"May I hunt, lord?" Swein asked, holding up his unstrung bow.

"We do not have time to wait while you amuse yourself," I said. "We must reach Nottingham before nightfall."

"I'll run ahead through the wood alongside the road," he said. "I move quickly. I may find us a deer or a boar."

Jocelyn laughed from his belly, startling his horse. "You'd be lucky to find a dormouse in these woods."

"I must practice my bow," Swein said, attempting another angle in his argument.

I looked down at him. "Go, then, if you must. But you must find us at the other side of the wood, upon the road. We will wait for you until midday."

He nodded his thanks and ran to the south, crashing through the undergrowth, and vanished into the gloom.

Jocelyn stared at me. "And that is the last you shall see of him."

"Possibly," I said. "He has told me enough to make a start."

In truth, I felt wounded by his betrayal. I had offered him the chance to squire for me. Knights from the best families in England offered me their sons that they may learn from me the skill in battle that had made me famous. And the filthy commoner had betrayed his oath almost as soon as it was uttered.

"I will have to find another squire," I said to Jocelyn. "When we get to Nottingham, I am sure there will be some lads or grown men who would leap into the arms of my employment."

"A squire for you and some general servants," Jocelyn said, whom I kept armed and equipped at my own expense. I loved him like a son and he loved to spend my money.

The robber's ambush was sprung was when we were about halfway through the wood.

Jocelyn, riding ahead of Anselm and me as usual, came galloping back to us from beyond a bend in the road. He cared greatly for horses, his own mounts he loved, and would never sweat them unnecessarily.

"A line of brush has been dragged across the road," he said. "Less than half a mile away."

I looked around into the shadows of the wood to either side. The wind rustled the young leaves above. It was not possible to see more than a few yards through the dense coppiced ash poles stretching away.

"Surely, robbers would not attack two knights and a squire?" I looked to Anselm for confirmation, as if he would know.

"It was a hard winter," Jocelyn said, shrugging. "And the hungry peasants grow bold."

"Perhaps the brush has been there a while," I said to him while drawing my own sword. "Perhaps the men are already far away with their spoils."

"The travellers in front of us this morning must have passed through the wood," Jocelyn said. "This trap was laid for us. They are out there. No doubt they are heading back to us here through the trees."

"Get our shields," I said to Anselm.

The good lad was already moving, sliding from his saddle to go for the packhorses behind when the first arrows came flitting in.

The first I saw cut the air where Anselm had been sitting. The second I felt as it smashed into my shoulder, hard enough to throw me from my horse.

I smashed into the road and knocked the wind from my chest.

A broken arrow shaft stuck out sideways from my upper arm. I must have snapped it as I fell.

Someone was shouting. Jocelyn.

My dear grey courser bolted. As always, my sword was still in my hand.

"Run for the trees," Jocelyn cried.

It was good advice. If surrounded, choose a place, attack it with all your might and break free of the encirclement. More arrows thumped in. I was exposed, vulnerable. I rolled to my feet and staggered toward the trees after Jocelyn and Anselm.

Without my hauberk, I felt naked. An arrow slashed through a bush next to me and clattered into a coppiced stand of hazel.

There were men there. The robbers had driven us from one side of the road into the arms of their fellows, who came screaming out of the trees with spears and axes.

The pain in my shoulder vanished. Three men converged on me, their faces contorted with the rage of battle, the first thrusting a long spear underarm, up toward my belly. The man on my left was big-boned but thin. He attacked with an old sword that he swung at my head as though he were splitting a log, his yellow teeth bared, spraying spittle into his beard. To my right, a young fellow screamed a wordless, high cry and thrust at my legs with his staff, hoping to trip me or smash a knee.

All my life, I had been either fighting or training to fight. I was always strong, quick, and skilful. Ever since I was first killed in the Holy Land, my physical abilities had been even greater. The men rushing me were full of desperate rage, fully committed to killing. My left arm was numbed and practically useless. I was unarmoured. But bringing death to my enemies was my purpose in life.

I flicked the spearhead aside with my blade and stepped inside the thrust, the point sliding past me and I thrust my sword through his guts, stepping close enough to him to smell his sour breath. I pushed him away off my blade. As I did so, I sliced the leading edge across his body, spilling the thick ropes of his guts out into the leaf litter, leaving a trail of offal as he went reeling away. The stink of blood and hot shit filled the air. The swordsman was following up his missed swing, grunting with the strain of changing direction when his weight was all in the blow itself. I twisted and ripped my point through his throat. He let go of his sword and clutched his destroyed throat, staring at me as he staggered backward. His mouth was a black hole. Blood sprayed from it and his neck as I turned on the boy with the quarterstaff, who was backing away shouting something in a confused scream. I ran him through the heart and his blood pulsed out as he fell back, dying. He put his hands over his chest as if he could hold in the blood. His face turned white. In the moment before his eyes closed, he knew he was about to die.

Jocelyn and Anselm had been fighting other men. The memory of it, the awareness of their combat nearby while I had been fighting my own battle, came back to me.

Those men they had fought were dead, too, a pair of them lying in a swathe of bright green nettles. Blood spattered the young leaves. Jocelyn and Anselm stood together, breathing heavily. Their swords were bloodied. Neither my knight nor his squire appeared to be injured.

The bowmen on the other side of the road had fled or were hiding, no doubt horrified by the swift deaths of their friends.

"The boy was begging for his life," Jocelyn said stepping behind me. "When you ran him through."

"He was?" Dark blood flowed from his chest, soaking his plain tunic.

"Look how young he was. Not more than twelve or thirteen, perhaps."

The smell of the blood was overwhelming. My mouth watered.

"You are wounded," Jocelyn said, pointing at the arrow sticking from the top of my arm.

"Cut it out," I said. "Anselm? Are you well?"

The young squire was staring at the blood on his sword, his eyes wild when they turned to me. "Lord? Yes, lord." He gulped.

"Did you kill your first man?" I asked him. The two dead men in the nettles where Anselm stood had their heads slashed and bashed in.

"I am not certain," he said, voice shaking and looking to Jocelyn, who shrugged. I understood. Most men are confused by battle and they say it quickly fades from memory.

"Anselm fought very well," Jocelyn said. "He kept his head, parried, moved in the proper fashion. Just as we have trained. Yes, he did very well."

"Well done, lad. We shall discuss every detail later over ale and wine," I said. "Firstly, you must catch the horses before their fellows take them away. Jocelyn will help you after he removes this arrow."

Jocelyn took his dagger, sliced away my clothes and held the point against the flesh where it was drawn in, around the broken shaft. "Perhaps we should wait until we can get you to Nottingham. There will be monks there. If you are blessed, perhaps even a barber."

"Cut it out, you coward," I said. "Be quick about it."

Jocelyn licked his lips and hesitated. "The monks—" he started.

"For the love of God," I cried. "Go. Assist Anselm with the horses. Those bowmen will marshal their courage soon enough."

Relief flooded his features. "Are you sure you can manage yourself?" he asked. "You will make a mess of your arm."

"I will heal," I said, staring at the blood still welling from the dead boy's chest. "When you catch the horses, clear the brush that closed the path. I shall come and find you there."

Jocelyn followed my eyes. I caught his look of disgust and horror before he turned away and hurried down the road.

I took my dagger and wiped the blade upon my surcoat. My left hand I placed upon a sturdy trunk and twisted my shoulder so I could see the entry place of the arrow. Likely, it would be headed with the barbed broadhead type. I would have to cut away much flesh, slicing down to the bone, in order to free the path that the barbs must take. Without knowing how the arrow was oriented, I did not know where to cut the line. So I started in along the shaft, pushing the point of my dagger against the skin. It depressed a long way before the skin gave way with a sudden, wet pop. The pain speared through me and I was worried because it hurt and yet that was the least of it. I recalled that I had experienced much worse, many times over. Steeling myself, I sawed down, slicing through the flesh. Blood welled out, hot and fragrant. I was thirsty. The pain burned and sweat pricked out all over my body. I glanced around, checking no man was near. The wood was quiet, even starting to fill with birds flying back. Crows cawed overhead, drawn by the scent of fresh death and a pair of pigeons clattered away from them.

Blood had obscured the wound. My water and wine were on the horses so I had to continue by feel alone. I sawed down until the tip of my dagger was tapping against both the bone and the point of the arrowhead. The tip was lodged in the bone itself. I paused while I vomited a little then felt around with the dagger to find the orientation of the barbs. I sawed my way back out, above them. Blood flowed freely and I dropped my dagger twice as my hand was slippery with it. When I felt I had enough flesh cut away, I wiped my hand upon my surcoat, gripped the shaft and pulled. Agony shot through me. It was as though I could feel every bone in my body.

I cursed myself for my weakness, ground my teeth and yanked the thing out with a cry loud enough to terrify even the crows. The blood gushed out while I held on to the tree for a long moment. I knew I was not yet done. I peered closely at the arrowhead. The point had bent, compressed from hitting my bone but otherwise seemed whole. Anything not of your body that remains inside a wound would encourage corruption. I had seen it many times in others. I thrust my fingers inside and felt around. There was a scrap of my linen shirtsleeve inside that I had mistaken for a long blood clot. When I was close to certain, I sat for a moment.

Anselm and Jocelyn would be waiting. Other travellers would be along the road soon. I walked passed the bodies of the three I had killed. Already, the death smell was overwhelming.

The crows had returned and a brave few stood upon the earth, watching me.

The bearded man, so full of fury in life, looked at peace but for his ruined throat. His eyes were still open though one eye was white and the other red. I stepped around the trail of quivering, gelatinous guts joined to the spearman and knelt by the boy I had stabbed in the heart. I tried to avoid looking at his face. His blood was drying up and his body growing cold.

I had to hurry. I looked out along the road. No one was around. I slit the boy's dirty clothes and exposed the wound. He stank but I had to have blood if my arm was to heal. And I needed my arm to kill William.

I dug out a few clots from the wound, sank my lips to it and sucked in the blood. It had been so long since I had tasted it. The blood from inside him was yet warm and that warmth spread through me until it burned with a wondrous heat. Like hot sunlight on a cold day. Like cold water from a spring after a hot day. I drank until my belly was heavy with it and then I drank some more.

A noise. I looked up, my hearing improved by the magic of the blood. A figure moved in the trees on the other side of the road, knew it was spotted and fled, slipping through the wood. The man moved with skill, making barely a rustle or snapping a twig. But the blood allowed me to hear him crashing away like a boar.

I wiped myself down, collected my sword and followed the road.

At the edge of the wood, with our horses, Jocelyn and Anselm waited.

And beside them, his bow at his side, stood Swein.

3

THE LADY MARIAN

"THE LAD LOOKS TERRIFIED," JOCELYN SAID to me in French as we rode the final miles to Nottingham.

We were well on our guard, dressed for war in mail with our shields slung and helms at hand. The shadows grew long before us along the road. Every few yards there was another blossoming bush in the hedgerow perfuming the evening air. I prayed that no enemy lurked beyond them.

He was speaking of Swein, who had shocked Jocelyn by returning to us after all. Swein walked beside Anselm's rouncey, a way behind us, with his head lowered and his face unseen inside his hood.

"He saw me," I said, keeping my eyes on the hedgerows.

I doubted we would be ambushed again. There were people about on the road, heading to Nottingham from the countryside. Most walking, a few driving a cow or a sheep and one with a tired old pony pulling a cart loaded with shit-stinking chicken crates. They all gave us space, taking off their caps and staring at us going about so armed. Knights were one thing. Knights armoured for war meant trouble and the sight of us no doubt made them fear war would follow. My shoulder had fully healed, the blood doing its work in moments. Yet, I would not be caught out again. Let the peasants fear.

"He saw you?" Jocelyn asked. "You do not mean he saw you drinking?"

"At the end, he was in the trees." I kept my voice low, though I thought Swein would likely not understand French. "I suspect he believed he was well hidden."

"You saw that it was him?"

"It must have been him," I said.

Jocelyn shook his head. "If it was, why ever would he have returned?"

I looked at Jocelyn. "You saw me drink, once, when you were a boy. Yet you returned."

"That is different." His mouth wrinkled up as if tasting something foul.

"It is," I allowed. "Well, whatever his reason, he is here now."

Jocelyn looked over his shoulder. "Have you considered that he led us there? That he disappeared at precisely the right moment? That he was one of the archers? It may have been him that shot you."

"Of course I considered it," I said, irritated that he thought me so foolish. "Yet the fletching on the arrows that were shot at us was grey."

"So?"

"Swein's are white," I said.

Jocelyn pursed his lips. "Perhaps he borrowed his friend's arrows."

"Perhaps. But if he had been a part of it," I said, "why did he come back?"

Jocelyn thought for a while. "Could he be William's man after all?"

I considered it. "Could be."

"What are you going to do about it?" Jocelyn said.

"I do not know," I admitted. "Watch my back?"

We arrived with the sun low in the sky and the air growing cool. Nottingham was a thriving place. It was not a market day, nor a holy day nor a Sunday and yet it was busier even than Derby. The castle sat high on a natural sandstone cliff edge on the southwestern corner of town, covering the approach road. The town arced along the northern side of a bend in the wide, meandering River Trent.

While we found rooms, I sent Anselm up to the castle to ask if the sheriff would see me and if so, when I could call upon him. We handed the horses to the grooms at the stable, along with dire warnings should they not be properly cared for.

Swein was nervous, peering out of the stable into the street. "I should not be here."

"You are unlikely to see the bailiffs, are you not?" I lowered my voice. "Even if they claim to know you, I shall state you have served me for two years. Swein is not the name they know you by, so do not concern yourself. If anyone tries to take you from me I shall bash his bloody skull."

Swein attempted a smile but his face was white as bleached bone. I was sure he had seen me, he was afraid of me and yet he stood bravely before me. His will was strong, even back then when he was so young.

Anselm returned.

"Sir Richard," Anselm said. "They told me that the sheriff wants to see you immediately." Anselm was good enough to speak in English, which we rarely did when alone. He spoke thusly so that Swein would understand what was being said. I resolved to do the same and speak in English whenever my new squire was in hearing.

"The sheriff wants to see me tonight? Not the morning? Very well, you all eat and drink and I shall be back later."

Jocelyn offered to send Anselm to serve me, as befitted my station or even to come with me himself but I wanted them to rest. I needed them all to be strong for the fight against

William.

The castle at Nottingham was a fine, neat place, built atop an imposing sandstone cliff with the River Leen running at the base. Not a huge river and not a large castle but a formidable place to assault none the less.

After waiting at the gate for what seemed to be a long time, I was escorted through the outer gate, the bailey and inner wall into the castle keep and the Great Hall.

The sheriff's men were drinking at the tables in the gloom. A couple of well-dressed knights sat at the top table. There were no women, other than a couple of servants moving about. It was quiet. The men's eyes followed me as I was led through.

The sheriff was not there.

He was up a flight of stairs at the end of the hall, sitting at a table in his solar, attended by two clerks and a priest. They were gathered about the table behind stacked rolls of parchment and scratching away at a fresh section when I was introduced.

The sheriff, Roger de Lacy, looked up from his work and stared at me, confused for a moment. He started and lurched to his feet.

"By God," he said, pushing his clerks aside and coming around the table. "By God, Richard, can that truly be you?" He peered at my face, narrowing his eyes.

I had been expecting a reaction of some kind, because of my complete lack of ageing. I had no way to explain it. How could I say that I had been killed and resurrected by unknown means at the age of twenty-two?

"Roger, I am so pleased to see you again," I said.

He had greyed and filled out. He was bulky underneath his superbly rich cloth and his belly stretched his tunic tight. His face was deeply lined and his eyes were tired and sagging. But the young man I had known many years ago was still there and he had aged better than most men. Especially one who was never active in the martial sense. Roger de Lacy was an enormously able administrator and a wily politician but he had rarely taken up arms. As a local representative of the king, his position as sheriff had infested him personally with the unpopularity of King John.

"Richard, I do not understand this," Roger said, stepping slowly toward me, peering at my face. "Do my eyes deceive me? You have not aged a day. How long has it been?"

"I am told that I have retained my youthful aspect."

"Retained your youthful aspect?" Roger grabbed a lamp from his desk and held it close to my face. I blinked at the light. "You still look like a twenty-year-old boy. Ten years ago, I could forgive it but now we are almost fifty. What sorcery is this?"

"What can I say?" I said, pushing the lamp away from my face. "I have been blessed. No doubt the years will catch up with me all of a sudden. Now, tell me, Roger, how do you yourself fare?"

He shook his head, put the lamp down and took my arm. "I am beset on all sides by madmen," he said, fervently. "And that was why I was as delighted as I was surprised to hear you had come to my gate. Take a stool, come on. Will you take a drink? Of course you will. I have some very fine stuff, the finest. Come, take your seat, take a drink."

I took both, gladly. The power of the blood was fading.

"Beset by madmen, you said?" I asked, glancing at the young priest, who was not introduced.

A servant came in the small side door, poured for us and retired without a word.

"You come to me dressed for war," he said, looking me up and down and I was suddenly aware of my stench. "Is there news I must know? Do you have word for me from your lord? I must say, I am astonished Hugh has finally allowed you to leave your lands."

"The archbishop did not grant me leave," I said. "I came of my own volition. I have no news of the war, nor knowledge of it. Indeed, I was hoping that you could inform me."

"I am honoured," he said, waving his clerks away. The priest lurked but Roger shot him a look and he also backed out. "So you came simply to discuss the war?"

I took a drink. "This wine is wonderful."

He snorted. "It costs a fortune. How I wish the king had not lost Gascony. I heard you were there?"

"I am sure that you did."

Roger laughed. "I never believed what they said about you." He looked at me closely again. "Not until you walked through that door. Is this why the archbishop keeps you locked away? Because of your disgusting eternal youth?"

"I am sure he has his reasons. But whatever they truly are, it is beyond me. You must see him more than I do."

"He is almost always with the king," the sheriff said, clearing his throat. "Or in York. Or seeing to his own lands, which continue to be acquired, here and there. On occasion, he has honoured me with his presence on his way to or from York. So, Richard. If he has not let you off your leash, why are you here?"

"I hear there is trouble in Sherwood."

He nodded without meeting my eye, drinking. "There is always trouble in Sherwood."

"Oh?" I said. "There is no new figure arrived in the shire, no outlaw leader?"

He looked up sharply. "I do not remember you as a man who dances around your meaning. What do you know, Richard?"

"A tinker came to my hall. He had come from somewhere up north and he said there were murders happening in Sherwood. A new leader, uniting the outlaws and robbers."

"These people are always banding together for a time. Leaders never last long."

"Is there a reason you are ignoring my question, Roger?"

He sighed and stood up, crossing to his narrow window. Night had fallen outside. "I am not certain you should become involved in this. In fact, I know that you should not."

"What is it?"

He turned to face me.

"I first heard about this fellow the summer before last. Some of the men living in the forest fled. A handful fell into our hands. They all told the same story. A new man living deep in the green wood at some special place. None of them could agree on where in the wood it was but they all said he was a knight. A nobleman. Nonsense, of course. They all claim to be some disposed, wronged hero when they are in fact a burglar from Bodmin. Nevertheless, whoever he was he was scaring men that I would have placed money on being beyond fear. I sent my best bailiff, John, to Mansfield to find out if there was any truth to the rumours. He was to go from there into the centre of the woodland." Roger paused to look out the window again.

"And?" My heart thudded against my chest.

"My chief bailiff never returned, nor the men I sent with him. John the Bailiff was a good man. Not kind, not at all, but he was sharp and I relied upon him. He had his ear to the ground, despite his head being so far above it. But they disappeared. Then the bodies of villagers and outlaws starting washing up dead in the fall rains. Washing up against Cunigsworth Ford. Others were found in the Rivers Meden, the Maun and in Rainworth Water. A dozen, all told. Men and women both, even a child. Killed from being savaged about the neck."

I gripped the table as sweat broke out all over my body. My muscles tensed, I resisted the urge to leap up and throw over the table.

Roger nodded at my expression. "Yes, like you, I too thought of the massacre of Ashbury Manor."

I took a slow breath. "Why did I not hear of this?"

"The forester and his deputies claimed it was all the work of a wolf or a bear. The wounds were well washed by the waters and the skin was clearly torn, not cut. And the bodies were bloated and many corrupted so it was simple enough to claim it was thus. Most of all, the victims were largely outlawed folk so no one other than their families was concerned by the deaths. God knows, the king and his court had enough to concern themselves with. But the people around here were afraid. Praise God, it went quiet over winter and I prayed that was the end of it. I even began to believe it had been wolves or some sort of enraged bear.

"Last year I had to go to the king, down to Windsor. It was a rather unpleasant summer. The barons forced the king to sign their ludicrous document. When I returned to Nottingham, I found my men had kept to the castle and the town, fearing to venture into the wood. The forester was drowning in drink, sitting on his behind and doing nothing but fining and harassing those who live outside the woodland but still inside the boundary of the legally afforested area. Nothing would get that man into the trees again, he said."

"Was he just afraid?" I asked. "Or had someone bribed him?"

"Is the fear not enough?" Roger asked. "In the short time I was away down south, the Knight of the Greenwood had tightened his grip. All the villages and farms in and around the wood were paying their tithes to this king of the outlaws. All were calling him the Green Knight or the Knight of the Green or some such nonsense. And the warden was collecting no fees. No forest courts were held. The foresters were out there giving the money to this leader, as were the agisters. The verderers were scared witless. The woodwards and the rest had disappeared. Everything was going to this outlaw leader."

The king's forest warden and his deputies the foresters set up forest courts and made inspections of forest lands. They were, therefore, the Crown's least popular servants as they received forest income, levied fines for violations of forest law and extorted every penny. Permission was required before forest land could be cleared and cultivated and the Crown received rent in perpetuity for that land. The right to pasture animals was controlled and would be withdrawn by the foresters, in the king's name, for the slightest offense. Of course, they might just look the other way if you paid them what they asked for. If an individual offender could not be identified in the forest courts, the forester would gleefully impose the required fine on the entire family, village or community.

It was not just the warden and his deputies who made up the forest bureaucracy. Each forest had verderers who reported to the king rather than the warden. They were elected locally, often held the post for life and did little other than rake in money so the posts were coveted, fought over and as corrupted as Judas. The agisters collected the fees from everyone who had permission to keep cattle and pigs in the forest and they creamed money off the top.

The king granted deer parks, chases and warrens to his barons and those lords employed woodwards, warreners, reeves and beadles in private offices all over the forest, each the master of his specific domain.

There was barely any oversight by the king's justicar and the officials were as corrupt, exploitative and self-interested as it was possible to be. No commoner who lived in a forest wished to be under forest law. But such is the way of things. A forester's rampant corruption was inevitable and unavoidable. They lived to line their own pockets. An appointment to most of the posts meant you would be set for life.

Which is why it made no sense that they had given up all that. No sense at all, unless the Green Knight was someone of astonishing power. Someone who could terrify all those officials. It was a wonder the great lords of the land had not done something about it.

"By God," I said. "But what about the Church? The priests in the villages. They would not stand for this. Does the archbishop know about this?"

"I wrote to him," Roger said. "More than once. He finally said that he had written to his men and that I was overreacting. The local deacon was not concerned. The Prior and monks at Newstead Priory claimed to be perfectly happy with their situation."

"I do not understand," I said. "The Church was unconcerned with the loss of their local authority?"

"No, indeed," Roger said. "Now I believe that the monks, the priests, all of them had been frightened or bought into silence. But this green fellow is most certainly stealing from the poorest and the wealthiest in Sherwood and taking it all for himself."

With every word the sheriff spoke, I was more certain that the Knight of the Greenwood was William de Ferrers. There was no longer a modicum of doubt in my mind. Who else could terrify an entire shire into compliance without raising alarm in the outside world? It was remarkable.

"Did the archbishop offer nothing in the way of help?" I asked. "He has the ear of the king, after all."

"King John is negotiating with the Pope and Philip the King of France and, therefore, has no time for your petty local issues. So our wise archbishop wrote to me. He finished with something that I shall attempt to quote to you verbatim. I suggest you keep your own counsel in this matter, he wrote, and if you cannot then the king will have to take an interest in your existing position for the Crown."

"I do not understand," I said. "He thought that you were at fault?"

Roger chuckled and took his seat back at the table. He drank down a cup of the Gascony wine. "All England knows you are a terror on the battlefield, Richard. But you will never make a courtier."

"No, thank God. Tell me his meaning, then."

"It was a threat. Be silent about the events in Sherwood or I shall remove you from your position."

"He has the king's ear to such an extent?"

Roger shrugged. "Hugh is the Archbishop of York. He and the Archbishop of Canterbury vie for influence. The Marshal, of course, remains the most powerful loyal baron and I know that the great man struggles to resist the ambition of both archbishops." He broke off. "I heard the Marshal's son was your squire?"

"Anselm, his least important son. A good lad. He is Jocelyn de Sherbourne's squire."

"So you retain a following of sorts," the sheriff said, "despite being held back by the archbishop."

"Jocelyn and our squires are all I can afford to keep," I admitted. "And if the price of everything goes up much further I shall have to sell my horses, send Anselm back to his father and call myself a beggar."

"Of course, of course, times are hard indeed, very hard," Roger said, as if he had ever known anything close to privation. "I wonder, though. Do you think you could attract more men? Perhaps if you had the coin to pay them?"

"My reputation cannot be so tarnished that hungry men would not take my coin," I said. "What are you asking me?"

He rubbed his eyes, sighing. "Last year I commissioned a knight to scour the wood clean of this infestation. A man named Sir Geoffrey of Norton."

"But I know this man," I said. "He fought beside me on the walls of Acre when we were young. A solid knight. Somewhat headstrong but he had the strength to justify it. He had a marvellous voice. I think he was injured at Arsuf and returned home."

"Indeed? Well, he was not so young when I found him. I paid him and two knights, a half dozen squires, and twenty bowmen to go into the wood."

"He is dead?"

Roger sighed. "It was his intention to catch the outlaws in the villages and homes of their families over winter. They rode into the wood to roust out the outlaws and force them to give up their master or, at least, the camp and to burn it. Bring the man out of hiding."

"A good plan."

The sheriff shook his head. "Three days after they left here, two surviving bowmen dragged themselves to the Priory before succumbing to their wounds. The Knight of the Greenwood, the Green Knight or his men ambushed Sir Geoffrey. There was a great slaughter. I had hoped to receive a ransom for the man but it has been four months and we have had no word. I hesitate to conclude that the worst has happened and so I hold out hope for his survival. It is likely that they are holding him until they need his ransom. But whatever the truth of it, his commission was a failure."

"And you want me to take his place," I stated. "To finish what Sir Geoffrey began to do."

"As soon as they told me you were at my gate, I knew that God had answered my prayers. But with times being as they are, I am afraid that I have no money. I can hire few men. One or two perhaps, if they are desperate enough. You shall have a commission and a warrant to arrest or slay the Green Knight but I do not know how you would accomplish this task. It is too much to ask, I know."

"Roger," I said, leaning forward. "Surely if you know me at all then you know it is a task I had assigned myself before ever I came to see you," I said. "It is a task I would carry out without your commission, without even your leave. For the Green Knight must surely be William de Ferrers and I am sworn to end his days with the edge of my sword."

He looked at me for a long time, judging me, perhaps or deciding whether to tell me something. Before he did so, his brows knitted together and he glanced at the main door to his chamber.

The sheriff coughed and said loudly, "Shall we descend to the hall for a little food? I am utterly famished, are you not?"

He spoke as men do when they wished their servants to attend to them, instead of calling for them directly, so I expected the door to the corridor to open. The sheriff looked nervous.

When no servant entered, on a whim I jumped to my feet, stepped to the door and yanked it wide open. It was an instinct that had served me well before and would continue to serve me for centuries. I half imagined that Roger had betrayed me and that armed men were about to burst in through that door and slit my throat.

Instead, a young woman stood there, caught leaning forward at the waist listening at the gap between door and frame. Huge eyes stared up at me. Her lips formed a plump circle of surprise.

I believe my own expression would have been rather similar.

"Marian!" Roger shouldered me aside. "What are you doing, girl? Lurking about in the corridor?"

She stood up straight, closed her mouth and stared at Roger with loathing.

The girl was extremely beautiful. Startlingly so. Her eyes were clear, her hair shining and dark and her skin was perfect.

"Lurking?" she shot back at him. She thrust her chin up and set her shoulders back, straining her dress against her chest. She may have been young but she was no girl and my loins stirred for the first time in many moons. "How can I do anything other than lurk in this God-forsaken place?"

Roger looked shocked. Hurt, even. "Marian..." he mumbled.

She stared at him for a moment longer, her cheeks flushed. The girl scoffed at his hesitation. With a final glance up at me, she spun on her heel and strode off, clattering down the stairs.

The sheriff stared after her, frozen to the spot.

I cleared my throat. "Your daughter?" I asked him.

"No," he said, his face turning dark. "Come, let us eat."

Later, we sat full of meat and ale, his men drinking at the tables in the hall. But it was not a joyous hall to drink in. The food was poor, little more than onions, meat, and bread in various combinations. At least it was plentiful.

The subdued atmosphere I had noticed among those men while walking through the hall earlier now made sense. They had lost Sherwood to murder and sedition. They did not understand what was happening but they knew enough of their enemy to be afraid and that fear had kept them in the castle for months. They were ashamed.

We talked of the war. Which barons were where and what each was doing, what the king's plans likely were in fighting them. Lots of rumour, plenty of martial opinion offered though little of any value. My hauberk felt like a hundredweight on my shoulders. My gambeson underneath was stifling. It was foolish of me to wear it indoors and yet I could not rid myself of the feeling that I was at war and at risk, even inside that fine castle.

After a while, Roger's head was nodding. He had drunk an astonishing amount of ale before calling for wine. His misery was profound and I suspected that the cause of it was more than the presence of the Green Knight nearby.

"The girl," I said. "Roger, listen. You called her Marian. Who is she?"

Roger was rather unfocused but the mention of her name woke him up. "That girl," he said, grimacing. "That damned girl. She is the daughter of Sir Geoffrey of Norton."

"What is she doing here, Roger?"

He took a long time to answer. His words were slurred, his movement sluggish. "No family," he said, stopping to burp. "If Sir Geoffrey is truly dead."

"How can he not be?" I asked. "Do you really think William de Ferrers is the type of man to ransom another? And anyway, surely the girl is of marrying age? She must be twenty years old or so."

His face clouded over. "What do you mean? What do you mean by saying that? You filthy bastard. Just because you have that face, you think she wants you? You're finished. You stay away from her, you accursed demon." He reached for me and I gently pushed his hand away and held it on the table. His strength was as a child's, compared to mine. I wanted to snap his wrist. I wanted to grab the jug of wine and smash it into his face. I wanted to sink my teeth into his flesh and tear it apart.

His men were watching closely. The hall was quiet. Forcing a smile, I released his hand.

"I meant nothing by it at all, my lord sheriff." I stood and bowed a little. "I wish you a good night, thank you for your generosity. I shall return tomorrow to discuss how I can help you with the Green Knight."

He waved his hand at me and grabbed another greasy bird off our plate.

Oftentimes, you find that the longer you know someone, the greater the chance that their character will disappoint you.

"I will show myself out," I said to the old servant at the hall door who struggled to his feet and lit a lamp. He held himself as if he had once been a soldier or at least a bailiff used to violence. But he was well past it.

"My lord says I must–" the old man stammered.

"You will stay here," I said, clapping my hand down on his shoulder. He winced. "I would not want an old man such as yourself to risk falling down some steps, unnecessarily."

"But–" he said.

"Ah, yes, I would appreciate borrowing your lamp," I said. "You are too kind. Now sit down."

I had a quick look around the keep but I could not find the girl. For some reason, I expected her to be skulking around. But I was bored and tired so I gave up.

I was almost out of the keep when Marian stepped out of the shadow of a side doorway near the doorway into the inner bailey.

I pretended to be surprised.

"Come with me," the young woman whispered.

I hesitated and looked around. It was still quiet and very dark.

"I will," I said. "But you should know that if the sheriff's men see us together I do not think Roger will be pleased with you tomorrow."

"I care nothing for what that monster thinks," she hissed. "And neither should you. This way, hurry."

There was a narrow stairway up to the floor above. Along the corridor a short way, she turned the handle into a small parlour. I followed, ducking inside after checking there was no one watching. The room contained a table with a lamp, a couple of plain chairs and not much else. Beyond was a bedchamber.

"Do not trust a word that he says," Marian said, planting herself in the centre of the space. I stood with my back almost against the door.

"The sheriff?"

"Whatever pretext he summoned you on, do not take him up on it."

"Actually, I came to see him," I said. "He is an old friend."

Her face closed up. "A friend, is it? What sort of friend would lie to you?"

"What lies did the sheriff tell me?"

"That my father may yet live."

I stopped myself from saying that her father would have lived up until William needed blood to drink.

"So you know differently?" I said. "I might have expected that a young woman would pray her father be returned to her."

"Oh, do not be an imbecile," she said, her pretty face twisted in contempt. "I could not bear it if you were simple. I loved my father. He was the kindest, sweetest man who ever lived. But he was a fool with money and he trusted far too readily. He took up this foolish mission though I begged him not to."

"I knew your father," I said. "He was indeed a good man. A capable knight. He could not have known the evil he was up against."

"But the sheriff knew," she said. "He chose my father because he wanted me. The sheriff wants me to be his wife."

"You are speaking madness, girl," I said. "Roger is already married. Has been married for years. He has children grown."

"He has sworn his undying love for me," she said, standing up straight. She pointed at me. "There, right there where you are standing he fell to his knees and begged me to marry him. He would divorce his wife, he said. He would have her charged with adultery and a divorce would be simple. He would put a child in my belly, a son who would inherit. He would disinherit his own sons for me, declare them bastards. He would give me the world if only I would marry him."

Some men went mad with lust but it was difficult to believe Roger would risk so much, even for a girl as lovely as the one before me. "Was he drunk?"

"When is he not? I refused him, so the sheriff sent my father off to die but now pretends that he lives."

"How does your father being alive help him to marry you?"

"He sent off my maid and my friends," she said, emotions other than anger creeping into her voice. "One night he forced his way in here, then into my bedchamber. He forced his fat body upon mine. I should never have opened that door to him but I knew enough what to expect to keep a dagger on me all the time. A dagger held against a man's loins is as a miracle cure against his ardour, did you know that? I keep the door barred every night. He cajoles and begs me to move to a chamber nearer to his. I am certain there is a passage through the walls into that chamber, I hear the guards allude to it. It is where he brings his women."

I still struggled to understand. "Yes, but how does your father's life help the sheriff more than his death would?"

"If my father is alive then I am a guest of the sheriff. If my father is dead then I become a ward of the king, who can marry me off to who he likes. And whom he likes would probably not be Roger. Although I suspect the sheriff fears that the king will take me for himself. None of these prospects fill me with joy."

"I do not doubt what you tell me. And I am sorry you have been subjected to this. But I doubt that your father can be brought back to you. The man they call the Green Knight is not one to hold prisoners for long. Sir Geoffrey was a good knight. His shield saved my life once. He stood guard over me after I slipped upon the top of the wall at Acre. I owe him my life."

She screwed up her lovely face. "What madness do you speak? How can you have fought with my father? He was a young man when he took the cross. It was many years before I was born."

"Twenty-five years ago, I would say." It felt like a different life. I had been truly young back then.

"How can this be? You are surely no older than twenty-five years yourself." She wrinkled her nose.

"Forty-seven," I said. "Thereabouts. In truth, I stopped counting years ago."

"I had hoped and prayed that you would take me away from here," she said. "But you are a witless fool and a liar, just as he is. Why would you even say these things? Am I supposed to be impressed? Go away. Leave me to my fate, then. It is God's will, I suppose."

I forced myself to laugh, lightly, as if I was unconcerned by her words. "I swear to you," I said. "I know that I have a youthful aspect. But I knew your father. He had the most beautiful voice. He would sing and a crowd of battle-hardened old soldiers, drunk and rowdy by the fire would fall silent and weep."

She paused and looked up at me. "My father has not sung since my mother died. Ten years ago."

"Then I am sorry to hear that."

She stepped closer to me, tilting her head up. She smelled good. Her neck was exposed to me, the beat of the great veins either side of her throat warming her skin, sending her scent up to my nose. It was the smell of honeysuckle flowers, sunshine on ripe wheat and hard apples. The scent of her neck was different to the scent of her hair and the warm musk of her breasts beneath her clothes. It was the smell of life, youth. Fertility.

"You are truly that age? But your skin is so smooth." She reached up as if to touch my face then pulled her hand back to her breast and held it with her other hand against herself. Her lips were parted slightly, she breathed lightly. She sucked her bottom lip between her teeth and frowned. Her eyes were huge and bright, flicking, searching all over my face.

I was beginning to understand how Roger de Lacy had become obsessed with the girl.

"What did you mean, you hoped I would take you away from here? I cannot carry you away from the sheriff's care. How could I do it?"

"He is not your liege lord, is he? You could defy him. And I am free to go where I please. I am no prisoner."

"He is the Sheriff of Nottinghamshire and Derbyshire. He is the king's representative in the shire where I hold my land. I cannot defy him, he would take grave offence. And anyway,

I have nowhere to take you. I ride into Sherwood Forest, into the deep wood, to finish what Geoffrey began. There will be battle, girl."

"Do not girl me," Marian said. "I will take care of myself. I have been without maids or servants for months. I will not get in your way."

"It simply cannot happen. I do not expect all the men I take with me into the wood to survive. I will not lead you to your death, Marian. And I cannot send you to my home, especially if I am not there to protect you. The sheriff, if he is as infatuated with you as you say, would simply go there and take you back. All that would change is that I will have risked my position and my chance to take revenge on the man who has slain your father."

For a moment, as she took a deep breath, I thought she would explode with anger. Instead, she sighed a great shuddering sigh and slumped into a chair. She held her head in her hands upon the table.

"I understand. And thank you for listening to me. But I do not know how much longer I can fend him off," she said, her words muffled by her hands.

She was truly desperate. If Roger had tried to force himself upon her once then it was likely that he would do so again. The young woman was desperate indeed and she had asked me for my help. I did not want to make Roger my enemy. I did not want to be distracted from my task.

I approached where she sat. Her head snapped up and she watched me warily as I sank to one knee before her.

"If what you say is true," I said and held up a hand to stall her protests. "I swear that I shall do all I can to help you. Consider me a friend, lady Marian. But now I must go."

4

BROTHER TUCK

I RODE FOR THE WOODLAND two days later. With me were Jocelyn, Anselm, and Swein.

The sheriff had supplied me with provisions and even a few shillings for the paying of bribes but he had provided me with no men. He had, in fact, been distant and surly to the point of rudeness since that first night. No doubt, one of his men had seen me conversing with Marian after all, or even entering or leaving her chambers.

I had gone to see the Warden of Sherwood in his large Nottingham house. The man was too drunk and terrified to be of any use and I had no patience for sobering him up just to beat the truth out of him. He had given me the name of one of his deputies, however, and his village.

"How can the sheriff expect us to succeed without providing us with a few more men?" Jocelyn was unhappy about the venture, as well he should have been.

"Indeed," I said, absently.

If I were thinking more clearly myself I would have known something was up with the sheriff's strange lack of support.

Instead, I was thinking of Marian.

It was a shaping up to be a lovely day. Bright, warm. The blossom on the crab apples lit up the hedgerows. Fat bees flew about, happy after their long slumber wherever it was that bees went over winter and drunk on nectar.

We rode at a slow pace along the road north from Nottingham, toward York far to the north. The woodland of Sherwood started on the right hand of the road. So close to the town it was well used and coppiced in the under layer and free from brush. It was a light, peaceful, pleasant woodland.

I knew, however, that the place grew dark and impenetrable just a few miles to the north. Inside the deep wood, at the centre, there were few people other than the outlaws. Outside the couple of villages, there was little more than a few charcoal burners and swineherds, if indeed, William had allowed them to continue to live there.

"Or even a servant or two," Jocelyn said. "With our lack of men, we need Anselm to be fresh for fighting so Swein will have to do all our armour maintenance and fetching water and cooking."

If Swein heard him, and he must have done, the young man said nothing.

"Swein must also save his strength," I said. "We will need his bow. We will scrub our own armour when needed and fetch our own water. Come, Jocelyn, you have been on campaign before."

"This is no campaign," he said. "This is madness."

"Yet you come," I said.

"Of course," he snapped. "I have as much right as you to revenge what William did. More, even."

"Then pray that we succeed," I said.

"What about Anselm?" Jocelyn asked under his breath. "Do you really wish to risk the life of the Marshal's son?"

"His fifth son," I said. "Anselm will never receive a thing from his father, except the weight of expectation. He must make his own way in the world, just as his father did."

"In other words, you do not care if he dies."

"Do not direct your anger at me," I said. "Save it for William and his monsters."

Jocelyn rode on ahead. I wanted both us and our horses to be rested, so we stopped at midday to eat the food we had bought in Nottingham and to water the animals. The meat was freshly cooked in the castle kitchens and the bread was freshly baked. We ate largely in silence, other than the sound of Swein slurping and smacking his lips.

Jocelyn stared at him. "He attacks his food like a bull charging a gate," he said in French.

Swein froze and stared, aware of an insult when he heard it, no matter what language it was spoken in. His hand tightened around his hunk of bread, squeezing it together. "What did you say?"

Jocelyn smiled and answered in English. "Speak not with your mouth full, you uncouth swine."

"Jocelyn, attend to your food. Swein, be not so eager to take offence. Turn and watch the trees for enemies, string your bow. Have you forgotten that we are in enemy lands, or close enough? An arrow could find its way into your back at any moment here. This may be the last meal any one of us eats. We must rely on each other. Our enemies are out there. So I will have no more of that, not from any of you."

That sobered them well enough and I finished eating to the sound of blackbirds chirruping in the hedgerows and the sun warming my face.

"They say in the tavern that the sheriff has himself a lovely piece all shut up in his castle," Jocelyn said as we dressed in our hauberks.

"Is that so?" I said.

"They say she is a great beauty. Young and unmarried."

"Indeed?"

Jocelyn stared at me. "I knew it," he wailed. "You have seen her."

I said nothing, strapping my belt around my surcoat.

Jocelyn was outraged. "You spoke to the maiden, I know you did. I can see it upon your face. What was she like?"

"She was a girl," I said. "Old enough for marriage, I suppose."

"Describe her to me," he said.

"You should find a wife," I said. "As soon as is possible."

"That is what I am doing," he said. "Tell me about the girl. Has the sheriff deflowered her yet?"

"For the love of God, Jocelyn," I said. "We have more important things to discuss. Mount your horse."

The road was deathly quiet, other than the birds and the ceaseless breeze in the twigs of the branches above. The leaves shimmered with an infinite variety of greens upon the browns and black.

"Not far till the village of Linby," Swein said, walking by the horses with his bow at the ready and his arrow bag over his shoulder. "Track comes up down there, then you go into the wood a ways. They cleared out a good few acres for planting years back. Paid old Ranulf a tidy sum for the pleasure. Not bad land, so they say."

"I hope this forester is still here," I said. "Or at least, uncorrupted by William's influence."

"If not, we can just talk to the villagers, right?" Swein said.

"You can trust nothing a peasant says to you," Jocelyn spoke in English. Swein's head jerked up but he said nothing.

"Nor will I," I said. "William twists people to his will, in one way or another. Whether his reach extends this far, we will discover. But you will be respectful to these people. They will have suffered. We will ask for ale and bread and we will eat. And I will ask the questions. Do they know you here, Swein?"

"Some might," he said. "That good or bad?"

"I do not know."

Soon after, we took the track and rode through the trees until they receded into a few small fields upon either side. A spring trickled along the side of the road, growing ever larger. We rode into the village. I counted six houses, arranged roughly in two rows leaving a road down the centre. There was no church or chapel. A pig snorted from somewhere.

"Where are they all?" Jocelyn asked.

"Hearth fires still burning in the homes," I said. I could smell them, along with fresh oat cakes.

"They are all hiding," Swein said.

I strode for the largest house. "Jocelyn, Anselm, stay out here and watch the trees. Swein, come with me."

The ground was muddy and there was pig shit everywhere. I ducked inside the dark house. It was dry inside and smoky. "I am looking for the forester," I shouted. "The warden's deputy. I am come from Nottingham. From the sheriff."

The fire crackled in the central hearth. A slowly bubbling pot swung atop it by a long chain to the rafter above.

Swein shrugged.

Outside, I looked to Jocelyn who waved his left hand low, toward the trees behind the house I was in. It was a sign we had worked out while campaigning for King John. It meant there were men hiding there. Jocelyn must have glimpsed shadows in the trees. His other hand rested on the pommel of his sheathed sword. Anselm stood by him, looking everywhere but where the men were and failing to appear relaxed.

"I have come from Nottingham," I shouted into the trees. "I come to talk. I am not here for outlaws. I am not here to impose fines nor to inspect boundaries."

The only answer was the wind in the leaves.

"I will pay silver for any man who will sit and speak with me," I shouted.

Pigs squealed again. They had been herded into the house next door, one with the door closed. No doubt, the owners sat inside, trying to silence their animals, fearful of my intrusion. It was as though I had wandered into enemy country yet it was not ten miles from Nottingham and not nearly as deep into the wood as I had to go.

Twigs crunched and Swein placed an arrow on his bow cord and peered through the trees. I held out my hand to forestall him. A man of about forty years stepped through. He was dressed surprisingly well, in a dirty but well-made surcoat over a bright blue tunic. His face was deeply lined, cast in the shadows from his cap. When he drew near, he looked at me most unhappily.

"Never know who's coming, these days," he said, looking at me dressed head to toe in mail. My helm was upon my horse but otherwise, I was ready for war. "I am Ranulf, the forester here."

"And I am pleased to hear you say so," I said. "For it is you that I have come to speak to."

"Ah," he said, looking over his shoulder. "And you are?"

"Thirsty, thank you, Ranulf the forester. Shall we drink some ale in your home?"

He pulled off his cap and scratched the top of his head. The hair was thinning and he had some sort of weeping sore on it. It reeked of wet cheese. "The thing is, my lord, I think it would be best if you spoke to the warden instead of me."

"What a wonderful idea," I said. "Sadly, the poor man was too drunk to speak. When I sobered him up, all he did was weep and vomit until I allowed him a little wine. For a short while, he babbled about a terrible Green Knight in Sherwood stealing the king's revenue and how I should seek out his loyal forester, Ranulf of Linby who would know everything about this knight. What village is this?"

"Linby," he allowed, glum and defeated. "Best come in, then. I suppose."

"Wait here," I said to Swein. "Watch all ways." Swein nodded, eyes already darting about.

Back inside his neat home, Ranulf poured his rancid ale and invited me to sit on a bench at his table. He would not meet my eye but stared at his lazily bubbling pot.

"By all means," I said. "Ask your wife back in here to continue making your stew."

"She is not my wife," Ranulf said. "And the fewer folk seen talking to you, the better it will be for all of us here."

"Seen?" I asked. "William's men watch you?"

"William?" he was confused. "You mean Will?"

"The Green Knight," I said. "Whatever you name him. Where is he?"

Ranulf shivered. "I have never seen him. His men, though. His men come. They take what they want."

"Why do you stay here? Take your woman and go to Nottingham."

"They would kill me. Men have run. They do not get far. They do not die well."

"I can help you," I said. "I will kill the Green Knight and his men."

"You?" Ranulf swallowed. "You and your three men? Forgive me, sir, but you must not understand what you are facing."

"So tell me. What are his men's names? Where do they live in the wood?"

He lowered his voice. "I beg you, please, leave now."

"You are afraid."

"Of course I bloody am," Ranulf said. "Every moment you are here risks my life and the life of everyone in this village, forsaken as it is."

"Perhaps you should be more afraid of me." I spoke softly.

He stared at me, confused.

"You have failed in your sworn duty. You have failed to manage the people of the forest. You have attended no courts for, how long, two years?"

"Two years of Hell upon the earth," Ranulf's voice shook. "Would you rather I had died?"

"Not I but the king demands you do your duty in his forest. Tell me all you know and I will speak for you, help you to avoid punishment."

"Punishment?"

"You may be treated with leniency and allowed to go free with just the loss of a hand or perhaps both hands."

He laughed. "I have lived in terror, day and night, since those monsters came. Nothing you can say will frighten me any further. I will tell you because I have not forgotten my duty, no matter what you say." He drank down his ale and wiped his lips. "Will the Red. Much the Miller. Brother Tuck, the Bloody Monk. And the rest."

"The Green Knight's men," I said.

"Aye, sir. Some of them. Each one of them worse than the last. Mad, terrible, the lot of them."

"Will the Red is red of hair?"

"Red with blood, sir," Ranulf said.

"Did you say one of them is a monk?" I asked.

Ranulf scoffed curling his lip. "He dresses like one. He claims he is one, from the priory just up the way. Maybe he is. But he don't act like one."

"And the third man is a local fellow, too, I take it?" I said. "From the mill down the river?"

"The Miller," Ranulf said. "They call him that as he likes to grind folk up. He carries a hammer. Smashes flesh and bones into pulp in front of others. As a warning, like."

I wondered whether William finds such men or creates them himself. Perhaps his blood makes men evil. Or perhaps it is his way with words.

"Where do they live?" I asked.

"Deep in the wood," Ranulf said. "I have not ventured that way in over a year. But there are caves there. Cabins. Plenty of places for the outlaws to hide. They are all loyal to the Green Knight. Loyal or dead themselves. It was give yourself up to them or become their prey."

"They take people," I said. "To drink from?"

"Drink?" His voice cracked. He nodded. "They took my wife, here in this room, took her then sucked blood from her body and—" He banged the table. "I have been a craven."

I said nothing about that because it was the truth. "Tuck, the Bloody Monk. Does he claim to be from the priory at Newstead? Does he live there still?"

Ranulf nodded, his eyes wet. "Take me with you," he said.

I looked at the cooking pot. "What about your woman?"

"She is an old creature. I allowed her to live here when they took her sons."

"You do not want her to come with you when you leave with us?"

"She is nothing to me," Ranulf said.

"Yet I see just the solitary bed," I pointed out.

Ranulf's face coloured. "The nights are cold."

"I will collect you when I return. I go to the priory to find this Bloody Monk."

"Do not," Ranulf's voice shook. "You shall be killed."

"Monks do not frighten knights."

"They are monks no longer," Ranulf said. "They are much changed."

"You will wait here until I return," I instructed Ranulf. "I will not take you back to Nottingham unless your bedfellow comes with us. I will be back tomorrow."

I spoke with such confidence. Although I knew what William and his men were capable of, I still underestimated his brutality.

That night, our small campfire crackled in the darkness. I was hungrier than I remembered being for years and tore into my bread and hard cheese.

"If we are to rest," Jocelyn argued. "We should do so in the meagre comfort of that shit stinking village."

"The forester believed the place was watched," I said. "I'd not sleep soundly in a hovel that could be burned in a trice."

"But you'll sleep out in the open?"

"Of course," I said. "I can hear enemies coming. I can see into the darkness. We are much safer here. Sleep, all of you. We will approach the priory at dawn."

"You mean to attack?"

"A priory?" I asked.

"You said the forester claimed it was taken over by William's monsters. Why would we not attack it?"

"Even if I trusted the word of a craven," I said. "How can we four mount an attack on such a place?"

"It is a small house," Swein said. "Compared to many such places."

"Seen many priories, have you?" Jocelyn asked.

"A few," Swein said. "This one never had much more than a dozen monks."

"Have you heard of this Brother Tuck?" I asked.

Swein nodded.

"Strange name, is it not?" I said. "What on earth can it mean?"

"Well, spit out your words, lad," Jocelyn said, knowing Swein considered himself a man grown.

"They say he was a bad man, even before. A glutton, a thief, and rapist but he took to the clergy and somehow avoided the noose. He is one of them men what is always jesting and laughing but he does it to make men feel afraid. It makes men nervous, have you met men such as that, Sir Richard? Anyway, I heard they call him Tuck because he tucks into those he kills with great passion. Tucks into them as a man does with a hearty pie."

Sitting beside Swein, Anselm's face was illuminated by the fire. The lad looked horrified. "Tucks in, as in eats them? But I thought they drink the blood, not eat the flesh?"

"Drinks the blood and eats the flesh, with a right savage manner." Swein shrugged. "That is what they say." His face was drawn and his eyes looked through the fire and into the past. "There were a bunch of other monks at the priory. The Green Knight's men killed all the ones who would not follow him. And those that did became like Tuck. Drinkers of blood. Everyone stayed away from the priory after that."

We sat and listened to the fire crackling.

"In the morning," I said. "We will ride to the priory, arrest this Brother Tuck and take him quickly to Nottingham, stopping to collect the forester and his servant. When we get Tuck to the castle, I shall have him reveal all about William's lair. Then he shall succumb to his wounds, dying in agony."

I could feel Swein looking at me and he nodded once when he met my eye.

"Finish eating, sleep. In the morning, we fight."

Jocelyn could be a prickly and proud man. But he was good at heart and generous. He woke himself well before dawn and came bade me sleep myself, for which I was grateful. We rose as the sky was growing bright in the east and a light rain fell. We broke our meagre camp and rode north, for the priory. It was not far from the road and on the edge of the wood rather than deep within but we were parallel with that darkest part of it, between the rivers.

When we arrived at the boundary of the priory, I saw what Swein had meant. Set back from the road in a large clearing, the place was little more than a small timber hall, in a poor state of repair and some equally tumbledown outbuildings scattered around it. There was no wall, nor even a proper fence and the hedgerows were ragged and full of gaps.

The ditch around the boundary was full of leaves and overflowing with stinking, green water. The fruit bushes were wild tangles. Although the gardens were bare, the orchard was overgrown and everything was untended and filthy. The air stank of old death, like a battlefield a week after the fighting had ended. Underneath it all was a faint smell of smoke, suggesting someone, at least, lived nearby.

The path up to the hall was muddy. There was spattered shit from dogs, sheep and deer, all washed together by recent rain into a rotten slop.

"It looks deserted," Jocelyn said.

"Your pardon, sir," Anselm said. "There are fresh tracks upon the path. A man or two or perhaps three, not more than a day old."

"Up to three men in there?" Jocelyn said, drawing his blade.

"How many monks did you say became like Tuck?" I asked Swein.

"Not sure," my new squire said, shrugging. "Half a dozen?"

Jocelyn coughed. "I believe I will wear my helm after all."

"As will I," I said. "You two young men guard the horses. If any man so much as approaches you while I am inside, no matter how far distant that man is, sound the hunting horn, do you hear me?"

"Blow the horn at the sight of any man," Anselm said, fingering the hilt of his sword.

While I pulled my helmet on top of my mail coif, Swein set to stringing his bow, which he did with a longer cord tied to both ends. I disliked the helm as it restricted vision and hearing so much. Yet, I was entering an enclosed space that was likely to hold at least one of William's monsters and I wanted as much protection as I could get. Jocelyn and I both chose to leave our shields because the rooms and corridor walls could impede us and because we were attempting to abduct a man and needed a free hand each.

Jocelyn and I stood at the heavy door.

"Should we knock?" Jocelyn said. I could hear his smile even through his enclosed helm.

I tried the latch. It clicked up and the door swung outward. It was unbarred.

"Perhaps they think they are safe," I said.

"Perhaps we are falling for a ruse," came Jocelyn's muffled reply.

"Quiet now," I whispered, drawing my sword.

I eased the door wider.

The hinges caught and juddered. I stopped the door but it was too late. The uncared for iron hinges screeched their unmistakable sound, echoing through the house, loud enough to wake the dead on Judgement Day.

"That's that, then," Jocelyn said.

"Silence," I hissed. I could hear sounds within. Men's voices. Laughter. Even singing. "Do you hear that?"

Jocelyn shook his head.

"Sounds as though they are yet awake and drinking," I said. "Just like monks."

"Let us sober them up with a sword through the spine."

"All but Brother Tuck," I said. "We need him alive."

We stepped inside and I waited for my eyes to adjust to the gloom. The building was partitioned with internal walls, painted plaster over the wattle and daub. A short corridor, two closed doors on either side and one door at the end, right in front of us. Once, it had been painted in bright colours but now everything was filthy. Brown stains spattered the walls. The floor oozed underfoot. The stench of death, old death and fresh blood filtered through my helmet.

Voices echoed around. Even Jocelyn, through his helm, coif and under-cap could hear them. Three to five men, I guessed. Easy enough if they were monks, hard odds if they were fighters and worse if they truly were men imbued with the strength of William's blood. I would take no chances.

Pushing in front of Jocelyn, I stepped to the door. The men were on the other side. I considered whether it was worth opening the door and attempting to talk, first. Perhaps I could avoid bloodshed. After all, who knew who these men were, really? On the other hand, we were dressed as if we had come to kill and their first response might be to attack, in which case I had handed our enemies an advantage that should have been ours.

Jocelyn hissed in irritation and nudged me on my back. I half turned to him.

The door opened inward.

A young monk stood, door in hand, staring up with profound shock at the sight of a huge, armoured knight intruding into his revelry. He was unarmed, wearing a filthy robe. His tonsure had mostly grown out. But his eyes were hardening into rage and I thought I saw William's madness in them.

I smashed his nose with the mailed fist of my left hand and barrelled him aside, knocking him down. I stabbed my blade through his eye, grinding the edges against his eye socket

The hall was as filthy as a pigsty. A milky grey light came from small, high windows, two holes in the thatch above and a few fat tallow candles stuck about the hearth. The floor was covered in smashed pots, bones and rotting things. It reeked of excrement and rotten flesh.

Of the five men who sat about the dying hearth fire, four leapt to their feet, knocking over their stools and a bench. They were dressed like the man I had stuck, in filthy robes, as if they were monks that had climbed fresh from a grave. Their age was difficult to determine through the grime on their faces but they moved fast enough. And I knew men who were ready to fight when I saw them.

The fifth man remained seated, with his feet raised upon the back of a quivering, naked old man. His pale body smeared in black filth and old blood, curled up in a ball. His beard was matted, his head bald.

The man with his feet up was bulky, with a fat, red and grinning face, reclining like a lord in a great chair. He was their leader. He was the man I had come for.

"Ha," that fat man shouted, pointing at me. "Take them, I want that fancy armour."

The other four circled wide, staggering in their drunkenness but moving like wolves circling an ageing ox, their eyes fixed upon Jocelyn and on me. I moved to my left to take the two there and Jocelyn went right. I hoped that he knew these men were William's and that despite their pathetically weak bodies and their inebriated state that they would likely be faster and stronger than he would.

I circled, crushing potshards underfoot, stepping through mud and a mass of flesh. The men laughed, though they were unarmed and attacking an armoured knight. They were mad and I chose to slay them. I knew which was the man known as Brother Tuck.

Deciding, I charged the nearest man. My first step was onto a dismembered wrist and my ankle rolled and twisted. Seeing my stumble, the men whooped and charged into me.

I ran the first man through his guts but the both of them bore me down with their fury. I ripped my blade out, spilling blood and bile but both pummelled my helmet with their bare hands. Their blows were like hammers, one was upon my back, knees pushing me down into the filth. I could see nothing and tasted the bloody filth oozing through the eye slits in my helm. They were trying to drown me in it.

I heaved myself up, throwing down the man upon my back. My sword I rammed up into the chin of the other, driving it up through into his brain. My sword jarred against the inside of his skull, scraped, and caught on the bone as he went down. The other one leapt upon me again, tearing at my helm. I elbowed him in the head, spun and backed away and swung my blade at his head. He jerked back but I caught him in the neck, slicing deep and sending him sprawling. I staggered after him and cut the other side, severing his head from his body.

My helm eye slits were half filled with oozing grime. I swiped out as much as I could and peered about the room.

Jocelyn was stepping back, keeping both men away from him. Both men were bleeding from the head. An ordinary knight would have stood little chance but Jocelyn was a superb fighter, his defence with the shield and footwork were outstanding. And the monks, for all their brutality, were not trained in war and nor were they freshly fed on William's blood. So I left Jocelyn to fend for himself a moment longer and instead looked for Brother Tuck.

His feet splashed through the filth toward me, a cry of incoherent rage bursting from him as he charged. The monk must have had his fill of William's blood. He moved like an arrow, shot from a bow. I got half out of the way and raised my elbow as high as his neck. The great mass of the man crashed into me and past me, the impact of his crazed rush smacking into the small space of my mailed elbow. A normal man would have received a crushed windpipe but not William's monster. It was, though, enough to send him sprawling into the filth underfoot. I followed his fall, bore him down and kicked him as he landed. I stomped on his back, popping ribs. I forced his face into the blood-drenched mud. His hands clawed at it, sliding in the slime. He grasped what appeared to be the lower leg of a small child, torn off at the knee. Perhaps he thought to use it as a weapon against me. I ground my heel into his hand.

Across the hall, Jocelyn cried out. I feared he had been wounded but it was a cry of victory, as one of the monks fell, his head cleaved top to bottom.

The final monk, finally seeing sense, turned to flee.

I charged to him, crunching and splashing, and speared him through the back of the neck.

Jocelyn panted from the exertion, muffled by his helm, nodded and waved that he was well. I returned to my prisoner as he was rolling onto his back. I kicked him hard in the balls. Hard, like I meant to kick through to his heart. Hard enough to rupture his stones, I hoped. He racked and jerked in silence, all wind kicked out of him and curled up into a tight ball.

"Get the rope," I said to Jocelyn.

Jocelyn was breathing very heavily and he had somewhat of a wild look about him. The kind of look a man gets when he has faced his own mortality. I realised that his fight against the monks had taxed him. I resolved to not allow Jocelyn to face William's men alone ever again.

We bound Brother Tuck tightly. He reeked like an animal. He growled and spat. I had to thump him in the face and head a few times to keep him still while we bound him wrist and ankle and at elbows and knees. I balled up a rag, stuffed it in his mouth and tied rope tight around his head to hold it in place.

"Quickly now," I said. "We must ride for Nottingham."

"What about that fellow?" Jocelyn pointed to the hearth.

The old man with the matted beard lay curled and shaking in his filthy nakedness. "I had forgotten about him."

"You cannot mean to leave him," Jocelyn said.

"For the love of God," I said. "You watch that one. Keep him on his knees with your sword at his neck."

I removed my helm, placed it upon the large chair, and rolled the creature over. His face was caked in ordure. The stench from his mouth was like rotting meat and befouled eggs. "No," he mumbled through smashed teeth. "No, no, no..."

"Jesus Christ Almighty. Jocelyn, they have put out his eyes."

The broken old man shook all over. "Who? Who?" he mumbled.

"Who am I? I am Sir Richard of Ashbury. Who are you? Do you live hereabouts? Can you hear me? Can I take you to your family?"

"Prior." He swallowed. "I am. Prior. Gregory."

"Sweet Christ, he's the prior, Jocelyn. Hear me, prior, you are saved. We shall take you with us back to Nottingham."

His shaking grew violent and he reached out a hand to me. I grasped the wrist. The fingers and the thumb had all been hacked off and left to fester. The hand was black. I eased his hand back and sat him up. His other hand was missing no more than the thumb but it too was mottled with black corruption.

"Kill. Me."

"I cannot imagine how you have suffered, good prior." I stroked his disgusting head. "But know that your tormentors have all been killed but one and he is not long for this world. Before he dies he shall know suffering as you have known it."

"Bless. You."

"Say your prayers, prior," I said and drew my dagger. When he was done, he mumbled that he was ready and I ended him rightly.

I wrestled Brother Tuck onto a steady packhorse and bound him to it while Jocelyn calmed the beast. I advised Tuck that if he caused me too much trouble I would simply remove his head and after that, he lay largely still.

Wary of the possibility of pursuit, we rode hard for Linby, Ranulf the forester's village.

Upon arriving, we found that every soul there had been slaughtered.

5

ENGLAND INVADED

NOTTINGHAM WAS ABUZZ when we returned. I naively assumed they had heard of the slaughter so close to the town.

I was wrong.

"What has happened?" I asked a groom as we walked our horses up to the extensive castle stables. "What is all this everyone is saying about the French?"

There were fine palfreys, much finer than my chestnut riding palfrey than I had brought with me to Nottingham, unused. He was getting old and his gait was never particularly civilised but the palfreys in that yard clearly belonged to a great lord. It was a joy to see the ambling palfreys, their skin full of juice, their coats glistening as they paced softly, gently exercised by the grooms.

There were even two destriers, the most expensive and desirable warhorses for knights. The fine beasts graceful in form and with goodly stature, quivering ears, high necks and plump buttocks. I could not afford one, let alone two. The grooms were taking great care with those dangerous beasts. A destrier was trained to bite, kick, rear and ride right over people and those horses were well known to kill more stableboys than smallpox.

I had to wave coins around to get anyone's attention. A lad found us a corner and set to work while we unloaded.

"The French, lord, the French, have you not heard, lord?" The boy could hardly get his words from his mouth he was so excited. "The French have invaded, lord."

Anselm and Swein shared a look. I hoped that they were becoming friends and allies.

"Invaded where?" I said. "When?"

"London, probably," the boy said, grinning. "The king is riding there to throw them back into the sea."

"London is not by the sea," Jocelyn pointed out.

"Well, wherever, then," the boy said, unconcerned.

I dragged Brother Tuck from the courser, who stomped and whinnied at me.

"You are happy now?" I said to the beast.

"He is not happy, you fool," Jocelyn said as he pushed me aside. "He is angry at you for making him carry that filth." He brushed the courser's grey-white coat down himself, whispering in his ear and neglecting his own war-trained stallion so that mine would be mollified. "If the French have truly landed, Richard, then we must ride to meet them."

I cursed under my breath. "You may do as you wish. I am staying to destroy William. I have waited twenty-five years for him to turn up and I do not mean to squander this chance. Truly, Jocelyn, you must do your duty."

Tuck, bound tightly at my feet, squirmed and groaned. I kicked him in his belly, hard and he curled up in silence.

"And what about your duty?" Jocelyn asked, brushing my horse.

"The archbishop considers me disgraced," I said. "He will not want me where all men, especially the king, can see me and remember Gascony. All his life Hugh de Nonant has fought and clawed his way upward and his life is built upon his reputation."

"And what do men say about me?" Jocelyn grumbled. "Your disgrace is mine by association."

It was true but it annoyed me to hear him be so ungrateful. "Men say that you have dutifully stayed loyal, like a true knight. Like the Marshal himself would have done."

"The Marshal would never have served a lord as lowly as you," Jocelyn said.

I laughed. "True. You never had to stay with me. And you may go and fight the French if you wish it. I will publicly release you, if you wish to join whatever forces the king musters. You will win great fame, I have no doubt. Now is the time to achieve your greatness."

He said nothing while he saw to the horses with our squires and I guarded Tuck, who became fitful every time he recovered from my blows. I hoped that he was almost-but-not-quite dying of thirst and suffocating. I had so many questions for him but no time to ask them so he would have to wait.

"Whose horses are they?" I said to the stable hand, pointing at the magnificent destriers and fine palfreys.

"Why, they're the archbishop's, sir," he said, looking at me as if I was a madman.

"The Archbishop of York?" I grabbed his shoulder.

"Yes, sir," the lad was frightened by my intensity so I let him go.

Jocelyn stared. "Did he say—"

"Yes. My liege lord is here. I must go to the castle. Watch the monk every moment. You do it yourself Jocelyn, allow the squires to do all else but you be sure this monster stays bound."

Tuck was awake and he squirmed violently and shook himself, moaning from deep within his fat belly. I readied another kick but Jocelyn placed a hand on my arm.

"I think he wants to tell us something," Jocelyn said.

"I do not have time for this," I said and untied the monk's gag and withdrew the sopping rag from his mouth. It reeked worse than dysenteric bowel water. I held my dagger against his neck.

"Please," he begged. "Blood. I must have blood."

I stared hard at him. "I heard how you like to jest. I am not amused." I moved to replace the rag.

"I will die." His eyes bored into mine. They were shot through with blood and I would have sworn he was afraid. "I swear, if I do not have blood then I will die."

"What do I care if you do?" I said.

"You need me," Tuck said, his foul mouth gaping like a landed fish. "Need me to talk. About him. About the Lord of Eden. If I am dead, you will never know. A drop is all I ask. Just a drop."

I looked at him, confused that he thought I would stoop so low as to feed him blood and I jammed the sopping gag back between his yellow teeth. He wailed and groaned. I shoved him onto his face to tie the rope about his face. His thrashing about was scaring the horses and drawing attention.

"Be still. Lie still, I say. Very well, here, then," I said, standing and looking around. "Here is your blood for you, if it will cease your caterwauling."

Tuck looked up from the straw, pathetic hope in his eyes.

I kicked him hard in the teeth and nose, rocking his head back. He lay still.

"You killed him," Jocelyn hissed.

"No, no," I said. "It'll take more than that. But I pray he'll lay quiet now."

The horses started and the nervousness spread around the stables. I held up my hand, apologised to the grooms and squires for the disruption, and explained that the man I had abused was my lawful prisoner. The muttering and grumbling continued. It does not do to disturb rich men's horses.

"Sir Richard of Ashbury," Jocelyn said quietly. "Making friends wherever he goes."

"Roll that thing onto his face so that he does not drown in his blood."

"What if he does die?" Jocelyn said. "How will we explain that?"

"I have bigger concerns," I said. "Anselm, clean my armour and have my sword straightened and sharpened. The point may require regrinding. See to it yourself that it is done properly. I go to meet the archbishop."

The castle was a heaving with men, dressed in an array of colours, all talking of the new turn in the war. Most would be Roger de Lacy's personal knights and squires, men that owed him service. Some few wore the archbishop's livery. I was escorted through the castle and into the hall, where I expected the sheriff to be holding court but instead, I was taken back to the sheriff's solar, announced and ordered in immediately.

The archbishop stood by the narrow window. He turned as I entered. He was just as I remembered him. Tall, broad shouldered, going to fat but still full of strength. His skull looked as thick as a bullock's but his eyes were shrewd black pinholes.

"My lord archbishop," I said, inclining my head momentarily.

His eyes were shining with inky blackness. His eyebrows knitted together over his slab of a nose. He did not look happy to see me.

"Roger, how are you?" I said to the sheriff, who looked deeply unhappy. He was surrounded by parchment and his clerks and priest buzzed about him. "So, I hear England is invaded."

"Richard." The sheriff glanced up at me from his seat, no expression on his face. "You have returned." He looked back at his parchment.

In the far corner, a wiry, tall figure leaned in the shadows. One of the archbishop's men, I assumed, though I could not make him out.

"What in the name of God are you doing here?" the archbishop said, his voice deeper and fiercer even than I had remembered. "You were to stay in that hovel you call a home until I summoned you."

The archbishop was one of the most powerful men in the kingdom and my liege lord, yet I had to fight the urge to leap forward and smash his skull against the wall. "William is here."

Roger and the archbishop exchanged a glance.

"So you say." The archbishop snorted.

"You doubt it, lord?" I said, surprised.

"I do doubt it," he said. "I doubt it very much. As I doubt your sanity and your good judgement in coming here in a time of war."

"I have done as you asked and stayed in my lands," I said. "But my home was attacked. The attackers were sent by William."

The archbishop nodded. "They told you this?"

"Yes," I said, bending the truth.

He scowled. "They said they were sent by Earl William de Ferrers?"

I took a breath. "They did not use his name."

"Ah," the archbishop nodded, glancing at the man in the corner as if inviting him to join him in mocking me.

"It is William," I said. "He is hiding in the deep wood. He has killed or subdued or driven off the outlaws. He is extending his tendrils into the villages. Soon, the roads will be unsafe."

"Absurd," the archbishop said. "Utterly absurd. You were always a little touched, Richard and now you have lost your mind."

"Will you tell him," I said to the sheriff.

Roger rubbed his grey head and sent his clerks away. They closed the doors behind them. "No," he said. "The Archbishop of York is correct. The trouble in Sherwood is the typical outlaw banditry and we shall clean them out in time."

I stared at him. "I disbelieve what my ears are hearing. You and I discussed this. We agreed it was William. Before I left to discover more."

Roger stared at me. "I was mistaken."

The archbishop smirked from across the room.

The sheriff was bitter about that girl, Marian. I had forgotten her and forgotten Roger's enmity before I left. Had he been hoping that I would be killed in the wood? Was that his plan all along? Or had the archbishop poisoned him against me, for some reason?

"And what did you discover?" the archbishop said. "You come into our presence with a filthy face and stinking of mud and manure."

"I rode to question the forester," I said. "In his village. He confirmed the new ruler of the wood was a knight."

The archbishop laughed. "They always claim to be a lord, do they not, Roger? What arrogance. Jumped up peasants strap on a stolen, rusted sword and think themselves equal to a king. Richard, you have no head for these kinds of things, you know this. You are a mighty warrior, every knight in England knows it. But you are a step above simple minded when it comes to the hearts of men. That forester is as corrupt as they come. Ranulf, is he not? The warden tells me the man has been keeping the fines he forces from those living in the forest. He was spinning you tales, son."

There was more to it, of course. I could have explained how the poor folk of Linby had all been slaughtered by William's men merely for speaking with me. I could have told them about the destruction of the priory and the torture of the prior. But some instinct caused me to withhold the existence of Brother Tuck. Perhaps it was the hot rage that spiked through me at the archbishop's moronic, offensive words.

"Do you mean to insult me?" I asked him.

The shape in the corner moved out into the light. It was the archbishop's man.

Only, it was not.

It was a woman.

She wore a hauberk, covered with a black surcoat. She had no mail coif on her head but wore a padded cap ready to take one. She was broad at the shoulder but narrow as a sword blade. I would have taken her for a man but for the fine features of her face and her huge, dark eyes. Some men have a womanish look about them. Other men are as beautiful as a Spanish princess and yet I was certain the figure in the corner was a woman. I could smell her. She reeked like a knight does, of horses and leather. Yet her sweat-stinking linen undergarments smelled strongly of woman. She stared at me with defiance, anger and amusement filling her eyes. The confident stare of one warrior facing down another.

"Insult you? By speaking the truth?" The archbishop growled. "Do not stare so, Richard. This is my bodyguard, Eva."

"Bodyguard?" I said and laughed. She stiffened, like a cat that is ready to pounce. The archbishop held out his hand to her.

"She is more capable than any man and you will watch your tongue. I trust her with my life and she has my full confidence, in all things."

It was suddenly clear. He was swyving her. Every man knew of the Archbishop of York's love of young girls. He usually kept his dalliances to servants and peasants, those who would not cause a fuss and whose families would be easily bought. I had assumed him too busy and too old to keep up with such things but clearly, he had found a new perversion. Dressing up his fancies as knights. I wondered if she screwed him while wearing the hauberk. I would imagine the mail would chafe. Perhaps that was what the old goat enjoyed.

"I understand," I said.

"No, you do not," the archbishop said, scowling. "You will go south. We must slow the Prince's invasion."

"I cannot go anywhere, did you not hear? William has made himself King of the Wood not thirty miles from here."

"Then he will wait," the archbishop shouted. "The very kingdom is at stake. Your personal squabbles are irrelevant."

"Squabbles? He murdered my wife. Slaughtered my brother, his family. Uncounted others. He must be brought to justice."

Roger and the archbishop exchanged a long look.

"You have my sympathy," the Archbishop said. "Certainly, you do. And rest assured, if William de Ferrers is truly in the greenwood, we shall roust him out, Roger and me, shall we not, sheriff? And he shall hang for his crimes. If he is there. But in the meantime, the Prince of France has landed an army upon our shores and he is aiming for London."

I was defeated. I knew my duty. There was no way out of such a command from my lord. It was a perfectly reasonable request and not one that the king would have any sympathy with if I brought my case to him. He would never even hear it.

"The king marches to meet the French?"

The archbishop coughed. "Indeed, he does not."

It should not have surprised me. King John was a capable enough leader of armies who could steal a march on anyone, if he so chose. But he was a far cry from the audacity and vigour of his brother Richard, who was called lionhearted for good reason.

"Where does the king go?"

"North."

That did surprise me. "He is running away?"

"Did I not tell you he is slow, Roger? Give him a castle wall and tell him to get over it and no army in all Europe will stand in this man's way. Give him a simple puzzle and he will stare at for a week, like a dog calculating a dice roll."

The sheriff looked horrified at the insult. The ridiculous, sham bodyguard, Eva, smirked.

"Very amusing, my lord," I said. "The king goes north to deal with the barons there before he faces the French."

"There," the archbishop said. "Not so difficult after all, is it. The rebel barons are giddy with joy. The Scots, in league with the French, have invaded the north of England. The French had sent a few knights and plenty of marks but the Prince has landed with thousands of men. The rebels feel assured that victory is theirs. The king's army is made from the men of us few loyal lords but the bulk of it are mercenaries. And mercenaries have to be paid. The king will isolate and crush each baron on his way north to deal with the Scots. One by one, he will fine those traitor lords for every mark and shilling they have squirrelled away, if they wish to keep their lives and their lands."

Roger and I nodded in agreement. It was a sound and necessary strategy. The Scots could be beaten. They were a rabble, who were used to fleeing at the first sign of resistance. They counted on the lack of forces in the North.

"And," the archbishop continued. "When the king has enough gold to pay for his army for a season or two, he will come south and defeat the French."

"By which time," I said, "the French will be in possession of London and a dozen castles in the south. It could take a year or two or more to grind them out of each one."

"Which is precisely why you must go south and slow the French advance."

"Me alone?" I said it in jest. "Certainly, I can defeat a thousand men with a single lance."

"You should not attempt wittiness, Richard, it does not become you."

"Tell me what men you are giving me."

"None," Archbishop Hugh said. "You will ride south for the Weald, in Kent. South of London. The king has a loyal servant with lands there. His name is William of Cassingham. You will go to him and together you will slow the invasion."

"How many men does he have?"

"It is uncertain," the archbishop said, looking at Roger.

"At least two hundred," the sheriff offered the figure reluctantly.

"Two hundred knights," I said, amazed at the audacity. "Against ten thousand?"

"Ah," Roger said. "Two hundred archers. Not knights."

"Dear God," I said.

"Yes, quite right, son," the Archbishop Hugh said. "Put your faith in God."

"Why me?" I asked, appalled. I was being given an impossible task. All I could do was pretend to obey and then lay low. Perhaps I would ride to the Weald, find this man and stay back from the fighting while he was crushed. No one could say I was shirking my duty if the Kentish archers were all dead.

"Most loyal knights are flocking to the king," the sheriff said. "We all must throw our lots in with him now. If the French win, if the rebels rise to power, we shall all lose our lands and everything we hold dear. Even our lives."

"What the sheriff means to say," the archbishop said. "Is that you are a great knight. You have fought in countless skirmishes, raids, sieges and even pitched battle. You have the vigour and countenance of a man half your age, with the experience of one twice as old. Who better but you?"

"And unlike many knights," I said, "I cannot say no."

"Indeed." The archbishop stood in front of me, almost of a height with me but bulky beneath his robes. "Think of this as an opportunity to regain your position. When you do this for him, the king will be willing to overlook any past rumours that surrounded you in the past."

"You give me your word that this will happen? That I and my men would be welcomed at court?"

"What do you want at court?" my lord said, looking horrified.

"I can teach John's sons the lance or the sword," I said. "Anything suitable that pays well for me and my men."

The archbishop relaxed when he realised my ambitions were so meagre. "What men?"

The sheriff spoke up. "He means Jocelyn de Sherbourne."

"Ah, your son, of course. Yes, of course. Yes, yes. No, you shall be welcomed by the king, of course, and I will myself extend your lands and find you a better place to live than tired old Ashbury Manor. So full of dark memories and tainted with death. You could even bring that beautiful daughter of yours back into the world. She is still of childbearing age, is she not? She would dearly love to converse with ladies of her rank once more, I am sure. A suitable husband could be found. And is your boy married yet? He will have wealth enough to find a proper wife."

"You lay it on thickly," I said. "But I will take you at your word, as witnessed by the sheriff here, is that not correct, Roger?"

"Yes, yes," he said, waving his hand at me.

"Every day is vital, Richard, every single day. You will ride in the morning. I will see you provisioned. Eva, give Richard his money, will you."

The woman moved like a wolf, stalking toward me with her eyes fixed upon mine. I felt that I was the prey.

"Here," she said, her voice deep but clear and strong. She dumped a heavy purse into my hand and slid back.

I hefted it and held it up. It was good to feel such riches, heavy in the palm of your hand. "I will ride at first light for the Weald and there I shall find this knight Cassingham. We shall fight the invasion with our two hundred peasants until the king comes. This Cassingham knows to expect me?"

"I would not say that he expects you, precisely, no," the archbishop said, walking away from me. "In fact, you may need to encourage him to stay and to fight the French."

"We have prepared you this letter for him," the sheriff said, handing it over. "It has both mine and the archbishop's seal upon it."

I had been given an impossible task but I could see no way out of it. What could I say? I laughed and nodded, tucking the letter away.

"One final thing," the archbishop had the good manners to at least look embarrassed. "You must take Eva here with you."

I could not understand for a moment. "A woman?" I looked at her. "I care not that you bristle, so, girl. My lord, I cannot escort a young woman through England when it is beset by war."

His great forehead knitted together and his voice became a growl. "She is more than capable of taking care of herself. And you will do as I command."

"Very well," I said to her. "I will come for you at the Castle at first light. Do not be late as I shall not wait for you, not at all, do you understand me, woman?"

"Perfectly," she said, her lips tightening, curling up at the edges.

I knew that I had to abandon her.

As I was led through the keep, the bailey and the outer gate, I felt a deep, profound fury at the thought of William slipping away once again.

The sheriff had insisted that I be escorted all the way out of the castle. No doubt, he wished to keep me well away from Marian so I was accompanied by three of his men. Burly fellows with stout clubs, no doubt very good at keeping townsfolk in order. I could have killed all three in the blink of an eye but, of course, Roger knew I would not create a disturbance for the sake of the young woman. But it confirmed how much he was concerned for her.

I looked for her but did not see her until I was well outside the walls.

At the bottom of the pathway up into the castle main gate, a short, stocky servant with stick-thin legs swept the path outside a large, newly built two-story house. It was by that time very dark so it was strange that she be working so furiously when she should have been resting. Bent-backed and swaying, she swept ineffectually, glancing around from deep within her hood. I assumed she had lost her wits.

"Sir Richard," the old lady hissed as she sidled up to me keeping her back to the gate and the guards standing inside far up the slope. She peered out of the shadows of her hood.

"Sweet Jesus Christ," I said. "It is you, Marian."

It took a moment for me to recognise her because she was dressed in a peasant's garb that was far too large for her. Her clothes were bulky and lumpy around her abdomen, like she was a deformed old crone.

"Keep your voice down," she said, her eyes glaring up at the castle walls.

I drew her into the shadow of the house. "What in the world are you wearing?"

She grinned. "My maid Joan brought me some clothes. I have stuffed my own garments inside to make me appear fat. Rather ingenious, is it not"

"It is madness," I said. "How did you get out?"

"I am no prisoner," she shot back. "Well, not precisely. I simply have no place to run to."

"You went through all this to speak to me?"

Her eyebrows knotted together over her nose. "What? No. No, I wish to come with you."

I drew her deeper into the shadows as two squires strode by, their arms full of linen. "I am going to war."

"I know that. I heard them speaking. I had to warn you and beg your help. Please, you must get me out of here."

"Warn me of what? What did you hear?"

"They wish to get you far away from Nottingham. I think they are expecting that you will die."

"You have warned me and you have my thanks. Now you must return."

"I shall not return. If you do not take me, I shall run anyway. I have food, wine." She tapped her bulky body. "My good, kind friend Joan will take my place, calling out through the door if asked. She is old and fat but she has the voice of a girl. She will slip away back to her own rooms at dawn before I am discovered to be gone."

"If he is truly infatuated with you, his men will bring you back."

"I must act. I must at least try. I cannot simply sit and wait and allow myself to become that man's wife."

"Would it be so bad?" I ventured. "To be the husband of an enormously wealthy lord?"

She set her jaw. For a moment, I thought she was going to hit me. Instead, she softened. "Will you not be a true knight and save a maiden in need of rescue?"

"The ballads are not true to the world. You will find that out in time."

Marian leaned into me, looking up with her big eyes. "They all say how you are a true knight. That you risked your life to save that of the Lionheart. That you risked your life to rid the holy land of an evil band. That you fought bravely for King John in Normandy and Gascony, storming wall after wall—"

"Stop, stop, you think I am so weak as to be won over by flattery? Do you take me for a fool?"

She straightened up. "Yes," she said. "The sheriff is lying to you, using you, sending you into harm's way. Would taking me with you not be a way to set even the score against him?"

I looked at her then up at the castle. Then back at her again.

"Hide your face, look down. You will have to spend the night in the stables."

Jocelyn had paid generously for the stable boys to look the other way. No doubt, word of a blood-soaked monk tied up in the stall would get back to the sheriff by morning but he had troops to muster so I hoped I could be away the moment the gates were opened.

"Who is this?" Jocelyn asked.

"You wanted me to hire servants, did you not?" I said, ushering Marian into a separate stall to Tuck's. The horses were yet nervous of the man but Jocelyn had worked his magic on them and they stood quietly and slept. My grey courser was even laying down to a deep sleep.

"Men servants," Jocelyn said. "Not an old scrubber woman."

I was silently gleeful at the prospect of his regretting those words when he saw the young lady. I felt her resist my hand as I guided her into the stall by the grey but I pushed her gently inside.

"She is joining us and we will have not another word on the matter until we are on the road. Not another word until then, do you hear me?"

Jocelyn understood something was up and he must have died to ask what. I whispered to the girl that I would find her some clean straw and a blanket.

"The monk was groaning," Jocelyn whispered. "I had to knock him about the head. He sleeps now but when he wakes I fear his cries may wake the dead."

"He is perhaps dying of thirst," I said.

"Thirst for blood?" Jocelyn asked, with a heavy emphasis.

"I have only felt I needed it when gravely wounded," I said. "Other times it is an urge I am able to resist."

"You can resist," Jocelyn whispered. "But this fellow appears unable to last much longer. Come and see for yourself."

"It is too dark," I said. "What would I see?"

"He has the appearance of a corpse," Jocelyn said. "I paid a couple of grooms to bring water, wash the fiend and change his robe for a peasant's garb while I stood guard."

"Good man," I said.

"But I saw that his skin was green and mottled, fetid and taught. As if he were dead."

"Yet he breathes."

"I do not like it," Jocelyn said. "And the grooms were as disgusted and disturbed as I was. No doubt word will be spreading that you keep this creature. No, I do not like this, Richard."

"You will like what the sheriff and archbishop said even less."

Of course, I should have known that Jocelyn would embrace the chance for glory. To save a kingdom, single-handed, was all Jocelyn ever wanted. That and fame, riches and a well-bred wife to give him sons while he spent every day out hunting. Not too much to ask of God.

"We must be together at the gate and ride out through it the moment it is opened. We shall be miles away before the archbishop's woman realises she has been abandoned."

"She is supposed to watch you for him," Jocelyn said.

"Of course. But why not send a man? Surely, he must have expected me to reject her and he will somehow later use it against me. Bah, I have no mind for these things. Go, eat, find the squires and send them to me. We must buy up supplies for the road. The prices will be as high as Heaven but the archbishop has bought me with these coins."

Marian slept curled up on the straw without complaint. It was as we mounted at dawn that Jocelyn realised that the old scrubber was, in fact, a great beauty. I thought his eyes would burst from his head but he controlled himself and we rode out as quickly and quietly as we could.

Brother Tuck was almost dead but I bound him in sackcloth and carried him over my shoulder. I told the porter I was taking one of my men home for burial. He did not believe me but he let us through the gate.

Our little company headed west. I meant to stop at home on the way South.

Not five miles along the road from Nottingham stood a knight with his horse, a very fine black courser, waiting for us.

"Is it a trap?" Jocelyn said, drawing his sword and looking all around at the fields beside the road for signs of waiting ambush.

"Of a kind," I said. "That is no knight. That is Eva, the archbishop's bodyguard."

6

THE WEALD

WE RODE EAST FOR THE MORNING, as I wanted the sheriff's pursuers to think I was heading for Derby and my own land. But well before midday, I instead took us through a narrow track that led roughly south. We weaved our way through wooded hills toward the River Trent, where I knew of a little-used ford used mainly by drovers.

If we avoided trouble right away, we still had two hundred miles or more to go before we made it to Kent. I had decided immediately to avoid London because I was afraid that the French would have taken it by the time we got there. So we would continue to edge west of south from Leicester, perhaps to Cirencester and cross south of the Thames high upstream, then hook around London and keep on east, all the way to Kent. It was the end of May when we left Nottingham and the damp, misty morning turned warm and stayed that way.

A strange company we made as we set out that first day. Eva, the archbishop's supposed bodyguard, had impressed me by stealing the march on us, presumably sneaking out from one of the town gates in the dark or earlier and spending the night out by the side of the road. The archbishop had clearly meant for her to spy on me and she meant to carry out that duty with no regard for her own wellbeing. Women are born to bear pain and they do so better than men, yet they do not endure discomfort with the same fortitude.

Her woollen cloak hung heavy with dew and under it, she wore her full hauberk, black surcoat and a fully enclosed great helm hung from her saddle. It was clear from the way it clung to her when she moved that her hauberk fit her perfectly. There was no doubt that it had been made for her, fitted exactly to her shape, rather than some lad's cast off. It was excellent quality and would have been a significant investment for any knight. In her case, the archbishop had presumably paid for it and he was wealthy beyond the limits of my imagination. At least, before the king had bled him dry over the years.

"I had hoped to leave you behind. But as you are here, well, of course, you are most welcome to join us," I said, feigning acceptance of her outmanoeuvring of me.

"Just as your lord commanded you," she said, looking me square in the face before mounting her fine horse.

She barely spoke a word all morning. I did not ask her questions and she volunteered nothing of herself. She rode well and her gear appeared well worn and well cared for. Barely any rust at all. I doubted I could give her the slip easily but I intended to get rid of her as soon as I could.

Jocelyn was tight-lipped, confounded by her sudden appearance and her arrogant style of dress. But he was barely aware of Eva. Marian had caught his eye.

She was wrapped in my cloak, with the hood up over her own, sitting very well in the saddle of the ageing palfrey I had provided for her. That palfrey was old when I bought him years before but still he had cost a small fortune for his gait was as smooth as a maiden's belly. Aged as he was, I rarely taxed him with my weight but he was an ideal mount for a young lady. Marian had seemed touched by my generosity, offering to ride one of the packhorses instead and I warmed to her even more. She wore the servant garb, still stuffed with clothing and food and the Lord knew what else so she looked as round as a ripe apple. Even with her face down and in shadow, she could not hide her beauty.

"My lady," he said, easing his horse close beside hers. "I am Sir Jocelyn de Sherbourne. It is a great pleasure to meet you. Of course, these are somewhat unusual circumstances. I wish only to say I swear that, wherever it is that we escort you, I shall protect your life with my own."

From the back of the palfrey, Marian looked up at Jocelyn from under the rim of her borrowed cloak. "What a brave and honourable knight you are, Sir Jocelyn. I have never felt safer than I do at this moment. I am so glad that you are here beside me."

I thought his chest would burst. His cheeks coloured and his tongue was suddenly tied. I spurred past them to Anselm, Swein and the wrapped, writhing body of Brother Tuck.

"Anselm, Swein, we must deal with this monk before we get to Leicester. He may die of thirst before we can arrive. But even though he is weak and dying, he may yet retain his unnatural strength."

"Where should we torture him?" Swein said. He was bareheaded, having put his hood away once we were away from the town. "Me and Anselm can take him off into the woods?"

"Anselm will stay with the others," I said. "Swein, you will come with me. Can you sit a horse?"

He looked up at me through his tangle of blonde hair. "Climbed on an ox, once."

"You will lead the packhorse, then, but you must hurry. We will head for the large copse up ahead, do you see?"

"On the little hill?" Swein said.

"Hurry on ahead, run if you need to and I will catch you," I said. "Oh, and be sure to take a cup with you. Do not untie that monk."

"I'm not daft, my lord," he said and picked up his pace.

"Anselm, keep an eye behind for any sign of pursuit. And listen, son. You keep an eye on that Eva woman. If it seems like she's going to grab the Lady Marian then you raise a cry, you understand? Be ready to race after her. She rides like she fancies herself a horseman but I wager she'll not out ride you on that grey lightning." He took the praise well, though he was grinning as he fell back alongside Eva. I waited for Jocelyn to draw near. "Sir Jocelyn, might I beg you for a word?"

"Of course, Sir Richard," he said, throwing his chin up and riding ahead with me out of earshot.

"My hope is we slipped the damned sheriff's men but while I am up there sorting out the monk, be mindful that you might get company."

"Worry not, Richard," Jocelyn grinned. "I'll not let them take her." He patted his sword.

"You bloody will let them take her," I said. His face fell into a scowl. "What will you do, draw blood over her? He might send a dozen men after that girl, do not be a fool."

"God will grant me victory," he said. "I have sworn to protect her."

"Listen, son," I said. "Understand that standing by your word could mean her coming to harm."

"My word is my word," he said, rather offended. "I have a noble name that I must uphold. And I have a noble heart."

"You have a stiff prick and a soft head. If the sheriff's men come for her then you give her up. If your noble heart is set on her you can try for her hand when we return. Roger cannot marry her until he rids himself of his wife."

"I heard what they were saying in the town," Jocelyn said. "He means to have her, marriage or not, at any cost."

"Do not make an enemy of the sheriff and get yourself killed over a girl you have spoken a dozen words to."

"It is you who have made yourself an enemy," he said. "Yet again. It seems to be the only thing you are good at. Why did you abduct her if you mean to simply hand her back?"

"I did not abduct her, she is a free woman. She is simply riding the same route as we do."

He looked over his shoulder. "What about that ridiculous woman? Is she here to grab the Lady Marian?"

"I doubt it. She was surprised to see her, did you notice? And she is the archbishop's plaything, not the sheriff's. Still, she may get an idea about stealing the lady back to Nottingham, so I instructed Anselm to keep one eye on her. You do the same. That horse of hers looks fast but I am sure that she would be no match for your horsemanship. Now, I am going to question the monk before he dies."

I caught up with Swein and we picked our way into a copse upon a slight hill across the field. In a second field beyond the copse, the folk it belonged to looked to be out together as a family, hoeing about their green crops in the late spring sunshine. I hoped they would be too far to hear any cries the monk made.

We secured the horses and I dragged Brother Tuck from the packhorse and dumped him beneath a stand of hawthorn.

"String your bow and stand back over there to the side with an arrow nocked and ready," I said to Swein, who obeyed swiftly and without question. The young man impressed me more every day.

The stench of rot and death billowed out when I unwrapped the sackcloth from Tuck's body. His ankles were bound together, as were his wrists and I had tied his arms to his fat body.

He groaned and writhed. The man's skin was greenish and waxen. His eyes were closed but they darted about underneath the bulging lids.

I slapped his face, hard.

His eyes sprang open and he lunged for me with his mouth. I dodged back. He flopped like a fish onto his face. He snarled and drooled, his jaw working into the mulch.

"Brother Tuck," I said. "I will give you water if you control yourself."

He snarled and twisted within his bonds. I yanked him from his front into a sitting position against the trunk of a hawthorn, the leaves green and the uncountable berries turning bright red above. Tuck's eyes rolled, bloodshot and unblinking.

I poured water from a skin into his mouth. He gagged and coughed on it, spraying it everywhere. He cried and groaned as if I had burned him with fire.

"Swein, you will not need your bow, for now."

"Is this some plague," he asked, coming near behind me. "Something to do with the Green Knight's blood?"

I sat on my haunches, watching Tuck twitching and gasping. "In the Holy Land, William made many men loyal to him. They would drink his blood, once every week on the Sabbath. It gave them great strength and speed and resistance to pain and hunger."

"That is what this is," Swein said. "That is what he did to the men in Sherwood, the ones I tracked to your hall."

"The ones who attacked my hall, yes," I said. "But that is not what this is."

"What is this, then? Lord?"

"I do not know. But I do know what he needs."

Swein sighed. "Blood."

"Take your dagger and cut yourself where you think best. Your arm, perhaps. Drain some into the cup you brought."

The young man stood very still.

"I do not wish to make you angry, Sir Richard," Swein said, stopping and starting. "But can you not use your own blood? I am not afraid to bleed, you know, I don't mind a bit of a scratch, like, but I don't know, lord, I just don't know about this."

"You do not wish to give any to him," I said. "I understand. I am not angry. But I cannot use my own blood."

"Very well." He hesitated. "I do this because I want the monk to tell us where the Green Knight is. And after he tells us I want to be the one to kill him."

"I understand," I said, promising nothing.

As Swein sliced the back of his forearm, Tuck's head snapped up. His nose twitched and his lips curled back. He began to growl.

I drew my sword and held the tip to his neck while Swein collected the blood. "Hand it to me," I said after a few moments. "Stand back and ready your bow once more."

Swein wrapped his arm and when he was set, I raised the cup to Tuck's mouth. "Hold still or I will slice open your neck rather than feed this to you."

The words calmed him long enough for me to pour the thick, hot blood into Tuck's mouth. I wished it were I that could drink it. Tuck drooled and gulped it down, licking his lips.

He let out a shuddering groan and sank back against the tree, unmoving.

"Did it kill him?" Swein asked.

Tuck's mouth moved, twitching and his eyes opened, focusing on me. The sweaty pallor on his skin seemed immediately less, a little red came back into his cheek. His lips formed a word, a whispered croak.

"More."

"Speak and perhaps I shall allow you to live."

"More."

"Tell me about William," I said. "The Green Knight. The man who gave you his blood. Who did this to you? What do you men call him?"

"God." He grunted out what could have been a laugh.

"Where is his camp?"

"Blood."

"What made you this way?" I said. "Why are you dying without drinking blood? What did he do to you to make you this way?"

Tuck grinned and leered at the cup.

"Perhaps we should take simply his head," I said to Swein. "Are you sure you wish to be the one to do it?"

Swein nodded. "I will send an arrow through his skull."

Tuck's eyes swivelled between Swein and me.

"Fine, then." I stood, holding the point of my sword against Tuck's chest. Swein planted his feet and drew back his cord.

Tuck screamed, "No!"

"But you have no use to me."

"I will tell you." Tuck's throat must have been raw, his voice was like gravel.

Swein eased his bow cord. I squatted and gave Tuck another taste of blood. His eyes became clearer. His skin took more colour and he breathed easier.

"Tell me how he made you," I said. "Why are you suffering in this way?

"I drank the blood of the Lord of Eden," Tuck said, his voice still raw but almost human. "I am now a son of Adam." He grinned.

"But that is how he has always granted his power," I said. "The power of the blood simply fades over time. Over seven days."

Tuck giggled. "That's for the initiates. I'm special. He changed me for eternity."

"And his men would drink normal blood to make it last longer. But why are you suffering like this?"

Tuck nodded. "Now I must drink blood, every couple of days. More than that and I get weak. Sick. By the seventh day, I die. But as long as I drink mortal blood, my gift will last until the end of days. The end of days, I say. Now, give me blood."

"That seems a rather simple cure for your evil," I said. "All I need do is starve you? But how is that change made? What is the method? You get no more of this cup until you answer."

I placed the cup beside me, well out his reach.

He stared at me, his eyes mad, red-ringed and twitching.

Without warning, distant shouting came through the trees from the road.

"Watch him," I commanded Swein, who nodded and pulled a touch of tension on his bowstring.

I ran to the edge of the trees and looked out across the field to the road, which ran from left to right along the boundary.

Jocelyn and Anselm were cantering to the left, back the way they had come. Marian and Eva continued heading to the right.

The shouting came from six horsemen, riding two abreast, who approached Jocelyn and Anselm along the road from the left.

Clearly, we had been pursued and we had been found. The sheriff's men had found Marian.

Those men-at-arms were all in full mail, helmeted, some had shields on their arm or slung on their back.

All six of the sheriff's men drew to a stop in front of Jocelyn and Anselm. Their leader raised his hand to halt his men. Marian and Eva rode on at a walking pace, Eva with one hand on the bridle of Marian's palfrey. Both women looked over their shoulders, tense and ready to spring ahead.

"Let them through, Jocelyn," I whispered, urging him from afar. "Let them take her, you romantic idiot."

I watched, too far away to be heard or to interfere, as Jocelyn drew his sword.

"Bloody fool," I said.

"Sir Richard," Swein shouted from the trees behind me.

I spun, sword up ready to strike at Tuck. Instead, the disgusting fiend was sitting exactly where I had left him. He had the cup of blood to his lips, draining the last of it, his hands at the farthest reach of his bonds.

"Should I kill him?" Swein shouted, half drawing his bow.

"No," I said, running toward the monk. Tuck looked up, blood all around his grinning mouth. I clouted the top of his skull with my pommel, hard enough to cave in the skull of a normal man.

He fell, dead or just nearly. I knew not which.

"Bind him, cover him, put him on your horse and follow me," I shouted at Swein as I ran for my own, unwinding his reins. I led the grey courser out of the thin trees at the edge of the copse and rode out across the field, taking stock of what I had missed.

Blows had not been struck. But three of the sheriff's six men rode around Jocelyn while he remonstrated with the leader and the remaining two men. Jocelyn shouted an order to Anselm, who wheeled his horse around and chased the three men along the road. Those three mounted men were going to take Marian. Anselm looked like a child next to the big men. At least, he had both hands on his reins, sword sheathed.

Marian, on my ancient palfrey, could never have escaped from them and I doubted that Eva would be capable of outriding a man. So the only course of action for the women would be to surrender to the three men-at-arms closing on them along the road.

Eva turned her horse and drew her sword, placing herself between Marian and the approaching riders.

It took me a moment to realise that Eva was going to fight. The idea was absurd. That mad young woman was facing down proper soldiers. Just because she wore the garb of a fighter and had the hilt of a sword in her hand, she thought she could challenge three mounted men-at-arms. By so doing, Eva was in danger of getting herself or Marian hurt or even killed. Men-at-arms were not known for restraint or good judgement.

I spurred my horse and he sprang forwards, released into a gallop. I aimed for Marian, sitting still upon the palfrey, looking at the riders who bore down on her. Anselm rode hard on their heels. I was near enough to hear the hooves of their horses thudding against the packed earth of the road and though I closed the distance rapidly, I was too far away to stop what was happening.

The three riders slowed and reigned in and surrounded Eva. One of the men rode right around Eva and closed to Marian. That man reached out of his saddle to grasp the bridle of Marian's palfrey.

While the other men shouted at her to stop, Eva raked her heels against the flanks of her black courser and the fine animal leapt forwards as fast as a cat. Eva slapped the flat of her blade on the top of his helm, hard. He yanked his own mount back, in panic and anger. Forgetting Marian, he drew his own sword. His eye slits must have been knocked out of alignment, as he waved his blade wildly while shouting.

The palfrey was not trained for combat and the frightened horse shied sideways away from Eva and into the man-at-arms. With a backswing, that blinded, angry fellow hit Marian with his sword.

The girl screamed and fell from her saddle. She hit the road surface and lay still. The panicking palfrey stepping and stamping all around Marian's body, afraid of the shouting around him.

After a moment of shocked silence, the tension on both sides erupted into action.

Eva cried out a challenge, pushed forward and barrelled the blinded swordsmen from his own horse. He fell, arms flailing, his sword spinning from his grasp.

I was closing but still too far to intervene.

The other mounted men drew their own blades. A second of the three attacked Eva from behind, pushing his horse onward, with his sword ready on his shoulder and his shield up.

Anselm urged his rouncey on and slashed that horse's rump with his blade. The animal sprang forwards, trying to throw the pain of the wound from its back. Instead of attacking Eva, the rider dropped his sword into the long grass at the side of the road and held tight to his reigns while his mount leapt away into the far field.

Jocelyn and the three remaining sheriff's men galloped toward the confused melee from the left side of the road. I reached it before them. Shouting at everyone to stop, I forced my courser into the third man's smaller rouncey and simply pushed him out of his saddle.

Eva leapt to the ground, stamped her foot on the fallen man and then pushed Marian's horse away, showing no fear as the animal half-reared. Eva stood guard over Marian, sword out, helm down. She looked like a knight.

I spun to meet the other remaining men as they reined in. Jocelyn and the leader of the six men stopped together. That leader bellowed at his men to stop fighting.

"And stand back," I roared. "All of you. Keep your distance. Put away your blades, for the love of God."

The sheriff's men calmed themselves. Everyone but Eva sheathed their swords. For a moment, the only sound was the hard breathing of men and horse.

"Sir Richard," the leader called to me. "So good to see you." He unbuckled his helmet. It was the sheriff's friend and loyal servant, Sir Guy of Gisbourne.

"Check the girl," I said to Anselm, who leapt from his horse and ran over while we waited. "She fell hard." I glared at Gisbourne, saying nothing.

Sir Guy attempted to hide his discomfort, sitting up straight as an arrow, sweat running down his brow.

"The lady's upper arm is cut, Sir Richard," Anselm shouted, his voice breaking. "Her head is bruised but not broken. She is too winded from the fall to speak but she breathes."

"You are lucky the girl is not dead," I said to Sir Guy. "Your man there was a hair's breadth from being a murderer."

"I know," Guy said, anger flushing his face. "He will be punished. I am relieved the young lady is uninjured."

"Uninjured?" Jocelyn was spoiling for a fight, his blade in his hand. "She is hurt, you fool. Blood has been drawn. Justice demands—"

"Jocelyn," I said. "Please attend to the Lady Marian." Jocelyn wanted to argue but his lust for the girl overcame his love of a fight. He swung his leg over his saddle and hurried to her, fussing over her like a mother for her firstborn child.

"I apologise for my men's enthusiasm," Sir Guy said, attempting a smooth smile. "Yet you must understand why I am here. Truly, I regret this misunderstanding and placing the girl in danger. But the fact is, the young lady must now return with me to Nottingham."

"She will not," I said.

"I cannot return without her," Sir Guy said.

"And yet you must."

Sir Guy looked at me and past me at my men, such as they were. "We outnumber you," he said.

"We outclass you," I said. "Do you really wish to trade more blows? You will lose men, perhaps even your own life. You would risk harming the lady even more than you already have."

"I cannot return without her," Sir Guy said, desperation edging his voice.

"The sheriff will punish you," I said, nodding. "He must have been angry. He must have threatened you with all manner of consequences should you fail." Sir Guy's silence confirmed my words. "She is free to go where she wishes. And she does not wish to go to Nottingham."

"She is a ward of the crown, entrusted to the sheriff's care."

I eased my horse close to his and lowered my voice.

"No, she is of age," I said. "She is eighteen years old and free. You understand, Sir Guy, that I must defend her freedom. I will do so."

"I have no wish to fight you," Sir Guy said, lowering his voice so that his men could not hear. "I saw you slay half a dozen knights in just a few moments in that campaign. I never believed the rumours about you and the blood but I understood why they said it. You move with unnatural speed, Sir. So I tell you that I know I am no match for you. But the sheriff will not accept that I had her in my grasp only to allow you to leave. You know what the sheriff is like."

"Strangely, I did not know until now," I said and glanced over my shoulder. "Take the woman Eva back with you. Lay the blame upon her in some way."

Sir Guy's face set hard. "I'll not go near that woman."

"Why?"

"She is the archbishop's," he said. "I will not cross him. And she is unnatural."

"How so?" I asked, glancing at her.

"Can you not see? She dresses as a man. She fights in the yard, invites challenges from squires and knights alike." Guy spat.

"Oh? How does she do?"

Guy hesitated. "I will not take her back with me."

I shrugged as if I did not care what he did or did not do. "You cannot have Marian. You will not take Eva. So keep riding. Chase about the country looking for me." I raised my voice. "Find somewhere quiet to spend a few days. Come back to Nottingham having lost me. Having never found me. Your men will want to save their hides also. I will pay you and your men a few shillings to tide you over for the next few days. Why not find a nice tavern somewhere and spend it on drink?"

Guy's men sat bolt upright and stared at him.

Ultimately, I suspect, it was fear of my sword that kept him from forcing the issue. Being known as the Bloody Knight sometimes had its uses.

Swein returned across the field with Tuck bound up across his saddle. I had to stop to gag him once more, which was a dangerous business now he was full of vim once more.

"You did not kill him," Jocelyn said, surprised and offended.

"I am not finished with him," I said. "Your little encounter with Sir Guy rather interfered."

After we patched up the Lady Marian, we went on our way.

We spent the night in local lord's tumbledown hall. The place had a sagging roof and the thatch was brown, wet and stinking. The lord was off with the king but his steward was generous enough, considering the way things were in England.

I could never have predicted but Eva and Marian seemed to make a friendship of sorts and they slept alongside each other. I suppose that Eva felt protective of Marian and the young lady was glad to have Eva's attention in spite of the woman's strangeness. Marian was otherwise alone in the world.

Jocelyn did his best to contain his desires for Marian and his anger at me, for taking him away from his own vengeance, from his chance at a stable life with a good woman and his confusion as to why I carried Tuck with me. Jocelyn was full of unspent forces.

The next day he rode on ahead, keeping clear of the girl. And me.

That morning, I fell in beside Eva as we rode and before I spoke, I shared a companionable silence with her. Anselm rode on one side of Marian, babbling at her. Swein led a horse on the other side, looking up at her almost continuously.

The weather was warm and I could not bear to wear anything more than a shirt and tunic. The sun was wonderful. Blossom burst forth among the uncounted shades of green in the hedgerows. The fields were sprouting their green shoots of wheat and rye and the people were out hoeing the rampant weeds from between them.

Eva was not nervous of me, nor of what I would say and she rode without even glancing my way. It was admirable.

"I was most impressed with the way you protected the young lady," I said to her.

She nodded her head slowly, as if to say, "Of course you were."

I pursed my lips, wondering how to get her to speak of herself.

"I suppose I also wonder why the archbishop's bodyguard would fight the sheriff's men in that way for some unimportant girl," I asked.

She fixed me with her hawkish eyes over the long, straight nose. "If she is so unimportant, why not let them take her?" Eva spoke as if she was a lady who was halfway to becoming a commoner. I guessed that she was somewhat like me and came from the impoverished rump of the knightly class.

"I would have done so, had they not charged in so." I was not sure if I meant it.

"They would never have tried it but they saw you were not there and they thought to seize their chance while they could."

"Sir Guy says that you sought to challenge his men in the training yard?"

She laughed but with little joy. "Did he tell you how I beat them all?"

"Surely not," I said, for it was not possible.

"Try me yourself."

I had to laugh. "Where are you from?"

She scowled, staring straight ahead. "Nowhere."

"You are certainly English," I said. "But where were you raised? Who is your father? Does he know that you ride like a knight? How long have you been training?"

"So many questions," she said. "Let me ask you some, first."

"Gladly," I said. "But you must offer something yourself. First."

"Very well. Yes, my father does know that I fight and ride like a knight. Now, tell me what you are doing with that man tied up in the sacking."

"He is no man," I said. "He is a murderer and when we are south of Leicester he will tell me what I need to know. Then I will cut off his head."

She looked at me then. "You should not trust a man like that to talk. You should kill him now."

Eva spoke as easily of killing as an old soldier might. "How old are you?" I asked her.

"How old are you?" she shot back.

"Forty-seven, I think."

She laughed, her face lighting up. Her mouth was suddenly wide and her eyes shone. She was a striking looking woman. "My father said the same but I did not believe it. How have you stayed so young? What is your secret?"

"Perhaps God rewards my service in the Holy Land. Who is your father?"

"Hugh de Nonant. The Archbishop of York."

I did not know what to say.

"I see."

"Do you?"

I thought about what the archbishop could be up to by sending her with me. Was she telling the truth? Why would he clothe her in such a way?

"He dresses you as a knight?" I asked. "By your presence does he hope to unsettle the men he speaks to?"

She was silent and I chance a look. Her face was drawn tight over her bony face, her lips pressed together. I gathered I had given a great insult.

"Do you mean that you truly can fight?" I said. "As well as a man?"

"Better," she said. "Better than most men. Better than most knights."

I suppressed a laugh, as I did not wish to anger her any further.

"Where did you learn to fight?" I asked.

"It is your turn to answer my questions," she said and she was quite right. "They say that when you were fighting for King John, in Gascony, you would drink the blood of the men you slaughtered. High on a castle wall before the army you swallowed the blood from a knight's severed neck and threw the body down to the defenders."

"I see the tale grows in the telling," I said.

"So you deny it?"

I sighed. It was a beautiful afternoon. By speaking of such things, it was as though I was spoiling that glorious, holy thing. The most wonderful thing in all the world. An English summer day.

"We scaled the walls but only a few of us made it inside. I fought my way down the other side and chased a fleeing group of knights and squires into the ground floor of a corner tower. They were pressed together tightly, I thought I could trap them, kill them. But I was drawn inside. They shut the door behind me, thinking to kill me. There were twelve men in there. Men and boys. I was alone. Surrounded. They were behind me and halfway up the spiral stairway. I killed them all. I cannot remember precisely why I needed to be so thorough. I can recall a few of the survivors, on their knees, begging to be taken prisoner. But when the battle rage is upon you, what can you do? Certainly, I was very gravely wounded. My face was torn open, I could feel my cheek opened and flapping like the sole of a shoe. My knee had been smashed. I'd had my helmet torn away and my skull felt cut and crushed by heavy blows. I would have died. So I drank."

She looked confused. Disbelieving. As well she might.

"You were dying so you drank the blood of dead men?"

"It heals me," I said. "So long as the blood is somewhat fresh. It heals me completely, quickly and thoroughly, leaving no scar. I know that may surprise you. That you will not believe me. But it is the truth. And that is how they found me. They broke into the tower from above, came down the stairs. I looked up over the body I held to see a group of Monmouth's knights crowded on the stairs. Of course, as I am sure you know, Monmouth and my lord the archbishop are enemies, of a sort. Before the day was out I had been denounced, the priests had proclaimed me possessed by a demon or the son of Satan or some other form of evil. They demanded my death."

She looked closely at me, perhaps judging whether I was playing some game. Plainly, she doubted wounds so severe could be healed.

"How did you escape the accusations?" Eva eventually asked.

"There was no crime committed, as such. I denied it. I had fought bravely. I had won the walls. The king sent me home, hoping that the scandal would blow over. God knows, he was right. He has had enough of his own in the years since that it is no more than a rumour."

"A rumour that is true," she pointed out. "How long have you been this way? What does it have to do with the monk in a sack on that horse?"

"It is your turn to answer my questions," I said.

She declined.

It was two weeks of riding to get to the Weald, on the southeast corner of England. We went west and south, then headed east once we were south of London. An interesting journey. I did not press the woman for details and, little by little, Eva revealed her story.

One night, sitting quietly together by the hearth in a hall in Wiltshire, she spoke more about her early life. The firelight flickering orange over Eva's strong features, making deep shadows in the hollows beneath her cheekbones.

"The archbishop is your lord," she said to me. "So you well know his nature. I have often wondered how many brothers and sisters I have in England and France. And Rome, too, no doubt and in every other village in between."

I laughed politely. Yes indeed, I knew what the archbishop was like. And I knew that I was also a bastard, though not raised as one. Not quite.

"My dear mother was just a young girl when my father became infatuated with her," Eva said. "So she says. She was the youngest of a poor knight up in Northumbria and they had very little, other than too many children. And mother was a beauty. Beautiful but weak of body and mean in spirit. I suppose now that they somehow thrust her under the archbishop's nose. He used her, and then when she fell pregnant he put her away. Her brother took us in. And I was born in the cold, up north. And foisted onto my uncle, who was a knight."

"Who was he? Perhaps I know him."

"Perhaps you do," she said. "And that is why I will not say."

"Fair enough," I said. "How did you end up working as the archbishop's bodyguard?"

What I really wanted to ask was why she was telling me everything about herself and how much of it was true. What was her game? Was she really who she claimed to be? Was she still going to spy on us, report to the archbishop?

Surely, I thought, I should not expect her to slip a knife into my ribs one night.

"I am not sure why or how it started. But I loved to play at knights and Saracens with the boys. Even though mother and my uncle beat me bloody so many times. I would hide away, in the stable or go out into the wood and swing a stick around."

"I was the same," I said.

"Were you beaten when discovered? No, you were encouraged. As I got older, the boys did not like me playing with them. My cousins and the other girls would mock me. When I was eight or so, some of the manor and village boys caught me and gave me a hiding."

"A gang of boys can be the evilest thing that walks the earth," I said. "I wager your mother was pleased you'd had some sense knocked into you."

"She was dead by then," Eva said, dismissively. "She died in the winter. Died of her bitterness. She was abandoned by the archbishop and then no other man was good enough so she died bitter and lonely. I did not miss her."

"Your beating did not cause you to give up," I said, nodding in approval.

"I hunted those boys," she said, the firelight glinting in her eyes. "One by one, over weeks. Days, perhaps. Time passes differently when you are young. I took the first boy, Thomas, in the woods by his den. I left his face a pulp. He would not admit who had done it but everyone knew. The other boys knew. They were on their guard all the time but still I got them. John the Pimple was their leader. He must have been twelve years old. He seemed a giant to me. He was canny. Wary. I had to stalk him for days. He thought that he was safe in his father's workshop after dark. He was wrong."

"You seem to be proud even now," I said and she snapped her eyes to mine. "And you bloody well should be." I banged my ale mug against hers and she smiled.

It was the first smile I had seen on her face. It was quite lovely.

"So you were sent away?" I prompted.

"Quite the opposite," she said. "The boys' fathers were livid. My aunt and the women were horrified. But my dear uncle began training me as he would any squire."

"Good God," I said, trying to imagine what my own people would say if I did something similar.

Eva nodded. "The first year or two they all tried to dissuade him. The priests, his wife, the villagers. My uncle never wavered. He told them all to shove off. There were a few of the boys also training. We were quite poor. They would never speak to me, let alone train with me."

"Sounds like an isolated way to grow up," I said, recalling my own chaotic upbringing amongst dozens of pages and squires. "Lonely."

"I was never happier," she said, a smile creeping back onto her face. "Over the years, he taught me the lance, the sword, dagger. Wrestling, riding."

"Ah," I said. "A wonderful existence." For these were the best things in all the world, as well as women and wine.

"Until my uncle went away to fight. He never returned. His wife, everyone else, forced me out. My cousins were triumphant. I had nowhere to go but to the archbishop."

I winced. "I am sure that he loved that."

"He denied that I was his," she said. "At first. He tried to force himself on me. But I fought him, tripped him and threw him down. I thought he would kill me but instead he was impressed. He had one of his men test me with sword and shield. After that, he indulged me. In a certain amount of secret, of course. But even though word got out, everyone is afraid of the archbishop's ire."

"And then he took you into service as his bodyguard," I said.

"You must know what he is like," she said. "He knows that I fight well. Better than most men. But he has me by his side when he speaks to certain men."

"Certain men?"

"Men such as the sheriff," she said. "And other men that the archbishop likes to fluster with my presence. Most of his vassals and almost all of his priests and monks. He enjoys seeing the indignant expressions on their faces, he has told me. He enjoys making them uncomfortable and dares them to make mention of my presence. Dares them to challenge him. But he has never taken me anywhere near the king or his courtiers."

"And he asked you to follow me," I said. "When we left Nottingham. He knew I would not take you willingly."

"Yes," she said, not meeting my eye.

"And you were to do what? Watch me?"

She drank more of her ale. "To see that you did your duty and went to the Weald. He told me to do everything I could to keep you there and I was to stay with you. But if you went north or anywhere else, I was to find the archbishop immediately and tell him. He suspected you would go into Sherwood, or return to your home. I think he hoped that you would flee overseas."

"Would he mind you telling me this, do you think?" I asked, confused as to why he would want me so very far away from Sherwood.

She shrugged. "I do not care what he thinks. I serve him because I know no other who would have me. Have me as a squire or in service as a man at arms." She eyed me over the rim of her cup.

"I would," I said. "I would have you serve me." Of course, I did not have the income to support more men but I was somewhat drunk and her eyes were large, dark, and beautiful.

"You would?" she said, orange dancing over the black irises.

"Of course," I said. "I saw how you defended Marian without a thought for yourself. You stood over her, ready to fight to protect her, though you barely knew her. You ride well, you have your own equipment and you care for it diligently. You would make a very fine man-at-arms. But my lord is the archbishop and he would never allow me to take you on."

"I see," she said. "I understand."

"So we shall not ask him."

We crashed our cups together and drank, smiling.

During the journey south, Eva was taciturn with all of us, except those nights when she and I would sit, drink and talk quietly. I enjoyed teasing words out of her, enjoyed her company very much. I suppose it was because I so favoured her with my presence that Jocelyn resented hers. He thought that her manner of dress was an absurd boast, an affectation that was offensive to any true man-at-arms. Jocelyn continued to hold her in contempt until the day he humoured her with a practice sword fight using a sturdy stick.

She rapped him on the head and the fingers before he realised what he was up against. She was like a willow and as fast as the strike of a night viper I had once seen in Acre. Jocelyn, with his sturdy bullock's shoulders hunched low behind his shield, hammered her into submission. Eva was a fine fighter but Jocelyn was simply beyond her.

Still, she had more than proved her worth to him. What is more, because he was already infatuated with Marian and because Eva was illegitimate he had no lust for her. He accepted her as another squire.

Anselm seemed to be terrified of her. Presumably, he was either in love with her or saw her as competition. Possibly, it was both.

Swein mistrusted her and kept his distance, without ever explaining why.

For Marian, she was a great comfort, being both a woman and a person she could ask about practical matters such as where to pass water while on the road and other issues particular to ladies.

Marian proved herself stoical and strong willed. The first few days she was close to tears from the soreness of riding and the discomforts of the road. Even my old palfrey's gait would make you sore if unused to riding. But she never complained, not once in my hearing. Jocelyn waited upon her, tended to her every whim, helping her on and off her palfrey, to and from buildings. He cut her meat and poured her ale. He laughed at her jokes and sang to her. He berated an innkeeper to heat gallons of water so that she might bathe and spent my money to pay for it. I had the bath next, though, and I did not begrudge him for his attempts to woo her. To what extent it was working, I had very little idea. Marian often behaved strangely around me, as if she were wary of being close to me. She was deeply disturbed by the writhing creature I carried with us.

All the while, Anselm taught Swein the practicalities of being a squire. We even allowed him to train with a sword, every now and then. The young man was not bad, although he was rather old at sixteen to be beginning his learning and we kept him to swinging a stout stick lest he hurt someone. Untrained swordsmen always want to swing their swords like axes, going for power over speed and control.

But Swein's true talent was the bow.

One fine evening outside Devizes, we stopped to spend the night at the edge of a meadow under cover of a stand of oaks. Swein declared that he must shoot some arrows.

"You have duties," Jocelyn said from a low log by the young fire, rubbing at a flake of rust on the hilt of his second-best sword. "See to them before you play."

"If I don't practise the bow then next time I shoot in anger I might miss," Swein said, taut with contained anger. "You have to practise the bow, Sir Jocelyn, you just have to. What if you need me to protect you and I miss?"

"What did you say?" Jocelyn said, climbing to his feet, his blade flashing in the evening light. "Did you defy me, boy?"

"Jocelyn," I said, tired of his nonsense. "You go ahead, Swein."

Swein grinned in triumph while he strung his bow and bent it, pulling the cord back repeatedly without nocking an arrow.

"You have to warm the bow," he said over his shoulder, aware of how I stared at him. Bows and arrows fascinated me.

His arrows were precious to him and he looked after them as if they were newborn babies, always checking on them, keeping them dry and protected in their arrow bag. He twisted up a big bundle of shoots, wildflower stems, and long grass and laid it in front of a tussock at the edge of the meadow.

He stood fifty yards away and shot a few arrows into it. Every shot was on target.

"Good thing too," Swein said when he came to collect them. "I can make a new bow from a stave, if I have to. And I can make a cord out of almost anything. But I can't make an arrow. Just can't do it. Every single one of them is precious. If I miss the target then chances are I ain't ever going to find that arrow. Not in woods like these."

"So will you let me have a shot with it?" I asked. His face fell and I laughed. "I am only pulling your leg, Swein. But can I try the bow? I always loved shooting a crossbow. Is it much different?"

Swein handed it over and I tested the pull. It resisted. Pulling it back to my cheek was an enormous effort. "Good God," I said. "Jocelyn. Jocelyn, quickly come and try this bow."

I will never forget the look of wonder and blossoming respect upon Jocelyn's face when he attempted to draw Swein's huge bow back to his cheek.

"How can you pull this thing?" Jocelyn asked Swein. "Over and over again? You are as scrawny as a baby bird."

Swein scowled and disrobed for us, taking his undershirt down to his waist. He turned his back and flexed the thick muscles across his back and shoulders.

"Good God," I said, poking at his flesh like I was at a market. "You have shoulders like a destrier."

"A lifetime of using a heavy bow," Swein said over his shoulder. "Every year when I was a boy, my dad used to make me a bigger bow. Took me all summer to get strong enough to pull it with ease. Then next year he'd do it again. It's the only way to get strong enough to pull these big war bows."

Eva cheered from by the fire, asking Swein to remove the rest of his clothes. Marian laughed, clapping her hands and gave voice to her agreement. Swein covered himself up again, his fair-skinned face glowing red. Jocelyn was surprised by Marian's somewhat lewd outburst but there was lust in his eyes, for what man does not want his lady to be a secret harlot?

From the shadows under the trees, the writhing form of Tuck groaned. I sighed and motioned for Swein to follow me.

Brother Tuck had to be fed every couple of days with a few drops of blood. Swein, driven by his desire for revenge – whatever it was he was revenging –gave up his blood gladly. Anselm dutifully contributed when Swein's arm began looking like a ploughed village field.

We removed the sacking wrapped around the rancid smelling figure. He was growing thinner every day, which was good because he was easier to move and contain. I kept his eyes bound but undid his gag. His mouth was fouler than a city gutter.

"Hurry," I said, holding Tuck down.

Swein slit his own arm, held it high and squeezed a trickle into Tuck's gaping maw. Tuck groaned and slurped it down, making noises like an animal.

I bound him up again, looping him to the branched trunk of a solitary yew so he could not get away unseen in the night. Or worse, worm his way into our camp.

Jocelyn scowled at me as we returned to eat. "Why do you keep him? How long has it been? Ten days? It is madness. Either take the monk for trial or, at least, drag him away and slaughter him yourself."

"I will," I said.

"When, Richard?" Jocelyn said. "What are you waiting for?"

"He is the only one who knows where William is," I argued.

"So question him and be done with it," Jocelyn said. "Carrying him with us is absurd."

"Tuck is raving mad most of the time," I said. "I keep him on the verge of starvation lest he causes trouble when at full strength. Keeping him bound, gagged and covered up drives his wits further from his mind. I cannot question him upon the road. But when we reach the Weald, I will find a secluded place. I will bind him and I will give him a pint or two of blood. That should bring him back to himself so I question him fully. But we cannot do that here. What if he gets loose out here?"

Jocelyn looked unconvinced. Everyone else refused to meet my eye.

"Alright, listen. When we reach the Weald, I will question Tuck and then I will fulfil my promise to that poor old Prior," I said to everyone. "Will that suit you all?"

It was difficult to hide his presence when we rode through towns. He had befouled himself so many times that we submerged him in a river and rubbed his disgusting body against pebbles and sand to clean at least the outside of his clothes.

His presence greatly disturbed Marian. It was many days before she accepted that he could only be kept alive by blood. I explained everything to her. She found a kind of comfort in the fact that her father had been slain by immortal, powerful monsters rather than mere men. Marian had heard the rumours of a darkness in the greenwood, everyone in Nottingham had. It was a nameless evil far worse than the normal outlaw bands. But no one would tell her anything. The sheriff had kept her ignorant and isolated and only ever repeated the lie that he expected her father to be ransomed any day now.

None of them understood why I kept Tuck. Why I refused to question him until we got to the Weald. In truth, I did not clearly understand it myself at the time. But Tuck was the single strand that might lead me to William. And he had been made into what he was by my brother's blood.

My blood.

The roads were infrequently travelled, especially in the south. Everyone loyal to the king had fled or was locked away in one of the many castles that John controlled. We met many men fleeing from the French forces but no one had any useful information, merely rumour and fear. Some men said the king was coming, others that he was in London and others that he had fled for Scotland.

Still, we met no French. Nor did we meet English forces other than the occasional group of men scouting about for their lords. Few men loyal to King John were brave enough to travel deep into Kent.

We asked for directions and arrived in the Weald at the beginning of June.

Kent was a beautiful place. Rolling green hills and rich villages. It was perfect land for farming. It lay between London and the ports of Dover and Sandwich and the routes to France and the rest of Europe. It was the richest land in England, as well as the key to the entire country.

The Weald, however, was a semi-wild land in the centre of that most civilised part of England. It was heavily wooded and hilly, where the rest of the shire around the coast was cleared and heavily farmed. The soil in the Weald was thin and difficult to grow crops on. It was grazed by sheep and cattle in pastures dotted between acre after acre of dense woodland. The ash and oak and beech woods were cut and provided fuel for the towns of Kent, for London to the north and the many charcoal makers working throughout the deep wood.

When we reached that land, we asked for the village of Cassingham and learned that was on the far side of the wood, halfway to Dover. We came from the west and would have to travel miles from one side of the wooded Weald to the other.

We never got that far.

Within the first few miles, walking slowly through that tangled, remote woodland we were surrounded by men armed with bows.

The road was completely deserted, twisting through the dense tangle of old wood, coppiced ash and thick layer of green summer growth. There should have been people around. There were villages, farms, shepherds, swineherds and charcoal burners all over the Weald but I assumed that the Wealden folk had fled or gone to ground after the French invasion. It was approaching the middle of June 1216.

"Do you feel as though you are being observed?" Jocelyn asked me as we rode, our horses' hooves thudding softly on the dry ground.

"I do," I said, peering into the gloom, glad that we were all armoured. All of us that had it to wear. I looked back to Anselm and nodded to him that he was to watch Marian. The lad sat up straighter in his saddle and placed his horse beside hers.

"But is it Englishmen," Jocelyn said. "Or is it the French?"

I fingered the hilt of my sword.

"It's just the Green Man," Swein said, brightly, from behind us. He sat awkwardly on top of his stocky packhorse, like a dog riding a cow. He was an appalling horseman but he loved being in the woods.

"What in God's name are you blathering about?" Jocelyn said, still looking sideways, trying to see further than a half dozen yards away.

"The Green Man, isn't it," Swein said. "That feeling you always get when you're in the woods. That feeling of being watched? That's the Green Man. He lurks, watching. Up to no good."

"A peasant superstition," Jocelyn said, lowering his voice. "It is more likely a man of the usual colour. Perhaps we should ride hard, leave him behind."

I knew he meant Swein, not the watching man.

"It's not superstition," Swein said. "You can see where he's been, all the time. He leaves his mark."

"What mark?" Jocelyn said, attempting to scoff.

"The knots in tree trunks," Swein said. I turned but his face was completely serious. "Knots in tree trunks is where the Green Man has just pulled his face back inside the trunk, after watching you. The tree bark flows like water but the moment you look at it, it turns to solid bark again, only the ripples are marked upon the tree. And he loves the yew most of all."

"The yew?" I said. The trees are massive but squat things with dense, very dark green leaves that are like flatted needles. There was one or more yew outside every church in England.

"The yew is the archer's favourite tree making bow staves," Swein said, stating the obvious. "Because it is the tree of death. The Green Man lives inside every yew, in the darkness under the leaves, between the trunks. Why else would they be green all year round? You know the leaves are deadly, right? You have to keep cattle away from yews or they'll eat them and die. The berries are the colour of bright pink blood and anyone that eats them, man, dog, cattle, dies coughing up bright pink froth. The Green Man is death, he lives in the yew and his magic, his sight, his murder goes into your bow. That's the truth. Every archer knows."

Jocelyn was silent. We looked out. I listened hard, sure I could hear footsteps and sure I could smell bodies on the air. But perhaps, I thought, it was my imagination. It was difficult to smell anything over the stench of Tuck.

"Do not be absurd," Jocelyn said eventually but his heart was not in it.

Marian laughed from behind us, breaking the spell. "The Green Man is a story," she said. "The songs say the Green Man when they mean to say birth or death and rebirth. You know the poems, do you not? Where the leaves burst from his face and eyes, as though he is spring itself, come to life only to be so full of vitality that he dies, that he cannot breathe. Like he is himself a form of folksong. Like a wood in summer. Suffocating in its own abundance. That is all. He is no more a true man than is the sound of a river or the wind in the trees."

Jocelyn whispered to me, "Do you know what she is saying?"

"Of course," I lied.

"Fascinating," Jocelyn said over his shoulder. "Just fascinating, my lady."

"Halt!" A man in the centre of the road said.

I yanked on my horse's reins so hard I hurt the animal. Jocelyn drew his sword.

"Hold it there," the young fellow in the road before us said, looking at Jocelyn.

The man was not tall but he had somewhat of a commanding presence.

I opened my arms wide. "We will not harm you," I said and leaned over to pat my horse's neck.

"Calm yourself," I whispered to Jocelyn. "Watch the trees. Be ready."

"Harm me?" the young man on the road said, grinning. "I am not afraid."

I looked closely at him. The man was strongly built, with a large face. He was dressed in rough country clothes and no armour but he wore a sword at his hip.

"Fine, fine," I said, allowing him his swagger. "We are simply passing through. I am travelling through this land, heading toward Dover. On the road there I believe I will find a village called Cassingham."

"What you want in Cassingham?" the young man said.

"I am looking for a squire named William of the village called Cassingham," I bellowed at him.

"What do you want him for?" the man said, eyeing me warily. "You for King John? Or for the French?"

Leaves rustled and twigs snapped in the trees to either side and there were shadows moving amongst the dark green. Whispers, too, perhaps and definitely the wood smoke and sweat smell of men.

"Who are you for?" I asked the young man.

"I asked you first," he shot back, knowing that I had spotted his men surrounding us. If they were archers then we had no chance.

I stuck out my chin and slipped my hand around the hilt of my sword. It felt good in my hand. I glanced round at Eva behind me. She nodded, her own hand at her hip, reins held ready, her horse high and sensing the tension of the rider. Swein slid his hand toward his bow staff. Jocelyn had his fine horse under masterful control but the beast was quivering, expecting to be charged at any moment.

"I am a loyal and proud servant of the rightful king of England," I said, watching the man closely. "King John."

"Thank God," the man said, relaxing and then he cupped his hands to his mouth and shouted. "They are loyal to the king. Show yourselves."

There was a great rustling and stomping from the thick undergrowth all around on both sides of the road. I was shocked to see more than a score of men push their way through the bushes and stride into the road.

The twenty men wore gambesons and iron caps. A couple had mail coifs. Some were armed with spears, a handful swords and every one of them carried a huge bow and a quiver of arrows. They simply stood and looked at us, many of them smiling at our discomfort.

Jocelyn and I shared a look. We were surrounded and outnumbered but I did not feel as though we were being threatened. But they were certainly enjoying themselves at our expense, the damned commoners.

"Perhaps you'd be good enough to point me toward Cassingham," I said. "Can we reach it before nightfall?"

"You probably could," the fellow said walking toward me. He seemed relaxed, amused even, so I let him come close. "But William of Cassingham ain't there."

"Where is he then?" I asked and the men around us chuckled.

"Why, he's right here, sir," the man said, indicating himself.

I was not expecting a great knight but still I was surprised. The stocky fellow was young, in his early twenties perhaps, with big eyes, a huge nose, and a wide mouth. Although his features were too large, it was not an unattractive face. The man was unarmoured, even less so than his men and his clothes were of poor quality. Strange attire for a man who was supposed to be a squire but then again, a landed country gentleman was one step above a wealthy peasant. At least he wore a sword at his hip, though the scabbard was battered.

"You're William of Cassingham?" I said. "I am Sir Richard of Ashbury. The Archbishop of York sent me to you."

Cassingham stared at me for a moment then laughed. His men laughed with him.

I ground my teeth and fought my anger back down. "Something amuses you about that information?"

"My apologies, Sir Richard," Cassingham said. He reached up under his cap to scratch his head, sighing. "I am not mocking you. I wrote to the king, to the Archbishops of Canterbury and York. I wrote to the Marshal. I begged for help in facing the French. They have thousands of knights and they are destroying this land. My land. Our land. We have held out in the hope of making a fight of it here, of throwing them back into the sea. But it has been more than a fortnight, waiting for more men. We have fallen back from them, this far into the wood. All the while, we have been praying that an army was heading this way." He looked at me and my small group and laughed loudly. "And then we get two knights, their squires, and their wives. If I say that I wished for more, you will forgive me, sir, that I take refuge in bitter jest."

Jocelyn shook with anger at the man's disrespect but he managed to hold his tongue.

I fought my own anger down and looked closer at the young man called William of Cassingham.

He was filthy, unshaven. His men were lean and their faces were drawn. He had bravely stayed and stood ready to fight. Had no doubt been fending off French raiding forces.

"You wished for more," I said to them, nodding and they nodded with me. "Of course you did. And I wish I was an army of English knights come to save you. I wish that I were here two weeks before now. And I wish I was a great lord in his castle, as rich as the Marshal and married to an Iberian princess who squirts the finest wine from her tits." They laughed, so I scowled at them.

"Wishes are for children. The king is occupied with conquering the rest of his kingdom from the rebel barons. You asked for help. Here I am. And here I will stay and here I will fight with you. We cannot win the war. We cannot take back Kent. But perhaps we can kill a few wagonloads of the bastards before they kill us. Now. Where are those bloody bastard French, eh?"

"In London," William Cassingham said, beside my horse. "In London, where Prince Louis of France has been proclaimed King of England."

7

THE POISON PLOT

"HOW LONG DO YOU MEAN to keep this up before we can go home?" Jocelyn whispered into my ear in the darkness. "We have been here in the Weald, testing God's will for weeks. For how long do you expect us to get away with this? Look, the guards are even staying awake all night now."

"Precisely," I whispered to his shadow. "So be quiet before the French hear you."

Jocelyn and I lay in the sheep shit and long grass at the edge of a pasture, looking down into the French encampment outside the town and castle at Dover.

Dover was and is the closest part of England to France. The narrowest point of the English Channel at just twenty miles. On a clear day, it is perfectly possible to look from England across the water to the coast of France. Fishing boats bobbed always out there, along with the bigger, fat bellied trading ships running along both coasts.

On that morning, the sun was not yet up so all we could see were shadows in the blackness but the sky to our left was taking on the blue of a clear summer morning and all was becoming clearer.

Jocelyn was quite right. We had been harrying the French for weeks. Most of the summer, in fact. The French camp outside Dover was the largest target we had taken aim at. But Prince Louis and his large, well-equipped forces had taken the royal castles at Rochester and Canterbury, and all the towns of Kent, in a matter of days. London, always siding with the rebel barons, had thrown open the gates to him and welcomed him as the new King of England.

Yet for the entire summer, and despite taking the whole southeast of England, the French had simply avoided the castle of Dover.

The castle was said to be the key to the Kingdom of England and it had been since the dawn of time. Since the Saxons, King Arthur and the Romans, there had been a castle atop those white cliffs. In 1216, though, Dover Castle was vast, modern and well supplied with men and stores.

It was designed to bar the way to any French assault and yet Louis had made a mockery of the whole idea and simply ignored it for the summer. The loyal men inside Dover were enough to guard the walls but not to present a challenge if they ventured outside of them.

Then, when Louis was sure that King John was not coming for him, he had finally invested in Dover. Or, at least, he had sent his men to do so while Louis languished in John's palace in London.

"There must be thousands of men down there," Jocelyn said softly.

"Possibly," I said.

"Hundreds, at least."

"Let us go back to the men," I whispered and we slithered back down the hill and into the trees. It was so dark in the scrubby wood that I saw little more than outlines and shadow and my eyes saw better in darkness than most.

We had forty men waiting for us, led by William of Cassingham.

Each man was an archer and each had a pony. The beasts stood dozing, a few chomping quietly and there was the occasional gushing patter of horse piss on the leaf litter.

"All is quiet in the camp," I said to Cassingham, seeing the glint of his open-faced, old-fashioned helmet. "This is your last chance to call off this raid. We cannot be sure our man will come out to me. And the chances are your men will be caught."

Cassingham laughed in the darkness. "They have not caught us yet."

His men laughed quietly.

In the middle of June, Prince Louis had marched his army all the way across southern England to the ancient and royal city of Winchester and captured it. After not contesting London, King John had declared Winchester to be his capital, the seat of his authority.

John had fled rather than fight a battle he would lose. It was probably a sound military decision, based on the reality of the situation over his personal pride.

But it had greatly disheartened the men of the Weald.

"What do you reckon on our chances, lads?" Cassingham said, half turning to the shadowy men near him. They chuckled again. A good sign of their trust in their leader.

William of Cassingham had rallied the men of the Weald and called them to him when their lords had gone over to the rebels or the French or simply fled. And Cassingham alone had organised the defence of the villages from the roaming bands of foraging French forces.

His band of archers could see off all but the strongest of French groups. The men were mostly freemen farmers but there were villagers and tradesmen too. But they were all skilled with the bow and many with sword and dagger. A dozen had fought in the Holy Land or claimed to have done.

Few on either side were ever killed in those first scraps with the French and rebel soldiers because no man in his right mind stands to be shot when archers are shooting at him. And why attack a defended village when there were plenty that stood defenceless and deserted?

When the French had landed, Cassingham's men drove sheep and cattle away from the edges of the Weald and deeper into the wooded hills and valley pastures, away from the roads and off the trackways. They carried and carted off sacks of grain and barrels of ale to hidden stores or places that could be better defended.

And it had worked. Cassingham and his men were by the middle of summer already confident of keeping their families fed in the coming winter.

But the fear was that the French would overrun the Weald. And they could, if they wished. But the men were outraged by the invasions of the French into their homelands. Villages were emptied, farms abandoned and the people came to Cassingham's places, looking for protection.

None were turned away.

Cassingham was nobody. A country squire barely out of boyhood. Too poor to equip himself properly. Too beloved in his parish to feel able to leave to it to the ravages of the French.

And yet his legend was already growing.

When all men of noble birth had fled, he alone had stayed and led.

By the end of July, the French had returned to the southeast corner of England. They would take Dover, and then they would be free to receive all the reinforcements that France could send, completely unopposed and unthreatened. Then, no matter how many rebel barons King John brought back under his banner he would never have enough men to stand. King John's Flemish mercenaries would stay with him only as long as he had the coin to pay them.

All Prince Louis had to do was take Dover and then wait for John to run out of money.

And then the French would rule England forever.

"The most important thing is speed," I said to Cassingham and to the rest. "We must be in and out before they know they are being attacked. We need our head start or their superior horses will overtake ours."

"There is no need to say it again," Cassingham replied. "We all know what to do."

His confidence was reassuring and I did not doubt him but I found his disregard of my advice irritating.

"I pray that you do," I said and called for Swein, who brought my horse and my armour. Anselm brought to Jocelyn his and we shrugged ourselves into them.

Cassingham had his men kneel and pray with his priest. I stood to the side. Jocelyn kneeled with Anselm.

For all their talk and quiet laughter, the men were tense. Cassingham was quite right that they all knew what to do. It did not change the fact that they had never done anything quite like this before.

"The French were sleeping?" Swein whispered to me while the priest babbled on about faith and protection.

"A few guards, I believe. But the camp was quiet."

"Sir Jocelyn thinks this attack is a mistake," Swein said, his voice low.

"He does. What does Anselm think?"

"He thinks that whatever you decide to do is the right choice."

I smiled in the dark. "What do you think?"

"I think I should be in Sherwood."

"As do I," I said. "We will return very soon. Tuck is almost recovered enough to talk. If he can tell me what I need to know and if this raid goes well then I might consider my task complete and return to Nottingham. As long as Cassingham does well."

"He will," Swein said. "They all will."

"Oh?" I was amused by his certainty. "So you are an expert in warfare now, Swein?"

"I know archers," he said, defiantly. "I've seen these men shoot. And Cassingham leads them well."

I thought the same thing but then I had seen twenty-five years of war, on and off, and I had seen the best and the worst of leaders.

"Why do you think Cassingham leads well?" I asked Swein. The priest was finishing his prolonged prayer, asking God to bless their dutiful service for the king.

"When he talks, it seems like he knows what he is doing," Swein said slowly, struggling to put his thoughts into words. "And when he does something, you know that he has done the right thing. In the right way."

It was a garbled but fair assessment. "And do you think that Cassingham relies on what other men think?"

"He listens when his men suggest something or ask a question," Swein said, pondering it. "But he seems like he always knows what to do anyway."

The men murmured an Amen and stood to prepare themselves.

I clapped Swein on the back. "Good," I said to him. "Be sure to remember that when you are a leader."

"Me?" he said.

Cassingham returned with Jocelyn and Anselm. "Sir Richard," Cassingham said. "My men will be in their positions by the time you and Sir Jocelyn get to the camp."

It grew lighter with every moment. Colour coming into the world.

I mounted my horse. Jocelyn and Anselm climbed upon theirs and I nodded to Cassingham and Swein, who would fight with the other archers, him being close to useless on horseback. I hoped he would be able to cling on to the back of one as we fled.

I walked the horse from the clearing to the road that wound up and then down toward the camp. It was dark. My heart raced. Like Jocelyn, I was not convinced that an attack on a heavily fortified enemy camp with thousands of men was a good idea. I was afraid that I would be captured. I was afraid that Anselm would be killed and that his mighty father would punish me, or at least, never forgive me. The Marshal was the one man whose opinion I respected. And the most powerful man in England, aside from the two kings.

The French camp already stank. The wind blew the cold salt smell of the sea to keep the excrement stench from overwhelming the senses. And even though only a fraction of their forces had arrived at Dover to begin the siege, it never took long for thousands of bodies to befoul the land and air for miles around.

The light wooded hillocks at the landward border of the camp would no doubt be cleared and occupied when the rest of the French arrived. But for now, it would cover our forty archers as they crept within long bow range and would protect our coming retreat.

It was light enough to see the silhouette of the vast castle, a dark shape on the brightening sky. The castle occupied a high mound of chalk that ended in the famous white cliffs on the seaward side. The land descended down to the town on the right, built on lower ground with easier access to the beach.

Between the castle and us stretched the edges of tents and frames of shelters and the siege engines they were quickly throwing up. It was a warm night, despite the cool sea breeze.

It was less than three hundred yards from the shadows to the camp but it felt like the dark moment stretched out like a black cloak, on and on, to the sound of hooves drumming on the thin soil covering the chalk trackway.

The first challenge came out of the dark.

"Stop there. Who are you?"

"Friends," I said in French, pulling to a halt.

"But who?" Two men approached in the gloom. "Name?" They seemed rather bored, which was good.

They also held spears, which was unfortunate.

"Sir Richard of Ashbury," I said,

"English?"

"A knight loyal to King Louis of England," I said. "As are my squires."

I dismounted slowly, groaning and sighing as if I had been riding all night.

They backed away from me, their spears held ready. I wished I could see their faces but they were clearly wary.

"Why are you here?" the closest man asked. He was a seasoned man-at-arms who could be trusted with gate duty.

"I have ridden hard to bring you news of King John's army."

They stiffened. "Tell me, now."

"How dare you speak to me in such a way," I said, feigning anger. "Bring me Sir Geoffrey and I will speak to him here."

The spear-bearing man-at-arms was becoming visible as the dawn grew. He glanced at his fellow spearman.

"Hurry, man," I said. "Come on. If I am an enemy, then how do I know that it is the steadfast Sir Geoffrey that is captain of the gate tonight?"

That appeased the senior man-at-arms somewhat. "Very well. You will come with us, Sir Richard and we shall rouse Sir Geoffrey."

I was certainly not going to walk into the French camp. "I do not obey your orders. You will bring Sir Geoffrey to me here and I will gladly speak to him."

They were confused and suspicious, as they had every right to be. What tired man would refuse shelter and refreshment after a long ride? But their natural deference to their betters asserted itself and the man-at-arms went to find Sir Geoffrey, leaving just the one to watch over my two men and me.

There were other French moving just inside the entrance. Rough ditches had been dug either side of the road and a bank thrown up as the beginning of a defensive palisade. They need not have bothered, for King John had neither the men nor the inclination to contest the south.

Jocelyn and Anselm dismounted, likewise making a show of easing their aching bones. Anselm walked our horses back and forth along the road. He was supposed to ensure they were ready for when we had to make our escape.

It grew lighter. More men woke in the camp and I cursed the man-at-arms for taking his time to grab the knight on watch. Jocelyn was tense beside me, attempting to appear nonchalant.

"What if Sir Geoffrey is not coming?" Jocelyn muttered.

"Any knight will do," I said.

Jocelyn nodded at the camp entrance, the gap in the ditch and palisaded bank stretching away ever clearer in the predawn light.

Sir Geoffrey was a small man, roused from sleep. His clothing was tousled and his cap was pulled down over his head.

Unfortunately, he had brought two large, armoured men with him. Neither wore their helm, at least nor carried a shield but both had swords at their sides with hauberks and mail coifs over their heads, much as my own men and I were attired.

"Who are you?" Sir Geoffrey said, looking me up and down. "What in the name of God are you doing waking me? Come on, out with it."

"King John approaches with his army," I said, speaking loudly enough for the men beyond the entrance to hear me. "Ten thousand men, two thousand horse."

Sir Geoffrey was stunned. His men stared in shock.

"Preposterous," Sir Geoffrey said, looking sideways at me. "You are lying." His men stared back and forth between us. "Take them."

"Jocelyn," I said. Before the word was out of my mouth, my man's sword had cleared his scabbard. He grasped the head of the man-at-arms' spear with a mailed fist and thrust his sword through the man's mouth into his head.

Sir Geoffrey gaped but his armoured men stepped in front of him and came for me.

The second spearman ran for the camp, raising a cry of warning. Jocelyn made to go after him.

The armoured men were wide-awake, battle-scarred veterans and they moved apart to surround me as I drew my blade.

"Joss, take the lord!" I shouted. Jocelyn changed his target to the noble Sir Geoffrey who was likewise attempting to flee.

The bodyguard nearest me charged at me while the other turned to protect his master. I had only one to contend with, so I turned his thrust, stepped inside it and slammed my body against his, grabbing the wrist of his sword arm. I crashed the pommel into his face, then again as he reeled away, pulling him back to me. As he fell, I pushed my point through his nose, grinding against the bones of his face. He was screaming until the blood poured down his throat. I tasted it in the air as he coughed it out.

Jocelyn had tripped Sir Geoffrey and was fending off the other man. Cries were coming from the camp. It seemed to be suddenly brighter. I ran to the armoured man and, having no time for niceties, thrust into his spine so hard that he was thrown onto his face. My blade pierced his mail and I felt it push into his backbone.

The blade snapped. It broke two-thirds of the way to the point, which clattered away onto the road and the rest was too bent to get it into the scabbard so I tossed it away.

Jocelyn dragged up Sir Geoffrey and together we got him onto my horse. He was dazed and bleeding from the head. Still, I had to hold my dagger to his throat as Jocelyn thrust him up to me from below.

Frenchmen came charging out after us as I embraced the knight in a bear-like grip, holding the point of my dagger against his neck and my other hand on the reins.

The whole sky to the east was faint blue and the world about us was tinged in blue-grey as Jocelyn and Anselm mounted. Both of them turned to defend me from the two dozen men that staggered out of the camp toward us, tired and uncertain but armed and willing to kill.

The arrows slashed down, just beyond us. A man was shot through the head, another the chest. Arrows clattered off the road. One that bounced off a stone in the road snapped and hit my horse, spinning but still with enough force to draw blood from his leg.

I urged the grey courser on along the track, between my men and up the hill toward the cover of the trees, holding Sir Geoffrey to me.

Jocelyn, Anselm and I stood our horses side by side on the brow of the hill. I glanced behind at the top of the hill. There were a dozen men lying dead or dying at the entrance and still the arrows arced in.

Dozens of men stood out of range. A score of knights gathered at the edge of the camp, more arriving and mounting with every moment.

"Run," I shouted. "Go now."

Most of the archers fell back to their ponies, mounted and began streaming away through the trees. Crows flying up, cawing in panic at the clattering of hooves and shouting men. A few kept shooting, covering the retreat.

When the knights realised that the rate of the arrows was falling, they advanced, shields up. Arrows bounced off them.

"We must go," Jocelyn said.

We rode hard. The final ten archers behind us were the best riders on the best horses.

They kept pace with us, or almost but the French knights caught up, their huge, powerful horses charging up behind us.

We made the first ambush just in time. The road bent around a low hill, the wood was a dense tangle either side of the track.

The pursuing French were slashing at our rearmost archers when the first arrows smashed into them. Our archers had left their horses on the other side of the hill and were only a few yards from their targets. The force of the arrows crashed into men and horses, the arrow shafts shattering and cracking in a cloud of splinters. Riders were unhorsed. The others fled.

On we rode, falling back through three more planned ambushes. We rode, through field and heath at a trot and at a gallop. We led them away from our defended villages and broke off into smaller groups, seeking to confuse them.

The pursuers gave up at sunset.

"Your friends have given up on you, Sir Geoffrey," I said as we looked out at the riders filing away back to Dover. "Which means you and I can have a nice little chat."

After another night and half a day, when we were certain the French had truly given up, we returned to Cassingham's village in the Weald. The Kentish squire was given a hero's welcome by the men we had left behind to guard the families.

The day after our escape, I bound the French knight Sir Geoffrey up in the small shelter I had built away from the camp proper. I had made sure the place was well out of earshot and down in a dank hollow.

I had built the structure around a deep-rooted stump of oak. It was dark and damp, despite the bright summer's day outside coming through the doorway and the gaps all around the sides. The walls had been made from green saplings and the floor was merely earth with dirty straw atop it. A row of three sturdy posts on either side of the stump held up the sides of the roof. The place was crawling with spiders.

I had built it as a place to hold Brother Tuck.

"This is no fit prison for a knight," Sir Geoffrey said, puffing out his little narrow chest. "You will get your ransom. I demand a house befitting my station."

"What do you think," I asked Cassingham. "He is your prisoner."

"Don't speak French all too well, Sir Richard, truth be told," Cassingham said.

"He demands a finer gaol. Are you certain that you do not wish to ransom him?"

Cassingham, by way of answer, stepped to Sir Geoffrey and looked down. "We know what you did. We know you raped that girl in Rochester. No, you'll not be ransomed, sir. We may send them your balls. But the rest of you will never leave the Weald."

"What did he say?" Sir Geoffrey asked me in French. "Tell him I have wealth. I can pay whatever price he sets."

"I would not be so quick to offer that," I said. "We know that you raped that young girl outside Rochester. Everyone there knows it."

"I deny it," Sir Geoffrey said, his voice shaking.

In the far corner of the hovel, I found the bound form of Tuck and dragged him into the light before Sir Geoffrey. A thick rope ran between the oak stump and the scrawny form of my starving, mad, bound prisoner, Brother Tuck.

Cassingham stood just outside the door, leaning on the frame with his arms crossed.

"You see, Geoffrey, the only thing you have to offer is the stuff flowing through your veins. I have had a problem with our monk, here. He refuses to tell me what I need to know, without me giving him a proper drink. One that will bring him back to himself."

I took Tuck's sack from his head and the monk's twitching eyes fell upon our new prisoner. Tuck growled behind his gag.

"Silence," I said and cuffed his head, thumping him down to one side. "You see, Sir Geoffrey, Brother Tuck has knowledge that I need. And he is remarkably resistant to torture. Show him your hands, Tuck."

The monk held out his shaking, bloody hands. I had removed the tips of most of his fingers. Even the thumb and forefinger of his right hand but still he protected his master's secrets.

Sir Geoffrey recoiled and horror crept up his face as he realised he was being held by madmen.

"I have promised Tuck that he shall have as much blood as he can drink, should he answer my questions."

Tuck gurgled and heaved, his eyes bulging. He was laughing.

Sir Geoffrey pissed himself, which was the proper reaction.

"Please," Geoffrey said. "I will tell you everything."

"No, no. You misunderstand me," I said. "I do not need anything from you but your slow death."

"King Louis has given me Rochester," Sir Geoffrey swallowed. "And other lands hereabouts. If you ransom me, I can assure you that not only will you receive a significant payment, you shall have lands of your own under me when the war is won."

Cassingham and I looked at each other. "You think you will win?" I said to Sir Geoffrey. "You and Prince Louis?"

"Yes, King Louis." Geoffrey stammered. "That is to say, Prince Louis of France. I know his plans. I will tell you, I swear it. All his plans."

"His plans?" I glanced at Cassingham. "He plans to take Dover Castle before winter. Then he in spring he means to take the rest of John's castles, one by one until John is forced to flee or is captured. Then Louis will be King of England, for ever."

Tuck giggled behind his gag, his eyes bulging.

"Quiet, you mad bastard," I said to him. "Am I not correct, Sir Geoffrey? Of the siege, it looked to me that half of Louis' men will guard the town of Dover while the other half invest the castle. The engines being assembled were mangonels and perriers. It looked as though a huge tower was being made, with wattle sides. Louis has sent his fleet to sea, perhaps back to France, lest it be trapped by John's ships if they decide to attack. You had men digging in the front of the castle. No doubt, you intend to undermine the great barbican. A sound plan, I am sure. Is there anything I have interpreted incorrectly? Is there anything of substance that you can add? You see, you are not here to tell me anything. You are here because the good folk of Kent want a little justice. And, also, because I need your blood to feed to my monk."

Tuck giggled again, drool soaking through the bonds at his mouth and down his chin, glistening in the gloom.

"Do not despair," I said to Sir Geoffrey. "You will have a few days of bleeding yet."

I took out my dagger and the knight screamed.

The French siege of Dover Castle dragged on. By August 1216, they had already breached and captured the castle's barbican. A great success for them but then they still had the gate beyond to take. Later, one of the mighty gate towers was brought down by the mangonels but still the French could not get through the castle's defences.

Dover Castle had cost a fortune to build and John had invested thousands in enhancing the place during his reign. Clearly, it had been worth every mark to the crown. It was the only place in southern England the French had failed to take.

All the while, our Wealden archers denied the French foragers access to stores inland. We ambushed, captured and killed dozens of them even when they began riding in force. Eventually, the foragers avoided the Weald altogether and we had to venture out into the rest of Kent to disrupt them. Our efforts certainly helped. Late in the year, the storms grow strong and regular enough to disrupt the short crossing from the French coast. The French would be without resupply from the sea for the autumn and winter and so the besieging forces grew desperate to take the castle before the bad weather forced them to become self-reliant.

At the start of October the garrison, led by the brave lord Hubert de Burgh, still held out, throwing back every assault on the walls. The longer the strength of the French was focused on Dover, the longer King John would have to strengthen his own forces.

All that time, I tried to put the pieces of Tuck's mind back together. An impossible task, though my hope was I could do enough to find out where William de Ferrers was and what his plans were.

But I waited too long. I had already kept Tuck in a state of starvation and isolation for three months. And it took three months more of feeding Sir Geoffrey's blood to Tuck to get anything close to coherent answers from him.

Even then, his mind was so ravaged that almost everything he said was incomprehensible. I had to keep Sir Geoffrey alive an awful lot longer than planned. Tied up in the dark with Tuck, being bled every day to feed him, Sir Geoffrey lost his own mind.

Cassingham was a hard young man but it was too much for him. His honour would not allow him to be part of my torture of Sir Geoffrey, the severity of whose continued punishment went beyond the law and common decency. Cassingham spent his days and weeks leading his men on raids against the foraging French and spying on the siege from afar. Swein rode with them and I was pleased, for the young man learned much about that particular kind of warfare.

All that summer and into the autumn, Jocelyn could barely tear himself away from Marian's side. But when he was with her he found his tongue tied and his jokes and witticisms were painful to behold. Although I met her only rarely, Marian seemed formal and distant with Jocelyn, far more than she was with any other person, noble or common, man or woman. Whether that meant she could not stand Jocelyn or that she was in love with him, Jocelyn could not decide. Neither could I, for that matter.

Whenever we could, we knights and squires trained Cassingham's men in the art of war. Most of them could shoot an arrow through a barrel hoop at a hundred paces but few could ride or fight effectively with a bladed weapon. No doubt they were good in a wild scrap for they were strong and fearless. But any idiot can swing a blade around. It was restraint they needed to learn, and control and how to defend. Even the ones who knew the sword had to be taught how to properly align the edge of the blade and how to cut with a draw or a push rather than hacking as if chopping wood. And these self-proclaimed swordsmen were the worst. When a man believes himself knowledgeable on a subject not all the true experts in the world can change his mind. It must be beaten out of him with rapped knuckles and clouted skulls.

Eva had learned proper martial techniques from knights and though she had rarely used them in anger, she could instruct just as well as any of us. Many of the Wealden men would scoff at the idea over their ale, or make bawdy comments but they would listen and gravely obey her in the cold light of day. Especially after she knocked them on their arse five times in a row.

After a long day of hard training in early October, I sat with Eva on the edge of a high pasture watching the sun falling over the trees. We shared a jug of ale and some bread. She wore a cap with her hair gathered up inside it.

We had taken off our mail and gambesons and sat in our undershirts, our bodies hot and stinking. She smelled much like a man did after a day of work, only it was different. Better. Whenever she was without the weight of her mail on her, I could not help but notice the swell of her breasts beneath her clothes. She rubbed and scratched at her chest. Through the open side of her shirt, I caught a glimpse how she had bound her breasts down with a wrap of linen.

"They are an impediment," she said, unsmiling.

I realised I had been staring and looked at the sunset once more, my face no doubt taking on the colour of the clouds. I began to mumble an apology. She waved a hand at me, telling me it was unimportant. She was not offended.

"I imagine it would be," I said, coughing. "Though it does not seem to slow you down nor restrict your skill. You are better than many a man I have seen named a knight."

She nodded, accepting what she knew to be true. She fingered underneath the side of her linen wrap. The skin beneath was as pale as moonlight.

It was a sort of madness, her carrying on as if she were a man. Without first her mother's brother and then the archbishop to pay for her, keep her hidden, and suppress talk, she would never have managed to carry it on. Of course, I would never have said such things to her. The woman was as prickly as an old holly tree.

But I liked her. She was the only person I knew, other than Emma, who would speak to me properly. She and Emma, though they were so different, shared a directness of speech that was so rare. Without Emma's effortless courtesy to temper it, Eva's bluntness was mistaken for rudeness and she found herself without many friends. I liked especially how she never seemed to want or expect anything from me.

"How is Marian?" I asked, keen to change the subject.

"Ask her yourself."

"You were well trained to fight," I said. "But never to converse, I see."

She snorted her derision. "Says you, Sir Richard, who speaks to no one unless it is to command or to terrify them."

I stared at her, wondering if that was truly how she saw me. "Perhaps you have the right of it," I said, drawing a suspicious look from her. "Marian will not speak to me."

Eva shrugged. "You frighten her."

"Me?"

"You frighten everyone," she said, peering over at me.

"Is it Tuck?" I said. "I do not wish to keep him there. I know what they say about him. About me."

"Yes," she said. "Of course it is Tuck. And Sir Geoffrey. It is wrong. It is madness. But it is not simply your torture of those two. Nor is it your nobility that scares them, for you are barely rich enough to warrant your title."

"What a kind thing to say," I quipped. She ignored me.

"Everyone knows that you are different from normal men. They have seen how you move. They have seen you lift a barrel of ale, without effort, by yourself. The story of you snapping that bow is whispered. Then there are the rumours. No one knows why you were disgraced. I certainly have said nothing. But the folk here say you were known as the Bloody Knight. That you drank the blood of the dead while on campaign in Gascony. They say you fought with the Lionheart and that you are sixty years old though you look like a man of twenty and the secret is that you drink the blood of maidens. That last part, I suspect, is one reason why Marian stays away, despite how she truly feels about you. But every day that you keep those two locked up together only further confirms it."

"That I am the Bloody Knight?" I said. "I do not care what these people say about me."

"You should kill Tuck," she said, her eyes cold. "He is mad beyond saving and evil. His presence is poison. And what you are doing to Sir Geoffrey in there is evil too. He deserves death. Not what you are doing to him. That is true whether people are saying it or not. Surely you see that?"

I looked in her eyes. Her face was dirty with grime and sweat. The skin beneath shone with health and vitality, stained brown by the sun.

"I will kill him tomorrow," I said. "Both of them."

"Good," Eva said. "Is what I am saying unknown to you?"

"No," I said.

She sighed. Her face was softer, more open than I had seen it before. "I wish I had been taught how to make conversation."

I thought of Emma, for the first time in months. That I had not thought of her surprised me, because usually she was never far from my thoughts. But it was because I knew what she would have said about my abduction and preservation of Brother Tuck and my treatment of Sir Geoffrey.

"You tell the truth," I said to Eva. "And the value of truth is greater than the art of conversation."

I stood, finishing my cup of beer.

"Where are you going?"

"I will end those men now," I said, standing. "Why put it off any longer?"

For a moment, she looked tempted to come with me. But even her warrior's heart balked at two grimy executions in the dark.

Mine certainly did.

"And I am not sixty years old," I said to her as I walked into the wood, treading the familiar path to the dell with my greenwood gaol.

When I stepped inside with my sword already drawn, Sir Geoffrey wept. His lips muttered a prayer. He was filthy, thin as a bow stave and his beard and hair were matted and wild. His arms were lined with half-healed cuts and scars where I had drawn his blood for Tuck.

"Sir Geoffrey," I said. "You raped a child. You and your men killed loyal Englishmen. But your punishment has denigrated us both. This ends now with your death."

"Oh, thank God. Thank God."

He was still muttering when I drove my blade through the base of his skull.

I dragged Tuck from his corner and unbound his eyes and mouth.

Tuck wailed at the death of Sir Geoffrey. In his mad, lonely state, Sir Geoffrey had been Tuck's only friend.

I felt a sudden weariness and horror at what I had inflicted upon both of these men.

"The time has come, Tuck," I said.

"To be free?" he asked, looking up like a dog at his master's homecoming.

"In a way," I said. "I know now that I have wronged you. That I damaged your mind by starving and confining you. Damaged beyond repair. You have told me nothing. You are not capable of telling me what I need to know. So now I will free you from the bonds of William's blood. If you have any sense of God left in you, take a moment to pray before I end your days."

"No!" Tuck screamed. "I will tell you. I will tell you."

"It is too late."

"The king, the king!" Tuck shrieked. "The Green Knight will kill the king."

I hesitated. "What new madness is this?"

"Not madness, my lord, not madness. A man. The big man. He came to Eden. He came to the Green Knight. He begged my lord for poison. My lord said no. The big man said he would pay any price. My lord agreed that he would do the poisoning himself, if the big man would name the man to be poisoned. The big man was quiet. But Tuck heard it. Tuck hears all. Tuck is a good monk. Tuck says his prayers. Tuck likes to do a shit at vespers but don't tell the Prior, don't tell the old prior or else Tuck—"

"Who was the big man?" I cut in.

"Didn't know him. A man. Big man," Tuck said.

"Who was the victim?"

"The what?" Tuck looked startled, confused.

"The big man's target. Who was the Green Knight going to poison?"

"Oh, that," Tuck giggled, covering his face. "I told you. I told you. The king, of course. Bad King John. King John is to die, I heard it in Eden. My lord will do it when next the king comes to Nottingham."

I leaned against the wall, smelling the damp, earthy fungal smell of the greenwood posts. Tuck was mad. There was no doubt. He was deluded as to where he was and what he was doing. But because it was William de Ferrers he was talking about, I thought it might be true.

"Listen to me, Tuck, you must tell this to the sheriff. Or to the Marshal, yes. Yes, that is what I will do. You must come with me." I cursed myself for killing Sir Geoffrey too soon. He could have been witness to Tuck's words. "You must say to them what you said to me."

"What I said to you?" Tuck asked. "I behave myself. I only drink when my lord commands."

"You must tell the king that the Green Knight means to poison him in Nottingham."

Tuck's face fell into the deepest horror that a man could show. "I told?"

"You told," I said. "But I will protect you from him. I am your new lord now, am I not?"

"What did I tell?" Tuck said.

I sighed and spoke patiently, as if to a young child. "You told me that your master, the Green Knight, is going to poison King John in Nottingham."

"No," Tuck said. "No, I did not. I would never. I could not. I never said. Anyway, it'll be some other great lord what does it."

"Who?" I said. "Do you mean Hugh de Nonant? Or someone else?"

He ducked his head down and rocked back and forth. "No, no, no."

"I will get you all the blood you need," I promised. "But you will tell the Sheriff of Nottingham or William Marshal what you told me."

Tuck's groan started from somewhere deep in his bowels, like the lowing of a cow. Quicker than I had ever seen him move before, he leapt up, tearing through the rotting rope around his arms and leg.

Before I could bring up my sword, he threw me aside and rushed Sir Geoffrey's body. I assumed he was going for the blood but instead he crashed his head into the central oak stump. The hut shook. Tuck cracked his head twice more before I recovered my wits enough to drag him away. The ancient oak had cracked and so had Tuck's skull. His nose was split, smashed flat. I could see shards of bone and the pink stuff of brains flecked in the wound before the blood welled out, filling his eyes.

I thought that perhaps he could recover from such an injury, if I could get some blood down his throat immediate.

But I would not. I knew Tuck. After so many months breaking and then nursing his broken mind. I knew he was telling the truth about the poison plot. And I also knew that no court would take the words of the man as anything but raving lunacy. And the thought of dragging him across the country again was more than I could take.

I forced pity from my mind. This creature had committed tortures and terrors against the innocent and even against the holy. The suffering I had inflicted upon him was fair, even if he had been serving as a proxy for my revenge against William.

About to warn him once again that he was about to die, I decided not to bother. I did not see what difference it would make.

I killed him and cut his head from his body though I doubted he could rise again. I buried Tuck and Sir Geoffrey both, in the wood by their summer prison, hacking through roots with my sword.

Then I gathered my men and the next morning before sunrise, we set out for Nottingham.

I had to warn the king that he was to be murdered.

8

THE DEATH OF THE KING

"I AM HERE TO SEE THE KING," I said to men at the gate of Newark Castle in Nottinghamshire. The town lay behind the castle and to the north over the wall I could see the top of the church tower as I stood before the gatehouse.

Newark was a small but sturdy castle built on the banks of the River Trent, rising it seemed straight from the waters. Upriver to the west, the sun was low in the sky above the wooded hills, casting a smear of orange light on the rippling surface. The castle was square and compact and still looked like new, having been built in stone only twenty years or so before. We approached from the south and crossed the bridge that the castle guarded.

A stocky man-at-arms with a mace hanging on his belt came forwards and looked me up and down, taking in my filthy, mud-spattered clothes and rusting armour.

I had ridden all the way from the Weald prepared for war, not trusting to the safety of the roads. Potentially saving the life of the king and catching William in the process was worth days of sweat and discomfort and we had arrived at Newark by the middle of October.

I hoped that the hard riding had not permanently damaged our horses. Sometimes it took them days or weeks to fall ill and die. Jocelyn was already close to weeping for his precious bay courser.

"And who are you, sir?" The man-at-arms said and looked beyond me as if to query why a lone knight could possibly be important enough to want an audience with the king.

"Sir Richard of Ashbury." I wanted to bash his face in with his own mace but I was too tired to put him in his place. He was the sergeant of the guard and served the crown rather than the local lord, so I had to pay him the proper respect or I would end up in gaol instead of before the king.

Still, mention of my name had a satisfying effect. Colour drained from his face. The two guards behind him whispered to each other, glancing at me.

"Are you staying at the inn, Sir Richard?" Though his tone was more respectful, he looked pointedly at my legs. They were caked in black mud.

The town and castle were packed full of the leaders who followed the king from place to place though the bulk of his army was camped miles out of town. The common loyal men and mercenaries spilled over into the villages for miles and tents were up in fields all around.

"I know that I am unfit for the king's company but please impress upon the king's men that I have urgent business. I have knowledge of the highest importance. Knowledge that must be heard now, or the king's life—" I broke off, fearing I sounded like a lunatic. I cleared my throat. "I have hurried hard. There are no rooms where I might clean and dress for court. Hence my appearance. I shall wait nearby with my men. But I must be seen. Ideally, by the Marshal, if he is here, or William Longspear or Ranulf of Chester."

I pointed to Jocelyn, Anselm, and Swein who waited with the horses pressed against the base wall of the castle wall below. They all looked miserable and exhausted, the horses' heads low as they dozed. I had pushed them all hard on the ride north.

The sergeant cast a final, withering look at me and went away in conference with one of his men.

"Don't want much, does he," I overheard them say as they passed through the gate.

Night was falling when the sergeant returned and allowed us to lead our horses into the castle courtyard and stable our horses. Newark Castle was essentially a large irregular square with a large hall, stable, chapel and other buildings inside. The outer walls were thick enough for chambers, storerooms and quarters on all four sides and there were, in addition, five towers plus the gate tower. There was enough room to house scores of knights with their retinues of squires, pages, grooms, servants, and chaplains but even still, it was now full to bursting.

The castle stable was heaving with the fine horses of the king and the courtiers. The beasts were spilling out from the stalls and the grooms struggled to find places for them. Most were riding horses that the great lords paid fortunes for. The court was never in one place for more than a week and being with the king meant a whole day in the saddle every second or third day. But there were knights' horses there too, straining at the excitement of being near strange mares. We kept well away from those creatures. Everyone knew enough to avoid a trained warhorse, even I would retreat into doorways to avoid being bitten or kicked by beasts who were as violent as a drunk man-at-arms or a wronged wife. One huge, black-coated stallion with heavily muscled hindquarters steamed in the cold, quivering in a high state. Barely contained, it snorted and moaned, lunging at the mares nearby while the grooms strained to contain the chaos.

"Whose horse is that?" Jocelyn asked no one, as if his heart ached with longing for the magnificent animal.

The sergeant escorting us shrugged. "Came in with a bunch of lords last night. He's not one of the king's," he said. "But if he claps his eyes on it, no doubt he'll want it."

"Some rich fool," I suggested. "With more money than sense."

"That is Geoffrey of Monmouth's horse, my lord," a passing groom said, his eyes full of wonder and terror.

"There you go then," I said, for I had heard how the young Monmouth was enormously rich but not at all a fighting man. "The idiot will like as not get himself thrown."

"What a waste," Jocelyn muttered, talking about the horse and not the loss of the courtier.

"Wait here, if you please, Sir Richard," the sergeant said. "They will send for you."

My men all fell asleep in the corner of the yard amongst our equipment and supplies. Our precious horses were tended to and they too lay down to sleep where they could, on mounds of straw and covered with blankets. I hoped that they would all recover soon. The men were young and the horses expensive and well cared for by the castle and royal grooms so I trusted that they would.

I sat on my cloak on the floor, leaning on my saddle and wishing I could drink blood. Just a little bit. I wanted my strength back. I wondered if anyone would miss the smallest groom.

I woke.

"Sir Richard," a servant with a lantern stood in the darkness before me, the flickering light illuminating a miserable old warty face. "My lord will see you now."

Still half asleep, I followed the servant through the castle until he told me to wait through a door somewhere deep inside. Squires, priests, and servants hurried up and down through every corridor and the place resounded with shouting and the clashing of feet. The room was an antechamber with nothing but two stools and a side table, a slit window on the wall opposite the entrance door and a door on each of the other doors. It was bare but clean and I sat on a stool, a shower of mud flaking off the links of my mail. I was aware of the sour stench of my body.

One side door opened and two lords walked in. I jumped to my feet. I did not know them but by their dress, they were vastly rich and therefore powerful men.

"You are Richard of Ashbury?" one man said. He was about thirty years old and plump, soft of the body. But he had the eyes of a murderer.

"I am."

"You lie," the plump man said, his lip curling. "Richard of Ashbury fought with the Lionheart. You are little more than a boy. I should call my men to throw you in the Trent."

I overtopped him by a head. I ground my teeth and held myself still until my rage subsided. Striking the fat little lord would no doubt mean my death. "I am Richard of Ashbury. I have a youthful countenance. I am known for it."

"That is true," the other man said. He was probably younger than thirty but his bearing showed no deference to the other man. This one was a fine looking fellow and stood straight and tall. Indeed, he looked familiar but I was tired and I could not place him. "They say you made a pact with the devil in exchange for your strength in battle."

"They do that, yes," I said, shaking my head. "Often I decide to take it as a compliment instead of an insult."

There was fear in his eyes for a moment before he laughed. "I am William Marshal," he said. "It is an honour to meet you." He noticed my confusion. "Ah, my father is the Earl of Pembroke, the famed William the Marshal. I am merely his firstborn son and barely worthy of his great name." He smiled but there was a hint of bitterness under his levity.

"Of course, my lord," I said. "Forgive me, I have ridden far to bring news."

It was also the fact that the last time I heard of the Marshal's son, he was with the rebel barons. Clearly, he had been pardoned and welcomed back into the king's arms. The great William Marshal was the king's most powerful supporter, despite how badly the king had treated him over the years. The king owed the Marshal more than a few favours and I supposed Marshal the elder was calling them in.

In fact, all his five sons but Anselm had been with the rebels and they had all suddenly changed sides.

The plump lord interjected. "You do not mean that you believe him, William?"

William Marshal the younger peered at his fellow lord. "Richard of Ashbury, this is John of Monmouth."

"I have heard of you," I said. "I am glad that you are here."

"Heard of me?" the pudgy little goat turd said. "What have you heard of me?"

"Simply that you were raised at court. I knew your father, in a way. You are a favourite of the king. That is good, for I have news that concerns his safety."

John of Monmouth sneered. "You could be anyone."

"Bring me to a man who knows me," I said, fixing young Monmouth with a stare. His lordly father had been the one to engineer a scandal about my blood drinking. His son was not my enemy but still, he shared his father's blood and, it seemed to me already, his father's character.

William Marshal nodded. "Your lord is Hugh de Nonant. The Archbishop of York."

"Perhaps not him," I said. "Someone else can confirm who I am."

"You see?" Monmouth said, sneering. "He lies."

"Why not your liege lord?" Marshal said, placing a hand on Monmouth's arm.

"I am not sure that I can say," I said, keeping my face set hard lest I give anything away. "I have information that should be heard by as few men as possible. My lord would force me to tell him and that may not be in the best interests of the king."

"What in the name of God are you blathering about?" Monmouth said. "Are you feeble minded? Are you drunk?"

The son of the Marshal rubbed his nose. "How is my little brother? Is he well? Is he learning his duty?"

"Your brother?" I was tired. "Oh, Anselm? Of course. He is here. In the courtyard, sleeping in the stables. He is very well. He is a very fine squire and there is no doubt he will make a good knight."

"Ah, that is good to hear," William Marshal grinned. "I have not seen the boy in years. I will have him brought to me. I am glad to hear he will make a good knight in time. The Lord knows we need good fighters right now and I fear we will need them still when he comes of age."

"Anselm is already a good fighter, my lord," I said. "We have been fighting for the king in the Weald. Anselm has fought this whole summer. I have lost count of the number of Frenchmen he has killed."

Satisfyingly, the Marshal was shocked. "He takes after our noble father then. Good."

"Yes, yes, how very proud you must be," fat little Monmouth said. "Yet another witless killer, just what England needs. What vital news do you bring? The messenger said it concerns the king's life. Was that all nonsense? If all you hoped for was a chamber for the night then you shall be very much—"

"Poison."

Monmouth gaped.

William Marshal froze. His whole body went rigid and his eyes darted all over my face, searching for something.

Neither man spoke so I continued.

"A while ago, I captured a prisoner. He was from Nottinghamshire but he only gave up what he knew shortly before he died. He told me of a plot to poison the king."

"Who was this man?" Marshal asked, his welcoming, conversational demeanour abandoned. He was intense. Fearful, even.

"A monk from a priory in Sherwood. A monk who had abandoned God. And common decency. He was with an outlaw leader when that outlaw was propositioned by a lord to carry out the poisoning. It was to be the next time the king passed through Nottingham."

"Who was the lord?" William Marshal said, his eyes boring into mine.

"The monk did not know him," I admitted. "But he said he was a big man. A big man and a lord."

Marshal the younger pressed his lips together.

"And you say this monk is now dead?" fat little Monmouth said. "So we have your word alone?"

"Yes."

"How convenient," Monmouth said, sneering. "But I suppose something must be done."

"Word of this must reach the king," I said, glaring at both of them. "It will reach him, immediately, one way or another."

Young Marshal was irritated by my presumption, glancing at Monmouth as if weighing a decision. He chewed on his lip for a moment. "I suppose the word of this monk can be trusted?"

I nodded. "He was not trustworthy. He was a criminal. He lost his mind well before his end. But I knew him well enough to know he was speaking truthfully. He expected nothing in return. It was not to save his life or to make any gain. And I would not have ridden this hard and fast to bring this news if I did not think it was worth relaying. I may have made a pact with the devil but I am not a fool. I know that I put myself in danger by telling you this.

I know I expose myself, to mockery at least and possibly worse. But I felt it my duty to come. If the king was killed and I had done nothing..." I was tired. I wanted blood. Or, at least, a large cup of wine.

"Sit, Richard, please," Marshal guided me onto a stool. "I understand."

He called a servant, ordered me brought food and wine and also that Anselm and my other men be found a place to sleep that was better than the stables.

"We will speak to the king himself," Marshal said to me, his friendliness restored although I detected that his manner was forced and likely had been from the moment we had met. "Yes, yes, we will speak to the king and as few others as we can. Wait here, eat, rest."

As they left, Monmouth looked at me with anger but he no longer mocked me. In fact, he regarded Marshal's retreating back with a sort of brooding wariness.

I could make no sense of their true feelings but reading my enemies' intentions was always a problem for me in my first one or two centuries.

That night I had no strength to ponder it so I ate, drank and slept sitting with my head upon the table until a squire shook me awake.

"What is it?" I said, bleary eyed and grabbing the man by the arm and pulling him down toward me. "What is happening?"

"Marshal the younger sent for you," the squire said, shaking with fear. "You have an audience with the king. Please, my lord, please do not hurt me."

I looked down and realised I had my dagger pressed to the inside of his thigh.

"Sorry, son," I said, putting it away. "Take me to the king."

Once he checked his balls were still attached, the squire led me through the castle again. It was dark. The young man's lantern was a candle surrounded by translucent, waxed parchment and it gave off a meagre, smoky light. The keep was quiet, though still clerks, knights and priests shuffled by us carrying lanterns and candles of their own.

At a door guarded by two sturdy men-at-arms, they took my sword and my dagger and I waited while the squire went inside. After a few moments, young William Marshal slipped out of it, closing it softly behind him. His face was grave.

"The king wishes to see you," Marshal the younger whispered, his eyes fixing me with an unreadable stare. "I warn you that he does not believe in you. And my father is with him. And also your lord, the Archbishop of York is there."

As if I was not nervous enough at facing the king, the knowledge that Hugh de Nonant would be present made me fret indeed. I was as certain as I could be that my lord was in league with William. How could I possibly accuse the man while he was in the room. It was close to a disaster.

"I see," I said.

"There was no avoiding it once the king got wind that you were the bearer of the warning," young Marshal said, a strange look in his eye. "Perhaps you should play this threat down, Richard and avoid the archbishop's ire? I pray, though, that you are given leave to pursue this plot up in Sherwood, eh? Anyway, you must go in. And I must get away." He smiled, patted my arm and opened the door for me.

Candles flickered from the motion of the door and shadows danced over the three great men inside. It was a solar, a day room given over for use by the king, with other chambers unseen beyond. A roasted meat smell rolled over me. My stomach churned from hunger and nervous excitement.

The king himself sat at the far end of the long central table. John, by the Grace of God, King of England, Lord of Ireland, Duke of Normandy and Aquitaine, Count of Anjou. The titles came to mind, I had heard them announced so many times and they had a familiar rhythm, as if they were an old prayer. But no one spoke them aloud anymore. He held almost all those titles by claim but not in fact.

There he was, the man who had kneeled in Westminster Abbey seventeen years before and sworn to observe peace, honour and reverence toward God and the Church all the days of his life, to do good justice and equity to the people he ruled, to keep good laws and be rid of all evil customs.

He was eating, his head down, slurping up wine from a shining cup and sucking grease off his fingers.

On one side of the room stood the Marshal himself, the Earl of Pembroke, the greatest knight who ever lived. He was over seventy years old but stood straight and tall and was still an intimidating man.

On the other side of the room loomed the archbishop, my liege lord. Massive, bulky, wearing fine, glowing church robes resplendent in white with gold crucifixes. Above his finery was his bull's head face, red and angry.

I did not know in which order to address them, nor what to say. So I stood in the doorway, hesitating like a maiden crossing the bedchamber threshold on her wedding night.

"Come in, you Godforsaken fool," the archbishop roared. "And shut the damned door."

The king paused in his eating to take a drink of wine. He glanced up at the archbishop. "You are the least holy man I ever met, Hugh."

"Thank you, Your Grace," the archbishop said, his voice rumbling from his chest.

The king smirked into his goblet and waved me over to him. I approached on the opposite side to the archbishop, nodding at William the Marshal who gave me the faintest hint of acknowledgement. He wore a fine sword at his side. He wore brilliant green over bright red.

I reached the king's side and knelt. King John sat in a huge, solid chair carved from oak and stained a brown so dark it was almost black. He paused for a moment and looked down at me, fixing me with that stare that he had. His eyes were pools of ink. Always, he bored into your soul with those eyes, searching yours for plots and threats and signs of disloyalty.

The moment that King Philip of France had heard the Richard the Lionheart was dead, he had invaded Normandy. That had been seventeen years before and John had been fighting, in one way or another, for his kingdom ever since. The kings, dukes, and counts of France had turned against him. His own barons had jostled and provoked him.

Since taking his oath, John had fought and lost in Poitou, Gascony, Anjou, Brittany and Normandy. He had invaded and subdued Wales, Scotland, and Ireland. I had fought for the king in most of his campaigns and had watched his struggles and his failures take their toll. But in the two or three years since I had last stood before him, the king had aged a decade or more. He had grown remarkably fat. His face had a yellow tinge. He seemed old, older than I would have believed. I remembered right then that he was of a similar age to me, almost fifty. His black beard had gone grey. His hair had receded and his cheeks had sagged. There were lines around his eyes and bags under them. The rebellion and the invasion were sucking the life from him.

"You are truly in league with the devil, Richard," the king said, searching my face. "Are you getting younger with each passing year? Dear God, your face makes me sick to my stomach."

He waved me to the bench alongside the table and I eased myself onto it. The table was laden with plates, half eaten pies and roast birds and fishes. It was very late to be eating such a meal. I wondered if the king had lost his wits or if he had completely succumbed to gluttony. Judging by the great mound of his belly and the fat under the beard at his neck, I guessed it was the latter, at least.

"So," King John said after cuffing his mouth. "Someone is trying to poison me?"

It took all of my will to not look at the archbishop so I just sat there, dumb.

The king glanced at the archbishop. "Would you look at the state of your man, Hugh?"

"My apologies, Your Grace," the archbishop said. "He did not come to me first or I would have never allowed him into your presence like this."

King John waved him into silence. "Richard is a man of action, a bringer of death and terror to my enemies, is that not right, Richard? Yes, I can well forgive a little filth at my table. I live with the reek of horse sweat in my nose, do I not? So, out with it, what is this plot against me?"

"I know little of any plot, Your Grace," I said. "Simply that an outlaw of Sherwood has been tasked with poisoning you when you returned to Nottinghamshire."

The king regarded me. His dark eyes were unfocused. Whether through overindulgence in wine or through age taking his sight, I knew not. The candlelight danced as servants came in to take away dishes and bring more. The king did not offer me any, for which I was glad. He slurped away more wine.

"What do you think, Hugh?" the king said, still watching me.

The archbishop sighed. "I think that someone is playing my dear Richard for a fool."

The king nodded and glanced at William the Marshal, the Earl of Pembroke.

"Almost certainly, this plot means nothing, Your Grace," Pembroke said with confidence. "Almost certainly the plot does not exist. And even if it did, there is no chance some outlaw could ever attempt to get close to you. But would a little prudence not be in order? Perhaps we should take care with your food and wine while we are in the shire. It would hurt us none to do so."

King John looked up at the Marshal through heavy lids. "Do you mean to say that you do not take care with it now?"

"Of course, Your Grace," the Marshal said smoothly. "I only meant to post guards over the wagons. And in the kitchens."

"What a lot of fuss over nothing," the king said, wafting away the threat with a bird's thighbone. "Do I not carry my wine with me, everywhere I travel? The food is procured locally but prepared by my own staff, is it not? Well then, how could I ever be poisoned? Richard, how could you ever imagine some vile peasant outlaw could ever get anywhere near my royal person?"

"It is not a peasant, Your Grace," I said. "This new leader of the outlaws was once an earl of England. He–"

The archbishop spoke over me. "He thinks the outlaw is William de Ferrers."

The king looked between the Archbishop of York and me. "You killed him in the Holy Land."

"Your pardon, Your Grace but William de Ferrers escaped," I said. "I looked for him for years but I never found him."

"That is because he died," the archbishop growled, his huge thick robes rustling like parchment. "He died in some shit stinking hole in the middle of some shit stinking land, you imbecile. You think that he still lives simply because you failed to kill him yourself? What arrogance. You have no proof that William is the outlaw that plagues Sherwood. You simply wish it to be true. Please, Your Grace, I cannot apologise enough for wasting your time with this."

The king held up his hand. "The latest outlaw chief in my forest, yes. I remember that he has been preying on the Great North Road, has he not? Taking coin and messengers. Taking travellers. Churchmen. What is being done about this?"

The king addressed the archbishop, for he was the most powerful lord of the north.

The archbishop bristled. "Sheriff Roger de Lacy has sent men to clear Sherwood but they were all lost. The year before last, I believe. The sheriff has sent almost every man of his to you for the war."

"I know what de Lacy has sent me, you fool, and I asked what is being done about the outlaws." The king burped and rubbed his fat belly, sighing with satisfaction.

"I cannot answer for the sheriff," the archbishop said. "But I believe he has not the men to do anything until you win the war."

The Marshal, behind me, snorted quietly but the king did not seem to mind.

"You believe the outlaw leader is William de Ferrers?" the king asked me.

"I am certain of it," I said. "His followers know him to be a nobleman."

"All these peasant leaders claim to be some exiled lord of somewhere or other," the archbishop said. "It is preposterous."

The king yawned and rubbed his eyes. "What do you say, Marshal?"

"It does not matter who the outlaw is," the Marshal said. "He threatens the road north. I agree with you, Your Grace. Sherwood must be cleared, immediately."

The king nodded as if he had suggested such a thing be done. "You make other knights nervous, Richard."

"I do not mean to, Your Grace."

"Have you stopped slurping up the blood of the slain?" he asked.

"I have, Your Grace," I lied. "It was the momentary madness of battle, after I had taken the walls for you."

He waved down my justifications. He had heard them before. "They say you are cursed. When men see that your face is ageless then they will know that they are quite right. My armies are crushing the barons, one after the other. Soon I will be ready to drive the French from England, for the last time. But things balance on a blade's edge. I cannot bring you into my armies again. But your magnificent abilities can be of use to me. What's say I find a handful of men who would fight under you. What would it take, Marshal?"

"To clear Sherwood? Richard could do it with twenty knights and squires and say, fifty bowmen. I am sure we could spare them."

"There," the king said. "Would that suit you?"

I could not believe my luck. The king would give me the men I needed to destroy William.

"It would, Your Grace." I bowed my head.

"Fine, you do that and then we will see about you serving me once again, what do you say? Yes, yes, of course, you say yes. Go now. Let me sleep. Someone see this man out. Marshal, you will organise the men for Sherwood? Yes, yes."

I was led out. I would have the men. My revenge was at hand.

I rushed to tell Jocelyn the good news.

That very night, the king was taken ill. A bloody flux, they called it.

I was nervous but everyone seemed sure the king would recover. He often had digestive problems, so they said. So we prepared our equipment, cleaning and sharpening. I met a few of the men that I would be leading. They seemed good enough. I had not been sold a duck after buying a pig.

Two days later, in the castle stables, I was seized by a half dozen men. I did not fight, for they were John's own men. They escorted me through the castle, downstairs and, to my complete surprise, they threw me into the castle dungeon.

"But why," I shouted as they closed the door. "For the love of God, you bastards, tell me why. What is happening?"

One man held the door open a crack, his candle casting his face in yellow and black dancing shadows. He spoke four words before the door slammed with an echoing boom.

"The king is dead."

9

OUTLAWED

I STEWED IN THAT BLACK DUNGEON, not knowing it was night or day. Barely knowing if I slept. A few times, I was brought water.

"What is happening?" I asked the gaoler but he ignored me.

Once or twice, there was bread.

I measured time by the level of piss and shit in my bucket but since I barely ate and my lips were cracked with thirst, I was not sure if I had been there two days or two weeks. It was like being buried alive. All I had for company was the scurrying rats and my memories. I saw, awake and asleep, my wife murdered over and over. I saw the men I had slain. I saw the gallons of blood I had spilled in a massacre in the Holy Land.

No wonder Tuck had lost his mind.

I woke to the searing light of a single candle and was brought up into the world again. Outside, it was dawn. A thin, steady rain gusted down in waves of countless tiny needles. It felt wonderful.

I expected to be brought to the archbishop or to the scaffold.

Instead, it was Jocelyn and Anselm waiting in the rain in the castle courtyard, holding our horses at the ready. Swein was there too, his old brown hood soaked and heavy on his head. He grinned at me over Anselm and Jocelyn's shoulders. My armour and weapons wrapped and loaded upon my horses.

My men gave me wine and a chunk of tough cheese and I followed them out of the castle gates, holding my tongue until we were gone.

It was strangely quiet. More than subdued, as would be expected, Newark felt deserted.

Guards looked away from us as we rode out and off from Newark Castle, heading west along an empty road. The swollen Trent flowed by to the left, down the hill, rain patterning all over the mud-brown surface.

"Tell me," I said to Jocelyn after we were well clear of the castle and town, pulling to a stop in the rain right on the road. There was no one around.

"The archbishop had you taken into custody before the king was even cold. We could do nothing. His household knights took the king's body away to Worcester for burial. And immediately all the great lords fled in the night. They raced each other to be the first to reach Prince Henry, who is all the way down in Salisbury or thereabouts. They will be there by now, I don't doubt."

I looked back at the castle. "The archbishop had me taken. And then I was just left there?"

Jocelyn and the others exchanged a look."

"You are charged with treason," Jocelyn said. "But no one knows precisely why or any detail. You were supposed to be held."

Treason. The word hung as heavy as a roll of lead.

"They think that I murdered the king?"

"No man says it is murder. He died of the flux. He has been long on campaign. He ate too much and drank too much wine and he fell ill and died."

"But it was William," I said. "The king was poisoned. It was just as I said. Just as Tuck said."

"We tried to tell them," Jocelyn said. "Anselm told his father and his brother."

"You did?" I asked the young man. I knew he was terrified of both of them. The Earl of Pembroke frightened everyone by his fame alone. And the elder four sons of the Marshal were all mad enough to have joined the rebellion, however briefly and Anselm was confused and intimidated by disloyalty. "You have my thanks, Anselm."

"That is not all he did," Jocelyn said. "Tell Richard what your older brother did."

"He gave me gold and silver," Anselm said, rain streaming down his face. "For bribing the guards."

"It took us a couple of days to find out who were the right men to pay off," Jocelyn added. "And they made Anselm swear to wait until the archbishop and the last of his men had themselves left."

"What treason am I supposed to have committed?" I asked.

"The precise charges are unknown," Jocelyn said. "But I heard it was because you abandoned your task in the south."

"The grooms are saying it's because you are swyving the archbishop's daughter," Swein said, grinning. "Stole her away from him."

"I see," I said. "How do they know about Eva?"

Swein shrugged. "Servants talk, lord."

"It is simply a means to do away with you, lord," Anselm said. "My brother said the archbishop wants you to stay away from Sherwood. And your lord knows you would obey the Marshal rather than be loyal to him, if it came down to it. In an open war between the two Royalist factions."

"The archbishop and the Marshal are enemies," I said, seeing the extent of their rivalry for the first time. "What will they do now?"

"Think about it, Richard," Jocelyn said. "They are going to crown Prince Henry as the new king. Do you know how old Henry is?"

"Young," I said.

"He is nine years old, Richard. And whoever controls the boy controls the kingdom," Jocelyn said. "The king's loyal barons have been fighting a war of access to the Prince for years. Every maid, page, and lady within a mile of the boy are in the pay of Anselm's father or your lord. Or both. Or some other baron."

"So goes the rumours," I said.

"We spoke to my brother about it before he left," Anselm said. "He told us all."

"So freeing me does what?" I said. "What does the Marshal want me to do?"

Jocelyn pointed south, as if we could see my liege lord. "The archbishop has brought the charges against you himself. With his resources, the archbishop will win. You will be denied the right of appeal through trial by combat and you will be killed. The archbishop is disposing of you. Legally, perhaps, but he has declared you an enemy. The Marshal wants you to fight for him instead."

"For him and for the Prince and the kingdom," Anselm said, proudly.

"So I am fleeing justice," I said. "I am making myself an outlaw?"

My three men looked at each other. I was struck by how they seemed to be friends, companions, comrades. One was the son of a great lord, one a knight who would have a fine career without being sworn to me and one was an outlawed commoner. Any of them could have fled while I was locked up. I would have been convicted and no man would have condemned them for breaking an oath to a treasonous lord. Instead, they had not only stood by me but had worked hard to break me out and save me from the fate that the archbishop had arranged.

"Richard, we have no choice but to flee," Jocelyn said. "But you are not fleeing justice. You would be found guilty. Do you want to be tried when you cannot win? Is temporary outlawry not the better choice?"

"Temporary?" I said, grasping the word. "Are you certain of that?"

"No," Jocelyn said, glancing at his squire.

"My father is certain that he will make things right," Anselm said. "He will soon be in a position to help you."

"So long as he seizes control of the boy king before the archbishop," I said.

"The archbishop is known for governing well, for making his own lands richer and for passing on his wealth for others. The barons all want to be rich," Jocelyn said. "Yet we are still at war with the French. There are two kings of England, one French and the other a young boy. The barons will want a warrior in charge. They will turn to the Marshal as they have before. He is the steadiest hand in the kingdom. He wants you. He will have you. Legally. We simply need to wait it out."

"A perfect time to go to Sherwood," I said. "I will be out of sight and we can dig William out of his hole like the parasite he is."

"For the love of God, Richard," Jocelyn cried. "Will you forget William for once? How can we four take him? We do not all have your strength. You think only of yourself. What about your house? You manor? My sister? Have you considered her at all? Emma has been running your manor all summer. What happens to her when your property is seized?"

"But the archbishop is not here," I said. "His attention will be on young Henry, you said so yourself."

"Come, Richard," Jocelyn said. "He has a practice of taking lands. From his own men. From anyone. He has men who do this for him. Men learned in the law, from London. They will be acting upon the archbishop's orders to take everything you own. Anselm's brother told us."

"I will fight them," I said. "We shall man the walls of Ashbury and fight off any man who comes."

"That is your answer for every challenge," Jocelyn said. "A blade will not work in this case. Will you kill men acting within the law of the land? Will you cut down men armed with writs and lawfully charged bailiffs? You will never climb your way back from outlawry then."

I sat and looked at the soaking land around me. The hedgerows hanging heavy with water. Fields running with tiny rivers downhill toward the Trent through the lines of alder and willow along the banks.

"You are right. Let us go and collect Emma and everything we can carry. With no income and nowhere to go, I will not be able to take any servants. They will have to serve their next lord."

"Only until we return," said Jocelyn.

I prayed that he was right.

It was two days before we arrived at Ashbury to collect Emma and put my affairs in order. By that time, we had almost dried out and the sun struggled through.

The thought of abandoning my manor was unsettling. Approaching my home along the familiar lane was something I had done countless times but every detail was imbued with significance. We forded the stream that had burst its banks at the bottom of the hill and flooded the woods at either side. It had always been a boggy area, surrounded by bladderwort and bog myrtle but when I was very young I had tried to catch sticklebacks as they darted over the pebbles.

All woods are wet places. Even in a summer drought, go into an English lowland wood and you may immediately plunge your fingers down into cool, wet earth, full of fat worms, perfect for tempting fishes and making girls scream. Two or three spade depths and you are into sucking black water amongst the tangled roots.

The pigs from the village snuffled at the edge of the wood and hedgerow, gobbling up the acorns and beech mast, roaming under the loose guidance of the local swineherds.

In the hedgerows around my manor house, I had encouraged my men to plant blackthorn. I loved blackthorn though my servants and villagers thought the wood half-evil or, at least, magical and, therefore, to be mistrusted. Perhaps they were right. The wood certainly burns like the devil.

That stuff was dense and hard and made the best walking sticks and poles for sword training. It kept the sheep and cattle out of the gardens. I always enjoyed the way it blooms before Easter and before any leaves grow so the white blossom explodes over the bare black branches. In autumn, my servants picked great basketfuls of the blue-black berries harvested and boiled them with fat game from my woods. That day, I noticed that no one had picked the berries.

Snails clad in their yellow and purple armour spotted over the sodden timbers of my gateway as I rode through at midday. Bert the Bone's pack of elderly dogs howled and bounded around me as I dismounted, scattering the chickens.

Would I ever see any of it again?

Although it had been well over ten years since we built it, the palisade around Ashbury manor house still felt new. I had dug out the ditch and piled up the bank alongside the rest of the labourers from the village and beyond. Those that did not know me had not liked it. They thought I was showing off, making them look bad by throwing more muck than they did. And also, that I was there to keep my eyes on them continuously so that they would work harder and take few breaks.

My own servants had explained to them that I simply enjoyed a physical challenge. That I liked being up to my knees in mud, seeing how hard I could work, testing my strength and endurance. I well remembered being struck by how well they knew me and I felt immoral for having to abandon them to an unknown fate.

"Some of you stood by my family after the tragedy that occurred here twenty-five years past," I said to my gathered servants in the hall.

It had turned into a warm, bright autumn afternoon and the doors and windows were thrown open and the golden light flooded in across the men and women standing together.

"More of you came after, trusting that there was no curse in this place and no curse on me. I am sure that some of you do believe me cursed, because of what they say about me. And that I have a youthful countenance though I am as old as a grandfather. Well, perhaps you are right. But no matter what you believe in your hearts, you have stood by this place and you have each done your duty. You have served me and I hope you feel I have served you well in return. I have tried to be fair in my judgements. I have tried to give to you as much as I could."

I was pleased to see nodding heads and hear murmurs of assent. I took a breath.

"It is also a lord's duty to be often away from his home. And whenever I have been on campaign or on other business, you have continued to serve faithfully under good stewardship. This past summer you have done without me once again and I am certain you have followed the Lady Emma's commands as if they were my own. Indeed, you all know she makes a better job of things than I ever have." They laughed yet it was unfair of me to seek refuge in levity. "But now I must go away again. Only, this time it will be different. You know that we are in a time of war, our land divided. I have had a disagreement with my liege lord, Hugh de Nonant who is also the Archbishop of York. He has brought a charge of treason against me."

Their astonished muttering rose to cries of alarm and I waved them down into low murmuring.

"I am told by other great lords that my enemies conspire to find me guilty, no matter the evidence I can bring before judges. And so I must flee. In fleeing, I condemn myself to outlawry. My property will be confiscated. That means this house and these lands will be sold by the crown. Soon, you will have a new lord. You must serve him well, whoever he is. With no income from these lands, I can take none of you with me. But, I swear to you, I shall return. I shall defeat my enemies and I shall claim back my home. For now, I ask only that you all help me and my family to prepare for our absence. With the steward, we shall work out how what is left can be shared amongst you all, rather than fall into the hands of the next lord of Ashbury. God be with you all."

They clamoured again and begged me for more words but I could not face them and I pushed past into the courtyard.

"That was the longest I ever heard you speak in my entire life," Jocelyn said, grimacing as he walked out with me. "You are not very good at it."

"Pack your things," I said. "I must have a word with the prior."

I walked through Ashbury's fields, then the Tutbury Wood and waded the Stickleback Stream to go to speak with Prior Simon before leaves for outlawry.

Simon was young to be a Prior, as I understood it. But he had been at Tutbury since he was a little boy. He had always shown a great aptitude for monkish things. The young Simon had even travelled away somewhere or other to study for a few years.

The man, when elected Prior by his brothers, had become a nuisance to me. Always he was seeking to improve the lot of the priory, which in practice meant pressing me for more money or for more rights or privileges. Money that I never had.

His monks worked hard for him. He was a Godly and practical man both and I admit that I admired his resolve and his aptitude.

I never liked him as a man.

"Where will you go?" Prior Simon asked in the privacy of his own house.

"Away," I said. "Just away."

"You do not trust a man of God to keep your secrets?" the Prior said, with absurd familiarity.

"It is better for you and everyone else if you do not know, surely?" I said, attempting to keep the irritation from my voice. "I came simply to ask that you do what you can to help everyone through this period."

"Of course, Sir Richard," the Prior said. "It is my God-given duty to do so. Do not think of it as a favour to yourself."

His self-aggrandising and pretentiously pious answer made me want to smash him in his chinless face.

"Before you flee into the wilderness," Prior Simon said, shifting closer in his seat and lowering his voice. "You should unburden yourself. Your life's tragedies weigh upon you, I know that they do. I have seen it."

He leered at me, his lips wet with anticipation.

I considered tearing his throat open and drinking him dry.

"Whenever thoughts of my life's tragedies occur to me," I said, speaking truthfully. "Or if feelings of anguish intrude upon a waking moment, I simply do not think on it any longer. I ignore the thought. I push away the feeling. Such things are too much to endure."

My answer seemed to excite him.

"God wishes you to face your sin," Prior Simon said, placing his sweaty palm on the back of my hand. "That evasion is your guilty heart. God wishes you to be unburdened of your crimes. Tell me and feel free."

"I am guilty. I have sinned," I pulled my hand from his sweaty grasp and stood. "And yet it is not my own crimes that concern me but those of enemies. And I will be the instrument of God's vengeance upon the guilty."

"Which enemies do you speak of?" Prior Simon asked, his eyes looking up at me, voice wavering.

"All of them."

Two days of activity at Ashbury later and we were heading south once more. There was only really one place in all England that I could hide and also give me a chance to fight my way into a king's pardon.

I had to go to Kent.

There was little news of what was happening elsewhere in the kingdom. It seemed everything was happening far away. Whether our king was to be King Louis the French prince or King Henry the child.

Emma had taken our sudden flight with good grace. All her life, God had thrown bad luck at her. Her father had died when she was a baby. Her mother killed, violently when she very young. Brought up with Jocelyn by family she barely knew. Married young to an older man, whose seed had been weak. Pregnancies came to bloody ends. Her husband died leaving her nothing but debts and a manor that was overrun by Saracens. When Jocelyn had failed to claim his Poitevins inheritance, she had come to Ashbury with him. Through it all, she had remained remarkably accepting and had not turned bitter. She prayed often. Perhaps that was her secret.

I tried to speak to her of it, our first day riding.

"Good grace?" she said to me, her eyes flashing. Suddenly, she looked very much like her mother. "Taking it all with good grace? How else am I to take it, Richard? How could I have changed anything with public anger? Or displaying self-pity? When I say I am going to pray, it may mean that. Or it may mean I am weeping in the darkness. But what difference does it make how we accept God's will? You are a knight with a disagreeable temper. You charge your lance at anyone who offends you and then you end up friendless and alone, just as I am."

She spurred off to ride beside her brother, who threw me a look. For a moment, I was reminded of him looking at me that way many years before, when he was a small boy after I scolded him for his wandering attention.

"But I was thinking about being a knight," the young Jocelyn would protest, as if the content of a daydream was relevant.

I had failed them both. When they were children and since they had come to me, penniless and desperate. All I had needed to do was find each of them a good match. Both had plenty of promise for any prospective knight or young lady. But I was poor and friendless through my own lack of grace. And I had been lonely and I had welcomed their company. I had never truly wanted them to leave. I had been selfish. Taking them into outlawry with me was a new low for them as it was for me.

I had to make it right, somehow. I urged my horse beside theirs.

"And what are you two talking about?" I said, grinning, certain they had been cursing my name.

"I am not convinced that our destination is the right one," Jocelyn mumbled.

"Yes," I said. "I know. But you know why we must go."

"Because," Emma said. "You are almost entirely without friends."

"Correct," I said. "It is curious, is it not, that if the archbishop had not previously forced me to Kent then I would have nowhere to go at all. It is most fortuitous."

"Fortuitous?" Emma said. "That your liege lord wishes you dead?"

"You know what I mean," I said. "You call me friendless but I know one man who will welcome us."

"You hope," Jocelyn said.

"I do," I said. "I might even pray for it."

From the corner of my eye, I watched them both smile, just a little.

"But the truth is," I said. "I would go south no matter what. Whether I had the fortune to know Cassingham or not. My only hope now is for a pardon from the king. From the regent. When I have made war on the French. I will have a great victory and then no man can deny me my place as a faithful lord and knight."

Jocelyn sighed and nodded. "But I swear," he said. "Sometimes your arrogance borders on madness."

Never a truer word spoken.

***

It felt like a long ride. I could not wait to get stuck in against the French. I did not declare myself anywhere that we went and I stayed out of the towns. Emma, who rarely rode and almost never travelled, was exhausted from the start. She never complained. Not to me, anyway. Jocelyn was giving up a lot to throw in with me. But he strove to be a good knight who did his duty by his lord. And, I suspected, he had his heart set on returning to Marian who awaited us in the Weald.

But I worried that Swein chafed at fleeing south again.

"This will be the last time," I said to him one night, sitting out under the stars. "I will make things right and when we go back north, we shall destroy William. Together."

"Yes, good." Swein poked at the fire with a long, blackened stick. He did not seem pleased at my promise. "I understand."

"Do you no longer wish to attack Sherwood?" I asked. "Has your heart gone out of vengeance?"

"No," Swein said, looking up at me. "Those men will pay for what they did. But I have missed my fellows in the Weald. You are not an archer, my lord. You wouldn't understand. Just chatting with others who know their business as well as you do, or even better."

"I can't shoot a bow," I said. "But my trade is the horse and the lance. My passion is the sword and the shield. I know well enough what you mean. I am pleased you found good company. I pray we find them well."

"They'll be alright, Sir Richard," Swein said, with the certain confidence of the young.

Of course, he was quite right.

Cassingham and his band of archers had kept up their attacks on the supply lines of the French.

He had set up winter quarters in a hall in a village deep in a wooded part of the Weald. One of the many manor houses that some lord had abandoned in flight from the French. We had found our way to him, village by village, as if they were stepping-stones through a river. Cassingham's men had built defences and stocked stores inside, enough for hundreds of hungry mouths through the coming winter.

We arrived late one morning in November and were welcomed like old friends. It was all rather heart warming. Marian and Eva stood together in the cold, Marian with a huge smile on her face. Eva scowled at me.

William of Cassingham rushed to meet us and welcome us into his hall.

“I apologise for bringing more mouths to feed, William,” I said.

“We have had plenty of food from the French,” Cassingham said, grasping my arm. “And even if we were starving, I would feed you, Sir Richard, from my own plate in order to have you fighting with us. Come inside, let us eat. You must tell me what is happening beyond London. We hear little.”

Later we were seated, full of food and halfway drunk on stolen French wine.

We were crammed against each other at the top table.

Cassingham sat opposite me, with Emma seated on his right, then Jocelyn opposite Marian and Anselm. On my side sat Marian, and then beyond her Swein and Eva sat at the far end, not speaking.

Marian seemed to have grown ever more beautiful since I last saw her and many eyes, it seemed, were drawn to her as well as to Emma.

Whereas I was very aware of Eva at the far end. I wanted to speak to her but it was difficult to do so at the best of times.

“That was a fine thing to say when we arrived, was it not?” Swein whispered to me, leaning over Marian like the bumpkin that he was.

“Cassingham is only a country squire,” I said in a low voice as I pushed Swein out of Marian’s face. “But he has more of the true knight in him than many a rich lord, I assure you.”

Swein’s eyes shone as he looked over the rim of his cup at Cassingham. Marian’s did the same and I wondered what I had missed while I was away. I glanced at Eva who sat with her arms folded across her wonderful bosom. Jocelyn stared at Marian like a drowning man stares at a rope.

“What has happened with the siege?” I asked Cassingham who sat opposite.

“The French have abandoned Dover for the winter. The French brought down the gate, beyond the barbican, and they stormed the breach soon after you left for the north. Every attack they made was thrown back. The defenders made a timber wall inside the destroyed section of wall and there they fought back assault after assault. The fall rains came in late October and the French, dispirited, signed a truce. They would lift the siege and attack no more for three months and the garrison promised to not attack them in the same period. The French have now dispersed into the castles they took in the summer and also into London, which still celebrated Louis as king of England.”

“I am astonished that the people yet support Louis,” I said. “I will never understand those merchants of London.”

“But the heart is going out of the Lords and merchants of London who supported Louis in the summer,” Cassingham said.

“Why do you say the fight is going out of the rebel barons?” I asked. “How can you know, stuck down here? In this lovely wood.”

Cassingham laughed. “It is not all of them. But the barons were at war with King John. It was King John that took their wealth and their lands and did as he pleased. Already, many are cooling their support for Prince Louis, who is granting lands as king of England to his own French lords. Already, so they say, many of the prominent men of London are sending word to King Henry and to the regents William Marshal and the Archbishop of York."

"But who says?" I asked. "You are living in the middle of a woodland, William, how on earth do you know what the barons of London are thinking?"

He grinned at my ignorance. "A handful of their servants have come to us. They are proud Englishmen and women. Many in London suppose that their lords might as well be French as English, so long as their rights are respected and their profits continue. Which is a fair argument for a merchant in London. But many here have been wronged and it is our duty to see them right."

Marian beside me stared, enchanted, at Cassingham. "If ours were a just world, you would be lord of these lands after you throw the French back into the sea."

She tossed her hair back over her shoulder, exposing her neck.

Cassingham blushed. "My lady, you are too kind. But I am far too lowly to hope for so much."

"Anselm will put in a good word for you with his father, won't you Anselm," I shouted down the table.

"Yes, Sir Richard, I will indeed," the lad said, speaking with absurd slowness and at far too great a volume yet still not entirely disguising the slurring.

"Jocelyn, do not allow your squire any further wine and punish him tomorrow."

"Oh, I will indeed, Sir Richard," Jocelyn said, mimicking Anselm. He clouted him round the head.

"Even though the lad cannot handle his wine, I am honoured to have him fight with us," Cassingham said. "It makes the men proud. They feel they are fighting on the side of right."

"It makes me proud too," I said. "When I was a boy, his father was at the peak of his fame in the tournaments. They say he bested five hundred knights across Christendom. Can you imagine such a thing? We would charge about the courtyard, legs astride a stick, shouting, I am William the Marshal, no, I am William the Marshal."

Jocelyn laughed. "As did we, twenty years later, in the Holy Land. Truly."

"What makes him such a great knight?" Swein asked, turning abruptly to me. "My lord, if you don't mind me asking? Sorry, my lady." He elbowed a boiled turnip into her lap and she swatted him away, laughing at his eagerness and ineptitude.

When she turned away, I noted how lovely and soft her neck looked. I could almost smell the blood beneath her skin.

"William the Marshal?" I said. "He won, first and foremost. He would never have been more than a minor son of a minor lord, had he not won his riches at tournaments. Then he went to serve the old King Henry and he served him with absolute loyalty, even in the final days when all the king's sons rebelled. Did you know the Marshal unhorsed King Richard the Lionheart? Only man who ever did. Of course, he was just Prince Richard back then but still. He could have killed Richard, had he wanted, but instead William Marshal killed his horse, just to prove the point. But then he served Richard with complete faithfulness. Then came King John."

"Who treated him appallingly," Anselm said, loudly.

"Give him more bread, Jocelyn and shut him up. And King John mistrusted the Marshal and treated him badly as Anselm says. And again, the man does his duty and puts the king and the kingdom first before himself."

"That is not to say he has not feathered his own nest every step of the way," Jocelyn said to Cassingham. "He has played the games of power as skilfully as he ever did in the tournament."

"Yes, yes," I said.

"But how did he win so much?" Swein said. "Was he a big man in his youth?"

"Not especially," I said. "I have heard it said that he claims only to have a hard head. His single greatest talent, his one God-given ability that sets him above all others is that he can take a blow from the mightiest arm and yet stay on his feet and keep fighting."

"An ability that is rare for a man," Emma said. "Yet present in all women." I laughed, as did Marian but the others looked disturbed. "I am speaking poetically," Emma explained to Cassingham.

"Ah," he said.

Jocelyn took up the tales of the Marshal. "After winning a tourney in Normandy once, the blacksmith had to lay his head on his anvil and hammer his helm back into shape just so he could remove it from his head."

We traded stories about the Marshal while his fifth-born son lay slumped and snoring on the table. The meal had lasted until nightfall. More and more, I turned to Marian's lovely neck beside me. She smelled wonderful and the wine had thinned her blood and caused the skin of her face and neck to become flushed with a fetching pink hue.

I felt Eva's eyes upon me.

When it was late, she came and dragged Marian up from the table. I fell into Eva's dark eyes but the women said it was time to retire. The ladies shared a bedchamber attached to the hall but when they were gone, I could think of little else but Marian's neck and Eva's magnificent bosom. I remembered her sweat and her linen wrap from the weeks before.

That first night, I slept in the hall but I knew I had to get away from people. There was too much temptation. I wanted blood, to taste it, to feel it in my mouth and in my guts and limbs.

"I must find somewhere to live," I said to Cassingham. He himself occupied the bedchamber at the rear of his hall and, as far as could tell, he shared it with no one. "Somewhere away from anyone else."

The village houses were fully occupied but two men offered to give theirs up for me as I was a knight and they were no more than freemen farmers. I declined, though I was touched by their generosity. Cassingham had clearly put them up to it so I stressed to him again that I wanted somewhere miles away from the village.

What I did not tell him was I wanted somewhere that I would be no danger. Far from Eva and from Marian and everyone else.

And I wanted somewhere private.

Somewhere that I could feed.

***

When Cassingham understood just how alone I wanted to be, he pointed me toward a cabin up on the side of a hill a few miles north from the village along the valley.

It was an abandoned oak cabin in an oak wood, in need of serious work. It had until a year or two before been a hunting lodge and belonged to the lord who owned the wood. The lord had died and his heir had been so caught up in all the unrest that he had never claimed it.

The wood was mostly oak but had a dense understorey of holly and coppiced hazel. Along the ground were straggly remains of blood-red crow's foot, almost died back for winter and a thick carpet of bright green dog's mercury. It was a working wood but empty of workers. The winding route up to the cabin was along a disused charcoal burners' path.

The hazel and ash had clearly been used by the charcoal makers but still, the oaks ruled the wood and acorns were everywhere underfoot. The local swineherds were about with their pigs who snuffled up and crunched acorns for miles around. The leaves were falling or fallen by the time I moved in, the architecture of the oaks revealed. Winter woods are stark, the lines and angles are skeletons bared to the bone, like the corpses of crucified men. The bones of the wood stood out like ruins.

My cabin was a sturdy place built from thick oak boards and beams, put together when the locally felled oaks were yet green. The single door faced south into the valley and through a cleft in the hills, I could see the sheep grazing the grass on the other side. The cleared area in front of the cabin let the sun warm my plank walls on the few warm days, causing sap to bleed down from joints and pegs and filled the air with the scent of life and summer, though the days were drawing in.

It was a steep valley, or as steep as it gets in the Weald. Out of the windows beside the door, I could look at the stream nearby that provided my water as it ran down the hill to the river flowing along the valley floor. Buzzards sometimes swooped along the length of the valley, often high up but also shooting low, hunting mainly at dusk. One dawn I watched a buzzard drinking from the stream, flicking the water up into its mouth and shaking water from its great dark feathers.

I would lay in bed and listen to the constant sound outside, through the walls and roof. Whether it was the rain or wind in the trees or the trickling of the stream, it was a never ending, reassuring humming of the world. At night, it would be the owls hooting in the branches high above. In the daytime, the blackbirds would flit between the holly and the ash, ever agitated, perhaps afraid of the coming winter. Always, over it all, were the rooks.

Rooks, birds of carrion and harbingers of death prefer elms, the taller the better, but a big group had made their nests in an oak glade close to the cabin. Even at night, I would hear them in their nests cawing in the darkness, jostling and pecking, stretching their wings. Each pair bedded down together in their nests, safe from the madness of crow society for the span of the night. Whenever there was a high wind, I used fallen rooks nests for kindling.

Rooks have a thundery call, like the rough accent of the backwoods Sherwood folk or the voice of any man who hailed from north of the Humber. A rasping, raucous, leathery old cry halfway between a hoarse complaint and a throttle shout of greeting. It reminded me of the men swarming up on scaffolds when churches and castles are being built. Bawled conversations consisting of endless oaths and laughter. Rooks are the most sociable of birds and they like people's company as much as they do their own. They were pleased that I had moved in.

Of course, this only confirmed my own darkness and unpopularity. Wealden folk, if they are proficient with a bow always shot rooks on sight. If not, they will go as far as sending boys up the trees to smash the eggs or throw down the chicks for the dogs to gobble up. I would not allow such practices for my rooks.

As the winter grew colder, the birds ate worms, pests and anything that crawled. Only at harvest time was it they prey upon farmer's grain and it seemed unfair to punish them for taking a little of what they needed.

"They enjoy my company and I theirs," I explained to Cassingham one time, who looked at me like I was mad beyond measure.

"But what about rook pie?" he asked, aghast.

"Any lad shooting my rooks can expect a hiding."

Swein gleefully told me that the men called me rook master. No man was stupid enough to say such things to my face, no matter how drunk he was. Though I gladly took up their name of the Crow's Nest for my woodland home. It was perfect and their name for it, created by them from fear and spite, made me care for the place even more.

The cabin itself was full of little mice and enormous spiders, who all came out to creep around in the darkness as I lay alone with my thoughts.

Scattered throughout the oak wood were wide flat clearings dotted with a collection of blackened stones, many shattered by the long heating from whatever it was charcoal burners did. They made excellent areas for practising the sword, once I had stamped down the bracken, stitchwort, dying foxgloves and saplings.

The cabin was damp and took weeks to dry through, burning through great mounds of fuel. I stuffed up the windy cracks with moss and clumps of wool.

I built a stable, of sorts, for my horse. It looked awful but I was mightily proud of it and I prayed it would not only survive the winter but also keep my dear horse safe and warm too. I would have happily brought him into the cabin, had it been warm enough.

Mostly, I chopped wood and brought food up from Cassingham's village.

As well as preparing for a lonely winter, I had other plans. I intended to ride north to the nearest French occupied town that remained unfortified. And I would bring myself back a Frenchman to feed on. I could keep him bound and gagged, much as I had done with Sir Geoffrey for Tuck. I would feed off him, taking a little at a time. And if the man died, I could bury him in the wood, unseen and I could take another man and another.

When the winter was over, I would be stronger than I ever had been. Strong enough, perhaps, to take on William by myself.

* * *

After Christmas was well over, I rode north and spent many days exploring the tracks and routes that I could use to bring a man back to my cabin unobserved.

There was a village a dozen miles away. French knights had been there, they told me, and forced rent from the villagers. Their English lord had run away and left them to their fate a year before and they had no one but Cassingham to protect them. But even he and his men could not be everywhere. The French were due to return to collect further payments in kind, the villagers told me, begging me for help. All I could do was advise them to pay what was demanded and then I rode away.

But not far. There was a wood nearby. A mixed wood of elm, hazel, ash, oak, and elder throughout. Elms stood together in circular thickets where goldcrests and chaffinches sang.

There I hid and waited for the French to return. I lay shivering in the bare branches of a wych elm, watching a family cutting back a portion of their ash trees. Wych elm trunks often branch near to the ground, which makes them perfect for easy climbing. When I was a boy, I used to try to get girls to climb up them with me so we could be secluded in the wide boughs.

That day, though the branches were bare, I lay high up and well-hidden. I kept one eye on the family at work below me and one eye on the distant road, praying for a visit by a Frenchman full of warm French blood.

Coppicing must be done in winter, or at least before the sap rises in spring. I watched that family collecting every piece of the wood they cut down. The poles had a thousand uses. Thatched roofs required rods to secure the stacked bundles of thatch. Poles were used for making and setting eel and fish traps. Even the brushwood trimmed off the sides of the poles was gathered up by the children into tight bundles, bound together from twisted lengths of bark or from nettle twine. Those bundles would be used to get a young fire burning quick and hot. They piled fallen leaves over the cut stumps to protect the hazel shoots in spring from the browsing of deer. Moss showed everywhere, vividly green and shining around the stumps. The children chatted incessantly while they worked, recounting old scores and battles won by them against their enemies, the children of another family nearby.

Two days, I waited, shivering in the trees, hoping that the French would come raiding or raping so that I might prey upon them. My poor horse was miserable, though I covered her with a thick blanket and walked her about when it was quiet.

The French did not come. On the third morning, angry, hungry and eager for the taste of hot blood in my mouth I returned to my cabin.

On the way back, in the afternoon and almost at my oak wood, Eva found me.

She was beside the track, hacking at a fall of deadwood with an old, bent practice sword. Her black courser stood behind her, dozing, a thick blanket over him.

"Eva," I said, totally surprised. "How did you know where I was?"

"You can't do anything in the Weald without someone seeing," she said. She was wrapped up in a cloak with her hood up over her cap but her cheeks were flushed pink with the winter's chill.

It was an awkward, wild part of the wood with the hill rising steeply above, too steep to harvest the wood. Dead trees up there had fallen down over one another in tangled jumbles, slumped like piles of corpses after a siege. Leaning trees, partly-felled by great storms or the toppling of their elderly fellows, are called widow makers. When felling an already-leaning tree the immense forces on the trunk can cause it to suddenly twist and spring out at you, knocking you flat and sending your axe spinning into your face. A half-fallen tree though providing a haul of dried, seasoned wood, is dangerous. It is neither alive nor dead. It has no future but destruction and yet it will fight it all the way down. And it will betray the unwary.

Did Eva suspect what I was up to, I wondered. Was she ambushing me? Was she going to try to kill me?

"Why are you here?" I asked, fingering the hilt of my dagger.

She could not meet my eye. "You have not been seen for many days now. Not since Christmas. Some of us were wondering if you were well. Perhaps the French had come up here to raid."

"No one is travelling," I said. "And if they did I would kill them. This strikes me as strange?"

She sighed. "Life in the village has become somewhat tedious," she said. "I have no conversation and no man will train with me."

I relaxed, slightly. "You do not converse with Marian? Have you fought over something?"

"No, no," Eva said, irritated with my misunderstanding. "She only has time for Jocelyn, Cassingham, and Swein. And I knew you would be hungry. I brought you bread and cheese and wine."

"I suppose you better stay with me tonight," I said, ungratefully cursing that God's will had confounded my search for blood. "It'll be dark soon."

"What a generous, gracious knight you are, Sir Richard," she said and we rode single file back to my home.

"Where were you going to stay if I had not come along?" I asked her.

"Do not think me some helpless maiden," she said. "Finding a sheltered spot and starting a fire is simple enough."

"If you say so," I said. A part of me wondered if I could murder her and drink her blood.

Although she was a stranger and not well liked, she was far more popular than I was. If she disappeared, then men would know who to blame. Of course, it would also have been completely immoral and I would never have done anything like that. The very thought was unworthy. Shameful, even. But I felt empty and weak and I wanted instead to be filled with power.

"I am stiff," I said when we had stabled our horses. "And there is daylight yet remaining. I will stretch my limbs and warm myself with some sword practice before eating."

"I will join you," she said, shrugging off her cloak.

We sparred in the open space between the stable and the cabin before going inside. She had improved and I was impressed by her ability. I had trained with dozens, possibly hundreds of squires and knights in my time. Eva was skilful. She was as strong as a young man was and had a long reach.

Her greatest attribute was her quick mind. She anticipated attacks. Her footwork was superb.

We sparred and clashed shields and I let her rap me upon the helm. Somehow, when we were breathing heavily, our breath misting the air, I made her laugh.

Twilight came. The gradual softening of the bleakness of the day turned into the still blackness of night. We had no candles outside and no lamps to fight by, but even while the western sky was a deep blue we could see by the light of stars in the crow-black blanket of night right above. When we became two shadows fighting each other, we could put it off no longer and went inside.

It was cold. I built up the fire while she sat on a stool at my rough table, not speaking but drinking down ale. I felt her eyes on me. The silence stretched out.

While the fire grew, I poured out a little of the water I had drawn that morning into the washbowl by the hearth. We had trained together, as men did so I decided to honour her by continuing as if she was a man. At least, that was what I told myself. With my back to her, I shook off my hauberk and continued to disrobe until I was naked and I washed the sweat off my body.

She moved behind me, rustling as she stood but I did not turn. I heard her shrug and shake herself out of her mail, which swished and thumped as she dumped it on the table. Even though my heart thudded in my chest, I admired that she had kept her steel off the damp floor. Then her doublet dropped and I wondered how far she would go.

Still not looking, I dropped to a knee to lay thicker sticks upon the fire. They caught as one and the flames lit up the room as bright as a yellow sunrise.

I stood. Her skin glistening and beaded with the cold water, she unwrapped the final circuit of the linen strip that enclosed her torso. As it came clear, her breasts spilled out, full and heavy and round. They bounced a little as they came to rest, freed from the binding.

She took the cloth from the bowl, bending at the waist, her back and flanks catching the firelight and shining along the hard muscles. There was not an ounce of spare flesh upon her, nothing but the whipcord of ridges and pits that came from hard training and never enough food. She was muscled like a knight and with her long limbs and square shoulders could have passed for a young man. But underneath that frame hung her huge breasts. She stood and washed them, wiping the cloth about them so they lifted and fell. She wiped her ridged flanks and under her arms, sighing and tossed the cloth into the bowl.

Fixing me with a stare of defiance, she thrust her hands on her narrow hips and stuck out her chin. She was shining like a statue of bronze, her belly flatter and harder than mine was, running into the shadowed triangle beneath. Her eyes began searching my own body. She smiled.

"Good God," I said, bewitched by her beauty.

She shook her head, laughing but not probably not with joy. I was unsure what to read from her eyes, dark and flashing.

"Good God, I said again, praying for words or thoughts to enter my mind. I knew what was going to happen and I welcomed it but I wanted to preserve the moment for eternity.

She sighed. "You are utterly witless."

Thankfully, she was not.

Making love to her was perfectly wonderful but a somewhat strange experience. Her body was hard. Her backside was small and all muscle. And she was strong. Strong of body and strong willed.

After pushing me down and sitting astride me, she issued curt commands throughout, telling me where to place my hands. I found it difficult to keep them from her voluptuous breasts, they being the only pliable part of her and also a sight in themselves that would have made St Paul spill his seed under his bishop's robes. She pushed my hands from them and into the moistness of her body and she made me grasp her by the neck. My own pleasure in the act appeared to be of secondary importance to her own. I can only suspect that my face wore an aspect of ecstatic bewilderment throughout.

At the end, she ground herself down against me, throwing her hips back and forth, flinging her black hair, and arching her back. I held tight to her as she gasped and lay against me, hard but for the giving softness of her chest.

"You may plough me until you are yourself finished," she whispered and rolled onto her back.

It was mere moments until I hurriedly withdrew and spilled my seed upon her belly. I collapsed beside her in a state of exquisite surprise.

I was cleansed. Complete. Whole, for just a moment.

It was dark but for the light from a smoky candle on the table. The fire I had started had died into nothing.

She wiped her stomach with the corner of a blanket and rolled over and leaned her hot skin against mine. "Build the fire."

She took a blanket and went outside to piss while I built the fire. When she came back, she cut bread, sprinkled it with salt and brought it back to the bed with the cheese and a skin of wine. The bed was narrow and she pressed herself against me after passing me the platter.

The fire grew and threw light on us. It all felt rather domestic. I was not sure what was happening or why it was happening now but I was contented enough to live with it. We ate in silence. I could smell her body and I waited for her to begin to talk, to tell me about herself. I knew well that women loved to speak in the darkness. I was ever happy to listen and even to join in on occasion but rarely could I speak much myself. They always wanted more than I could give. I was never good at that sort of thing.

"May I sleep here?" she asked after we had eaten.

"Of course," I said. "I would be happy with the company. It has been a long time since I had the pleasure of—"

"Good," she said and lay down, stretching out alongside me. In just a few moments, she was snoring.

Not knowing what else to do, I lay beside her and wrapped her in my arms. In her sleep, she pushed her sinewy body against mine while I held her magnificent breasts. Somehow, I slept too.

And slept late. She woke me at dawn by whispering what she wanted and then doing it to me until I woke enough to return her passion. She wrapped her legs around me and sighed when I rolled on top of her.

A voice called from outside. "Richard?"

It was Marian. I froze. She was calling through the door and her voice carried through the thin walls.

"Richard, Eva did not return last night. Jocelyn said not to worry about her and also that I should check with you. Have you seen her?"

Eva lay under me, her hand across her mouth, eyes filled with mirth.

"Yes," I shouted back. I hesitated, wondering what else to say. The silence stretched out.

"I see," Marian said and she stomped off without another word. Hooves pounded on the hard earth as she cantered away.

I lay down to Eva's laughter. "You've done it now," she said.

"Done what?" I said.

"Broken her heart."

"What in God's name are you talking about?"

"Did you not know?" Eva seemed genuinely surprised. "You really can be witless, Richard. For some time now, Marian has had her heart set on marrying you."

I leapt from the bed, pulled on my shirt and flung open the door into the frosty morning. I called her back. Her horse was already gone and she did not return.

The sun shone over the hilltop and shone through the wood, catching the crisp bare blackthorn branches, dark holly leaves and skeletal oaks standing their guard around my cabin. The winter sun throwing flashes of silver frost and outlining every twig and leaf, illuminating every blade of grass, existing in its own right even when attached to the whole plant and tree.

As I called Marian, the rooks in the wood erupted with the most raucous of choruses.

The great black birds swooped in the dawn light and cawed on the wing, as if they were mocking me. Crows take flight before the dawn, swooping through the dark like spirits. Is it the crows' duty to wake all the other bids? If all the crows were to die, would all the other birds wake later, after sunrise?

"Richard?" Eva called me from the doorway of the cabin, blankets wrapped around her. "Come back to bed."

While the raw chorus of dark birds in the canopy sounded above, I noticed the warbling, sweet, delicate trilling of robins, chiffchaffs and blackbirds in the understorey and bushes.

I gave up my hunt for blood. I did not take a Frenchman and feast upon him. Instead, I exhausted myself with chopping wood, practising the sword, caring for our horses and ploughing Eva.

It was a long winter. When the snows came, I chopped wood for fully half of every short day just to keep us from freezing overnight.

A tawny owl would cry from a favourite tree nearby. On still nights, his fellows could be heard calling back from far away through the wood, keeping in contact like archers waiting to spring an ambush.

Those nights I spent with Eva were long and pleasant, huddling under blankets by the fire. I cannot say I grew to know her but we grew comfortable around each other.

By the time of Lent, I was sure she had no secret motive, that she was not working for the archbishop. As sure as I could be, at least.

We rarely spoke of the past. Never of the future. For a while, I wondered if she would bring up marriage but she never did so I said nothing of it. Whether it was her intention to get with child or not, she did not do so. I could not tell if I was relieved or disappointed but I think she was a little sad.

Of the others, we saw very little, although Eva forced me to visit them as often as the weather allowed when we went down to collect more salted pork and flour.

Jocelyn courted Marian, without success. At least, they did not marry and it seemed to me that he grew impatient and angry, driving her further from him. What advice could I offer him, me who knew so little of women? Nevertheless, I tried. One night before Easter, we sat drinking together by Cassingham's hearth fire after mostly everyone else had fallen asleep.

"These stupid moths," Jocelyn said, giving me a significant look. "Waking from their winter slumber only to plunge straight to their deaths. Why would they do this, do you think?"

I had the feeling his comments were somehow aimed at me. No doubt, a part of him was hoping to stay in the Weald and keep trying with Marian rather than attacking Sherwood. And I knew what part.

"Moths are in love with the moon and the stars, son," I said. "They are creatures so mad with lust that they will fly into anything that remotely resembles it, even a candle flame or campfire. They want light. They want it so much that they do not mind if it will lead to fatal disappointment."

"Disappointment?" Jocelyn said, laughing. "Is that what you believe is waiting for me? That I am a moth to a flame? Listen, Marian is a perfectly suitable woman and I am a suitable husband. Or will be as soon as I win myself land. If any man here is a moth, it is you with that woman. Mark my words, she is the archbishop's, body and soul. She comes from his seed, you fool. She will give you up. Betray you. Betray us. Mark my words."

"You are wrong," I said, dreading even the thought of it.

"Calling me a moth," Jocelyn said, scoffing. "You are the moth."

Marian was always civil with Eva and with me but there was no doubt we had both offended the young lady by abandoning her to spend the winter with each other. She spoke to me very rarely.

We went into the village for most of the holy days, important saint's days and feast days. Every time I saw him, Swein chafed to get north. He and Marian both wished vengeance upon the Green Knight and his band of evil men. They drew together, as far as their stations allowed. Swein could make her laugh, which was more than Jocelyn would ever be capable of.

"When can we return to Sherwood?" Swein asked me one cold March day in Cassingham's hall. The others were with me and we shared the last of the stolen French wine, which was souring into vinegar but was better than no wine at all.

"I have been long thinking on that," I said. "In order to hire enough men to scour Sherwood, we need money. And in order to overcome my outlawry, we need a glorious military victory. And the French can provide both."

A large part of me wished I could stay in the Crow's Nest forever, swyving Eva, chopping wood. Getting old. Perhaps my seed would one day grow in her belly and we could live as man and wife. I said nothing of the sort to Eva, fearing scaring her away from me. She never mentioned marriage or a future together so I assumed she was not interested in one. So it was all just a dream. I had been playing all winter, pretending to be a commoner, pretending to be a husband and half-hoping to be a father. It would never happen.

Instead, duty beckoned. William had to receive the punishment he was owed. The monster had even slain the king. When the blossoms bloomed all over my wood, I knew it was time for me to fly the nest.

In late spring, the French returned to Kent in force. Cassingham gathered his men from all over the Weald.

It was time to fight.

10

THE GREAT DOVER RAID

"THE FRENCH ARE COMING," I said to the assembled leaders in Cassingham's adopted hall in early May 1217. One of his men had come charging in that morning. The fellow upon a steaming horse with word from the coast. The news he brought with him had stirred the hornet's nest that was the Weald.

"They mean to take Dover once more but this time, they shall finish the job," I said. "Your man's report is clear. The siege engines are being carried ashore. The first are already being assembled. We must strike now before the fighting men join them."

Jocelyn rapped his hand upon the table. "Sir Richard is right. The longer we wait to take action, the stronger their position becomes."

Cassingham and his men were disturbed, exchanging glances.

"We have been taking action," Cassingham said. "For many months have we been fighting the French while our king fights the barons of the north and the west."

"Skirmishes and minor ambushes," Jocelyn scoffed, waving his hand.

Cassingham's lip curled into a snarl.

I stepped in. "You have performed magnificent deeds," I said, raising my voice so all in the hall could hear me clearly. "You have harmed the enemy with raids, you have stolen his supplies, you have protected villages. Punished crimes. But now is our chance to destroy him. To truly change the course of the war. If we do this, Prince Louis will be denied Dover Castle, for months at least. We can destroy his engines, kill his engineers."

"It would delay only," Cassingham pointed out, "you say it yourself."

I carried on, unperturbed. "They have unloaded their supplies at Dover. Supplies of food, wine, oil, bolts and swords, engines and horses are being brought ashore as we stand here and speak. If we destroy them, Louis will be without the things he needs to fight the war. He may have thousands of knights and bowmen but what use will they be if he cannot move them, supply them and fight them where they are needed?"

"If we do this," Cassingham drummed his fingers upon his table. "The Marshal could move to isolate the barons. Without the promise of reinforcement from Prince Louis, he could invest in a siege."

One of Cassingham's captains spoke up. "Our men in London say the barons have taken the city of Lincoln."

"But not the Lincoln Castle," another said. "That, the rebel barons yet besiege."

"Precisely," Jocelyn said. "Many of the barons and their men are gathered in a single place."

"We must move quickly," I said, encouraging them to see it all. "We must strike at the French and then the Marshal must destroy the barons before Louis can recover his supplies. Speed is the key to this lock. We must strike now and we must send word to the Marshal right away."

"Send word that we mean to attack the French camp?" Cassingham asked.

"We must send word that we have destroyed it. The riders must go out immediately. Today, if possible. Tomorrow at dawn if not."

There was a minor uproar that Cassingham waved down.

"How can we give word of a thing that has not happened?" Cassingham said, aghast.

"But it will have happened," I said, "by the time that word reaches the Marshal."

Cassingham did not like it. It seemed immoral to him. As though he would be lying to the Regent.

"It is a moot point. We cannot attack a camp of that size," Cassingham said. "Even if it is undermanned we would be hugely outnumbered."

"You are always outnumbered, Cassingham," I said, grinning. "All of your men, all of last year, all this past winter. It has never stopped you before. This is not so different to when we took Sir Geoffrey last year and led them into the woods."

"That was a mad chance," Cassingham said. "We never expected it to work as well as it did. It should not have done. In our favour was the fact we were on the far edge of the camp, we killed barely any of them and led them to where we were strongest. Carefully prepared ambushes, in the woods. It was little more than a gesture. And still they hunted us for weeks, we were always on the run. And even then, Sir Richard, we planned that raid for days. Now you ask us to muster hundreds of men and to mount an attack on a fortified encampment the moment we arrive at it."

"It is the only way, Cassingham," I said. "If we delay even a little, there will be hundreds of knights, hundreds of bowmen, thousands of men and our chance will be gone."

"You wish only to better your own standing in the eyes of the regent," one of Cassingham's captains said. "You are accused of having a hand in King John's death, are you not, my lord? You would risk all our lives for your own ends."

Jocelyn leapt to his feet. "How dare you?" he cried. "Who said that?"

I stood too, slowly and waved Jocelyn down.

Crossing my arms, I looked around the room, into as many eyes as I could. All were silent. I found my accuser, recognising the captain as one I had fought beside before and saw him shrink under my gaze.

"We should each of us be thankful to God," I said. "When duty and glory align. I fight for our young King Henry. Which man here says I do not?" I let the silence fall. Eyes flicked about. "We can win glory. William of Cassingham will win fame. Sir Jocelyn, too. You men who are not knights or not of noble birth, you will win whatever riches you can take from the French. And you will win the chance of a great story to tell when you are old and fat, about the time you saved England from a false king and his pillaging armies. You men are the finest archers in all England, or so you like to tell yourselves. You decided to fight with William of Cassingham when your lords ran and hid in the king's castles. One day soon, this war will be over. What will other men say of the Wealden Archers? Will they tell of a band of big-mouthed oafs who sat through the war with their arrows shoved up their arses? Or will they sing songs of the common men who threw down a French prince and pissed in his face? Come with me, or stay here. The choice is yours. If you stay then I will simply have to keep all the spoils for myself."

We rode for Dover at dawn.

***

Cassingham knew that I was right. Once we were committed to making the attack, we had to carry it out and get away before the French arrived in force.

All the first day while we rode through the Weald with over a hundred archers, I allowed Cassingham to take charge and admired how he harried his men, harangued them for their slothfulness, inspired them, bawled them out, praised them and kicked their backsides into a frenzy.

They knew him. They loved him. Me, they still did not know and few of them liked or trusted me. I was a knight, from far to the north. Some of the Wealden archers had fought in Gascony, Normandy, Ireland, Wales and the Holy Land but most had never left Kent. Amongst those men, outsiders were mistrusted. And I was an outsider amongst outsiders.

It was safe to say that the men under my temporary command obeyed me with some reluctance.

Watching them that day I noted that Swein was welcomed and accepted, despite his Yorkshire accent and youth. He was a brilliant bowman, through and through and when he talked, men listened. He had matured over the winter. His clothes were better than they had ever been and he had taken or purchased a gambeson and a decent helm with a huge nosepiece. Still, he wore a hood over the top of it but, at least, he had found a new, green one.

The second day we met with other groups in the woods outside Dover. We were almost two hundred and fifty of Cassingham's men waiting in the darkness before the dawn a few miles from the edges of the French camp.

Cassingham and his captains, who it seemed now, included Swein who was supposed to be my squire, checked their men's equipment and kept up their spirits in the dark.

"Hope it don't rain," Swein said to me, looking up at the grey clouds rolling in from the sea on the dark sky.

Wet bow cords lose their potency. But I doubted Cassingham's huge band of archers would be shooting many arrows that day. We wanted the rains to stay away so that we could burn the French camp.

There was no way to hack that many siege engines to pieces. So we carried oil and most men carried bundles of kindling. With any luck, we could get in amongst the siege works and make such a blaze that they could not put it out before their vital equipment was destroyed beyond repair.

But only if the rains stayed away.

"I might even pray for it," I said to Swein and he grinned.

"Do not mock prayer," Cassingham's priest said, overhearing. "Not this day, Sir Richard. God will not be mocked."

"I never mock God," I said. "Only men who believe that He cares about their whining."

The priest cursed me under his breath as Swein laughed.

"This is why you never have any friends, Richard," Jocelyn said. "Most men do not take such things lightly."

"But my man Swein here takes God as lightly as I do," I pointed out, "and he has made plenty of Wealden friends."

"Swein is a commoner among commoners," Jocelyn said, grinning. "And he can make conversation on subjects other than war, which is more than you will ever achieve."

Swein had the good grace to laugh. I did not.

"You are in fine fettle this morning," I said.

"We will win a victory," Jocelyn said. "And perhaps even take a knight or two as my prisoner. And this time, I shall ransom him and finally put some marks into my purse. I shall be on my way." He looked back along the dark road toward the village of Cassingham as if he could see Marian from all those miles away.

Eva had wanted to come with me before we left.

"I know that you wish to test yourself against real foes," I had said. "And know that all your training has made you a fine man-at-arms. But you should stay with the Lady Marian. There will be few enough wounded men left behind to protect her, should the French raid here while we are away."

"Do not condescend me," Eva had shot back. "I know I am a fine man-at-arms. I want to kill Frenchmen."

"And that is why you are needed here."

Even though I knew she was stronger than most men, certainly better with sword and shield than any of the Wealden archers, still I treated her as though she was a weak and feeble woman. In time, the poor woman would pay for my condescension of her.

But Eva had stayed with the Lady Marian. Already I missed her long, hard limbs and her hot skin against mine. I would much rather have been naked and abed with her than lurking in the dark woods dressed for war.

Cassingham called his men to him.

"Some of us have been here before," Cassingham said to them. "This one, though, will be the biggest raid any of us has ever been on. You all know what you must do so I will not repeat it. I merely remind you that if we succeed in our task this morning we may save the garrison in Dover Castle. And if we save them, we may save all England. Our battle cry will be King Henry."

Their murmuring grew towards a shout and Cassingham growled at them to shut their idiot mouths until we attacked.

They knelt for prayer and for once, I joined them. While the priests wittered away, I asked God to make my enemies stupid, weak and fearful that morning. Please, Lord, I said, let the French have drunk themselves insensible last night on their fresh wine. God likes it best when you ask him for very little.

Cassingham and I divided our forces into three groups and agreed on the signal for starting the attack and the signal for withdrawing.

I would attack the centre of the camp. Cassingham would lead his men around the left flank and come in from the north. The third group was on my right hand, attacking the southern side of the camp. That group would attempt to hold that entire side of the camp and also to watch the town for any counter attack from French forces garrisoned there.

My group would drive into the centre of the French, straight for the largest of the siege engines.

I had eighty men under my command. They were nervous, excited, grim. They tested their bows, checked their swords, daggers and other weapons. I did not give them a speech. They knew their jobs.

We led our horses toward our group's mustering place outside the French camp, under cover of the thin trees, already much cleared from the year before. The French camp was unseen over a rise but I could see the battlements of Dover Castle's highest towers, dark against a lightening sky. A light mist drifted through the deep green, grey of the morning, settling dampness over the shimmering nettles, goosegrass, grasses, sedges and ferns. Ferns were everywhere.

I drew next to Jocelyn. "If this succeeds then we will have to ride north. We will have to bring the news to the Marshal."

"What about the messengers you made Cassingham send?" Jocelyn asked.

"They were vital but they will not be believed."

"And you will?" Jocelyn shot back. "You are outlawed."

"They will believe you," I said. "You are known to be a true knight."

Jocelyn scoffed. "A true knight? No man of import knows me as anything."

I did not argue. "Anselm will tell them, won't you, son," I said over my shoulder.

"Yes, my lord."

"So you better not get yourself killed this morning, you hear me, Anselm? I do not give you permission to die. Stay behind Jocelyn or you and Swein will guard the horses."

"Yes, lord."

"You too, Swein. I know these men are your friends, now but I want you with me when I go into Sherwood."

"Don't worry about me, Sir Richard," Swein said. I could hear the grin on his face. "This ain't my fight."

"Quite right."

We gathered just as the light was growing and waited for Cassingham's signal to attack. The other groups all had to get in position so that we could all attack at once.

The trees about us were young, well coppiced and much of the brush had been cleared. Along the floor was the last throws of the intense mauve-blue haze of bluebells in the wood. There had been an extravagant profusion in my oak wood because the deer grazed the undergrowth, the boars chewed and stamped down bushes and saplings leaving the ground layer clear for the strange plants to flourish. Outside Dover that morning, the pink campions and goosegrass spread along the ground, ringed by a wide layer of bright green nettles in the deep shade at the edges beneath the trees.

The woods were full of birds singing in the dawn. Rooks and crows gathered above our heads, scaring the pigeons and blackbirds into flight. We waited for the signal to attack.

"How do they know?" Swein asked me, pointing to the carrion birds. "That they will feast soon, I mean."

Before I could answer, a Kentish priest growled his own opinion. "Because they are evil."

"They are wise," I said, ignoring the holy idiot's huffing. "They have seen from their own experience that when men gather like this, blood is spilled."

Swein nodded, accepting this truth.

"They are beasts," the priest said. "They cannot be wise. It is blasphemous to think otherwise."

Jocelyn glared at me. He was right. It was no time for an argument with a priest, no matter how much I enjoyed them. I held my tongue and wondered if I would get a chance to drink some blood of my own, along with the crows.

We waited for the signal.

On the horizon, beyond the camp, the familiar silhouette of the great castle resolved out of the darkness. Upon its huge mound, the castle looked down upon the landing area for the ships below the famous cliffs. Southwest, to my right, was the town, on much lower ground and overrun by French.

The messengers had told us how the beach below the town was covered with fat cargo ships pulled higher than the tideline up the sand and shingle. Many of the ships had already been unloaded. I half dreamed that we could go down there and burn them too but I knew we had to be realistic. We were but two hundred and fifty men against perhaps two thousand between the siege camp and the town.

I mentioned my thoughts to Jocelyn. He called me mad for even thinking it.

"How do you get down to the beach?" Swein asked, cutting in.

"Jocelyn is quite right. It is beyond us," I said. "We would have to attack between the forces of the camp and the town, being trapped between both. The cliffs are low by the town but it is still a steep, narrow slope down to the beach. Then we would have to burn the ships and fight back up that slope. I saw it from afar last summer when we scouted the camp. The lowest part of the cliff is thirty, forty feet high. We would never make it back up while under attack."

Swein laughed. "Now that would be a feat worthy of a song."

"Indeed," I said. "It would be a beautiful thing, though, would it not?"

"You have a strange idea of beauty, Richard," Jocelyn said.

A thin drizzle started, then stopped. Then started again.

"These God-forsaken peasants," Jocelyn muttered in French. "What is taking them so long?"

"Be patient," I said, fingering the hilt of my sword.

"Perhaps they have run away," Jocelyn whispered. "What can they be doing?"

The men around me fiddled with their clothing or pissed where they stood. Anselm went a few paces back to take what must have been his fourth shit of the morning.

Swein chuckled to himself and spoke in a low voice. "How can you even take a shit while wearing a coat of mail?"

"It can be awkward and messy, squatting in a hauberk," I said. "But all you need do is hold your small clothes aside. And anyway, it is preferable to shitting yourself during the battle."

"Does that happen?" Swein whispered, amused, no doubt, at the idea of knights soiling themselves.

"It happens very often," I said. "Would not be a battle without the stink of shit. I seem to remember doing it myself once or twice."

"You do it every time," Jocelyn said.

"Shut your mouth."

In truth, I was growing nervous at how light it was getting. It was only a matter of time before the watchers in the French camp saw us. They would see hundreds of men spread in a broken crescent about the edges of their camp, crouching in the shadows of the brush. No doubt, we would run into the first French work parties at any moment, coming to chop wood and cart it back to the camp.

Jocelyn fretted too, mumbling to himself. "What is taking them so damned long?"

A hunting horn sounded far to our left.

Cassingham's signal.

I nodded at our man, standing at my shoulder and he blew his horn just as the third to my right sounded, halfway to the town.

"Thank Jesus for that," Jocelyn said and jammed his helm down over his head.

Leaving a few lads to bring up and guard the horses at the palisade, we streamed into the camp on foot. The place was laid out much as the previous summer. A rough circle half a mile away from the castle, which rose high on its mound with the mighty walls and tower after tower around it. The town of Dover was half a mile to my right, lower down the hill.

The camp in front of me was protected by a narrow ditch and a low bank, topped with a half-hearted attempt at a palisade of steaks. Roads crisscrossed inside between the rows of canvas tents. Latrines and piss-trenches lined the downhill side.

On the far side of the camp, beneath the walls of the castle but outside of bow range were the great war engines that the French were building. Black struts and beams stuck up into the dawn. Mostly half-finished and dwarfed by the walls of one of the greatest castles in the land but still impressive structures.

They were our targets. We would have to fight our way clear through the entire camp to reach them. And, more to the point, back out again.

All of a sudden, I was struck by the madness of it. I saw our attack through Cassingham's eyes and the eyes of his men. But I had cajoled and browbeaten them into the attack and it was too late to back out now. Withdrawal without first attacking them would have been disastrous, leaving them free and full of confidence to chase us down.

Most of the men with me were archers in the prime of their life. There were a handful of boys with us, and a couple of priests and at least one woman had snuck along with us, too. It was not Eva.

The men who were supposed to be guarding their gateway were lax indeed. If there were men watching the approach at all, then they had fled at the sight of us and had not even paused to spread the alarm.

We had declared our presence with horns but we did not cry out yet as we streamed into the camp. We saved our war cry. But we made plenty of noise as we shouted instructions to each other.

"Walk," I shouted to my eighty men as the ones in front starting pulling further ahead. "Save your strength. Stay together, stay together."

French men pushed aside the flaps of their tents, blinking in the overcast dawn light, looking confused. These first few men received arrows for breakfast or were cut down with our blades.

We were quite deep into the camp when the first proper, martial French cries came, their shouts of warning, their own horns sounding and warning bells started clanging.

A line of bleary-eyed soldiers jostled each other into place, blocking the roadway between the tents. We had to get beyond them. There were a dozen, then twenty and thirty of them. Many were without mail armour, some without even gambesons and others had no helmets but there were plenty enough armoured men-at-arms there to frighten my men back from them.

We had to cut them down before they inspired more men into making a stand. Although the camp was barely populated, we were still vastly outnumbered and the French organising against us would be our undoing. We had to break them.

"Stay together," I shouted, drawing my sword and pointing at the line ahead. "And kill them. King Henry! King Henry!"

I ran ahead, trusting they would support me. Arrows cut the air right by me and felled every man in the line before I could reach them. An arrow at close range can pierce mail, especially the cheaper sort and some of the men wore none at all. The arrows thudded and slashed into their bodies. They cried out, some screaming. A few turned and ran but were brought down by arrows in the back. Most of the fallen were wounded but not dead so I finished them off, stabbing them through the necks and eyes and armpits. Jocelyn and Anselm came up beside me and together we made short work of those unlucky survivors. French who had been coming to their aid backed away, looking to make a stand elsewhere or, hopefully, flee to safety.

"With me, with me," I shouted to my wonderful archers.

We made our way further in. There was no chance of us killing them all. Indeed, we did not wish to do so. We wanted only to scare them away so that we could do our burning of the engines and the food and wine and shoes and arrows and other supplies.

I had insisted to Cassingham and his men that we needed to leave the French a route of escape, toward their fellows in the town garrison. But they were not fleeing as swiftly as I needed them too.

"Burn these tents," I said to my men. "Stir up some camp fires. Get the boys to start blazes here. Let's scare them back into the town, come on. Make a noise, you bastards. Show them who the men of Kent truly are. For the Weald! For Cassingham! King Henry!"

They took up the cry, shouting for their homeland, for their leader. They kicked over tents and lean-to's and threw burning brands into them. Fires flickered and grew. Black smoke drifted across the dawn light. The rain stayed away.

The gathering French ran. In ones and twos and then, seeing that so many of their fellows fled, dozens at a time swiftly followed. They ran for the town, plodding down the hill.

"To the engines now, to the engines, men, with me, with me," I cried. "King Henry!"

The engineers, those experts who constructed and then operated the mangonels and other engines, were proud men. They were men who brought down castle walls, towers, and gates. They were men who brought down counts and dukes and kings. A few brave fools defended their half-built mangonels from the trenches they had dug about their engines. They shouted challenges, brandishing huge mallets and iron spikes and long, heavy wooden levers.

"Leave," I shouted at them. "Go join your friends."

Reason said that I should have killed them anyway, because if they were dead then who could build the replacement engines for the French? But I admired the way that they stood defiantly in the face of such odds and I offered them the chance to live.

Instead of taking it, they mocked my men and were full of contempt, for they could see how poorly dressed we were and they knew us for the peasant rabble we were.

But these peasants were deadly beyond any that could be found in France.

"Kill them quickly," I told my archers. The men cheered and they murdered the engineers in moments. The bowstrings thrummed and the arrows crunched through the clothes, skin, flesh and bones of those men. The arrows ripped through them like the hand of God had smitten the engineers. After the single volley, the archers leapt into the ditches to finish them off by hand.

"Good God," Jocelyn shouted to me. "Why do we not have archers with us every time we fight? With a thousand of these men behind us we could conquer all France."

The Wealden men in earshot roared their approval and Jocelyn's standing was immediately improved among the peasantry.

"Shut up and burn these machines," I shouted. "Burn them now, burn them well. Come on, hurry. This is why we are here."

I took a dozen men and we kept up the madness of the attack to keep the French away and afraid. We whooped, cried, kicked over barrels and tents, and threw down everything that was upstanding and tore up anything planted in the earth. My men doused the timbers of the machines in oil and set fires about them. The flames licked up and took hold.

But something was not right.

There was no great store of food and weaponry and equipment.

"Bring me a Frenchman," I shouted and they dragged a wounded engineer over to me. He seemed young but it was difficult to tell as he had taken a cut across the forehead and his face was covered in a torrent of blood.

"If you ransom me," he said, wiping his eyes and peering up at me. "My father will pay you handsomely, my lord. He is a rich burgess, a craftsman in—"

"The best you can hope for," I said, "is that I end your life swiftly. If you do not tell me true answers to my questions, then I swear to you that I shall throw you onto that fire."

He started shaking. "No, no, no, please, I know nothing, I know—"

I slapped his face. Too hard, knocking him senseless for a moment.

My hand was covered in his blood. I fought down the urge to lick my fingers and suck the blood from his face. My men were all around me. I had to fight it down.

I grabbed him. "Where are the supplies?" I asked him. "Where are the stores of grain? Where are your barrels of oil?"

"On the ships," he said, gibbering and whimpering. "The beaches ships. Not yet unloaded. We need the grease, also, to coat the parts before we assemble the gears..."

I stared down toward the sea.

"What is it?" Swein asked beside me. "What did he say?"

"The supplies are on the ships."

The men's shoulders slumped.

"A partial victory is a victory still," I said though I did not believe it. The smoke billowed up into the air, catching the sea wind and drifting across the camp.

An English voice shouted from over by the burning engines. "A counter attack! They are coming, knights and soldiers are coming this way."

I ran to the men who were calling, shouting at them to fall back to me. It was all falling apart. We were going to be driven off and I would be robbed of the great victory I needed.

"Where?" I shouted, looking toward the town.

"There, my lord," the men shouted, pointing up the hill.

I laughed and clouted them about the head.

"You great, bloody fools," I shouted. "Those are Englishmen. That is the castle garrison, riding out to fight with us."

And so it was.

They were glorious to behold. The knights of Dover Castle streamed from their castle gates on their fine horses and down the steep slopes towards us. Lances held aloft, pennants streaming. They had dressed for war quickly.

I called for my horse and Anselm ran back and brought it up to me. I rode up to meet them as the sun broke through the layer of low cloud.

There were twenty or so knights and twice as many squires, all mounted.

Their leader advanced his destrier to me. "I am Hubert de Burgh," he called. "Constable of the Castle."

He was a small man, rather young for his position but he came from the best stock and his entire family were loyal followers of King John. His oldest brother had taken half of Ireland and another brother was the Bishop of Ely. Sir Hubert was dressed in magnificent armour and cloth but his horse looked thin and weak. Horses suffer in sieges.

A few of his knights and squires stayed with him but most of the others rode by us, toward the French camp, to join in the slaughter and the destruction.

Hubert de Burgh and I spoke from horseback.

"My lord," I said. "I am Sir Richard of Ashbury. I have heard nothing but fine things of you, my lord. We were all mightily impressed by your resistance to the French last year."

The Constable frowned. "You are Richard of Ashbury? Are you the son of the Sir Richard who fought beside the Lionheart?"

I sighed. "My lord, we have come to raid. We are only two hundred and fifty. Freemen of the Weald, for the most part. We cannot hold this position, not for very much longer."

"I can see that," Hubert de Burgh said. "And we are too few to risk becoming too much embroiled in your fight. We do not have long. We cannot be caught out here. But we came to hold off their counter attacks while you burn as much of the damned place as you can before their master arrives."

"Our scouts and spies told us the camp was full of supplies but in fact, much of it remains onboard the ships below. I mean to go down there and burn them."

"Good God, man," the Constable said, looking down toward the distant beach. "We cannot help you to do this."

I pushed my horse closer to his. "Your men can hold the French back from the town while my men burn the ships."

"But you have no time," the Constable cried. "Prince Louis is about to land."

"What do you mean?"

"Look," Hubert de Burgh shouted, pointing out to sea. "Are you blind?"

The sun was near its zenith. The day had half gone in the blink of an eye while we had fought and burned. Out to sea, beyond the roofs of the town and further along the coast to the southwest, crept a scattered line of dark shapes.

"Ships," I said.

"Prince Louis," de Burgh said. "The false king of England. He is coming. He is coming here. And he is coming now."

"Then we had best move quickly," I said and dragged my horse around to tell my men to gather so that I could tell them the change in plans. I was half expecting them to tell me to stick my ship burning idea up my backside and I wondered what I could promise and threaten to get them to risk being killed or captured.

But when I turned, Swein was already shouting at the men. They were gathered about him as he stood atop a wagon. He had his bow raised in one hand and one foot up on the sideboard of the wagon.

"... and we're going to go down there and we're going to send them back to France with their arses on fire. Now, grab your kindling and every arrow you can find. For the Weald!"

The men shouted as one, "For the Weald!"

Swein turned, saw me and grinned. He leapt from the wagon and strode over to me as I dismounted.

"I suppose it would be churlish of me to ask you hold my horse," I said.

Swein laughed.

All men are afraid of battle, unless they are mad. But some men can also enjoy it. Many great warriors do not love the madness of battle. But the very best do in fact revel in it. Not in the way a madman does but with the certainty and surety of a man who is doing the thing he loves. Much as a blacksmith does when fully occupied by his art or a carpenter consumed by the procession of his carving or when one is riding a horse at a full gallop and you fall into a state of perfectly flowing clarity. For some few of us, the madness of war makes perfect sense. I was always one of those few. I was surprised to find young Swein amongst our number also.

"Find two men to take a message to Cassingham that we go for the ships," I said to Swein, for he knew the men more than I did and I trusted him to pick the right ones.

"I will."

"And tell the rest to bring all the kindling and fire that they can carry."

Anselm looked after the horses and with four men and all the boys, he held by the edge of the French camp under the castle walls. Other than Anselm, all were archers and they would keep any roaming bands of French away from our few mounts.

The Constable led his forces down the hill away from the camp and toward the town below. There were hundreds, if not a thousand or two thousand men down in the town and still more filed down to their fellows from the camp. The Constable let them go and his men spread out, ready to charge down any attempted counter attack.

We were about sixty as we trotted down the path to the beach. What unburned skins of oil we had remaining were slung about a few shoulders. Others carried bundles of twigs or smouldering brands and all of us carried tinder.

The younger men ran forwards and shouted back what was ahead and below but I saw for myself soon enough.

A dozen, fat bellied traders' ships in a row high up on the golden sands. Just as the messengers had asserted. It was a narrow beach, with the tide high and licking at the sterns. The salt spray of the sea blew right up the cliff.

The path ran down along the crumbling, chalk cliff face switching back halfway down. The cliff was angled enough to grow bushes and great clumps of sedge. It was narrow but we could make two abreast for most of it and we ran down as fast as we could.

Seagulls swooped about us, crying and squawking. It was nesting season and the gusting clouds of black smoke above had wound them into an even greater frenzy than gulls normally felt. Beyond there were more wheeling birds in mixed flocks of sanderlings and dunlin.

One of the men paused to take aim at one of the birds, being cheered on by a comrade at his elbow. I kicked the archer up the arse, cursing them for their delay and both of them picked up their feet and scarpered down the slope.

The sailors and guards had seen us streaming toward them and were already leaping from their vessels and trudging away down the sand, leaving the vessels unprotected.

I pulled off my helmet so my voice would be heard above the surf and wind. "Five men to each ship. Each group needs kindling, fire and oil if there's enough." I shouted to Swein and Jocelyn, who began organising and directing the men as they came down off the slope. "And kill any bastard who tries to stop us."

I did not dare to hope that we would burn all the ships before we left. Likely, we would only get a couple going with a blaze so big that it could not be put out. As our men split up to take the ships, I trudged toward the nearest one, keeping a look out up behind us.

On the top of the cliff below the walled town, men were massing. Heads and shoulders looking down at us. Whether they were French or surviving English townsfolk, it was hard to say. They made no move to interfere, they simply watched. Many heads swivelled away from us to down the coast. From so low on the shore, with the enormous ships blocking my view, I had no sight of the fleet of Louis' ships. But I knew they must be close.

"We have to be quick, Swein," I shouted as I came into the shadow of the nearest ship. The hull was covered with tiny shells and green stuff, although much had been scraped off and was lying about in the sand. The hulls of the older of the beached ships were chewed and gnawed at by gribbles and shipworm.

The sailors had set up little campfires. There were ropes strung everywhere, hanging laundry and supporting sailcloth shelters. There was the usual camp detritus underfoot, discarded smashed pots and animal bones amongst the driftwood. No sailor used driftwood for fires unless he was desperate. The flames of a driftwood fire burn green and blue, haunted by the spirits of the drowned.

The men had been lazing about for a couple of days, no doubt getting their fill of the supplies before their master Prince Louis of France showed up. I would be willing to bet the ship masters had been busy selling some choice stuff to the townsfolk, too.

Swein leaned over the side of the nearest ship and cupped his hands to his mouth.

"There's oil here," he shouted to the men. "Pass the word, this ship is full of oil. Come and get it. Pass the word."

Jocelyn, his helm under his arm, shook his head. "You are the luckiest sod who ever lived."

"I have been called many things in my time," I said. "But lucky is not one of them."

"Not in life," he replied. "Clearly, Richard, you are not lucky in life. Merely in battle."

"Is that what this is?" I said. "A battle? Come on, you lazy oaf, let us make a bonfire big enough for Louis to find us. Use some of this driftwood."

We slung casks of oil between Swein's ship to the farthest ship in either direction.

"This is taking too long," I muttered, as the fires started to catch inside the ships.

Oil is all very well but much of it will not burn until it is heated. There were hundreds of small casks of almond, poppy, and olive oil that the men were pouring all over the decks. There were stinking ones full of rendered animal fat that they smashed and dumped into the flames. But our fires would have to burn big and hot before they caught.

"Come on, hurry, lads," I shouted up at them. "Pile the fires high and let us go."

"Sir Richard," men were calling me from up above the ships near to me and pointing frantically up at the cliffs behind me.

Our men were up there, waving and pointing and calling. Black smoke billowed above them. They were jabbing their fingers out to sea and jumping up and down.

"Time to go," I roared. "Swein, get them out of here. We fall back now. Leave the fires unburnt, come on, to me, to me."

I walked backwards, waving the men off the ships.

Swein shouted the orders and the word was passed down. They did not have to be told twice. They leapt from the smouldering ships and ran back to the cliff. We counted them all back in and Swein and I were the last to trot up the steep cliff path. The gulls squawked and dived at us.

At the top, I saw how close the French fleet was. They bobbed so near, their sails half full and men packed the decks and were shoulder to shoulder at the rails, staring at us while the spray frothed under the keels.

My men were tired and covered in soot and oil.

Looking down from the cliff, the beached supply ships had small fires glowing in the holds, the smoke from them blown flat by the offshore wind.

"God damn those French ships," I said. "Everyone, we fall back."

Hubert de Burgh rode up, scattering my men as they fled back toward the French camp. "Sir Richard, the French grow lively. They are emboldened by the arrival of their comrades. We cannot hold them and I will take my men inside the castle once more. On behalf of everyone, I humbly thank you for your efforts today. You have set Louis back by months, I pray."

"The leader of these men was William of Cassingham," I said. "A squire of the Weald. He brought these men together, he leads them. Remember him, my lord, when the war is done."

"Truly? William of Cassingham, you say? Then I will certainly remember him," de Burgh said, "and you also."

His men were urging the Constable to flee when a crossbow bolt thudded into the flank of one of their horses. The knight wrestled the horse from panic and rode away for the castle.

Hubert de Burgh's squire rode up and held out the Constable's helmet. More bolts clattered in. They were being shot from long range, down by the town walls. There was a gusty wind and there was little hope for accuracy but the French had found their courage and it was truly time to flee.

"God be with you," the Constable of Dover Castle shouted through his helm and he and his men rode off.

Anselm and his lads were rushing to us with our horses.

"Thank God," Jocelyn said as they approached. "Come on, Richard, we're the last men here."

"It is a shame about those ships," I said. We were so close to wiping out tons of vital supplies. I had a mad urge to run down there and stoke the fires.

Jocelyn clapped me on the shoulder and shoved his helm back onto his head. He fumbled with the chinstrap. "It was a good effort. The whole camp is burning, or near enough. This was a successful raid. Now, let us go."

"I suppose so," I said.

We mounted and turned, ready to weave our way through fire and crossbow shot, back to our men.

There was a roar, like a great rushing wind and I turned back in time to see the closest ship, the oil-laden ship, go up in a white-hot burst of fire, like a dragon had incinerated it. The flame grew and grew and it seemed as though the very air burned, shimmering and wild. I felt the heat of it through my armour and doublet and clothing from hundreds of yards away.

As if by some signal, the other ships also ignited, one after the other, with great rushes of light and heat and in moments, every ship upon the shore was engulfed in a terrible inferno.

I had never seen anything like it.

"Like looking into the unquenchable fires of Hell," I said, hearing the rising passion in my voice as I spoke.

"Come on, Richard, you mad fool," Jocelyn shouted. "Or we shall see the real thing for ourselves."

We rode out through the smoke, with bolts clattering about us and Cassingham's archers sending their own arrows back toward those who were coming out to see us off.

As our full force gathered on the road back to the Weald, we found the French garrison suddenly losing heart. The men slung their crossbows over their shoulders and slumped back to Dover.

"What has plucked their goose, so?" I asked.

Cassingham himself told us when we met up with him under the cover of the woodland. By then, the sun was low in the sky. The day had almost gone without me really noticing the time passing. Such is the way in battle.

Cassingham was grinning, clapping every man on the back as he came to us. His priest was praising God, for we had won a great victory and, though we had many wounded, we had not lost a single man.

"Are we pursued?" I asked, for my fear was that our exhausted men, without mounts, would be overtaken and slain.

"It seems not," Cassingham said, hands on his hips.

"Why not? What about the reinforcements?" I said. "They were practically on top of us. I could smell them over the smoke."

"The French ships abandoned their landing," Cassingham said, laughing. "Our brave King Louis must have thought twice about landing amongst that inferno."

"Praise God," I said, mad with the flush of victory. "Now is the time. Jocelyn, Anselm, Swein. We must take the women and ride north. With this victory, the Marshal as Regent will surely grant me a pardon. Then we will take Sherwood and destroy William de Ferrers and his band of blood drinking bastards."

It seemed so simple.

11

THE BATTLE OF LINCOLN

"WE WILL NOT BE SAFE HERE," Eva said, crossing her arms in the doorway of the small hospital, the small dormitory where travellers could stay when visiting or passing by the priory.

Eva and Marian would stay there, at the Priory of Tutbury, near to Ashbury. After riding north from the Weald, I had nowhere else nearby that I could take them. Nowhere that I could trust. Nowhere that was not under the influence of one great lord or other.

Thankfully, Emma had elected to remain safe in the Weald. She told me she had decided to stay. There was no discussion. She did not seek my permission nor approval. Cassingham had sworn holy oaths upon a local relic that he would defend the lady's life and her honour.

"You expect me to trust your words because you grasp a box with some old saint's rotten knuckle bones inside?" I had said to Cassingham in his parish church before I rushed north.

"Blasphemer," Cassingham's priest had hissed at me, his words echoing from the plastered walls. "You should fall to your knees and beg forgiveness from the holy bones of Saint Bertha."

"You can shove Bertha's bones up your holy arse," I said. "Now leave my presence immediately or I shall drink your blood."

When Cassingham gave him no support, he backed away and then fled, condemning me and my offspring to terrible punishments.

"You are not welcome in the houses of God," he shouted from the doorway. "The Lord shall cast you down onto your belly and you shall be smited by His mighty hand."

I laughed loudly and the priest slammed the door behind him.

"The men love how you fight," Cassingham said, unimpressed with me. "But many people here will be glad to see you return to the north."

"Take care of Emma," I said, grasping his shoulders and looking hard into his eyes.

"I swear I shall," he said. I believed him.

Marian and Eva, on the other hand, would not stay in Kent. But I could not risk taking them into the arms of my enemies. Before riding directly to the Marshal's gathered forces I had to hide the women somewhere safe for a few days. If I was arrested or killed, they could be seized too. Once I was sure of their safety, I would collect them from the priory.

Strictly speaking, Tutbury Priory was on land granted by my family yet it was Hugh de Nonant who held ultimate authority. But he had not visited the place nor shown any interest in twenty years. It was a small house but it had always been attached to the lords of Ashbury.

"No one will know you are here but the monks," I said, confident that Eva was concerned over nothing. "You will be safe in this hospital. The monks will keep an eye out for you."

"It is precisely those monks that we will not be safe from," Eva said, throwing her chin out. "And I know where their eyes will be looking."

"I have seen you fight," I said and reached up to stroke her face. She slapped it away.

"You are making a mistake," she said, crossing her arms.

"My family has kept this Priory since it was founded," I said, gently. "The new prior has been here since he was a boy, on and off. They are not dangerous."

"Not to you, perhaps," she said. "You are a man. A lord."

"They are men of God."

"They are men. And I cannot stay awake all night, every night."

I sighed, desperate to be away. "It is only for a few days."

"You are a fool," Eva said, unwilling to part on good terms and she would not kiss me.

Jocelyn fared little better with Marian, who was angry at being left behind. She wanted to come to Lincolnshire with us and I spoke to her too before we left.

"I must have the Regent's pardon before I can return to the world," I said to Marian at the gates of the priory while Jocelyn waited, already mounted, out on the road. "If I remain an outlaw I could be killed on sight. Once I get the Marshal to agree, I will return for you both and we will take the fight to William, I swear it. But none of that can happen unless it is I that tells the Marshal to his face that I have won a great victory for the king. Jocelyn and me both, that is."

"You come back quickly," Marian said, pointing her finger up at my face. "And you bring Jocelyn back to me. And Swein."

"Good Lord, girl," I said. "I promise nothing."

Though I was in a great hurry to be off, I pulled young Prior Simon to the far side of the gate and extracted oaths sworn upon Christ's bones in Heaven that he would keep the women safe and well cared for. Just words to me but binding for him, I believed. To make sure and secure an earthly loyalty, I made a small donation with what little coin remained to me and promised more upon my return. It was in his financial interest to keep them well and monks loved nothing more than money. Foolishly, at the time, I did not follow that thought through to its inevitable conclusion.

"What is happening at Ashbury?" I asked the prior in his house. "I hear there is no new lord yet."

"A steward arrived," Prior Simon said, not meeting my eye. "Sent by the archbishop. A hard man but a lively one. Full of jests but not kind, I fear. John is his name. Tall as an oak, he is. He brought a couple of servants with him. Rough types but they have not caused any trouble and I pray that they will look after your manor until you can make your proper return to us."

"What about Cuthbert?" I asked.

"Ah, your old steward has gone to live with his daughter's family in the village."

"That God damned bastard bishop," I said.

The Prior looked up at me while attempting to look down his nose at the same time. I wanted to smash that nose and suck out the blood but I need him to keep Eva safe so I swallowed my pride instead.

"I apologise, Prior Simon, I spoke without considering first," I said, with as much contrition as I could muster.

The Prior, who I had known since he was a boy and given money to keep him and brothers in their house for decades, grudgingly forgave me.

Then he betrayed me.

It was two more days of hard riding from Derbyshire to Lincolnshire, something like sixty miles. The roads grew ever busier with scouting and foraging groups and levied men coming to muster with their lords.

The Marshal's royalist forces were pouring into a camp around the village of Stowe in Lincolnshire. The village was barely ten miles north from the great city of Lincoln, where the rebel barons had concentrated their forces.

When I reached the camp, the men-at-arms guarding the road by the camp forced me to surrender my arms in the name of William Marshal, the Earl of Pembroke and Regent of England. I told them that I had a vital message that the Regent must hear.

"Are you alone?" the chief knight among them asked. It was strange to them that a noble knight would have no retinue.

"I am," I said, not telling them that my men waited in a woodland a few miles away.

They took me at once, through the great mass of men and horse, all the way into the Marshal's presence. His quarters were in the tumbledown hall outside the village. The roof was sagging and the place reeked of damp, despite the warmth outside. A fire smoked away in the centre of the hall, which was crowded with lords, priests and attendants and the immense noise was like a pot filled with angry bees. The Marshal's men escorted me through that chaos and into the presence of the great man himself, who turned from his conversation at the top table to peer at me as I was introduced.

I recognised many of the men around him. There was his son, also called William

Marshal, who had helped Anselm to free me from Newark Castle, smiling yet raising his eyebrows in silent remonstration. Also, there sat young Geoffrey of Monmouth, smirking at me as if he knew what was in store for me. He was an odious little shit but the size of his lands guaranteed him a seat at the table. I recognised William Longspear, the illegitimate son of the old King Henry and brother of Richard the Lionheart and King John. Longspear was as tall as me and a great knight and leader, though he had commanded over the disastrous defeat at the Battle of Bouvines a few years before. Ranulf of Chester sat beside him, the great lord and slayer of Welshmen. There were also a dozen or more bishops and priests in all their finery, scowling at the mention of my name. Those holy men I did not recognise.

Those great lords and priests looked at me with surprise and waited for the Regent to make his response.

"You do not much understand subtlety, do you, Sir Richard," the Marshal said as looked up at me. "Do you understand that I must have you arrested now?"

Geoffrey of Monmouth snickered, and looked round at the others. Only the priests shared his glee.

I froze. "I had hoped my great victory in Dover would prove my loyalty to the Crown."

The Marshal sighed. "You never needed to prove it to me, Richard. But there are ways to do these things. Our good friend the Archbishop of York would use it against me if I did not have you seized."

"I apologise, my lord," I said. "I cannot allow you to do that."

"I am sorry, I believe I misheard," the Marshal said, blinking up at me. "What did you say?"

"How dare you," the pudgy Monmouth declared in a shriek, slapping the table hard enough to wobble the wine. "Good Lord, man, you should be hanged for such treason."

"Be quiet, Geoffrey," the Marshal snapped, without bothering to hide his irritation.

Monmouth collapsed into his seat and hung his fat head. Longspear laughed.

"My Lord," I said, dropping to one knee by the Marshal's chair and speaking earnestly. "There is no man alive who I respect more highly than you. As a knight, as a warrior and as a loyal servant of the crown, you have no equal. So understand that when I say I must be allowed to destroy William de Ferrers. He is hiding in Sherwood, he is killing or enslaving the good folk of the king's forest. He is so close I can almost taste him. He is preying upon the king's loyal forces, you know this, my lord. And it must be I who slays him. I have sworn it. I swore it twenty-five years ago. I am begging you to allow me to fulfil the oaths I have made to the innocent dead."

The Marshal stared at me in disbelief.

"Everyone, leave us." He spoke softly but somehow everyone around him heard his order and fell silent. The great lords and knights stood and filed out, taking everyone in the hall with them in a cacophony of muttering and clattering feet.

Geoffrey of Monmouth stiffened and leaned in to the Regent. "My lord, I beg—"

"Get out, I said," the Marshal shot back at young Monmouth, steel in his voice.

Geoffrey stomped out, glaring at me over his shoulder.

A couple of silent men-at-arms stood at the back wall ten feet away, ready to defend their lord. As if any man in their right mind would attack William the Marshal, even as ancient as he was. I noted how his upper arms were thick with muscle and his shoulders were broad though the rest of him remained slim and straight.

"I have never been entirely sure of what to make of you, Richard," the Marshal said as everyone left, leaning back into his chair. "You can fight, anyone who has seen you has attested to that. But since your return from crusade, you have had little ambition."

"The Archbishop–" I started.

"Yes, yes. Your liege lord has kept you repressed," he said. "Yet if you had any ambition to change the facts of your situation, you could have changed them."

"When I returned from crusade?" I said. "I did not know that you even knew my name, my lord, let alone that you had any interest in me so long ago."

"I take an interest in all promising knights," the Marshal said, grandly. "But after a year or two of inaction, I ceased to expect anything from you. You were content to slumber in your hall, living a quiet life. There is nothing wrong with that. I expected you were growing old. But when you mustered for the king's campaign, I was astonished to see you looking so young. And now, what has it been, more than ten years later and I see you have not aged a day. No wonder the men turned on you when you were caught slurping up the blood of the dead. Do not deny it. Men whom I trust told me themselves that they saw you. Your perversions are a matter for God and for yourself, as far as I am concerned but the men did not like it. The old Monmouth, he did not like it. They were jealous of your fame and then they were jealous of your eternal youth and your ability. And instead of protesting more than a little, you were content to hide yourself away again. It smacks of a certain moral cowardice, does it not? But perhaps you were right to hide. And now that I see you once more, I am struck that there must be some truth to the rumours."

"That I have made a pact with the devil?" I asked.

He stared expectantly at me.

"May I sit, my lord?" I asked.

The Marshal stood, grabbed a jug of wine and two cups and sat down himself again. Not in the chair at the centre of the table but on the bench at my end. I sat opposite and he poured us both a cup of wine.

"My true father was Earl Robert de Ferrers," I said.

The Marshal spilled a little of the wine he was pouring. He set the cups before us. "I see."

"I only learned the truth of it while I hunted William near Jerusalem. And then he confirmed it to me himself when he had me captured."

"He captured you?" The Marshal said, for I had never really spoken of that part of the story.

"But for a moment," I said. "After I had slaughtered most of his men. But the truth is that William and I share the same father. And I do not know why but both of us aged normally, until the day we were each killed. He died at the Battle of Hattin and when he rose again, he was immensely strong and he did not age a single day after that. And his own blood, when ingested by other men, granted them increased strength also. And speed and endurance and it seemed to addle their brains. They believed him Christ reborn. It may not have been the blood that made them believe. William has a way of twisting men's minds."

"And you believe yourself to be the same as he?" The Marshal said, looking warily at me. "With magic blood?"

"I am the same. William and his foul beasts killed my wife and then they killed me. I was being buried by my surviving servants when I awoke."

"Yes, I heard this part, I recall it now. Sometimes, you know, Richard, these things happen. Your servants should have called in a physician."

"I was dead," I said. "I died and I rose again. Since that day, I have had great strength. I have not aged a day. See for yourself. I was twenty-two years old. Today I am forty-seven or so."

The Marshal stared at me for a long time. "And what did you have to do to gain these gifts?"

"My pact with the devil?" I asked. "Nothing. I was killed. I awoke, like this. That is it. I met no devil. William believed it a gift granted by God. It often seems more of a curse. But what can I do? This is what I am. They call me evil for drinking the blood of my enemies, men already slain. Well, I admit it. What other evils do I do? I do not kill the innocent. I seek to do right by my lord, my family, my household. I support the Church. And I loyally serve my king and his regent."

He drank while he observed me closely. "What of this blood drinking? Why do such a thing?"

"The desire for blood is always in me," I admitted, speaking freely to the most powerful man in England. "But I resist it. I do not kill for it. It seems that every time I drink, the desire for it only grows. And it rarely lessens. When I drink, my strength is increased even further. My speed of arm and mind both rise. And with blood, my body heals from terrible wounds in mere moments. I have been run through with blades, pierced by arrows, sliced and cut upon the face, arms, body and legs and yet I have no scars."

"And William de Ferrers has these same... abilities?"

"He may be stronger than I. In fact, I am certain of it for he has no compunction about taking blood from men, women, and children. He revels in it. In the Holy Land, he scoured the countryside taking families to feed upon. To drink dry and then discard. This increased his strength and also allowed him to make an army of men. Knights and men-at-arms who would be unremarkable in combat were it not for their ingestion of William's blood. He is most certainly doing the same in Sherwood."

The Marshal drummed his fingers on the table. "But why? Why here and why now?"

"Who knows what his plans are or what his ultimate goal is? In the Holy Land, he was on his way to creating an army. He wanted to carve out his own kingdom. Perhaps he has similar plans for England."

"Do not be absurd," the Marshal said. "This is not Palestine but England. One man cannot overcome a kingdom, no matter how much blood the fellow drinks, no matter his own strength. Nor how many blood-swilling swine he ensnares."

"I do not believe he is one man alone," I said. "I believe that there is, at least, one man working with him. The most powerful lord in the north of England."

William Marshal wiped his mouth with the back of his hand. "There is no doubt," he said after a long pause, "that the Green Knight of Sherwood is in league with the Archbishop of York. I had my suspicions when it was my men and the men of other lords who were disappearing on the Great North Road by Sherwood and yet the archbishop moved freely up and down many times in a year. When he had you arrested, I knew for certain."

"And I knew for certain that it was he that planned the king's poisoning," I said. "It seems strange but William de Ferrers poisoned his own father."

"Robert de Ferrers was killed by poison? But why?"

"My brother Henry killed William's wife and child in the Holy Land," I said. "I now know Henry was no true brother. We shared only our mother and he well knew it when we were children. In the disorder after Hattin, he slaughtered William's family. It drove William mad. He returned after a couple of years."

"The Massacre of Ashbury," the Marshal said. "It was always said there was no reason behind it."

"Reason enough for a madman," I said.

"And now you wish to continue the slaughter," the Marshal said.

"I want justice," I said.

"You want his death."

"More than anything," I admitted.

"He should be tried," the Marshal said, looking at me intently, judging my reaction. "This is England, not some Saracen backwater. We should bring William de Ferrers to justice. But perhaps the kingdom requires certain men to face a quieter fate. A simpler solution, for the good of the realm."

"You believe me," I said, not realising he was getting at something else. I was quietly thrilled, as I never expected anything but derision.

"No," he said. "I cannot believe the half of it. Magical blood? You are some form of lunatic, I do not doubt. But there is enough truth in your words to reinforce my own conclusions. The Archbishop of York is colluding with an outlaw band in Sherwood. The archbishop, I believe, poisoned King John. The sad truth is, the archbishop may have saved England by his treachery."

That gave me pause. "What are you saying?"

"John may have triumphed in the field, eventually. He was a competent enough commander of men. But I can do better without him. And with him out of the way, I have reissued the articles of the barons in the name of Henry, with a few corrections, of course. I have pardoned all men who come back into the king's peace. Once we throw out the false king Louis, England shall be at peace with itself once more. And all because John is not here to poison his own well."

"That may be the case," I said. "It does not excuse the fact that the archbishop is a regicide."

"Of course it does not," the Marshal snapped. "Do not top it the morality with me, you blood slurping madman."

William Marshal was my lifelong hero. Still, I felt an urge to twist his head from his shoulders and drink from his severed neck. I closed my eyes and allowed the anger to pass.

"How will you prosecute the archbishop?" I asked. "I would be happy to speak my evidence at a hearing."

The Marshal laughed at my naivety. "I can never prosecute him. Even if I thought that such a thing would work, which it would not, England has enough open fighting amongst itself. All I can do is isolate him from the king and continue to outspend him."

"That seems somewhat uncertain," I pointed out. "Would a knife in the dark not be the better option?"

"Perhaps. And yet who would do such a thing?" he asked, speaking lightly and taking a drink of wine without looking at me.

I understood what the Marshal wanted from me.

"A man who would expect little in return," I said. "Merely a warrant to clear Sherwood of outlaws. And perhaps a very small payment. I am nearly out of money."

"I doubt he would let you near him," the Marshal said, looking at me once more.

"Perhaps I know someone who could," I said, wondering what Eva would say. She did not like her father but I feared she would feel somewhat displeased about me murdering the man, let alone helping me to do so. "Or perhaps I could take him on the road, as William has done with so many other travellers."

"Spare me the details," the Marshal said. "I suspect that the archbishop is content to wait until my death, as old as I am. He's playing a game that will last longer than the players."

"He must be of an age with you, my lord," I said, thinking back to when I first met the archbishop. He was already old, or seemed so to me at the time.

"I suppose that he is," the Marshal said. "Yet he wears it well. Like you, he seems to have not aged in the last ten or fifteen years."

The silence drew out as we stared at each.

"He has not aged," I said, deliberately.

The Marshal rubbed his eyes and leaned forwards to pinch the bridge of his nose. "Can it be true, what you say about William's blood? The truth now, Richard, is it not some conjurer's trick? You wear some secret eastern face paint or perhaps you are the true Richard's son?"

"I swear it," I said. "I will swear any oath, holy or otherwise. William's blood, my blood, can arrest ageing if ingested. But how precisely, I do not know. Only that it seems to be effective. And I believe that for it to continue to work the archbishop must be drinking blood regularly. The blood of who, I do not know but a man of his power could be using servants or, come to think of it, those that William takes into Sherwood."

"Good God." The Marshal looked all of his seventy-plus years. "What can he and de Ferrers be working towards?"

"It seems our purposes are one and the same," I said, planting my hands on the table. I would kill William and if I had the chance, I would kill the archbishop as well. And I would reap the Marshal's reward. "I am ready to leave for Sherwood immediately."

"Do not get ahead of yourself," the Marshal said. "Sit down. I have to take Lincoln first. And you will help me."

"You must have hundreds of men here," I said, warily. "You do not need me."

"I have close to four hundred knights," he said. "But you are worth ten more, at least."

Frustration boiled up. "I am honoured to hear you say so yet—"

"And there is your wife's son, Sir Jocelyn, plus the three squires and a score of archers you have in the woods a few miles away. My youngest son is with you also? Yes, I have exceptional men who saw your approach and shadowed you all the way from Nottinghamshire. All of you would be most useful. In fact, I have a task for you. Do not argue. You fight for me at Lincoln and then I will see you restored to your lands and you will have your warrant for Sherwood."

"And a manor for Jocelyn."

The Marshal stared me down. Then he sighed. "Fine. Now, listen."

The walled town of Lincoln was in possession of the rebel barons, led by Thomas the Count of Perche. The castle of Lincoln was in the centre of the town and that, however, was in the possession of royalists, men who had been loyal to King John and had continued to be loyal to young King Henry.

The Marshal, after he had heard from our Wealden messengers that the French had been repulsed and delayed by our daring raid at Dover, had decided to take back the town of Lincoln and save the brave garrison of the Lincoln Castle.

"He was greatly impressed by the Dover raid," I said to the archers. "So he wants us to fight for him here, too. In a way, that makes use of your abilities."

"And what is our task?" Jocelyn asked, impatient as always.

We stood in the shade of a copse of alder where my men had made their own camp. There were hundreds of such groups of men all over the fields all around us to the north and the west of Lincoln. There seemed to be a few mercenary crossbowmen about but few enough English archers.

I wanted to let our men know what they faced. They were strangers in this part of

England.

"We're to fight our way through to the castle," I said to him and to others, gathered together now in the Marshal's lively camp. "The Marshal wishes us to scale the western wall of the town while his main force attacks the north gate. Once inside we will gain entry into the castle, freeing the garrison to attack from the rear while you men shoot down into the town. You will have only as many arrows as you can each carry up to the walls. There are thousands of men-at-arms in Lincoln so I suggest you choose important targets. The Marshal prays that our disruption will distract and distress the defenders. There are hundreds of crossbowmen in the city. If they are within range, the Marshal suggests we consider shooting them instead. And we are to exploit whatever opportunities present themselves. You men know I am no archer. I will leave the details up to you, Swein."

The archers exchanged nervous looks.

"Perhaps you fellows are regretting following us into the north. But out of all Cassingham's men, you twenty wanted glory and wealth the most. I allowed you men to come with me because Swein asked for it and because he swears you are all gifted archers and brave men. I know you expected to be fighting in the woods, against outlaws, not storming the walls of a city and fighting knights. But this is your opportunity. Fight well and you will be rewarded. When the city falls, you will be amongst the first to take what you can from the fallen and from the rebel citizens."

A few of them, at least, began nodding and standing straighter. I would leave it to young Swein to inspire them further.

"You truly expect the city to fall just like that?" Jocelyn said to me. "We simply scale the walls and attack thousands of knights with a score of archers? No offense, my friends."

Jocelyn was making out as if he was angry but I could tell he was excited. He was eager to prove his worth. I had not yet told him what the Marshal would give him were we to succeed. I did not want him to risk his life more than necessary.

"I admit, it is a difficult task," I said. "But they are sending us a local man, a mercenary named Falk. And long ladders for the wall. So we will complete our task and we will all win glory for ourselves. And then we will finally destroy William. Then you can marry Marian, Jocelyn and be lord of your own manor. Your dream come true, son, and all of it within grasp."

"I very much like the sound of that," Jocelyn said, smiling.

Swein scowled and turned away to speak to his men.

I bet you do, I thought. "You know, when all this is over, I might even ask Eva if she would like to stay with me."

"Not marriage, surely?" Jocelyn asked. He could not imagine marrying so far beneath himself.

"Why not?" I said. "She likes me."

"Now you are dreaming," he said and we laughed.

God must have been laughing too.

***

Two days later, on the twentieth of May 1217, my men and I stood ready across the fields from the western walls.

Lincoln was a magnificent city. Lincolnshire is one of the flattest parts of all England, a wet, boggy, flat place. Yet there is a great limestone ridge running straight as an arrow through almost the whole county up to the River Humber. That great escarpment is cut through by the River Witham and at that point stands Lincoln. Lincoln was also the crossroads of two of what were England's greatest roads. Ermine Street ran straight south all the way to London and the Fosse Way ran southwest diagonally across the country to Leicester and then down to Cirencester and beyond toward Dartmouth. On the northern bank of the river stood the walled city of Lincoln, which spread from the bridge at the bottom, up the steep escarpment to the plateau of the ridge above. On the edge of the escarpment was the castle, on the western side and the great cathedral on the eastern.

Its location and geography were the reason the rebel barons had taken the city. It was of vital strategic importance. By controlling Lincoln, they could control not only the county but also control access to the rest of England.

And that was one of the reasons the Marshal wanted to take the city back. But really, he wanted a great military victory to finish the rebellion and King Louis for the last time. Crushing the thousands of men in Lincoln would break the resolve of those who held out for their rewards from a victorious King Louis. They had to be persuaded that England was now under the command of the greatest knight who ever lived and that they had no hope.

Win Lincoln and we would win England.

Yet, the city would be a tough place to crack. The rebels had got inside because the citizens had thrown open the gates and declared themselves for Louis. Storming it by force would be a different matter.

We stood at the edge of a copse of alder on the western side of the city looking across fields and a scatter of isolated houses to the walls, the castle keep behind them and beyond the tops of the stunning towers of the enormous cathedral. The walls of the city fell away on the south, down the escarpment towards the River Witham. It was a huge place.

"We have to take that?" Swein said, gawping. He and the archers from the Weald had never seen Lincoln. It was only forty miles southwest to Nottingham but in those days, you never went to a place unless you had good reason to.

"No," I said, misunderstanding him on purpose. "Those men have to take the city. All we have to do is get up on the walls."

To the north, across the fields of the ridge, we could see the Marshal's army as it approached Lincoln's north gate. He led about four hundred knights with their attendant squires plus another thousand armoured, non-noble men-at-arms and a thousand or so levied men who were lightly armoured. Most were making the final approach on foot. Those who yet rode would dismount before they got within bow range of the north wall.

The Marshal's forces included four hundred mercenary crossbowmen who approached in front of the knights. The crossbowmen would cover the assault by keeping the heads of the defenders down behind the walls while the ladders were scaled and the walls assaulted.

Bands of mounted soldiers roamed around outside the walls on all sides, no doubt there to cut off any attempts at escape and to relay any clues to troop positions. Down the escarpment on the other side of the river, there were more horsemen and groups of soldiers, although who they belonged to I had no idea. They were too far away to be concerned with. Battles always draw gawkers.

The rest of the Marshal's forces were held in reserve to the north. No doubt, he hoped he would not need them, or perhaps he feared to cause too much damage to the beautiful, wealthy city. But I knew they were there if needed.

In my group, we had four men-at-arms, including myself. I led Jocelyn and Anselm who were armoured like knights. Swein commanded our twenty archers, armed with their huge bows, laden arrow bags, and swords or daggers. Between them, they had a pair of ladders twenty-five feet long. They looked spindly to me. I prayed to God that they would hold us as we scaled the wall.

We were being escorted by my last man-at-arms, a mercenary named Falk. The Lincolnshire man was a commoner who had risen to knighthood over a brutal career fighting from Wales to the Holy Land and wherever there was state sanctioned murder to be had. He was rough of manner and ugly as hell, a rolling lump of a man. His blade was a dirty great falchion, nocked and rusty but sharp as sin. His surcoat was emblazoned with a griffon design but it was partly hidden underneath a thick layer of grime and old blood. I was glad to have him.

The Marshal's forces charged onward, out of sight. The shouts of battle grew.

"Let's be off, Richard," Falk said and spat out a quivering glob onto the trunk of the tree beside me.

"We move quickly," I said to the men. "Even if they see us, we keep going. Even if we do not have surprise on our side, even if they shoot crossbows down at us. We are getting up that wall."

Those of us with helms jammed them on. We tightened our buckles and straps, knots, and we trotted on foot out of the tree cover and cut straight across the field. To our right, the ground fell away steeply down to the river. There was a road down there that ran parallel to the river with houses all along it, leading to the river gate.

It seemed a long way to the wall. A long way to be completely exposed.

Please, God, I prayed, please do not let them see us.

We crossed into the final flat meadow field, an open expanse that led right up to the base of the wall. There was a narrow postern gate there but we would not waste time attempting to break it down. Surely it would be sealed with rubble and boarding.

Our target section of the western wall loomed up higher and higher the closer we got. The top of the castle keep, with it's loyal, royalist garrison still holding out, poked up behind. The crenellations like the shattered, rotten teeth of Falk, panting beside me like an old dog.

There were heads up on the top of the castle tower, between the gaps of the crenellations, but they were all pointed northward. I prayed that those men were still loyal to their young king and would be spurred into taking up arms and joining us.

And if they were not, I meant to force them to do so.

It would only take one of the rebel heads inside Lincoln, on any of the long section of wall, to glance our way for the cry to go up.

Jocelyn next to me panted. His shield, like mine, was slung over his back. Our hauberks were heavy. But I rarely tired. Jocelyn was about thirty years old but he was strong and he trained every day that he could. Anselm was dressed as we were but he was so young, he could run all day and not tire. Falk was lumbering beside me, panting like Jocelyn. The man was battered and scarred and he ran with an awkward, limping gait but he kept up with us.

The lightly armoured Wealden archers trotted along with their ladders, their faces grim but focused on the wall ahead.

I expected a face upon the wall to turn. A shout to cry out. A horn to sound. Arrows and bolts to slam down into us.

But we reached the base of the wall, unnoticed and unopposed. We lined up in the clumpy, long grass, backs to the wall, looking up.

Panting, the men looked down the line to me.

I jammed my mailed fist upward, indicating the top of the wall.

The archers hoisted their ladders against the bottom of the crenellations at the top of the wall, about ten feet apart. We wanted to come up both ladders together.

I moved to mount the ladder nearest to me. Jocelyn grabbed me.

"Wait for the men to go first," he said.

I knew he was worried that the ladder would snap under my weight. And more to the point the top man would be the first to cop a rock or bolt to the face or be run through as he clambered over the top.

But I knew that a fall from such a height would not kill me as it might a normal man. Also, if the ladders did break after other men had climbed then I might be stranded. Without me to lead them, they would struggle. And I had to have a victory. It had to be mine. Personally. I had to be free to kill William.

I shrugged Jocelyn off. "You wait until last. Your task is to protect Anselm."

Though I could not see his eyes through his helm slits, I could imagine the look in them.

"Falk, you get up the other ladder," I said.

"You do not command me," Falk said, his crude voice muffled by his helm. Nevertheless, he leapt upon the ladder. It bowed and creaked under his weight. The fifth rung snapped and he fell, catching himself on the other rungs, his weapon and armour clanging and clattering. The men holding the ladder wrested it back into upright position, dragging the top against the stone at the top of the parapet high above. Falk clambered back up.

"Go softly, you fool," I hissed at him and swung myself up my own ladder.

I trod as lightly as I could. My breath was loud inside my helm. The ash poles of the ladder creaked and cracked. I wondered if I should have left my shield behind rather than wearing it strapped upon my back. It would no doubt catch on the top but then while I fretted away, I had reached the top. My hands at the top of the stone. My instinct was to hesitate, to peer over to see what awaited me.

But speed was vital. If there was a man there then I could not wait for him to leave or turn away. I had men mounting the ladder behind me. It was a matter of go up and over or go home in defeat.

So I threw myself up, onto the edge of the wall, grasping the far side with outstretched arms.

My wrists prickled and my heart was in my mouth, expecting a sword blade or an axe to come chopping down to sever my arms.

I pulled myself up so I was face down on the top of the wall, the crenellations rising up each side of me. Hiding me, or so I prayed, from anyone looking along the wall. I was laying stretched out, imagining a blow aimed at the mail covering the back of my neck. I wriggled forwards and heaved. The corner of the top of my shield caught on the crenellation and screeched as I pulled myself in and fell on the other side in a jumble of arms.

A shadow fell across me and I drew my dagger.

Falk was there, standing over me. "You know, they told me you moved like a warhorse on the charge. I see they were lying, as usual." He laughed inside his helm and stomped away along the wall to the north, fiddling with the chest strap holding his shield to his back.

I rolled to my feet as our archers clambered over. I helped the first two to make a more graceful entrance than I had, then left them to help the rest over.

I looked inward, across the castle bailey and over the other castle wall into the city. The castle keep was on my right and the magnificent cathedral towers were right ahead, in the centre of the city.

The attack on the north gate was already raging. Arrows and bolts clattered and flew. Men shouted and pushed from atop the north wall. I could not see down into the city by the gate, for all the buildings in between, but I could hear them well enough.

I slung my shield upon my arm and walked south along the wall to the point where it made a right angle turn toward the castle keep.

Everyone else, the squires and archers, went north after Falk.

Two men climbed from inside the city farther along the wall. When they saw me, both froze. They were well-armoured men-at-arms, wearing great helms and I was sure they would attack. Instead, they stopped atop the wall by the steps.

"Who are you? What are you doing here?" The first man shouted in French.

"A loyal servant of King Henry," I roared and drew my sword, bringing my shield in to cover my body.

The two men looked at me, looked at the archers streaming away along the wall behind me, then up at the castle keep. And then they ran back down the way that they had come.

I turned to the sound of cheering. The men at the top of the keep were cheering my minor victory. I took the right angle junction of wall and hurried to the wall of the keep. There was a small, very thick, iron-banded door there. I hammered on it, hard, over and over.

"You in there," I called. "Time to get your swords wet."

The men at the top shouted down.

"Who are you?"

I removed my helm and shouted back. "Sir Richard of Ashbury. William Marshal, the Regent of England, has sent me to request that you men join him in attacking the traitors holding this city."

It did not take them long to open the door and join me. There were twenty-six men at arms in all who came out to fight. They were led by a young knight named Sir Stephen of Cranwell. The young man and his fellows were spoiling for a fight, their eyes mad with desire to smash into the men who had taken their city and their families and kept them besieged in the small keep for so long. They had been fully armoured and prepared all day, in case the fight spilled into their keep.

"You will all listen to me and do as I command," I said. "But only until you are unleashed upon the enemy. Then you may each prove your worth as you see fit."

Sir Stephen was wound as high as a young stallion but he nodded in agreement.

"Have you fought in a real battle before?" I asked as we moved off.

He scoffed at me.

"Do not worry," I said. "Remember your training, all of you."

They were greatly offended. I recalled how young I appeared to those who did not know me. They thought I was topping it the grand knight when I was younger than they were.

You just wait and see, I thought.

I led them north along the wall toward the section where Falk had halted our archers.

The castle wall surrounded a roughly rectangular bailey that sat against and inside the larger city walls. Inside the bailey were the usual hall, stables, workshops and open ground for training in the centre. That bailey took up a full quarter of the upper city, with the cathedral opposite it taking up a huge area across the open square between the two great structures. The lumpy Falk had led my archers and men northward from where we climbed in, all the way to where the castle wall led inward to the centre of the city.

There, at the northeast corner of the castle bailey, was a circular bay atop the wall where our twenty archers plus the rest were gathered under the shelter of the battlements.

Sir Stephen and Falk exchanged a terse greeting and I peered over the wall.

The noise of battle is like nothing else in all the world. The noise was like a storm wind howling through a woodland. It was like the crashing of ocean waves onto a rocky shore. And it ebbed and flowed like both. So much so that it was possible to understand at what stage a battle was at by the sound alone. The early stages of a battle were composed of individual shouts and insults and the sounds of feet and hooves running to and fro. Toward the end of a battle, the air would be filled with groaning, moaning, weeping and men begging for aid, for a priest, for their mother.

In Lincoln that day, I heard the sound of battle in full swing. The clash of iron upon iron. The thud of iron on wood. Horses hooves stamping. Bowstrings twanging, crossbows clacking, arrows splitting the air, tapping, and clattering against stone and wood. The loudest noise was the shouting. The noise that thousands of shouting men can make is breathtaking. A cacophony of insults, orders and incoherent cries of rage as men try to murder other men and to stay alive themselves that build to a roaring the likes of which exists nowhere else on earth. It is a humming of discord that fills every octave, rising, falling, and rising sometimes into a strange and beautiful harmony, just for a moment, before crashing into a thousand cries once more.

I peered over the parapet toward the north gate.

There were hundreds of men in the street below, from right underneath the wall all the way up to the north gate. The walls were yet being fought for, with our loyal fellows still climbing over the walls one by one all along it.

Our men were pushing them back, though. The walls were being taken.

"We should attack from the south," the young Sir Stephen yelled into the side of my helm.

"Shut up and get down," I said and dragged him into the cover of the crenellations. "We will do so but not yet. We must wait until they are committed. We have to time it correctly, do you understand? The timing is all-important. We must shock them with our attack, shock them into breaking their will. They are far from that yet. Now, where are the men guarding the castle?"

"What do you mean?" Sir Stephen said.

I cursed God for sending me a fool for an ally. "The men who kept you all from breaking out."

"Honour kept us from breaking out. We could have fled at any point over the wall and away in the darkness. But we knew we must hold. There are men-at-arms always by the bailey gatehouse, however, if that is what you mean?"

I shouted to Falk. "Gatehouse for the bailey?"

"East wall," he said, shuffling over to me. "Near the southeast – keep your fat heads down, you sons of Kentish gravelkind bastards – near the southeast corner of the bailey by the tall square tower, do you see?"

"I do. And that is our way off this wall and into those men below."

"And here I was thinking you were going to leap off this wall into the middle of them and just sort of slay the lot of them," Falk said.

"Do not give Richard ideas," Jocelyn shouted.

A hunting horn sounded and then another and more joined. Over and over, they sounded while we poked our heads over the parapet.

The rebels were falling back. They had lost the north gate.

"They run," Sir Stephen shouted, so elated he jumped to his feet and shouted down at them. "Yes, run, you sons of meretrices, run all the way back to London. Run back to France and drown along the way—"

I kicked his legs out from under him but it was too late. His men, taking his lead, leapt to their feet and began shouting.

We were spotted immediately. Men pointed up as they filed past.

"Cease your shouting," I yelled, as did Falk and Jocelyn.

"They are not fleeing," Jocelyn said as he dragged down the ones nearest him. "They are falling back in good order. This is part of their plans."

"What did you do to Sir Stephen?" the nearest man growled from behind his helm. I wished to tip him from the wall. Instead, I ignored him and he jerked from a metallic ping against his helmet. He ducked down.

Crossbow bolts clattered off the stones and we crouched low again.

There were bowmen scattered across the city in the roofs of the tallest, largest buildings. Some sat on the thatch and tile, most had hacked their way through the bottom of the roofs and were shooting from inside, well hidden and well protected.

"Archers?" Swein shouted.

"No, do not waste your arrows," I said. Crossbowmen and archers were hardly worth bothering with when we had so many knights upon the field. "We must take the bailey gatehouse."

"They are stopping at the square," Falk said, dragging me away from my part of the walled, circular corner of the wall. Bolts fell around us but he paid them no mind. "Look." Falk pointed south along the wall to where the rebel men were falling back to.

"They have built a wall," I said.

"I heard you was a sharp lad, Sir Richard," Falk said. "There's not nothing get past you, is there."

Between the wall of the castle bailey and the corner of the cathedral, the rebels had built a wall from carts, barrels, house timbers and whatever else that could be jammed and hammered together. The knights, squires, and men-at-arms clambered carefully over certain lower sections and then took up places on the far side.

"Hardly the walls of Jerusalem, is it, Falk," I said.

"Don't need to be, does it," he said, pointing east along the length of the cathedral. Along that road were gathered dozens, no, hundreds of horses. They were held by grooms, pages, and squires but as the mass of men fell back, I watch knight after knight hurry to his own horse.

It was immediately obvious what the enemy intended to do.

"Good plan," I said.

Falk grunted.

"What is it?" Swein asked.

"Our enemies down there are preparing to charge the flank of the Marshal's men," I said. "They will wait and wait and then they will smash into our tightly packed men-at-arms when they reach the palisade."

"Charge like that will crush our lads," Falk said. "Kill a lot of men, make the rest run off. For a bit, anyway. Good plan, aye."

I thought about it for a moment. The bolts kept coming, clattering about us.

"We have to clear a section of the palisade for our men," I said. "If they break through quickly then we still have a chance."

Swein's archers looked deeply unhappy. So much so that I laughed. I laughed at their misery and their fear.

I stood and walked to the centre of our circular corner. At once, the bolts came at me. One glanced from my helm, then another. It was good iron and my hauberk was as expensive as I could possibly afford. The rings that made up my mail were thicker, smaller and denser than most men would wear. The better the protection the heavier it was, which cost men speed and mobility and made them tire faster. But with my strength and stamina, those were not concerns I shared.

A bolt or arrow could still bust a ring apart and enter my quilted, linen doublet underneath and if it pierced that and somehow entered my body deeply, then as long as I could find some blood to drink before I died, then I would live.

My helm was enclosed but for the eye slits and breathing holes, yet an arrow could find its way in or buckle the metal. My greatest concern was blindness, however, as I was unsure whether I would be able to regrow an eye, even after ingesting blood. So I turned my back to the city. Almost every bolt shot at me missed but the ones that hit me and bounced off my mail still hurt. An awful lot. But I had to make those talented but inexperienced archers believe that they would live through the day. They might not have my armour but perhaps I could give them a little of my courage.

"Our enemy is luring William Marshal into a trap. The Regent's men are chasing headlong into a barrier that is built clear across the space between this wall and the cathedral. That wooden wall will be manned by hundreds of armoured men. When the Marshal's forces are pressed against the barrier, our enemy will charge his horses down to take our lads by the side and by the rear with lance and with sword. We will not allow that. We are all going out of the bailey gate and we are going to sweep that wooden wall of its defenders. What do you say, do you want to shoot some knights up the arse from ten yards away?"

They cheered and followed me down the wall toward the gatehouse.

"You have bolts stuck in your hauberk, Sir Richard," Swein said from behind me.

"Well, bloody pull them out, lad," I said.

We had to fight our way out into the street. No man was killed, we just shoved them out of the gate towers and cleared the arched gateway of men huddling in it. The gateway was wide enough for two wagons to pass through abreast of each other. I shouted at them all to get out and pushed and shoved them away.

No one there had any idea who we were, or if we were a threat. Even when we burst out of the bailey gateway amongst them, they assumed that we were on their side.

A battle is a confusing place. You can see no more of it than your immediate surroundings and the mass of men around is always surging and changing. And attacks on castles and towns are even more restricted, by buildings and by the funnelling effect of the streets. From approaching along the wall, we had had a rare view of it from above and so I understood as much or even more of what was occurring than the enemies on the ground.

By that point in the battle, they were thoroughly engaged along their front. Behind the makeshift palisade, squires and servants waited with water, wine, and food for the knights. Wounded men drifted away. Fresh men waited their turn at the front.

I wondered when the rebels would spring their trap and charge the Marshal's flank. If I was commanding the mounted knights then I would save it until the latest possible moment until the king's men were exhausted. The charge could be disengaged and repeated but the first shock of it would be the most important moment of the battle. It was impossible to hear anything but the shouting and the clamour of battle. Perhaps the charge had already been launched.

Few of the enemy paid us much mind. Some of those that took note of us backed away, with the instinctive wariness of men when facing the unknown. A few seemed very interested in our presence, nudging each other and pointing.

"Alright, you men," I shouted to those under my command. "We may have to make a start."

I lined my men up in the open gateway of the bailey, archers and men-at-arms together and told them what I wanted them to do. All the while, I hoped that we would not be attacked in the rear from inside. I had seen no one in there behind us but it pays to expect the worst while you hope for the best.

Sir Stephen, his pride wounded but not his person, assured me that his men would perform admirably.

"I have no doubt," I shouted over the roar of battle and clapping him on his shoulder. "What fine fellows you all are. Make your fathers proud."

A group of men-at-arms approached us, their shields up and walking together shoulder to shoulder. Six of them, well armoured behind their shields. Swords drawn.

They knew that we were enemies.

"Hurry, Swein. Ten men shoot there and ten at our six new friends here," I said and stepped back against the wall of the gateway.

The archers shuffled together as closely as they could and drew their huge bows. Half aimed at the rear of the men fighting up on the palisade.

The others aimed at the six men who were only ten yards away.

Our archers called out their chosen targets to each other and then released, almost as one. Twenty of the great war bows sending their heavy arrows into knights and men at arms.

I had never before that moment truly appreciated the power of those things. Months I had been around the archers of the Weald. I had tried my hand at a few of the weapons and I was always astonished that these mortal men could pull them back as far as their ear and further and then do it over and over again.

For sport, the archers would compete to see who could shoot the farthest. Invariably it was the strongest men who had the heaviest, thickest bows who would win. Other forms of competition were to see who could shoot five arrows into a target the fastest. But the war bow was not meant for long range shooting. Nor was it meant for shooting quickly, as arrows were very precious things indeed and every one would have to prove its worth.

The war bow instead was meant for shooting at close range and punching their iron arrowheads into anyone who stood in their way. The arrow shafts themselves were huge things, longer than my arm and thicker than my thumb. Most of their arrowheads were shaped into stubby points, diamond shape in cross-section, designed to force its way into a ring of mail and, through the force of the bow, burst the ring of iron mail apart and carry on through into the man. Of course, under the mail, a man would wear a gambeson, a coat of many layers of linen over the body and arms and cap of the same material under the mail coif worn overhead, with the helm over the top. Our legs were also padded under the mail leg coverings that were like iron trousers, held up by thongs attached to the waist.

An arrow that broke through a mail ring would very likely be stopped in those layers beneath. Some men even wore another thick, padded linen gambeson worn over the chest and back which might stop a blow from ever reaching the mail beneath. But over everything would be a colourful surcoat, adding another layer primarily for protecting the iron from the elements, as well as for decoration and recognition in battle. But a surcoat could also help to catch the shaft of the arrow and stop it penetrating further.

All these layers in combination were counted as armour. And armour worked. If you were a fighting knight, that was the reason you bought the best armour you could afford. You would spend a fortune on having it made to your measure, with the best rings and made by an armourer with a good name. Your armour would save your life against blows from edged weapons, especially slashes and cuts. It could save your limbs and ribs from being broken. Mail worked. Often, when wearing the full harness with every layer included you felt as though you were invulnerable.

The weakness of mail was in stopping penetration, which is why the lance was so powerful a weapon and so feared. The weight of a horse on the charge, pushing a spear point into your armour would run a man through. Our swords could be thrust into mail, though you needed a mighty blow and a lucky one to break through a hauberk.

The other way through was the head of an arrow, whether shot from a war bow or a crossbow. An arrow could never have anything like the penetrating power of a lance. Although I had seen men wounded and killed by arrows and bolts, I had also seen men with ten and more arrows sticking from their armour who swore they could feel nothing, as the arrows had been stopped before pushing into their skin even a little.

So, while I trusted that our Wealden archers would disrupt the enemy and perhaps panic them, I was fully expecting that my knights and men at arms would have to step in front of the archers after the first or second volley and hold the gateway. The archers had orders to fall back up the stairs and shoot from the crenellated walls above down onto the men who attacked we real soldiers.

The six knights who approached held their shields out, just in case we were enemies. I can only assume they thought to push us off our spot or to ask us what on earth we were doing and where we had come from. If they meant harm, they would have charged us, heads down. I expected our archers would drive them away with arrows in their shields.

Instead, they murdered them.

Ten yards was spitting distance. The thick ash shafts thumped into the six knights. Two fell back as if struck by charging horse. Arrows pierced the eye slits of those two men. One dropped, dead, as if he was struck down by a vengeful God. The other screamed like a child, the yard-long shaft waving around.

A third man took an arrow to the centre of the thigh, ripping through his mail and flesh and into the bone, no doubt shattering it. He fell to the side with a cry loud enough to tear his throat to ribbons.

Another man took two arrows to the shield, the force powerful enough to stop him dead, he dropped his sword, clutched the shoulder of his shield arm, and backed away. Another knight took a blow to the top of his old pot helm with an impact that knocked him senseless and staggering like a drunkard. The final man had been rocked by something or other so vigorously that he reeled backward and then sat down on the cobbles, dazed though seemingly unharmed.

Our other ten archers shot into the rearmost ranks of the men upon the palisade. I turned and peered past the gatehouse wall in time to see armoured men there falling backward. One man flung his sword aside as he fell with an arrow shaft sticking from what must surely have been his spine. Other men fell where they stood.

There was not much of a reaction from the survivors, who were fixated upon the Marshal's men charging the other side of the barrier. Crossbow bolts and arrows flew in from either side but they were shooting in an arc, at high angles and without much force.

"Again," I shouted but they needed no urging from me and they were already shouting their targets to each other and nocking their next arrows.

"Blue coat, left."

"Mine's the tall lord."

"Bare head, far right."

"Fat arse."

"Shiny helm."

After they called their men they bent their backs into the next shots and heaved back the cords to their ears and further. I jumped back, well out of their way.

This time, all twenty of them shot into the backs of the enemy fighting.

At a distance of around twenty yards, shooting into their rear, it was like a magic spell.

Ten men dropped in an instant. Wounded men screamed and their cries added to those of the first lot down. The survivors edged away, looking over their shoulders.

The noise from the battle was intensifying. More of the Marshal's men were coming and no doubt, the rebel trap, the heavy horse charge into the flank, was ready to be sprung.

"That got their attention," Falk shouted. Faces and helms across the square were turning to face us. "Right lads, up the wall you go."

"Wait," I shouted. "Stay here. Keeping shooting, keep shooting."

I wanted to see how much carnage they could wreak. Some knights peeled off the palisade and edged toward us.

"Drop any man who comes near," I shouted to Swein but so the archers could hear me. "But keep shooting that wall. Keep killing them."

Arrow after arrow ripped into the men of the palisade. No knights could approach us without coming under the hail of iron.

They were edging away, afraid of the murder we did. Men who stopped to help their comrades were shot. Men who thought to stand were driven away. There were ten down, then twenty and then I lost count of the men who had fallen. Some of them were already dead. More and more, the enemy was aware that they had foes at their rear. The word was shouted between them to get away from us and we had cleared the nearest end of the palisade.

It was magnificent.

"Getting low on arrows, Sir Richard," Swein shouted.

"Stop shooting," I commanded. "Get behind us, not up on the wall. Save your last arrows. If they start using their heads, we may need to scare away crossbowmen."

I got the knights and men of Sir Stephen's castle garrison lined up with us, shoulder to shoulder across the width of the gateway.

I stood in the centre of the line with Falk on my left and Jocelyn on my right. Anselm tried to take position beside Jocelyn but the knight pushed the squire back and rapped him on the top of his helm with the flat of his blade.

Before us, the rebels were gathering to assault our position, where we were so few and they were so many.

"Stay together and stay in the gateway," I shouted. "If any of you breaks our line then I will run you through myself. Do you hear me? Tell me you hear me, you men."

They shouted they did.

"King Henry!" I cried. "For King Henry!"

The men took up my cry. We slapped our blades upon our shields, clapping in time. A few of us shouted insults and jeered, which was a fine thing to hear. It showed our enemies and each other that we had spirit, that we welcomed the fight.

Our challenge was answered at once by a growl of the knights who had been cowed by our archers. They saw our bowmen had fallen back and they surged forwards to finish us off. There was a roar as they rushed onward, twenty, thirty, and then fifty men advancing on us.

My heart raced with the thrill of it. Every sense alive to the clangour and stench of the battle. I felt strong and light. I wanted blood. I wanted to strike the heads from every man before me and I wanted to drink the blood from their necks and devour their flesh.

They charged, so close I could hear their heaving breath and the rattle and rustling of their clothing, their swords bashing their shields as they ran, their shoes slapping on the stone cobbles.

Occasionally, in battle, it seems as though you are in a dream. Can this truly be happening, you wonder, can I be here while this terrible thing occurs?

Coming straight for me was a huge, tall, broad shouldered knight. He was dressed in a bright blue surcoat, stained with fresh blood that was not his own. His shield was half blue and half black. His mail had been scrubbed to a shine, his helmet was silvery like a mirror. The man's sword looked particularly long and very wide at the base, a sword, perhaps, made for thrusting through armour. I was the tallest in my line and perhaps I was clearly the leader of our little band and he had sought me out, jostling his fellows aside for the glory of killing me himself. His men beside him were finely armoured also, in similar colours of blue and black. Perhaps they were from the same place, the same family, even.

And then they were upon us. We stepped into the attack to take their first, mightiest blows on our shields.

My knight in blue made as if he was charging up with a powerful thrust at my head, which meant that his true attack would be anywhere but there. And he checked his thrust at the last moment, slamming his shield into mine so as to force it up and he shoved his blade low, to strike up below the bottom of my shield and into my groin and thighs.

He was strong, his weight was like being knocked by a horse. But I bent my knees, took the force of his strike and forced his shield back. I thrust his sword away as it snaked up toward me and counter attacked with a strike of my own, which he deflected well with his shield.

My strength might have been greater than his but I was as limited as anyone by the strength of my blade. If I struck with all my might, I knew from experience that I could snap my sword blade, or, at least, bend it out of usefulness. I thrust and blocked, waiting for an opening.

More men arrived behind the first line and pushed them against us.

I struck blows against the blue knight, jabbing against his armour. My shield was being chipped to pieces. Jocelyn and Falk by my sides fought their own shoving battles. My helm was smacked and then again by someone, somewhere.

My anger grew. Frustrated, I pushed back, hard. My feet I jammed into the gaps between the rutted cobbles and heaved against them. I could not be resisted. I pushed the blue knight's shield aside and stabbed my blade into the inside elbow of his shield arm and pushed the blade through into his flesh. I reversed the blade backhand into the side of his helm, ringing his head like a hammer on a bell and I followed up with a lunge up beneath the bottom of his helm, sliding up against his coif and smashing into his chin. I twisted and thrust again as he reeled back and I forced him away further, twisting and ripping my blade out downward, tearing his throat. Blood gushed out and he staggered back into the melee.

Another man forced his way into his place and then I edged back to my line and fought again.

Falk breathed heavily, his breath whistling inside his helm. Even Jocelyn was tiring. The men we fought could afford to rotate out of the attack when they tired and the man behind would take his place. Yet we had no replacements but a score of archers and a squire behind. Our line was a single man thick. While we stood firm in the centre, the men to either side were pushed back by the weight of numbers.

Soon, all I heard was my breath in my ears and the muffled shouts and grunts of desperate men. I could taste blood on the air. I wanted it. I needed it. I wanted to break away from my men and take on the whole army. I fought on while Falk and Jocelyn took their first steps back. I had to go back with them to avoid breaking the line.

I had no breath to shout anything to inspire my men to fight harder. Then again, they already fought for their lives, what more was there?

Yet they would break at any moment, I knew, I could feel it in the way the line moved. They were beyond the limits of their endurance.

Perhaps I could give my men a chance, or brief respite at the least, if I fought my way out, break through the enemy and so cause them to react to my actions. As I thought it, I did it. I shoved aside the three men surrounding me and stepped forward into them.

A mass of armoured men surged toward me, seeing a fool and an easy kill or a good ransom. There were dozens of them, in rank after rank and I realised I had made a mistake. There was nowhere to break through to, any more. It was a sea of armoured men all the way to the cathedral. Perhaps I would not kill William after all.

Perhaps, after all I had seen and all I had done, I would die at the gate of Lincoln Castle.

I hoped, prayed, and pushed forward, swinging my blade like a madman. I pushed them back, smacked heads and arms, I aimed for hands to smash and knees that I could stamp on. I took blows to my helm that clouded my vision with ten thousand swirling stars and still I kept moving, spinning, shoving them back, breaking out further from my men and hoping to bring the enemy knights with me.

My arms felt broken. My shoulders burned. I could see almost nothing.

I was alone. Arrows smashed down about me. The knights around me backed away, struck by a hail of shots from above. They held their shields up over their heads and I struck them from below.

And then the enemy melted away.

The attacks on me grew lighter and fewer for a moment and then they were gone. I straightened my helm, lined up the slits with my eyes once again and watched them running full tilt down the steep hill, down the road toward the river and the bridge that crossed it. Hundreds of men squeezing together between the buildings.

The Marshal's men had cleared the palisade and were over it, chasing the fleeing rebel knights and men at arms.

A group of knights swerved toward me, their blades drawn.

"King Henry!" I cried, throwing my arms wide and backing away. "I fight for Henry. For the Marshal."

Still they came at me until Falk rushed to my side, yanking off his helm.

"Hold fast, you fools. This is Richard of Ashbury."

They left me alone and I stood while my men approached, exhausted, battered, and wounded, to watch the flight of the enemy.

Swein led his archers down from the wall where they had saved me by shooting down into the attackers that had surrounded me.

"Good fight, that," Falk said, still wheezing.

Jocelyn clapped me on the back. "Let us go capture ourselves a few knights, shall we?"

"You go," I said. "You and Anselm, make some money. Oh, and find me a good sword. Mine is quite ruined."

I looked around for a body that I could drag into the shadows.

* * *

Swein and his archers were plundering the dead and retrieving their arrows from the men they had shot in the battle. It was only fair that they took whatever else they could.

Jocelyn looked at me as if to say that he knew what I would be doing and he did not approve of it. But I cared nothing for what he thought. The air was full of blood and I needed it. I needed it.

While the dead were plundered, the living were chased through the city and captured for ransom by whoever took them. Knights were found hiding in cupboards, cellars and roof spaces. Many were drowned in the river while in flight over the bridge that led out of town.

Those who escaped on horses fled south. Those that fled on foot were largely rounded up by the Marshal's knights, held in reserve on the south side of the city for just such an eventuality. Inside, the city was plundered from top to bottom.

Noblemen, knights, men-at-arms, squires, pages, crossbowmen, archers, grooms and servants lost their minds once they had taken the city and all plundered it three ways from Sunday. Everything of value within the city was stolen, no matter who it had belonged to. Wine and ale casks were smashed open and men grew drunk and sang. Of course, it is often the way when a city falls though I was surprised to see Englishmen carrying it out upon an English city.

As soon as the day after that first mad evening, men were referring to the plundering as the Lincoln Fair. As in, do you see what I got at the Lincoln Fair? And, prices were low at the Lincoln Fair this year. Their glee, I felt at the time, to be somewhat unseemly, although I would never be one to judge on account of how I spent my own first evening after the battle.

When the looting mobs had rushed beyond the bodies at the gatehouse, I dragged the corpse of the blue knight by the ankles through the gatehouse and into the bailey. He felt heavy as a horse and I was tired but I was also thirsty so I moved him rapidly. I dragged him over the cobbles into the bailey and then quickly pulled the body into a dark armourer's workshop and stripped off his helm.

He was younger than expected. Perhaps not much over twenty. A young knight who fought like an experienced one. I wondered if he had been English or from France or elsewhere.

I took off his coif, seeing that I had, in fact, split it entirely through at the throat, breaking open the mail rings with my blade. It was sticky with blood. I salivated and checked that I could hear no one in the bailey. Pulling down the mail at his neck, I bent my mouth to his wound and sank my teeth into the sticky, congealing mass.

I drank down the hot blood, it gushing into my mouth. It spread through me, like climbing into a hot bath, like warm spiced wine after a winter trek, like a dream coming true.

Something was wrong but I did not know what it was until the young knight groaned and moved.

I jerked away from him as his eyes opened and tried to focus on me. His right arm rose slowly toward me. I slapped it away.

I had never killed a man just for his blood before.

But I had not had my fill, and I meant to have it.

I sank my teeth back into his throat and held him still while I drank down his blood, sucking it from his body. He coughed a spray of blood and without looking, I held my hand over his mouth. His body wracked with spasms while he died. I drank until my belly was full to bursting and sat back.

If I were discovered again drinking blood after a battle, it would mean the end of my position in England. My name would be destroyed. I would have to go to the Holy Land, take a false name, and fight as a mercenary. Any chance at revenge would be over. I wiped my mouth, stripped the surcoat from the body, and stuffed it deep into a dark corner of the workshop.

The knight would be recognisable, I supposed but I would do what I could. I hefted up the anvil from its block and smashed the knight's face in until it was a cavernous, bloody mess. I took his rings and tossed his scabbard behind the workshop when I snuck out.

I kept to the shadows. Few people were in the castle bailey. Two servants walked from the keep door, hurrying out through the gate, no doubt eager to join in the plundering.

No one noticed me.

I gave the rings to Swein, who said nothing but understood. Perhaps he thought I was buying his silence but I was not. In fact, I wished to reward him, for he had done exceptionally well and he deserved a rich reward. Not least for sticking by me, no matter what.

The blood surged through me. I felt stronger than ever. The day's exertions had flowed from my limbs and I stood and listened while the Lincoln Fair was in full swing. I thought I should probably join in, as money is always useful. But I had no will for it.

I saw the blue knight's face staring up, sightless, before I crushed his face in.

Was it even murder, I wondered? He had been trying to kill me in the battle and he would surely have died from his existing wounds in time anyway. But no matter how I justified it to myself, I felt like a genuine murderer for the first time in my life.

But he was dead and I was not going to confess to the crime, nor would I admit it to some priest. They were all in some man's pay. Like every other horror I had seen and done in my life, I would simply push the thought of it away and pretend it had never happened. And if I never spoke of it to God then perhaps He would forget as well.

The next day, I found the Marshal's tent, which he had erected to the north of the city while he oversaw the cleaning up and sorting out and tallying the costs and gains from the action.

The hangover from a battle is a strange thing. The aches and pains start in on a man, his elation at surviving a slaughter becomes melancholy that he himself has killed, or known a man who died or perhaps he did not perform well or committed a crime in the anarchy after. Men sat slumped and quiet talking of things to come, sharing bottles and hiding their spoils.

While I waited outside, along with two dozen other men on their own business, Falk approached. He had not changed out of his armour, had not removed his blood-soiled surcoat.

"Good day, yesterday," he said as he stomped up to me. "Reckon that's the war over, then."

"You think so?" I asked.

"Got to be, Richard," Falk said. "We killed or captured most of the leaders. There's not enough loyal to Louis to carry it on. And the Marshal, you know what he's like, he'll sue for peace on almost any terms, just to be done with it, mark my words."

"I do," I said. "And now I will speak to the Marshal, accept my warrant and go clear Sherwood of outlaws."

"The Green Knight," Falk said, nodding.

I was surprised he had heard about him.

"Course I bloody have," Falk said. "He's taken enough of my men off the road, last year or two when we went up to York and Scotland. I hope you take the bastards and skin them all alive, the Green Knight especially. Green Knight, what a laugh. Rip his tongue out."

"I will," I said. "Nothing can stop me now."

Sometimes, you say something and as you speak, you know you are mocking God.

"There's a messenger in the camp looking for you," Falk said. "Looks like a priest. Monk, I reckon. Poor lad looks like he's shitting himself. I said I'd dig you out for him. The lad's gone down to the cathedral to wait there."

I had a terrible feeling and I left word that I would be back to see the Marshal as soon as

I could.

There was blood everywhere before the cathedral. It was massive, stretching to Heaven above me, like God Himself staring down in judgement on what I had done. I dreaded entering that holy place. I was not sure I could take it but I did not have to.

The monk hurried over to me from somewhere out of the way by the side of the cathedral. He led his tired pony. Both beast and rider were covered in dirt and sweat, suggesting a hard ride.

I recognised him as a brother from the Priory.

"Brother Godfrey, is it not?" I said.

"Sir Richard," the young man mumbled, would not meet my eye. "Prior Simon sent me to find you."

I stepped up to him, grasped him by the front of his robe and dragged him close to me.

"Speak. Tell me all. Quickly, man."

"The women. The women, the Lady Marian and the other one. They were taken, my lord. Taken in the night."

12
INTO SHERWOOD

"WHERE IS HE?" I demanded at the gate of Nottingham Castle, two mornings later.

"We are not to let you enter, Sir Richard," the captain on the gate said, swallowing hard. He had an open-faced helmet on his head and I imagined what would happen to his warty nose if I smashed my mailed fist into it.

"I am going through that gate," I said, advancing upon him. "And the three of you are welcome to try to stop me. But you should know I am in a killing mood."

The captain stepped back a full step. "I am merely doing as commanded," he said.

"Please attempt to stop me," I said. "I beg you to draw your swords and try, please. I want to feel my sword slicing through a man's flesh."

The captain and his two men stepped aside and I strode through. They followed after me at a distance, keeping pace with me and whispering accusations at each other. Servants scattered from me. Entering the keep, two of Roger's clerks stared at me down the corridor. They clutched their scrolls to their chest, spun on their heels and fled with their robes flapping about their scrawny ankles.

I pushed through the doorways and climbed stairs until I came to the Great Hall. It was almost empty but for a few men sitting at the table. The chief amongst them I recognised.

"Guy of Gisbourne," I shouted. "Where is the sheriff?"

He stared for a moment then leapt to his feet. "Sir Richard," he said. He looked to one of his men who nodded and ran off through a door at the back of the hall.

"Where is he?" I said, striding forward toward the top table behind which he stood.

Guy spread his hands. "Please, Sir Richard, there is no need for you to be angry. Sit, I beg you, let us drink together and talk."

"They say you are a brilliant swordsman, Sir Guy," I said, placing my hand upon the pommel of my new sword. "I would love to see how you fare against a man who would test your ability. Shall we wager? If I beat you, then you tell me where the sheriff is."

Guy swallowed and placed his hand on the hilt of his own weapon, shifting back away from the table. "And if I win?"

I summoned as much contempt as I could muster and I threw back my head and laughed.

His face flushed red and I watched with satisfaction as the rage filled the man. I had insulted him gravely. I wished to beat him into submission and draw the truth out of him like blood.

He stepped back further from the table and drew his sword.

Three men rushed into the hall from the back door. I recognised them vaguely as Guy's men.

Alone, I could beat Guy into submission without killing him. But with four men, I would risk killing a man who could tell me where the sheriff was hiding.

I decided to frighten them into subjugation.

Without drawing my sword, I stepped forward to the huge table, bent my knees into a squat and, with a roar straightened, and heaved the massive oaken thing up into the air, longways onto the end nearest Guy's men. Plates and cups slid and flew and smashed. I hurled with such force that the massive, ancient table spun and crashed down on its top, scattering Guy's men aside. The sheriff's chair fell backward with a bang and the benches clattered away.

While Guy stood in shock, I ran to him and seized him by the arms, pinning them to his side.

His eyes were wide as platters and all colour drained from his face.

"Where is the sheriff?"

"Sherwood," Guy said, his throat tight.

Guy's eyes flicked behind me.

"Stay where you are," I shouted. "I will rip his arms from his body."

Guy, his neck tight, nodded at them and I heard them back away from me.

"So he's in Sherwood," I said, my nose half an inch from his own. "I could have guessed that. Where in Sherwood? Where has he taken them?"

"Taken his men? He knew not where."

"What are you blathering about?"

Guy frowned. "He goes to find the Lady Marian. He took ten men before dawn, leaving me and a few of us here to guard the castle and the town."

"Find Marian? But he is the one who took her from me."

Relief washed over Guy's face. "He did not. The Green Knight took her."

"The sheriff is in league with the Green Knight."

"He is not," Guy said and I squeezed him. "I swear, I swear it, on God's teeth, I swear it."

"But the sheriff is in league with the archbishop," I said.

Guy peered at me warily. "The archbishop is here often," he said. "But they are two of the most powerful lords of the north, why would they not be?"

"The archbishop is working with the Green Knight," I said.

Guy simply gaped at me.

I shoved him away and turned around. The three men at arms stood with their swords out. I ignored them and straightened the sheriff's fine chair. I sat myself down in it and thought.

"The archbishop sent a steward to Ashbury after I was outlawed," I said to Guy as he inched around to where I was. Guy waved his men back and pulled a bench upright, quite far away from me. "The new steward was a big man, a very big man named John. I did not think of it at the time but after the women were taken, I recalled the sheriff saying he had sent his chief bailiff, a man named John into the Greenwood. John the bailiff was a big man, correct? And he's the sheriff's man?"

"Bigger than you," Guy said. "Little John they called him. But he went into the wood. He never came out."

I nodded. "I understand now. He was not the sheriff's man after he came out. He was William's. William de Ferrers, the Green Knight. He has made the bailiff, Little John, into his own man. And somehow, William has sent his man to Ashbury, on request of the archbishop. But how did the sheriff know that Marian had been taken?"

"He pays a man who lives near Ashbury. He sends reports, every now and then."

"Reports of me? Who is this man?"

"I would rather not say," Gisbourne said.

"My dear Guy," I said. "I am sorely tempted to cut off your head and then kill your men here. Are you on my side or are you not?"

"He is the Prior of Tutbury. A monk named Simon."

"That sneaky little bastard," I said. "He told the sheriff Marian was there, and the sheriff sent a man to take her, am I right?"

"He sent me," Guy said, sullenly. "Only, when I arrived she was already taken by the new steward, this fellow John."

"You bunch of sly, traitorous bastard dogs," I said. "You have been conspiring behind my back."

"I do only as I am commanded by the Sheriff of Nottingham and Derbyshire," Sir Guy said. "I am a loyal servant."

"You are as cowardly as a woman, Guy," I said. "And as faithful as a snake. Be thankful your head is yet attached to your body. Tell me, where was the sheriff going first, to look for Marian?"

"Linby, first, then on to Newstead Priory."

"He will find both places empty of life," I said. "Where would the sheriff go next?"

"On to Blidworth, I should think."

"Then I ride to Blidworth," I said.

Guy leapt to his feet. "I will accompany you," he said, then paused. "That is, if you agree, Sir Richard."

"Your lord commanded you to stay here, did he not? All Nottingham is entrusted to you."

"My men can be trusted," he said. "Can you not, boys? If the sheriff's good wine is so much as looked at then I shall cut off your hands myself, do you hear me?"

"Fine," I said. "But you do as I say at all times."

"I swear, Sir Richard," Guy of Gisbourne said, the lying sack of shit.

***

"First, we find the sheriff and his men," I said to my own assembled band. We were all mounted, on the road north of Nottingham and were ready to set off. It was midday and I ached to be gone already. "Then we will combine our forces, find William and his monsters and save Marian and Eva."

We were Jocelyn, Anselm, Sir Guy of Gisbourne, Swein and sixteen Wealden archers. Four of the original twenty had elected to return to Kent with the wealth they had taken at the Lincoln Fair. The sixteen that were left were young men all, good fighters, excellent bowmen. I was glad to have them but I feared I was leading them to their deaths.

"Any man who wishes to return to his home is welcome to do so," I said. "I have a royal warrant to defeat the outlaw band and we will all be rewarded. But none of you should think this will be an easy way to make money."

"Sir Richard," Swein said. "My men want to save Marian and Eva as much as you do. The women spent the whole winter with us. There's not a man here who would not give his life for the Lady Marian."

"They are your men now, are they?" Jocelyn said.

"They are," Swein shot back.

"And you consider yourself a man," Jocelyn said. "But if you think the Lady Marian looks upon you as anything but a boy then you are very much mistaken."

Swein reached for his bow and I rode forward, pushing my horse in between the two of them. I kicked Swein's horse on the rump and it jerked sideways. Swein, being such a poor horseman, fell from his saddle and landed hard.

The archers, all mounted, sat up straighter and a couple put their hands to their daggers.

They were Swein's men indeed.

I had not meant for him to fall but I could not apologise now without appearing weak.

"I will have no fighting in this company," I shouted, making some of the horses nervous, and their riders too. "We will be fighting for our lives this very day. Save it for William's men, you flaming bloody fools. Get up on your horse, Swein, and try to stay upon it."

"I told you peasants make poor horsemen," Jocelyn said.

I glared at Jocelyn. "You are supposed to be a knight. Act like one." His smirk fell from his face. "And get rid of that absurd lance, will you, man? We are riding into a woodland, you will find no place for a charge."

"I am a knight," Jocelyn said, sticking his nose in the air. "And the lance is a knight's weapon."

Swein clawed his way to his feet, his eyes full of murder as he looked up under his cap at me. I hoped I had not made an enemy of the lad by shaming him in front of his men.

"Swein, you know the Greenwood better than any man here," I said. "Please lead us onward to Blidworth. Let us move quickly, we have less than a half a day's light left."

The lad mounted and nodded, somewhat mollified.

Sir Guy raised his eyebrows as we rode out. "Not a word from you, Gisbourne," I muttered and he lowered his head to hide his smile.

We knights and squires had good horses, capable of comfortable gait. But the archers and Swein had their sturdy, short-backed ponies. They could keep pace with us but they were much jostled. All had complained bitterly in the long, fast journey north and then every day that they had mounted since. Although, I had to admit they had all grown into their saddles, learning to move with their mount and as we rode north from Nottingham I was pleased to see them riding fairly well and without complaint. For I would need them in fighting form the moment that they dismounted.

"Your so-called squire grows big for his boots," Jocelyn said as he rode close beside me. He spoke in French and, even then, he kept his voice low.

"You will stop this absurd rivalry with the lad," I said. "What has gotten into you? You are a famed knight and he will only ever be a commoner. No doubt, he will end his days on the end of a rope yet you treat him as if he is a threat to you. I know, son, you are afraid for Marian, of course, you are but why release your ire onto Swein? What has he done to deserve it? We need him, he was an outlaw in these woods. And, as you are too blind to see it, those archers are indeed his men. Did you see him when we raided Dover? Did you see him leading them in Lincoln? They were Cassingham's men once but the lad has brought them over to himself. They are here with us because of him. If you truly want Marian back, then you will treat Swein as a friend, not your enemy."

Jocelyn said nothing for a long while and I waited for him to argue. Instead, he eventually agreed. "You are right," he said. "It is just that he and Marian have been often found talking together and laughing together. I could never make her laugh. I am ever awkward with her."

"He is an outlawed son of a freeman," I said. "She could never marry him. You must be patient with her. She will know that you are a good man and would make a good husband, you will see."

Jocelyn hung his head. "She is likely dead, is she not? Or at the very least, she is raped by those beasts."

I thought that Jocelyn was probably right. "More likely they have taken her to William, who will drink from her," I said.

"But his men," Jocelyn said, his face twisted in anguish. "His men will take her, will they not?"

"All that matters is that we get her back alive," I said. "And Eva too."

We rode into Linby. It looked the same as the last time we were there after Ranulf the forester had talked to me in his home and then been slaughtered for it. The whole village had been butchered, with bodies in the houses and in the gardens. It was still deserted. The bones of the dead had been dragged away by the beasts of the woodland. There was no smell of smoke. No animals squealing and being hushed. A pair of goldfinches flitted through the open doorways.

"The sheriff and his men's horses came through here," Swein said, dismounted and looking at the disturbed ground. "No sign of a fight, as far as I can tell."

"Onward to Blidworth," I commanded Swein. "Every man be ready from here on out. Keep your eyes open."

"As if we weren't already," one of the archers muttered.

We picked our way along the track from Linby toward Blidworth. The sun slid behind a cloud but the wind was still warm. The overwhelming scent of immense clusters of elderflower filled the air with their heady smell, so strong that it was unpleasant.

Once out of the village the trees grew close to the track. The woodland by villages is always coppiced and often free of tangled undergrowth. No animal larger than a field mouse is found in such domesticated wood. It was late May. Blossom bloomed in the hedgerows and at the edges of the wood. The whitebeam blossom formed loose domed clusters of small white flowers. Hawthorn shrubs and small trees were more numerous than any other. The dense masses of flowers form white in May but I knew they would turn pink as they matured, as if in the promise of the vivid red berries that they will become, turning the colour of old blood by Christmas. I wondered if I would be alive to see it.

Bullfinches flitted through the branches, crying out at our intrusion with their mournful, single-note call.

And yet for all the new life in it, the woodland outside of Linby felt deeply threatening. I imagined all manner of men and beasts waiting just out of sight and sound in the darkness between the dense trunks and green understorey.

"How far to Blidworth?" I asked Swein, who rode at the fore of our band.

He glanced at me. "Not far," he said. "Half of half a day on foot?"

"A quarter of a day," I said. "So, seven miles?"

"Sounds right," he said, shrugging.

"What is this place like?" I asked.

"Just a village, Sir Richard," Swein said. "A village like any other in Sherwood. A village subject to the king's laws of the forest. Subject to the whims of the warden, foresters, and the verderers." Swein spat off the side of his horse to show me what he thought of those men.

"Like that man Ranulf," Anselm said, from behind me. "He was a landowner in Linby. What did the folk of Sherwood think of him?"

"The folk of Sherwood?" I asked. "Like Swein alludes to, Anselm, the folk of Sherwood are the same as the folk of anywhere. They moan and gripe about the laws that govern them and likewise complain about the loyal servants of the Crown who must enforce them."

Swein shook his head. "The laws are wrong, my lord, they are wrong. Outside of the king's forests, there are laws, traditions long held. Inside the forest then there is another law. A law where a man is sentenced to maiming or even death for simple actions like trespass or the killing of a deer. I ask you, Richard, what kind of law is it where a skinny old doe in winter, not a day from a natural death, is equal to the life of an Englishman?"

"No fair law," Anselm said.

"The king's law," I said. "Now hold your flapping tongue still for a moment, will you? Who is the verderer at Blidworth? Not Ranulf too? He did not seem important enough to be forester and verderer both."

Swein looked at me strangely. "Did you not know? It is your friend, Sir Guy of Gisbourne." Swein jerked his thumb behind us.

Anselm started to turn about. "Do not look at him, Anselm or I will take your eyes."

Swein grinned. "He's a right evil bastard, that one, my lord."

"He is the verderer at Blidworth?" I asked. "Why would the sheriff not take him to his own village?"

"Perhaps because all the verderers in Sherwood are corrupted," Swein said. "The sheriff is supposed to have no legal authority in Sherwood but he and his friends have seen to it that every post, from warden and verderer to forester and on down has been one of the sheriff's men."

"But the verderers are elected by the county courts?"

"And who rules them, my lord?" Swein asked.

"It is true," Anselm said. "Swein has told me much about this. I think I shall have to speak to my father."

"For the love of God, Anselm," I said. "You are a good lad and a fine squire but you will never change the way of these things. Men's hearts are corrupted and so their hearts corrupt their posts. So the priests tell us." I lowered my voice. "Now, fall back slowly and warn Jocelyn to watch out for Sir Guy. Speak softly, out of Guy's hearing, draw Jocelyn away. Warn him that Guy may have been left behind to lead us into an ambush."

Anselm's eyes widened, all noble thought of justice for the peasants forgotten. He moved to the edge of the path and slowed his horse to do as I asked.

"An ambush?" Swein asked, scanning ahead.

"Do you know of any likely places?" I asked.

He scratched his nose. "A few, perhaps. There is a dell, a couple of miles from Blidworth. The rocks climb high above the track. And the village has fields on all sides but the houses are in two rows, either side of the road. Men could hide there for us to enter, trap us between the buildings."

"And between here and there is all woodland?"

"I recall a patch of moorland on the high ground up ahead."

It sounded as though we might be ambushed anywhere. I wondered if I was overreacting. Perhaps Guy never considered it important enough to mention. Certainly, if his post existed only to increase his personal wealth and to keep Sherwood as well as the county in his sheriff's hands, then there was little reason to bring it up.

And yet why would Roger leave his best man behind in Nottingham? As Guy had said, his men would look after such a quiet, stable place as Nottingham. Guy was quick enough to volunteer to accompany me into the woodland. Had I been manipulated? Was the sheriff even in Blidworth at all? Perhaps I was being led far from where Marian and Eva really were.

"Every man who has a helmet," I said, turning my horse to face the archers. "Put it on. String your bows. Loosen your arrows. Distance yourselves further from each other. Watch ahead and to either side. Sing out if you hear or see anything at all. Do you all hear me?"

Sir Guy showed no obvious sign of distress at our preparations.

Thus arrayed, we continued on.

I myself chose to go without my helm to preserve my exceptional sight, hearing, and sense of smell. However, I did not pretend to myself that my powers of healing would cure an arrow through my head and I remained rather concerned as we proceeded.

I was thirsty for blood. I wondered idly what Swein would say if I asked him for some of his own, as he had fed Tuck. He would probably not agree.

In the narrow band of moorland between the wood, we went single file, in three separate files moving parallel to each other. The central one I led along the path. Jocelyn the left and Swein on the right.

We sprung no ambush.

At the dell, we found a mix of ash, alder, goat willow, holm oak, strawberry tree, suckering elms, spindle tree, dogwood, elder and white poplar woven together in a rich limestone scrub by a scramble tangle of wild hops, dog-roses and brambles that could have hidden a thousand crouching monsters. I sent archers up and around both sides to discover any waiting bowmen.

There were none.

We approached the village of Blidworth with caution. As we came out of the wood, to either side of the track was a large strip field with rows of barley. The sun was setting over the woodland behind us, sending our long shadows before us as we rode up the hill toward the village, which remained out of sight over a hump in the road.

The clash of iron came on the wind.

I pulled up, straining to hear.

The men, needing no instruction, reined in behind and beside me.

Jocelyn turned his helmeted head toward me.

"I hear the sound of battle," I said. "Up ahead."

"The sheriff has found William," Jocelyn said.

"Or the other way around," I said, speaking quickly. "Jocelyn, you and Anselm lead your five archers up the left through this field. Swein, you take six of your fellows and take up position to the right of the village. Sir Guy, come along with me and these five fine fellows here. We knights to close in from three sides, each covered by the bowmen. And if any of you archers shoot me in the back, I shall rip your giblets out. Move now, quickly now."

The archers all dismounted and the three groups spread out from one another, the outer two circling through the fields to either side of the village.

Unslinging my shield, I advanced my horse slowly forward on the track, right up the hill toward the centre into the main street. Sir Guy rode beside me on his sturdy little rouncey.

The sounds of battle grew as I reached the top of the rise.

Inside the village, men were dying.

The sheriff's men were fighting for their lives.

Two rows of houses, a wide street ran through in between the rows. In the centre, a small group of knights and men at arms fought back to back. Bodies, limbs, and entrails lay at their feet in pools of blood. Their horses were lying dead or dying all over the village, some still kicking their feet and thrashing, blood streaking down their flanks. In the rear of the village, one horse walked slowly left to right, dragging her entrails along the dirt behind her.

A group of men attacked them with darting and jabbing with swords, swinging blades in scything motions. Seven of them, with another man standing apart. All wore iron caps. A couple had spears, another a quarterstaff, and a couple with clubs. Most wore filthy gambesons, the rest in those green tunics. They moved like William's monsters.

They were laughing, jeering, and cheering each other on.

Sheriff de Lacy was in the centre of those men, covered in blood, without a helm, parrying attacks with a bent blade. The men with the sticks were darting in, clouting the sheriff's men with them and dancing gleefully out.

Sir Guy of Gisbourne, all credit to the man, cried out, "Roger!" and spurred his horse straight down the track toward his master and friend.

"The sheriff's men are the centre group," I shouted to the archers and raked my heels back.

My horse had been trained fairly well for the charge. He was often nervous and in high spirits around any sort of excitement and this time, he did not fail to be himself.

He swerved away from the track, trying to avoid the stench of blood and shrieking of the dying. I could not control him so I allowed him to veer to the left.

As he moved aside from the track, the arrows shot past me and sank into the jeering attackers.

A couple of the shots hit their marks, making that wet-solid sound of meat being punched through by steel. Those men went down, staggered and knocked back.

All the attackers broke off, spinning about, looking for the archers.

Guy bore down on them, his sword point forward and low, ready to spear it through the nearest man.

But Guy of Gisbourne had no true notion of the speed and power of the men he faced. What was a charging horse to the power of men filled with William's blood?

The three nearest men charged forward and swarmed Guy's horse, knocking it aside and bearing the beast down, with the rider crashing hard into the street. His sword spun aside, glinting as it momentarily left the long shadow and reflected the blood-red setting sun behind me.

I left my horse and ran toward Guy, the sheriff, and his men.

Arrows slashed through the air from behind me, most hitting home, smacking into the men.

More arrows from the left and right, shot from the flat, slapping into William's men, who snarled and jeered.

The three nearest broke off from Guy and his horse, which was bleeding from the neck, the coat shining and sleek with it.

The boldest of the men wore a gambeson with a mail coif and he was faster almost than even I could see. He swung a rusted falchion at my head as I drew near, which was a terrible mistake on his part. A falchion is a single edged meat cleaver and wonderful for cutting open the flesh of non-armoured opponents. Whereas I was in full mail, shield, helm, and he should have retreated immediately. Instead, I took some of the weight of his blow with my shield, rolling with his wild swing to guide it past me, then pushed his blade away, throwing him off balance. I thrust at his open side, piercing him through the gambeson under his ribs and he screamed, reeling away. His two men were on me, one with a sword, and the other with a sturdy club. Both had arrow shafts sticking from their body.

They were savage and quite clearly trusted their speed and strength to overcome their paltry arms and armour. After all, they had just butchered the sheriff's men, who had been all armoured as well as me. But they had not encountered my speed before.

I gutted the swordsman and took a huge blow to the side of my helm from the club, which shattered the wood and knocked my eyes out of alignment. I could see enough to pull the back edge of my blade through the swordsman's throat.

The falchion-armed man I had run through ran away back to his fellows, as did the man with the broken club.

I straightened my helm in time to see William's creatures fleeing from the centre of the village. They spread apart from each other and away from the sheriff and his two surviving fellows. At first, I assumed they were fleeing from us, from me.

Instead, they were seeking cover between the houses so that they could approach the three groups of archers. They leapt over the wattle fences to the pens and gardens and rushed my men.

They stayed away from me.

Most of the archers stood and shot their arrows but a few scattered away from the rushing men. Swein loosed an arrow into the head of the man charging him, dropping the man at the last moment. The young outlaw ran from the next man and dived into the barley, his archers filling the pursuer with arrows.

Across in the other field, I turned in time to see Jocelyn take the top of a man's head off just as Anselm was borne down under another.

Footsteps slapped behind me and I swept my sword out, cutting into the arm of a charging man and knocking him aside. I was on him, stamping down on his hand and driving my sword through the base of his neck.

I was struck on the back of the helm, sending me staggering. I whirled and lashed out but I was hit again, high on the back near my shield shoulder. I caught a glimpse of a man's face twisted in fury, wielding a heavy blacksmith's hammer.

No mortal man can strike with such force. I was thrown from my feet into the dirt. I fell awkwardly, my shield under me and my sword arm flung out to the side.

I was blind, stunned, starting to panic when the hammer smashed down on my elbow.

The pain was incredible. The crunch of the bones was like a white-hot lance spearing through my body and into my brain. Even as I screamed and writhed, my instinct took over and I rolled to my left, over my shield arm and kept rolling so my shield was across my body. The hammer crashed into my shield with force enough to crack it.

My ears were ringing, I could not see.

I kicked out, purely on instinct and connected with a leg, a knee that crunched.

The man fell on me, pinning my shield to my body. I was afraid, I could not feel my arm.

Had it been cut off?

The body on top of me was not moving. I shoved up with my shield arm and threw him off me.

Screams, shouts, and clashes sounded through my helmet and I rolled to my feet, agony spearing through my arm once more. I wheeled about, shield up from the figures around me. I had to tilt my head back and look sideways to see out of my eye slits.

"Richard, Richard," a voice shouted.

"Jocelyn?" I cried back, spinning around, trying and failing to lift my sword arm.

"Richard, we are victorious. Now sit down before you hurt yourself."

They had to hammer the side of my helm back into shape to remove it from my head. I laid my helm on the stone threshold of the nearest house and Anselm tapped a bad dent from the side with the pommel of his sword.

"There," Anselm said, laying his sword down. "I believe that is it."

"Get this thing off me," I shouted. "Hurry up."

When Anselm eased the helm from my head, I reached up and shoved it off, grinding the edge against the tender part of my skull.

"You took a bad hit, there, Sir Richard," Anselm said, touching my scalp.

I slapped his hand away and stood up, swaying and blinking around.

We had won. William's men were mostly dead. Of the living, the sheriff and Guy sat together, side by side on the threshold in the doorway of the nearest house, holding on to each other. Both were covered in blood.

The centre of the village was drenched in the stuff, red soaking into the packed earth.

Jocelyn stood guard over two survivors, two men bleeding and bristling with arrow shafts.

One man had two arrows through the neck and mouth, as well as three through his chest. The man had his eyes closed, breathing slowly and holding himself perfectly still upon the floor.

The other man was not much better off. Five arrows had pierced his shoulders and upper back at various angles. The left side of his scalp from the crown to the ear had been sliced off. It was a flat, red slab, shorn of hair and skin down to the bone. Blood leaked freely from the wound, soaking the entire left side of his body. His face was white yet he looked around with clear eyes, fully alert.

Surrounding them stood Jocelyn, his shield and sword ready. Four archers stood back, arrows nocked upon the strings, five others stood with their blades out.

My sword arm was broken, very badly. My elbow was smashed and with every movement, I shivered.

"How many did we lose?" I asked Anselm as I stepped gingerly over to Jocelyn.

"John Redbeard and Bull," Anselm said. "Struck dead in an instant. These men, their speed. Their power. It is astonishing."

I was surprised that we had not lost more but still their deaths angered me. "Jocelyn," I said. "Stand ready."

Cradling my right arm with my left, I stood and looked down upon the pair of survivors.

"Who are you?"

The man with the arrows through the neck and mouth blinked up at me, unable to speak. He glanced at his friend. That man smirked and spoke for them both.

"My name is Much," he said. "The tongue-tied fellow here is Will."

"Ah," I said. "You are Much the Miller? And he is Bloody Will?" I shook from the pain in my arm and the anger at the men before me.

"Will the Scarlet, so he likes to be told. His name's Bill Scatchlock. Though you certainly is bloody now, ain't you there, Will?" Much was putting a defiant face on things but he was losing more blood every moment and he would not last for very long.

I wanted to kill them immediately but I needed them to speak. "Where is William?"

Much the Miller stared up at me, nodded at the one with arrow shafts through his face. "Right here next to me."

"Another William. The former Earl of Derbyshire. Where is the Green Knight? Whatever he is calling himself, you know who I mean."

"Robert, his name is," Much said. "Sir Robert. He's nobly born, he is."

"That was his father's name," I said. "His real name is William."

"Christ almighty," Much said, staring up at me, his eyes bulging. "You know what, lord. You don't half look like him, you know. Are you his son?"

"Where is he?" I said, shaking with the effort of containing my anger.

"Might be here, might be there," Much said, pausing to spit a little blood onto the street. "Never know with him. Who are you to him, then?"

I kicked Much in the stomach and bent to the one called Will the Scarlet. With my one good hand, I grabbed the shaft sticking through his mouth and yanked it out. The barbs caught on the man's back teeth and those were ripped from his jaw.

Blood and teeth gushed out and Will bent over lest he drown in it. I braced the man against my leg, grabbed the arrow coming from his neck and yanked that one out. The barbs tore a great chunk of his neck as it came free, leaving a tattered and wet sucking hole.

I sank to my knees, grabbed the back of Will the Scarlet's hair and held him up on his knees while I drank down what remained of the blood within his body.

It was like fire, that blood, like fire and ice and the first flush of the night's wine in your belly, multiplied beyond counting.

And it was more. More than I remembered, better than the knight dressed in blue back in Lincoln. It reminded me of a cave in Palestine when I had drunk from my brother William. It was not the same. It was not as powerful but it was a faint echo of that blood. I drank until the spurting blood turned to a trickle. It did not take long.

I stood, letting the drained body fall. My elbow itched and I straightened it out, extending it as it popped back into shape. I sighed as the pain left my arm and my head and all my weariness fled from my limbs. My vision and hearing snapped into a sharpened point, colours warmed and glowed, edges popped.

"You are full of William's blood," I said to Much. "The Green Knight, you drank from him. Tell me all you know of him, now."

"What can you do you me?" Much said, smirking. "No matter what I say, I'm going to end up like Bill, there, ain't I?"

"You will certainly die," I said. "But if you do not tell me then I shall remove the skin from your face, take off your hands and feet, smash your teeth out and leave you here to die slowly. Or I can take off your head. Which would you prefer?"

Much glanced at the body of Bill. "What do you want to know?"

"Where is he?"

"Eden," Much said.

"Do not play games with me," I said, through gritted teeth. "Where is he?"

Much grunted. "Eden is the name of the place. The Green Knight rules it, as Adam ruled the first Eden before God and woman betrayed him. We sons of Adam live within the walls of Eden. Sir Robert lives in the sacred dell beneath the palace."

"What palace? There are no palaces in Sherwood. Are there?"

"The Palace in the Green," Much said. "In the green heart of Eden."

"Where is this Eden?" I said, barely holding to my remaining patience.

"Up beyond Mansfield," Much said, jerking his head back. "Not really a palace, I suppose. It's a hunting lodge what belonged to some fat lord before Sir Robert took it over. The old lord run off years ago, no one went there, not for something like fifteen years or more. No servants, nothing. Nothing but deer and boar for miles all around. And us. The sons of Adam. We gone back to the way things was, back at the start of the world."

"And how were things then? Adam was a homeless outlaw, was he?"

The mad creature nodded. 'The Green Knight came to us to gift us his gift. To bring us all back to our own land. We who was thrown off it by lords like you, who took everything from us and demanded more. Well, not no longer. Now we're the ones who have the power of life and death. We overcome it. We are the hunters and now they are the prey. Them, you, and everyone who ain't us."

"This is no more than the typical William nonsense that you are spouting," I said. "You hear me? I say he has filled your head with nonsense, man. Tell me this. You were living in the wood as an outlaw? And he took you and gave you his blood?"

Much nodded. "He done that but he done kill me first, then he saved me after, when he saw that I was a man who believed in the world being the way it was in the beginning, once again. I will help you return the earth to its true self, upon my oath, I said to him. And when I was empty of blood, he filled me up with his. His blood of fire, poured into me, flooded through my veins like quicksilver. It was the greatest gift a man can receive. See, the Christ come down and he told us we had to wait for eternal life, had to wait to have it in Heaven when we wake on the day of the last judgement. But that was a lie. The Christ lied to us. We can have it now. We can live forever. All we have to do is let the Green Knight into our hearts. Obey, faithfully, and we live for eternity, here on earth, with all the pleasures that God has given us. All of it flows from the Lord of Eden."

"You murder innocent folk for their blood," I said. "That is not Heaven upon the Earth. That is base. That is plain murder."

"It ain't murder if we don't kill them," Much said. "We only kill the ones who refuse to open their hearts to the Lord of Eden. And them what offend us. And when we want to see their blood and bone smashed flat and ground up into a pulp. Blood and bone, marrow and flesh, ground up all nice and lovely. A taste worth killing for, ain't it not? If we're going to talk more, lord, I might be needing a little drink. Maybe just a cup's worth off the floor, hereabouts? I can drink it right off the ground before it drains away and dries up. I'm right parched."

"Where are the two women he has taken?"

"Two? Got to be right many more than two. More like two hundred, ain't it, Bill? Oh, sorry, Bill. Poor old Bill. Poor old, dead Bill."

"Two women of noble birth, taken recently," I said. "You must know of them. Where are they?"

Much shifted his weight. "Don't know what you mean."

"I'm going to take your eyes and slice the skin off your face for that," I said.

"No, no, I know I heard what was what," he said. "John's got them all locked up."

It was all I could do to resist caving his skull in. "Where? This is your only chance to speak all you know."

He nodded, grinning. "Do you know a man named John? Little John the Bailiff?"

"Go on," I said.

"You know him?" Much said. "He's a bad one, lord. You stay away from him. He's a giant.

A giant bastard, too. He's not right in the head, that Little John. Not right at all. Not fair, neither, not fair at all but he's lord of Mansfield, now. The Lord of Eden granted him the village and fields, just like he done with Blidworth and dear, dead Bill."

"The ladies?" I said, holding myself still lest I shake the words out of him. "The noble women he took."

"Yes, yes," Much said. "I heard all about it. He's bragging about what he done. He went away for a few weeks. Then he come back with them women. He's got them in Blidworth. In the church. And I heard about you. The knight who is coming to save them. Well, big old Little John is in Blidworth. Waiting. Waiting for you and your men. All set up. You'll go charging in to save them and you'll be surrounded. They're going to get all of you in one go. He's a clever one, that John. You got no hope against him, let alone the Lord of Eden himself."

"You have spoken," I said. "You have told me many a useful thing. I will allow you to have a drink. And perhaps I will even allow you to live."

"My eternal thanks, my lord," Much said, looking about, as if fearing a trick.

"First, before I allow you to drink, just tell me. You say the Lord of Eden lives in a hunting lodge north of Mansfield?" I asked.

"That's right," Much said, licking his lips.

"And he warned you to expect me?"

"Expect you, lord? Well, perhaps I was told all about you. Perhaps they been talking about you showing your face round here for months, now. I don't rightly remember. Maybe there is a plan for you and maybe there ain't. Maybe you'll be gutted, lord. Maybe you'll be cattle, lord." Much grinned. "One thing I do know is, you won't get past Mansfield. None of you will." He giggled.

"My thanks," I said. "You are a murderer of the innocent. You have slaughtered entire villages. I wish I had more time to make you suffer properly but this will have to suffice."

I forced him onto his face, snapped the arrow shafts off and held him down while I smashed his limbs with his own hammer. He screamed loud enough to wake the dead. With my foot upon the back of his head, I smashed his feet and his knees. I smashed his hands and his arms. The skin split apart in a half dozen places at each joint. Bone shards ripped through his skin like bright red shards of pottery. His muffled screams were incoherent wails. I crushed his spine and his ribs and still he bucked and wept.

I rolled him onto his back, seeing he yet lived. William's blood keeping him alive and awake beyond what mortal men can endure. Still, he cried and begged me to stop so I smashed his jaw and teeth into a quivering mass that tumbled into his throat and stoppered his screams. And still he writhed around, living through an ordeal. I thought to leave him like that. I even considered trickling blood into his ruined throat to see if I could prolong his torment. But as I looked about for a cup and a likely body, I saw the archers and my other men staring at me in profound horror. At once, I found myself without the heart to continue torturing the man. I almost felt shame but not quite.

I turned to Jocelyn. "Even if it is a trap, our women will be in Mansfield. If not, they will be in this hunting lodge to the north. This place William names Eden. We should leave immediately."

Jocelyn stared back, dismay on his shadowed face. Confused for a moment, I looked around me.

My men were turned away from the violence I had done, their shoulders hunched, collected in small groups on the outskirts of the village. Jocelyn stared at me, Swein and Anselm were turned away.

I realised then that I had drunk from the body of Will Scarlet, in the open, in front of everyone. In front of Jocelyn, in front of Swein's archers. In front of Anselm Marshal. I had devoured blood before Roger de Lacy, Sir Guy, and their two surviving men. My wounds had healed before their eyes. No wonder they either stared at me or looked away in horror.

My secret was truly out. The stories told about me were revealed to be true.

I felt a wave of hot nausea before I realised that I did not care.

"Richard, it is almost dark," Jocelyn said, his face in shadow. I knew from his tone that he thought I had gone too far, that I had thrown away my future but in that moment, I cared not what Jocelyn thought.

"So?" I said. "We can travel at night, we have done so many times. It is imperative that we move quickly. Perhaps we can beat this trap before it is set."

"Richard," Jocelyn said, lowering his voice as he stepped up to me. "You may not know weakness or fatigue. Especially after gorging yourself on the blood of evil men. But every other man here does. We must rest. There are wounded to take care of. Not least your friend the sheriff. And Sir Guy."

"Fine," I said. "Swein, tell the men to take turns on watch. One or two up high, upon the thatch. The rest of them get fires going inside the houses. Eat, drink. Rest. We will leave well before dawn. We will need the darkness."

Swein exchanged a glance with Jocelyn and nodded to me, going off to carry out my instructions.

We dragged the bodies out of the village, separating the sheriff's dead men from William's creatures, and led the nervous horses in.

My men lit the hearth fire in the largest of the abandoned house in Blidworth. Most of us gathered inside, to rest and eat. After checking the archers on watch at the edges of the village, I came inside and sat by the fire on low stools beside the sheriff and Guy. Both men stared at me, saying not a word. Roger seemed miserable, no doubt hurting physically but also wounded in his pride. He had failed in his rescue mission.

Roger was wounded all over. His mail had been pierced and rings torn apart into a gash at one shoulder. The way he held himself suggested that he had broken ribs and no doubt his skin would be a mottled, purple bruise from neck to ankle. If he ever made it back to Nottingham, he would be abed for a week or more.

"Roger," I said to the sheriff. "Before dawn, you will take your two surviving men back to Nottingham, along with Sir Guy."

My tone, perhaps, shocked him out of his silent contemplation and his wariness of me.

"I am the sheriff. You do not command me where to go, nor when. You vile fiend. How dare you?"

"Roger," I said. "You must understand that you will not be the sheriff for very much longer. The Marshal is Regent now. Your agreement with the archbishop, whatever its nature, has not worked in your interest. The Marshal will win the struggle for power. The archbishop will be dead. You will be removed from your post."

"Nonsense," Roger said to me. "Nonsense," he repeated to Sir Guy. "The archbishop has power that you cannot—" he stopped. "Well, perhaps you can conceive of his power. But he is the richest man in the kingdom. He has—"

"He has made a pact with the devil," I said. "He has conspired with William de Ferrers, the Green Knight, this Lord of Eden, to murder King John by means of poison. The archbishop has schemed with you to grant William the run of the king's forest of Sherwood in return for what favours? Immortality for the Archbishop and riches for you. And for the hand of the Lady Marian. So cheaply bought, Roger? What else were you offered? A bright future for your children? A position at court? A castle or two?"

He twisted his face and mumbled. "And a divorce. He would free me to make Marian my wife."

I shook my head, amazed at his folly. "Well, it will all come to nothing. The only reason I have not killed you so far is because we were once friends. Or were we? Perhaps I was never anything to you. How long have you and Hugh been scheming like this? Since before John was king?"

"If you murder me," Roger said. "Then you would have to kill Sir Guy and my two men."

"Would I? Perhaps if I was going to remain a lord and a knight after all this, I suppose I would. You know, in fact, you will all spread the tales of my drinking blood, of my torturing a prisoner and the rest. I think it really would be best if I killed you all. By freeing you, I am only doing myself a disservice."

Roger failed to hold my gaze. "What do you demand in return for our silence?"

"Nothing," I said. "I will let you go because it is the honourable thing to do."

They stared at me and traded looks.

"You are in league with the devil," Roger said, warily. "We all saw you. How can I believe you wish to act with honour?"

Sir Guy did not meet my eye but he nodded.

"You do not believe me but I am trying to be a good knight," I said. "And anyway, it does not matter what I do, your time as sheriff of any shire in England is over. The Regent will replace you. Do not worry, the Marshal is not a vindictive man. He will allow you to return to your lands and live. You, Sir Guy, will have to decide whether you stay in Nottingham. I am certain the new sheriff will want a man who knows the shire. Or perhaps Roger can find you some quiet employment on his own lands."

"I will tell them," Roger said, quivering with indignation or perhaps with fear. "I will tell everyone that are the monster everyone always said you were. I will swear, and so will my men, that we witnessed you murdering prisoners and drinking their blood. You will be charged with murder. Stripped of your lands but properly, this time."

I nodded. "You may say what you wish," I said. "They will not believe a disgraced man. But if they do, it does not matter to me. I do not want my lands. I am not going home. You have nothing to threaten me with, Roger. And I am done with you. Get some rest before you ride."

Roger de Lacy stared for a moment, gathering strength for an argument. Instead, he sighed.

"All this for a woman," he said. "A stupid, stuck up little girl holding on to her precious maidenhead as if it was the Holy Grail. The Green Knight can have her, the filthy little bitch."

My mailed fist smashed his face and threw him down. I felt the bones of his cheeks crack and a number of his teeth break loose.

When I left before dawn, Roger was breathing but had not woken. His face appeared to be rather a mess. Sir Guy swore he would take Roger back to Nottingham, though it was doubtful de Lacy would be much use for anything ever again.

"You know," I said to Guy as I mounted. "That was a courageous charge you made for your friend."

"Bloody stupid," Guy said, rubbing his neck. "You evil bastards have the strength of the devil."

"That we do."

We rode north, for Mansfield. The village of the giant they called Little John. The man who had taken Marian and Eva. The man who waited for me and my men to come to him.

I was going to cut off his head and I was going to drink from his severed neck. And I was going to do it before my men, not caring that the rumours would get back to the lords of the land.

For what I had said to Roger was true. I knew that once I had gone into the depths of Sherwood that there would be no going back for me. For years, I had denied it but I was not a knight like any other and I could keep up the lie no longer. After I killed William and destroyed his followers I would leave England forever.

13

HEART OF EDEN

"SURELY, THIS ENTIRE ABDUCTION WAS meant as a means of luring you into Sherwood?" Jocelyn said as we rode slowly in the darkness, his voice low. "All of us, in fact. Of killing all of us in a single attack. There must be a better way of approaching this problem."

We rode in almost complete darkness, finding our way down the path to Mansfield by feeling the overgrown hedgerows on either side of the road.

"I would have been in Sherwood a year ago if the archbishop had not kept me away," I said. "Him sending me away was for William's purposes. Taking Marian and Eva, I do not know what that could be other than a warning, or as a means of staying my hand should I corner him once more."

Jocelyn's voice grew louder. "That man you tortured told you explicitly that the ladies are bait on a hook."

"He was a fool and a liar," I said, whispering. Our horses were so close that our knees bashed together. "We can trust nothing that he said."

"You will believe anything so long as you think it leads to your vengeance."

"Our vengeance, yes," I said. "Yours and mine both."

"Even if it means risking Marian's life? And Eva's?" Jocelyn was as impassioned as he could be while keeping his voice down.

"William knows that by taking her, harming her, he will enrage you into attacking him," Jocelyn said. "And we are."

"If he was going to kill them, why not do it at the Priory? Or anywhere else and leave the bodies to be found? And why would their deaths enrage me? Marian is a dear girl and I know you are smitten with her but she is hardly anything to me. And Eva. She shares her bed with me but not her heart."

"Come now," Jocelyn said. "You care for that woman much more than that."

"Perhaps," I said, for of course I cared for her. "But William cannot know that."

"William knows you will come to rescue a lady in distress," Jocelyn said. "You said that even when you were a boy, you always loved the ballads where the knight rescues the lady. William knows that you came for me and Emma in Palestine. He is playing you like a harp, Richard. Both of us. We are riding directly to where he wants us to go."

"I do not say you are wrong," I said. "But what else can we do?"

"All I want," Jocelyn said. "Is to get Marian back. I do not care if she decides against marrying me. Who can blame her? Who can blame her when I have so little to offer for our future? But I must do this thing. And not because it is like living some blasted ballad or poem, do not say it is. I do not wish to be a tragic hero and I do not expect her to throw herself into my arms. But I do care for her. I do. Truly. And I will get her back. I will save her. No matter the cost."

Our men ahead slowed down and we reined in a little

"You know," I said. "I have been thinking about my own future."

"You do wish to marry Eva," he said. "I knew it."

"No," I said, even though I would rather have liked to do so. But she was better off without me. "Far from it."

"What future, then?" Jocelyn asked, shifting in his saddle.

"I must move on," I said. "After I kill William. And the archbishop. I shall have to go away. Take the cross, perhaps. And I was thinking that I would renounce my claim to Ashbury. You will get the place anyway, when I am dead, you are my heir and you have been since soon after you came to me."

"For God's sake," Jocelyn whispered. "Do not throw your future away for me."

"You are a good man," I said, for I knew he wanted Ashbury. "But unless I fall in battle, I will not die. Never, Jocelyn, do you not see? I will never age. How long will my servants put up with me? Leaving will be for the best, that much I have decided. And of course, Ashbury must go to you. Just promise me that you will take care of your sister. And please take care of the servants, the labourers, and the village. Or allow Emma to do it until you find her a good husband and then let Marian do it after she marries you."

Jocelyn grunted. "I pray we find her soon. Wait, what should I do about Tutbury Priory?" he asked.

"You may pull down the Priory, stone by stone," I said.

He chuckled. "You cannot mean to give me Ashbury, Richard," Jocelyn said quietly though he could not keep the excitement from his voice.

"I do. And I will," I said. "I have decided. You will have the wealth and position you need to get a good wife. The Regent knows you, he will use you well. You can get a knight or two of your own, take on a couple of squires, a page, a groom, a servant. Your very own shit-bucket carrier. Everything a country gentleman needs to live a full and proper life."

"Richard," he mumbled. "I do not know what to say."

"No need to say anything," I said. "Even just thinking about it has made me feel happy.

We will get the women back, kill William, I will go away and then everything will be right in the world."

Swein, ahead of us, held his horses on the side of the road until he was abreast of us, a dark shape against the darker background.

"Perhaps I can make a suggestion about how to attack the village of Mansfield, Sir Richard."

"Oh," Jocelyn said, his words full of his smile. "The peasant has been studying strategy."

"I have," Swein shot back. "Studying by observing William of Cassingham. Perhaps if you yourself had—"

"Enough," I said, tired. "What do you suggest, Swein?"

"You mean to ride into Mansfield at dawn, with all our forces surrounding the village and trap Little John and his men. But that way risks Marian's life. And Eva's. They can hold a knife to Marian's throat and we will be able to do nothing about it."

"You see another way?" I asked. Stratagems always intrigued me because I could never think of any by myself.

Swein's voice grew excited in the darkness. "Why not send in a single man, or perhaps a pair, disguised as beggars. Or monks? Or some other sort of travelling folk, perhaps a man selling pots. That way we can discover the lay of the land, the positions of the enemy and where the women are being held. Then we leave and relay said whereabouts back to you, my lord. That way, we could creep in tomorrow night, snatch the women and flee with them without notice. We can ride hard for Nottingham or some other place of safety. Lincoln, maybe. Hide the women with Anselm's father or some other great lord. Then we can go back for the Green Knight."

I waited for Jocelyn to pour scorn upon the suggestions, yet he did not.

"I commend you for your creativity, Swein," I said. "And your ideas might work against mortal men. But we are facing men who can see and hear and smell better than you. And these blood drinkers would see a stranger as a walking meal. A beggar or pot seller wandering into their village at dawn would be nothing more to them than a pleasing way to break their night's fast. And if we took the women and attempted to flee then they would catch us. A mortal man could outpace a horse over a day in a woodland such as this. These men could catch us before we got away from Sherwood."

Swein took a deep breath, ready to object and to argue for his ideas. I spoke over him as he began.

"Yet you make some good suggestions. You have a natural capacity for cunning and no doubt have a long future ahead of you as an outlaw. Let us push on. In order to do what must be done, we need to be at Mansfield before it is light. And dawn approaches."

I crept through the shadows between houses just as a rosy dawn grew in the east. I would have been quieter without my armour and I would have seen and heard better without my helm but I simply could not bring myself to go without either.

The village of Mansfield was quiet. Like Blidworth and Linby, the folk were clearly dead, enslaved, or terrified into silence and abject misery. The houses were quiet. The few fires, from the faint smell of the dry smoke, were burning low. There were no animals in the pens by the houses. There were few crops growing in the gardens. The middens still stank, of shit and rot, corpses and old blood.

Jocelyn and Swein had both argued that it should be them sneaking in alone. Or that I should take archers with me, at least one or two, who could watch my back while I stole back the women.

Once, months before, Jocelyn had accused me of being so arrogant that it bordered on madness. Confidence turns to arrogance when your view of yourself becomes warped beyond truth. It becomes madness when your view of the world itself is warped and that night, my madness had reached a new height. I told my men that I alone was strong enough to fight my way out if anything went wrong. I believed that no man, not even William's men, could stand against me. Had I not proved myself better than them at every turn? What a ludicrous notion.

My anger and my fear played their part in robbing me of my reason. My anger at William and his men for taking Eva and Marian paled in comparison to the anger I felt at myself for putting them at risk. My fear that they would be hurt was almost overwhelming. That fear was greater than I was willing to admit even to myself.

Secretly, I was also hoping that I could find and rescue both women by myself. It would be a way of redeeming myself to both of the women and to myself but I did not admit such vanity to my men, of course. So I browbeat their objections down and, like a mad fool, went into the village alone.

The top of the church caught the first dim light of the morning, the sandstone glowing softly as if catching the light from the air. The door was half bashed in, hanging awkwardly, like a broken tooth.

If Much had been telling the truth, that was where they were.

I picked my way carefully, slowly. Breathing lightly, still I could hear my own breath hot in my ears. Every step I took further into the centre of the place, the more I doubted that Marian and Eva could truly be held inside.

What did William want from me? What was I walking into? I realised that, whether riding into the village at daylight or sneaking through in the dark, I had been drawn into William's web once again. But how could I do anything different? What move could I make that would confound him?

But why did I even need to? I had been caught up in the schemes of Swein. That lad admired and aspired to cleverness. To stratagems and gambits.

I did not. I wanted the women back. William – or his man John – had them.

All I need do was kill any man who stood in my way.

I kicked down the wattle fence before me and strode into the village.

The black rectangle of the church door beckoned. I jogged up the steps and yanked open the broken door, which gave with a shriek of wood on wood, loud and jagged enough to wake the dead.

Inside was dark. It reeked of death. Of rotting flesh and blood that was fresh.

Muffled movement at the far end.

Ambushers or prisoners, either way, the makers of the noise had to be approached. I stepped forward and there came a cry, a stifled cry from that end.

The blackness at my feet was complete. My helm restricted my sight even further. I held my shield up and strode forward, sword point before me.

A woman's voice, her throat tight with terror, cried out.

"Help!"

She was at the far end of the church and I ran forward toward it.

And I tripped.

Like a blundering fool, like a child in a game, I tripped over a rope set for the purpose. It caught on my ankle and my momentum carried me forward and down.

I fell hard on my shield.

Then they were on me.

William's men sprung from the darkness on either side, with a weighted net and ropes at the ready. They struck blows on my back and my head with sticks and bludgeons and staves, over and over.

My sword was not in my hand when I swung it, so instead I swung my fists. I struck out with my feet, my elbows. But they were so many and I was struck about the head so often that their blows knocked me senseless.

I fought, of course. Though I was blinded and knew not which way was up, I wrestled and thrashed and heaved and struck down one after the other.

But the men set upon me were freshly fed with the living blood of the villagers. I was dragged out into the street.

A knife found its way to my throat. The cold iron nicked my skin, drawing blood and searched around under my jaw.

I was utterly certain my throat was to be cut. My final thoughts were wondering what my final thoughts were going to be, and thinking about how paltry those thoughts were. I wondered if I should instead think of my wife or her children, Jocelyn and Emma but I thought of how I had failed them all and failed the two women I had set out to rescue and I hoped that Swein, Anselm, and the men would get away.

But the knife instead sawed away at my chinstrap and my helm was twisted from my head. I blinked in the slight glare of the predawn sky.

There was a great giant of a man there before me. A head taller and twice as wide as I.

"He said you was a great knight," the huge man said. "He said you was to be feared. Never to be fought, not even a score of the sons of Adam could face you. But I know knights. You all want to save a lady from a dragon, don't you? Well, I'm the dragon. And you ain't saving no one, my lord."

With his giant's strength, made unnaturally strong by William's gift, he brought a cudgel down onto the back of my head.

* * *

When I awoke, I was on my back, on the cold ground.

My head was throbbing with every breath. It felt as though my skull was caved in at the back. A tender mass of broken bone shards and swollen skin.

There were men around me, voices, the stench of blood and death.

It was dark, still. But the sky above was pink with the morning and quickly turning to blue.

I was in chains.

They clanked as I raised my hands to feel my head only to find my hands bound to my body. My legs were likewise wrapped.

My mouth was stoppered with a rag tied tight.

"He lives," a man's voice said.

"Thank the Creator for that," another man said and I was kicked in the side of the head.

The pain shot through me. I ached all over and wondered if my arms and legs were broken. My sight was impaired in some way as the figures around me were blurred and smeared. I realised I had blood in my eyes but I could not move my hands up to wipe my face.

Still, I saw the big man move into view above me. He faced away from me, down the street and bellowed.

"You men out there. As I'm sure you can see, I have your master Richard of Ashbury in chains. Attack me or any of my men and I will slit his throat. I see a single arrow. I hear the twang of a single bow. I slit his throat. I see one of you following us, I slit his throat."

The big man, Little John the Bailiff, turned and mumbled to one of the other figures.

I guessed there were at least a dozen men around me and a few moved off toward the church.

Jocelyn would not give up on me, I thought, he would not back down. Neither would Anselm. They would keep their distance.

Swein and his archers, I did not know what they would do. Swein wanted revenge for the hurts he had suffered at the hands of the men about me, or their friends. Whether he would seek to avenge me when it was a lost cause, I could not guess.

But Jocelyn, surely, would attempt to save Marian and Eva, no matter if I were dead or alive.

Two women were dragged from the church. I could not see properly but both had heavy hoods tied down over their faces. They had been dressed in filthy old robes. The women whimpered under their hoods as they were brought to Little John.

I writhed and tried to sit up but the men guarding me struck me and a filthy old man sat upon my chest, a rusty dagger held to my throat.

"You want these women?" the giant shouted out. He glanced at me and grinned through his thick, black beard. "You want both these women, do you not?" He laughed. "You follow me and both of them will get this."

John grabbed the woman nearest to him and wrapped one mighty arm about her from behind. With his other hand, he stabbed a knife up into her throat and sawed back and forth.

Rolling over, I threw off the old man on my chest, his dagger slicing deep into my cheek, all the way through until it clashed against my teeth. But the other men pinned me down, held me on the ground and allowed me to watch the murder.

Blood gushed from beneath her hood. It poured out, soaking John's arm and the woman's robe. Her body sagged against him and he held her to him.

A great cry of anguish sounded from outside the village.

Jocelyn or Swein watching from afar, afraid that it was Marian rather than Eva. We always fear the worst, when those we love are concerned.

Little John shoved the body of the woman into the hands of his men, who gathered about her with two buckets. They between them held her upright, pulling her hooded head back so that the blood spurted into the buckets. When the pulse faltered, they picked her up and held her body so that the feet were higher than the head, draining as much as they could.

"Can we string her up, John?" one of the men said.

"No," John said, his voice like the falling of a tombstone. "We ride for Eden. Bring the body."

I was picked up by rough hands and heaved onto the back of a horse, face down and I was tied onto the beast.

The woman who yet lived was wrestled onto a waiting horse and slapped around until she ceased struggling and complied.

The body of the woman was tied onto another horse near me. As they tossed her on, the horse shied away and the body slipped. They grabbed it and shoved it back on top with a stream of curses. The hood fell away for a moment.

As the men and horses filed out of the village of Mansfield, with me along with them, I knew I had failed. The feeling was worse than any wound I had suffered.

But in any case, the woman who had been stabbed was not Eva.

And it was not Marian, either.

Little John had murdered some other woman, for my watching men's benefit. What it meant, I knew not. Perhaps Eva and Marian both lived. Or perhaps they were already dead.

It seemed I was being taken to William and to the place they called Eden.

I had imagined myself storming William's lair. In my fantasies, I had been sometimes alone, sometimes charging at the head of a mounted band or with archers' arrows flying past me to bury themselves into William's monsters.

Never had I expected to be dragged there in chains.

My wounds were bad. My skull pounded with every step of the horse.

To distract myself, I attempted to count Little John's men by the sounds of their voices and the smell of them. Not all of them spoke and they all stank of blood, so it was difficult but there was a score, at least. The horse I was tied to was a swaybacked old mare with mud splattered all over her coat and shit all around her hindquarters.

The sun rose to its midday peak above the green leaves overhead. My view was of the track beneath the horse, her mud-caked hooves and a short way in front or behind at the men who had captured me. All flowed past me in a flickering of dappled sunlight. A jay's blue wings flashed as it swooped through the dappled splashes of sunlight.

Soon, the woodland gave way to open fields and then a hard-packed track surface. I must have dozed for a while and was woken by the horse's hooves clattering on flat cobblestones. I peered about me, wincing from the wounds, remembering my failure.

Our procession had reached a stone pathway, the surface was large, irregular pebbles with flat tops embedded into a hard surface. What we called a pitched path. It was quite common in castle courtyards or the homes of the wealthy but was completely strange in the middle of the wild greenwood.

Looking ahead, I was shocked. The trees all around me had thinned and ahead was a high timber wall across the path with an open gateway in the centre. It was a hunting lodge. One of the few I knew were deep in Sherwood that the king could use as a place to stay while he hunted deer and boar.

The lodge was a rambling stone and timber complex that seemed to grow from the wild profusion of vines and scrambling plants climbing over the walls. The woodland around it had been cut back, coppiced and cleared of brushwood but still the trees were huge, gnarled and ancient.

The men around me were strangely silent, the only sounds were of hooves and leather shoes upon the stone pathway that took us through the gate and into the huge courtyard of the lodge.

Pillars of limestone, carved at the top and bottom supported a gateway in a thick timber wall that stood at least ten feet high. The outer face of the wall was plastered and painted with leaf patterns though it was crumbling everywhere. The wall seemed to extend a long way in both directions before turning to make an enormous square enclosure. The weathered limestone columns had turned green and were pitted from the climbing vines around them.

"You are honoured, little man. As you pass through these gates, you are leaving England. And you are entering Eden," Little John said from beside the old horse. I knew he was talking to me. "You will obey the law of this land or else I will have to punish you. I trust that you will behave yourself? Good, good."

Beyond the gateway, there was a massive open space, all of it paved with the solid pitched surface of flat cobbles. But filled with a great mass of living green plants. Servants tended to them. The cobbled surface had been pried up all over the place to reveal the soil beneath.

Ahead was the main hall, a long, low single storey building of stone on the bottom half and timber on the top.

Many of the other buildings were constructed similarly. To the right of the hall was a big storehouse or barn, roughly built but sturdy. Between the hall and the barn was a thick hedge of raspberry bushes, tangled and overgrown. Beyond the barn, I could just see the corner of what was clearly a huge stable.

The other side was obscured by the horse but I caught a glimpse of workshops. The walls of all the buildings were covered with vines and climbing plants.

It was tough to see far because everywhere was overflowing with plants, crops, bushes and trees.

John clapped me on the back with his meaty palm, hard enough to knock the wind from me and make my head swim.

Little John leaned down to speak into my ear, his hot breathing reeking of death. "We have a special place reserved just for you. Cost us a fair old bit of trouble, getting hold of all that iron. But then what my Green Lord wants, my Green Lord gets, right? Anyway, hope you like it, Sir Richard, as it's the last place you're ever going to live in. If you can call it living."

He laughed. A big, belly-shaking, rumbling laugh that scared birds from the trees above. His men laughed with him, the silent spell broken.

I was struck upon the back by clubs, wrestled from the horse, dumped onto the ground and struck again. Powerful hands dragged me to my feet. Blades were held to my throat and the men pushed me forward through the courtyard of the lodge complex.

I got a better look at the main building as they dragged me toward it. It was a squat hall built from the local sandstone with a timber and tile roof on top. Other buildings around the courtyard were a mix of timber and others stone.

The truly astonishing, peculiar thing was that beside and between all the structures was an abundance of green leaves. Overgrown hedges and sprawling young trees grew against every building. There were apple trees and wild raspberry bushes. Clumps of cereal crops were planted around lines of grape vines.

Before the front wall of the main hall was a wild garden of herbaceous plants and weeds. I recognised henbane, hemlock, monks' wood, foxglove, datura, and hellebore.

I could see little order to anything and the growth seemed overgrown and almost wild.

Throughout the enclosure, amongst the crops and herbs, were William's servants. Men, women, young and old. They were slumped like slaves, their faces pale and their eyes dark. They clutched hoes, rakes, and scythes to their chests, glancing up at us from under their eyebrows.

"Walk," William's men said and shoved me on through toward the hall. Little John strode before me, sending the slaves scurrying in panic.

They dragged me into the building, yanking open the door. Instead of a grand open space, it was a long corridor down the centre with doors along each side and a single door at the far end.

"Guess what we got in here, then?" Little John shouted. He stomped past the first pair of doors then banged on the ones after, hard enough to rattle the beams locking them shut. "These are the cattle pens. Our cattle are the folk of Sherwood, the outlaws, the villagers. You hear me in there? They serve us or they feed us. Don't you?"

I prayed that Marian or Eva would be there but saw neither. Surely, if they lived, William would have a special place for them.

Although, I recalled how William had rounded up the locals in Palestine and penned them in a single large room underground. A young Jocelyn and Emma had been flung in with the Saracens and forgotten about. They were the children of a Frankish noblewoman and yet for William they had no more value than any of the other Saracens that he and his men used for harvesting blood.

Palestine was a land of war, a land of Saracen heathens who the Pope had declared enemies of God and Christ, so in a way, William's scouring of that land made a perverse kind of sense, to himself at least.

That he could get away with the same thing in the heart of England, making slaves and cattle of good Christians, astonished me.

Through the door at the far end of the corridor, they pushed, dragged and beat me down a stairway into a deeper darkness. It went down, under the ground. There were caves everywhere in Sherwood. It was one of the ways outlaws escaped detection and found shelter in the greenwood. The place Little John called Eden was built on limestone and the caves beneath the buildings were either natural or had been hacked out.

The roughly carved spiralling steps led down and down further. The stairs bottomed out into a short corridor carved from the limestone bedrock and they pushed and beat me along it. Little John squeezed his bulk through the cramped space and at the end he threw open a heavy door. I was beaten down again then dragged inside, leaving a trail of blood on the floor behind me.

The final room, our destination, was long, wide, low and carved directly from the limestone bedrock. The space was lit with lamps and candles in alcoves cut into the walls. All around, those walls were carved with shapes of acorns and oak leaves and attempts at rich, leafy woodland canopy. The leaves were arranged so that here and there, the gaps between appeared as pairs of eyes.

The chamber was dominated by a central altar. The top was a solid piece of thick, dark oak, like some kind of giant table top. It sat atop four wide limestone pillars. The wide edges of the altar were carved into the shapes of bones and skulls, arranged in the shapes of writhing bodies. The skulls eyes had their mouths opened as if they were crying out or perhaps preparing to sink their crazed grins into living flesh. The limestone pillars supporting the central oak altar top were carved like bones. Both the wood and the stone were stained with dark red and brown.

Lines were carved into the stone floor, long parallel lines, leading from one side of the room to near the altar, where there was a bowl-shaped pit cut from the floor. They were discoloured with a dark residue.

On the far side of the room beyond the altar was a heavy door with iron bands reinforcing it, of the kind used on a treasury, strong room or dungeon.

And there was a cage. On my side of the room, near the door that I had been dragged in through. A strongly built, black iron cage with wooden pillars at each corner holding it in place. The side of the cage was open.

It had been prepared for me.

They cracked me on the head again and set about stripping me of my armour. They took my hauberk, coif and all my mail, punching me repeatedly to keep me disoriented and weakened. They took my gambeson and all my padding. While I was yet dazed they threw me into the small cage.

"Do you like this?" Little John said. He banged the bars above my head. "We had it made just for you."

I looked at my cage. The flat iron lengths made a cage about five and a half feet tall and a couple of feet wide and deep. I could only stand with my head bent low, the top of my hunched shoulders touched the top of the cage. My shoulders were almost touching the bars of either side.

Outside, on each long edge, the cage was fixed to the floor and ceiling by sturdy oak pillars.

"I hope that you do like it," Little John said. "Because you will never leave this cage." He laughed, phlegm spraying past his black beard.

"When I get out of here I shall smash your face into pulp," I said. It hurt just to speak.

Little John laughed but his eyes were shining pits. "Here is your prisoner, my lord," he shouted, sneering.

The massive door at the far end of the room, beyond the central table, crashed open. A massive force had flung it open from the other side.

William.

My brother, my enemy, the man I was sworn to kill. He strode from the room beyond, wiping the corners of his mouth with a rag. His black hair had grown long and he had a neatly trimmed beard. He wore a dark green tunic, a white shirt underneath. He looked in the prime of his life, had not aged a day since I had seen him last, in a cave in Palestine. I had crushed his chest with a blow that sent him crashing across the room and set the place ablaze. William had escaped, from the cave, from the Holy Land and from my life.

And there he was again, standing behind the central altar, tall and straight, broad-shouldered and slim. The master of his domain. While I was filthy, beaten and hunched in a cage.

"Brother," he said, tossing a rag to one side. "Finally, you are here. I am relieved. You do not know how tiring it has been without you."

I had been waiting to face William for so long. Yet in my imaginings, it had been me in the position of power and William cringing in chains.

I found that I did not know what to say.

"Come, Richard," William said. "You must accustom yourself to the feeling of defeat." His voice had a sonorous, resonant tone that washed over you like a wave. He fixed you with an intense stare when he spoke. His men were all staring at him, transfixed by his every word.

"Just kill me quickly, will you," I said, wincing. "I do not think I can stand to listen to more of your mad ravings."

Little John smashed his huge fist into the bars of my cage, rattling the thing. "Mind your own words," he said. "Show respect. Or it'll be me smashing your face into to a pulp, tough man."

"John," William said, calmly. "There is no need for threats."

"But he won't even need his face to give us his—" John started.

"Silence!" William roared.

My ears rang in the silence that followed.

William continued in a softer voice. "Richard, you look quite broken. Please, rest for now. I shall have blood brought to you so you may heal."

"I would rather you choke on it," I said, though I wanted it. "I will have no part of your murders."

"Murders?" William said, as if shocked I could suggest such a thing. "Who ever said anything about murders? The blood is from the living, freely given."

"Freely given?" I said. "From those slaves out there? Spare me your lies."

"There are no slaves here in Eden," William said, spreading his arms wide. "This is Paradise upon Earth, brother."

"You have killed and murdered across the land," I said. "Your men have slaughtered and enslaved whole villages. You poisoned the King of England, you mad fool. You have created a Hell upon the Earth. Just as you do everywhere you go." I took a shuddering breath. The back of my head, where John had cracked it, felt like it was made from porridge.

"I poisoned King John?" William said as if he was genuinely confused. "What on earth can you mean? It was the bloody flux, was it not?"

"You would know," I said, bitterly. "You, more than any man. The archbishop and you conspired. You poisoned King John or you sent a man to do it. I noticed your poisonous garden outside this place."

"Ah," he said, smiling. "Have you ever wondered why so many woodland plants are poisonous?"

"Wondered?" I said, not understanding the question. "God made it so."

William sighed, like a priest teaching me Latin. "Yes, Richard, but why?"

I was irritated. William had a way of twisting words and minds. Even mine. "You think you can know the mind of God?" I said.

"Of course," he spoke with sudden passion. "Why else would He create us in His image if not to know His mind? We must take back our rightful place, as lords over mankind."

"We?" I said.

"You and I are not made as are mortal men," William said. "God made us immortal, as was Adam in the Garden of Eden."

I had never paid much attention to the priests. "Adam was not immortal," I said.

"Of course he was," William said. "And how was Eve made? From Adam's body, just as we make more like us from taking from inside of ourselves."

"We use blood," I said, astonished by the way he twisted the word of God to match his own mad needs. "Not our ribs."

"It is a story meant to reveal truth," William said, lecturing me in that priestly tone. "The sons of Adam lived for hundreds of years. Clearly, you and I are from the same stock. Neither of us has aged a day. Not a day since God brought us back. Since then we have both suffered wounds that would kill even the strongest man. I have gouged chunks of flesh from my own body and watched it grow back together. I have consumed gallons of poison, chewed deadly leaves and walked away."

I wished I could tear him apart. "Which of those plants did you use to kill your king?"

William threw up his hands. "My king? Mine? I swore no allegiance to that fool. Why should he have remained king when he could not hold on to his kingdom? I could protect England far better than he ever could. And, in fact, I will protect it. I shall be the greatest king that England has ever known. Imagine it, Richard, a strong crown year after year, decade after decade. I will rule for centuries and England will be the greatest land in Christendom. I will make the Pope one of my men. Imagine what I can do with the Saracens."

I stared at him in disbelief. His eyes seemed to shine with the flicker of the candlelight, boring into me, searching me, and almost pleading with me to see what he was seeing in his future.

"You are mad," I said. "You will be a king? The King of England? Absurd. You mean to poison so many lords that the crown comes to you, is that it?"

"Hardly necessary. When I have built my army, with your blood, we will simply take the kingdom from the young Henry. Who can resist us?"

"The Marshal," I said. "Longspear, Ranulf of Chester."

"Oh, Richard," William said. "You have so much to learn. The Marshal is old and mortal. His alliances will fall when he does. I have many men in place, helping things along."

"Men like the Archbishop of York," I said. "I know you are working together."

William laughed. "Together? The fat fool has had his uses, though he has been misbehaving. Keeping you away from me, Richard. I think he is fond of you."

"What in God's name are you talking about?" I said.

William pursed his lips, looked around the room and pointedly ignored my question. "This is a sacred oak grove, Richard. An ancient place. A holy place."

"We are underground," I said, leaning back in my cage. What could I do but listen to his madness? "This is no grove."

"The roots of the oak are its strength," he said, indicating the sinewy carvings on the walls. "And in the oak is the strength of our faith."

"Madness," I said. "Just madness." There was blood in my mouth. I spat it out.

"Did you know that the Tree of Knowledge was the oak? Eve's knowledge was that from death comes life. She knew why the tree bore the fruit. So that it would live again, after death, just as you and I do, Richard. We are the children of Adam. You and I alone. We are the inheritors of God's first creation."

"You and I are?" I said. "Is that why you freely murder everyone else?"

William nodded. "Those that take on our blood after losing their own become sons of Adam also."

"Your man Much the Miller told me. As did Tuck. Before I killed them, as I killed so many of your precious sons of Adam. And when I get out of this cage I will kill everyone else here. Then I will kill you."

He stared at me for a long moment.

Then he laughed.

William ran his fingers over the surface of the thick oak top to the central table before him. It was a huge thing, dark and solid as iron, three inches thick. Only God knew where he had got such a thing but it was as thick as a castle gate.

"Here is the altar where we both reap and sow our gift of blood," he said, his voice resonating and echoing from the walls. "Sin is poured out here at the Altar of Oak and the blood of Adam is given in its place."

"Come closer," I said. "Come and open these bars and I will drink yours again. Then you shall reap what evil you have sowed."

"Oh?" William started as if I had wounded his heart. "And what evil have I sowed?"

I laughed in disbelief. "King John, for one."

William shrugged. "What is a mortal man compared to us, Richard? We are the inheritors of Adam's gift. God has renewed His gift, through us. Only, you refuse to recognise the truth. You persist in your attempts to live as a knight and a lord of your pathetic manor. Why is your ambition so small? You could join me and together we could take a kingdom and remake the Garden upon the earth. And yet you never will. So this is how I must use you. In a cage. I will use you. Use your blood. I pray that you never forget that you brought this on yourself."

I stared at him, feeling tired. Tired and close to defeated. "You may believe that nonsense. Use me? Never. I will not allow it."

William tilted his head. "You do look weak. You have not been drinking enough blood, have you, Richard. Enough for now. You are tired. So rest, drink as much blood as you can stomach. It is important that you are healed and that you stay strong. I will have it brought to you. See to it, will you, John?"

William turned to leave.

"My lord," Little John said, taking a hesitant step forward. "I must speak to you privately."

William turned back. "You may speak in front of my little brother," William said. "After all, what can he do from in there?"

John nodded his huge skull. "His men followed us through the greenwood."

A thrill surged through me at his words. Of course, my men would not abandon me. Thank God for Jocelyn.

"So?" William said.

"Well," John replied. "It is just that they are out there right now, my lord, keeping watch on us."

"And what exactly do you think they can do to us?" William asked, laughing. "Do you believe them to be a threat?"

"There are a dozen or more. A score, perhaps. Who knows what mischief they could get up to? They could take one of my men on the road. Or they could go and tell the location of Eden."

"Tell?" William asked, glancing at my cage as if inviting me to join in mocking John's ignorance. "Who would they tell?"

"Don't know," John shrugged, looking down. "The Marshal?"

William sneered. "That old man is not long for this world," he said. "But I know how much you love to kill, John, dear boy. Go and murder Richard's men. Kill all you like, drink them up. If you feel like bringing back prisoners then we can always use more soldiers or cattle for our pens."

John nodded and turned to leave, as did William, in the opposite direction.

I knew Jocelyn and Anselm, Swein and his archers were fine fighters. But they had no hope against men imbued with William's blood.

My men were as good as dead.

"William, wait," I shouted, heaving on the bars, ignoring the pain from my bruised limbs. "What is the meaning of all this? Why not just kill me now? Do you mean to torture me? Why am I here?"

William turned back, sighing as though I greatly inconvenienced him.

"Why are you so dense, Richard? How can you be so quick of limb but slow of mind? I am tired,' William said. "I am so tired of giving up my blood to make more of my faithful men. But your blood is the same as mine. We grew from the same seed and our blood is the stuff of eternal life. Now I finally have you. You were meant to come last year. I sent a bunch of bumbling incompetents right to your door so that would you find your way to me. And then our friend Archbishop Hugh stuck his fat face in between us and sent you far away. He knew I wanted you. He was trying to strong-arm me, can you imagine? I will show him soon enough."

I stared at him. "I had forgotten that you were always mad. Your words are nonsense. Forget I asked."

William shook his head. "I have taken one of Hugh's bastard daughters. His favourite, by all accounts. But you know the woman I mean, do you not, Richard? You came running here for her, just as her father will. It took a long time but praise God, you have returned to me. Now I can extract all the blood I want from you and use it to build my army. We will pour good, clean blood down your throat by day and by night we shall milk you dry, brother. Rejoice, for from your lifeblood, from your gift, you will make an army the likes of which the world has never known. We will take the North, we will take the boy king and then his kingdom. Now, is that clear enough? Ah, but I get ahead of myself. Please, sit, rest. I will have your food and blood brought in. See to it, won't you, John?"

William nodded, strode back through his heavy, iron-bound door and slammed it shut behind him.

Before he did so, he called into the dark chamber beyond.

"A thousand apologies. Now, where were we, Lady Marian?"

14

TREE OF KNOWLEDGE

MY CAGE WAS STRONGER THAN I. The bars were flattened iron strips, half an inch thick. They crisscrossed each other so close that they formed squares barely wider than my fist. Where they crossed, they were riveted together.

As soon as I was alone, I gripped every piece of iron in that cage in turn, pushed, heaved, and sweated trying to bend it. I braced my shoulders against one side and pushed at the other with my arms, feet, knees.

The small door was the most obvious weak point. But the cunning smiths had reinforced that section. The hinges were hidden behind plates on the outside of the bars. The door overlapped the bars perfectly and the bolts securing it ran the whole depth and width of the cage where they were locked into the stone floor and the timbers on either side.

Nothing would budge.

All I managed was to tear off a couple of the more important fingernails and leave my shoulders and hands bruised.

I sat. The strips of bars on the bottom fitted into recessed, carved sections in the stone floor.

There were other lines carved into the stone, lines that ran from the cage floor and out into the cave, meeting in a carved depression by the table in the centre.

I wondered what they had been thinking of constructing when those lines hard been carved into the stone. Perhaps, I thought, they had intended a larger cage or one with a triangular point stretching in front but I could not conceive why they would do such a thing.

As I have mentioned before, I have no gift for creative thinking, nor logic neither.

All I really noticed was that the base of my cage was comfortable and I settled into it.

Little John said the thing had been made especially for me. I supposed I should have felt honoured to require such a thoroughly impregnable gaol.

I strained to hear of any noise coming from the room beyond, where William had called out to Marian. Had he been making a jest, in order to wound me? If Marian was in there, where was Eva?

William had said he held her so that her father would come to save her. But why would he? She had betrayed him by fleeing with me and staying by my side and in my bed. Surely, he would not come to save her.

Unless, she had never betrayed him at all. Perhaps Jocelyn had been correct. Perhaps Eva had always been spying on me for the archbishop, sending to him messages of my whereabouts and intentions.

But I could make no sense of it.

I reflected upon my own stupidity for some time. I considered carefully how inadequate was my ability for planning. I ruminated on the sour knowledge that I had only ever succeeded in ventures requiring a sword and shield and an enemy standing directly before me.

Jocelyn was not a complicated man but I was sure even he could outwit me. Anselm came from the best stock yet retained a perplexing innocence, even in the face of brutality and the knowledge that I was an unnatural, blood-drinking fiend. The lad was a fine squire but his trusting nature meant that a commoner like Swein could bend Anselm's ear on the supposed plight of the common man and the lad's heart would bleed for the imagined suffering. And even such a credulous fool as he was a wiser man than I.

And Swein. A man of no more than eighteen years, who had received no education, no training of any sort other than the bow and probably the plough until a year before. Even a man such as he possessed greater skill at reading men's intentions that did I, a lord over twice his age, with decades of fighting experience.

There was no way out for me. If they ever opened the cage door, I could attempt to fight my way out and I would. But I had no illusions they would be taking chances with me.

Upon stripping my armour and weapons, they had also removed every sharp object from about my person, so puncturing a large vein and bleeding my precious blood everywhere was out of the question. I was relieved because I had no desire to take my own life. I wanted to live. I still wanted to kill William. It was the only thing I had left.

I rubbed my wrist against the edge of the bar in front of me. Perhaps I could grind the skin away until I bled enough that they would remove me from the cage and then I would fight my way free. But the edges of the flattened bars had been forged or hammered or ground smooth.

Defeated once again, I slept.

When I woke, it was to the sight and feel of sword blades held against my throat. The blades had been eased between the bars by three of William's men, their faces leering down at me.

"What are you doing?" I asked, holding perfectly still.

"Don't you try nothing," one said, in an almost incomprehensible northern dialect. He was probably Cumbrian, which was barely one step up from a Scotchman.

"What could I possibly try?" I asked, astonished that they would send in three men who were clearly slower and dimmer than even I was.

"We know you're a tricky one, lord," one of the others said, a young lad no more than fourteen.

The third man, older, nudged him, hissing. "You don't got to call no one lord in Eden, Nobby."

"Oh, right you are, Sid."

The first man, their leader, cleared his throat to gain the upper hand. "You hold still while we feed you, right?" He nodded at the boy, Nobby, who withdrew his sword and bent away behind myself and came back holding a basket.

"Here you go, lord," Nobby said.

"He can't see it," Sid said. "And he ain't no lord, not no more."

Nobby giggled.

"So," I said. "You're the mighty soldiers of your lord William's great army, are you?"

Nobby grinned.

"We are," Sid said. "Or we will be when we're turned into sons of Adam."

"He's making mock," the first man, the Cumbrian said. "You might be a lord and all. But Big John said you can't talk to us like that."

He pressed the point of his blade against my Adam's apple. I pushed my head against the bars and twisted away but I had nowhere to go and he drew blood. There was a look in his eye that suggested an inability to control himself.

I grabbed his blade with both hands and pushed up as hard as I could.

The blade bent where it met the underside of the bar. It bent a long way and then snapped, clattering to the floor of my cage. I swept it up, holding the half-blade in my bare hand.

I shoved it through bars of the cage and on through the Cumbrian's neck before he could jerk away.

Sid swung his own sword from out and sent my broken blade crashing down, out of reach beyond my cage.

We all watched as the Cumbrian held his hands to his throat, that familiar confused expression on his face as the hot blood flowed out through his fingers. The smell filled the air along with the cries of his fellow.

"What are you doing?" William was out of his room, charging over to my cage around the central altar. "What in the name of God are you cretins doing?"

"John asked us to feed the prisoner," Sid said. "Little John, so it was. He said to keep the lord under our sword points while we gave him his food. But he done broke Tom's sword and shoved it up him."

"So I see." William looked at me as if I was a misbehaving child. "Well, get a bucket under him before we lose it all in the floor. Tom, can you hear me, Tom? Do not look so worried. Once you die, you shall finally be one of us. You should rejoice. Look at me, Tom, you will die and then you will live forever. Let yourself go, brother."

"Why save his life?" I said, standing as best I could in my cage. "Let the fool die. He is incompetent. Is this the sort of man you wish serving you? He is not worthy of my blood."

The giant, Little John lumbered in, ducking under the lumpy, rock-hewn ceiling.

"Incompetent?" William said. "He is a little too keen for my favour but that is no bad thing. You were loyal, Tom, were you not? Why would you kill this man, Richard?" William eased the man to the floor as he spoke. Tom yet held his hands to his throat, though the life in his eyes was fading. "He was bringing you food. He was helping you. That is it, Tom, let yourself die, there's a good man. Do you know, Richard, why you killed him?"

"He is your sworn man," I said. "That is enough."

"You killed him because you are a murderer," William said. "Just as much as I am. Only, I am also a creator. I am building a new world, a new Eden. Without me, all you can do is destroy. I am helping you."

"You are building a manor in the king's wood," I said. "And filling it with slaves. Do not delude yourself that you are doing anything great."

"Have you not seen our Eden?" William said, indicating the world above us. "I have made my own Garden, as described in the Book of Genesis. The Lord God made all kinds of trees grow out of the ground. Trees that were pleasing to the eye and good for food. In the middle of the garden were the tree of life and the tree of the knowledge of good and evil. Well, we have trees aplenty but the tree of life is here, it is our blood. The tree of knowledge is that which we grow in ourselves."

"This is no Eden," I said. "This is a hunting lodge, belonging to some baron that you have ousted. Growing crops, all crammed inside the gates, does not make an Eden."

"There were the four rivers of Eden and we have our own four around our Eden here. We have our Pishon, Gihon, our Tigris, and Euphrates."

"You mean the rivers of Sherwood?" I asked. "You have utterly lost your mind."

"No," William said. "It is you who has failed to grasp what we can make of this place. This wild place, where those from the world of men fear to enter. We who dwell here live as Adam did in the Garden. Without sin, without death, without fear."

"Without sin? All that you do here is sin."

William shook his head. "John, draw us plenty of blood out of Richard. This will be as perfect a time as any to do this."

"To do what?" I asked but I knew, really.

"Lash Tom to the altar," William commanded and the men that crowded the small room lifted up and then eased the dying form of Tom the Cumbrian onto the table in the centre of the room.

Little John leaned his face against my cage. "I don't suppose you will be going to give up your blood willingly, this first time?" His voice rumbled low, from deep within his guts.

"Try to take it," I warned him. "Open my cage and you shall see what happens."

"Ah," Little John said. "I do so enjoy fighting talk." He laughed and grabbed a short spear from one of his men. "Come on lads, time to earn your keep again."

"I will shove those spears up your arses," I said, as the men with spears manoeuvred themselves about my cage. My heart raced, watching the iron spearheads catching the lamplight.

They thrust through the bars from all angles. There was little I could do to stop them though I made as good a fight of it as I could. It was not a matter of will, or strength or speed. I was so very limited by the manner of my confinement. It was, indeed, a matter of geometry.

With my palm, I broke the shaft of the first spear that lanced through toward my chest. But I was stabbed in the back.

I pinned another spear against the bars with my shoulder but another gouged out a lump from my thigh.

I was speared through the shoulder, the legs. Blades sliced my scalp and my chest.

The pain was white fire, slashing through my flesh. I was cut a dozen times. I growled, shouted, and slammed against the bars, swearing I would kill them all.

They laughed and stabbed me again.

"Enough," William's voice crashed over their jeering. "We have enough."

They stepped away, clapping each other on the back for their good work. I hunched on all fours in the bottom of my cage, watching the blood drip from the wounds of my head. The drops splashed down between my hands into the shallow pool of blood under me, dark red on sandstone and black iron. My breath would only come with my chest juddering, betraying the weakness and despair I felt.

The blood pooling under me ran into the carved lines in the floor. The blood collected in them, like drainage ditches or gutters, then rolled, and flowed through the bars out into the cavern.

Of course, that was what they were. Channels, catching the blood and funnelling it away from me and into a bowl-shaped depression carved low into the floor by the table.

Upon the table Tom, the Cumbrian lay dead, or as close to it as made no difference. His throat was destroyed and the skin of his face was white as chalk. Tom did move, his fingers flexing and his mouth gaping open and closed like a fish slowly suffocating upon the riverbank. The huge, solid oak table was drenched with his blood.

William himself kneeled by the pool that collected my own and scooped out a cupful. The cup he used was wooden, ornately carved with intertwining oak and vine leaves, big enough to hold a pint or more.

"Behold," William said to me, holding the cup up. He moved to the other side of the table. "Hold him," William said to his men. "We must move quickly while he retains the strength to drink."

William held up the back of Tom's head and gently poured the blood into Tom's mouth.

The Cumbrian coughed and blood – my blood – sprayed out of his mouth but William continued pouring, holding Tom's head. Other men held him down and ropes wrapped around him at chest, hip and knee. Still, Tom writhed and still William poured it in, his face as rapturously proud as a mother spooning porridge into her baby's mouth.

"Dear God of Eden," William said, his sonorous, echoing off the carved stone walls. "The God of the Green. The God of the oak and the vine. The God of the rivers and the earth. Take this acolyte upon your holy altar and find him worthy of your gift. The Oaken Altar, carved from the Tree of Knowledge, is ready to accept this sacrifice. This man has given his essence and poured out his sin here at the Altar of Oak in the place of the blood. The sacrifice of his life and his blood is offered up to you, freely. We pray to you, the God of the Green, that you sanctify his sacrifice with the gift of eternal life so we may welcome this man who is called Tom into our brotherhood and into our immortal band as a son of Adam."

When all was gone, Tom fell back, twisting in his bindings.

William peered at Tom and then pointed at me. "We must have more blood," he said.

For a long moment, I was afraid they would slash me open further. But my blood had not stopped flowing. My shirt was drenched with it. It ran down my arms and down my legs, into the channels and the bowl by the table was filling up.

Twice more, William poured a pint of my blood into Tom until finally, William was satisfied. He stepped back, wiping his bloodied hands on his bloodied tunic.

"That should do it," he said. "Now, we wait."

I looked up across the room, holding myself still so my wounds would not gape open and further. My breathing was loud in the small space. My head ached. I had a raging thirst.

"That was not such a bad thing, was it, Richard?" William said. "You do look quite a mess. I shall have my men bring you water and so on. See to it, John. And now, Richard, you will watch the magic that our blood works. Our blood, with its power to bring life to the dead. To raise them up to be stronger, faster, all but invincible. And immortal."

"You make them like us," I said, my voice weak, for I knew from Tuck some of what was done.

It struck me, then, how what I had inflicted on Tuck and Sir Geoffrey—the rapist Frenchman who had been my prisoner in the Weald—was in some way being revisited upon me. It was God's punishment for my crimes. A man who injures his countryman, as he has done, so shall it be done upon him. Fracture for fracture, eye for an eye, blood for blood. It was the Lord's justice but I had brought it down upon myself.

"I make them almost like us, brother, almost," William said, a small smile in the corner of his mouth. "Our blood fills up their veins, once their own are emptied. They will not age, it is true, if they ever wake from their slumber. Sadly, they must then consume blood themselves or else they will die. One day, I shall discover a means of freeing them from such bonds. But until then, we must feed every man with blood every other day, or he begins to lose his strength. In a week or so, he will die. That is why we must keep these people in the pens above. We have tried the blood of pigs and cows and sheep and goat but nothing works, not fully. Human blood. It must be. So to build my army I must build my feedstock. A man slaughtered and drained will provide seven or eight pints but he can do so only once. From a living man, we can draw off a couple of pints every other day. It is a wonderful system. One blood slave can feed one of my men, day after day. Is it not wonderful? Do you see what we can do here? What we can do to all England? We have no limit on what we can accomplish. But it all starts here, in Eden. So you shall heal and grow strong and then we shall speak again."

William nodded, smirked and strode back through into his chamber beyond and slammed the heavy door shut behind him.

They brought me water, wine and cloth to wipe some of the blood from myself. I took it all without fighting, for I needed it.

"Here," John said, thrusting another cup through the bars.

I took it without thinking, such was my thirst, and threw it down my throat. I gagged.

"This is blood," I said, stupidly, though I had still swallowed what I had in my mouth. From one of your faithful servants?"

"Do you wish to heal your wounds or do you not?" Little John said, that smirk across his lumpy great face.

He was quite right. William knew me well, even then when we were so young.

I drank the whole thing. It was quite beautiful. That thick liquid, sliding down my throat. When it hit my stomach, the ache was like the longing for a lost love. The warmth spread through my body, caressing me from inside, glowing and tender.

My flesh drew together, the bleeding stopped. I sighed and leaned back against my bars, holding the empty cup to my chest.

"Enjoy that, did you?" Little John said, his grinning head up near the stone ceiling. "Lovely stuff that, ain't it. Funny, you wouldn't think a scrawny bitch like that would taste so sweet. That's right. That was your Eva's blood you just drank." He laughed so hard his whole body shook, his great barrel chest sounding like a bell.

My head snapped up. My sight burned with clarity. Every filthy pore on his face was as clear as a mountain stream. The sweat on his brow, the lines around his eyes, each of the night-black hairs of his beard.

"Don't worry," Little John said, his lips wet and sneering. "We ain't killed her yet. We ain't done nothing to her but drained her of a little blood. Our lord don't like us fiddling with women. And anyway, she scared the lads off from raping her after what she done to poor Alf. See, we need her alive and whole, right? We need her to make sure her old dad comes here to rescue—"

I threw the cup at his face. I could not extend my arm and I had to fling it through the square space between the bars but I had a belly full of blood and my eye and hand worked in perfect harmony.

The wooden cup flew like an arrow, at the perfect angle, and cracked him on the bridge of his nose.

Little John screamed like a girl, throwing his head back and his hands up to his face. Blood streamed from his nostrils and his eyes watered.

I laughed so hard that I thought the wounds in my head would open up again.

"You will pay for that," John said, his voice nasal and swallowing his blood as he spoke.

"No, your bitch will pay for that. You hear me, you lord's bastard, your precious woman is going to pay the price for that."

"My precious woman?" I said, still laughing. "Is that truly what you think?" And I laughed harder though my heart ached.

John kicked the bars of my cage, his huge strength rattling the thing in its timber frame.

"You don't fool me," John said, blinking through his tears and the bars above my head.

"I would wager there is little that does not fool you, John the Bailiff," I said. "You are as thick as two short planks. Is your great head no more than solid skull all the way through?"

He roared and kicked my cage again. The iron bars shook and shifted before settling back.

I wished to rile the monster further, hoping that he would inadvertently break my cage loose from its moorings. Instead, his fellow men drew him off, muttering about disturbing their lord and glancing at William's door.

"You will bleed and bleed," John said, his huge voice lowered to a rumble. "You will bleed for days and months and years and we will make an army from your blood. You will be in here when England falls. You will be in here when Ashbury burns to the ground. You will be in that cage until you are mad with grief and weak as a woman. You are nothing now, not a lord, not a knight. You are cattle."

His men drew him away while John sneered down at me. Then they were gone.

All of them, they left me alone in that underground chamber with no one to watch over me and no one to watch over the other body. Tied to the table was their comrade, Tom the Cumbrian, covered in blood. His own was mostly outside his body, yet he had a belly full of mine working inside him.

The candles guttered and the room grew darker. The first thrill of the blood faded away and I sat and observed the body of the brute called Tom, wondering if he would ever awake and what he would be when he did.

William's followers were a mix between his monsters, changed forever, and those who were not. No doubt, William would feed those who were not changed forever with his own blood when he wanted them to be strong for a short time. Perhaps he fed them from his own veins, on every Sabbath, just as he had decades before in the hills of Palestine.

I did not know how many of each type of follower William had in the lodge he named Eden but there were enough. With the group that had taken me in the village, the men who guarded the wall as I was brought in and the other faces I had seen in the overgrown courtyard and grounds, I would guess two or three dozen. Thirty or even fifty men, all brutes, some of whom were possessed of strength similar to mine. Some had been soldiers.

I prayed that Jocelyn would flee Sherwood, find William Marshal, the Regent, and beg him for a force large enough to take Eden.

But Jocelyn was not a man to back down from a fight. Not when the woman he wanted to marry was in danger.

Of course, Jocelyn would be certain of gaining victory. He was convinced that the moral rightness of a man's character would endear him to God. Surely, a knight on a mission of such importance would receive God's strength.

But then, Jocelyn was never very bright.

Just as I knew that he was sure to make the attempt, I also know an assault on Eden was doomed to fail.

Sure enough, as I slept curled in the bottom of my cage, he and the rest of my men hatched a plan. A plan destined to end in disaster and death.

"Tom? Tom?"

I woke. Some time had passed but whether it was day or night, I had no idea. Without sunlight, the measure of time is almost impossible. The candles had guttered but William stood on the far side of his altar table, leaning over the body of Tom.

Little John stood by William, holding up a lantern. Other men shuffled around the edges of the ornately carved room.

I had slept heavily and I ached from the prolonged confinement of my limbs. My back cracked as I stirred.

William patted Tom's face.

"He is dead," William said. "The true death. The final death. My brother's blood did not work."

All eyes in that cavern turned to me.

I yawned. "Good morning, my dear friends," I said. "Which of you shall I kill today?"

The men did not like that and they stirred into anger.

"Perhaps," Little John said, his rumbling voice hesitant. "Perhaps, my lord, his blood is not like yours after all."

"Perhaps," William allowed, his head tilted to one side. "But look at him. That man in that cage is fifty years old, thereabouts. Is that not proof enough of his blood's potency."

"I need a piss," I said.

"Could it be," John said. "That your blood can change another man, my lord, but Richard's does not?"

William appeared thoughtful. "No," he said. "It is the same blood. Our father's blood. This time, it simply did not take. It has happened to me too, has it not?"

"It could be that he lacks the will to put his magic into the blood," John suggested. "You, my lord, you wish us to be changed. And so we are changed. Our base bodies are transformed into the bodies of the sons of Adam, through your will. And that man in the cage does not possess that same will."

William pursed his lips. "You could be correct," he said. "But all we can do is try again. Get this lump of flesh off my holy altar. Cut him up and feed him to the blood slaves."

"But—" John started.

"Bring my brother food and ale," William said, glaring at John. "And blood. Then we will try his blood on another potential."

William went into his chamber opposite my cage. John and most of the men left by the other door, carrying the body.

"I need a piss," I shouted.

One of William's minions jammed a bucket against the outside of my cage.

"Put it inside," I said to the men. "I will stand as far back from the door as I can, I swear. I swear upon God's bones. Upon the Christ's Holy balls, you pathetic little bastards."

They decided to not believe me so I pissed through the bars. But they did bring me bread and pork and ale and a cup of some poor soul's blood. I devoured it all, praying for the chance to use the strength I would regain.

And then they dragged in Eva.

Rope bound her at the wrist. Her face badly bruised. Both eyes black and her nose broken. She wore no more than her shirt, black with filth and brown with blood. She shivered and when her eyes met mine they were full of a cold fury.

Little John yanked her to behind William's altar and held her there. William and John loomed over Eva though she was not a short woman.

"Shall we try this again, Richard?" William said. "It is my belief that you will try harder to keep this woman alive than you did poor young Tom, who you had already murdered."

"I am sorry," I said to Eva, my face pressed to my bars. "I am sorry that I allowed you be caught up in this."

Her eyes glared from her swollen face but she did not speak.

"You seem to believe very strongly in your importance, Richard," William said. "But I would have taken her anyway, even if you had not been swyving her."

William looked across to Little John.

"Now, my lord?" Little John asked, grinning.

"Indeed," William said, glancing to me. "Bring in our latest guest. We would not wish him to miss this."

There was a commotion in the hallway outside the room, coming from behind my cage. Raised voices, stomping feet.

The Archbishop of York strode in. Huge, angry, dressed in his colourful finery as a lord, not an archbishop. His massive belly snug under a blue coat.

Already he was roaring at William to release Eva.

"You fiend," the archbishop shouted. "You black-hearted monster. How dare you do this to me? To me? You summon me as if I am your servant. My men have been seized at the gate and taken away by your damned brutes. How dare you—" He froze. "Eva? Is that my Eva? What is happening here? Good God Almighty, you release her you little shit.

"Ah, Hugh," William clapped his hands together. "I am so glad you could join us."

"You fool," the archbishop said. "You do not know what you have done. Release my girl, right now. And then we shall speak."

"But of course," William said.

He cut Eva's throat.

William was so quick that even I barely saw it. He drew his dagger and slashed through one of the veins on her neck, beside her windpipe.

Eva clapped her bound hands to her neck. Blood welled through her fingers. Her knees buckled but William held her up, grinning at me.

I yelled and rattled the bars. "I will gut you," I shouted. "I will murder every one of your brothers. I will burn Eden to the ground. You will burn in the eternal fires of Hell."

Archbishop Hugh, himself one of William's spawn, moved almost as quickly as William had. But Little John was there to stop him, charging from beside the altar to intercept. John was even taller, even wider than the archbishop was and he grappled the older man until more of William's men could pin him in place. They held the big lord back while he roared and strained to free himself, his eyes bulging and veins standing out on his temples.

Eva stared at me in accusation. Her eyes filled with rage, sadness, and terror, her mouth working as she fought for breath, fought for life.

"Now," William shouted over us. "Richard, perhaps you would be willing to honour this woman with the gift of your blood? We can cut you open again, or you can volunteer your blood freely?"

"Give me a knife," I said, not caring that he was forcing my compliance and that I was giving it to him.

One of William's men was waiting by my cage with a short, slim dagger. Two more of the men, one on either side, pushed their spears through my bars and held them near to my throat.

I sliced the knife through my wrist. It was sharp as a razor and, in my own keenness, I cut too deep.

Blood gushed out in a spurt. I had shed so much blood already in my life but the sight of it made me nauseated. I held my wrist to the channels beneath me. The blood pulsed, pulsed and covered my hand and filled the stone.

"What a good brother you are," William announced. "I very much hope your blood works on this woman. If it does not then I will have no use for you. Perhaps I will keep you for myself, simply to drink from you. Perhaps I will feed you to the pigs."

"It will work," I said to Eva. "Drink from me and live." More of my blood pumped from my wound.

Her knees buckled and she fell. Already her shirt was soaked, glistening and slick from neck to knee. William allowed her to drop to her knees and held her there with the fingers of one hand twisted through her hair.

"No," Eva whispered. William had cut one vein but not her windpipe but I saw, rather than heard her speak the words. "No, please."

"You will die if you do not," I said.

"Eva," the archbishop said, fear and compassion in his voice. "My dear. You will drink and you will become one of us. It is not so bad. Trust me, my dear, it is better than a mortal life."

William's men still held the lord, spears and daggers at the ready. Little John standing at his side.

"Actually," William said, as lightly as if he were discussion the weather. "I have never made a woman before. I am far from certain that she will survive the giving of the gift. Woman is the reason it was taken from mankind in the first instance. We shall discover God's will in her death or her rebirth."

"She will survive," her father said, eyes fixed on her blood as it soaked her shirt.

"Indeed, you will, my dear girl," William said, clapping her on her shoulder. "Listen to your dear old father. Your life with us will not be so bad. You will never carry a child but from what I hear that would not suit a warrior such as yourself. Did you know, Hugh, that she killed three of Little John's men when they took her and the Lady Marian from Tutbury Priory? Three. This woman."

"And she cut Alf's stones off," John said, grinning.

"Indeed she did," William said, smiling down at her. "Their first night as our guests, a couple of the acolytes could not control themselves and let themselves into the ladies' quarters. Your magnificent daughter, Hugh, she took Alf's knife and castrated him. John had to drain the screaming fool to shut him up. Ah, what a brother you will make, girl. Someone get a pail and collect this precious stuff before it has all leaked from her."

While he spoke, I squeezed the blood from my wrist. It filled the channels and flowed down to the bowl.

Eva slumped forward. William allowed her to fall flat onto her face but his men whipped the blood bucket away before she knocked it over. Her head cracked into the stone floor and she lay still, dazed, weak. Dying.

William's men lifted her body and stretched her out upon the table. She was drenched with blood. They bound her to the top at knee, hip and across her chest.

Little John filled the wooden cup with my blood and passed it William, who lifted it over his head.

"Dear God of Eden," William began, his voice filling the crowded space, the echoes coming close, one upon the other. "The God of the Green. The God of the oak and the vine. The God of the rivers and the earth."

"Just get on with it," the archbishop said. "Spare us your sacrilegious, unholy nonsense."

William's men hissed at the archbishop's contempt for their practices though they were absurd and confused and bordering on pagan. Nothing at all like the holy word of God.

Little John lifted Eva's head and William poured the cup of my blood into her mouth. She coughed and writhed and I was sure she was drowning but William had judged the timing correctly. Eva gulped down most of the first cup and the second.

"Now we wait," William announced. "It is in the hands of the God of the Green."

"If she dies," the archbishop said. "I will have you killed." The big lord turned to me.

"And you will die too, you thoughtless great oaf."

"I tried to keep her safe," I said, objecting out of reflex though I knew I had failed miserably.

"I was keeping her safe," the man said. "I was keeping her safe by sending her with you. Do you not understand?"

I did not.

"You have been useful to me," William said, tilting his head to one side as he regarded the archbishop.

"Useful?" the archbishop shook with emotion. "We have helped each other. It has been a fruitful alliance."

"I have given you gifts," William said, studying Hugh. "I have weakened your enemies."

"And I have given you this place," the archbishop said, gesturing at the room around us. "I have allowed you to take Sherwood for your own. You would be scurrying around in the gutter if it were not for me."

"Is that how it is?" William said, pursing his lips. "And here I thought I had welcomed you into our brotherhood when I gave you eternal life? Instead, you have worked against me at every turn. You hold one hand out to me while the other you hold behind your back, holding a dagger."

"Every bargain that we made," Hugh said. "I have fulfilled."

"Is that so?" William said. "Why, then, have you worked so hard to keep my brother Richard away from me?"

The archbishop glanced at me in my cage. "Yes. Very well, I sent him away to the Weald instead of sending him to his death, to you. Do you hear me, Richard? I tried to save you from your brother. When you defied me, I even had you bloody well locked up in that castle to keep you from blundering in here."

"But why?" I asked. "Why would you try to save me?"

Hugh's face twisted. "How can you ask me that? Have I not loved you like a son for these many years? Have I not defended you against your enemies? Why, he asks me. You ungrateful swine."

"But why not tell me?" I asked, astonished. "You could have warned me that this was a trap."

"I tried," he said. "God knows, I tried. I could do no more. If I told you how I was in league with this man, you would have turned on me. You two have this mad desire to slay the other. I sought only to keep you apart. And to keep my wonderful daughter from this monster. He heard about her, somehow, asked me about her. I knew I had to send her far from Sherwood. I had a mad hope that the two of you would run away together for good."

I shook my head, disbelieving what I heard. "But why then did you send that man Little John to be my steward in my absence?"

"I sent no one, you fool," Hugh said. "If I wanted to take your lands I would have done so. No, I meant to leave Ashbury in the hands of your faithful steward but this black-hearted monster sent his blood-guzzling slaves here to wait for your return. It was that man there, not I. No, not I. They call you the Bloody Knight. They should have called you the bloody fool."

I felt winded, as though I had been thrown from a horse. I clutched the bars, my muscles straining as I attempted to prise them apart. The man was right. I was a fool.

William laughed at us. "Your concern for my brother is very touching. Truly, I am almost overcome with your fatherly assistance. Nevertheless, Hugh, you betrayed your word. Where was your love for me, Hugh? Me, who made you into a son of Adam. I became your father. You should have been faithful to me. And you will suffer for your betrayal, oath breaker."

"And you also lied to me," Hugh bellowed.

"Never," William said, feigning that he was offended. "My word is iron."

"A lie of omission, then. You never told me that once you turned me into an immortal, I would father no more children," the archbishop shouted.

William threw his head back and laughed. "How many bastards did you have already? I thought you would be grateful. You could shoot your seed into as many girls as you like, until the end of days, and never be troubled by another unwanted child or its needy mother."

"I love my children," Archbishop Hugh said. "I wanted centuries to father a thousand of them."

William laughed in his face. "My dear Hugh. How can this gift be otherwise? Richard and I were given the gift of eternal life but God took our seed from us. It is the same with everyone that I make. Of course, he takes it away. The only way we can make children now is by making more men like us. You, Hugh, you ask too much of God. And, more to the point, you ask too much of me. You have served your purpose. And now you will die."

"You cannot," Hugh said, struggling with the men holding him. "You need my men. My wealth. You need me to control the new king."

William shrugged and strolled toward Hugh. "I have turned enough of your men that they serve me now. Already they brought me boxes of your gold and silver. As for controlling our new young king, you have failed miserably. William Marshal is the Regent, not you. I have made other arrangements, many of them with members of the Marshal's own family. You have nothing to offer."

"How dare you?" The archbishop's eyes searched the room for allies or a way out. His men were all silent. William's men, now. Still, the man tried to save himself. "You are mad if you think you can find any other lord of my standing willing to do good for you."

William advanced, his dagger in hand. "Now, Hugh, all you are good for is a gallon of blood, a hundred pounds of meat and as much again in offal."

"No—" the big man said but he was held fast and said no more as William sliced through the throat of Archbishop Hugh de Nonant.

Little John and the rest held the big man as he writhed and groaned and shook. William gripped the hair on top of Hugh's head and cut and sawed through the skin, the veins, tendons, windpipe and gullet all the way back to the neck bones, working the blade back and forth with his face twisted in anger.

"This is what happens," William was snarling through gritted teeth. "This is what happens to those who defy me."

The archbishop's cry of defiance was cut off as William's blade sliced through his windpipe, the momentary whistling sound of air escaping from his neck was stoppered by the gushing blood. Hugh's eyes darted about, looking for help. He looked to me but I could not help him. Even had I not been caged, I was not certain I would have moved to help. He had plotted to poison his king, after all. I stared back at him until he squeezed his eyes closed.

William's men scurried forward to collect the stuff as it spurted and fell from the wound that grew wider and wider. Much of it poured into the stone channels in the floor and they collected it from the crater by the altar. After a few moments, Little John and his men threw Hugh's body face down on the floor. His blood continued to flow from him, running into the basin in the floor.

William stepped back, panting not from the effort but from the rage he was feeling. William nodded at me and I thought I was to be next. Instead, they bought a cup of the bishop's blood to me. I did not hesitate. I drank to heal my wrist and to be strong enough to fight my way free whenever the opportunity came.

The archbishop's blood, coming as it did from William, was more powerful than mortal blood. It coursed through me like fire in my veins. I felt like I could bend iron bars with my bare hands. Instead, I sat and focused on controlling my breathing while the strength filled me.

They dragged out the huge body of Hugh. William retired and the men washed much of the remaining blood from the floor.

Then I was alone again. Alone, with guttering candles and the body of Eva upon the slab.

"Please God," I prayed. "I wish I treated your priests better. I am sorry for that. I will try harder if I ever get the chance to. But please do not take Eva. She is a good woman. Well, she is not as bad as many of us. She is a good fighter. Let her wake. Let her wake and remain herself. And let her free me from this cage. Then I will cut off the head of every man in Eden, for you, Lord. Amen."

God rarely listens. Or, perhaps he does, for I have always been lucky. And what is luck, if it is not God either helping you or getting out of your way?

In the end, though, it was not Eva that freed me.

15

TREE OF LIFE

BEFORE THE POWER OF HUGH'S BLOOD faded, I worked to free myself from my cage.

The thing had rattled within its frame when Little John had struck it. I was sure that I could break it free of the timber supports if I thrashed around enough. But that would stir William, from the room beyond, and whatever other guards were close by. If I were to succeed in knocking my cage over then I would simply be in a cage laying on its side.

The one chance I had was in prising open the bolted door. It was half the height of the cage and narrow but almost the full width of one side.

"Hold on to life," I said to Eva. "Do not give up. I will get us out."

I pushed and pulled on the bars of the cage door, heaving and shoving, looking for some weakness.

I could not budge it.

Eva groaned and writhed on the oaken altar. The veins stood out on her temples and forehead. Her fists clenched and her back arched, straining her bonds.

"Do not die," I said. "Please, Eva. Come back to the world, woman, come back."

She thrashed her head left and right and groaned. Her eyelids flickered, opened, closed again.

"Stay with me," I said. "If you live then I will look after you. You will always have a place with me whether you want to share my bed or not. I'll see you right. I'll take care of you."

Eva fell still. Silent.

Was she dead? Her chest did not seem to be moving.

Footsteps approached and I pretended to sleep. My one prayer was that someone would open my door to pass me a bucket or some such. More likely, if a man approached alone I could grab him though the bars and force him to open by threatening his life.

I listened to footsteps shuffling into the cave. The person stopped still in the doorway for a long moment. I expect he was looking at Eva's form, the bloody linen shirt clinging to her cold chest and flat belly in the candlelight.

They approached my cage.

I readied myself. I would never get more than a single attempt at it.

A low voice whispered. "Richard? Richard? By God's eyes, do not be dead, Sir Richard or I will kill you myself."

There, just beyond the bars of my cage door, was Swein. He was cloaked in green and dressed in one of the green hoods that William's men wore.

His face, mostly in shadow, lit up with joy when he saw what must have been my astonished, ecstatic face. I had a hundred questions about how the sneaky little bastard had gotten inside undetected but they could wait.

"Draw back the top and side bolts," I whispered.

He slid them back out of the floor. They both screeched as they ground iron against iron. I cringed, looking at William's door and over Swein's green-clad shoulder at the entrance to the underground room.

"Where is everyone else?" I asked him as I eased myself through the cage door. I straightened, suppressing a mighty sigh of satisfaction as my back cracked.

"They await us beyond the gate and walls," Swein whispered. "We must find Marian and flee before I am discovered. And before they discover the men we stole the clothes from."

"You killed some of William's men?" I whispered.

"Outside the walls of this place," Swein said. "Arrows in the face. You say these men are powerful but I don't know what all the fuss is about."

"Listen," I whispered. "Most of William's men are ordinary. They live in the hope of tasting William's blood and gaining temporary strength. Just like those you killed back in Ashbury and the men whose clothes you now wear. There are a few, though, I am not sure how many who are very strong. Made strong as long as they drink blood, like Tuck. You must not attempt to fight those men."

Swein nodded. "An arrow to the head kills them, too, though?"

"Yes, praise God," I said. "Now, let us go. First, let us take Eva."

"Surely, she is dead?"

I stepped to the massive, thick altar and felt her chest and cheek. "She is bone cold," I said, my own heart racing. "But I think she breathes."

Her neck was thick with blood but I felt underneath the black scab that had formed over the slash through the great vein. The scab flaked away.

Underneath, the skin was whole.

"Oh, God," I whispered. "It worked."

"But where is Marian?" Swein said, his eyes wild and dark inside his hood.

"In there," I said as I untied Eva's bonds. "With William."

Swein stared at the heavy door. "Is it locked?"

"I doubt it," I said. "Give me your sword and I will go inside and kill him."

"What is he doing to her in there?" Swein said, his eyes bulging.

"Give me your sword, quickly." Without waiting for him, I pulled the blade from his scabbard. It was an old thing. Sharp at the edge, though nicked. The iron not particularly hard and it had been straightened so many times I feared it would snap at the first contact with another blade.

"Can you kill him?" Swein asked, mistaking my hesitation for doubt of my own abilities.

"Be ready to take Marian," I said. "And I will carry Eva. What is your plan for escape?"

"Put a sword in your hand and stay behind you," Swein said.

Eva groaned and rolled over toward me. I steadied her before she rolled right off.

"What is happening?" Eva mumbled.

"You are alive," I told her keeping my voice low. "We are escaping Eden. Can you stand?"

She sat on the edge of the thick altar top, swinging her legs off.

"I am thirsty," she muttered, wiping her mouth.

"I will get us both some blood from the first man I kill," I whispered, holding her shoulders. "Which will be William."

Her head snapped up, clutching at her fully healed neck. "They made me one of them." She looked at me, eye to eye, a dozen emotions fighting upon her face.

"No," I said. "Well, yes. But you will not be mad, as they are. You are made from my own blood. Perhaps that will make a difference. And you shall have me to look out for you."

She squeezed my hands upon her shoulders.

"We must hurry," Swein whispered. "Hurry, hurry, speed is the key. We do not have long."

"Eva," I said, "do you feel like you could stand?"

We helped her to her feet. She pinched the front of her shirt away from her body. It was halfway stiff with blood. "I feel like I could kill."

"Good," I said, praying that she would be strong enough to help me rather than weak enough to hinder our escape. "Give me room to move," I warned them both. "But if you can get around us while we fight then you can grab Marian."

"Marian is in there?" Eva said, frowning. "Since when has she been?"

Something that William had said came back to me. That an acolyte had tried to rape the ladies in their chamber. I grabbed Eva's arm. "Have you seen her elsewhere?"

She shook me off. "Marian and I were held together, in a chamber of the house above. Until they brought me here. How long have we been here? What day is it?"

Swein and I looked at each other.

"He called to her, as if she was within, when I first arrived," I said. "The evil sod was toying with me. Marian was never in there. That petty, spiteful shit."

"How was she?" Swein whispered, eyes shining in the lamplight. "Was she well treated?"

"I suppose so," Eva said, looking down at herself. "Considering."

"So William is alone in there," I said, staring at the heavy door. "

"Let us go get Marian," Swein said. "You can always come back for William."

"I may never get another chance," I said, my voice low but growing louder in my desperation. "I can go in there and cut off his head while he sleeps."

"If he wakes, though. You two clashing swords will wake this whole place and the rest of us will never get out," Swein said, standing up to me like a man. "Is that what you want?"

"God give me strength," I prayed and I passed Swein's blade back. "Stand aside."

Eva and he moved away while I leaned across the huge, bloody, stinking oak altar top. The thing was three feet wide and six feet long. The wood was about three inches thick and the wood was as dense as iron. I heaved it up. It barely shifted. I heaved again, it grinding against the stone supports beneath, juddering loudly.

Swein hissed a warning, frantic that I would make enough noise to wake the dead.

I took a breath, bent my knees and heaved up, lifting with my lower back. The great thing rose with me, with my body along it, one arm on the far edge, the other on the edge near me. I tilted it up, spun it carefully around and waddled over to William's chamber door.

Once, many years before when the lodge had been built, William's room might have been the lord's treasury, or perhaps a dungeon gaol cell for woodland miscreants. Indeed, it was a room able to be secured from entry or exit. The door was thick oak, reinforced with iron bands.

William had removed the oak beam that locked the door from the outside but he had neglected to remove the iron cleats on either side of the frame. I eased the altar top into those long iron hooks. I shoved it upright, checked it was secure. The oak altar top covered the door from halfway up, almost to the ceiling.

From the other side, the door rattled.

"Open this door," William commanded from the other side, his voice barely audible through the many inches of solid oak. "Whoever it is, I swear I shall forgive you when you open it up."

"I shall come back for you, William," I said.

He roared and smacked his fits into his door. The altar shook but held.

I shouted through the door, "Perhaps not today, William, but know that I shall come back for you and I shall—"

"Quiet," Swein hissed. "You will wake all of Eden."

On the opposite side of the room to William's chamber, the other door scraped open and I heard a man's voice.

Swein and Eva froze, as surprised people tend to do, staring at the doorway.

Running past Swein, I snatched the sword from his hand, leapt over the stone legs of the altar and closed the distance as the door opened.

Two of William's men pushed their way inside.

Both carried a spear but neither expected to find any trouble. The first got my borrowed blade through his neck. He fell, his bucket and spear clattering as he did so.

The man behind turned to flee but I continued past the first man and slammed into the second, crushing him against the rough stone wall. His spear bounced between the walls of the corridor, rattling loudly.

I stamped on his face and neck and chest until I was sure he would never rise again.

Swein and Eva had good sense enough to come after me, eager to flee. I waited for them, listening along the long corridor for any signs of life.

William pounded on his door from the other side. His blows were massive, like the kicks from a horse, but so was his bloodstained altar top.

It held.

"Is it day or night?" I asked Swein as he drew near.

"Should be getting light soon," he said. "Your blade is bent."

The bloodied tip had bent a hand's width from the point. I placed it against the wall and pushed it straight as I could.

"Jocelyn waits beyond the walls?" I asked him. "With horses for all of us?"

Swein nodded. "My men are hidden in the place they fight best," he said. "In the trees."

"Watch the corridor," I said to Swein, handing him the sword.

I picked up the first man by the shoulders. He was one of the ones who had provoked me before.

I drank from the wound I had slashed through his neck. His head flapped back.

After I had a few mouthfuls, I held him out for Eva.

She stared at the blood on his neck and licked her lips.

"Decide now if you wish to live or die," I said to her. "This man is dead. He will never need his blood again. You, on the other hand, must drink in order to live. Drink from him and find such power that you have never known. You will be able to defeat any swordsman, survive deadly wounds. But only if you drink."

William pounded on his chamber door again, shouting words we could not quite make out.

I held the dead man up for Eva. Her lip curling, she bent her neck to the bleeding wound and sucked the blood out. She gagged but kept swallowing.

Eva gulped it down, jerked her head away, eyes shining. "God," she said. "Holy God Almighty." Her chest heaved while she stared at her hands, flexing them open and closed. "Is this how you feel all the time?" Her eyes were wide.

"Someone comes," Swein said from ahead down the corridor.

Eva and I took up a spear each and ran forward to where the corridor turned into a twisting stair. Footsteps and voices came down.

Swein whispered to me. "Sounds like four men? Should we wait here, take them as they come around the bend?"

I could not wait even a moment more to kill the men who had captured me, humiliated me and used me as if I was cattle. Without considering, I ran up past Swein with my spearhead held up and out and I came upon the first man. One of Little John's armoured fellows, as were the three men above and behind him upon the stair.

Their mail had been stolen from better men. Most of it did not fit the wearer and was often rusted, split and then tied bound together with thongs or strips of cloth.

The first man wore no amour on his legs so I slid my spear up into his groin, twisted the head and pulled it out. He shrieked and fell past me, down to where Swein and Eva could finish him.

The next man barely had a moment to flinch before I ran my spear up into his chin. My blade bit into the bone. With surprising swiftness, he grabbed the shaft and attempted to yank it from my grip. Instead, I pulled him down, sending him tumbling by me. The third man had time to draw his sword and he swatted my blade away, slipping inside the reach of the point and thrusting down toward my unarmoured head. I shortened my grip, yanking the spear shaft through my hands until my lead hand was just behind the iron, so I held it almost like a dagger. I slipped aside the sword thrust, charging up the steps, grabbed his sword arm and stuck my own blade through a rent in his mail between shoulder and neck. The spear shaft bounced off the wall and I missed my strike. He drew his own dagger and managed to rake it up my arm before I could thrust into his throat.

The man above had retreated back up the stairs.

I took the sword from the dying man at my feet and charged upward, Swein and Eva behind me.

My fear was that the man would shut us behind some sturdy door but instead, he fled along the corridor up there, shouting for help.

At the top of the stairs, it was daylight. Morning filtering through the holes in the tiled roof of the old, stone built building. It was filled with that acrid stench of old urine, shit and unwashed human bodies.

The corridor had closed doors every few feet along it, four on either side, with one at the far end. The fleeing man banged on the farthest two doors, shouting that those inside should wake up, then kicked open and ran through that far door. It opened to reveal a rectangle of green beyond, lit with the pale blue of a summer dawn.

"Where is Marian?" I called to Eva but already she ran beyond me to the second door on the right. She lifted the bar across the middle of it and bounced it aside.

The two doors at the far end opened, one after the other. One of William's men poked his head out, rubbing his eyes, another came out with a sword already drawn.

"We must hurry," I said and went after Eva who threw open the door before she rushed inside.

At the far end of the corridor, one of the men shouted back inside his door to the others inside that room.

Swein pushed past me into the room after Eva. I stood in the doorway and peered inside as Eva helped Marian, grabbing her hand and pulling her toward the door. The room was dark and fetid and it reeked of piss.

Marian cried out at Eva's appearance. "What has happened to you? Dear God, Eva, what has happened?"

Eva had fresh blood covering her from nose to neck and old, dried blood caking her from neck to knee.

"I am unharmed. We must run, now," Eva said and yanked her out.

William's men tumbled out into the far end of the hallway until there were seven men stalking toward us along the corridor.

"Stay in there for just a moment longer, my lady," I said to Marian and I checked my stolen blade. It appeared to be a good one. "Swein, Eva, stay with Marian. If I fall, kill as many as you can and run."

William's men filled the far end of the corridor, coming on, two by two next to each other, in four rough rows. They had bunched up, one behind the other, far too close to each other. Bad for them, good for me.

The first two men looked nervous, as well they might.

I sprang forward, slashing at them, shouting. I drove them back toward their fellows. They waved their swords at me and they were fast compared to normal men but they were not practised swordsmen. I lunged low, slid sideways and thrust, gutting the one to the left, who fell to his knees, shrieking and trying to gather up his guts back into his body. I drove my blade into the man to the right. A killing blow for a mortal man, yet he shrugged it off and came back at me, almost taking me by surprise. I had to remember to put them down in a way they could not resist. So I slipped my blade across his throat, slicing his windpipe and neck veins.

The five men still in the fight were brave. Fanatical, even. I was used to fighting in full armour, with a helm and a shield and my inexperience with fighting in no more than an undershirt began to show.

One threw himself upon my blade, ran himself through on it and twisted himself to the side. It caught me by surprise and almost worked but I ripped the blade from him. Still, the man behind him cut me on the forearm, rather badly. I was lucky it was not on my hand or my fingers.

The cut on my arm released even more of my anger. It was like when a bowman is at full draw, with the cord at his cheek, and then he pulls it back even further to beyond his ear.

My sword flashed in the dim light, thrusting through the clothes of the men attacking me. I knew I was shouting as I killed the last few but I could not recall fighting the rest. I cut the last two down in short order, blood spurting from veins I had slashed through. Seven men lay dead or dying in the corridor, groaning, weeping. Blood soaked the floor and those that could move struggled to slurp it up.

"Come, let us flee," I shouted.

"What about the other prisoners?" Swein said, coming out of Marian's gaol, his eyes full of horror.

"There is no time," I said, trying to calm my rage. "William's men will be gathering outside. William could free himself."

"I know some of these men," Swein said, throwing over the beam to the nearest door to him and heaving the door open. "Outlaws like me, taken and locked up. Men who were taken when my father was killed."

Inside that room, it was dark. Two filthy men in rags shuffled out, blinking at the light.

"Come out," Swein shouted. "Hurry, you fools."

"Leave them," I urged Swein. I could hear men moving in the courtyard.

Marian strode up to me. "You must help them, Richard," she said. "It is your duty." She glared at me, hands on her hips. She was filthy. Her hair was matted. She stank like a pig.

"God give me strength," I said. "You sound like Emma."

"Well then," Marian said. "You should most certainly do as I say."

Together, we got all the doors open. While the others helped the stinking blood slaves, prisoners and servants out of their prisons, I picked up one of the men I had slain and I drank from a wound in his wrist.

The prisoners groaned in terror and disgust, edging away from me.

"He is a friend," Swein swore to them. "He is not one of them, he is freeing you."

I ignored them, caring nothing for what those foul peasants thought. I dropped the body into the pooling blood beneath and I looked out the door. Morning was growing brighter. The gate ahead, the gate into Sherwood and freedom, was barred.

William's men stood upon the wall and before the closed gate. The wide, clear path between the gate and my doorway was clear of men but I could hear them rustling in the bushes and trees to either side.

"It will be an ambush," I said to Eva at my shoulder. "I shall fight my way through, draw them out. You and Swein follow, kill any who oppose us." I glanced at Eva. "You should drink some more blood. You will need the strength."

"No," Marian said, hearing me. "No, God. You mean they made you into one of them?"

Eva just shook her head without looking at either of us. "I am strong enough," she said. "And full."

"Suit yourself," I said. "Be sure to move quickly and leave these dying weaklings behind. Some will get away, probably, if we leave the gate open behind us. We cannot carry them."

"Wait," Swein said. "You could draw the Green Men away from the gate. Give the prisoners a chance."

"No," I said. "I am not doing that. I want to live. Look at these men and women here, look at them. You freed them but without horses, they will all be recaptured within a day."

"There are horses," Marian said. "We saw the stable. It is behind this hall, there is a score of horses, perhaps more."

"Set a fire," Swein said. "In the storehouse to the left of this hall. Burn it down. That will give them something to do."

"You and your foolish stratagems," I said to Swein, shaking my head, and I glared at Marian for good measure, for she was almost as bad as he. "I go for the gate, you follow as soon as it is open. Get to the horses and ride as hard as you can. Go north, then west. We will raise more forces, come back in a week or two and destroy this place."

Without waiting, I charged out into the courtyard.

There were men there. Men in green, perhaps a score. Some were armoured in mail shirts or coifs. Many had open-faced helmets. All were armed.

I felt naked without my armour. Without a helm. Without even a gambeson. It was terrifying.

All I could do was put my chin to my chest, hunch my shoulders and run through them. Without the armour to weigh me down, I did, at least, move with a speed that astonished even myself. The men in green leapt aside from me, shouting warnings at each other.

Men upon the wall by the gateway shot their bows at me from less than twenty yards but I ran so fast they had little hope of hitting me. An arrow bounced from the pathway into my legs, missing me but almost tripping me. I took the wooden steps up to the wall in two strides, leaping up with my sword up and cutting down the three bowmen at the top.

The men who had scattered at my charge now moved back to the courtyard, shouting at me and each other, gathering their courage. I leapt down from the wall, put a shoulder to the timber and heaved up the great beam out of the cleats across the double door gate. My back itched, so sure was I that I would catch an arrow, a bolt or a spear while my back was turned. I gave half of the gate a mighty heave and it swung open.

I span about in time to parry a wild blow and split the fellow's skull down to the nose. His friend went down with the very top of his skull sliced off by a half-pulled backhand blow.

I wished that I could retain such strength as that at all times. No wonder William and his men had built a blood farm. It was intoxicating stuff. A small part of me dreamed of a time when I could drink blood every day, for the rest of eternity and fight back whole armies with my bare hands.

But more men were coming. I edged away from the gate, my back to the timber wall. They moved to follow me but more stayed back amongst the vines in full leaf. I had to get them away from the gate so Swein and Eva had a chance. "You cowards," I shouted. "Kill me. Capture me. The Green Knight will be ever grateful to you."

That brought a few toward me. A horse whinnied from behind the hall, beyond the big timber storehouse.

"I am going to slaughter your horses," I said.

A few more came for me.

"I have William's treasure," I cried. "I am making off with his riches."

Many more moved to cut me off so I ran along the path away from the gate further into the compound, I ran beside the wall, past the storehouse toward the stables.

Two men twisted out from behind the wall of the storehouse. I put them down, injured but it took a few moments and the men chasing me were almost upon me.

I checked my run, span and swung my sword in a wide arc, screaming like a madman. The three closest to me jumped back, scattering from me.

I turned and ran to the stable. It was huge, built to house a lord's hunting parties. Stone at the foundation and lower wall with a long timber roof, open on the sides. It was packed with horses. The grooms were already running away when I shouted at them to move, to get away or die. I ran into the central isle. It was dark inside. The horses and ponies were scared, shying away and tossing their heads. I kicked open as many stalls as I could as I moved down the stable building. My pursuers shouted at each other to surround the building and as I opened the stalls, the men gathered at either end of the long structure. When I had run in, I had conceived that the horses might bolt, throwing Eden's men into more disorder, perhaps making a herd of panicking horses that we could flee amongst. But of course, the horses were afraid to leave their pens.

Instead of fighting my way through the men cautiously edging into each end of the stable, I pushed past a big stallion, going for the open side of the stable. It had the short back and powerful rump of a charger and I was tempted to leap upon its back, or push it into the aisle and slice its rump into bolting through the men. Instead, I shoved the fine beast aside and clambered out over the outside wall of the pen.

On the other side, I took a breath while the men came to cut me off again. I hoped I had already caused enough disruption for Swein and Eva to fight their way through to the open gate. I prayed that Jocelyn and Anselm were ready with mounts and that the archers could cover our escape just as they had done in the raids on Dover.

I charged the men closest to me. These fellows were well rested and prepared for me. But I was becoming tired and I was slashed in the arm and a blade slashed a glancing blow along my skull over my ear. I killed or put down four men and ran along the path back toward the gate. William's men were following but avoiding contact, fearing me now, perhaps, more than the Lord of Eden's ire.

I rounded the storehouse, into the courtyard by the gate, and ran into a cacophony of shouting and the clash of weapons.

The prisoners, William's blood slaves, were streaming from the hall. The ones who could move faster than a walking pace were already out of the gate. Others were supporting each other, limping, wincing at the light of the dawn and from the effort of walking.

Eva stood by the open gate, laying about her with her sword at a group of green-clad soldiers by the stairs. She was magnificent. Always, she had been fast and skilful but now she was strong and relentless and even faster than before. Three dead men were at her feet and three more circled, probing her defences.

Swein, however, was wheeling backwards from two men parrying and ducking, his sword bent. He was bleeding, moving slowly, breathing heavily. For all his gifts, he was no swordsman and was fighting William's monsters. It was a wonder he yet lived.

Just by the doorway to the hall, Marian helped an old man and a couple of broken fellows out into the air, concern for them all over her face, though she herself was filthy and struggling. I cursed her stupidity. I cursed her compassion that was going to get her killed, after all that we had done.

More of William's men came from deeper within Eden, from the far side of the courtyard and from around the sides of the hall, to shove the blood slaves back toward their gaol. One of William's brutes punched two prisoners to the ground and went after more. Another cracked a stick into the side of a young woman's head and pulled her to the ground by the hair. He was set upon by the woman's friends who he threw down as if they were children.

The men pursuing me gathered by the storehouse at my back, arguing with each other about how best to attack me.

I decided to save Swein first, then Eva and then Marian.

"Sir Richard!" Little John strode around the far corner of the hall, crashing through the vines and fruit trees.

The man had somehow found mail and helm to fit his giant frame and his monstrous head and he had a sword drawn. Though the mail was tight across his belly and it was split on the inside of his arms and tied together, and it was short at the wrist. The helm was an old fashioned one with an open face and a nose piece but he wore a mail coif underneath to protect his head and neck.

Little John was a huge man, filled with rage and the strength of William's gift but he was not a knight. He was a bailiff, used to breaking the heads of commoners. I was tired but I thought I could take him.

With him were three men dressed in mail that fit them perfectly and all three held shields painted with the same red and white stripes. Those men were trained fighters, presumably come over from some lord or mercenary company and though they looked like children beside Little John, they were just as dangerous as he.

John pointed his sword at my face as he strode toward me.

"Leave the blood slaves," John shouted. "They will not get far. Kill that one there and the rest will fall."

He smashed his way through the prisoners, knocking down and stomping on a man and woman who had been too slow to move aside. Others scattered from him, falling down from fear and in their haste to get away from him.

There was no time to fight him. I could not kill every man in Eden. Even if I fought John and his men, it would leave at least a score for me to kill or drive off, perhaps twice that many.

The altar table would not hold William for long and his men could have already freed him even if he was unable to break through alone. I glanced at the hall doorway, by Marian, and imagined William suddenly appearing there.

I considered fleeing into the storehouse and setting a fire as some sort of distraction, as Swein had suggested. I wondered if I could flee through the gate and draw Little John away from the prisoners out to where the archers could take them. Backing away from John's approach, I searched for stratagems, for some clever trick of the kind that Swein liked.

But Swein fell. A cut sliced him upon the arm and then another and he cried out and fell, fighting as he went down.

The red rage came upon me and I decided to just kill them all.

John's soldiers spread out as they approached. The men who had pursued me from the stable spread out behind me, near the storehouse.

The prisoners fled as best they could. I willed them to run while I fought.

I chose the soldier on the farthest right and, feinting left, I charged him. Like a good knight, he braced behind his shield so I crashed into it with my shoulder. It hurt, badly but I knocked him down and while he was flailing, I trod on his sword hand and stabbed the point of my blade into his armoured neck. It may not have split the rings of mail there but I leaned on the pommel as I drove it down, crushing his windpipe.

Little John charged me like a bull and I had to leap over the fallen man and dance away like a coward, lest I be felled myself. A thicket of berry bushes blocked my way behind me but I leapt through a raspberry bush, hacking and tearing through the tangle. I found two of William's men on the far side, shocked by my sudden appearance. I cut almost all the way through the neck of the first man and the second I speared through the lower back as he turned to flee, all the while I kept moving.

Two of John's soldiers hacked their way toward me through the bushes but the idiots got themselves and their shields caught on the tangled branches. The nearest man looked down at himself to see where he was snarled up. I hacked my sword down on the crown of his helm as if I was splitting logs. The metal on metal sound clanged and he went down as if he was a candle that had been snuffed out. But my sword broke, right at the cross guard. I stared at the handle like an idiot though I had known for a long time that using my full strength in a fight was often a bad idea.

The other man-at-arms dragged himself through the bushes and aimed a clumsy strike at my head. I raised my hand to block it. Only at the last moment did I realise that my sword was nothing more than a handle. I ducked and the blade cut no more than the air an inch above my head.

Little John, unseen beyond the dense thicket, roared at his men to kill me and to feast upon my corpse

I dropped my ruined weapon, grabbed the man-at-arm's sword arm and snatched his sword from his mailed hand. The man thumped me with his shield but it was no more than irritation and, with my bare left hand, I guided the point of my blade into the eye slit of his helm and shoved it in. He screamed and jerked back, at the very least blind on one side and hopefully dying.

More men were crowding into the overgrown thicket of mulberry and gooseberry. I hacked my way free, coming out beside the storehouse.

One of William's men turned to shout that he had found me and I cut his head from his body while he was still shouting. It was one of those rare times where the body of the beheaded man does not yet know it is dead and the man, without a head, stood upright, hands out to balance itself. The body took a full step forward even while its head rolled away from it. I am sure it fell soon after but I did not see how many steps it took. For I turned to defend myself from the great beast that charged me.

Little John, his face contorted in rage, swung his sword overarm at the top of my head.

I was tired. No mortal man, no matter how much he trains, can keep up intense combat without periods of rest. And even I was breathing heavily, sucking down air like a drowning man. I had cuts all over my body, some of them bad and one on the side of my skull that I was sure would be ugly. My blood leaked out all over. I was desperately thirsty, for water and blood.

I got my sword up to deflect the strike. And I moved aside to get out from under that wild, brutal blow.

But I was slow and my arm was weak. Little John's blade knocked mine aside. His sword missed my head but cut into my body, smashing my collarbone and driving me to my knees.

A strike that like, with that kind of force, while it might not sever a vital vein or organ, can be enough to kill a man outright. The shock of the blow will travel through your bones, through the centre of your body, jar your brain inside your skull. The power of it can shut off the flow of your life like twisting a tap.

I knew it was bad. Looking up at his red, furious face as he yanked the sword out of my body, I could see just how he would hack it back down into my neck the second time. It was curious how I had time to think. I had time to rue being killed by an untrained brute after having defeated so many skilled knights in my life. A bailiff, of all people, a man who wielded a blade with all the finesse of a butcher. His grip was all wrong. His edge alignment was appalling.

And yet I could not move. I was done. Defeated.

John dropped his sword and stiffened. His face twisted and he jerked and clutched his chest. He twisted and fell to the side, his mouth opening and closing, trying to see behind him. He staggered a few steps, wailing like a skewered boar and he crashed to his side in a clatter of iron and bone.

It was Eva. She had run him through the arse with one blade, striking up beneath the hauberk that was far too short for him. Then she had seen a long rent in the side of his mail and stabbed her second blade up under his ribcage and into his chest. The hilts of her blades stuck out of his arse and his ribs.

She helped me up. The poor woman was covered in blood from head to toe, shivering in her undershirt and bare legs. She shook from exhaustion and excitation.

"Drink some blood," she snarled in my face and she snatched up John's dropped blade. She stood guard over me while I staggered to a headless body next to us.

William's men – seeing John fall, seeing Eva's power, and me rising – retreated from us.

I sucked a mouthful of spurting blood from one of the big veins of the body near me, lifting it with my right arm. My left shoulder was barely attached to my body. A piece of long, tattered skin found its way into my mouth and I almost vomited it back up. But I kept drinking. I needed it, all I could get. Even then, I felt like I was dying.

The scream from the courtyard was chilling. I dropped the body and with Eva's help, ran round the bushes into the space between the gate and the hall.

The prisoners had mostly all escaped from the hall. Some lay dead, others were being held or beaten by William's men.

But in the centre was the man himself.

The Green Knight, the Lord of Eden. My brother. William.

His eyes were wild, he was angrier than I had ever seen him. His fists were bloodied and swollen. His mouth and jaw were red with fresh blood.

There were dead all about him.

He held Marian by the hair.

"Come here," William snarled at an old man, who limped over to William, tears running down his face. "Here, Geoffrey."

"Please, not my daughter, please," the old said.

It was Sir Geoffrey of Norton. Aged, thin, his hair almost gone and what remained was white and brittle. But it was he. A man I had drunk with, fought with when we were young. I was astonished that Marian's father yet lived. He and his soldiers had been ambushed so long before that no man in his right mind had believed him so. Yet there he was, begging for Marian's life.

Of course, that was why Marian had dawdled so long. That was why she had been helping a decrepit prisoner instead of fleeing for her life. She had found her father, finally, against all hope.

There was movement among the fallen. Swein crawled through the bodies of soldier and slave alike toward William. But he was ten yards away and heading for nowhere but the grave. The lad was drenched in blood, pale and moving far too slow. Even if he reached William, there was nothing he could do.

Eva steeled herself to attack but she could barely hold herself upright. Her teeth were chattering in her head. I was leaning on her but she was also holding to me.

The blood I had drunk was working in me but still my left side was useless. The blow had cleaved through me deeply and there was no way I could use my left arm. I could not even feel it, it hung by my side like a leg of lamb on a butcher's hook. I needed more blood, more time.

"You shall watch what happens to those who defy the Lord of Eden," William shouted in Marian's ear. Still holding on to her hair, he stepped forward and ran his sword through her father's throat.

Sir Geoffrey jerked as the blade gouged out his neck and the old men fell.

Marian screamed as William threw her upon her father's body.

"Do you see?" William shouted at her then he addressed his men. "Take all their heads and we shall stick them upon the walls of Nottingham Castle. We will show England what it means to be the sons of Adam. John, where are you, you great fool?"

"Brother," I shouted. "Little John is dead."

His head snapped round to me.

"And," I continued. "Now it is your turn."

I finished in a fit of coughing. Blood spattered from my mouth. My wounds were greater than I had thought.

"Brother?" William said. "You are no brother of mine. I would have given you a place in our new world. Instead, you wreak this pointless havoc. What a waste."

He grabbed up Marian again, forced her to her knees and held his sword across the back of her neck. She knelt among the bodies of men that William had killed to reach her and her father.

Eva stalked forward and I took a step with her but my legs gave way. I needed blood.

"Stop," William said. "Eva, my dear, you are one of us, now. And if you take another step, I shall remove your friend's head. Richard, I will very much enjoy peeling off chunks of your flesh. I wonder how long you could live without skin. We shall find out together."

Eva turned to me, looking over her shoulder. "Drink my blood," she whispered. "Then kill him."

I shook my head. She was shaking all over. To take her blood would surely kill her and William would kill Marian anyway before I could reach her.

William's men gathered, their bravery regained.

"Return all the escaped blood slaves to their pens," William commanded and they moved to obey. "Close the gates, and then form groups to round up the ones in the wood."

From nearby, bowstrings twanged, the air split to the whooshing sound of iron in flight. Arrows smacked and thudded into William's men. A dozen. One after the other. Thrashing and cracking, splitting flesh. A half dozen men fell, others scattered away from the gateway and the wall.

William shouted, pointed at the wall of Eden.

Swein's archers had scaled that wall from the outside and shot down into William's men. After that first volley, they loosed another, and another, each man shooting as fast as he could. The wet thud of iron splitting clothes and skin and flesh sounded, again and again.

From the open gateway, a group of four archers ran forward, drew back their bows and shot as one, straight across the courtyard toward William.

My shout of warning got no further than a strangled cry as my own blood filled my throat. I wanted to warn them that they would hit Marian.

Four arrows plunged into his chest, knocking him back and down.

At once, Marian crawled away to her father.

Eva turned to me, a triumphant smile on her bloodied face.

William could never be killed by arrows, I tried to tell her but all that came out was blood.

Jocelyn rode through the gate on his magnificent bay courser, the brown coat shimmering. Jocelyn was fully armoured, the long shield covering his left side, his lance in hand.

William leapt up, ripping the arrows from his chest, spurts of blood and lumps of flesh coming with them. He lifted one of the bodies at his feet as if it were a leg of lamb, bent his head to it and drank.

More arrows thumped into William's men. Those who could move fled for shelter. Those felled by the arrows suffered more shafts shot into them.

William snatched up a shield and stalked toward Marian. I supposed he knew that his best chance of escape lay in taking her hostage, using her as another shield while he rode for freedom.

I struggled to my feet and lurched toward him. I was in no state to run and I knew William would reach Marian before I could get to her.

Jocelyn knew it too. As soon as the arrows hit he had raked his spurs back and his courser leapt forward. It was a magnificent charge to behold from across the courtyard. The horse was well trained and perfectly attuned to the rider. Jocelyn's form was faultless, his lance point under the finest control. Beast and man charging as a single entity, existing purely as a means to drive an iron point into a small target with the greatest possible force.

William stopped before he reached Marian. At first, he was shocked. But amusement spread across William's lips as he turned to Jocelyn's charge.

I shouted a warning but before the blood was out of my mouth, William had leapt to the side, raised his shield to deflect the lance and swung his sword low at the horse's legs.

Although he was a mere mortal and could not match William's speed, Jocelyn had anticipated just such an evasion and had already moved the tip of his lance to where he expected William to be.

The lance caught the Lord of Eden low in the chest. It spitted him through, knocking William down as if a giant had swatted him, the iron point driving right through the skin, the bone and out the other side, the ash shaft pushing through and through William's body.

William, though, contorted with rage and twisted as he fell. The shaft knocked Jocelyn from the saddle. Jocelyn fell, hard and William snapped the lance shaft at arm's length, then pushed the remainder through his body, reaching back to draw the final splintered part out.

Jocelyn rolled to his feet, dazed and placed himself between Marian and William, drawing his sword.

I staggered toward William as he slashed the throat of Jocelyn's beautiful horse and shoved it aside. William darted forward, smashed Jocelyn's sword thrust aside with his bare arm and picked up Jocelyn in his armour by the throat, wrapping both hands around his neck.

I screamed, blood spraying from my mouth, as William snapped Jocelyn's neck.

He tossed Jocelyn's body aside like a ragdoll just as I reached them. Thrusting at full stretch, I ran William through the side of the body and William jerked away, blood pouring from his chest and his side. The weight of his body slid off my blade and I stalked after him. William was afraid. He backed away across the courtyard, bent over his wounds. Arrows thumped down around us and I was aware that I was between the archers and William, blocking their shots but I meant to kill him myself. I was going to peel off his skin. I was going to make him suffer. I would take his eyes. I wished I could tell him but I could not speak. My vision faded and I knew I had to catch him before I succumbed.

Shouting behind me. I glanced over my shoulder in time to see Little John, lumbering forward like a dying bull, hack Eva down as if she was not there, his sword cutting into the side of her head. She had her sword up to block the blow but his strength and fury were too much and she fell. Her body hit the cobbles hard. I prayed she would hold on to life until I could reach her.

John, the monster that he was, had recovered from Eva's fatal blow. Someone had drawn the blade from him and the giant was coming to kill us all.

I turned back for William, reeling, unsteady on my feet. A horse charged right by me in a clatter of hooves and a roar of anger from the rider.

Anselm, defending Marian from John, rode his sorrel rouncey at the giant. Dear, brave Anselm sat perfectly in his saddle and held his sword straight, in line with his arm, to pierce the man's huge head. But Little John roared, moved like lightning and smashed his sword into the rouncey's face before Anselm's point could reach him. The beast reared, throwing Anselm down onto the cobbles. His horse trod on him, crushing his chest and falling on him, legs kicking.

Little John stomped past Anselm and lumbered toward me, his blade high over his head, arrows sticking out all over his body, his face and neck covered in the blood he had drunk to heal his wounds. He was roaring with fury, spitting curses in a shower of blood.

I charged him. Using everything I had left, I stabbed my blade straight through the rusty mail at his chest, snapping the rings and breaking my sword blade in his heart. He fell to one knee and I smashed his face into pulp with my bare hands, breaking my knuckles, lacerating my skin. I ripped off Little John's helm, tore up a loose cobblestone and caved his skull in until his head was tatters and shards and a quivering liquid mass.

"William," I said, dragging myself to my feet. "Where is William?"

My injuries caught up with me at that moment and the ground rose up to crash into my face. The world faded into darkness.

It was Marian who saved us. Despite losing her father and almost losing her own life, despite the horrors of the carnage around her, she knew what to do. She was a sharp young woman and knew from travelling with Tuck, from the rumours about me and of course, Swein had told her about my drinking of blood. She knew well enough what I and her friend needed. God bless Lady Marian, for she cajoled the archers to give us blood from the men I had slain. Those poor archers later told me how they held a severed arm over my gaping mouth and squeezed the blood into me. It was only a few moments after that I came back to myself.

"Where is William?" I was saying the words before I was fully conscious. Marian had already left me to see to the other wounded.

"He ran, Sir Richard," an archer said, his face grim. "Don't worry, sir, we'll track him for you. Here, drink a bit more of this blood, my lord. Tom's getting you a fresh leg to drink from."

Eden was a bloody mess. The survivors were dazed and those that could continued to flee from the carnage out into the wood where they gathered together for safety.

"Jocelyn," I cried, recalling the horror of his charge. The archers helped me over to my man.

Jocelyn lay on his back in the centre of the courtyard. I gently pulled Marian aside from him. I removed his helm to give him my blood.

His eyes were already unseeing, his skin growing cold, his neck twisted unnaturally. I dripped my blood into his mouth anyway and reached under his coif to massage his throat. He was too far gone to swallow. He was beyond saving.

I sat back. I knew I should have felt anger at William and at myself but all I felt was a great sadness. Tears flowed down my face but I felt numb, as I usually did. The feeling was too great to be felt until later when the weight of his death truly hurt me. For months and even years after, I would turn to an empty room and begin to address him only to remember that he had fallen there in Eden. He had been my son, my sworn knight and my closest friend.

"I am sorry," I said to his lifeless eyes. "I am so sorry, son."

He had given his life to protect Marian and so doing had saved the rest of us, too. Marian threw herself upon his chest and wept, telling him he was a true knight. The truest, bravest knight who ever lived. He would have liked that.

I left Marian weeping for Jocelyn and went to find the others.

Swein lived. Though the young man was wounded, the cuts were not deep and two of his archers dragged him into a sitting upright and got a cup of ale into him.

"Will I lose my arm?" he asked, his face grey. "Please, I need my arm. I have to draw a bow. I have to."

"I suppose you are right," I said. "You are no good with the sword. Drink my blood, heal yourself."

He did not want any part of it but Swein wanted to live even more. He was young and full of life and he was unwilling to trade his future for his principles, such as they were.

Swein drank and healed completely.

Next, I ran to Eva. The poor woman had been hacked down with such force that her skull was cracked front to back along one side. Her hair was hacked off on one side, the remains stuck to the scalp by the shining dark ichor. I lifted her up from the blood-drenched cobbles. Her skin was white where it was not covered in blood. Yet she breathed. Her eyes flickered when I called her name and tilted her head. Faithful Swein brought blood from the fallen and I poured it into Eva's mouth. She coughed and swallowed it down. She fought her way back from death once more.

"What happened?" She coughed and grasped me, her fingers like iron.

I was relieved she did not remember the blow that had felled her. Recalling one death is bad enough. Near to us across the courtyard, Swein and Marian called for my help.

"Recover your strength," I urged Eva. "I must see to Anselm."

A pair of Wealden archers rolled the dead horse off Anselm's body and dragged him out from under it. They called me over, weeping in desperation.

"Please save him," Marian said, wiping her tears and many others pleaded for him, also.

The young squire struggled for breath through his crushed chest. But before he took his last breath, I trickled my blood into his mouth.

Like Swein, Anselm did not want it and he squeezed his lips shut.

"This will heal you," I said to him. "It will not change you into one of them."

Sadly, I was not entirely correct about that. I was giving out my blood left and right, thinking simply to save my friends and sworn men. But I had no thought of the consequences that ingesting my blood might have. A seemingly permanent side effect that I did not discover until later.

But in the courtyard that day, Anselm recovered from his grievous wounds instead of succumbing to them.

Everyone recovered but poor Jocelyn. I would have his body taken back to Ashbury to be buried. He would have made a good lord, I think and a good husband. But it was not to be.

While the Wealden archers under Swein's command hunted down the surviving sons of Eden, I found myself a new sword, a fresh horse and began the hunt for William de Ferrers.

The Lord of Eden had fled while Little John had attacked. Most of William's men were tracked and killed by Swein's remaining archers within the first day but William had slithered away into the wood like a worm. The Wealden archers tracked his trail too but he had melted into Sherwood.

Still, I followed. I searched. I scoured the wood and the hills. I kicked my way through barns and outbuildings. We searched the fens and marshes of the east. Some archers I sent south, others west while I went north to the Humber. After two weeks I had to admit that I had failed once more.

William was truly gone.

16

CAST OUT

"WE CHASED HIM FOR DAYS. I sent men in every direction. Your son, Anselm, was of great help as he can read the signs and tracks of men very well. I exhausted a number of horses chasing word of him. God bless those Wealden archers and the rest of their efforts. But every trail led nowhere. Then, many days after the scouring of Eden, there was a series of bloody murders in Grimsby. There was no doubt who had done them, as the bodies were rent at the neck and a couple of women went missing. By the time I arrived there, William was gone. Some said they recognised my description of William in a man who had been seen in the town but no one knew what ship he had boarded. So I fear it is beyond doubt that he has fled the country by now," I said. "From Grimsby, he could have taken any number of ships into the North Sea. He could be in France, Frisia or Denmark and from there he can go anywhere in Christendom. And beyond."

"That is a terrible shame," the Regent of England, William the Marshal said to me. "After all that you went through, to lose him at the last moment. A terrible shame. But you must not blame yourself, Richard. That man is a snake and a coward and he crawls upon his belly back to some hole instead of dying like a man. No, do not blame yourself."

It was the end of September 1217 and two months since we had destroyed Eden. We sat together, alone, in a small day room of the royal castle of Dover. The chamber and the castle belonged to King Henry. But since the king was yet a small boy, he was not in attendance. We sat by a narrow window overlooking the sea. Outside, the gulls cried their endless cries, wheeling and battling through the sky. The cold wind blowing through the window tasted of salt spray and reminded me of the battle I had fought outside. There were few remains of the ships I had burnt but still there were charred timbers here and there on the shingle. It felt good to remember fighting with Jocelyn at my side.

"I will find him," I said. "I have sworn it so many times that it may sound meaningless but I will find him, my lord and I will ensure he pays for his countless crimes." My shame at allowing him to escape was almost overwhelming. If only I had known then how long it would take for me to fulfil my oath.

"Of course," the Regent, William Marshal said, nodding to emphasise his sincerity. "Well done to you, nevertheless. You scoured him out of Sherwood. But, the Archbishop of York's tragic death at his hands leaves the kingdom with a chance to heal the wounds caused by the past few years."

The Marshal looked at me carefully, judging whether I had killed the archbishop, as I had agreed to do. William had killed him but I was willing to take the credit if it meant gaining a few more of the Marshal's favours. I had family and friends who had to be rewarded for their loyalty.

"I am glad to hear it and I sincerely hope that with his death, you can bring peace to the kingdom," I said to the Regent. "The whole kingdom, that is, including the men of the king's forests."

"Good God, not you, too," he said, scowling. "My son has been nagging me about the king's forests without let up. Penalties too harsh and rights not granted and officials corrupted. What have you done to him, infesting him with this absurd concern for the welfare of the residents of the forests?"

"I care nothing for those residents," I said, which was not at all true. "But you should know, my lord, how close to disorder the forests are. The penalties for the smallest of crimes—"

"Yes, yes," the Regent said, waving his hand at me. A tiny gesture but full of his almost total authority. "I have heard it all a dozen times, from Anselm and from a score of other men. Do not fret, we will issue a charter to remake some of the laws. Enough to keep the common men quiet and happy. And your friend Roger de Lacy will retire to his estates and keep out of everyone's business for the rest of his life if he knows what is good for him. I hear his wounds were so grave that he will likely be bedridden until the end of his days, which is probably what he deserves. I have given the post of Sheriff of Nottinghamshire to Geoffrey of Monmouth. A noble lad, if somewhat arrogant. My hope is that a position of genuine authority will be the making of him. The chief bailiff is Sir Guy of Gisbourne, who has agreed to remain. It will be beneficial for Geoffrey to have an experienced man who knows the land and the people."

"That is good," I said but of course, I did not mean it. Geoffrey was a petty, vile little tyrant and I felt sorry for the common people of that fine country. "When does the French fleet sail?" I asked. "They look ready to go."

The Marshal's voice, always steady, rose in anger as he spoke. "They bloody better well sail tomorrow or I shall burn the lot of them. Louis, Prince of France has sailed already, tail between his royal legs." William Marshal allowed himself a small smile. He looked old, thinner even than the last time I had seen him, but still he had a core of steel. "Had to pay the little shit ten thousand marks to get him to sign the treaty saying he had never been the king of England."

"Ten thousand marks," I said, whistling.

"I know," the Marshal said, grimacing. "But it was worth the price to be sure he can mount no objections and will not pursue any claim to Henry's throne. Not to the Pope or to his father or anyone. Henry will be the king of England. And none shall challenge him."

"I am sure that with you to guide him," I said, "Henry will make a fine king."

He waved that way as flattery. "If you would stay in England," William the Marshal said. "I would find a duty for you. Not simply instructing the king with sword and lance but with a proper place in court. He is a bright young fellow but he is rather godly. Already, the priests gather and whisper soft, holy words into his ear. I admit, I am afraid that when I am gone they will have him building churches rather than castles and raising cathedrals over armies. The boy needs soldiers around him to harden him into a man of action instead of a man of God."

"You honour me, my lord. I wish you knew how much it meant to hear you offer me such a thing. But I must find William," I said. "And cut out his heart." My own heart ached that it was not so.

"I understand," William Marshal said though he seemed a little irritated. Most men did not say no to the Marshal. "I am sure you will do him the justice due to him."

"A thousand deaths are not enough for William de Ferrers," I said, unable to keep the emotion from my voice.

"No, indeed," the Marshal said, solemnly. "But one will do, will it not?"

We shared a cup of wine and I was shown the door.

"And I must thank you," the Marshal said, grasping my shoulder before I left. His grip was like iron. "For leaving Ashbury to my son."

"Anselm earned it," I said. "And he will make a very fine lord and a good knight. It is not my place to say so but you should be proud of him."

"Be sure that you never tell him this," the Marshal said, lowering his voice. "But Anselm is my favourite."

The Charter of the Forest was first issued by William Marshal in the young King Henry's name on 6 November 1217 and again in 1225. Amongst the articles rolling back the extent of the afforested areas, limiting the powers of the foresters and verderers were declarations I was certain had come from Anselm's discussions with his father, based on the injustices experienced by Swein.

There was an article granting that every free man can conduct his pigs through the king's wood freely and without impediment. And if the pigs of any free man shall spend one night in the forest, he should not be so prosecuted that he loses anything of his own.

Another article removed the punishments of death or the loss of limb for anyone taking venison. Finally, an acknowledgement in law that the life of a common man was worth more than the price of a deer.

And, finally, there was a general pardon for any man who had been outlawed for a forest offence. The king commanded through the charter that they should be released from their outlawry without legal proceedings after swearing that they will not do wrong in the future in respect of the forest.

So, Swein would be a free man once more.

The Charter of the Forest was drafted as a companion document to the reissued, rewritten Articles of the Barons. To differentiate the lesser Charter of the Forest from the other, the document dealing with the relationship between the barons and the crown was referred to as the Great Charter or Magna Carta.

The Marshal died a few years later, after seeing that his work was finally done. He had guided England through the greatest crises it had ever known. He had secured the succession and surrounded Henry with fine men.

Anselm was the fifth son. What was remarkable was that he did inherit his father's title in time. Every one of his elder brothers inherited the title in turn and then died without producing an heir. Poor Anselm himself died, aged forty-five and left no heirs of his own. The great estates of the Earl of Pembroke were divided amongst Anselm's four sisters.

The extinction of the male line is remarkable. I often wondered just how far William de Ferrers had seduced the lords of England. William Marshal's eldest son had been with the rebel barons before being welcomed back by his father. Was he one of the sons of Eden even then? That would explain why the young Marshal had freed me from the dungeon of Newark Castle. Had his Lord of Eden commanded him, so that I might run into Sherwood to be captured?

Perhaps the eldest of the brothers had brought his siblings over to Eden to be turned. Only Anselm remained beyond his grasp. And I had fed Anselm with my own blood, enough to bring him back to life. Had I saved the young man merely to condemn him to a life without the joy of children? Still, he died in his own bed with his dear wife at his side. Not a bad way to go.

But it was later when I understood these things clearly and by then it was already long past. We must accept what we cannot change, even if we were entirely at fault.

Despite the collapse of the Marshal family, King Henry ruled England for an astonishing fifty-six years. His reign was not necessarily a very successful or happy one. He fought his own wars against a new generation of rebel barons, including Richard Marshal. I was not in England for any of it, or else I would have happily slaughtered those selfish nobles. England would only be beaten into submission by Henry's son, Edward Longshanks, the Hammer of the Scots who was crowned in 1274.

But back in late 1217, I said my final farewell to the Marshal in Dover. Then Eva and I rode for the Weald.

We made it just in time.

***

My dear Emma and William of Cassingham married on the steps of the parish church in Cassingham. Emma wore a loose dress so that her swollen belly did not show too much. But everyone there, including Cassingham's priest, was already so in love with her that they felt nothing but joy for the husband and wife.

So many people came to celebrate their union, I was astonished, although I should not have been. Cassingham was by then a living hero to the Kentish folk. He had protected them from the predatory French and everyone wished him well. And Emma was the kind of person that decent people loved. They flocked around her, every face grinning and winking and wishing them well. That was a kind of love and joy that was beyond me by then and, truth be told, probably always had been.

After the short ceremony on the steps of the church, there was a great feast in the village. Swein and Marian had both travelled to the Weald with Eva and me, for the marriage and also so that Swein could accept his pardon and swear allegiance to the new king.

Swein and Marian would return north, to Sherwood, right after Emma's marriage and get there in time for winter. That celebration was the last time I saw either of them. We stood in the centre of the village, drinking ale and eating with gusto.

"The Marshal has awarded you some fine land in Sherwood," I said to Swein. "Now you have sworn allegiance to young King Henry, I suspect you will be returning there for good? Settling down?"

"Someone has to look after the good folk who live in the wood," Marian said, a twinkle in her eye. "And that will be me and Robin."

"Who in the name of God is Robin?" I asked Marian.

Swein rubbed the back of his neck and scuffed his shoes. "There was a man called Swein, up in Barnsdale where I'm from. He was a bit of a hero of mine. But Robert is my real name," Swein said. "My dad and my friends always called me Robin." He shrugged.

Marian looked at him with deep affection in her eyes. I remember thinking that it would be difficult for her to marry him, an outlaw commoner, but hoping that they would be happy in whatever way they could. Of course, they did marry. Who knows, perhaps they already had.

"You do not look like a Robert," I said, looking up and down his lanky frame. "Or a Robin. A heron maybe. Or a stork."

As it turned out, the man who once called himself Swein went back to Sherwood and that small band of Wealden archers went with him to take up their own lands they had been awarded by a grateful Crown. Sherwood had been badly depopulated by William's activities and the decent farmland was crying out for quality men to work the land again.

I have no doubt that Swein - Robin — meant to be a good farmer and to live a dutiful life within the law. However, within a few years, he was an outlaw again. Not only that, he became the leader of the outlaws of Sherwood and they fought to keep the new Sheriff of Nottingham in check. Luckily, he had that core of Wealden archers who became Sherwood freemen, to help him.

Geoffrey of Monmouth would turn out to be a deeply unpleasant, spiteful character. Of course, once he saw her beauty, Geoffrey became infatuated with Marian and he abused his position as sheriff trying to take her for himself.

Robin's love of disguises and stratagems came in handy over the years as he and his men looked to combat the corruption of the new sheriff and his men. Despite the sheriff's best efforts, nothing could separate Robin and Marian. He was another soul I had saved with my blood who never fathered a child. Despite that, I am happy that their life and adventures have grown into legend. Most of all I am well pleased that they found each other.

"It gives me joy beyond measure to see you smiling and big with child," I said to Emma before I left England. "And I am so sorry that I could not protect Jocelyn. He would have been so proud of you."

Two days after her wedding, we sat close together on a bench at the top table in her new home, a large country house with a good hall and many chambers off either end of it. The fires burned hot, driving out the moisture of autumn. The servants brought Emma a steady supply of warm wine and morsels to eat. It was clear they were devoted to her, as were the other wives and older women of the village who sat in the hall, working and gossiping and throwing smiles her way. I was glad she would have women around her once again, especially once she began her lying in before the birth.

"I know you are sorry about Jocelyn," Emma said and reached up to rub her hand on my cheek just as she had done when she was a tiny girl, sitting in my lap in the Holy Land. "My heart breaks a hundred times a day when I think of him. I wish that he could share in my happiness. But he died a knight. You say he died saving Marian's life? He dreamed of such a death, ever since he was a boy. A death like in the songs. But still, my heart breaks. I think he would have made Marian a good husband."

I was not certain that the young lady would have taken Jocelyn even had he lived but I said no such thing to Emma and simply nodded.

"William the Marshal will see that Cassingham gets an annual payment every year for the rest of his life," I said. "And he has granted you both land and the rights to cut and sell wood in London. You will both do very well and so will your children."

"I swear that I do not mind you have left Ashbury to Anselm rather than to me," Emma said, smiling. "Still, I wish you would stay in England. Let William go. Do not waste any more of your life chasing after him."

"He has killed so many people that I love," I said. "I must pursue him, even to the ends of the Earth. And I cannot live in England any longer. For years already, they have been whispering about my eternal youth. I hid away as much as I could but how long can I live as Richard of Ashbury before I am driven out? In ten years, I will be almost sixty. What about ten years after that? And all the while, I will look like this. At least by leaving now, it can be in a manner of my own choosing rather than being hounded out by an angry crowd that believes I am in league with Satan. And I am not made for this land, I do not deserve to stay. I am not a good man, I know that now. I am a killer. I tortured a man, prolonged his wretched life and I did not feel guilty for it. I bring death to my enemies but also I bring my curse down upon those around me. I cannot fight it. I must go away. The Holy Land is the only way. I can move from place to place, selling my lance and sword. It is not a bad life. Bloody, perhaps. But better suited to my kind of evil."

"You are a good man," Emma said, firmly. "You are. I know it, even if you do not. Do not submit to the thought that you are the same as that corrupted lunatic."

"We have the same blood," I said.

"You think that is what makes a man or a woman good or evil?" Emma said, growing angry. "You are not a perfect knight from a ballad, Richard but you fight for the right things. You try, at least. You saved so many of those people in Sherwood. All those prisoners, I heard there were dozens. Just as you saved Jocelyn and me when we were children. You burned yourself almost to death in rescuing us. Would you have done such a thing if you were evil?"

"You were too young to remember," I said, certain that she knew of the fire from Jocelyn.

She fixed me with her beautiful eyes. "I remember everything."

"I pray that is not true," I said, recalling the horrors of that cavern.

"I remember being certain that we would never get out of that cage," Emma said, her eyes looking through me. "I remember the people screaming and the smoke. Jocelyn held me, sheltered me from the flames. He said to me, over and over, to close my eyes and that all would be well soon enough." She took a deep breath. "And then there you were. My father. You used your body to hold back the flames so we could get out. I remember your skin turning black and cracking. But still, as soon as I saw you I knew you would save me. And you did."

I had saved her by giving her some of my blood. Never had I considered that my blood might have been the reason she had brought forth her previous children before their time. Even the fact that she had ever conceived a child at all seemed counter to William's assertions about infertility. But perhaps it was because she had been so young when she drank that she had overcome it. Obviously, I said nothing whatsoever about this to her at the time, while she was great with child. I prayed that she would bear the child to term.

I took a deep breath. "I had no idea that you remembered anything of it at all. You were so young. I thought you would not remember me at all. And then I abandoned you."

"And it was years before I forgave you for that. But even then, we never doubted that you would welcome us when we came to your door. You never once begrudged us anything. You bought Jocelyn finer horses and armour than you had yourself. You welcomed into your hall men and women that you despised so that I might have the proper company." She laughed.

"You are not an evil man. A fool for women, perhaps."

I took her hands. "I always hesitate to call you daughter. But if you were truly mine, I could not be prouder of you. Nor could I be happier."

"You are my father," Emma said, smiling her lovely smile. "In every way that matters. And you always will be."

Kinder words were never spoken and I remember them fondly. On dark, bitter nights over the centuries, I have recalled them and they have made me warm. For all I have done wrong and all I have lost, at least I did some things right.

Before I left, I took William of Cassingham aside. "I like you, William. I always have. But if you treat her and her children with anything other than profound respect then I shall return to England and cut out your heart, do you understand me?"

He looked very grave, swallowing but he looked back across the hall at his new wife before he answered. "Once, I loved fighting. I wanted to win a knighthood and be a great man. Now, all I want to do is make her happy."

I never saw Emma again. But I do know that she lived a long, good life with Cassingham and three healthy children, taking care of her own family and of the people of the Weald. It is my belief that she lived the life that she wanted and that she deserved.

And so it was that I left England once more. I left behind my land. And my name.

I left with Eva. When she drank my blood after being drained of her own, she had become immortal, like me. The difference was that she had to drink blood every few days or she would grow weak, get sick and die.

After Sherwood, she had taken days to accept her fate while we hunted William. She never spoke very much and I fretted about what she would do. At times, she was angry and I knew not to speak to her. Other times, usually in the dark of the night, she would become disheartened and sit curled up into herself. I never knew whether she would welcome my embrace or angrily punch me away. I blamed myself for what happened to her, for leaving her at the priory was an inexcusable blunder.

At the time, I had convinced myself I was protecting her and Marian but really I wanted the women out of the way while I waged my war. Eva could have fought beside me on the walls of Lincoln and been safer than she had been at the priory but for all she had shown her ability, she was a woman and I had put her away. She had warned me, I had ignored her and she was the one who had paid the price.

I remembered how it felt to die. I remembered the fear and anguish that resounded after waking again like an echo in an empty hall. I remembered that the horror of it faded in time, like all things. So I gave her time. Whenever she would allow it, we slept entwined and I wrapped her in my arms through the darkness.

Eva had left the land of the living and dying. The consolation was her enormous strength and speed. And, I think, that at least I would be beside her.

Before heading south from Derbyshire that last time, we stopped off at Tutbury Priory in the dead of night.

I banged on the door of the prior's house. It took the young man a long time to answer, it being between matins and lauds. I knocked quietly but insistently.

He was muttering under his breath when he yanked the door open.

"This had better be—" Prior Simon started. He froze, dropped his candle and attempted to slam the door on me.

I placed my foot in the door. "My dear prior," I said into the shadows. "You sold out the innocent young women left in your care, do you recall?"

"I had to," he said, backing away. "They forced me to do it."

I pushed the door open, stepping inside, into the light cast by a single candle lit on the prior's bedside. "They paid you."

"It is my duty to do what is best for the priory," Prior Simon said, then gasped as Eva stepped into the room behind me with her dagger drawn.

"I will kill him," I said over my shoulder. "Then you drink his blood."

"No," Eva said, pushing past me. "I will kill him, too."

The prior's scream was cut off before he could utter it. We filled his robes with rocks and slid his drained corpse into the fishpond and we watched his body plopping beneath the black waters.

"The monks are waking for prayers," I whispered to Eva and we rode south for the Weald. She wiped the blood from her chin and nodded.

After Emma and Cassingham's marriage, we went to Dover to catch a boat to Calais before the autumn storms ruined the short passage.

"I have to drink blood," Eva said to me while we waited on the cliffs of Dover looking down at the fishing boats bobbing far below beyond the beach. The thriving town was behind us. Down on the beaches, it thronged with fishermen and traders.

"You do," I said to Eva, standing close to her.

"I must drink blood every day or two in order to stay strong. Or I will become ill like that creature Tuck, ashen and green of skin and raving mad. So, in order for me to live, others must die. I know what you have said, that some men deserve death. I do not disagree. But there are not enough of them to keep me alive."

The sky was clear and light blue though the wind was growing colder every day. Though it was yet daytime, the crescent of the moon hung above the massive walls of the unconquered castle, higher up the cliffs to the north.

"You have never been to the Holy Land," I said, facing south. "You have not seen the rest of the world. Everywhere on this Earth, there is war. And anywhere there is war will be blood enough for the both of us. And whenever there is not, you will drink my blood," I said, looking out at the choppy waters of the English Channel. "You can drink from me every day if you prefer. No one has to die for you to get blood."

She scoffed. "So you wish me to be as dependent upon you as a baby is on its mother."

She spoke half in jest yet the word fell heavy upon us. She had died, my blood had brought her back but she would never now create life from her womb. Eva was the first vampire that I ever created with my own blood. She would not be the last. Just as my seed was barren, all vampires that William and I made over the centuries were infertile. William had told us the truth, in that at least. Years later we discussed our first months together. Eva said she had half hoped we would have a child from our many couplings. It was never to be but already, in Dover that day, we were accepting of it. In fact, it drove us together even more because we thought that we would have no one in our lives but ourselves. We were wrong about that.

"I swear, Eva," I said to her on the white cliffs. "I swear that I will stand by you. Through all of this. Through whatever it is that we face out there in the world."

"We are leaving the land of the living," she said, reaching out to take my hand. "Destined to live on, ageless, undying. But never truly part of the world."

"Don't be ridiculous, woman," I said. "Our life is going to be full of wonder and beauty. And plenty of fighting."

"Is this some sort of marriage vow?" she asked, looking up at me.

"Yes," I said, squeezing her hand. "If you will have me." I held my breath. People said that I gave little away of my true thoughts and feelings but Eva was so much more difficult to read than I was, I am sure. Especially then.

Eva nodded, almost to herself. "Do we not require witnesses?"

"Who would we have to witness our union?" I said, smiling. "We are leaving England, so why would we need them? And anyway, whoever they are, we will outlive them. The only witnesses worthy of us are the sky and the sea and the moon above us."

"Well," Eva said, smiling, finally. Her face came to life. "Alright, then."

We sailed for France. We travelled to Italy, to Cyprus, to Outremer where the last Crusader kingdoms held on to their lands. We travelled to Constantinople and then back to Italy and France. We went to Spain and spent many years living in that fine land, fighting in the endless struggles amongst the Spanish kingdoms and against the remaining Moors.

We fought for one lord or another in many battles. I earned my keep as a guard for many a merchant. Sometimes Eva disguised herself as a man. When she could, she fought openly as a woman, though often that was difficult. Other times she had to put up with posing as an ordinary wife. We had to run from a number of towns and mercenary camps.

To obtain blood for us both, we killed men who deserved to die. Criminals, mainly and we fed well while punishing the guilty wherever we went. For a while, we kept a tavern in Acre and even tried farming, growing fruit and felling trees. We always went back to what we knew best, for I knew by then that I was not truly a good man. I was not a true knight. Killing and torture and blood by the bucket load were entirely my nature. But I tried at least to always be good to my woman. A sword in my hand by day, Eva in my bed at night and a belly full of blood as often as I could get it. And so we were contented.

Always, though, I knew that I would find William again somewhere, someday. It was many years later and the place was farther east than I had ever travelled before, to the grandest and most civilised city in the world. A centre of learning and culture the likes of which the world had never seen. The citizens were the most literate, the most highly educated, most cultured on earth. A city that was both a crossroads and destination for trade between China and Syria, Russia and Arabia. East and West. The greatest city of the age, Baghdad.

Amongst the beauty and riches, I encountered William once more. But he was fighting with the most terrifying warriors and agents of destruction the world has ever known. William had finally encountered an entire people whose love of mayhem and murder rivalled his own.

The Mongols.

VAMPIRE KHAN

The Immortal Knight Chronicles Book 3

Richard of Ashbury
and the Mongol Invasion of Persia
1253 to 1266

DAN DAVIS

Part One
Constantinople
1253

THE BANNERS OF THE KNIGHTS whipped and snapped in the wind, framed by the vivid expanse of blue above. To my right, timber stands held the cheering spectators beneath the banners and blocked my view of the mighty walls of Constantinople on the horizon.

Through the eye slits of my helmet, I could see little enough. Straight ahead across the field, the line of knights struggled to contain their horses. Beside me, on my left and right, the men of my own side held their lances ready. Our horses stomped and shook their heads as the riders fought their beasts into submission and growled threats at them.

My destrier trembled. He was a monster. Too big and too slow for most knights and long in the tooth. Do not ride him into battle, a Burgundian man-at-arms had joked with me when I had purchased the animal, hitch him to a plough instead. But the beast rode as straight as an arrow in the charge and feared nothing. And he had a terrible anger when roused and would tear chunks from another horse's neck in a fight.

My enemies that day were twenty knights from France, Navarre, Aragon, Acre and elsewhere. My side was twenty knights from all over Christendom. The tourney was a French invention but it had spread immediately to the English, who knew a good thing when we saw it. And it had, over the years, become popular in many kingdoms of Christendom. That day outside Constantinople we even had two knights from the Kingdom of Poland, three from Bohemia, and two from the Kingdom of Sicily.

And me. A knight of England, who had no lord and nothing to offer but his lance and his sword. My coat and shield were black, emblazoned with a single red chevron.

The others were a riot of red, blue, green, white and gold, with blazons of crosses, stripes, lions, eagles, and chalices. Lances raised, pennants flapping in the wind like a flock of exotic birds.

It was best to enter a tourney with a companion or two, at least, who will fight alongside you and watch your flanks while you watched theirs. Some tourneys had companies of ten or more men fighting as brothers. While I, close to friendless in a strange land, had to make do with two young Breton knights who pretended they were granting me a favour by allowing me to fight with them. They seemed to ride well enough and they swore they had broken lances in Picardie and Paris. The damned whoresons barely spoke to me because they thought I was poor and landless. Well, they were half right. Eva, my wife, said it was because they were afraid of me but then she said that about everybody.

Much of the noise, muffled already by my helm, faded away as the watching crowd fell into hushed anticipation. That meant they had seen the order given and were watching the trumpets raised.

My horse stamped a foot and quivered.

The trumpets sounded.

Across the field, the line of knights contracted as each man tensed into hunch behind his shield and raked his spurs into his horse's flanks. I did the same, urging my destrier forward. The magnificent beast sighed with relief as he could at last give way to his instinct. Still, I held him to the trot and he would only reach a full charge as we met the enemy. He was a fine horse.

Beside me, the mounted knights leapt forward, pulling ahead as the men forgot everything we had discussed and urged their horses from dead standing straight into the charge.

If we did not meet the enemy line as one, then the most advanced of our knights would perhaps face two lances instead of one. My side would lose men to the initial charge and make my own fight all the harder.

And yet I made no attempt to keep up with them. I looked left and right, my view through the eye slits bouncing around. Already, our entire line was ragged. The centre, other than myself, was pulling ahead and the sides were lagging behind, but it was not a spearheaded charge.

Ahead, beyond the two Bretons, the knights against us lowered their lances and couched them. Both sides picked their final targets.

Mine was the man I had lined up against at the start. A knight of France named Bertrand de Cardaillac. A truly massive man in green and gold, newly arrived in Constantinople. Sir Bertrand was said to be a great knight with a reputation for brutality and no other wanted to face him, leaving me free to take the key position in the centre. I wanted his wealth. I wanted his horse and his purse.

And I wanted to see how good he truly was.

Two knights of Aragon flanked him, and they had together formed a temporary company for the tourney. As long as no other interfered, it would be my Bretons and me against Sir

Bertrand and his Aragonese.

But the Bretons wanted his wealth, too, and they forgot their duty and aimed at him rather than the Aragonese on his flanks. In so doing, they narrowed the gap between their two horses and blocked my line of approach. What were they hoping to achieve? They had made it into a charge of three against two.

Stupid bloody fools.

My horse was annoyed and confused but I urged him on, faster, and lowered my lance. The crashing of lances on shields began to ring out up and down the line.

The Bretons in front smashed into the knights of Aragon. My supposed comrades were a mere lance length beyond me but even had they not deserved it, I could have done nothing to save them from their fate. It was three knights against the two impetuous Bretons.

And both Bretons were struck, hard.

I held my course as the crashing of dozens of wooden shields and lances echoed across the field, horses, and men crying out in triumph or fear.

Bertrand, the French knight, smashed through one of my Bretons, unhorsing him. Even through all the noise and the steel of my helm, I heard Bertrand shouting in triumph at his strike. His voice was as throaty as a bull's and as he roared he half-turned to watch the Breton tumbling sideways from his saddle.

As the proverb says, pride goes before destruction, and I thanked God for prideful knights.

The blunted tip of my lance caught Bertrand de Cardaillac on the side of his helm. It was a hard strike, though of course the man's head was knocked away at once, reducing the force compared to a hit to the chest or shield. But the blow knocked the knight from his horse, all sense gone. His arms stiffened and jutted up in front of him as he fell, dropping his lance and throwing his shield arm up and to the side. His helm, too, was ripped from his head. I heard but did not see him crash into the hard earth and I prayed he would not die.

A knight from Aragon lunged at me with his lance as we passed but I saw it coming and leaned away, making a show of my lack of concern. Still, it was closer than I had expected and scratched the paint on my shield. I prayed he would be disconcerted by my bravery rather than encouraged by my incompetence.

By then the lines were through each other and the knights of both sides wheeled about to reform. Dust thrown up by the galloping hooves drifted across the field. A few men were down in the middle of the field. Bertrand de Cardaillac was on the ground, unmoving. I searched for another target and found both Aragonese knights already moving their horses toward me with intent displayed in their movements. The enemy line opposite was unformed and yet already they were charging. The knights of my side were not content to wait either.

Already, the tourney would be every man for himself. Every man and his fellows, if they stuck by each other.

"With me," I shouted to the remaining Breton knight, while he raked his spurs into his horse's flanks and the beast jumped into movement.

"God, give me strength," I muttered and urged my destrier into the fray. The noise of battle sounded once again, with shouts and the clattering of wood rising above the pounding of hooves on the hard ground.

My Breton clashed awkwardly with the Aragonese and both fell in a jumble, dragging their horses down with them.

Steady beneath me, my horse ignored the wildly kicking hooves and kept on toward the mounted knight aiming at me. As his blunted war lance thumped on my shield, my lance point bounced low and connected with his thigh and then his hip, knocking the lance from my grasp. My shield blocked my view but I continued past and drew my sword, turning about as swiftly as I could.

Few knights had made it through the melee in the centre and most were positioning themselves to fight from horseback with swords or other weapons. Broken and forgotten lances lay strewn about the dusty ground where the horses stomped and turned as groups of fighters formed. Sweat dripped into my eyes and my breath sounded like bellows in my ears. Already it was becoming difficult to know who was fighting for what side and the dust flew up, obscuring the men.

I pushed my way between two groups as the Aragonese knights, all on foot, came together with their swords drawn, one shield between the three of them. Bertrand de Cardaillac, massive as he was, looked dazed, blinking about him as though he had no idea how he had come to be here, with powdery pale earth caked to his big sweating face. The Aragonese knights, unlike my idiot Bretons, were doing their duty by holding him upright and guarding him while he recovered his senses. They were looking for a horse or at least a way out and away from the clashing men and kicking destriers around them.

I rode straight towards the three of them.

With cries of warning, the two knights tried to drag Bertrand away in two different directions, one on each arm, and so succeeded only in holding him steady and right in my path. My dear old horse reared his head but his powerful chest collided with Bertrand and knocked him down with more force than I intended. Thanks to God, he fell to one side and my horse avoided stamping on him.

I pulled up just beyond and dismounted while the other two ran back to protect him. Robust fellow that he was, he was already trying to get up.

"Yield," I shouted as I approached on foot. I held my shield low and my sword point down.

The Aragonese came at me, circling to either side in an attempt to surround me and attack.

I charged the one without a shield, deflected his thrust on my shield and barged him to the ground faster than he could retreat. While he was stunned I banged the edge of my blade across the eye slits on his helmet.

"You are mine," I yelled at him.

I turned at the sound of approaching feet and my sword point caught the charging knight on his mailed knee. The man screamed and went down, whimpering, all the fight gone out of him.

All around me, the tourney field was slowing down as men yielded. My side was victorious, despite my useless Bretons falling at the first charge and a ragged cheer went up from the exhausted knights and the crowd on their stand at the side of the field.

The knights from Aragon and the French giant gave up their swords to me, hilt first. I would have their horses and armour or the value of them.

And that was good because I needed gold and silver.

I needed it to help me to travel to the North, across the Black Sea, into the lands of the Tartars.

My immortal enemy, William, was there. And I was going to kill him.

***

Later that day, as the sun rolled its way down to the west across the tourney field, I sat in the shade of my tent with all four sides open and pinned well back so that the breeze could cool my skin. There was plenty of space around my tent and the other knights and squires ignored me, other than an occasional polite wave. Somewhere out of sight behind the tents, a smith tapped away on steel, reducing dents from helms and straightening blades. A gaggle of little pages ran by me, laughing and shouting abuse at each other in language so vulgar it would have made a Flemish mercenary blush. The smell of roasting meat wafted from somewhere and it made me salivate, even though I had already eaten my fill.

In the shade of my tent, with the sweat scrubbed from my body, dressed in a thin cotton tunic, and wine in my belly, my body was comfortable.

But my mind was troubled.

"You will never be content," Eva said, sitting opposite me across the small, square table. She was dressed like a man and acting as my squire. She had learned over the years to control the swaying of her narrow hips when she walked and could mimic the swaying-armed strut of a young man. It would fool most men, from a distance, at least. "You will never be content as long as you live."

"I am content," I said, which was not true. "Those knights were just too poor. I should have collected more."

"More what?"

"More silver from them," I said. "More knights on the field. It was all over too quickly."

"You always want more," she said, shaking her head. "More fighting, more silver."

"More wine?" I said and refilled her cup from the jug.

"We have enough silver now," Eva pointed out.

"We should have more," I said, feeling the anger build. "I should have taken everything from them."

The squires of the two Aragonese knights had, to their credit, brought their masters' horses and armour to my tent immediately after the tourney had been declared. Both of the young men wept before me like women as they begged to buy back their horses and armour from me there and then. Of course, coin was what I wanted anyway, so I agreed.

Two of the destriers were ancient and worth little enough. One was of particularly good breeding but it was close to lame.

"I could sell them to a butcher and get more than what you beggars are offering," I shouted at them. "And when were these helms made? Were they worn at the Battle of Hastings? And the rings on the mail are thin and flat as a blade of grass. Are you certain that you serve knights and not paupers?" The squires cringed and wept harder. Blubbing about needing the armour for crusading. They begged, on their knees, for me to accept the paltry sums in silver that their masters offered and swore, upon the hands of God in Heaven, that it was all they had.

After accepting their modest bags of coins, the pair had wiped their eyes and strolled off talking about where to get some wine before returning to their masters. I swear they were laughing as they went and I was sorely tempted to give them both a brutal thrashing. But they were just doing their duty, the little sods.

"If you wanted more," Eva said to me over her cup, "you should not be so susceptible to tears."

"It was not the tears," I said. "All Aragonese are like that, bawling at the slightest hint of strife. How could I take their horses and end those men's Crusade? Now, they may continue on into the Holy Land."

Eva nodded. "And sit in Acre drinking wine for a year before going home to tell stories for the rest of their mediocre lives about how they stuck it to the Saracens."

I could not argue with that.

"Where is the damned French squire?" I asked, for the tenth time. "The day grows long."

"The word is that this Sir Bertrand is an arrogant lord," Eva said. "He will not take kindly to being carried off the field after his first charge. We know he was newly arrived from Acre and is on his way elsewhere, only delaying his departure to take part in that sad little tourney. Perhaps he will neglect to pay his debt."

"I would go and take it from him."

She wiped her lips. "Is it worth the trouble? We have what we need, now. Unless you would rather stay here or go elsewhere rather than North?"

"It is the principle of the thing."

"Oh?" she said, tilting her head. "You are principled now?"

"The principle is that the big bastard has wealth," I said, "and I want it."

Eva nodded over my shoulder, sat forward and lowered her voice. "Someone approaches."

"A squire?"

"The squire of Methuselah, perhaps."

"What?" I asked, confused, as I reached for my sword that was leaning against the table.

Eva shook her head, pulled her hood close about her face and ducked away to make herself busy with our gear. I left my sword where it was, within arm's reach.

"Sir, God give you good day." A man's voice called out as he approached.

I watched Eva. She made a show of wiping down the good saddle but tilted her head so that she could keep one beady eye on the man.

Slowly, I sipped my wine and I watched her. She watched him from beneath her hood, and I made ready to grab my sword if Eva gave me warning.

The man strode by the table, into my view and stopped across from me, standing behind the chair.

An older man, with noble bearing. His face was long and narrow but his jaw was square and his bones were big. No fat on his belly. A Templar and a knight, that much was clear, for he wore the white robe of a knighted member of that order and a sword hung at his side. Square shouldered and straight backed in spite of his advanced years, the old Templar looked me in the eye and held my gaze.

"You are the English knight Sir Richard, I am told?"

I said nothing, which was remarkably rude.

"My name is Sir Thomas de Vimory," he said. "I should say, sir, that you fought very well today."

I scoffed. "Hardly a fight."

He inclined his head. "It was a rather brief tourney, somewhat unconventionally contested."

I smiled at that. "This is not France. And no great lords wished to try their skill. It was a scrap between the dregs and the desperate as a brief diversion before they head east or west." I lifted my cup. "Speaking as one of the dregs, of course." I downed my wine.

My uncouthness made him uncomfortable. "Nevertheless, you came out of it quite well, did you not?"

I shrugged. "I defeated the poorest knights in Christendom and a coward who has not paid his due."

Sir Thomas the Templar pretended to be amused by my words as if I had been witty, but he was in fact disturbed. "May I speak with you about a most pressing matter?"

I indicated that he was welcome to take the other chair and I filled the cup sitting before him on the table while he did so and then filled my own cup.

"They tell me you are seeking to journey to the lands of the tartars," the old Templar said, taking a sip. The man sat as stiff as a board, with his hands flat on the table.

"Is that what they tell you?" I said, sipping my wine and feigning mild disinterest. The wine was very good.

For months, I had desired to travel north from Constantinople into the lands of the tartars but the merchants would not take me. Word of my intentions had spread, clearly, because it was considered a strange thing for a knight to want. And it was.

"And why, may I ask, are you unable to do so?" the Templar said. "It would appear that you have the means." He flattered me by indicating the quality of my clothing and my equipment.

I hesitated. "No trader will take me, for they fear the wrath of the tartars and those that are subject to them. I have no conceivable business in their lands. I am no merchant. I am no envoy. As far as the tartars would be concerned, a Frankish knight could only be assessing their military strength."

"And they would kill you for that."

"Most certainly," I said. "Without hesitation. They are barbarians, with little enough law between them and none at all for Christians."

Thomas nodded. "And so, you have no way forward."

In fact, I did have a way forward. I had spent weeks persuading one of the merchants to sell to me his boat, his contacts, and his merchandise. The man's two sons had died a year ago and his heart was broken. He was rather old already and with no heirs, he wanted no more of his trade. And so, I would dress myself in the garb of a merchant, hire on his small crew and take iron tools and sacks of grain north up the Black Sea, and bring back furs for sale in the markets of Constantinople. Once in Pontus in the north, I could journey into the interior, with the pretence of wanting to trade directly with the tartars themselves.

That was my way forward.

I took a sip of wine and looked closer at the knight. He was certainly well beyond his best years as his long face was deeply lined and his hair was grey. But his eyes were a clear and bright blue and his body was straight, wiry and strong. His hands looked like they could throttle the life from a man half his age.

Clever, too. I could tell, by the way he looked deep into my eyes, searching for the truth within me. Searching out dishonesty. Even a fool knows one should never trust a clever man. So, I said nothing of my plans.

"Perhaps," I allowed. "But I will go north, by one means or another."

I was sure that he would then, finally, ask me why. Why would any man wish to head into the lands of the vile and murderous heathens who had so thoroughly defeated every army who ever stood against them?

Yet he did not.

Instead, the Templar poured himself another cup of wine from the jug, as if we were friends, and looked me in the eyes once more. "I, myself, am journeying into the lands of the tartars," he said. "And I should like another knight to accompany us."

I nodded.

"I have heard talk of you," I said, putting it together at last, recalling a soused Burgundian squire gossiping about it a few nights before. I had not believed him at the time. "You arrived in Constantinople mere days ago. You are escorting a monk? Who comes from the King of France."

Irritation passed over the old knight's face but he composed himself. "Yes, indeed. William of Rubruck, a Flemish friar from the Order of Saint Francis, is entrusted with a letter from the King of France intended for a lord of the Tartars."

"What is in the letter?" I cut in.

He cleared his throat. "I do not know. Neither does Friar William. And yet, I believe it to be a simple courtesy, one king to another. Or whatever passes for a king amongst them." His face darkened and he trailed off.

"It is a large party, is it not?" I said.

"No." Thomas collected himself. "Indeed, no. Myself and my squire. A French knight and his squire. Then Friar William has his companions, Friar Bartholomew of Cremona. Another brother, a young Englishman like you, named Stephen Gosset."

It was the first time I ever heard of Stephen Gosset. It was not a moment that held any significance for me at the time, of course. How could it have done?

Only much, much later would I curse the man's name. Curse it repeatedly and with fervour, despite all the things that he did for me and for England over the centuries.

"No servants?" I asked, surprised.

He nodded. "The Friar has purchased for himself a young boy, named Nikolas, from here in Constantinople. And we obtained a dragoman in Acre, who knows the tongue of the tartars and, indeed, a great many others. But no others. We wish to keep our numbers down, for we know not how the Tartars will welcome us. We will be relying on their hospitality through our journey, both there and back, and also when we are guests of their prince at our destination."

"And what makes you believe you will be admitted into their lands?"

"It is known that the tartars allow free passage to envoys," Thomas said. "And we have already sent word and have heard that we would be welcomed."

"Forgive my confusion," I said. "But are you this envoy? Or is it the monk?"

Thomas pressed his lips together before replying. "Friar William wishes only to proselytise to the heathens. You see, he has heard from another monk that some among the tartars are Christians. In fact, he has heard how the son of the local prince is a follower of the Christ and so he wishes to go to them and beg to be allowed to preach amongst them and so bring more of the heathens the word of God."

I could not help but scoff.

Thomas the Templar tilted his head. "I do not altogether disagree. I would sooner the tartars be scoured from the Earth and sent to Hell." He took a breath. "But that is a base desire. The friar will be doing God's work."

"That may be," I said. "But it may also be that God wants them all dead. Not baptized."

The look on Thomas' face suggested his own desires would align with God's will if that were indeed the case. I was not curious as to why the old Templar would have strong feelings about the tartars. They were terrifying brutes. Savages who had emerged from nowhere, from the nothingness in the east decades ago. Wherever they met the armies and cities of Christendom, our brothers in Christ had been slaughtered, most terribly. Towns and cities reduced to rubble and the peoples slaughtered or enslaved.

The tartars had pulled back from conquest of all the kingdoms of Europe but no one I had spoken to really knew why. It is God's will, they would say. A phrase which has ever been no more than an admission of profound ignorance.

"So," I said, unwilling to let myself be deflected from my enquiry, "why are you accompanying the friar and his holy companions?"

"The King of France asked me to do so." Thomas said no more.

King Louis of France. A king whose grand Crusade had ended in disaster. His army defeated, utterly, by the Egyptians and he himself captured. The great king who almost shit himself to death and had to pay a fortune to the enemies he had come to vanquish. King Louis now squatted in Acre, one of the last cities held by the Franks in the Holy Land.

"Are you not too great a man to be sent on such an errand?"

"I am no great man," Thomas said, wrinkling his nose at the suggestion. "I am a humble knight in the service of God. No more. And this is no errand. My order protects pilgrims, does it not? I can think of no more appropriate duty than to escort these men in their own duty to spread the word of God to the heathen barbarians. And I was with the King on his crusade and he made a request of me, which I accepted. It is really no more than that."

"Of course," I said. It was a nonsense that he was spouting. A yard of yarn he was spinning. A Templar had no business heading into the wild north.

What his true intentions were, I had no idea. All I did know, was that he was a lying old bastard.

But then, so was I.

He had to ask it, finally. "And why," Thomas said, "if I may ask, are you seeking to journey north of the Black Sea?"

I leaned back on my ancient chair, which creaked beneath me as though it were in pain. I drank my wine, looking across the table at the old man. I tried to think. Never my forte. "You want me to come with you. That much is clear. You would not be here, wasting your time with me, if you did not. But why?"

"I witnessed your victories on the tourney field today. I asked about who you were, I was surprised to discover this rumour that you wished to head north. And, truth be told, we would be safer with another knight, and his squire, to protect us."

"And why ask me? There must be a thousand men-at-arms you could ask."

"None of your obvious ability, nor your renown, and your stature. They tell me you fought in a number of tourneys. I must confess, I am surprised at your youth. In fact, I was told that you fought in the crusade of King Theobald and Richard of Cornwall but that was clearly a mistake, considering it has been fifteen years and you are scarcely old enough."

I could not resist smiling at that. The first time I had fought the Saracens had been sixty years before.

Not that I could admit such a thing to the Templar. "I started young. And flattery will not deflect my question. I know of a dozen men more noteworthy than I. A hundred." I wagged a finger at him, still smiling. "Allow me to guess. No one else that you asked before me would consider going into the lands of the tartars. Only a madman would do so."

He returned my faint smile and leaned back. "Many men would have gladly joined us, in return for payment upon our return. Yet, I could never trust a man so desperate for silver that he would make such a journey."

"Why, then, do you go?"

"The King of France asked me to."

"You are a knight of the Order of the Temple. You are not subject to him."

"I said that he asked me. He made a request, which was granted by the Grand Master of my order."

"And, when you return to him, what will you ask for in return?"

"That is not your concern."

I nodded. "And your other man? The French knight. What of him? What is his name?"

The Templar's face clouded. "He was once highly favoured by King Louis. A favour he no longer holds."

I smiled at that. "Must have done something bloody awful to get this for punishment."

Instead of being offended, the Templar nodded slowly. "Nothing that could be proven. But have no doubt, Bertrand is a magnificent knight who won his name and fortune through the pursuit of war. Rich men surrendered to him on sight rather than cross swords with him."

At the mention of the knight's name, the realisation gripped me.

"What did you say his name, was?" I said, grasping the edge of the table. "Bertrand? Bertrand de Cardaillac? The coward I defeated on the field? He is one of yours?"

Thomas clenched his jaw. "We both travel with Friar William of Rubruck into the lands of the Tartars, yes."

I laughed in disbelief.

"Did he send you here?" I said. "Is this all some ruse in order to avoid paying his forfeit to me?"

The Templar spread his hands in the air. "I swear, that is not the case. When you performed so admirably in the tourney, your intentions for travelling north were mentioned to me as a rumour. I come here in truth to ask if our ambitions perhaps aligned. We could each help the other, and travel together. That is all. He will still have to pay you his forfeit, it is not about that. Indeed, Bertrand does not know that I am here at all and if he did then he would be dismayed, to say the least. Also, he does not believe we need any additional men. And yet, he has no say over who joins us."

"Sounds like more trouble than it is worth," I said. "It seemed as though, even though he was so newly arrived here, he brought with him a reputation for arrogance."

"Bertrand was well favoured at one time and won a number of victories in tourneys. I am surprised you have not heard of him."

"I have not been to France for a long time."

He smiled to himself at that. What he saw, sitting across from him, was a young man. I died when I was twenty-two years' old. I had found that if I claimed to be older than thirty years, men would be surprised, or disbelieve me. Thomas assumed that, for me, a long time was a year or two. As much as five years, perhaps. A fair assessment, for young men often feel that way regarding the passage of their own years.

In truth, I had been born eighty-two years before. Older than the ageing knight before me, certainly.

"Say I was to join your company," I said. "You have yourself and your squire. And you have another knight and his squire. How many men do you mean to take with you? It seems to me that your small party, as you call it, is not so small after all."

"You and your own man there would complete our company to my satisfaction." He paused. "As soon as you reveal your reasons for seeking the tartars."

What reasons would he believe? Not the whole truth, certainly. But he may accept a partial truth.

"There is a man," I said. "An Englishman. His name is William. Once, he was a knight. A lord. But he committed murders. Then he fled. For quite some time now, I have been seeking his whereabouts. I have heard that a man named William is living amongst the Tartars. Is favoured by them. From what I know of this man, I believe these stories tell of William."

Thomas' face creased in concern. "Vengeance? You want to wreak vengeance on this man?"

I could sense my opportunity fading.

"Justice," I said. "All I seek is justice."

The Templar radiated disappointment. "In the lands of the tartars? A man who, if he exists, can only be there on the sufferance of the tartar lords? No, no. Impossible. You would risk our entire company with your act of vengeance, should you carry it out. You, sir, shall not be welcome in my company."

I held up my hand until he allowed me to respond. "May I provide you with my intentions? I have heard how the tartars allow no foreign man through their lands, unless that man is a known trader or envoy, with express leave to travel. Any other man may be murdered with impunity, for the Tartars reason that such men can only be spying for their enemies. When I discover the location of this man William, I shall send word to him and to the local lord that I am present and that I wish to discuss his crimes. My request shall be a simple one. William has committed a number of specific crimes that I can list. If the tartars consent, I ask only for single combat with William. A trial by combat. If I win, or if I lose, there must be no revenge upon my fellow Christians and we should be allowed to leave, as freely as we arrived in that land."

"And if the Tartar lords decline your proposal?"

I held my arms out to either side. "What could I possibly do but accept their decision? I am no Assassin, seeking to murder a man in plain sight. Nor would I murder a man in his bed. I would leave, and wait for the day that he leaves the protection of the tartars."

"What did this man do to you, that would drive you to this... this risk?"

"He murdered my brother, my brother's wife and their children," I said. "And I swore an oath to see William brought to justice."

And he killed my wife and he killed my wife's son, who was also my dearest friend. William poisoned King John to death, as well as William's own father. And he killed hundreds of others, men, women, children. From England to the Holy Land, he had bathed in the blood of an uncounted multitude.

My brother, William de Ferrers. The evilest man who walked the Earth. And no man but I had the strength to end his life.

Of course, I could say none of this to Thomas. The Templar would think me a madman.

"I have seen men drunk on vengeance before," Thomas said, fixing me with his blue eyes.

"Justice," I said, before finishing my cup of wine and carefully placing it down. "And I am not drunk on anything. But if you believe I will be a detriment to your company, then I accept your wisdom with a good heart. I shall make my own way. Perhaps we shall see each other there?"

The Templar drummed his fingers on the bone-dry table top. "So, you do wish to join us?"

He said no more and waited for me to make my decision.

"When Bertrand de Cardaillac sends me the value of his forfeit," I said, "and swears that he will cause me no trouble on the journey, then I will join you." Behind me, Eva coughed. "Myself and my squire."

Thomas the Templar smiled and we agreed our terms.

The Sun was setting as he walked away between the tents on the field, heading back to the city.

"This is precisely what we wanted," I said to Eva. "Official leave to travel into the Tartar lands, with the concealment and protection of a monk and his party."

"Yes, indeed," she said, standing by my side.

"So why do I feel as though I have just been swindled?"

She snorted. "How do you think they will feel when they meet me?"

It was another two weeks, on the Nones of May 1253, that the party was due to set off from Constantinople by ship. We would cross the Black Sea for Pontus, in the North across that great body of water.

Before we could set off, however, I had two hurdles to cross. The most important task was to convince Thomas and the others to accept a woman in their party. The other was to avoid coming to blows with Sir Bertrand and, if possible, establish a peaceable rapport with him.

"What is the meaning of this?" Thomas said, staring at Eva as she and I arrived together at the Neorian Harbour.

On the north side of the city, the harbour was the centre of trade for the Venetian, Pisan, and Genoese, all of whom hated the other with greater fervour than any had for the Saracens. They all traded in taking furs, amber, and slaves, to the east and bringing silks, spices, and jewellery back to the city, and from there into the Mediterranean. The harbour was heaving with cogs and galleys, a forest of masts sticking up toward the cerulean sky. Everywhere, men loaded and unloaded cargo and the shouted mix of Italian dialects, Greek and French was interspersed with barks of laughter and cries of warning. It stank of the salt sea, rotting fish, and the exotic mixture of spice and strange perfumes. Wealthy merchants in fine clothes stood in groups here and there, arguing with ship owners and ignoring the sweating men who toiled in the sun repairing the vessels or carrying heavy loads.

Thomas was garbed in the clean, white robe and red cross of his order, and had been engaged in a heated discussion with a member of the ship's crew.

But he broke off the moment he clapped eyes on Eva. She was garbed much the same as I was. That is to say, in a tunic and wore a close-fitting cap with her dark hair tucked tight into it. A sword in its plain scabbard hung at her hip. With her breasts wrapped as tightly as she could stand, and her lithe, square-shouldered frame, she did not present an overly-ladylike figure and yet Thomas had spotted her at twenty paces. Then again, the Templars were supposed to be celibate so perhaps it was no wonder he had noticed.

"What is the meaning of this?" Thomas asked again.

"Thomas," I said, pretending to be somewhat slow on the uptake, "we have come in good time for the tide, I take it?"

The knight gestured at Eva. "Why is this woman here?"

"Oh, this woman?" I asked, innocently. "She is coming with me."

Colour drained from his skin. "She is not. Absolutely not. You will leave her here. By the docks, where she belongs."

I sighed. "You may never speak to her like that again, Thomas. Do you understand? And she is certainly coming with us. Without her, I could not possibly join in your endeavour."

He stared at me, then at Eva and back to me. Finally, he spoke to the crewman without taking his eyes off me. "If you please, Guido, could you board the ship and ask Friar William to join me here? Soon as you can."

The crew member stepped back, bobbed his head and hurried off.

Thomas seemed stunned, so I spoke into the silence.

"May I introduce my wife, Eva? Eva, this is Thomas, of the Templars." The old knight stared at me in confusion. "Thomas, Eva is my wife and my squire. She squires for me in battle. She attends to my every whim, both on and off the battlefield." I risked a glance at Eva and saw that she was irritated by my minor exaggeration where her obedience was concerned.

"You have lost your wits," Thomas said, after a long pause. He quite rudely ignored my wife. "You cannot take a woman into the lands of Tartary. Did you take a blow to the head in that tourney? Or were you never blessed with wits in the first instance?"

"I do not–"

"A woman?" Thomas cut me off. "A woman? As a squire? A woman squire?"

"I will grant that it is somewhat of an unusual–"

He placed his hand over his forehead in anguish. "You cannot believe I would allow a woman to join us? No matter how you garb the creature, no matter if you call her your wife."

Eva and I had known that it would be difficult to persuade Thomas to accept. In our time serving in various mercenary forces in Spain and the Holy Land in the previous decades, Eva had acted as my squire. Often, we pretended she was a young man and most of those who noticed that she was not, chose to say nothing. Indeed, it often became a shared secret within the company we served with. Sometimes, the men adopted her and protected her. They would share in jests at the expense of our superiors and delighted in assisting us in the deception. But someone important would find out. I would anger someone, generate some resentment or suspicion, and she would be turned in and no matter the good will I had built up, we would invariably be required to flee.

Fleeing from Thomas the Templar and Friar William when we were in the lands of the Tartars would not be possible. A lone man with a woman crossing the grasslands of the north, and no permission or reason to travel, would be a death sentence. And so, we had to drop any pretence from the start. By arriving to the ship as late as was possible, we hoped to give them little time to make a decision. Take us or leave us, I would say.

It was a slim chance, but our best chance. If it failed, I would have to become a merchant, as originally planned. I did not want that. One may as well attempt to make a horse into a duck.

"She is my wife," I said, turning to Eva.

She nodded at Thomas. "It is the truth. I am also his squire." Eva glanced at me. "And I can fight."

Thomas scoffed. "I think you had best take your leave," he said, addressing me alone.

Perhaps I should have considered who Thomas was before taking such a direct approach. He was no poverty-stricken man-at-arms, signing up to fight for one lord in a local land dispute with another in Castile. Thomas was a senior knight of the Order of the Temple, a man who had taken a vow of celibacy. Perhaps taken the vow as a young man. I had the impression that Thomas was a man who tended to keep the vows that he took and so it was likely that he knew very little of women. Perhaps had never known a woman. And what we do not know, we often fear.

"Our belongings are already on board the ship," I pointed out, as I had sent them along the day before.

"I shall see that all you own is removed from the ship and placed on the dockside," Thomas said. "You may wait here while that is done."

"It would be easier if Eva and I took our places on the ship," I said. "As agreed."

"Agreed?" Thomas said, his voice rising as he spoke. "Agreed, you say? We never agreed to you bringing this... this..."

"Squire," I said.

Thomas took a deep breath but before he could unleash it upon me, he was interrupted by the approach of a young man in the grey robes of a brother of the Order of St Francis, along with two more Franciscans. The young man in front was aged about thirty years. He was a big, burly fellow, with a clean shaved, red face and light brown hair. Fat beneath his robes and with a wide face now creased in concern as he approached.

At his shoulder, half a step behind was an even younger monk with fair hair and an old one trailed behind.

"What is the meaning of this commotion, my lord?" the fat monk called out as he approached. His French was excellent but surely this was William of Rubruck, the Flemish leader of the embassy heading north to the Tartars. If Thomas was a lost cause, perhaps I could persuade Friar William to accept a woman in the company?

Some monks were fair-minded, kind men. Others were lovers of reason who delighted in being convinced of this or that through clear argumentation. Others still were lecherous sinners. If William of Rubruck were any of these, it would be simple to have him take Eva and I both.

"Friar William," Thomas said, his good manners overcoming his anger so that he could make a formal introduction. "This is Richard, the knight who—"

"Of course it is," Friar William said, coming to a stop before me and planting his feet wide. The monk was only a little shorter than I. His barrel of a belly was close enough for me to reach out and poke. "But what is the argument regarding? Perhaps you have decided that you will not be accompanying us after all, Sir Richard?"

His disregard for formality gave me hope. "I would like very much to join you, Friar William," I said. "We were merely discussing a practical matter regarding my squire."

"Your squire?" William turned to Eva, who was of a height with him. She looked him square in the face. William looked her up and down and found nothing to be remarked upon. "What practical matter?" he asked me and Thomas.

The rest of us looked at Thomas, who cleared his throat before replying. "Friar William, his squire is a woman."

William of Rubruck was at first confused but he looked at her again with this new knowledge and became somewhat flabbergasted.

Eva was tall, square shouldered and slender. Her face was perfectly womanish, her mouth was wide and her cheekbones high and sharp. But her hair was hidden beneath her cap and her substantial breasts were wrapped beneath her tunic, and anyway, we see what we expect to see. And she was dressed as a squire.

"A woman?" William said, utterly confused. "Is this a jest?"

"She has served dutifully as my squire for many a year," I said. "And what is more, she is my wife."

William struggled to comprehend. The fair-haired young monk at his shoulder grinned from ear to ear while the elderly one wore an expression of pure horror.

The friar's powers of reason won out over his emotion. "I am sure that this sort of thing may seem... permissible in the Holy Land. But there are practical considerations. We simply cannot bring a woman. Where would she pass water, for example? How would she bathe?" He paused while he searched for other things that women do.

I grinned at him. "She will piss on the ground, like everyone else. How much bathing do you expect to do on the journey, Friar William? If she needs to wash, you can bloody well avert your eyes, like a decent man would. Can't you, Friar? Are you suggesting that you would look upon a woman's nakedness?"

"What? No, I most certainly would not. But that is—"

"Well then, there you go, Friar William, nothing to be concerned about at all, is there."

Our small gathering was attracting some attention from the people around the dockside, with workers slowing their toiling while they threw glances our way. Other men stared at us from a distance.

Thomas lowered his voice and addressed Friar William. "Perhaps you could leave the question of whether we need additional men-at-arms to me," he said. "While you and your brothers wait on the ship."

William frowned. "I seem to recall that it was you who argued you needed another man."

"That is true, however—"

"I would rather none of you accompanied me at all," Friar William said, lifting his fat chin in the air. "There is no requirement for impoverished brothers to bring guards into Tartary. To do so may indeed risk—"

"The King himself commanded—"

"I know full well what the King commanded, Sir Thomas, as it was to me directly that he addressed himself. I do not—"

This time it was the young monk at his shoulder who interrupted. "Friar William, if I may?"

William sighed. "What is it, Stephen?"

The young man smiled, as if unconcerned with the irritation he had caused his brother monk. "It is known that the barbarian Tartar welcomes women as fellow soldiers. Indeed, they say that when the men go off to war and to raid, it is the womenfolk who defend the homestead. The women fight with bow and lance, from horse and on foot. They say that the women are quite savage. That they fight almost as well as the men do."

William scowled. The elderly monk behind shook with indignation at the idea of it.

"Why do you tell me this thing, Stephen?" William said.

The young monk, still smiling, gestured at Eva. "Perhaps the Tartars will look favourably upon us if we have a woman who displays a similar martial inclination?"

"I have no desire to emulate their barbarian, heathen practises, Stephen."

"Of course not. Of course. And yet, if there was a chance such a thing were to ultimately help our cause, would not such a thing have value? For the greater good of spreading the word of the Christ?"

William nodded, almost to himself. "You may be right, Stephen. I do not like it. Not one bit. But you may be right."

The young monk grinned at me, very pleased with himself. I found his attempt at ingratiation to be profoundly irritating.

"Wonderful," I said, forcing a smile onto my face. "Shall we board now?"

Thomas held up a hand in protest but another voice cried out from across the dock, a loud hail from a deep voice, and Thomas' face fell even further. "Ah. Well, this should resolve the debacle. Here comes Bertrand."

The monks all sank, their shoulders rounding and both the young and old ones gathered closer to the bulky form of William, like goslings round a goose.

Sir Bertrand strode toward us, along with two squires. Even out of his armour, Bertrand was a huge man, taller than me by half a head. Half a massive, bullock-like head. In those days long past, I was often the tallest man out of a hundred. Tallest out of a thousand, perhaps. But, of course, there were many who overtopped me. Sometimes they would be a yeoman or townsman but often such men are dragged into the profession of war and most commonly of all they would be men of good breeding. Men with the healthy blood and good food of the nobility or knightly classes.

Most men-at-arms, of all heights, would be of relatively slender build. There was rarely enough food and wine to make an active man fat, even if he be wealthy. Those of us who were strong enough to fight for half a day from horseback and with sword and shield almost never had large muscles.

But every now and then, you would get a man like Bertrand de Cardaillac.

A man who towered over every other and also had shoulders like hams and a chest like a hogshead. Big boned all over, with blocks for knuckles and a wide face and a jaw like a ploughshare. The man's eyes were small and dark, darting about across all of us as if searching for a threat.

One of the two squires trailing him was almost as tall, though younger and not so large of stature.

"What is the meaning of this?" Bertrand said as he arrived. His voice was louder than a docker's mother but he spoke with the fine, haughty French of the nobility. "Is it true?" He squinted down at Eva. "Is this truly a woman? Or was your saintly little squire telling me lies, Thomas? Does not look much like a woman. Are you a woman, boy?"

I pushed myself in front of her. "How joyous it is to see you again, Sir Bertrand. I am Richard of Ashbury. Perhaps you recall our meeting on the field? Or perhaps not, you took a rather nasty blow or two, did you not? This is my squire, Eva."

He ground his teeth, his massive jaw working while he forced himself into a contemptuous, false jollity.

"Ah, yes. The lucky little Englishman. Thomas complained ceaselessly that he needed more men." Bertrand grinned while he puffed out his chest. "As if any other knight would be needed when you have Bertrand de Cardaillac?" He turned and grabbed his squire and pulled him in, throwing a massive arm around the younger man's shoulders. "And my dear cousin Hugues, of course."

It was obvious that the squire, Hughues, shared de Cardaillac's blood. He was somewhat of a younger, shorter, slimmer version of the bigger man. His expression was just as smug, though his eyes did not exhibit the shrewd, penetrating glare of his cousin's.

"Yes, indeed, what a fine young squire you have. And let me just say, sir, it was very good of you to eventually send me your tourney forfeit by way of Thomas," I said, fixing Bertrand with a stare.

"Ah, of course, I hold no grudges for a lucky blow from an inferior young soldier," Bertrand said, with a tight smile. His eyes told a very different story. "It was all merely a diversion in between doing my duty for the King."

"Indeed," I said. "Indeed, I heard you were with King Louis in Egypt. A sad business. Very sad. I praise God that the Egyptians released him so that he could raise his own ransom. Praise God, also, that you yourself survived the Crusade. You must be a lucky little Frenchman, indeed."

Bertrand shoved his squire away and jabbed a big meaty finger in front of my face. "And you? You are a jester, who calls a woman his squire. And I know why." He leered at Eva.

I had told Eva to hold her tongue. Impressed upon her the need for her to avoid angering Friar William and Thomas. She had argued that she should be allowed to speak for herself, as we would be persuading the pair that she could act just as a man would. Exasperated, I had told her for the tenth time that a true squire would know to hold his damned tongue.

Even so, I could never control her.

"Fight me," Eva said to Bertrand.

Every man, me included, turned to stare at her.

"Quiet," I said.

She glanced at me only briefly. "Bertrand de Cardaillac, if you doubt my abilities, you should fight me yourself. If you beat me, we will leave you be. But if I beat you, I join your journey to the Tartars with my husband, Richard. Right now. With swords. No armour. I am ready."

We had not agreed this. Bertrand was as large as a giant and a trained knight.

But Eva was very good with the sword.

And, of course, she was an immortal vampire with inhuman speed and strength.

The men arrayed about us stared at Eva in shock, until Bertrand laughed in her face. "You are both mad. Utterly mad."

His squire laughed like a donkey but the monks and the old Templar and his young squire were apprehensive.

"You are afraid," Eva said, her goading shutting the man up. "You fear losing to a woman."

He sneered. "I would never use a blade on a woman, even one as shameless as this one."

"Go on," I said, warming to the idea. "What are you afraid of?"

The others were in a state of surprise and confusion and struggled to give word to their outrage.

"I would slay you with a single blow," Bertrand said, although he seemed somewhat perturbed by her confidence, or by the very notion itself.

"Practice swords then," I said. "Blunted wasters. We have dulled, old blades and wooden cudgels with our belongings on the ship, if your squire will fetch them for us."

"That is it," Bertrand said, his lip curling in contempt. "You call yourself a squire. And so you can fight my squire. Yes, yes. Come on, Hughes. Fetch a pair of wasters, one for you. And one for this woman. You may then humiliate her."

He glared at me, expecting that I would put a stop to the madness. Little did he know that the madness was only just beginning, for him and for all of us. I simply smiled pleasantly up at him.

A space was made by the monks, knights, and spectators standing in a rough circle on the dockside.

"Get back," I said to those gathering. "Make room, there, you damned fools, unless you want to get your bellies cut open by a reeling squire."

Eva fastened her cap beneath her chin, handed me the sword and scabbard from her hip, and tightened her belt. "If these fools do not disperse, we shall be arrested for breaching the peace."

"Do not finish him too swiftly, they must see your ability," I said. "But do not toy with him too long, or the authorities may detain us. And do not kill him."

She gave me a look.

"Yes, yes, I know," I said, "but he will attempt to humiliate you. Do you recall what happened in Castile?"

"That was twenty years ago."

"So, you do remember."

"The boy was incompetent," she said. "I can hardly be held accountable."

"What about that knight in Aleppo?" I reminded her. "We had to run all the way to—"

She scowled. "Why do you nag at me like an old maid? Stop your prattling. Here comes the squire."

When they faced off from each other, the size disparity between the two of them was startling. The squire Hughues was a huge young man, with broad shoulders and a big head. He must have weighed half Eva's weight again. He was smirking as he advanced toward her.

Eva stood straight and held her blunted sword lightly, resting the blade on her shoulder as she slid forward in a most casual manner. A man finds it difficult to see an attack that comes straight toward him. One cannot effectively judge the distance.

She brought her sword back as she moved and then exploded forward with a thrust to his face. Hughues jerked back and managed to get his own blade up to parry the thrust away. But Eva had him on the back foot and she pushed cuts at him, low and high, while he circled away. The squire's face went from swaggering confidence to shock to utter confusion as he found himself desperately flailing and outclassed with every blow.

Eva whipped her blade onto his wrist, hard enough to cause him to drop his sword with a clatter upon the paved stone underfoot. In quick succession, she struck his knee, chest, upper arm and knee again. Hughues' leg buckled and she slapped the flat of the blade against the side of his unarmoured head. The squire fell, whimpering and clutching his head.

"Yield, I yield, for the love of God."

Eva stood back from the downed man and nodded at the crowd. Some were shocked, others laughed. Many were scowling as they filed away.

Thomas and Friar William were shocked but both held my gaze. The young monk Stephen grinned from ear to ear. The old monk was horrified.

Bertrand glared at me with open hostility. Through our squires, I had humiliated him once again in front of a senior Templar and a monk acting as the ambassador for the King of France. A noble like Bertrand was obsessed with his own status. Indeed, he was only taking this journey in order to regain the favour of the King.

I knew Eva had won us our place on the embassy to the Tartars.

And, as I watched Bertrand drag his squire away, I knew I had made a dangerous enemy.

Part Two

Pontic Steppe

1253

WE MADE SAIL ACROSS THE BLACK SEA for the province of Gazaria, a triangular peninsula at the north of the sea. On its west side was a city called Cherson. The region would later come to be known as the Crimea.

"Cherson is the city where Saint Clement was martyred," Friar William said to me on the deck of the Genoese galley that we sailed on.

"How interesting," I said, looking out from the side of the foremost part of the galley at the seemingly endless expanse of water. In the south of that vast inland sea, the air was often humid in the summer and under a deluge in the mild winters. Up in the north, the summers were blazing hot and dry, and the winters bitterly cold.

The friar and I were alone, other than the gruff but efficient sailors who adjusted the rigging constantly to best capture the strong but blustery, changeable winds in the sail above our heads. The great sheet of canvas rippled and cracked as the wind moved about its course, thrumming into life whenever the force caught it flush and the lines snapped taut as though a monstrous beast had been captured and fastened to the mast.

"Do you know of the lands to which we travel?" Friar William asked. "I am told that you know these parts, to some degree?"

I nodded. "I know some. A Venetian had agreed to sell me his cog and his contacts with the cities around this sea. I took the time to learn of who I would trade with."

"Hmm," he said, nodding. "A knight and soldier such as yourself becoming a trader. I believe that to be somewhat unusual." When I did not respond, he continued. "Do the Genoese and Venetians not guard their trade against outsiders?"

"If you have enough gold, you can buy acquiescence," I said. "Especially from those men for whom gold is everything."

"And you are wealthy enough to purchase a ship of such size? And to provision and crew it? And purchase goods to trade with it?" The friar, I would discover, genuinely embraced the chief madness of his order. The Franciscans were ostentatious with their vow of poverty and William of Rubruck lived what his order commanded. "You must have won a great many tourneys, sir."

"I have been accumulating wealth for a very long time," I said, shrugging. "Wealth enables any man, even a knight, to do what he will."

"I do hope you have not brought a great deal of coin or gold with you, sir," Rubruck said, fretting. "Such wealth would only confuse the Tartars as to its purpose."

"It would not confuse them," I said. "If they knew one of us had gold, the first barbarian we come across would try to steal it. Do not be concerned. I may sometimes act foolishly, Friar William, but I am not a fool. My wealth is kept safely with the various Italian houses, and indeed, with the Templars."

"Good, good," William said, waving away consideration of my fortune with his fat fingers. "And you say you studied what goods you should trade with the Tartars? And what the key cities of the region are?"

The Flemish idiot was beginning to annoy me. "What do you want to know, Friar?"

He turned away from the sea to look at me. His smile dropped from his face. "Why are you here?"

I said nothing.

He pressed me further. "It is clearly not for the payment, as Thomas claimed."

"No. Not for the payment. I was going north alone, with my wife, as a trader. But you already have leave to travel through the barbarian lands. And I know a man who serves the Tartars, or at least lives in their lands."

Friar William scowled. "A man? What man?"

"A man who committed crimes all across Christendom and Outremer."

He was silent for some time then turned to glare out at the horizon instead of at me.

"And you mean to punish him?" There was an edge to the Friar's voice. He was controlling himself.

"All I wish," I said, "is to request a trial by combat. If the Tartars who shelter him grant it, we shall fight. If I win, it is over. Finally."

Rubruck squeezed his fat fists as he struggled to control his outrage.

"And should you lose this fight?"

I laughed. "Eva will return with you to Christendom and find another husband, I hope."

"What of us, then?" He was certainly angry but pretending quite well that he was not. "What evil will your hatred and your vengeance cause for us and our efforts to convert the pagans?"

"Evil? Vengeance?" I shook my head, sadly. "No, no, dear Friar. There is no hatred in my heart." I was far from certain that was the truth but I was not feeling hatred in that moment. "I will do everything that the Tartars require to stay within whatever barbaric laws and customs they have. If they do not grant me the trial by combat, I shall acquiesce. I would not force the matter. I shall say to him that I will see him again one day in Christendom and there bring him to justice." I shrugged. "It shall be as God wills."

Whether I was lying to the monk or lying to myself, I do not know. Either way, my words seemed to mollify him somewhat. "I shall not allow you to endanger our mission."

"I understand," I said to him, for monks and priests can be placated as if they were women. "You are right. God comes first, always."

"God and the Church," he said, looking down his nose at me.

"Of course."

"And the Pope."

His order had only grown into such power due to their fanatical devotion to orthodoxy and their willingness to be the aggressive right hand of a pope who used the Franciscans to keep the perverted, wine-sozzled, acquisitive priesthood in line.

"Yes, Friar William," I said, grinding my teeth. "I assure you I am thoroughly conventional in every way."

He stood, bringing himself to his full height and full girth. "I shall be watching you very closely. Both you and that woman. If you threaten our mission, I shall be forced to expel you. For the greater good."

How very Christian of you.

I fought the urge to slash open his gigantic belly and tip him into the sea and instead grinned at him like a lunatic.

"You do not need to worry about me, Friar. I shall cause you no trouble whatsoever."

The cabins were tiny, fetid and dark. I could not stand up straight, not even close to it and Eva and I had to share a bunk that was not large enough even for her alone. Upon the deck, by the bunk, we had a single chest for our belongings and some hooks for a lamp and clothing. The cabins ran down on either side of the ship at the prow end, with the stern to midships taken up with cargo. For privacy, we each had a canvas curtain threaded through a rope that pulled almost closed across the small space. The walls of each tiny cabin were boards that were little thicker than parchment.

At least it gave us a modicum of privacy and so she could drink blood from my wrist every other night and thus remain in good health. Without drinking blood regularly, every three days at the most, her skin would progress from rude health into a pallid green, and her sharp mind would descend into savage madness. We had managed to avoid her going without blood for decades, other than a few times, now and then, when we had kept such close company that it was difficult.

Once, we were arrested attempting to leave Obidos after a fight in the street that was categorically not my fault. For a while, it appeared they were going to sell us into slavery and they left us chained up in a tower room given over to the purpose of holding undesirables like us. That little makeshift gaol was full of prisoners destined to be slaves. It was always well lit, and there was always at least one man staring at Eva, and often it was all of them. Lest we be further accused of practicing some evilness, she held off for three days, becoming sick and twitchy, sweating and groaning in her sleep. Once, I had starved a vampire monk named Tuck of blood, and my dear wife began to resemble that vile beast. Although I knew not to mention that to her at the time. When one of the prisoners saw her drinking blood from my wrist in the night, he woke up the rest with his outraged accusations. I beat him unconscious and warned the rest of them to mind their own business.

They stopped staring at her after that and we were released a couple of days later.

Outside Obidos, I swore to Eva that I would never allow her to be taken prisoner again as long as we lived.

Another oath that I would soon break. Another way that I would fail in my duty to protect my wife in the pursuit of my vengeance. For such a thing is so very easy to swear, and yet not so easy to avoid in the face of a hostile world. Taking Eva into the wilderness, into a land ruled by violent savages, and in the company of men who would happily do her harm, was contradictory to my duty. I should have foreseen how such a contradiction would end, but I did not, and so I brought her into the confined space of a galley sailing across a foreign sea.

Our company on that Genoese galley on the Black Sea was metaphysically divided into two distinct social tiers. Thomas, Bertrand and myself were knights and the friars William and Bartholomew were spoken to as if they were equals.

The two squires, the young monk Stephen Gosset, the friar's servant boy Nikolas and the dragoman, who was called Abdul, we never conversed with unless it was to issue them commands.

Eva did not fit in either station. She was a squire but also the wife of a knight. The monks and the knights, I am sure, thought of her as a woman merely playing at being a squire, in spite of her skill with the sword. And any woman who would do such a thing was not a true lady. The squires and servants, she made uncomfortable with her presence. For all of our company, she was a conundrum seemingly impossible to resolve.

But both Eva and I had encountered such difficulties before and the only way to deal with these things is to pretend outwardly that they concern you not at all.

Either way, we shared a bunk which was closer to the centre of the ship, closer to the hatch through which came the fresh air. The squires came next, then the dragoman, Abdullah and the boy Nikolas. Both of whom were as miserable and sick as otherwise healthy young men could be. But we needed no interpreters on the ship, so they were welcome to lay in their bunks, located hard under the prow. Their ceaseless groaning and vomiting was, however, most unwelcome and by far the healthiest place to be on the ship was up on deck.

"You deceived me," Thomas the Templar said as we leaned on the rail late on the second day. "With regards to the nature of your squire."

We were as alone as one could be on the galley, which was to say, surrounded by the ceaseless bustling of the crew but not within earshot of anyone important. A warm wind tugged constantly at us and the mist sprayed up from the ship's prow smashing through the choppy waves. To the west, the fertile lands shone green in the summer sun.

"I did not tell you my squire was a woman, that is true," I said. "And I apologise for putting you in that situation with the monk."

"Bertrand is angered."

"She thrashed his squire without breaking a sweat," I said, not bothering to hide my smile. "I am sure that he will come to terms with it, in time."

Thomas sighed. "You do not know the man."

I nodded, for that was true. But I was sure I knew the type of man that Bertrand was.

"Tell me, sir," I asked Thomas. "What did he do?"

The Templar hesitated. "What do you mean by that?"

I leaned further out, looking down at the white froth running in a torrent where the hull smashed through the water. "I mean, what hideous crimes did Bertrand commit for the King of France to send him on this God-forsaken lunatic's quest."

Thomas bristled at that and I thought I had pushed him too far. But he ground his teeth for a moment then sighed. "Do you know his family? He is the second son but the family has two castles and Bertrand has one for himself. Somewhere near Cahors. Good land. Rich land. Bertrand brought twelve knights and their followers with him on the crusade. All dead now."

"Bertrand was at fault?"

"For his lost men? The King was at fault. He threw away his army." Thomas spoke with deep bitterness. As well he might, for the catastrophe of Louis' crusade was agonising and fresh. "No, Bertrand escaped death or capture and has served the King in Acre since. That is where he lost the King's favour. Bertrand is not a man who does well in the close confines of a court. Give him a horse and an enemy and he will do God's work but when required to be Godly, he is unable to control his passions. He is full of sin."

"Which sin of Bertrand's did Louis take umbrage with?"

"Lust. Bertrand lay with a wealthy widow of Acre. She claimed that he forced himself upon her and yet a child was placed in her womb, so her word was disbelieved. However, the child was lost and the lady almost perished herself. Some said it was God's proof that the lady had been raped after all."

"She probably drank too much pennyroyal," I said. "Why was he not tried and convicted?"

"The local lords clamoured for it. Louis would not submit one of his men to their authority so he sent him away." Thomas rubbed his eyes while screwing up his face. "And I had been pressing the King for more knights to accompany me on the embassy so when he insisted upon Bertrand, I could do nothing but accept. Which he knew. What a fool I was."

In fact, it was I, Richard, who was the fool.

Because I saw it then, striking me as suddenly as a slap in the face. Thomas was old. Strong, and perhaps even skilled at arms, but of middling height and with a slender build. His Templar squire was young and so humble as to be invisible. Friar William was a big lump of a monk but monk he was. The other two Franciscans were either old and frail on the one hand, or full of little more than the idiotically mirthful joy of youth.

"You only wanted me to join you," I said, as realisation dawned, "so that I would help you to control Bertrand."

I laughed heartedly at my own dim-wittedness for not seeing it earlier.

Thomas scowled at my uncouth laughter. "I always wanted more men, within reason, but yes. When I saw your ability, your strength, and your stature at that sad little tourney, I believed that you could act as a force to temper Bertrand's passions. And that is one reason I am so displeased at your deceit." He cleared his throat. "She should not be left alone."

"You don't need to worry about Eva," I said. I had left her snoring away down on our bunk. I grinned at Thomas, hoping to put him at ease. "If anything, it is they who should be afraid of her."

Sheer bravado, on my part. I claimed that I was not worried about danger on the ship and yet I wore my sword at my side so I felt threatened on some level, even though I denied it. Despite my general caution, I did not know then quite how dangerous Bertrand could be. And God was listening to my dismissive arrogance.

"Your lack of shame is unbecoming," Thomas said.

I scoffed. "She is my wife. I need feel no shame."

"Not for laying with her," he snapped. "For your deception."

"Ah, yes," I said. "You regret my presence, then?"

"Yours? No. Your wife's? I fear it will only add to my burdens." He looked me in the eye. "Yet, on the whole, I believe I shall be glad to have you." A smile twitched on his lips. "If not merely for the chance to have courteous conversation."

"I have been called many things in my long life," I said. "But never before has my conversation been called courteous."

"Your long life?" he said, smirking at what he thought to be my youthful perspective. "When you get to my age, you may speak in such a manner."

I was unsure how he would react if I told him that I was eighty-four years old.

"It seems like a long time," I said.

"You speak of your quest for vengeance," Thomas said.

"I suppose I do," I admitted. "William has eluded me for years."

"What has led you to believe he is with the Tartars?"

I wished I could explain how I trawled the edges of Christendom for traces of William's evil. How I had been drawn to the holy wars with the Moors and Saracens and pursued tales of his particular brand of messianic, blood-fuelled violence. All to no avail. Nothing but faint echoes of William. Stories of an English, or Norman, or French knight who had drunk the blood of an enemy on the battlefield, or a townsperson in an alleyway. Tales of a spree of grisly murders in a region that remained unexplained, other than by the blaming of witchcraft, demons, Jews, or foreigners.

Decades of frustration while Eva and I had earned our daily bread by fighting for one lord or another.

And then there had come the tales of the Tartars. The barbarian horsemen from the East, raiding and doing battle with the Rus and Hungarians in the north and the Christian kingdoms of Armenia and Georgia in the Caucasus. The reports were confused and confusing. Some said it was little more than the usual raiding from those lawless people of the steppe. Others said that great armies numbering in the tens of thousands or hundreds of thousands had crushed Christian forces. Stories of cities being razed and people enslaved were not unusual, yet they told also of entire populations being slaughtered beneath their own walls. Lurid tales told of the Tartars killing in creative fashion, torturing defeated lords by crushing them beneath a table supported by writhing bodies while the victors feasted and drank upon it.

It sounded like William. If he was not involved already, I reasoned, he would be drawn to them sure as a lion is drawn to the stench of death.

"I knew William would seek them out," I said to Thomas. "He is himself a bloodthirsty heathen barbarian at heart and yet he believes himself to be in God's protection. And so, when I came once again to Constantinople, I asked the Venetians and Genoese to listen for tales of such a man in the company of the Tartars. It did not take long."

"And what did you hear?"

"That the Tartar prince, Batu, has a foreign Christian with him. A man named William."

Thomas nodded. "Many of the Tartars are Christian, so they say. We know that the great Batu is said to be considering a conversion to Christianity. And Batu's son, Sartak, is himself a Christian." He paused. "A Nestorian Christian, of course. So they say."

"So they say," I agreed.

Thomas' eyes flicked over my shoulder to something behind me.

I whipped around with my hand on the hilt of the dagger on my belt.

"All is well, sir," Thomas said, placing a hand on my arm.

Before he had spoken, I was already relaxed. For it was only the junior Franciscan, Stephen Gosset. The fair-haired young man lurked a few paces aft, glancing in our direction.

"What in the name of God's hands does that little turd want?"

Thomas coughed at my blasphemy. "I fear he wants to speak to me."

"Well, why does he not approach?" I turned and raised my voice. "Come here, then, lad. What in the name of God are you lurking about for?"

The monk hitched up his habit and ran down the hatch to the lower deck.

"I ask you, Thomas," I said. "Are monks the most useless creatures to ever crawl upon the Earth?"

"I believe he is somewhat afraid of you."

"Of me?" I said, in a voice raised due to my incredulity. "Why would he be afraid of me?"

Thomas sighed. "Truly, I could not say."

"Well, so, why did he want to speak to you?" I said. Although I could not say precisely why, I did feel somewhat rejected by the pathetic young English monk.

"I suspected he was hoping to leave the Franciscans and join my order, perhaps because he seeks excitement that the poor brothers lack. Stephen is quite fascinated with my tales. He has been hounding me for these months since we left Acre."

"Your tales?" I was confused. "Are you a secret troubadour?"

"Tales of my battles with the Saracens and the northern pagans," Thomas said, smiling. "And particularly of my battles with the Tartars."

"You fought the Tartars?" I was astonished. "Where? When?"

He opened his mouth but before he could answer, a muffled shriek split the air. I was already moving toward the source of the sound when the shouting started. An eruption of angry voices down below yelling with full-throated vitriol.

Eva.

I leapt through the hatch and down the steps to the lower deck. I pushed forward through the cramped, stinking crew quarters and then ran sideways between stacked chests of cargo with my head lowered under the crossbeams. My heart hammered from fear, from the knowledge that my wife was in danger, from the rising panic and rage that filled me, body and soul.

Right forward, in our passenger section, the narrow space between the cabins was filled with shouting men. Between them and me was the forward ladder up to the hatch above. It was dim, light filtering down from the daylight above and from lanterns hung in the cabins.

Bertrand was roaring, venting his spleen about something of enormous importance, while Hughues was shouting also. Another voice cut through; a high, unmanly voice.

I swung around the ladder and half-tripped over young Stephen, who was crouching in the shadows and watching the commotion from a safe distance. I swore and shoved him aside with my shoe, causing him to fall very roughly. I did not cease my forward momentum and instead leapt forward into the fray.

The large men had their backs to me, hunched over in the confined space. Hughues, the squire, had his dagger in hand while Bertrand had one meaty hand on the squire's shoulder and the other braced upon the beams above. What they were shouting at, forward under the prow, I could not see.

Moving with the rolling of the ship, I charged between the two men. Stamping my foot into the back of Hughues' knee, I pulled him back off his feet with one hand. At the same time, I drove my other fist into Bertrand's lower back. And then pushed against him with both hands. The huge knight fell against the cabin partition, cracking his head on a beam and cursing even as he fell.

I moved forward between them.

There was Eva. Facing me, standing with her back to the prow, gripping a dagger in one hand.

She was angry but appeared unhurt.

The servant boy Nikolas that Rubruck had purchased in Constantinople stood in front of her, little more than half her height.

"Get back," he snarled at me, speaking in heavily-accented French and brandishing a small, rusted eating knife. He had vomit on his chin and on the front of his tunic. "Stay back from the lady."

"All is well," Eva said to me, with a nod. She placed a hand on the boy's shoulder. "All is well, Nikolas." She patted him.

Friar William and Friar Bartholomew stood in the open doorways of their own cabins, canvas curtains pulled back, looking out at the scene with expressions of complete shock on their faces.

I turned as Bertrand began roaring in protestation.

"Your woman is mad, Englishman." The massive knight and lord dragged himself to his feet, his big face as red as a slapped arse. "She needs to be locked away. She needs to be taught a lesson. By God, I will teach it to her."

He jabbed his finger in the air while he held on to the ship as it rolled. Behind him, the squire Hughues got to his feet, clutching his face. Blood welled through his fingers and his tunic was already soaked at the top. I did not recall injuring him so but that is often the way.

"Did you hear me?" Bertrand said. He shuffled forward and placed a hand upon the hilt of his sword.

He drew a third of it as he approached.

My own sword was at my hip.

I did not draw it.

"Stop," I said. I forced as much volume, authority, and contempt as I could into the single word.

Bertrand paused.

"What kind of man are you to threaten a woman with a weapon?" I said, sneering. "Put your sword away."

"She is no woman, she—"

I roared him down. "Put your sword away, sir."

He shoved it back into his scabbard. "She must be punished," he said, in a more civilised tone.

"Tell me what you think happened," I said.

"Are you blind?" Hughues the squire wailed. "She has cut my face, you fool. She has cut off my damned face."

Bertrand growled at him to be silent and then turned to me. "My squire has been assaulted. There must be restitution."

"Why did she cut him?" I asked Bertrand.

Hughues stuttered. "All I did was—"

"Silence," Bertrand shouted at his squire. "Another word from you unbidden and I truly will slice off your face." He turned to me. "Hughues wished to make an apology to your woman. However, she attacked him with a blade, as you can see for yourself."

I sidled over so I could turn to Eva while also keeping an eye on Bertrand. "And what do you say happened, Eva?"

Her face was grim but her voice loud, clear and steady as a rock. "I was asleep in my bunk. I awoke to find Hughues leaning over me, his breath hot on my face and his hand on my shoulder, holding me down. He whispered at me to be silent as he placed the hand over my mouth while holding a dagger in front of my face. I took up my own dagger from beneath my blanket and lashed out. I decided not to slit his throat and instead pushed him from the cabin. Then he began to wail like an old woman and here we all are."

I looked around at the monks. "Are there any witnesses?"

They shook their heads and avoided my eye. Monks are men who are paralysed by violence. That is why they become monks.

Bertrand spluttered. "This is not a trial. You have no authority to judge guilt or declare innocence and my squire has been grievously harmed with no cause by that—"

"You are lucky, sir," I said, raising my voice so that it filled the ship. Then I waited while he frowned in confusion. "You are lucky, sir, that I do not cut off your squire's head and throw it and the rest of him into the sea this very moment." He began to object once more but I did not give him the chance. "You will take your squire up onto the deck and explain to him that ravishing a woman is against the law. And wash out that wound with sea water, lest it becomes corrupted and rots his head from the inside. Go now."

I turned my back on him and went to Eva. It was a risk to do so but I knew that such blustering men were, as a rule, cowardly in their hearts. And a coward loves nothing more than being given instructions to follow. Perhaps Bertrand understood my gibe about ravishing a woman was aimed at his own transgression in Acre and that served to confound his indignation. Whatever the reason, they stomped up the ladder, blocking the light for a moment and then they were gone, their shoes stomping away on the upper deck.

I glanced over my shoulder to ensure we were indeed safe, for the time being and noticed that behind the ladder, Thomas lurked in the shadows amongst a group of grinning crewmen. Catching my eye, the old Templar nodded once and moved away forward on the lower deck.

I asked Eva, with a look, whether she was well. She rolled her eyes and shoved her dagger into her belt.

The little slave Nikolas was still standing in front of my wife, between the two of us, staring at me with distrust in his eyes.

"Why did you place yourself in harm's way, boy?" I asked him.

He frowned and looked down. "I am sorry, lord," he said. His Greek accent was very thick but his use of French was perfectly fine.

"You have done nothing wrong. But what did you think you could do against two such men?"

He shrugged, still looking down. "Protect the lady, sir."

"And who taught you to do that?"

He was confused. "Taught me, sir?"

"Who trained you, instructed you, that it was a man's duty to protect women?"

The slave kept staring at his toes. "I am sorry but I do not understand, sir."

I looked up at Eva who merely shrugged.

Reaching down, I took hold of his besmirched chin and tilted his head up. "How many years have you, boy?"

He frowned. "Mad Alex said I was ten when he sold me to master William."

I had no idea who Mad Alex was but presumably a slave trader or former master.

"Show me that knife," I commanded.

He handed it up and I took it from him. It was perhaps two inches long, the edge on it as blunt as the handle, which was poorly wrapped in an ancient strip of leather that was coming apart.

I handed it back to him. "You have the heart of a knight, young Nikolas and you should have a knight's weapon. But you are too small for a sword. Until you get taller, you must use this."

From my belt, I took my dagger in its decorated leather sheath and held it out to him.

The blade was an excellent steel that held a wicked edge for months. But the real beauty of the thing was the ivory hilt. There was a glorious and deep carving on both sides of Saint George at full charge, driving his lance into the body of the dragon while it writhed around the wound in a most lifelike fashion. As if the dragon was snarling at the knight and about to bite his head off. As if the outcome of the battle between the man and the beast was far from a foregone conclusion. It had cost me more than I could spare twenty years earlier from a master smith in Antioch.

Nikolas reached up, slowly, hands shaking all the way and then clutched the sheathed blade to his filthy, narrow little chest.

Eva clipped him across the head, but softly. "What do you say, boy?" she said.

"Thank you, sir," Nikolas said and he ran off to his bunk.

I saw the dragoman, our interpreter Abdullah laying on his bunk and staring out at me. "Bloody Saracens," I said. "Where were you, eh? Grown man, laying there and doing nothing?"

Abdullah simply turned over in his bunk, facing away from me.

The two older monks were clucking over Stephen and examining his arm by probing it with their fingers while the young man winced. I recalled how I had injured Stephen in my haste to rescue Eva. All three of them at once caught my eye and scowled before turning away from me.

"Tell me, my love. Why do I make enemies everywhere I go?" I wondered aloud.

"We all reap what we sow," Eva said. "We will take turns sleeping from now on. While the other stands watch."

* * *

We arrived then in Soldaia in late May. The city stood at the apex of the triangle that is the Crimean Peninsula, on the south side, and it looked across towards Sinopolis. It was a trading centre at the extreme borders of dozens of lands. Thither came all the merchants arriving from Russia and the northern countries who wished to pass into Turkia. The latter carried vair and minever, and other costly furs. Others carried cloths of cotton or bombax, silk stuffs, and sweet-smelling spices.

The city was subject to the Tartars and every year had to pay a great tribute to Prince Batu, else their thriving city would be destroyed by the barbarians. However, they paid that tribute with false but prompt enthusiasm and so were left alone to do their trade, and to become wealthy even in spite of the payments they provided to their overlords. As far as I knew, the city prefects were more than pleased with the arrangement, despite being Christians under the rule of pagan savages.

Although some citizens were Genoese, others were their enemies the Venetians, and many more still were Rus and the like, those unpleasant folk with squashed features and cold-ravaged skin. There were Greeks in their hundreds or thousands for all I know, and Bulgars and other people from the diverse lands all about us. Who the natives were I have no idea, although it was probably the Greeks, as they had founded so many places on the Black Sea just as they had on the shores of the Mediterranean.

Others there, living as well as trading, were the Saracens. Chiefly, those that were Turks but also those from Syria and other far-off lands. And amongst them, and over them too, were the peoples who were from the steppe. Advising, guarding, and taking stock of all that went on there, with their cunning eyes and their tails of bowing scribes who made certain that the Tartar lords were not being cheated or plotted against.

"This is a strange land," I said to Eva as the ship bobbed outside the port. "Strange people."

"This is what you want," Eva pointed out. "Always seeking what is over the horizon, never settled in one place. You revel in strangeness."

I shrugged, uncomfortable with her accusations. "I go where William's trail leads."

She scoffed. "You go where your heart leads."

Reaching along the rail, I took her hand and peered into her suspicious eyes. "My heart leads only to you."

"I know what part of you leads to me," she said, lowering her voice. "And it is not your heart."

Nevertheless, she held on to my hand.

Looking around, I saw the man I wanted. "Abdullah," I cried. "Come here."

The scrawny man came forward along the deck, his bony shoulders bent inward. He was a young man, or young enough, but it had taken me days to realise the fact. He had the appearance of an ancient creature, beaten down by the regular blows of disappointment. Thomas had purchased him in Acre and claimed that, for all the man's obvious misery, his ability with languages was second to none. He was said to have detailed knowledge of the lands of the Tartars, their languages, and their customs. He also claimed to have once been a famed scholar at a great house of learning so he was likewise clearly a great liar.

"Abdullah," I said. "Why are you dawdling so, man?"

He cringed with every word and Eva leaned in close to me. "Speak softly, Richard. He is close to being a broken man."

"Oh, for the love of God," I muttered. But you should always obey your wife, other than those times when you do not wish to. I spoke to him with a courteous tone. "Abdullah, you wise young Saracen, come here and converse with me."

He shuffled over, looking out from under his long black eyelashes like a coy princess. "How may I serve you, lord?"

"They tell me you have knowledge of the lands here about. I hear that some of the cities and kingdoms resist the Tartars and are not subjected to their rule. Will there be people from those lands in this city of Soldaia which lays before us?"

He frowned, unsure of why I was asking. I did not explain it to him but, in truth, it was simple. You never know who might one day be your allies, and who may be your enemies. And my main reason was that I wanted already to plan my escape from the Tartars.

Should it ever come to that.

"Yes, lord. Beyond this city, unseen to the east, is Zikuia, which does not obey the Tartars. And to the east of there are the Suevi and Hiberi, who also do not obey the Tartars. After that, further around the coast of the sea but to the south, is Trebizond, which has its own lord, Guido by name, who is of the family of the emperors of Constantinople, and he obeys the Tartars."

I waved my hand. "I know about Trebizond," I said. "That is on the other side of the sea from us entirely, you bloody fool. What about the other way?" I pointed to the west. "Who in the north and the west is there who is not subject to the Tartar rule?"

Instead, Abdullah pointed to the northeast. "From the city of Tanais," he said, and began to sweep his hand across from east to west. "All the way to the Danube, all are subject to the Tartars. Even beyond the Danube, lord, towards Constantinople. Do you know of Wallachia, which is the land of the Assan and Minor Bulgaria as far as Sclavonia? All of them pay tribute, lord. All. Even more, they say that the Tartars, as you call them, have taken in the past years from each house one axe and all the iron which they found unwrought."

I had heard that the Tartars had subjected many lands but hearing it again when I was on the edge of their territory, was greatly disturbing. A barbarian, savage people, who had conquered and subdued so many. Wherever we ran to, should Eva and I need to run, we would be travelling amongst people who would hand us over to the Tartars in order to save themselves from their wrath.

Eva intruded into my thoughts with a question for Abdullah. "What do you mean when you say, as you call them?"

"My lady?" Abdullah asked.

"You said the Tartars, as we call them," Eva said. "We call them Tartars, yes indeed we do. But what do you call them?"

He bobbed his head, eyes wide. "A simple slip of the tongue, my lady. My lord. My French is truly woeful. I beg your pardons for my stupidity and ignorance."

"Your French is bloody disgusting," I said. "And your false obsequiousness is revolting, I command you to stop that nonsense. But if you do not tell me the truth about the Tartars, I shall be forced to rip out your tongue entirely and toss it to the dogs." Saracens have an almost spiritual terror of dogs. I have no idea why. But it often does the trick.

Bobbing his head, he explained. "The Franks and Latins call them Tartars. They name themselves Mongols."

"Mongols?"

"Mongols, lord."

"Then, who in the name of God are the Tartars?"

"Some other tribe, lord. Barbarians, like the Mongols. In fact, there are a great number of tribes from the grasslands, stretching back into Asia and all of them have been subjugated by those that call themselves Mongols." The young Saracen grew ever more confident as he spoke. His voice became clearer and louder until it was almost as though he was preaching. "The Cumans are now the westernmost people who we call Tartars and these are the lands of the Cumans who we must cross to reach Batu, in the north beyond them. The Cumans fled the Mongols, and the Hungarians gave them sanctuary. But something went bad. It was all a trick, perhaps. The Cumans attacked the Hungarians, and the Mongols subjugated the Cumans. Further into the east, tribe after tribe is subject to the Mongols. One subject tribe is the Uighurs, whose script the Mongols use for writing in their own language. They do this because the Mongols are the most barbarian people of all the tribes of the East and were so ignorant that they had no form of writing of their own."

I stopped his babbling, confused by everything he said but that last, most of all. "Do you mean to say the Mongols were the most barbaric of all these savages and yet they conquered them all?"

He smirked. "The Mongols, so it is said, were so impoverished, lord, that they lived in the worst land in all Tartary, in the harsh mountains. And they had to sew together the skins of field mice to make their cloaks. But there was one amongst them, many years ago, named Chinggis, who became the leader. A giant, so they say. And he was so strong in the art of war that he conquered all, and none could conquer him in turn. And now they rule from Cathay, in the east, to Hungary in the west. All the tribes fight as one, now. They have armies of tens of thousands and even a hundred thousand or two hundred thousand horsemen."

I burst out laughing. "What utter nonsense."

He frowned and winced, and began to protest. But I cut him off and sent him on his way.

Eva was displeased. "You should listen to him."

"He is a fool," I said. "But I am the bigger fool for asking him. If we need to run, we will simply go west. Back into Christian lands. To the Kingdom of Hungary or the Kingdom of Poland."

Thomas' voice spoke over mine. "You mean to run, do you, Richard?"

The sneaky old bastard had crept up on me like a cat.

"Of course not," I said, not attempting to hide my irritation. "Yet it never hurts to make preparations for any eventuality."

"Unless I release you," Thomas said, "there shall be no running anywhere, at any time. Do you understand me, Richard?"

Eva placed a hand on my forearm.

She was right, and I swallowed my anger.

"I swore no oath to you, Thomas," I said, with as much calmness as I could muster. "Nor to Friar William. Not even to the King of France. But I shall do as I have said, which is to travel with you to the court of Prince Batu and there challenge William to a trial by combat. Between now and then, I shall protect you. From the Tartars. And also from other threats." I nodded over the Templar's shoulder.

We watched as Bertrand and then Hughues climbed over the side, down into the little barge which would convey all of us in turn to the busy shore while our ship awaited its berth in the harbour.

"He means to be first ashore," said Thomas. "Even though Friar William and Friar Bartholomew are the ones who demanded the barge so that they could arrange our onward transport without delay."

"Aye," I said. "That Bertrand is a strutting bloody old cockscomb. His arrogance will make further trouble in the north."

"His arrogance, yes." Thomas cleared his throat, managing to convey disapproval with the sound. "I trust that you will both remain on your finest, most courteous behaviour from now onwards."

I looked across the shimmering water at the city of Soldaia. It was the last outpost of civilisation before we crossed into the steppe and placed ourselves under the rule of the savages.

"Bertrand may be a prideful brute," I said, "yet he is a wealthy lord and a Christian. And yes, you are right that I also am arrogant, Thomas. And my sins are many. I am filled with wrath. But we stand here at the edge of the world and what lies beyond is all darkness. Bertrand is not my enemy. My enemy is out there, and he is the greatest sinner that ever walked the Earth."

***

We were not long in the small city itself. There had preceded us certain merchants of Constantinople who had said that envoys from the Holy Land were coming who wished to go to Prince Batu. This man Batu was the ruler of the Mongols' northern and western forces and was one of the most powerful and richest men in the entire world.

"But I am no envoy," Friar William said, to the group of Genoese merchants and prefects of the city who had prepared our way.

All of our party sat at a long table with those merchants in a very pleasant courtyard in the richest quarter of Soldaia, eating fresh fish cooked in olive oil. It was warm, both the food and the people smelled good and clean, and I was comfortable and happy. Eva, the other two squires, and the servants were somewhere in the back. Eva had returned to pretending to be a young man and strutted around with her head down beneath an oversized hood. I concentrated on shoving as much food as I could into myself while I could, and I knew Eva would be doing the same with whatever slop she had been served. We had years of experience with travelling and we knew to make the most of fresh, hot food and sweet wine while we could.

"You say you are no envoy?" The chief amongst the Genoese merchants was startled. "Yet, we have sent word to the Cumans that you are an envoy, Friar William."

William was inexplicably outraged, his cheeks quivering as he responded. "I publicly preached on Palm Sunday in Saint Sophia that I was not an envoy. Neither the King's nor anyone's, but that I was going among the unbelievers according to the rule of my order."

The Genoese and the prefects all stirred, exchanging meaningful looks. The leader shifted in his seat. "If you please, Friar William, may I caution you to speak guardedly, for we have said that you are an envoy. What is more, if you now say that you are not an envoy, you will none of you be allowed to pass with safe conduct through the Mongol lands."

Before the Franciscans could raise further objections, Thomas spoke up. "Of course, my friends. We understand perfectly."

Bertrand and I nodded our sincere agreement.

"We do not understand, sir," William said, his big face flushing red. "You say I must deceive our hosts with regards to our intentions? How can I do such a thing?"

"So, say nothing," I said, speaking with my mouth full of oil, fish, and bread. "Eat your supper, Friar. Try the olives."

"My lords," William of Rubruck said, heeding not a word. "It is imperative that we are not seen as envoys. For I do not wish to discuss matters of earthly power but to spread the true word of God and of the Pope in Rome. We have heard say in the Holy Land that your lord Batu may become a Christian, and greatly were the Christians of the Holy Land rejoiced thereat. And chiefly so the most Christian lord the King of the French, who has come to that land on a pilgrimage and is fighting against the Saracens to wrench the holy places from out of their hands. It is for this I wish to go to Batu, and also carry to him the letters of the lord king, in which he admonishes him of the weal of all Christendom."

"Letters," I said, and slammed my palm against the table with much force and the loud bang cut William off from his babbling. "Letters from the King of France to the Prince Batu. I ask you, my lords, does that not make us envoys, after all?" I looked around at everyone while nodding my head, and focused my attention on Friar William. "Yes, indeed it does, my lords, quite right, yes."

Thomas picked up from me, speaking over William's protestations. "You have our thanks, lords, for sending word ahead on our behalf, to your overlord. Our sincerest thanks. We shall say prayers for you, will we not, Friar William?"

And when they knew that we would not cause them diplomatic difficulties, the prefects did receive us right favourably and gave the three friars lodgings in the episcopal church. The rest of us were given use of rooms in the villa of an old Genoese merchant who bowed repeatedly and told us how honoured he was to have us as his guests, even while his servants removed the valuable decorations from our rooms behind him.

For the journey into the wilderness, they gave us the choice whether we would have carts with oxen to carry our effects or sumpter horses. The merchants of Constantinople advised William of Rubruck to take carts, and that he should buy the regular covered carts such as the Rus carry their furs in, and in these we could put such of our things as we would not wish to unload every day. They said that oxen would be the best choice.

"Oxen are so very slow," I said, to William and to Thomas. "With those lumbering beasts, we shall not reach Batu before the Day of Judgement."

Even Bertrand agreed with me, as he was eager to complete his task with as much haste as possible so he could return to his king that much sooner and so return to his favour. Ideally, Bertrand wished to get back to Acre before King Louis left the Holy Land or else he risked being forgotten by the court, and his ambition would be thwarted for years and perhaps forever.

But William of Rubruck, the incompetent great oaf, did not wish to insult our hosts by going against their recommendations. "Should we take horses it will be necessary to unload them at each stopping place and to load other horses," he said, "because you see my lords, horses are so much weaker than oxen."

We took the oxen, and so doubled the travelling time for that part of our journey. Eva cautioned patience and so I did my best to accommodate the slothfulness of that gluttonous heap of pompous dogmatism, William of Rubruck.

For all his many faults, he was not a stupid man. Naive, of course, in the worst possible way. But not stupid. He had brought with him from Constantinople, on the advice of canny merchants, fruits, muscadel wine and dainty biscuits to present to the captains of the Tartars that we met so that our way might be made easier.

"For, among these Tartars," Friar William told me, "no man is looked upon in a proper way who comes into their land with empty hands."

We set out on our journey from Soldaia about the calends of June 1253 with our six covered carts in which was carried our supplies, belongings, and bedding to sleep on at night. And they gave us horses to ride, one for each of us. They gave us also two gruff men who drove the carts and looked after the oxen and horses.

And so arrayed, we set off into the wilderness.

The path north across the landscape was wide, and well-trod and the weather dry, and hot. Our horses were not good. They were short and sturdy enough, but they could manage only a slow pace and had to be nurtured less they tire themselves into standstill before the day was over. Bertrand had immediately seized the best horse for himself, that is to say, the largest and strongest. Thomas had taken the next best due to his status, and Friar William, arguing that he required a sizeable mount due to his own bulk, took the next best.

Eva had given me a probing look on the first day.

"It is not worth the conflict that would result from arguing," I had muttered.

"And yet, if we must flee..." she then began, indicating our tired old nags.

I had lowered my voice. "Then we kill them and take their good horses."

Eva had relaxed. "Fair enough."

Through each day, we rode upon our horses while the six wagons—which were sturdy, four-wheeled things pulled by a pair of oxen each—trundled along behind us. Each wagon was tied to the one before it so that the two moody servants the merchants had provided simply had to drive the first pair and the others followed in turn. The wagons carried our supplies for the journey and also the many gifts that we had been strongly advised to bring for the Mongol lords, as such things were expected.

Riding on poor horses is tiring and we spoke little as we travelled. When we stopped to make camp, we drew up the wagons all close together and used them to corral the horses and to partly shelter against the wind. We made small fires for as long as it took to boil fresh water collected in the day to make it safe for drinking, and sat to eat the food we had brought from the city. There was no reason to stay awake for longer than necessary, so we each retired to our bedrolls. It was still warm at night, so sleeping wrapped in our blankets upon the grass was perfectly comfortable. Bertrand demanded that he sleep upon the bundles of furs we had brought as gifts on the back of one of the wagons. None challenged him, yet he appeared pleased with his petty victory over us.

Every other night, Eva would drink her fill of blood from a cut I would make across the veins of my wrist. Decades before it had felt strange, to be drunk from in such fashion but by then, our final years together, I paid it little heed. Her drinking of me gave me great thirst, for blood, water, or wine that I would need to satiate as soon as I was able. Yet, any weakness was not long lasting and she needed it.

Together, we lay entwined, her head resting upon my shoulder, or she would sprawl her upper body across my chest so that the good weight of the woman held me down. With her in my arms, I stayed awake for as long as I could every night to be alert for assault from without or from within. When I felt myself falling asleep, I would wake my wife and she would pinch herself into alertness and take over the watch.

What a remarkable land it was. Good land for farming but it was not defensible and yet it seemed to be peopled with groups from everywhere on the Earth. There were forty hamlets between Soldaia and the land bridge of the peninsula and nearly every one had its own language. All these places were subject to the Mongols, of course, and none of them mixed with each other. Among them were many Goths, whose language was Teutonic. I was told that there were Saxons thereabout, descended from men who had fled from the Norman conquest hundreds of years earlier. I greatly wished to meet these Saxons but no one knew where their villages were and I grew to suspect either they had all been killed or the entire story was a fabrication.

The guides were barely willing to exchange words with me but with much cajoling and with their words translated by the slave boy Nikolas, I winkled the knowledge of the wild land out of them. They told me that from Soldaia all the way along the coast to the city of Tanais to the east there were high promontories along the sea. And beyond the mountains to the north was a most beautiful forest, in a plain full of springs and rivulets. And beyond that forest was a mighty plain which stretched out to the border of the peninsula to the north, where it narrows greatly into a land bridge, having the sea to the east and the west. Once we were beyond that border we would be on the endless steppe, the grassland that ran from Hungary in the west to the ends of the Earth in the east.

Each time we stopped at sundown, I would ask Abdullah more about the people who populated the steppe and he would explain while some of us listened to his words, sitting upon the grass or on the backs of the wagons, while we ate what food we had in the moments before retiring for the night. The young Saracen slave grew somewhat confident when he spoke of such things, seeming almost wise at times, although we had to watch he did not get hold of the wine because he was a terrible sot.

"In the plain beyond us used to live Cumans before the Mongols came from the east," Abdullah said. "Once, it was the Cumans that forced the cities and villages hereabout to pay them tribute. The Cumans were once from the east, and there they were subject to the Mongols but had fled here to escape their subjugation. But when the Mongols came, the Cumans feared their retribution and they fled down into this peninsula for the first time. Such a multitude of Cumans entered this province that the people of the villages fled to the shore of the sea. But there was nowhere further to flee, and no food to be eaten, for the Cumans had taken it all. And so all these people ate one another. The living ate the dying, as was told me in Damascus by a merchant who saw it. Saw the living devouring and tearing with their teeth the raw flesh of the dead, as dogs do corpses."

None of us had anything to say to that. Bertrand scoffed as if he disbelieved it, but his big face showed he was as disturbed as any of us.

"What happened to the Cumans?" I asked.

Abdullah shrugged. "They were subjugated by the Mongols once again." He squirted a stream of wine into his mouth from a skin. The ancient, frail Friar Bartholomew leapt to his feet, hitched up his robes as he scurried over and slapped Abdullah about the head before yanking the wineskin from him.

Toward the end of the province were many large lakes, on whose shores were brine springs which the locals used for the making of salt. And from these brine springs, Prince Batu derived great revenues, for from all Rus they came to that place for salt, also many ships came by sea. The young Franciscan lad, Stephen, was most intrigued by the notion that a fortune could be made from salt and expressed that curiosity that evening at camp.

"Your interest in worldly wealth is unseemly," Friar Bartholomew said to chastise him, while Friar William nodded.

"It is not my own personal wealth that interests me," Stephen said, innocently, "I simply wish to cultivate a clearer understanding of the world."

Friar William scoffed. "Cultivate your need to practice simplicity and detach yourself from materiality instead."

"And not only that," Friar Bartholomew said, in a nagging tone while Stephen hung his head. "You must become more charitable."

I burst out laughing. No one else laughed with me but I thought I could see a hint of a smile on Stephen's face before he hid it behind a biscuit.

And so, three days after leaving Soldaia, we came across the Mongols.

When I found myself among them, they were so strange, so repulsive, and backward that it seemed to me that I had been transported into another century far into the past, or to another world entirely.

How long they had been tracking us, I could not say. That country was alien to me, and I could not read the land, could not see it, in the way that I have always been able to read the land of England, France and the rest of Christendom. Even so, late on that third morning, we saw riders on the horizon. We stopped our wagons and waited where we were, as was the proper procedure. A group of ten men approached on stocky little horses the size of ponies, with a few more riderless horses following behind.

It was early summer and the day was hot, the wind warm and full of the smell of grass, and fragrant herbs. As the sun was so high, most of our party sat beneath the wagons as it was the only shade anywhere in sight.

I wore only a cotton tunic, hose, shoes and a wide-brimmed hat and, despite the heat, I badly wished to put on my armour. When facing an enemy, I always wanted to be wearing my long mail hauberk, with a coif for my head, neck, and throat and then an enclosed helm to protect my head. Ideally, I would wear chausses, which were mail armour for my legs. And yet we three knights; Bertrand, Thomas and I, had agreed that appearing before the Mongols while dressed for war would be provocative and may cause us more problems than it would solve. I had argued hard for wearing our gambesons at least, with a loose tabard over the top to disguise the armour. Bertrand was ready to agree but Thomas insisted that it would be just the same, or nearly so, as wearing mail and that a tabard would fool no man, not even a savage.

"We will at least wear our swords, will we not, Thomas?" I had said.

"Even that may provoke them into some evil action," Thomas had countered.

"We cannot be defenceless," Bertrand had blustered.

"Put your faith in God, sir," Thomas had said, with a certainty that brooked no argument.

Bertrand had nodded his monstrous great head, scowling. "I do, Thomas," he said, a sound that was more growl than words. "I shall. But a knight should have his sword at his hip."

Even though I agreed with Bertrand, I was honour bound to side with Thomas and so we stood, wearing no more than light clothing, waiting for a group of brutal savages whose intentions were unknown. If I had been wearing my gambeson, the thick layers of linen would have made me sweat profusely under such a sun, but that was the price we paid for protection against sword and arrow. Without it, I was vulnerable to the arrows that I knew all Tartars carried.

While they were still some way off, I strolled as if I had not a care in the world to the side of the wagon where I had stashed my gear, and I leaned against the side. Eva strutted over and leaned by me, pulling her own hat down over her face. She hated the bright sunlight and kept her skin covered when out of doors, even if not attempting to pass as a man.

Nodding to her, I climbed up and reached over the side boards into the wagon and pulled my stashed sword up slightly so that I would be able to draw it swiftly, should I need to. Getting down again, I leaned my arm on the side of the wagon, ready to move. I watched the riders approach.

All of us were quiet.

"Remember to breathe," Eva muttered.

I let out a huge sigh. "I was not holding my breath," I said.

We had all been apprehensive about our first meeting with the Mongols since we had set out from the city. Even the brash Bertrand had grown ever quieter the further north we had gone. The friars especially so. The elderly Bartholomew was so terrified that I could see him shaking beneath his robes from twenty-feet away.

The servants clustered together behind us, beneath two of the wagons farthest from the riders' approach.

"Do nothing to anger them," Friar William called to us all from beside the foremost wagon as the riders approached. "I shall speak for us. Do not overrule me or we will appear divided to them."

Before even leaving the city of Soldaia, we had agreed exactly that. In fact, it was my recommendation that we maintain a united front. The friar was doing no more than betraying his nervousness by speaking so to us, which was understandable. The Tartars were conquering devils.

I had seen many strange peoples from far off lands during my travels in Iberia and Outremer over the decades. I had seen tall, dark men from the highlands of Ethiopia, who worshipped Christ with as much reverence as any priest. I had seen even darker men from beyond Ethiopia, brought to the Holy Land as slaves by the Saracens, who despised the black men and whipped them most brutally.

But no people I had ever seen were as hideous and vile as the Mongols. Their stink greeted us, even when they were a long bow-shot away and the smell grew overwhelming as they approached. A sour, foul smell such as a man gets when he has not washed his body for a year or more. A cloying, oppressive stench as foul as brewed piss, like a tanner's yard, but with an animal breadth and depth that filled one's nose like a poison.

They were all clothed in thick, long, light brown overcoats. The belts wrapped about their middles were decorated in brass, with slightly curved swords suspended from them, bouncing as they rode. Each man also had a short, curved bow and a huge quiver absolutely packed with arrows. Even in that summer heat, they wore trousers and thick, long boots. Most wore a sort of quilted hood with fur on the inside. A couple of them were bare-headed and they had the most bizarre hair. The entire scalp was shaved to stubble, other than the front and back, where the jet-black hair was tightly braided into thin, ratty strands longer than their faces.

All ten of them rode with a swagger the like of which I had rarely seen from the most arrogant of Christian lords. They spread themselves in a wide arc as they ambled up to us. Their other horses, twenty or more, trailed behind without ropes tying them together. The ten men spread out and those in front pulled to a stop a few paces from our wagons, while the others kept their horses walking.

Friar William stood and went to greet them, and young Stephen went at his shoulder. Old Bartholomew hung farther back but shuffled after them, as did Abdullah, like one of the Mongol remounts.

The riders on the flanks continued to ride slowly, surrounding us on their horses, staring at us with sneering contempt upon their faces.

And what faces they were. Wide, round faces, as though they had been stretched by a mighty hand. Eyes narrow and filled with animal cunning, and thin black moustaches twitching beneath squashed noses. Their complexion was swarthy from the sun and yet wind-ravaged about the cheeks. Each man wore an expression of the haughtiest contempt and scathing viciousness. These were men who had done evil things, and who had suffered evil things done to them in turn.

One of them spoke, suddenly. Barking his barbaric language in a harsh, throaty voice like a broken trumpet.

Abdullah bowed and turned to Friar William. "He demands to know whether we have ever been among them before."

William half-turned to Abdullah. "Tell him that we have not ever been amongst them. Tell them that this is indeed our first time here in these lands, yes. Tell him so."

Abdullah babbled his response back to the four Mongols who had reign in right before us.

I watched as the savages rode slowly by me, three on my side. On the other side of our group, three more rode around. Bertrand and Hughues were on the other side. Bertrand had one meaty hand clamped down on his squire's shoulder. That was good.

In the centre, Thomas and his squire stood straight and tall, as if he had done such a thing a thousand times. Such is the strength that faith can give to a man.

Eva looked down, hiding her face with the brim of her hat. I stared at the riders, half-willing them to attack me. The one nearest to me sneered and muttered something to the fellow behind him, and they both laughed. A savage, hacking noise.

My heart's desire was to leap at the man, run him down and smash his hideous face into pulp.

Instead, I stayed still and watched them position themselves around us. We were badly outnumbered, for there were six fighters on our side and ten on theirs. Also, they were mounted and had bows and swords ready, while we stood unarmoured and unarmed.

On the other hand, we had the wagons drawn up somewhat together, which would impede their charge or provide cover from arrows. Our horses were saddled and ready to ride, but I would not fight from the back of a horse who was not trained to it. You may as well save yourself the trouble of climbing on and instead throw yourself onto your spine and smash your face with a hammer.

"What is he saying, Abdullah?" William said, as the lead Mongol babbled on and on, whilst gesticulating wildly.

"He is asking for some of our provisions, lord," Abdullah said, his voice shaking.

"That seems fair," William said, turning to us. "A small gift, a token from us. That we might share bread. Yes, yes, that is perfectly right and proper enough. Stephen? Would you mind gathering together a piece of biscuit for each man, and I think one of the skins of wine. Yes, a whole skin, why not, let us be generous."

Stephen called over the boy Nikolas and together they rooted out a basket with ten or fifteen of the small biscuits, which were wheat breads baked twice so that they were as hard as rock and had to be soaked in water or wine or milk before they were edible. The large skin of wine sloshed loudly as Stephen manhandled it back to the Mongols. They took the wine very roughly, with no manners nor sign of gratitude at all, and drank with gusto, passing the skin between them. The biscuits they crunched with their teeth, biting pieces off and chewing with their mouths hanging open. After only a few moments, one of the men tossed the wineskin to the grass, empty.

The Mongols before William began gesturing wildly again while they babbled at William, jutting their outstretched hands to the wagons behind us.

"What is he saying?" William said, backing up against the onslaught of heathenish language.

"He insists that we give them more," Abdullah said. "Apologies, lord, he says we must give them more wine. Another skin."

"I am not sure that we have enough," William said. "Tell them we do not have enough."

The Mongols did not like what Abdullah said, and the lead man rode his horse slowly, right at William. As he rode, he spoke in a low voice.

"He says, lord," Abdullah said, "that a man enters a house not with one foot only."

"Well, he can keep both feet out of my house, if that is his attitude," William said, puffing up his big belly. "The impudence of the man."

Abdullah began to jabber away but William cut him off.

"Wait, wait," William said, holding up his palms as the Mongol bore down on him. "Stephen, please would you find another skin of wine for our guests."

I was already moving before I made the decision to do so. I covered the distance quickly but walked with as casual an air as was possible. I was unarmed and had no wish to alarm the heathens.

Clapping my palm down on Stephen's shoulder as he turned, I stopped him from moving away. Stephen tried to shake me off but I held him firm then pushed him back to where William stood gaping at me.

"What are you doing?" he hissed at me, eyes wide.

I planted my other hand on William's big shoulder and squeezed it, so I stood between and slightly behind the two monks, making a wall out of our bodies. I grinned up at the Mongol rider.

He scowled down at me and babbled some of his disgusting language.

"No," I said, shaking my head and still grinning like an idiot while the monks shook.

Our interpreter began to explain but I cut him off.

"I understand him, Abdullah," I said, looking up at the agitated Mongol. From the corner of my eye, I watched as others moved their horses closer. "And you understand me, don't you, you heathen bastard." I dropped my smile and raised my voice. "No more wine. No more food. Take us to your master."

He rode right up to us and turned his horse sideways with no instruction that I could see. With excellent horsemanship, he somehow got the creature to sidle into us so that its flanks were pressing against the monks. The beast was short but well-muscled, with a round belly. The stinking Mongol grimaced while he harangued us, and the monks quivered and tried to step back.

"Abdullah," I said without looking away. "Tell him to take us to his master so that we may give our gifts to him."

The interpreter jabbered away and I saw the Mongol's resolve fade. The heathen did not dwell upon his decision, but instead moved away, barking commands at his fellows.

When I turned around, I saw how Bertrand, Thomas, and their squires had taken positions between the wagons, a few paces behind me, ready to take action. That was a good thing to see. Friar William was angry at me for a while but the man had the intelligence and the humility to let it fade. Young Stephen, I fear, looked upon me with open wonder and admiration. I felt pity for him, for it is a small thing to stand your ground against those that you hold in contempt, but he was still naive, even then. Innocent to the darkness of the world.

He would not be for very much longer.

* * *

The Mongols asked whence we came and where we wanted to go. Friar William told them that we had heard that their lord Prince Batu was considering becoming a Christian and that we wanted to go to him. Also, that we had letters from the King of the French to deliver to him.

Then they asked what was in the carts, whether it was gold or silver or costly clothing that we were taking to Batu. I answered that Batu would see for himself what we were bringing to him when we reached him and that it was none of their business to ask. They made a big show of being offended but it seemed to me to be almost mere convention, and they accepted easily enough.

In the morning we came across the carts of a captain of the Mongols who was called Scatay. His carts were carrying the dwellings, and it seemed that a city was coming towards me across the wide plain.

Huge wagons, pulled by teams of oxen, rumbled over the grassland. More astonishing, however, was that every other wagon had a large, round tent on the back of it. It took me quite some time to come to terms with the fact that they dragged their empty homes up onto the flat backs of these enormous wagons and pulled them down to the ground again when they reached their new destination. The Mongols would move to new pastures for their herds, move from a river to a woodland, or from the plain to the hills, as the need takes them. Each lord had his own domain, however, these domains were so large that they could move regularly throughout a year and not camp in the same place more than once. They would usually spend winter in a single, sheltered place, near a woodland if they could, but would move with ease throughout the rest of the year. When the camp—which was called an ordus—was assembled, they would also erect pens and tethers for special animals and poles and lines for drying clothes, meat, and skins.

Some of their tents, called gers, were disassembled for transport and rebuilt at the new location. And that was how I saw the manner of their construction. The centre of the roof was a wooden ring, held up at a height of eight or ten feet or even higher by two posts. The circular wall was a lattice of wood, with long poles joining the centre ring with the wall. Over the top was pulled great sheets of whitened felt. And each building had a surprisingly strong wooden door. When complete, they were remarkably sturdy structures.

I was also astonished at the size of the herds of oxen and horses and flocks of sheep, though we saw but few men to manage them.

"Who is this captain?" I asked the Mongols, through Abdullah. "Is he some great lord?"

They were amused by my ignorance.

"Scatay has nothing," they said. "He has only five hundred men. There are ten thousand Mongol lords greater than he."

I felt the first inkling of the potential might of these terrible people. Still, I could never have imagined the true scale of their power until I saw it for myself, months and years later.

It seemed that there were many more than that, for each man had his own tent, and each tent had its own great wagon, with oxen to pull it. And each man had dozens or hundreds of horses. And some of the men had more than one wife, and she had her own tent, and her own horses and servants, and stocky children working as hard as a slave. So, five hundred men meant over a thousand people and more animals than I could count, roaming out of sight over miles and beyond the horizon.

We followed that mass of oxen and wagons and tents all day, moving through them at the edges toward the head of the procession where their leader's tents were. Late in the afternoon, the Mongols set down their dwellings near a muddy, wide lake. Their and Scatay's men came to us, and as soon as they learnt that we had never been among them before they begged of our provisions. Abdullah said to us that we must give something to Scatay.

The Mongols poked and prodded at us, asking for clothing and other items. I insisted that nothing be handed over to these heathens. Our dragoman explained again that we could in no way go to the captain, Scatay, without gifts and so we got a flagon of wine and filled a small basket with biscuits and a plate with apples and other fruit.

The Mongols were angry with our meagre gifts. Again, they demanded some costly cloth. We went with this in fear that they would take offense and turn us back, or worse but we could not give up all our presents to some lowly provincial captain or we would have nothing left for Lord Batu.

While the servants waited with the wagons, the monks, with Thomas, Bertrand and I, were invited into the chief Mongol's tent.

This was the largest ger in the camp, and it was located right in the centre of the others. We were warned to not step on the threshold when we entered, as this was a terrible taboo, and after I ducked inside I was impressed by the comfort within. Rugs covered the floor, other than a large hearth in the centre. On the far side, opposite the door, was a low couch where the chief man and lord of the ger sat. We were directed to one side and bade to sit. Opposite us were a gaggle of Mongol women and girls who were rather subdued but who also pottered about in a relaxed, domestic manner.

The captain, Scatay, was seated on his couch, with a little musical instrument in his hand, and his chief wife was beside him. What a hideous creature she was. In truth, it seemed to me that her whole nose had been cut off, for she was so snub-nosed that she seemed to have no nose at all. What is more, she had greased this part of her face with some black unguent, and also her eyebrows, so that she appeared most vile.

Then William begged him to accept the trifling gifts, explaining how he was not allowed by his order to own gold or silver or costly robes. That was why we had no riches to give him, only food to offer for a blessing. Scatay made a show of being displeased and yet he immediately distributed our gifts among his men who had gathered there to drink.

He asked us if we would drink kumis or mare's milk; for the Christians, Ruthenians, Greeks, and Alans who live among them, and who wish to follow strictly their religion, drink it not. They consider themselves to be no longer Christians if they drink it, and the priests have to bring them back into the fold as if they had denied the faith of Christ.

"Abdullah," William said. "You must have translated that incorrectly."

Stephen interrupted. "What he says is true, brother. I have read such a thing in the records of the Church of Santa Anna. The Christians of these lands have many unorthodox beliefs, due to the corrupting influence of the heathens and from not being one with the true Church."

William glanced between Thomas and Stephen before lowering his voice to answer. "You will explain to me later what you were doing in the records of a Templar church but in the meantime, you shall hold your tongue, do you hear me?"

A chastened Stephen lowered his head, cheeks flushing red.

"Tell him that we have enough of our own drink so far," William said. "But that if that should give out, we would happily drink whatever he gave us."

This seemed to satisfy the Mongol captain and he asked another question of us.

"What says the letter from your king, the King of the French?" Abdullah translated.

"Those letters are sealed," William said, stiffly. "And meant for Prince Batu only. But he can be assured that there is naught in them but good and friendly words."

He then asked, through Abdullah, what we would say to Batu with our own voices when we reached him.

William answered. "Words of the Christian faith."

The Mongol asked what these words were, since he was eager to hear them for himself.

Friar William expounded to him as well as he could through Abdullah, who seemed neither over intelligent nor fluent in the creed of the faith, he being but an ignorant heathen and follower of Mohammed. When the Mongol had heard William's pious drivel, he remained silent but wagged his head, entirely unconvinced.

"Ask him if Prince Batu has a Christian man who serves him," I said. "A man from France, or England. A man named William."

The monks grew agitated at my interjection and also Thomas hissed at Abdullah to say nothing. While the Mongols stared at us in confusion at our agitation, I grinned at everyone and nodded at those who would meet my eye.

"Let us maintain a friendly demeanour, shall we, my friends?" I said, smiling and nodding. "And, Abdullah, you will ask the Mongol my question for if you do not, I shall hurt you very badly by breaking your thumb and forefinger on both hands the moment we leave the company of these charming people."

Abdullah was a coward and so he did as I had requested.

"The Lord Scatay says that, yes, there was a man like that serving Batu Khan."

My heart was in my throat as I pushed for more. "And his name? Is it William? Did he look like me?"

The Mongol captain tilted his head and looked hard at me while he babbled.

"He says that William was the man's name but as for you men from Christendom, he cannot tell one apart from the other."

Thomas scowled, even as I grinned like a madman. "If you are quite finished with disrupting our royal business for your personal quest, sir?" Thomas said.

Then William and Thomas spoke to Scatay in the terms previously used, for it was essential that we should everywhere say the same thing. This we had been well cautioned by those who had been among them, never to change what we said.

The Mongols were wary to the point of paranoia about enemy agents observing their numbers, positions and internal political divisions, lest any and all these things be used against them. A particular worry for them, because that was precisely how they themselves operated. No other people, not even the devious Syrians, nor the ancient and corrupt Persians, had such an extensive intelligence network. And we Christians had almost no concept of such things, certainly not in such a widespread and formal strategic fashion.

Finally, the Mongols agreed to do as we asked, supplying us with new horses and oxen, and two men to guide us onward to Lord Batu. The servants from Soldaia who had brought us went back with their beasts.

Before giving us all this, they kept us waiting for a long time, begging of our bread for their little ones, admiring everything they saw on our servants, knives, gloves, purses, and belts, and wanting everything. We refused, over and over, every day while we waited to be sent onward, saying to every grasping heathen that we had a long journey before us and that we could not at the start deprive ourselves of necessary things. The monks explained with words, through Abdullah, while Eva and I explained by wrenching their hands and shoving them away.

It is true that they took nothing by force but they begged in the most importunate and impudent way for whatever they saw, and if a person gave anything to them, it was so much lost, for they were ungrateful. The Mongols considered themselves the masters of the world, and it seemed to them that there was nothing that anyone had the right to refuse. If one refused to give, and after that had need of their service, they served him badly.

No matter how much I explained to the servants to give nothing up, they were intimidated and I could not be everywhere at once. Thomas and Bertrand were determined to keep the peace, subject as we were to the mercy of the Mongols. Even Bertrand controlled his temper, for he knew he had to complete his embassy in order to return to the favour of his king.

While we waited with them, in their camp, they at least gave us to drink of their cow's milk, from which the butter had been taken. It was very sour. They called it aira. I did not like it but the Mongols valued it, so it was their way of offering us something, however small, as a token of acceptance.

Finally, we left this captain, and it seemed to me that we had escaped from the clutches of demons.

In fact, we had barely begun our descent into Hell.

For two months, from the time we left Soldaia to when we came to Prince Batu's ordus, we never slept in a house or tent, but always in the open air or under our carts. Travelling north and then east, we never saw a city, but only Cuman tombs in very great numbers.

In the evenings, our guide us gave us kumis to drink. Even though it is fermented mare's milk - an intoxicating version of the foul, sour aira - it was quite palatable. The Mongols loved that drink, indeed, they drunk it every day and took much sustenance from it. They loved alcohol in all forms, for life on those endless grasslands, exposed to constant wind and sun and rain, was dismal indeed and like the life of an animal and so they sought comfort, warmth, and distraction in their inebriation.

"Why do the Christians here fear this drink?" I asked Stephen, as I was fairly taken with the stuff, and the young monk seemed wise beyond his years. Whereas I have always had years beyond my wisdom.

"They are ignorant of the true tenets of the faith," Stephen replied, shrugging beneath his dirty robe. "And their blood is inferior to ours, which makes them stupid despite being saved." He giggled because he was drunk on kumis.

We hopped from one Mongol camp to the next, often at intervals of five days or so, as the oxen travels. Some Mongol captains were wealthy, where others were impoverished. And when we came among one particularly destitute ordus, which was confined to a barren and diseased territory, they were such horrible looking creatures that they seemed like lepers. There were no children running about as in other camps.

"Why in the name of God are they like this?" I asked Abdullah.

"Their lord displeased Batu."

During our journey to the royal camp of Batu, the Mongols rarely gave us food, only very sour and bad-smelling cow's milk. Our own wine was quickly exhausted, and the water was so muddy from the horses that it was not drinkable even with boiling. Had it not been for the barrels of travel biscuits we had, and God's mercy, we should probably have perished.

Not only that, the men who conducted us began robbing the monks in a most audacious manner, for they saw that the holy brothers took but little care with their belongings. Finally, after losing a number of things, vexation made the monks wise to the Mongols' ways and all precious things they kept on their person, as the rest of us had done for some time. Not only that, we none of us went anywhere alone, even to shit, else we would be mugged by our guides.

I was warned by Thomas and William never to hurt the Mongols who guided us, even in retribution for their uncouth, savage behaviour, because then we would likely be killed or abandoned¬, which amounted to the same thing. They spoke as if I was a child who had no self-control and I was greatly offended by their words of warning. Still, it was true enough that at times I found it difficult to resist murdering those arrogant bastards. I would happily have feasted on their blood, for they were miserable, thieving heathens with no honour amongst them.

They would never leave us alone, for in their minds they were the masters and we were outsiders. When we were seated in the shade under our carts, for the heat was intense at that season, they pushed in most importunately among us, to the point of crushing the weaker members of our party, such as Friar Bartholomew, who was frail and a poor traveller.

Filthy creatures that they were, whenever they were seized with the need to void their bowels, they did not go away from us farther than one can throw a bean. They did their filthiness right beside us while talking together, and much more they did which was vexatious beyond measure. I grew to hate them and hold them in deep contempt and disgust.

Still, I swallowed my disgust and even attempted to learn their hideous language. After many days, I began to understand pieces of what they said. One of my few gifts outside of the marshal traits is an affinity for languages, thanks to God, for if it were not so I would have died centuries ago.

Bertrand and Hugues were surly but subdued. The entire time, I made sure to never turn my back on them and watched them closely, especially whenever Eva moved apart from the group for momentary privacy. She dressed always in mannish clothing, was hooded or sheltered beneath a wide-brimmed hat and she reeked as much as a man, or a boy at least. Still, the men in our party eyed her in hunger. All other than William of Rubruck who, for all his faults, was an honourable and strong-willed man and old Bartholomew who either hated women or had no interest in women, on account of his advanced years perhaps or because he was that way inclined. Young Nikolas was at her side so much that anyone would think he was her slave rather than Rubruck's and though I am sure he sought her company from a need to feel mothered, he was also approaching an age where his thoughts may not be so innocent. On occasion, I would catch the filthy bloody Mongols discussing her while casting looks in her direction from a distance and those men, along with Bertrand, were the ones I feared attacking in the night. How she was able to withstand such ceaseless attention, I do not know, because it was enough to drive me to a state of heightened anxiety. I slept little and was ever ready to draw a dagger in defence of my wife.

"Any woman who ever leaves her home grows used to such things," she said one time, shrugging. "Their endless gazing means nothing. But any man who lays a finger upon me will lose his hand, his balls, and then his life."

"What a true English lady you are," I said in jest but I also meant it. However, my remark did not appear to amuse her one bit.

We crossed the great River Don, which was called the Tanais back then, ferried across on small boats. That river at that point was as broad as the Seine at Paris and the Russians had a village there, an outpost subject to the Mongols. It was the season when they were cutting the rye. Wheat thrived not there but they had great abundance of millet. The Ruthenian women arranged their heads like my own people did back in England and France, but their outside gowns they trimmed from the feet to the knee with vair or minever. The men wore capes like Germans and wore felt caps, pointed and very high.

The country beyond the Tanais was most beautiful, with rivers and forests. To the south, we had very high mountains, inhabited, on the side facing this desert, by the Kerkis and the Alans, who are Christians and still fought to resist the Mongols. Beyond them was the Caspian Sea.

At the end of every day, we ate quickly and retired early, sleeping beneath the wagons when it was still warm enough to do so. On the easier days, we would perhaps stay awake and talk. Once in a while, we would camp near to a lake or river and there would invariably be scrub on the banks. Enough to make small campfires for a little warmth and light either side of the long sunsets. On those nights with fires, we would drink more kumis than usual and would stay awake longer.

"Tell us of the battle again, sir, I beg you," the monk Stephen Gosset asked Thomas on one such night.

"Again?" Thomas said, warily. "I have never spoken of it. Not to you, brother."

We sat in a rough circle on the grass. The ground was still warm after a baking hot day, and the herbaceous smells of the dry grass wafted up from beneath us. A small fire flickered in the middle of us, providing almost no warmth but plenty of light. Without it, there would have been enough light from the cascade of stars sprayed onto the blanket of night above us. I sat beside Eva and chewed on the dried goat meat. It took all evening to chew through enough to feel even half a belly full. Eva scrubbed the hints of rust from her second-best sword.

"What battle?" I asked, speaking around my food.

Thomas waved a hand. "Young Stephen has an interest in war."

"An unseemly interest," Friar William growled from the shadows. "Most unseemly."

Stephen opened his palms in front of him. "Brother, I wish only to know more of the Tartars. My lord Thomas is the only man I ever met who has fought against them."

When a dribble of brown spit ran down my chin, I realised my mouth was hanging open.

"You fought the bloody Tartars?" I said. "When?"

Thomas took a deep breath. "Twelve years past."

"The second invasion of the Tartars," I said. "You were there when they smashed the Hungarians?"

"No, not there. I was in the Kingdom of Poland. There was another battle. A series of battles, in fact." He surprised me with a question. "Where were you twelve years ago?"

"Acre, I think?" I looked at Eva. She returned my gaze with no expression, or confirmation, while she rubbed at her blade.

"And no doubt a mere page at the time," Thomas said. "Bertrand?"

"Twelve years past?" he said, pausing to take a mouthful of kumis. "Chasing the girls in my father's castle. That was a year or two before he gave me a castle of my own, you see. By then I had already taken up my sword and won many—"

"What happened in Poland?" I asked while Bertrand scowled at me. "What series of battles? Against the Tartars? Why was your order up there?"

"Our order is everywhere that there are Christians. My brothers and I were stationed there to plan a crusade against the pagan Lithuanians. There was an important leader there, a great lord named Duke Henry the Pious. It was when the Tartars were attacking the Rus, once again, as they had done in 1223. Long time ago. Thirty years, almost."

"I remember it well," I said. Eva stared at me. "That is, I remember hearing of it. Please, go on."

"This Lord Batu led them. He conquered the Rus, all their cities by 1240. Tartar riders were seen everywhere across Poland, in the Kingdom of Hungary, even into the Duchy of Austria. Sometimes in groups of dozens, even hundreds. Not fighting. Rarely even raiding. Just watching. Learning the land, prior to the invasions."

"Clever," I said, for that was far from standard practice. We Christians had no tradition of that kind of preparation, as hard as it may be to believe.

"They gathered a vast army and led it against King Bela of Hungary."

"The battle at the River Sajo," I said, nodding. "King Bela led the largest Christian army ever assembled, so I heard. And they were destroyed by the Tartars."

Bertrand belched. "A hundred thousand Christians," he said. "A hundred thousand fools."

I scoffed, for that was an absurd number.

"Fewer than that," Thomas said, glancing at me. "But yes, it was a great many. I was not there but I spoke to men who were. Fifty thousand, perhaps. But they were not fools. They fought well, so it is said."

"Who says?" Bertrand demanded. "They were all killed."

"Almost. Not all. Some of my order were there, supporting, observing. The Tartars were led by Prince Batu, a most cunning and brutal commander. He battered, then surrounded all the forces, other than a few here and there. Some small number of my brothers watched the battle unfold across the plain, and so escaped the encirclement and related the tale."

"But you were in Poland," I said.

"I was. With seventy brothers from my order, as well as many sergeants and five hundred bondmen from our lands there. It took us time to assemble and gather to protect the great cities. Krakow, in particular. Duke Henry the Pious brought his army. It was a vast force. Twenty or thirty thousand but most of them villeins armed with little more than sharp sticks and the foulness of their breath. But there were thousands of men-at-arms, also. Five thousand mounted and armoured, at least, so they said."

"I did not know the lands there could field so many knights," I said.

"They are a good people. Strong in arms. Strong in faith. Worth protecting against the heathens."

"I do not doubt it."

"The Tartars sacked a town named Sandomierz. Then, in the month of March, they defeated an army of Poles at Tursko. It was extremely bloody, for both sides, but the Tartars won the field. A fortnight later, another battle, this time at Chmielnik, where the Tartars won again. Not only that, almost the entire nobility of Lesser Poland was killed in that battle. The Tartars sacked Krakow. We advanced with Duke Henry with his thirty thousand men. We were confident, for we knew that King Wenceslaus of Bohemia was coming to join his forces to Henry's and the Bohemians had forty thousand, so they said. Together, our armies would be sixty thousand men, perhaps more."

"How many were the Tartars?" I asked, before correcting myself. "The Mongols."

Thomas sighed. "After the battle, men were saying the enemy numbered a hundred thousand strong." He gave a snort of derision. "I doubt it could have been much more than a tenth of that. But whatever their numbers, they were all mounted. And that was why they were able to force the Poles to battle before the Bohemians could arrive. Duke Henry should have withdrawn, should have pulled back, denied battle. Should have allowed them to do whatever they wanted to his cities and the people. But he could not. A ruler cannot do such things. His lords would never have allowed him to do so. In any case, he had ten thousand mounted men, well equipped and on good horses."

"So the Poles had perhaps an equal number of mounted men as the Mongols," I asked. "Plus ten or twenty thousand on foot? Little wonder he was confident. Were the heathens mounted on these stocky little horses or did they have true war horses?"

Thomas took a deep breath. "I was like you, back then. We all were. We saw those small horses and the riders on their backs. Some of them were so close to the ground, I swear their toes brushed the grass as they rode. And many were mounted archers, with these short bows. And no matter the stories we had heard, how they would shower us with arrows while we advanced, we trusted our armour to protect us."

"What went wrong?" I asked.

"Nothing," Thomas said. "We were held in reserve, my brothers and our mounted sergeants and our bondmen soldiers. I had rather a good view from the right of the battle, on a rise, looking out across the fields of the plain. It was a cold day, and we had to keep our horses warm. Tartars roamed and wheeled about, coming close and pulling away again. It was difficult to discern their positions, where they were strong or weak. It was clear they had some sort of order to them but my brothers were convinced the heathens were a disorganised rabble. The Poles sent their levies forward while the thousands of knights waited for a chance to charge. But the levies came under attack from the mounted archers, who simply withdrew as the levies advanced with their spears. Of course, Duke Henry sent his archers and crossbowmen to engage with the horsemen but the Tartars did surprisingly well, riding in and out from all directions to pour their own arrows down on the Poles. Somehow, we lost hundreds or even thousands and yet the Tartars seemed almost untouched. And then, amongst all the wheeling of horse archers, their lancers appeared through a sudden gap."

"Lancers?" Bertrand said, his voice almost a growl. "They do not have lancers, Thomas. Have you seen a single lance amongst them?"

I silently agreed with the Frenchman.

The Templar ignored him. "There must have been a thousand of them, formed up in ranks and riding knee to knee. Their horses were larger than the others we had seen. The men wore mail and steel helms. They smashed into the ranks of the levies and crossbowmen from the flank and routed them immediately. Exactly what the knights were waiting for and they descended on the Tartar lancers. The Poles were elated. Finally, the heathens would pay for the destruction they had wrought. But the heathen lancers turned and fled at the sight."

"They did not stand?" I said, interested that the terrifying Mongols would be so cowardly.

"Ha!" Bertrand said. "They could not stand against the Poles. They would certainly die under the hooves of the French, am I correct, Thomas? Not the English, though."

Thomas was not amused. "The Poles are as fine as any knights in Christendom, and they were well led that day. But the Tartars fled, seemingly in panic. The mounted Poles charged until they were stretched out and separated into groups, the horse archers shooting into the knights and their horses which killed them and disrupted their communication. Further and further, they retreated and our army became disorganised as the lords of Poland tasted victory and charged again and again, but their lances found few targets."

"What were the Templars doing?" I asked.

"We were on the right, pushing forward in an attempt to keep pace with the greater body of the army. Pushing our levies along with us. Many of my brethren believed that the Tartars were about to be crushed, and they rode on, eager to be part of this great victory. None would listen to councils of caution."

Stephen Gosset spoke up. "You knew it was a trap?"

"Knew? No. Suspected. I felt only dread."

"Why?" Stephen asked.

"You are not a knight, Stephen," Thomas said. "You have not seen a battlefield. You cannot comprehend the disorder. Trumpets are used to sound a unified advance, or sometimes to initiate a more complicated manoeuvre. But men do not often obey, for one reason or another. And battles are loud. Louder than you could imagine. Chaos reigns. But the Tartars, for all their wheeling about and dashing hither and thither, were not disorganised. Their commanding lord sat far to the rear and never once approached the fighting. Instead, his men waved flags upon enormously long poles and the companies of Tartars would discern meaning in those flags. It seemed to me that they differed by shape and colour, and the height or distance from the top of the pole. Orders could thus be relayed immediately across the entire field of battle."

I could scarcely believe it. "These heathens? These men who cannot build a simple stone wall or a solid timber house? These men with their stinking, meagre food? They are utterly witless folk."

"My brothers felt then as you do now and urged our men on so that we could slay some heathens ourselves before they all ran away or were killed by the Polish." Thomas tilted his head back and looked to the darkness above. "Their retreat had been carefully planned in advance of the battle, for there was suddenly a huge cloud of dense smoke drifting across the field. The Tartars had lit enormous fires, with many green branches and pine leaves so as to make a thick smoke. Riders galloped across our front dragging piles of burning brush so that fires burned everywhere. Quickly, we could no longer discern the other side of our army. Soon after, was when they attacked."

"They turned around and charged?" I asked.

"From the front, yes. But also from the flanks. Thousands more of their forces had lain in wait. That part of the field, many miles from the first clashes, had been chosen by them and they had led us straight into it. By that time of the day, our horses were exhausted from charging. You know destriers and war horses have no legs for a prolonged pursuit. Knights were strung out over miles, even separated from their squires and friends."

"But man to man," Bertrand said, outraged. "Man to man, our knights would destroy theirs. Our weapons and armour are vastly superior. And our skill at arms is unmatched in all the world. Look at the Saracens, and they are far richer than these impoverished raiders."

"We were slaughtered," Thomas said. "Thousands of men at arms killed. Knights and great lords. Duke Henry himself was killed. Our defeat was total."

"Bad luck, that is all," Bertrand said. "Anyone can lose a battle like that. The important thing is that our knights are bigger, stronger and fight better, man to man."

Stephen, showing signs of arrogance even then when he was so young and naive, spoke up, his voice rising in pitch with indignation. "But they were outmanoeuvred by the heathens. The enemy fought with intelligence and wisdom and—"

"You know nothing, monk," Bertrand said, shouting him down. "What do you know? Nothing, you know nothing."

The dying fire cracked and popped as the lit branches collapsed into the coals.

Thomas said nothing for a while. "Have you ever seen a knight train a young page in the sword? The page will swing and thrust while the knight presents his unguarded chest or head only to dance aside, parry the blow and send the sword flying. Perhaps kicking the page in the rump while the other boys roar with laughter."

I snorted. "I have been both the page and the knight in that situation. Many a time."

Thomas nodded, slowly, staring at nothing. "We Christians were the page, against the Tartars. They toyed with us. I tell you this, as a knight who has been fighting at the frontiers of Christendom my entire life. I tell you, these Tartars. They are masters of war. And we are children."

And so we came to the ordus of Batu Khan.

After seeing a number of Mongol camps, I assumed Batu's would be simply a larger version. And it was. But it was much more besides.

It was a city, only one unlike any I had ever seen or even conceived of before. It was a city of tents. The great white tents of the Mongols, their gers. And what is more, it was a city that moved. Hundreds of enormous gers on the backs of wagons so big that their axles were the size of ships masts. Mongol women stood on their own wagon, in the doorway of their ger, holding the reins of the teams of oxen that pulled the massive wagons so that it was like seeing fleets of ships sailing across the great grass sea.

Each ger belonged to a woman, and she belonged to a man. One man may have many wives, but each wife controls her own household, with her children and her servants tending to their home and to the animals that the household owned. And there were many animals. Mostly horses. Hundreds and thousands of horses, everywhere one looked. But cattle, too, and other creatures. It reeked worse than any city in Christendom, worse even than Jerusalem or Paris, and possibly even Rome. A hot, shit-stench that filled one's throat so thoroughly that the fear was you would never get it out.

Batu Khan's ordus covered the land from horizon to horizon. And it seemed at first sight to be chaos and disorder. But, like Thomas' battle, that was deceptive. It was because I could not see what the Mongols saw. I could not understand their organisation, their hierarchies. But when their city stopped moving, each ger was set down in its proper place, to east and west. All doors faced south, as that was the holy direction for those people, and the Khan's ger had no other to obscure the view in that way. Their homes were set down by order of seniority but more than that, I could not understand, no matter how much Abdullah explained it to me. I suspect that he did not know himself but a scholar would rather lie and invent falsehoods than admit to his own ignorance.

The ger of Batu was not large enough to contain his court. The man was perhaps the greatest lord of the Mongols, other than the Great Khan Mongke. He was of the oldest generation and had proved his mettle by leading countless battles. And Batu was the eldest son of the eldest son of the legendary Genghis Khan, the first and greatest Mongol Khan. We were not the only visitors to the court. There were ambassadors from almost every kingdom and city from Central Asia to the Danube and so the Mongols were not impressed by us in the slightest and they made no special efforts for us.

We were made to wait, half-ignored, for two days, for the ordus to set itself down in its new location and then for the court to assemble. Not simply for the attendants and petitioners to gather but for the structure itself to be strung up.

In place of a ger, they erected a tent the size of a cathedral. Not in height, but certainly in length, made from poles taller than any tree and ropes as thick as any on the most massive of ships. It was large enough to hold a thousand people at least beneath the vast canopy overhead, and, at the head of all the assembled masses, sat Batu Khan.

Eva waited at where our wagons were parked, with the other two squires and Nikolas. She was under guard by the men who had guided us but still, I had no wish to leave her alone amongst thousands of barbarians.

"If they try anything," I said to her, "do whatever you must to resist them and scream bloody murder. Send the boy to find me."

She looked me square in the eye. "I will kill as many as I need to."

"Try to avoid killing them," I said. "If you possibly can."

"I promise nothing."

She made quips only when she was nervous.

I bent to Nikolas. "Are you well, lad?"

His eyes were wide and his mouth hung open. He had spent his short life inside Constantinople and the wonders of that place were like nothing to him. But the wide plains and vast sky had cowed him and now the city of tents, peopled by strange barbarians were more than he could comprehend.

"I am well, sir," he said.

"Listen, Nikolas," I said, and took a knee in front of him, placing one hand on his shoulder. "I must leave you and my lady, now. I will be going to see this Tartar prince. Can you keep a look out? Look for any trouble and should any trouble happen, you run and find me." I pointed north. "I shall be in or around that giant tent in the centre of the camp. The heathens may try to stop you, may shout at you. But you will not stop for anything, will you, Nikolas?"

Eyes wide, he shook his head and his hand drifted to the white, ivory dagger I had given him, which he now wore suspended from his belt so it hung on his hip like a tiny sword. I could see the beautiful carving of Saint George with his lance running the dragon through as it writhed in coiled agony.

He swallowed and spoke solemnly in his thick Greek accent. "I shall protect her with my life, sir."

I kept a straight face. "Do not fight anyone, Nikolas. You have the heart of a knight but not yet do you have the stature of one. You come find me instead, understand?"

Eva was afraid by the masses around us. She felt as trapped as I did, only now I was leaving her alone. I would not be far, as the crow flies, but we had rarely faced danger apart from the other for thirty-five years. I took her hand in both of mine for a moment. Her eyes spoke of their love and concern for me, and I felt the same.

We brought Abdullah with us to translate our words.

"They say to not step upon the ropes of the structure," Abdullah said, as our guides gesticulated wildly and babbled at us. "The ropes surrounding the entranceway represent the doorway and threshold of a typical ger. If any of us tread on the ropes, we will be removed from the camp, and banished forever. Another one of these men is disagreeing with his colleague, and claims that we would at once be executed in a most terrible fashion."

I shoved away the hands that pawed at me. "Tell them to cease their damned fool gibbering, Abdullah."

He said nothing of the sort. Mongols were everywhere around us. Hundreds of them, thousands. Some staring, others talking at us, many seemed to me to wish to do violence. With all my will, I remained outwardly calm. As well as I could.

We were all checked for weapons once again, and led in and seated together on the left side, sitting upon the patterned carpets laid thickly upon the ground. The monks were the ambassadors and sat in front of us, who were seen as the attendants. A hearth was at the centre of the tent, and a raised dais with benches to the north, opposite the entrance.

On the bench, sat Batu. A large man, broad-shouldered with a wide face and a massive forehead. His complexion was truly awful, grey and with terrible pimples and pockmarks. He looked to be in his later middle age, fifty or so, perhaps. Dressed just as any Mongol would be, in a voluminous tunic, and thick belt and trousers. Yet the cloth was shimmering, dark silk and embroidered with swirling patterns.

"Lord Batu," Friar William muttered.

"Prince Batu," Thomas corrected.

"Batu Khan," Abdullah said.

Friar William looked around at me, eyes wide. "He is of a size with my lord John de Beaumont, would you not say?"

"I would indeed," I said. To this day, I have no idea who he was talking about.

There were so many men within the vast space. Even though the sides of the huge tent structure were open, the air beneath the fabric roof hung heavy and stank of sour sweat. Across from us, were a small group of women, and some children were there.

We were given kumis to drink, and very gratefully did we receive it. Abdullah drank an unseemly amount until I squeezed his shoulder and whispered in his ear.

"Consume no more, you drunken heathen, else I shall gut you from beard to stones when we leave this place. Do you understand?"

William turned over his shoulder and scowled at me. "You shall do nothing of the sort," he said. "Not without my express permission. Nevertheless, Abdullah, if you do not control yourself, I shall be forced to abandon you here amongst the heathens when we return to the Holy Land."

"No, lord, no," Abdullah wailed, quietly.

Stephen hissed. "People are looking at us."

Many people were brought forward, close to Batu and there was much talking, and back and forth. Men from many kingdoms, in many modes of dress, speaking many tongues. Some went away happy. Others were grim-faced as they were escorted out from Batu's presence.

In time, it was our turn and they called us forward.

A herald or some such functionary asked us, through Abdullah, what we had brought in gifts for Batu Khan.

"We are but poor monks," Friar William explained. "Who have taken vows of poverty. All we can offer is some wine, and some foodstuffs, not as gifts but as blessings. Tokens of our good intentions."

The Mongol herald was horrified. "But you have many furs in your wagons. This will be your gift to the Khan."

"Those furs are for trading with," William said. "We are a long way from our own lands and all we wish is to survive through exchanging those furs, piece by piece, for food and other necessary items."

The herald was unmoved. "Those furs belong to Batu Khan, now. Come forward and speak your purpose here."

We were all required to take a knee, and then Friar William unleashed his holy nonsense upon the Khan. How he wished only to preach the word of Christ to the Tartars, and how him and his two brothers were praying they could meet Batu's son, Sartak who was a Christian himself.

Batu's face, already hideous and devoid of civilised niceties, darkened further when William's words were translated.

"The Khan says that his son is no Christian," Abdullah said, voice shaking. The Saracen was hunched over, his shoulder's rounded, like the cowering slave he was. "His son Sartak takes an interest in all gods, all religions, as is right and proper."

William was angry. "Tell him that there is only one God, and He is the God of the Christians."

Whatever Abdullah said to Batu, it was certainly not William's words, nor even his sentiment.

Batu Khan replied. "Do you wish to go? Or do you wish still to speak of your Frankish Christian words to the Mongol people?"

"We wish to spread the word of God, my lord," William said. "But there are many—"

Thomas stepped forward, in front of William, and bowed. "My lord," Thomas said. "We are also ambassadors from the King of the French. I carry with me a letter from him, to you." From within his tunic, William produced the parcel I had seen him hoarding for months and handed it to the herald. "The words are repeated in Latin, Greek, Arabic, and Persian."

It caused quite a fuss with the Mongols, and they busied themselves right there and then, with a group of squabbling scribes jostling to make a translation into their own version of written language. We were ignored while they did so and our group turned in on itself for a time.

William looked physically wounded by the shock. By the impropriety or the subsuming of his authority. "What are you doing?" he whispered.

"I pray you will stay calm, brother William," Thomas said. Bertrand stood with a smug expression on his face.

"That is why you are here?" I said to Thomas. "You came, not to protect these monks on their fool's errand but to deliver a message to Batu? Why not be open about it? These people accept ambassadors from everywhere."

"Quiet," Bertrand said. "You are no more than a hired sword. It is none of your concern."

I have always been slow on the uptake. But then, time does tend to be on my side.

"You are seeking an alliance," I said, astonished I had not realised earlier. "King Louis wants Batu's men to attack the Saracens? Is it to be a surprise assault, is that why this deception?"

Stephen Gosset, clever little bastard that he was, saw through to the heart of it. "The King's peace treaty with the Saracens," Stephen said. "If the Saracens knew about Louis seeking a pact with the Mongols, the Saracens would fall upon Acre at once, fearing to be trapped between two united enemies. And if you had travelled as an ambassador through Constantinople and Soldaia, word would have got back before we ever arrived to make the proposal."

"What do you mean, we?" Friar William said. "Are you on his side, now, Stephen? Are you renouncing your vows and joining the Templars, Stephen, is that what you and Thomas have been conspiring about? Ever since Acre?"

Stephen made no attempt to defend himself. William was dismayed and the monk shook with the hurt of it.

"Oathbreaker," Bartholomew said, looking down his nose.

After a good while, we were brought back before the Khan.

"Your proposal from your king is too important for me to decide," Batu said. "Your letter must go to the Great Khan, in Karakorum. Mongke Khan will hear your petition, and he will give me orders, which I will follow. For that is the proper way. And you must all go with this letter, so that the Great Khan may question you further, so he may make the best decision."

He nodded to the herald to signal that our audience was over.

Abdullah wailed and fell to his knees, muttering something. He was already so homesick that he had aged and grown frail, body and mind. I understood that Karakorum was a good deal further away but I had no true conception of the distance.

"Get up," I ordered, and dragged him to his feet.

"Batu Khan," I said, stepping forward with my arms held out.

This set them off. A dozen men took a half step forward and the herald grabbed the top of my arms from behind.

Batu looked confused and barked something at me.

Abdullah relayed it, between his sobs. "The Khan's decision has been made. If you argue, he will have you killed outside the tent. You do not know our ways and so he makes allowance for this. Otherwise, you would certainly be dead by now."

I knew I could survive terrible, otherwise-mortal wounds. But I knew I would not survive having my head cut off. Still, I had one chance to speak, to take action while I could before I was removed from Batu's ordus. If my brother was anywhere in Batu's lands, I could not be sent to some other city, nor could I return to Christendom.

"I am looking for a Christian knight," I said, undeterred. "A Christian knight, from England but he may say he is from France. He looks like me. His name is William de Ferrers. He is your man, so they say."

Abdullah was still translating when six men came forward and seized me by the arms and shoulders. While they heaved and yanked me, I allowed myself to be drawn forward and forced to my knees.

A heavily calloused hand grabbed my jaw and yanked it up. I looked into the face of Batu. It was his hand under my chin, and I shook it off by jerking my head back. He was lucky that I was blessed with self-control because I had a powerful urge to tear his throat out for touching me in such a fashion. When he spoke, his breath reeked of onions and the fumes of strong wine.

"You serve him?" Batu said, through the sobbing Saracen. "This Frankish knight William?"

"Never," I said, sneering at the thought.

Batu peered closely at me with his beady eyes. "Why do you seek him?"

"He has committed many crimes," I said. "Done murder. Killed a king, and a bishop, and countless others besides. Women, children."

Batu nodded as this was relayed to him. "I will ask you one more time. Why do you seek him?"

My life hung in the balance. The wrong answer would result in my execution.

"To kill him."

The Khan let go of my chin. His men dragged me to my feet while he peered at me. "You have the look of the man you seek. Why is this?" Batu asked me.

He had seen William with his own eyes. My heart, already racing, skipped a beat.

"He is my brother. It is my duty to bring him to justice. A trial by combat. That is all I ask of you, my lord."

Batu sneered, amused by something. He walked away, slowly, and took his seat while the others held me fast. "Your brother William is evil," Batu said raising his chin. "And that is why I sent him away. To the Great Khan."

"He is not here?" I said, almost wailing like Abdullah had done.

"He was. No longer. He is wreaking his evil somewhere in the east. At Karakorum. You monks can warm the Great Khan's ear with your droning prayers. You, old man, will bring the letter of your master. And you, brother of evil, will cut out the heart of the devil that is called William."

Part Three

Karakorum

1254

BY GOD, IT WAS A HARD JOURNEY. One of the hardest, and longest I have ever undertaken.

On about the feast of the Elevation of the Holy Cross, in September, a rich Mongol came to us whose father was a chief of a thousand men. He spoke and Abdullah hurried to tell us what he was saying. "I am to take you to Mongke Khan. The journey is four months, and it will be so cold that stones and trees are burst apart by the cold. You should think over whether you can bear such a thing."

I answered him without hesitation. "We will bear what men such as you can bear."

He tilted his head as he looked up at me and babbled while Abdullah translated. "If you cannot bear it, I shall abandon you on the road."

"You will not," I said and I felt Eva's glare from across the ger. It was all I could do to control myself but I spoke again, this time with restraint. "That is not right. We are not going of ourselves, but are sent by your lord, Batu Khan. Being entrusted to your care means you should not abandon us, or you are going against the wishes of your lord. You are the son of a great chief, so I hear, but what would Batu Khan do to you if you failed in your duty?"

The rich Mongol scowled. "If you can keep up, all will be well."

"It had better be, or you shall have me to answer to."

I do not know if Abdullah translated my words accurately but I suspect he did not.

Friar William clucked about me. "Must you make an enemy of every man you meet?"

"You sound like my wife," I said, which nobody found amusing, Eva least of all.

After that the rich Mongol made us show him all our clothing, and what seemed to him of little use for the cold he made us leave with our host. The next day they brought each of us a sheepskin gown, breeches of the same material, boots according to their fashion, felt stockings, and hoods such as they use.

The day after, we started on our ride, with pack horses for each of us. We rode constantly eastward for three months.

In the first stage of our journey, to the north of us was Greater Bulgaria, and to the south the Caspian Sea.

The cold was paralysing and the distances we covered were astounding. Every day, I grew less concerned over the danger of Bertrand's anger at me and lust for Eva and I thought that perhaps he had changed. Been cowed by fear of the Mongols, and weakened through hunger and exhaustion. And that was part of the truth. And then it slowly dawned on me that I had come to see that immense, hostile foreign land as my greatest enemy. And it was an enemy that could easily see us dead on the side of the road. If the Mongols abandoned us, or turned on us and forced us out, we could starve or die from thirst, encased in ice and buffeted by the relentless wind. And so I watched our guides like a hawk, day and night, wary of any sign that they meant us harm, or even if they meant us indifference.

After travelling twelve days from the Etilia, we found the Ural River, which flows into the Caspian Sea. The language of Pascatir was the same as that of the Hungarians, and they were shepherds without any towns whatever. In fact, from that country eastward, and also to the north, there were no more towns at all, all the way to the ends of the Earth, other than Karakorum.

One evening we sat huddled in a tight group in the lee of a little cliff. The soil of that part of the grassland had been blown away and the landscape was rocky with knolls rising up here and there, often with scrubby trees, all bent over from the wind. We indulged in the luxury of a fire but it was so cold we all sat almost on top of it, knee to knee and still shivering. Still, it gave us a few moments to speak.

Bertrand was angry at the world but all his anger was directed at his squire Hughues, who took it sullenly and then turned his own frustrations on Abdullah for his appallingly-feeble collection of firewood. Little Nikolas cringed away from their insults and harsh commands so I dragged him into my lap and wrapped my cloak around him. He felt as light as a bird.

Stephen seemed the happiest of us all. The world was a fine place to him. The young man had devoured the entire library at both of the monasteries he had spent his previous years in.

"It was from this country of Pascatir that went forth the Huns," Stephen said, excited and smiling, even though his words were terrifying to me. "Isidorus says that with their fleet horses the Huns crossed the barriers which Alexander had built among the rocks of the Caucasus to confine the savage tribes and that as far as Egypt all the country paid the Huns tribute. They ravaged all the world as far as France so that they were a greater power than are now the Tartars. With the Huns also came the Blacs, the Bulgars, and the Vandals."

"They conquered France?" I said. "The Huns were horsemen who conquered from here, all the way to France? And defeated the Romans?"

"And the Romans were a united people," Thomas said, looking very grave, his eyes full of meaning. "And Christendom now is not. What is to stop the Tartars from doing the very same thing, should they decide upon it?"

His squire, Martin, looked at him with his eyes wide. "Would our order not resist them?"

"We would unify against such a threat, should it come to that," I said. "Look at the Crusades."

"Yes," Thomas said. "Let us look to the Crusades. How successful have we been at winning back the Holy Land from the Saracen conquerors? There has been little enough unity there, not for a hundred years or more. No, we must find another way."

A gust of icy wind howled around the rock and the flames of our fire were flatted for a long moment. Our horses gathered closer together. I looked up at the top of the cliff above us, where one of our guides sat looking out at the horizon. He was fully exposed to the elements, and bare-headed, and yet seemed perfectly comfortable. I hoped he was simply idling at the end of the day, rather than plotting violence against us.

Stephen spoke up once the wind died down again. "What other way is there to protect Christendom from the Mongols, if not unity under the Pope?"

"A treaty," Eva said.

Thomas shifted on his arse, as Eva always made him nervous but never more so than when she spoke.

"That is why you agreed to be the envoy for King Louis," I said. "You have seen the Tartars in battle. You wish to facilitate an alliance with them, to turn their attention to the Saracens and save Christendom from attack. That is why a Templar is acting for the King of France." From the corner of my eye, I saw Stephen staring at me, a faint smile on his lips. "Turn your dim-witted gaze elsewhere, Stephen or I shall turn it with my fist."

Friar William became annoyed whenever he was reminded that far from being the leader of the group, he and his brothers were being used as a disguise for Thomas' mission for Louis.

"If we can but turn their leaders and enough of their people to Christ," Friar William said, scowling, "then they would never make war on Christendom."

No one bothered to respond.

Soon, we curled up for another long, cold night, listening to the howling of the wind. Praying for the night to end and dreading the coming of the morning.

We rode through that country from the Feast of the Holy Cross in September to the feast of All Saints in November. It was a blistering pace. Nearly every day we travelled, as well as I could estimate, about the distance from London to Dover, and sometimes even more, according to the supply of horses. Sometimes we changed horses two or three times in a day, while at others we went for two or three days without finding anyone and we had to go slower. Out of thirty or forty horses we, as foreigners, always got the worst, for they invariably took their pick of horses before us. They tended to give Bertrand and Friar William each a strong horse, on account of their great weight; but those horses rarely rode well. The monk did not venture to complain and tended to bear it all with good grace but Bertrand grumbled when he was tired and raged when his belly was full. The squires and servants were morose and silent, as they were experiencing the toughest challenge they had ever faced. I expected at least one of them to break under the strain.

Indeed, we all had to endure extreme hardships. Oft times the horses were tired out before we had reached the staging place and we had to beat and whip them, change our saddle horses for pack horses, and sometimes even two of us would ride one horse.

Times out of number we were hungered and athirst, cold and wearied. They only gave us real food in the evening. In the morning we had something to drink or millet gruel while in the evening they gave us meat, a shoulder and ribs of mutton, and some pot liquor. When we had our fill of such meat broth, we felt greatly invigorated, for it seemed to me a most delicious drink and most nourishing.

On Fridays the monks fasted without drinking anything till evening when they were obliged, though it distressed them sorely, to eat meat. Sometimes we had to eat half-cooked or nearly raw meat, not having fuel to cook it. This happened when we reached camp after dark, and we could not see to pick up ox or horse dung for the fires. We rarely found any other fuel, save occasionally a few briars. In a few spots along the banks of some of the streams were woods, but such spots were rare.

At first, our guide showed profound contempt for us and was disgusted at having to guide such poor folk but after a while, when he began to know us better, he would every so often take us to the gers of rich Mongols along the way, where the monks had to pray for them. The Mongols were never Christian themselves but sought out and accepted blessings from any and all religions.

Their great king Chinggis, the first Khan, had four sons, whose descendants were very numerous and all of them had a strong ordus. More than this, these offspring multiplied daily and were scattered all over that vast sea-like desert. Our guide took us to many of these, and they would wonder greatly at us and where we had come from. They enquired also of the great Pope; if he were as old as they had heard.

"What does he mean, as old as he has heard?" I asked Abdullah when this question was relayed to us within the shelter of the chief's ger.

"He has heard that the Pope is five hundred years old."

I laughed and received very hard looks in turn, so I controlled myself.

"I believe," Stephen said, because he could not help to impose his opinion at every opportunity, "that they are confusing the immortal title with the name of a single man. Tell them, Abdullah, that the man we call the Pope is a temporary bearer of that title. Just as their own leader is always the Great Khan."

They babbled back and forth for an age and I am certain they went away convinced we were ruled by an immortal king named Pope Khan.

These descendants of Chinggis probed us with endless questions about our countries, such as if there were many sheep, cattle, and horses. How many men could fight. Whether the women were strong.

"If you tell them anything about Christendom," I said to Abdullah the first time, "I will cut out your tongue."

"We must not offend them," Friar William had said, fretting.

"Tell them our lands are nothing but mountains, woodland, and swamp," I said. "Horses die there. And our women are dreadfully thin and worthless."

When we told them that beyond our lands was the Ocean, they were quite unable to understand that it was endless and without bounds. Their refusal to accept the truth that there was nothing to the west of Christendom was a clear sign of both their immense arrogance and their profound ignorance. It was more than two centuries before I discovered that they were, in fact, quite correct in their assertions but that was pure luck on their part and I give them no credit for that whatsoever.

After travelling east for three months, we left that road to turn due south and made our way over mountains that were like the alps continually for eight days. In that desert, I saw many asses called culam, and they greatly resemble mules. Our guides chased the creatures a great deal but without getting one, on account of their prodigious fleetness. The seventh day we began to see to the south some very high mountains, and we entered a plain irrigated like a garden, and here we found cultivated land. After that, we entered a town of damned Saracens called Kenjek, and its governor came out of the town to meet our guides with a false smile on his face bearing ale and cups, for they were subject to Mongke Khan. If the Saracens did not make a show of hospitality, they would surely be punished with extermination, for the Mongols would happily cut off a source of riches in order to make a point. And that was a lucky thing for us because the Saracens in that town looked at us Christians with murder in their eyes from the moment we arrived until we disappeared over the horizon.

I could see why they had settled there. In all that harsh land, that plain where the city lay was sheltered by the mountains around them. And there came a big river down from the mountains which irrigated the whole country wherever they wanted to lead the water, and it flowed not into any sea but was absorbed in the ground, forming many marshes. There at Kenjek, I saw vines, and twice we drank real wine, though it was sharp as vinegar.

We heard that there was a village of Teutons out there in the vastness, six days or so through the mountains out of our way so we never came across them in person but I was assured they were indeed there. It was a startling thought and only later did I learn that Mongke had transported these Teutons, with Batu's permission, so very far from their homeland. I should have known that they were not there of their own free will. The Mongols had no arts of their own, save those concerning the horse and other animals, so they pressed civilised men into service for them. And so it was with those poor Teutons, who were set to work digging for gold and manufacturing arms for their masters. Friar William did everything he could to persuade our guides to divert to them for a time so that he could pray with them, administer rites and do whatever else he could for their souls and so ease their hearts while they delved and travailed in a hollow existence. The monk was greatly anguished when they denied him, and he drew into himself further for many days as his mind dwelled on the suffering Teutons so close by.

From there on, we went eastward again staying close to the mountains. We had entered the lands of the direct subjects of Mongke Khan, who everywhere sang and clapped their hands before our guides because they were envoys of the great lord Batu, who was considered second only to Mongke in all the world. A few days later we entered more alp-like mountains and there we found a great river which we had to pass in a boat.

"They say that if any of us should fall in," Abdullah said, "the water is so cold that we will die immediately, even if we were pulled to the bank downstream."

I gripped the side of the boat so hard I swear my fingers marked the wood.

After that, we entered a valley where we saw a ruined fort whose walls were nothing but mud but the soil was cultivated there. No doubt the people had fallen foul of the Mongols and all their efforts to tame that land was slowly being undone by the elements. Days later we found a goodly town, called Equius, in which were Saracens speaking Persian, though they were a very long way off from Persia. Unlike the village of Teutons, these people were there by choice because they were all merchants who profited from the goods moving up to the royal road from their own lands in Persia. The Mongols were greedy for Saracen goods, and the merchants of Equius lived in relative luxury despite the harshness of the jagged landscape all about them.

Descending from the mountains we entered a beautiful plain with high mountains to the right, and a sea or lake which was twenty-five days in circumference. All of the plain was well watered by the streams which came down from the mountains, and all of which flowed into that sea.

Such a fruitful land was like an island of fertility in the desert. In that plain, there used to be many towns but they were destroyed so that the Mongols could graze there, for there were most excellent pasturages in that country. They had allowed a single town called Qayaligh to survive under the yoke because the Mongols valued the market there and many traders frequented it to take advantage of the Mongol's wealth.

Here we rested twelve days, waiting for a certain secretary of Batu, who was to be associated with our guide in the matters to be settled at Mongke's ordus. It was there that I first saw idolaters, who were properly called Buddhists, of whom I was told there were many sects in the east.

Even amongst such a diversity of people, our company was very much outside of the norm in those parts and we were regarded with suspicion and hostility.

"We must stay all together," I said to my people. "All of the time."

Bertrand scoffed. "I am not afraid of these weaklings. They are no more than dogs. I could slay a dozen at once."

"And how many dogs does it take to bring down a bear?" I asked. "No matter how strong you are, sir, we are outnumbered more than a hundred to one. If they decided to rob us of our belongings, who would we go to for justice? Our guides?" He had no answer. "We stay together, in pairs at the least, and in as large a group as possible. And keep your hands on your valuables. Weapons and armour especially. Nikolas, you will not leave my sight, do you hear me? Any one of these Saracens would snatch you up and take you home as soon as look at you."

There was never a restful moment, for me at least, as I stood watch over the company and turned away many a hostile ne'er-do-well and would-be pilferer with no more than my gaze and an occasional kick to the guts.

In November we left the city, passing after three days a vast sea, which was called Lake Ala Kol, east of Lake Balkhash, which seemed as tempestuous as the Ocean beyond Bordeaux in winter, though they swore it was indeed a lake. I stomped down to the shore across the frozen mud and moistened a cloth in it to taste the water, which was brackish though drinkable. And it was as cold as ice.

The cold in those regions was savagely penetrating, and from the time it began freezing in the fall, it never thawed until after the month of May. And even then, there was frost every morning, though during the day the sun's rays melted it. But in winter it never thawed, and with every wind it continued to freeze further, covering everything with an ever-increasing thickness of ice as hard as rock. And with the ceaseless wind, nothing could live there and we barely survived wrapped in furs and carrying all our food and fuel with us as we rode. Every once in a while, a terrible gale arises and blows hard enough to stagger a man, if he be unbraced or weakened. Bartholomew was blown from his horse and fell on the ice so that his arm needed splinting and he grew a lump over his eye as large as a goose egg. Little Nikolas was once blown a hundred yards down a slight hill and so I tied him to his horse for a while and later I took to holding him before me as I rode. His bones were so sharp that I had to feed him from my own rations to fatten him up, for the sake of my own comfort.

"You cannot fatten a boy's elbows," Eva said when she caught me as if she had not been secretly feeding him also, which she had and far more than I.

We crossed a valley heading north towards great mountains covered with deep snow, which soon covered the ground on which we travelled. In December we began greatly accelerating our speed for we already found no one other than those Mongol men who are stationed a day apart to look after ambassadors. In many places in the mountains the road was narrow and the grazing very bad, so that from dawn to night we would cover the distance of two stages, thus making two days' distance in one and we travelled more by the light of the moon than by day. I thought I had known bitter cold before but I was wrong. We would all certainly have perished had the Mongols not cared for us as if we were children or fools and they allowed us the use of their sheepskins and furs, which we all took most gratefully.

One evening we passed through a certain place amidst most terrible rocks. The pass we climbed had grown narrower and sharper, even as it grew colder, and the jagged rocks, dark but streaked with red, stretched up like walls sculpted by the hands of a vengeful God. Our guides stopped, though there was a wind that howled through us like a storm of ghosts tugging at our clothes, and they sent word through Abdullah, begging the monks to say some prayers by which the devils of that cursed place could be put to flight.

"What heathen nonsense is this?" Friar William said, his teeth gritted against the cold.

Abdullah had always been as thin as a spear shaft but he had shrunk on the journey so that he appeared to be a skeleton with skin stretched across it and when he spoke, his voice was flat. The dead voice, I always called it, the voice of a man who has no hope in his heart. "They say that in this gorge there are devils. The devils will suddenly bear men off. You will turn to speak to the man behind you and he will be gone."

"What do you mean, gone?" William said, warily. He had lost much of his fat by that time and looked like a different man.

The Mongols babbled, their eyes darting about, and Abdullah related it to us while the wind tugged at his words. "Sometimes they seize the horse and leave the rider. Sometimes they tear out the man's bowels and leave the body on the horse. These things happen on every journey through. They say we should expect to lose at least one man."

"They cannot give us commands," Bertrand said, bundled up in the best furs, which he had claimed for himself. His bulk had reduced but he had coped with the hardships with surprising determination. Then again, the man had been to war before. And it felt very much as though we were at war with the land all around, and with the sky above.

Friar Bartholomew roused himself enough to provide us with his learned opinion. "Heathen fools. God will protect us. Onward with you."

He was ignored.

"It may be a ruse," Stephen Gosset called out. The young monk had never faced such difficulties, nor anything approaching it. He had withdrawn into himself and his rosy cheeks had faded first into grey and then into a wind and cold-blasted rawness. He did not look so young as he had. "A ruse, so that they may kill one of us and then blame it on the demons."

None knew what to think about that. When one is cold, thinking clearly is a great challenge and brave men become cowards. Energetic men grow idle.

"For the love of God," I said, raising my voice above the wind and their prattling so that the sound echoed off the rocks and made the Mongols wince. "Will you monks just chant some prayers so we may get moving again."

We proceeded through the pass while the monks all chanted, in loud voice, Credo in Unum Deum. The three monks, frozen as they were, gave full-throated conviction to their singing. It lacked the finesse of monks raising their voices to God in their own chapels but our three had to contend with the howling wind and the echoes of the iron-hard rocks all around. That far-off, God-forsaken heathen pass resounded to the beautiful, clear voices of those men of Christ. For the Mongols, it was no more than a spell of protection, and they would have been as contented with Buddhists, Mohammedans, or their own shamans. Yet it seemed to me that Christendom had conquered that pass. That we had left a mark upon it, though the voices echoed into nothingness. My companions were confused by my joy, for it was a terrible place, but the voices of those monks warmed my heart, and my body, too.

By the mercy of God, the whole of our company passed through.

Again, we ascended mountains, going always in a northerly direction. Finally, at the end of December we entered a plain vast as a sea, in which there was seen no hillock, and the following day, we arrived at the ordus of the great emperor, Mongke Khan, lord of all Asia from the ocean of the east, to the Black Sea in the west, king of all Tartar devils that rode upon the Earth. It may be true to say that there was no man richer than he in all the world at that time, for his armies and those of his grandfather, had stolen the wealth of uncounted millions and brought it back home so that even the lowliest in Karakorum wore silk from head to toe beneath his furs.

I was far from impressed.

"What town is this?" I asked our guides, through chattering teeth, when I saw it with my own eyes, looking down on it from the hills.

Abdullah was horrified. "This is Karakorum, lord."

"Dear God," I said. "What a pigsty."

Perhaps I was overly quick to judgement. But after such a journey, I was deeply disappointed by the place. Of the city of Karakorum, other than the palace quarter of the Khan, it was not even as big as the village of Saint-Denis outside Paris. And the monastery of Saint-Denis was ten times larger than the Khan's palace.

There was a rectangular wall enclosing it, with two roads running right through to make a cross in the centre where most buildings were, and one corner was taken up by the palace and associated buildings. Dotted here and there about the city were a number of smaller enclosures, each surrounding a temple of some kind.

The important buildings, such as palaces and holy places, were of stone and timber and the houses in the centre, clustered along the crossroads, were two-storey homes for the most eminent inhabitants. But the majority of the people, and the visitors of a lower standing, lived in gers packed very close together within one quarter where all the ground was churned mud, frozen into rock-hardness.

There were two non-Mongol quarters in the city, one of which was inhabited by the Saracens, where all the markets were. I was full of contempt for the steppe nomads' inability to learn to operate something so simple as a marketplace. A great many Tartars of all sorts gathered in the Saracen quarter to do business, as the Great Khan was never far from the city and so it was always full with ambassadors from every place on Earth. These visitors frequented the Saracen markets in huge numbers, buying and selling goods from everywhere that there were people.

The other quarter was that of the Cathays, which is what we called the Chinese, all of whom were artisans making a great many useful things in iron, silver, and gold, and in timber and stone, also. For the Mongols were utterly ignorant of all civilised things and could make nothing for themselves. I assumed that they were all too stupid to learn such things.

"Yet they are not stupid in war," Stephen pointed out when I made my judgement of their failures in mercantile activities and skilled crafts.

"A man may be stupid in one way but not another," Bertrand pointed out, and he was living proof of his own statement.

"Please pardon my presumption, my lords, but would you yourself seek to become a silversmith or a merchant?" Stephen said.

"Of course I bloody well would not stoop so low as that, you impudent little monk."

Stephen bobbed his head as his cheeks flushed. "Quite so, my lord, yes indeed. And each Mongol man, whether he be lowly or wealthy, considers himself to be something like a knight, in that his trade is war, and so none of them would become anything lesser, just as you would not."

"How dare you!" Bertrand had roared. "These little fat shits are not knights, you ignorant villein."

Stephen had hitched up his robes and fled from Bertrand's presence while the man shouted after him. I had laughed at the sight of it but I did believe Stephen was quite right about the Mongols. Still, it made their one city a very strange place, cobbled together as it was from the skills and cultures of alien peoples so that it felt like no other town I had ever seen. The closest thing I could liken it to was, perhaps, a busy port in the Holy Land.

Besides these foreign quarters and the Mongol ger quarter, there were the great palaces set about Mongke's own, though what were called palaces would have been grand townhouses in any leading city of Christendom. The palace quarter was home and workplace for the leading administrators of the court and the entire empire of the Mongols.

There were twelve idol temples of different nations all over the city, two mosques in which was cried the law of Mohammed, and one church of Nestorian Christians in the extreme end of the city. Karakorum was surrounded by a mud wall about ten feet high that did little more than keep out wandering animals and, I suppose, provided the Mongols with a means of controlling the entry of people. The four gates in the wall were guarded at all hours of the day and night by hard-looking men.

At the eastern gate was sold millet and other kinds of grain, although there was rarely any to be brought there. At the western one, sheep and goats were sold. At the southern, oxen and carts were sold. And at the northern gate were the horse markets.

Even though it was so small, and even though every surface was covered in ice and the ground was so hard that a pick could never be hammered into it, the city of Karakorum stank. It was surrounded by herd after herd of horses and oxen, clustered together in tight groups against the winds and shivering in the bitter cold. Every morning, more would be dead. Frozen to the ground. But the Mongols seemed not to care overly much, for there were always more animals to be had and the ones that died were eaten.

The animal smell surrounded the city but within the streets, such as they were, it reeked from the dung-fuelled fires that burned in every hearth. And, God forbid, when you were inside a ger that was warm enough to thaw out the people within and heat their clothing. For then the stench of months of sweat and filth would fill the air like a cloud of pestilence so foul that I saw children vomiting from it. And the food and the drink that they consumed was always sour and bitter. The iron-hard ground was too solid to bury night-soil or absorb urine, so it was collected in buckets and thrown into great mounds here and there all across the city, within and outside the walls. Those frozen mounds grew all through the winter and I wondered what would happen when summer thawed those mountains of shit.

This, then, was the capital city of the great Mongol Empire.

Yes indeed, I was far from impressed.

But I was not there to be awed.

From the moment we were led in through the gate, I looked everywhere for William, or for any sign of him. The city was so small and there were so few men who could conceivably be from Christendom that I was certain I would clap eyes upon him from across a marketplace or along a street.

But William was nowhere to be seen.

Our guides, who had brought us from Batu, housed us all together in a single ger on the edge of the city near to the church, which pleased the monks mightily. They told us to wait in the city and that the Khan would send for us. Every day, someone would bring food and fresh water. It was never enough but it kept us alive.

And we were free to explore the city at will. No one guarded us.

After so many months of hard travelling, our company was suffering from terrible ailments. Feet were rotten, skin was raw. All of them had sores and weeping blisters. I was astonished that Friar Bartholomew had survived the journey and I was certain that he would die at any moment. Abdullah, for the first few days, seemed as though he had already died but he was young and recovered quite rapidly. All they wanted was to stay inside the ger, away from the wind and by the fire.

Myself, I could not wait to explore the city.

William was there somewhere, so close now. And I was determined to find him. Someone would know. Someone would talk.

Eva, of course, came with me. And young Nikolas would not leave her side, as he had become besotted with her. He had only fared well because Eva and I had taken rather good care of the lad, I suppose, but he was still on shaky legs and would have been better off resting like the others. Then again, knowing how bad-tempered most of our company was, I thought the boy might be safer out with us in the city.

Stephen Gosset decided that he would also accompany us and though he still irritated me, there was something about the young man. Some force within him that intrigued me as much as it maddened me. Though he suffered physically, he claimed that his heart was lifted at the sight of the Tartar city and he could not wait to speak to the peoples of the world.

"And how will you speak to them, Stephen?" I asked, not wanting him trailing around after me and getting in the way of my vengeance. "You should save your breath."

"God will provide," he said, grinning. "Between Nikolas and I, we will get by."

"Let him come," Eva said. "For he is indeed learned about the ways of strange people and may help us."

Stephen stood to one side, smiling at me like the village idiot.

"Say nothing to anyone," I said, sticking my finger in his face. "Lest you get yourself killed by these heathens."

"Oh, yes, they are heathens, sir, but there is the rule of law here," Stephen said, earnestly.

"There is the rule of law everywhere," I said. "And everywhere men are murdered."

I felt profoundly alien, wandering in that city. And I felt exposed and vulnerable and expected an attack at any moment. For months, we had been amongst Mongols almost exclusively, other than crossing paths with occasional surviving local peoples, or fellow travellers on the road, coming or going to Karakorum. Often, these were Saracens, who the Mongols loved to use for their experience with trade, and with money and transactions of all kinds.

But the road was sparsely populated, where Karakorum was full to bursting with arrogant Mongols of all stations, from lowly slaves to powerful men. All were bundled up in their heavy coats but one can always tell by a man's gait and by the quality of the cloth he wears on which rung he stands on the ladder of his society.

There were women, also. Dressed the same as the men, wrapped up so thickly that they waddled when they trudged through the streets.

"Such strange faces," I said to my wife as we watched a group of four Mongol women walking by us. "Their eyes, and the width of their cheeks. I will never fail to be amazed by their strangeness. Utterly unlike women from civilised lands, are they not?"

"When they are naked," Eva said to me, "they will look just the same as a Christian woman."

I blinked at Eva, unsure how to respond.

"You were wondering about their naked form," she said, helpfully.

"I most certainly was not," I said.

She needed only to shake her head, for she knew me well.

Stephen lurked behind us. "Your pardon," he said, stammering. "But how do you know about their nakedness?"

Eva threw him a look over her shoulder. "I saw our guides and other Mongol men stripped and showing their bodies to the open air, on a number of occasions during our journey. Despite the difference of their faces, their bodies were like any other man's."

"Ah," Stephen said, staring at Eva in wonder. "You are applying logos to the question, in order to come up with a reasoned conclusion."

"No, no, I disagree entirely," I said, while Eva rolled her eyes at Stephen's condescension. "The men are soft. Barrel-chested and strong but somewhat pudgy. Their legs are short and bowed. Eva, they are not like us at all. Who knows what the women's bodies are like?"

"Well," Eva said, sighing. "Why do we not find a desperate Mongol woman and offer her a few coins to disrobe before us?"

I nodded. "Stephen, how much do you have in your purse?"

He begged us not to make trouble with our hosts, and so we agreed to temporarily postpone our investigation.

"They are making mock of you," I heard Nikolas whisper to Stephen.

I swatted the young Greek lad on his furred hood. "You are too kind-hearted by far, Nikolas," I said. "But what makes you think I was making mock of Stephen? Anyway, keep an eye out for any harlots, will you, son?"

Our young monk prided himself on his wits and, as he could not divine whether we were indeed serious, he stopped speaking to us all the way across the city until we reached the Nestorian church. It was small and simple, no more than a rectangle and had no tower. Built from plain stone, plastered, and with a low wall all around making a small enclosure, it was not much to look at. The roof was a sweeping gable in the Chinese style, so it looked halfway to becoming a temple.

"Do you wish to enter, and pray?" I asked Stephen.

"I do not like this place," Stephen said, glancing around at the crowds heading this way and that behind us. "It seems to me that the people are watching us."

"Nonsense," I said. "Our strangeness is unremarkable here. Half the people you see likely feel the same way as you do."

He was quite right, of course, but I wanted him to remain calm.

We had in fact been followed by a group of men from our ger, across the city. By taking many fleeting glances, I had determined that they were, to a man, competent warriors. Too arrogant to truly blend into the masses.

But whose men were they? Did they report to Mongke Khan?

Or were they followers of William de Ferrers?

"Stephen," I said. "I need you to find out where my brother William is."

His face dropped. "Me?"

"Speak to the Christians. They will trust you, as you are a monk. Would you not like to find out why we are being kept waiting? If there is some reason that they tell us nothing about our status amongst them?"

"Is it not simply the bureaucracy of the Mongol state? Is it not as we were told, that we must wait our turn to be seen?"

"I do not know, Stephen. Is it?"

He lowered his voice, looking around. "Are we in danger?"

He stared up at me in alarm. I paused, waiting to see if he was serious, then laughed. "Try to make a friend or two at the church. See what they have to say."

"About us?"

"No, no. Do not ask them about us directly. Men love to talk. All you have to do is smile and nod your head and listen."

Stephen nodded, then his face lit up. "Perhaps Abdullah can do the same in the Mohammedan temples?"

I sighed. "Not a bad idea but we cannot trust him. The man is a drunkard, and when he is sober he is a miserable cur. Who knows what he would say or do for a skin of wine, especially for his own people. No, you will find out plenty from the Nestorians."

Stephen chewed his lip. "My brothers will not like me speaking to anyone without them present."

"Why did you come here, Stephen?" I asked.

"To Karakorum?"

"You followed Friar William because you believe you will rise in importance with your order once you return, is that it?" He did not respond to my question. "Is that all that you seek for yourself?"

His obsequious façade dropped for a moment. "And what do you have to offer me instead, Richard? An empty, dead-end mission of familial vengeance? Or is there something more to the two of you?"

I clapped him on the arm, hard enough to stagger him and leaned in. "You have only one way to find out, Stephen."

Most places excluded us, but where I could speak to people, I tried my best. Without a huge amount of gold, or the ability to bestow favours, I had little to bargain with. All my questions about William were met with indifference or denials. Occasionally, I would see hint of a knowing smile and I knew that if I could take that man into a dark alley and beat him bloody, I could make him tell me where my brother was hiding.

But I could not do such a thing and hope to live.

Stephen reported that the Nestorians knew of my brother and they believed he was not in the city.

"I could have bloody-well guessed that by now," I said when he told me. "Where is he?"

"No man will say."

All the time that we waited in the city through that winter for the Khan to grant us an audience, I was alert to the danger all around us. It chafed my nerves so that I grew evermore short-tempered and everyone avoided me.

"Just as I need blood, you need a fight every few days," Eva said one night. "Else you will make one with someone."

"I dare not make a fight here," I said. "It would mean death for all of us."

Residing in such a place, where every man was a possible enemy, is no way to live. Whether Saracen or Cathay or Rus, all other foreigners were still more at home than we were, and they were a danger also. Not just the people but the bleakness of the landscape wore me thin. The madness that the Mongols would erect a city in the face of such barrenness was an affront to me.

Most of all, my frustration at not finding William, nor knowing what to do about it, was driving me into madness.

There was a particular cold after midwinter that came on with a wind which killed an uncountable number of animals about Karakorum. Little snow fell in the city during the winter until that bitter wind when there fell so much that all the streets were full of great mounds of it and they had to carry it off in carts. Even in our ger, wearing all our clothes at once, we still shivered beneath blankets while the dung fire smouldered and gave off more foul smoke than warmth. Little Nikolas had already grown as thin as a bird that winter, and through the sudden cold spell Eva and I held him between us beneath our blanket so that he did not expire.

Without prompting, young Stephen wrapped himself in strips of cloth, tunnelled out of the ger and struggled out through the great drifts and howling wind to beg at the palace for succour, claiming that elsewise his fellow holy men would surely perish. His cleverness and courage brought us from the ordus of Mongke's first wife sheepskin and fur gowns and breeches and shoes, which we all took most gratefully. I would not say that Stephen saved all our lives, but he may have saved the life of Nikolas, for which I was most grateful, and also the life of ancient Bartholomew, for which I forgave him.

There was no thaw in all the time we were there, yet the wind blew all the snow away in time and the cold became somewhat less deadly. Just in time, too, because I felt certain it would be only days before I murdered someone and drank his blood in public. I was almost beyond caring.

It was in January 1254, as I was pondering whether killing Bertrand or Bartholomew would give me greater satisfaction, that we were summoned to court.

Finally, we would be presented to Mongke Khan.

And there I would demand to be told where he was hiding my brother.

"You will be silent," Friar William said to me before we left the warmth of the ger on the way to the court. "Say nothing of this vengeance of yours. Do you hear me? Nothing. We were blessed by God in the court of Batu when we were all forgiven by the prince after you spoke out of turn. The Great Khan will never be so generous should you break with etiquette in such fashion once more. Do not think of yourself, Richard, but think of the all the harm that you would do to us, should you cause us to be expelled, or worse. We could bring many of the Tartar lords into the Church if we have the opportunity. Think of why Thomas and Bertrand are here. If Louis the King of France can make an alliance or even an understanding with the Great Khan then think what could be done in the Holy Land against the—"

"I do not serve you," I said. "And I value neither your greater good nor your advice. So save your breath."

He was outraged but I had spent months listening to his prattle, and he still did not realise that he had only ever been sent to Batu as a cover for Thomas' true mission. And even after so long living amongst the Mongols, he failed to see that they believed in everything, every God as it suited them, and so they ultimately believed in nothing. For the Mongols,

Christianity was already available to them through the Nestorian Church and they had no need of Franciscans, let alone some distant Pope Khan.

Still, my irritation at his ignorance had been expressed only because I was dying to find my brother. It had been decades since I had seen him last, in the Forest of Sherwood. He was so close now, I could almost smell him.

After being officially ignored for weeks on end, our party was escorted most reverentially to the palace, such was the significance of the royal invitation.

Entering the walls of the palace compound, I strained to see the famous silver tree that a Parisian silversmith had wrought for Mongke. It stood in a courtyard at the entrance to the palace and it was a lovely thing to look upon. At first, it appeared to be a magnificent sculpture, dripping with fruits made of gold, the branches reaching into the upper windows of the palace. Yet it was more than that. The tree was also a device in the form of a fountain that dispensed different kinds of wine from its metal vines into basins below. At the top, a silver angel held a trumpet aloft that would play a sweet note and golden serpents wound about the trunk. Little birds and other creatures would bend and trill when the device was set in motion, which I saw only briefly that one time.

"It is a marvel, is it not?" Friar William said, breathily as we were ushered past it. "You see how it moves so, from some cunning mechanism within?"

"A little slave boy is encased within the trunk," I said. "Yanking on pulleys."

He thought I was being contemptuous to anger him but that was the truth, as I had heard it. It was still a marvellous sight to behold, even if it should have by rights been erected in Paris, if anywhere.

In an antechamber, the door-keeper searched our legs and breasts and arms to see if we had knives upon us, which we had already been told not to bring.

Then we were brought within the great hall of the Khan's palace.

The palace inside was all covered inside with cloth of gold, and there was a fire of briars and wormwood roots, and of cattle dung, in a grate in the centre of the hall. It was set out just as if we were in a Mongol tent, only the walls were stone and square rather than felt and circular. There were hundreds of people within, men and women of all stations, though mostly it was richly-dressed men. Some sat in silence, others carried on whispered conversations so that there was a steady hum of quiet muttering filling the air.

Mongke was seated on a couch and was dressed in a skin spotted and glossy, like a seal's skin. He was a little man, of medium height, aged about forty-five years, and a young wife sat beside him. And a very ugly, full-grown girl, with other children sat on a couch after them.

They made us sit down on a bench to the side of the dais, just as if we were in a ger.

Mongke Khan had us asked what we wanted to drink, grape wine or cervisia, which was rice wine, or carakumiss, which was clarified mare's milk, or bal, which was honey mead. For in winter they make use of these four kinds of drinks. It seemed at first to be rather courtly, and quite peaceful, and I was apprehensive about the coming moments. I knew I would have to force the issue and by so doing I risked my own death and that of my wife and the other men who were in my company.

But I had set myself on a path and I knew no other way to fulfil my oath to kill William.

While we awaited our audience, a series of other supplicants were brought forward to plead with the Khan. Mongols and men of other races. I dragged Abdullah to my side and made him speak in a low voice into my ear. All I wanted was the general gist of what was said by the Khan and by those brought before him.

The first few were discussions of disputes between the Khan's subjects, and also between his subjects and the kingdoms on the edges of the Mongol lands. Men sought guidance on whether to raid into neighbouring countries and the Khan appeared to tell each of them to maintain their own territories, to keep to treaty boundaries and to settle disputes with diplomacy rather than force.

It is fair to say I was shocked by the civility. Both that of the Khan and his honouring of treaties and that each man, many of them clearly great lords in their own right, took the Khan's judgements with not a hint of ire.

Until a young man was brought forward, along with a young woman.

The sight of the girl made me sit up as straight as an arrow.

She was remarkably beautiful. Most of the Mongol women were quite unpleasant to look upon. Their bodies were wrapped from chin to ankle in thick woollen coats, or great bundles of silk. And their heads were often crowned with elaborate headdresses made from lacquered wood and silks. For some reason, the Mongols found the forehead to be a most attractive feature, in both men and women, and so they shaved the front part of their hair. In the men, it made them appear rather savage and intimidating. In the women, it made them appear the same. And their countenances were often round and flat, and quite alien to me.

Some of them, though, were very fine to look upon. Their eyes could be astonishingly alluring, especially over high and prominent cheekbones. Many of those women had lips as soft and pink as a ripe apple.

But the young woman brought forward into the hall was something else altogether. She looked almost like a Christian, perhaps like one you might see in the lands north of Constantinople. Certainly, her skin was pale enough. And her face was narrow, not round, yet her cheeks were high and sharp and she had the flat face and narrow eyes of a Mongol. Her hair was as shiny and as black as any woman of the east. In her clothing, she was also like a Mongol, wearing a coat wrapped at her waist with a belt and on her legs, she wore trousers.

The man at her side was young, also, and a most strikingly handsome man he was. Not pale, like the girl, and his face was wider but his features were arranged in some particular combination of proportions that held one's gaze. A well-built fellow, too, broad at the shoulder like many a young Mongol warrior. It was no wonder that he had managed to win over such a wife as the girl by his side.

Neither was happy. Both held their handsome features still as they approached the Khan but it was clear that they were there against their will. Behind them, as they walked came a row of four sturdy fellows. Like a wall, warding against escape. I knew guards when I saw them, and they were certainly guarding the young couple.

While heralds made announcements regarding the couple, I turned and whispered to Abdullah. "What is this all about?"

Through the centuries, I have seen many a man deeply in love. A man profoundly smitten with a woman. But on only a few occasions have I been witness to the very moment that a man lost his mind to love.

Abdullah was staring at the young Mongol girl with his mouth hanging open wide enough to insert the rim of a goblet. His eyes were about ready to pop from his skull. His dark cheeks and neck were as flushed as a Syrian can manage. The man was breathing rapidly, with shallow breaths.

I elbowed his ribs, hard. "Cease your panting, you dog."

He recoiled, wincing and then glared at me. Calling a Mohammedan a dog is a very grave insult.

"Why are these young lovers here, Abdullah? What are they charged with?"

He pressed his lips together and rubbed his flank, but dragged his resentful, dark eyes away from me and watched the back and forth between the young man and the court functionaries. Mongke watched and drank more wine.

"He stole her," Abdullah said, after a few moments. "She was married. But the husband mistreated her, the foul creature. Beat her, perhaps. How could a man do such a thing? And then this one stole her away from her ger in the night. They escaped for many days. Months, it was. Riding across country from somewhere. But they were captured and brought here."

A tragic tale, no doubt. "But what case is the young man pleading? He broke a law, I presume?"

"He is saying that the woman wished to leave her husband but he would not let her and that she never agreed to the marriage in the first place. So, she should be allowed to return to her mother's ordus, no matter what happens to the young man, here."

"And?"

I felt somehow invested in the young couple's fate. Not only because of their beauty but I was mightily impressed by their stoicism as they listened to what would be their doom.

Abdullah jerked as if he had been shot by a bolt and his thin hand shot out to grasp mine. I shook him off.

"What do you think you're doing?" I said.

"They are both to be killed," Abdullah said, tears in his eyes.

"That is a great shame," I said. "A great shame. But why? The man, I can believe but surely the husband wants his wife back?"

Abdullah wiped his cheeks and whispered. "She was the newest wife of Hulegu. He is the brother of the Great Khan."

"Ah," I said. A powerful man had been wronged and shamed, and so the crown had to make an example.

"Hulegu is on his way here. Those men," Abdullah gestured at the slab-faced guards.

"They are Hulegu's men. They chased the girl across the mountains and the plains and they brought her to here many days ago, knowing their master would arrive in this season. And Hulegu is coming now. Mongke Khan has pronounced his judgement but will allow his brother Hulegu to carry out the sentence, as the poor woman is Hulegu's wife."

Some of those great Mongol lords had four or five or ten or even more wives. I suppose this Hulegu took it as a challenge to his authority that had to be repaid. Or perhaps his heart was so crushed by the rejection that he had lost his mind in a murderous rage. But Mongols did not think about things in the same way as we Christians did and attempting to understand their behaviour would ever be beyond me.

The young couple were led out, their heads held high but their eyes shining and full of deep despair. Abdullah sobbed once as they went by us.

Next, came an official embassy by a small group of Saracens. The hall fell silent and the Mongols all around us grew very still. It seemed to me that they all edged closer to the Khan and all eyes were fixed upon the leader of the Saracens.

He was richly dressed in a green robe, with some embroidered pattern in yellow and a conical hat wrapped on his head. The man was tall, broad-shouldered, with a well-oiled beard. By his bearing, he demonstrated his nobility.

"Who are these fellows?" I whispered to Abdullah.

The translator scowled. "They are Nizari Ismailis."

"Saracens, yes?"

Abdullah sneered. "They are rejecters of the true faith. Heretics."

I had no idea what he meant. "Heretics? They look like Mohammedans. Persian ones."

He was filled with contempt. "You know them as Assassins."

I was shocked. Even when I had first arrived in Outremer, decades before, the name of the Assassins had been whispered in fearful tones by the crusaders. I knew they were a sect that had strongholds in the mountains of Syria and Persia and that all the other Saracens hated and feared them. Were at war with them, in fact. Because they were so few in number, they could not wage war against the Caliphate in Syria, nor against the Persians, or anyone else. Not in a traditional sense. So, they resorted to the judicious murdering of the leaders of their enemies to further their political aims. They were said to follow their leader, the Old Man of the Mountain, with complete and utter devotion. Willing to throw their own lives away, without hesitation, without question, for their lord. They were said to be willing to leap to their deaths from a cliff, at the mere click of the fingers from the Old Man of the Mountain.

So, I had heard, anyway.

"Why are they here?"

"The Mongols accuse this Nizari envoy of sending four hundred fedayin to kill the Great Khan."

"What word is that? What is fedayin in French?"

"I do not know how to translate this word. It means a man who gives up his life. A sacrifice. But for the Nizari Ismailis, the Assassins, the fedayin are the men who carry out the secret murders. They are caught and killed. Sacrificed."

"Martyred."

"Yes, that is it, yes. Fedayin. The martyred."

"This envoy must be facing a terrible death, no?" I asked. "If he sent four hundred martyrs to murder Mongke, they must have something exquisite in mind for this fine fellow."

"He is to be sent back to his people," Abdullah explained. "To persuade them to submit to the Mongols, before they are destroyed by the army of Hulegu."

That name again.

Hulegu.

I would come to know it well.

I would come to hate it.

"I thought no one could defeat the Assassins," I whispered. "Due to their great fortresses in the mountains."

"That is what the Nizarite lord here is arguing," Abdullah said. "But Mongke Khan says his brother Hulegu will march with an army of three hundred thousand men and crush every fortress and put every Assassin to the sword."

I chuckled to myself. They certainly seemed to like throwing numbers like that around but three hundred thousand was ten times bigger than any army was likely to be. "Absurd," I muttered, shaking my head.

The magnificent looking lord of Assassins was dismissed, along with his attendees. As he passed by us, he turned and looked us over. His black eyes held my gaze for a long moment, and it was a look full of meaning.

What the meaning was, sadly, I had no idea.

And then, finally, it was our turn to come before the Great Khan.

"Come forward, refill your cups," Mongke said, indicating his benches so laden with intoxicating liquids and the servants who would pour any of them for us.

Friar William was still the nominal leader of our party and yet he was a man so filled with the traits of deference and agreeableness that he had become a monk. Instead of simply saying what he wanted, he aroused the Great Khan's confusion and contempt.

"My lord," Friar William said, grandly, "we are not men who seek to satisfy our fancies about drinks. Whatever pleases you will suit us."

I hung my head and held my hand over my mouth, lest I speak out of turn. All this time and the monk had not realised that the Mongols respected strength and assertiveness while they found excessive humility contemptible.

The Khan sneered and had us given cups of the rice drink, which was clear and flavoured like white wine. I sipped only a little, eager as I was for the audience to move on. However, while we sipped our drinks before him, the Khan had some falcons and other birds brought out to him which he took on his hand and looked at. It was a way of showing his contempt for us, and after a long while, he bade us speak.

Friar William stood once more, approached before the Khan and bent to one knee.

Abdullah lurked at the side and translated his words.

"You it is to whom God has given great power in the world," William said, raising his voice as if addressing an army. "We pray then your mightiness to give us permission to remain in your dominion, to perform the service of God for you, for your wives and your children. We have neither gold, nor silver nor precious stones to present to you, but only ourselves to offer to you to serve God, and to pray to God for you."

Mongke stared for a long while before he answered, and Abdullah turned to us and related the words.

"As the Sun sends its rays everywhere, likewise my sway and that of Batu reach everywhere, so we do not want your gold or silver." Mongke slurred as he spoke, clearly suffering from too much drink. He seemed displeased that we had come to him at all, and he waved a hand and barked orders at a secretary or some other servant. This man came forward and handed the Khan a curling square of parchment. The Khan gripped it in his fist, rather than reading from it, and waved the crumpled document at us while he growled his words.

"My cousin Batu has sent to me a copy of the letter you sent to him, begging for his support in your war against the Syrians. It is wrong that your King of the French did this thing. Batu is a great and powerful lord of the west but he is subject to me. I am the Great Khan and Batu will not make war without my orders. Just as your King would take great offence at some foreign lord seeking alliance with one of the King's princes without his authority, so have you offended me."

"My lord," Thomas said, standing up with a look of determination on his face. "My lord, if you please." He stepped forward and stood beside. "King Louis wishes only—"

Mongke snarled a response and slashed a hand down. Be silent.

Thomas squeezed his mouth shut.

And then, Mongke Khan turned and looked right at me.

It was no accident. It was obvious that he already knew where I was seated. It was me he wanted to see.

And Mongke himself spoke my name.

"Richard."

He mangled it horribly on account of his foreign tongue and his inebriation but it was unmistakably my name.

One by one, everyone turned to stare at me.

I stood up and stepped forward. "Where is William?" I said.

Mongke laughed at me, even before Abdullah interpreted.

"My cousin Batu sent word to me. I know why you are here. You are another one, like him. Another man who cannot die. That is true, is it not? You cannot be killed? Like your brother, you will never grow old. Answer me."

I took a deep breath and tried not to look at any of the others. It was silent in the great palace hall. "The years do not mark me, that is true."

Mongke nodded and sat up straighter. "You are a hundred years old, yes?"

Again, I hesitated. The Khan was testing me. It would confuse the others but I did not need them anymore.

Or so I thought.

"I am eighty-four years old," I said.

The monks and the knights, my companions, stirred in disapproval.

But the Khan nodded and asked further questions. Abdullah was confused and hesitant but he translated all the same.

"You must drink blood, yes? To give you life, and strength. You must kill many slaves to make such magic."

If anything, I was relieved. I had been on the right trail after all. William was known to the Khan and so Mongke would know where my brother could be found. Was he a prisoner? Was William off at the edges of the kingdom, huddled in a cave with dozens of followers? Or had Mongke given William an ordus of his own?

To get any answers for myself I would have to give the right ones to the Khan.

How much should I admit, I wondered? Was he testing me with his questions about blood drinking and killing slaves, or was he searching for answers for himself? How much had William told him? And what lies had been amongst the words of truth? I knew I could myself speak the whole truth about us and yet still end up dead at the end of the audience.

"I kill no slaves," I said. "And drink blood only when I need to."

Mongke found that amusing. "And when do you need to, Richard?"

I was never good at battles of wits. Many men would have found a way to appear to speak openly but in fact to tell the Khan nothing. Other men might have extracted information from the Khan with clever trading of information.

But I had no patience for that, and no head for it either.

"Drinking blood helps to heal me," I admitted. "When wounded."

Mongke Khan nodded again as Abdullah translated my words as if the Khan knew already. Or was pretending to know.

He waved at my companions. "And have you made all these men into blood drinkers like you?"

I was surprised. Friar William and Stephen, and Thomas and Bertrand were thoroughly confused but also outraged at the suggestion.

"None of them," I said. "They have no idea what I am."

The Khan did not seem to believe me. "And what are you?" he asked.

"In truth," I said. "I do not know. Only that my brother and I are the only ones in all the world."

He became angry as he listened to my words. "The only what, in all the world? What are you?"

"I am a man," I said. "With some gift given by God. Or a curse, perhaps. Just like my brother. You know why I came to you? All I wish is to be granted the chance to duel with my brother and so I beg that you summon him to your court from wherever it is that he is hiding.

He is a criminal. Through a trial by combat, to the death, God will grant justice."

The Khan had his cup of wine refilled, and he drank it down in a few gulps before cuffing his mouth with a silk sleeve.

"I already sent for your brother. Months ago." Mongke's ugly face screwed up as if he had detected a foul smell. "Your brother now serves my own brother, who is called Hulegu. They are camped outside the city. Both of our brothers will be in Karakorum tomorrow. And then your brother will kill you."

"Thank you, Great Khan," I said. "But my God will surely grant me victory in our duel."

The Khan laughed aloud. "There will be no duel, Richard. You will be executed."

* * *

They were angry with me. Inside our ger, Friar William ranted and raved at my deceit and manipulation of him. Bartholomew, of course, railed at me with what little strength he had.

I ignored them while I gathered my weapons, armour, and equipment. Eva did the same. We would put on our armour and throw the rest of our gear and supplies over at least two horses that we would steal.

Neither of us needed to speak of it to the other. We knew that, whatever happened, no matter how unlikely it was we would ever get away, we needed to prepare to run.

Before we made a break for wild flight, however, I had other plans to enact.

"Your underhanded plotting has quite ruined our hopes for converting the pagans," Friar William said, quivering with rage. "You are a liar, and a traitor, and entirely unchivalrous, sir. Entirely!"

"The Khan has given you leave to stay and preach the Gospel and spread the teachings of the true Church," I pointed out, speaking over my shoulder. "I am astonished at his generosity and you should be, too. I am the only one who will be killed."

Even the fact of my imminent death did little to mollify the monks. But that was monks for you.

After we were dismissed from the palace, we had been escorted back to our ger with just as much respect as we had been given on the way there. It is likely that the Mongols were not concerned about letting me loose within the city because they had no fear at all of me or what I might do. Such was their unparalleled arrogance, they no doubt believed I could not escape across the plains without being ridden down and rounded up. Nor would they have believed me capable of harming them, when every subject of the khan was a warrior. So little did they regard me as a threat, they did not disarm me or any of my companions nor take away our armour. As far as they were concerned, their city was a prison and each citizen a guard. Perhaps I was wrong but, as far as I could tell, we had been left to our own devices.

And devices were what I intended.

Unlike the others, Thomas seethed in silence. He felt that I had been most dishonourable, I am sure. Yet he looked at me with an odd glint in his eye and he did not rave at me.

"You endangered us all," Bertrand said, pacing back and forth behind me across the ger. "I should kill you myself for this affront."

"You are welcome to try," I said, without turning around.

Eva said nothing, merely packed our equipment with practiced efficiency.

"What will you do, Richard?" Thomas said when their anger had begun to subside. "Will you appeal for mercy?"

I snorted. "From the Tartars?"

"From your brother," Thomas said. "This William, who is arriving tomorrow."

I grinned and looked to Eva. She did not return my smile.

"The last time I saw William," I said, "I destroyed his home, killed all of his men, and one of my knights ran him through the chest with a lance. He will not grant me clemency."

Bertrand scoffed. "No man could survive such a wound."

The young monk, Stephen, had been silent since we had been led away from the palace and back to our tent. "Back there," Stephen said. "You claimed to be eighty-four years old. And the Khan said you drank blood. And you agreed that you did. I do not understand."

Bertrand jabbed a finger at me. "He claimed it because he is a deceiver and a liar. Do not trouble yourself what he claimed, brother."

"I heard stories," Stephen said, undeterred. "Of men who drink blood. Men returned from the dead."

"Stephen," Friar William said, full of rapprochement. "Do not speak of such nonsense."

Thomas was interested. "Where did you hear stories like that?"

"At the monastery," Stephen said.

"Nonsense," Friar Bartholomew said. "You are always gossiping with servants, like the jumped-up little villein that you are. Their tales are utter fancy."

"I heard a tale once," Thomas said, staring at me. "Of an English knight who fought with old King John. I heard it from a man who was there. Fifty years ago now, this would have been. Swore upon all that was holy that this English knight was caught drinking the blood of his enemies. That he had magic that healed his wounds when he drank blood. He was in league with the devil, they said."

I stood and turned around, my sheathed sword in my hand. "The Bloody Knight, they called me." I shrugged. "For a while, at least."

"Absurd!" Friar William shouted.

"I would hear your tale," Thomas said, "even if it is nonsense."

"As would I," Stephen said. "Please. I beg you, explain what is happening, sir. We must know it all."

Eva shook her head but I am a prideful man and I wanted to tell them.

Most settled onto the benches, while Bertrand, Hughues, and Friars William and Bartholomew paced and scoffed and poured scorn on my words, huffing and sighing as I spoke, shaking their heads and rolling their eyes at each other.

I ignored them, other than to raise my voice over their objections, while I told them all my tale. A rapid summary of my life, from the death of my half-brother and his family to the murder of my first wife. I told them of my searches for William, in Outremer and elsewhere, only to find him many years later in the dark woodland of Sherwood Forest.

I explained, as best as I was able, how William had given some of his strength to his followers by giving them his blood to drink. That it passed on a modicum of his speed, and his ability to heal, but only for round seven days or so, until they needed to drink.

In spite of their incredulity, I told them how he had discovered a method to imbue his followers with a permanent change. How he would drain a man of his blood, and then at the very point of death, have them drink the immortal blood.

"I knew it!" Stephen muttered a couple of times. The others tutted at him but he simply shrugged. "I mean, I knew it was something."

I did not tell them that William had done that very thing to Eva. That he had used my blood to turn her into an ageless immortal. And I did not tell them that she had to drink blood every few days or else she would grow sick and become raving mad.

"If this were true," Friar William said, scoffing. "and it is not true, of course. But if it was true, then it would certainly be the work of the devil himself. And so would you be, sir!"

"Hear him!" Bertrand said, inviting Hughues to share the monk's outrage.

"But how did it come to be?" Stephen asked. "How did you come to be as you are, sir? You and your brother? What did you do to become so powerful?"

"Do?" I said. "I did nothing. At first, I believed that it came from our father, my true father, the old Earl de Ferrers. When William poisoned him, he was said to have woken up before burial, only for my brother to murder him again with a blade. It sounded similar to how William and I both died and were reborn. And as both William and I grew from his seed, I believed it was that which made us as we were. As far as William was concerned, he always appeared convinced that his power was a gift from God. That he was a new incarnation of Christ or even of Adam."

This drew hisses from the monks. "Blasphemy," Rubruck growled.

"Indeed," I said, continuing. "The Archbishop of Jerusalem many years ago suggested that William was created by the Devil and thought it possible that God made me as I am so that I may stop him. What the truth of it is, I honestly do not know. All I know is that I am as I am. And William is the same. Many times, we have survived wounds that would have ended the life of a mortal man. And we go on, ageless."

Bartholomew sneered. "At least you are to be executed tomorrow," he said, with relish. His skeletal face pulled into a wicked grin.

"Not if I can help it," I said. Darkness was falling and it was time to act. Eva helped me into my mail hauberk while my companions objected, in anger and fear.

"What do you mean to do?" Friar William said, repeatedly. "Why would you need that armour? You cannot fight your way through an entire city, you raving lunatic. What are you planning? Your actions will have consequence for the rest of us so you must—"

"I mean to find my brother." My words stopped them all. I looked at my wife. "Before he finds me."

"Richard, no," she said, voice low and meant only for me. "We must flee. Now."

"Perhaps. Yet how far would we get on a pair of stolen horses? We are months away from any hint of safety."

"So that is it?" She was appalled. Angry. "We kill William, and are caught and killed? Or we are killed in the attempt?"

"We kill William," I said. "And capture Hulegu. I will hold a knife at his throat for a thousand miles and none will dare to attack us."

She simply stared at me.

"You have lost your mind," Bertrand said. "You will bring punishment down upon all of us. It is time to end your lunacy." He turned to his squire, then gestured at Eva. "Hughues, take her."

Before Bertrand had taken two steps, I rushed the huge knight and smashed my mailed fist into his nose, hooked my foot behind his knee and tripped him to the floor, falling heavily. I was armoured and he was not. He screamed and struggled beneath me but I hit him again and drove a knee into his guts. Still, he was strong and tough and I had to near-enough crack open his skull with my elbow before he was knocked senseless and groaning.

I rolled off, drawing my dagger as I did so as I expected Thomas and his squire to be following up behind. The squire had indeed moved to intervene but Thomas held him back, though both Templars glared at me with anger.

Eva had bested Hughues easily, ending up mounted on his chest, hammering punches into his face. Blood spattered over her fists.

"Eva," I called.

She climbed off of him, leaving the young man spitting blood and whimpering, tears streaming from his swelling eyes.

The monks were clustered together on the far side of the ger, with Abdullah and Nikolas, like a gaggle of hens.

Stephen Gosset alone was smiling, like the madman that he was. Grinning at Eva, his eyes shining with passion.

"Do not do this," Thomas said. "You have made a mistake by coming here, you know that now. Trusting these pagan monsters to help you do justice. Do not make your failure worse by giving them reason to take revenge on all of us, when you are caught. What is your strategy, anyway? How can you possibly think you could find and kill your brother when he is out there, beyond the city in that wasteland?"

"If they will be here in the city tomorrow then they must be close by," I said. "Camped just outside the city, perhaps only a short ride away. All their camps are the same. The lord's ger is in the centre of every ordus. I will go there, kill his guards and take this Hulegu Khan, brother of Mongke. He will tell me where William is. I will kill William and flee with Hulegu as hostage."

Thomas shook his head in disbelief. "You say you have strength and speed. And though you are quite mad, I believe in your abilities as I have seen them with my own eyes. But such a thing could never be done by one man alone."

"Not alone," I said, looking at my wife.

Stephen spoke up, the words spilling from his lips almost faster than he could form them. "But she is one of you, also, is she not? She must be. Surely, by God, she must be as he says. Do you not see, brothers? Eva is one of the immortals, such as Richard has described. You have seen her strength, seen it again just now, you see? It is the only way she could have defeated—"

Friar William strode forward and smacked Stephen on the back of the head with such force than the young monk fell to his knees, silently clutching his skull.

"It is true," I said, placing a hand on my wife's shoulder. "She is over sixty years old but she can kill better than any knight I ever knew. Together, we will do this. Come on, the sun will be setting soon. And Bertrand is coming to his senses. I would prefer not to kill him but I will do so to protect myself."

"Wait!" Stephen said from his knees, rubbing his head and climbing to his feet. "Wait, please, wait. What about the Assassins?"

I glanced through the door of the ger, the freezing air stinging my skin. The sun was low in the sky and the temperature was plummeting.

Thanks to God, there were still no guards outside our ger. I suspected that the Mongols of the city continued to keep watch on us wherever we went, trusting that I would never be able to get away. And I had no doubt that if we were seen fleeing for one of the four gates in the twilight, we would be arrested.

"It will be dark soon," I said as I closed the door and turned back into the ger. "Only then can we leave."

"I will take them a blessing," Stephen said, earnestly. "That is what we shall say to the guards outside the Assassins' quarters. You others shall be escorting me through the city."

"You cannot use God's name for deceit," Friar Bartholomew said, his voice tight and rising in pitch. "I will not allow it."

"We must remain on the side of truth, Stephen," Friar William said, with condescension. "If we are to do any good here, if we are to win any souls for Christ, we cannot jeopardise the trust the Great Khan has generously placed in us."

Stephen laughed in their faces. "Do you truly not see? Are you both so blind?" He waved an arm around to indicate the breadth of the city beyond the felt walls. "These barbarians hold every faith to be equal, and it is for each man and woman to choose which of these to follow. A man here may be a Mohammedan, with a Buddhist wife, and a Nestorian son. And none of them, nor any other soul they know, would find anything remarkable about it. Any of them can already choose Christ but in the manner of the Nestorians. When you tell them there is a better way of worshipping, the true way, that of the Pope in Rome, not a soul here cares one jot. They will tolerate your presence only because they love all priests and wish for blessings from any man who will give them. You are wasting your time. You came here for nothing. They have no space in their hearts for the true Christ."

The monks stared at him, open-mouthed. Friar William began to speak but Stephen cut him off.

"And even if they did, neither you, William nor you, Bartholomew, would be the men to turn them into Christians of the Roman Church. I have watched you, listened to you, these many months. More than a year, now, have I listened to you droning on about minuscule points of doctrine that none of these people could ever hope to understand, and both of you are too stupid to see it for yourselves. You have no hope here, none. You should return to civilised lands and do what good work with whatever years God will grant you with people who will listen to you. In truth, Bartholomew, I doubt that you will survive the journey home. But you must try rather than remain here, useless and pitiable, in failure."

Bartholomew gripped William's sleeve and his face turned grey. Neither monk spoke a word in objection.

"Now, leave me alone," Stephen continued. "I have no interest in following your orders, nor in my oath to obey the doctrine of Saint Francis. And so, I will use deceit to help Richard. And, in return, he will give me what I want."

"I will?" I said, amazed by his recklessness in disavowing his order. "And what is it you want?"

"You know what I want," he said, glancing at Eva.

"Eva is already married," I said, deliberately misunderstanding him.

He swallowed, glancing at her again as his cheeks flushed. "Not that. I want—"

"You will help me," I said, stalking over to him. "You will gain entry to the quarters of the Assassins, on pretence of your blessing." He backed away, until he bumped into one of the roof posts, eyes darting left and right. "And in return, I will refrain from tearing out your throat and drinking all of the blood from your scrawny little body. Is that acceptable?"

In a few moments, I was ready to leave.

"Bartholomew," I said. "Give Eva your robe so that she may disguise herself."

"I shall not!" he said, quivering.

"No," Eva said. "I will stay here."

"We must not separate," I said. "This could all fall into pieces at any moment. We must stay together."

"And who will watch them?" she nodded at the monks, and then at Bertrand and Hughues, both tied up on the floor. Faces bloodied and full of anger. "We leave, they will raise the alarm. No, I will stay. You will return."

"I will," I swore, then raised my voice. "If any of them give you cause for fear, you should run them through, do you understand?"

"It would give me great pleasure."

"Thomas," I said. "You will do nothing to hinder my wife, will you."

He looked me in the eye. "I shall do as honour dictates."

I turned to Eva. "Run him through first, my love. Stephen, come on. Abdullah, you are coming with me to translate." He was terrified but he did as he was told. What is more, he had already discerned where in the city the Assassin envoy had been quartered. It was the centre of the new city, in one of the many mudbrick houses built there. Most were two storeys tall, and some higher than that.

With a final glance back at Eva, I ducked outside. The cold attacked me and I pulled my Mongol coat tighter and tied the fur-lined hat under my chin.

Men were in the streets, hurrying to complete the day's business before retiring for the freezing night. Few of them gave us even a glance but I was nervous. Ready to fight.

"The Assassins are not to be trusted, my lord Richard," Abdullah whispered as we walked through the dark main street. The Sun had only just set and the sky looked like a pale blue silken shroud soaking up a pool of blood.

"Truly, Abdullah?" I said. "You are advising me that I should not trust the Assassins?"

Abdullah explained to the pair of stony-faced Persian fellows inside the entrance to the Assassins' quarters that the young monk had come to perform a blessing for the men within, and that I was his escort and assistant. They were suspicious, and I told Abdullah to simply say we had come with gifts for their lord. They let us further inside, opening the sturdy door from the antechamber and calling out for their master while we entered the building proper behind them.

I stepped through into a large central room with doors to either side and steps at the far side leading to the floor above. The room was well-lit with lamps all around the walls.

A dozen or so Assassins were busy within, carrying and stacking boxes and sacks in neat piles about the room. All wore thick woollen clothing, with trousers and some wore coats even though they were indoors. Servants busied themselves all around, with footsteps and banging and dragging noises sounding on the floor over our heads.

Their leader was called over, the fine-looking man I had seen earlier in the palace hall. He was no longer dressed in silks like a Persian lord but wore similar sturdy travelling clothes, like his men.

"This is Hassan al-Din," Abdullah said, introducing us with a clumsy attempt at formality. "And this is Richard of Ashbury."

Hassan surprised me when he responded in superb French. "It is an honour to meet you, sir. Welcome. How may I be of service?"

"You are leaving," I said, for it was obvious they were making preparations for travel though I was surprised that they would be free to do so.

He inclined his head. "At first light. Our embassy is completed and now we return to our lands."

"To Alamut?" I said. Every man in the Holy Land knew of the home of the Assassins, and half the men in Christendom, too.

He smiled but there was steel behind his eyes. "Why have you come here?"

"To ask you what you know of my brother," I said, unwilling to say too much right away.

He looked at me for a moment, his dark eyes glinting in the lamplight. Perhaps he was wondering whether to waste his time with me. "Your brother is William, yes? The Englishman who has bewitched Hulegu Khan."

"That is indeed my brother. In what way has he bewitched Hulegu?"

The elegant Saracen lord's mouth twitched beneath his glistening beard. "Your brother is a master of blood magic. This is well known. They say that he cannot be killed. And they also say that with his blood magic he has made Hulegu into an immortal with the strength of ten men."

I felt as though I had been kicked in the guts. But I should have known that William would use his blood to forge powerful alliances. He had done that very thing in England.

"He has made Hulegu into an immortal?" I said, half to myself.

"Well, sir," Hassan said, with a slight smile, "that is what people say."

"How do you know this?"

"We have ways to know. Hulegu is an enemy of my people, even more than the Great Khan Mongke. His brother Hulegu is set on turning his strength against us, to conquering all Persia and destroying our people. We were surprised when this Frankish knight William was welcomed into Hulegu's court and given so much power at the Khan's side until we discovered that he had promised everlasting life to Hulegu, his chief captains and his keshig. That is to say, his most elite bodyguards."

My own blood ran cold. "You say it is not just Hulegu who is immortal but other lords at his court also? How many others?"

"We have been unable to determine this precisely," Hassan said, apologetically. "His keshig bodyguards may number ten or so. And his chief captains may be half as many. But what does it matter how many? Unless you also believe in this blood magic?" He looked closely at me but continued when I gave him no response. "Our people have been meeting with increasing resistance from Hulegu's court for years. We have sent a number of men to kill Hulegu but all who have tried to carry out their mission have been killed. There is an inner circle of five or so senior captains around Hulegu, each a great lord of Mongols in his own right. The keshig bodyguards are great individual warriors, honoured with a place at Hulegu's side, night and day. With William a key figure at the court, we would expect his presence to be resented by the Mongols, and yet he is respected. Feared, even."

"They are right to fear him," I said.

I felt my plan crumbling beneath my feet. I felt confident that I could cut my way through a number of mortal men, even trained warriors such as Hulegu would have in his ordus, and protecting his ger. But a dozen or more with the power of our blood would be a terrible danger. I recalled with horror the efforts it took to bring down John Little the former bailiff of the Sheriff of Nottingham. He was a huge man but was not a trained fighter, and he had almost killed Eva, even though he had received a sword thrust to the hilt up into his guts from his rear end.

Hard to kill. Even harder to kill quickly.

What is more, the Mongols were on their guard against attacks by the Assassins. The precise method of attack that I intended to use to kill my brother was the one that they would be most prepared for. To infiltrate the camp in the night without being detected.

"I am deeply sorry. These were not the answers you wished to hear," Hassan said. "You are to be executed tomorrow, I believe. A very sad state of affairs." He spoke lightly, barely even attempting sincerity. "You wished to seek clemency from your brother?"

"I swore an oath to kill him. I cannot allow myself to be killed before I fulfil my oath."

"And how will you kill him, sir?" Hassan was amused but growing impatient. He and his men were ready to leave. "Even a hundred of our finest men could not reach Hulegu, nor any of his captains. Or, perhaps, you, in fact, claim to have the same blood magic as your brother?"

He knew. This Assassin lord knew, just as the Great Khan Mongke had known, that I was immortal, that I had the power that William my brother claimed.

The Assassin was sceptical, of course. But he wanted something from me, or else he would not have granted me so much of his time.

"I have no wealth," I said. "I cannot bring you men or fortresses. But, yes, I do have the blood magic, as you call it. I do not age. I am stronger than any mortal man. My body heals wounds that would kill any other man. Perhaps these things would be useful to you. After all, the Mongols have chosen your people for destruction, have they not? Surely, you could benefit from such power."

Hassan raised his black eyebrows. "You claim to have the strength of ten men?"

I shrugged. "I never truly tested the limits of my strength. Ten men? Two or three, certainly. Perhaps more."

He smiled. "In Acre, and in Tiberius, I have watched Frankish knights training in war. You have this contest which is called grappling, do you not?" As he spoke, he called out to his men and waved two of them forward.

The biggest two.

They dropped the loads they were carrying and strutted over. Both were well-built. One was thick-set and older and the other younger and wiry but with big hands and wide shoulders. Perhaps they were cousins or an uncle and nephew. Both listened while Hassan explained what he required of them.

"Grappling, yes," I said. "We engage without striking blows, and without weapons."

"As do we." He reeled off a few terse words at his men, who nodded and stepped forward. Hassan, smiling, stepped back. "No blows, no weapons."

Everyone else in the room hastily scrambled to the edges of the space.

The burly Assassins launched themselves at me with considerable enthusiasm. They each took a hold of me, one on each arm and shoulder, and tried to force me backwards, then the other way, and then they tried to throw me down to the floor. It took discipline to resist striking them both.

I planted my feet, bent my knees, and resisted. They held on and twisted and heaved against me, our shoes slipping on the tiled floor.

Pushing into their grasp, I snaked my hands up to the top of their arms, squeezed their shoulders with my fingers, digging them in hard, and heaved down. Both men gritted their teeth and the fat one growled but neither could resist my strength. One man after the other, their legs buckled beneath them and they fell to their knees.

They attempted to pull away and get up but I held them there and turned to Hassan. "I could demonstrate my strength further by tearing their arms from their shoulders?"

The Assassin lord was not pleased. "Release them, sir, if you please."

They glared at me as they stood but I smiled at them. "You have seen my strength. Now you must believe what they say about my brother and I."

Hassan pursed his lips. "Some men are born with great strength and perhaps you are one of those. And yet you claim also that your body heals wounds that would kill other men?"

I sighed, seeing where these tests were heading. "I am able to resist great wounds and heal quickly, yes. But the effect is far greater when I drink a man's blood after I am wounded, and that wound will heal so rapidly that one may witness the flesh restoring itself even as you look upon it."

"Well, this is something we must see with our eyes, is it not? This is a thing that would give credence to your words, no? We must cut you open." He drew a wickedly curved dagger from the sash about his waist. "And then, once you are dying, we will blood for you to drink?"

I am not taking a mortal wound for you, Saracen. I am desperate but not utterly witless.

"I will cut my flesh superficially, and you shall watch it heal."

"I have seen too many conjurors' tricks to allow you to administer a wound yourself," Hassan said, in an apologetic tone. "I shall do it, with my own knife, and then I shall know it to be true."

It was not so simple a thing to receive a wound anywhere other than my face, as I was bundled up in a coat and clad in my hauberk. But I stripped them off quickly and pulled up the sleeve of my gambeson and undershirt and indicated that he should perform a shallow cut into the meat of my forearm.

The Assassins all stopped their preparations and gathered around Hassan. I felt extremely vulnerable, and especially when turning my back on them to hand my sword to Stephen, who trembled so much he had trouble taking it from me.

One of the servants held a wooden bowl under my arm while Hassan held my wrist in one hand and placed the cold blade of his dagger against my bare skin with the other.

Then he paused, his face close to mine. The scented oils in his beard filled my nose.

"Do you feel pain?" he asked.

"Oh yes."

His cut was deep. Far deeper than I had indicated and his dagger sliced down, through the skin, and through the muscles, down almost to the bone. I winced, sucking air through my teeth and watched as my blood welled out and ran down my arm, dribbling into the bowl beneath. Hassan recoiled and let go of my wrist before any reached him.

Another of Hassan's men sliced open his own palm and squeezed his blood into a cup.

I glanced at Abdullah and Stephen, who were so close they were practically clutching at each other, united in their horror of what they were witnessing.

The smell of the Assassin's blood was intoxicating and when he passed it over I drank the contents of that cup like I was dying of thirst. It had been some years since I had consumed blood. It was like coming home after a long absence. Like embracing an old friend. It was fire in my stomach, dull ache and a burning warmth that spread and spread through my body, up my neck so my face flushed and down to my fingers and toes.

Hassan and the others around me muttered and stirred, staring at my forearm. A servant poured water over my wounded flesh and swiped away the blood with a cloth.

When the blood was cleaned off, the wound beneath was already closed, leaving just an ugly pink line.

"This scar will soon fade into nothing," I said, quickly pulling my hauberk back over my head and wriggling into it.

Hassan stared at me. "The reports of this William's blood magic. I had always thought it to be a conjurer's trick."

"Now you know," I said. "And this blood surely has value to you."

"How is this possible?" he asked. "What did you do to gain this power?"

I hesitated. "I did nothing that I am aware of. Certainly, I did not ask for it. Perhaps I was born this way. Whether it was through the seed of my father or by the hand of God, I know not."

He was suspicious, believing that I deceived him even though I spoke sincerely. The Saracens, and the Assassins most of all, were well versed in deceit and because it was in each of them, they saw it in everyone else, also.

Hassan pointed at the bowl of my blood that one of his servants held. "But if I drink this, I will become like you?"

"No. Not like me. And there is a cost."

"I will pay any price."

"Not that sort of cost. You must first be drained of much of your blood, and at the point of death, you must drink down a pint of mine. It takes half a day or so to bring you back from the brink of death and not all men survive. You may die. If you come back, you must yourself then drink the blood of men, or women, every two or three days, else you will become weakened, then ill, and then you will lose your mind in raving madness. And you will never be able to father a child, no matter how often you lay with a woman."

"A heavy price."

I nodded, taking my sword and other things back from Stephen.

"And you, Richard, you must drink blood every three days?"

I hesitated, for I was giving my secrets to an enemy. But if I did not take drastic action then William would seize me come morning and then I would be no more. Besides, all I would have to do to keep the secret would be to kill every man in the room.

"No. Not me and not William, either. We are different. We are stronger."

"Why? Tell me, good sir, what made you as you are?"

"I do not know," I said. He still thought I was lying. "Truly."

"The tasks that my men could achieve, if they had this power," he said, looking through me into a future only he could see. "We might even resist Hulegu's assault."

"I want you to help me kill my brother," I said.

He snapped back to me. "In exchange for your blood? We can do this. Yes."

"Tonight."

He gaped at me, then spoke to his men in a bust of rapid guttural words. They all laughed, and he allowed himself a smile.

"Tonight, truly, sir? It cannot be done."

"We could kill Hulegu, also."

"We certainly would. But such a thing is not possible."

"I will do it myself, then," I said.

Hassan al-Din, the Assassin lord, and emissary, hesitated. I could see that he was weighing up a series of choices. One of which was surely to simply kill me, and the two men with me. He could deliver me to Mongke or to Hulegu or William, in exchange for favours from those men.

"Perhaps I might suggest a different course of action? You should come with us, Sir Richard. Back to Alamut. We leave at sunrise."

"Mongke's men would bring me back and punish you all. Kill you all for such an affront."

"My men are all prepared for death. None of us truly expected to leave here with our lives and if we do not return then our master shall know the outcome of our embassy just as surely as if we told him with our mouths. But perhaps they would allow us to leave? The Mongols are truly evil and yet they value greatly the role of ambassador and seek always to deliver envoys safely through their lands, even if they are emissaries from mortal enemies. That is also why we are not closely guarded within Karakorum, even though my master has sent four hundred individual men to murder Mongke in any way that they can. I would gladly risk the lives of my men to bring you and your blood magic away from this place."

"No, that would not be successful. I have delivered myself into my brother's hands, like a fool, and he will not let me go."

"Emissaries are used to negotiating terms," Hassan said. "What do you have that William might want? Or do you have something that Hulegu may want?"

"Nothing," I said because it was true.

Hassan tilted his head. "Is there anything that you can get that William might want?"

"I have no idea what he wants," I said. "I have not seen him for decades, and I never knew him well. I have no way of knowing what he needs now. Neither him nor this Hulegu, who I have only heard of recently. How could I have anything that he would bargain for?"

Abdullah, standing against the wall, raised his voice. "You do." Every face in the room turned to him and he trembled, lowering his head. "Forgive me, my lord, your pardon, sir, your pardon."

"Spit out your words, Abdullah, for the love of God."

"The girl," he said. "The girl who was Hulegu's wife. The young woman we saw in the palace who ran away only to be captured. She is to be killed tomorrow, too. Hulegu wants her, does he not? And also, might she not know Hulegu's needs? And, if William and Hulegu are as close as they say, might she not know of your brother, too?"

Interesting.

"You just want to feast your eyes on her again," I said.

"Oh, no, my lord," Abdullah said. "I am thinking only of your interest, my lord."

I looked at Hassan, who was stroking his beard. "They are being held in a house on the southern road," he said. "Guarded, of course. We will not be allowed to see the prisoners."

"I will kill the guards," I said. "Seize her and force the girl to tell me Hulegu and William's secrets."

"Even if she does tell you something of use." Stephen stepped forward, lowering his voice. "You will not have time to act upon that knowledge before you yourself are seized. They let us go from the palace but only because they knew where you were. What if Mongke's men come for you at the ger tonight, and find you absent? A search of the city would not take them long. And even if Mongke washes his hands of it, you will be taken to Hulegu's men come tomorrow. You must secure an escape, and the only possible chance you have is with these Assassins. Then, you can take the girl when we flee and question her on the road. Hulegu will want her and will pursue her but you could throw her off your horse once you were done with her and Hulegu's men would find her again, then kill her as they intended."

"Impossible," I said. "There is nothing I have to offer the Mongols to stay their hand." I looked at the servant holding a bowl of my blood. One thing I could do was promise to stay at Mongke's court and turn him and a number of his own captains into immortals, as William had done for his brother. But the thought made me sick to my stomach. I would be making myself a slave in exchange for my life. "In exchange for letting us go free, I have nothing that I can offer them."

"But he does," Stephen said, pointing a finger at Hassan.

My breath frosted in the air. Night proper had fallen when I approached the door where the young Mongol woman was being held. It was a house, the same as the others around it, but the Assassin leading me—assigned by Hassan al-Din—pointed it out. Abdullah and Stephen followed behind.

The door was not barred. As I opened it and stepped through, the heat from inside poured past me out into the freezing night. A single large room filled with lamplight, with steep stairs up to the floor above on one side, and a door on each of the other walls. A small dung-fuelled fire smouldered in the central hearth, and the air was thick with smoke.

Hassan had suggested there would be a single guard inside, perhaps two.

Four men sat around the hearth, drinking together. They fell silent as I stood there in the doorway.

"Good evening, gentlemen," I said, cheerily, and clapping my hands together. "Is this the Karakorum brothel-house?"

They jumped to their feet, their hideous faces twisted in anger at my intrusion.

Quite suddenly, my own days and hours of frustration and fear rushed up to engulf me in a murderous rage. I was on the first man before he had time to recoil, and my dagger punched him in the neck, up to the hilt. Shoving him down before me, I leapt into the next man, who was caught between drawing his own blade and retreating. As he turned from me, I grabbed his long, greasy hair and stabbed the side of his throat. I thrust the blade out of the front of his neck in a shower of blood and the gristly mass of his severed windpipe slapped onto the floor.

I sensed an attack coming from behind and ducked as a sword blade was thrust toward the back of my neck. As I twisted away, it caught the back of my head and cut a gouge into my skull. The attacker might have expected me to retreat in panic, so I turned low enough to place my offhand on the tiled floor and leapt up at him, close enough to hug him while I slammed my dagger up beneath his chin. As I followed him down I drew the blade out and jammed it through his eye.

The fourth man had been expertly dispatched by Hassan's Assassin, who nodded at me while he wiped his curved blade on the Mongol's coat.

In the doorway, Abdullah and Stephen stood with their mouths open at the sudden horror before them.

The delicious smell of blood filled the air and my mouth watered.

"You are injured, sir," Stephen said, raising a shaky hand at my head.

I felt it. It seemed to be pouring with hot blood over my fingers.

"How bad is it?" I asked Stephen.

His face was grey. "There is a gash and, beneath, a... a flap, of skin."

That would not do. I bent to the first man, who was still struggling for breath as his life pumped away onto the tiles beneath his body. Without a word, I bent to his neck and drank down the hot blood that welled up from the wound.

"Good God Almighty," Stephen said. "That flap of skin has knitted itself back together, Richard. I watched it happen. Did you see that, Abdullah?"

A silence descended and hung over the room like a shroud.

The young Mongol woman stood at the top of the stairs, looking down on us like a princess. By God, she was a beauty. She was bareheaded and her shining black hair tumbled down in braids and was not shorn on top

Abdullah drifted towards the bottom of the steps, mouth agape.

As he started to speak, the young Mongol man pushed past the girl, a low growl in his throat, bare hands raised and ready to fight to defend his woman to the death. His eyes were steely but edged with that madness that shows a man is prepared to die.

I stepped in front of him with my hands up and out. "Stop!"

He jabbed his finger at me and snarled a stream of angry words.

"Tell him we're here to help," I said to Abdullah, and to the Assassin. "Tell him we are fleeing the city and we want them to come with us."

The two young Mongols exchanged a look. The man barked a question.

"He asks why."

"I want to kill Hulegu. And I want to kill my brother William, who serves Hulegu. And I want him and his woman to help me."

They did not hesitate.

* * *

We wrapped ourselves in Mongol garb and hurried back through the bitter darkness. Faint moonlight provided just barely enough light to see the edges of things, whenever the clouds and dung-smoke did not obscure the sky completely. Every crunching step on the iron-hard icy ground made me wince, and my head swivelled left and right as I strained to hear any approaching danger over the heavy breathing of my strange company. The city appeared deserted but all it would take to ruin us would be for a single alert Mongol to raise the alarm before I could silence him. Inside the houses and tents, voices and laughter spilled out into the night.

And I wondered whether I would return to our ger to find Eva safe and well, or whether the knights had overpowered her, or if the Mongols had come for us while I was away.

It was quiet as I approached, with the others behind me. Smoke rolled from the top of the ger.

I tapped on the door in the pattern that Eva would recognise.

The few moments before the door opened, my heart was in my mouth.

Thomas opened the door, his face blank. He nodded and stepped back. All was quiet within and Eva smiled, briefly. I was glad to see her, too.

Waving everyone in, I closed the door behind us.

"Quickly," I said to Eva. "We must make final preparations and be at the gate before sunrise."

"You will bring disaster down upon us," Friar William said, for the hundredth time.

"Save your breath," Stephen Gosset said as he helped me to pack our belongings, including some stale food, and speaking over his shoulder.

"These murderers breaking the law is one thing," Friar William said. "But you, Stephen, you are a brother of our order and you are bringing us into disrepute with your—"

"Be quiet, I said," Stephen snapped, turning on his brothers. "I have seen things this night that are bigger than your notions of reputation. Go home, tell the Pope that you failed to convert anyone, and leave me be."

The monks stared. Friar William recovered, shook his red face and took a deep breath ready to shout down the youngster.

"Quiet," I said. "Quiet, all of you. And listen."

They all broke off and turned to me.

"I am leaving tonight. Eva and I together. We are taking these Mongols with us. We will flee with the Assassins of Alamut, and go to their lands with them. In that way, I shall be free from the sentence of the Khan. Free to return and to fight again."

"Why would the Assassins welcome you?" Thomas said. "And why would the Mongols let you go?"

I hesitated. "The Assassin envoy, Hassan al-Din, has gone this very night to the palace of the Great Khan. He will make a trade for my life and together we will ride to Alamut."

"What trade?" Thomas asked. "What could they possibly offer that would be worth your life?"

"It does not concern you," I said.

"He is giving the Assassins his blood," Stephen said as if he was too proud of the knowledge to hold on to it. "He will make them into immortals, just as his brother has done for Hulegu."

"Good God Almighty," Thomas said.

"We should thank God Almighty," Friar William said, "that this power of his blood is nothing but a nonsense."

"It is true," Stephen said. "I have witnessed it with my own eyes. As has Abdullah. The Assassins have seen it, and that is why they are risking everything to protect Richard."

"How can you trust these Saracens?" Bertrand said, glaring at the Assassin who stood quietly by the door. "You are betraying God."

I scoffed. "You are the least devout man here."

"And yet he is right," Thomas said. "You cannot go with the Assassins. You will make yourselves prisoners, to be used and exploited by these heathens. They will kill you whenever they are done with you. And you cannot give them this power of yours... if it truly does exist."

"I need allies," I said. "I cannot defeat my brother, nor Hulegu and the other immortals that William has made, without men to assist me. Men with the strength to face William's evil." I pointed at the nameless Assassin in his Persian headwear. "They are the only men with such strength."

"It should be Christian men by your side," Thomas said.

"I wish it were so," I said. "But where are they? Will you join me, Thomas, and fight at my side? Would you bring Martin with you? Would you use the strength of your order to help me?"

Stephen stepped forward. "I will join you."

I laughed in his face. "I need knights, Stephen, not clerks."

He was deeply offended. "I have knowledge of the world that could help you. I gave you the means for your escape, did I not?"

I hesitated. The young monk had shown a certain gift for creative thinking. Something that I sorely lacked. "Very well, you will come."

"I will come also," Abdullah said, stepping forward and bowing his head. "With your permission, my lord."

"Why in the name of God would you want to come with me?" I asked, appalled.

He glanced at the Mongol girl, who sat by the entrance with the man's arm about her shoulder, next to the Assassin who watched us through his eyelashes. "I wish to be with my people," Abdullah said.

"The Assassins?" I said. "You are a Saracen, subject to the Caliph in Baghdad, are you not? The Assassins are the sworn enemies of your people."

Abdullah's eyes twinkled in the lamplight. "They follow the word of the Prophet. They are closer to me than the Christians, or the Mongols. And I can be useful to you. How will you speak with the Ismailis without me?"

I jerked my thumb over my shoulder. "Are you that smitten with the girl that you would risk death."

He lowered his head. "I simply no longer wish to be cold, sir."

"If you wish to serve me, I will not say no."

"He belongs to me," Friar William said, outraged. "He may not go with you."

"Try and stop him," I said. The monks cursed me but what else could they do?

Little Nikolas ran forward. "I, too, will join you, Sir Richard." He grinned up at me with his hand on the ivory dagger I had given him.

"No, son," I said. "It is not safe for you. Stay with the monks. Serve them well and in the Spring they will take you back to Constantinople."

His eyes filled with tears. "No, my lord, no, I will come with you. You and Eva. I will serve you well."

William and Bartholomew protested but I waved them into silence. "You are too young," I said to Nikolas.

Eva placed a hand on my arm. "Richard?"

I knew what she wanted but I did not want to have to look after the boy. He would be pestering us and slowing us down. And, absurd as it was, I found his obsession with Eva to be irritating. He was just of the age that his interest in her would not be purely a platonic one, and I felt like Eva was allowing herself to be exploited in some vague, ill-defined way. Perhaps it was as simple a thing as my feeling excluded, and that he took her attention away from me.

Whatever the reason, I found myself relieved at the prospect of being rid of him.

"The boy stays with the monks," I said. "It is fair to the Franciscans, who I am already depriving of one interpreter. Nikolas can assist them in Abdullah's stead. And besides all that, it is not safe for you, Nikolas. We will be riding hard, riding in a fashion that you are too small to do. Stay safe. The monks have been promised safety by the Great Khan. It will please me to know you are safe."

He half-drew his white dagger, gripping it tightly around the carving of Saint George killing the dragon. "Please, sir. I will make a good knight. I will serve you and become a brave knight and fight the Saracens."

I saw then how I had wronged him. Patronised him and given him false hope for something that he could never be.

All I could do was ruffle his hair. "Serve your masters well," I said.

Thomas grabbed me by the shoulder before I left. "I beg you," he said. "Do not give your power to our enemies."

"Come with me," I said. "You and Martin, both. The Franciscans do not need your protection. They have Bertrand and Hughues, and they do not even need them. The Mongols, despite their savagery in every other way, keep all ambassadors safe and well. No harm will come to them."

"I must return to the Holy Land," he said. "And the Kingdom of Jerusalem. When I get to Acre, I must tell King Louis, and the Master of my order, that the Mongols mean to make war on the kingdoms there. I must tell them how these Mongols may destroy our enemies, but they may take everything that we hold, too."

"Send Martin with the messages," I said. "Ride with us yourself. God knows I could use your wisdom. And your skill in battle."

"Yours is a personal quest," he said, glancing at the Assassin and the Mongol couple. "I serve higher powers."

"That is fair to say," I admitted, though I knew would miss him very dearly. "Then I wish you well. Perhaps, one day, we shall meet again."

"If your new friend Hassan al-Din is unable to make his deal with the Great Khan," Thomas said, "I will see you dragged back here to Karakorum before sundown."

We had to make haste, and our strange little group carried our gear, along with what supplies we could muster, to the south gate of Karakorum where the Assassins were already assembled in the pre-dawn light. It was intensely cold, and the ground was hard as iron and sheathed in frozen dew. After a nerve-wracking night and no sleep, we were all tired. And yet the fear of capture was so acute that I was jittery and ready to fight with a moment's warning.

As we approached the gate along the empty road, I was surprised to see wagons gathered by the gate, with the Assassins heaving their wares into the backs of them.

"I thought we were riding hard," I asked one of Hassan's captains, who had been watching for our approach. "To evade Mongke or Hulegu's men. These wagons will slow us terribly."

Abdullah translated for me. "They say that no matter how hard we ride, we could never evade pursuit, should the Mongols decide to launch one. All depends on Hassan's embassy."

"Do you think he will have been received by the Khan yet?" I asked, though I knew the answer.

The Assassin captain looked at me like I was a buffoon, though he was kind enough to explain. "Mongke makes himself insensible from excessive drink very early every night. And though he wakes early, it takes much time for him to bestir himself for the day's business."

I nodded, for I had known many man who lived lives taken over by drink. I had been one of them myself.

The Mongols who guarded the gate were well armed and armoured with mail and steel helms beneath their thick coats and furs. They watched us all very closely, holding lamps out and peering into the Assassin's wagons as they strolled through us all.

We would be caught, I was sure of it. The gate, such as it was, remained closed and I did not know how I could force it open. We had little chance of killing every guard before one of them raised a cry of warning that would bring hundreds or thousands more down upon us.

Not only was I not supposed to leave the city, I was harbouring criminals. The two young Mongols hid their faces beneath their fur hoods and held tight to each other.

I gathered the rest of my brood to me. Eva, Stephen, and Abdullah. In outer appearance, we were dressed much the same as everyone else; our thick overcoats hiding our amour or our robes, and our hoods hiding our faces. We kept our voices low and spoke barely at all.

Around us, the Assassins busied themselves. Hassan's captain stood by my side, watching the Mongols all around us from the corner of his eyes.

A guard approached, lantern held high, and the Assassin directed us away from him while he went to intercept. Another Assassin took control of our group and directed us to one of the wagons, where he invited us to load our belongings.

While the sky lightened, and preparations continued, they moved us between them so to hide us from the Mongols in plain sight. I noticed how the Assassins formed another group like ours, with the same number, and one of them was tall, like me. This group was allowed to be inspected by a guard, and then we were swapped for their position. Not for nothing were the Assassins said to be cunning in the extreme.

We waited for the gate to be opened and I was gripped with a sudden, mad fear that William would be standing there as it did so, backed by a thousand battle-ready savages. No matter how much I told myself it was merely a weakness of my own heart, I could not shake the fear.

As the sun rose, finally the gate was opened.

William was not there.

It was the harsh and barren landscape with the silhouettes of groups of horses huddled together against the freezing night dawn. I breathed a short sigh of relief but remained tense and anxious as we mounted our horses all together, with us fugitives in the centre and the Assassins shielding us from view as well as they could. We kept our heads down, in shadow within our hoods.

Finally, we rode out through the gate into the freezing valley beyond. Our immediate route was to follow the frozen river southward as it wound along the valley, edged by the sharp hills.

We went slowly. The horses were hardy but it was so cold it was a wonder they were willing to walk at all. The oxen pulling the wagons were subdued as if they could sense our tension, our fear. I had heard often how the Assassins were joyfully willing to die for their lord, but they seemed fearful also to me. Perhaps it was concern not for themselves but for Hassan al-Din, who we left behind at the palace with only one attendant so that he could secure our safe passage.

If Hassan were killed, or his deal refused, we would be brought back and I would be executed by Hulegu, who was arriving on the other side of the city that day.

That freezing morning, facing my imminent death at the hands of my immortal enemy, it is fair to say that I ached for my home.

England.

I had felt cold there, but the deep, crisp snows of English winter were nothing like the bitter, dry, howling winds of the foothills and mountains at the edge of the great grassland plains. I hated it, suddenly, hated the strange land, that was so lifeless and miserable that I understood at once how it could create such a foul people as the Mongols and other tartar peoples. England was green, with thick, dark, rich soil that crumbled between one's fingers. Soil that was deep, and always moist, and grew tall, healthy crops.

The hills of my homeland in Derbyshire were beautiful, steep and hard in places but civilised and on a human scale. My dear hills were so unlike the savage grey and black giants that jutted up into the bleached skies in the distance, like dungeon walls. I knew, deep in my bones, that God had lovingly sculpted Derbyshire and all England with his own hand, and had set the climate to make civilised men, and good women. A land hard enough to make us strong, and courageous but generous enough to breed within us a fundamental decency and goodness of spirit.

That land of central Asia seemed to be scoured by the hand of some demon, bordered by mountains thrown up out of the bowels of the Earth. Even the low hills that hemmed us in were an unnatural shape, with peaks like the edge of a curved blade, or the backs of giant serpents undulating across the landscape in a grotesque parade. Hot enough to kill a man in summer, cold enough in winter that many a traveller never awoke in the morning but lay frozen to the ground, as if the land wanted to devour him. A brutal place that bred brutal men. A people without the luxury of civilisation.

A pale sun dragged itself halfway into the sky to our left, casting long shadows across the stony ground. From our right came the howling, bitter wind that could cut through half a dozen layers of clothing, including furs, to numb one side of your body and drive painful aches deep into your bones.

All the while, I felt the presence of Karakorum behind me. Would it be a galloping army come to take me away? Would William himself lead them? Would I be killed here, in this God-forsaken nightmare land? What would happen to Eva? Had I led her into ruin, finally?

It was the end of the day, as the sun grew weak and rested for a moment on the distant mountains when I had my answer.

A shout went up and the procession of Ismailis halted and turned. I could see nothing behind us but more broken land and a sky turned pale as ice, with a sun falling away to the West as if it were glad for the shelter.

Riders.

My hand went to my sword, and Eva moved to my side so that we could fight together against the pursuing enemies.

Yet there were so few of them. Just three riders, in fact, with three more riderless horses following.

"It is Hassan," Eva said, squinting, for her eyes were far better in the half-light than any mortal's, and better than mine also. "With his attendant. The third man is... I cannot make him out, it is as though he is hiding."

"Thomas," I said, hardly believing my own words as I spoke them. "That is Thomas with them."

Stephen positioned his own horse behind mine and spoke up. "What in the name of God is he doing here?"

"Why is he hiding?" Eva asked. "Hunched so low as he rides?"

"He is cold," Stephen said.

"He is injured," I said.

And so it was.

I rode out to meet them, along with Eva and a group of Hassan's men.

"What happened?" I shouted as we came together.

"Mongke Khan agreed to let us all go," Hassan said. "All of you included. In exchange for me agreeing to call off all of the four-hundred fedayin."

Thomas was slumped over, barely conscious, and tied to his saddle. The horse was skittish, tossing her head and stepping sideways.

"What happened to him?" I asked as we took his reins. "Thomas, can you hear me?"

"Is he dead?" Stephen said as he rode up behind me against my orders.

"Almost," Eva said. "Look."

Thomas' lower body and legs were saturated with blood, as were the flanks of his horse. He seemed dead but the Templar groaned and feebly tried to fight us off while we cut him down from his horse. We carried Thomas and placed him on the back of a wagon, removing his clothing.

"Who did this?" I demanded, though I dreaded the answer.

"Your brother," Hassan al-Din said. "Used a dagger to cut him, here. See?" Hassan mimed the cut, low on the abdomen, from hip to hip.

Upon examination, the cut was not so wide as that, but it was bad. It stank of foul blood and shit, and only the frigid wind stopped the stench from being totally overpowering. It smelled of death and I knew Thomas would not be long for the world. Still, the Assassins moved to help us and Stephen poured their offered wine over the wound to clean it, then wiped at and soaked up the blood. Thomas shivered and his skin, where it was not bloody, was as white as bleached bone.

"Make a fire," Stephen said. "We must warm him. Hurry."

No one made a move to do so. All of us knew that it would do no good. Thomas had only a short while to live.

"My brother did this?" I said to Hassan, my own body shaking now, not with cold but from a white-hot rage that grew with every moment. "Sent him to me like this, just to taunt me?"

Hassan grimaced. "Mongke Khan agreed to the terms, and Hulegu could not persuade him otherwise." He pointed at me. "Your brother William calmed Hulegu and demanded to see your monks."

"He killed them?"

"William harmed them, demanding to know where you were fleeing to. Of course, they told him everything, immediately. They will live. As will the large knight who looks like a bullock."

"Bertrand."

"Hulegu himself demanded Bertrand tell everything about the King of France and the land of France. Precisely how many towns are there, how many sheep, how many horses."

The Mongols had asked us similar questions before. "Absurd. How can any man know such things?"

Hassan shrugged. "This Sir Bertrand made a sincere attempt to give them answers. Hulegu said that he would make Bertrand a great lord when the Mongols conquer France."

"Dear God," Eva said, looking at me.

"When did William do this?" I said, pointing at the dying Thomas.

Hassan looked back at the dark horizon. "Night will fall soon. We should make camp here." He called orders to his men, who immediately began to corral the horses and circle the wagons on the bleak plain.

I grabbed him by the arm, which alarmed his captains enough that they drew their daggers and made ready to strike. But they were utterly obedient to their lord, and he restrained them with no more than a look.

"Tell me what happened," I said, in a low voice.

"Hulegu and your brother arrived and your companions were brought to the palace," Hassan said. "The monks, the knights, the Templars. Even the servants. Hulegu was angry that Mongke had agreed to free you, and his traitorous wife, in exchange for my word to stop the fedayin."

"First, he killed the young Templar. The squire of this man," Hassan said. "Crushed the skull with his bare hands and drank his blood from the neck. His keshig were there. Evil men. While the body yet twitched, they passed it between them as if it were a skin of wine, many drinking from it before tossing it aside. The old knight here shouted curses and Hulegu's keshig held him so that he would see it all."

Eva shook with rage. "We shall kill them," she promised me.

"William spoke into the ear of Sir Thomas," Hassan continued. "And then cut him, like you see. He told me to take him to you. Take this old man to my brother Richard, he said to me, and the old man will tell my brother my message. I said that I would do so but that the old man would die before he could speak it."

I hung my head, for I knew at once what William intended. "And he told you I would have to turn him into an immortal in order to save his life. In order to hear the message."

Eva and I looked at each other.

Around us on the back of the wagon, the Ismailis placed lamps that cast yellow light over Thomas' body.

"And then, there was a boy," Hassan said, speaking reluctantly. "While William cut this Templar across the body, a slave boy attacked your brother with a white dagger. Stabbed him low in the flank."

"Nikolas," Eva said, her eyes shining in the dusk. "What did he do to Nikolas?"

Hassan's nose wrinkled. "You do not wish to—"

"Tell me," Eva said.

"William laughed at the boy, pulled the blade from his body without pain, and asked the slave from where did he steal such a fine dagger? The boy said it was a gift from the greatest knight who ever lived, Sir Richard the Englishman. William found this to be highly amusing." Hassan looked away from us. "They held him. William peeled the boy's skin from his face and chest using the white dagger. Played games with his pain. All the time, they were laughing. When they tired of it, two of Hulegu's immortals took an arm each and pulled him apart. The keshig tore his arms from his body." Hassan shook his head. "It was a very bad thing. Very bad."

Eva stood, her body shaking, her face set in stone as she glared back at the north.

"We cannot go back," I said, softly.

She did not look at me when she replied, irritated. "I know."

"Here," Hassan said, taking an object from inside his overcoat. He handed it over. Small, wrapped in a square of silk, cut from robes. "Before I was dismissed, your brother approached with this. I thought he was going to defy the Great Khan and kill me but instead he told me to give this to you."

I unwrapped the object.

My white dagger.

While the blade had been wiped clean, the carving of Saint George lancing the dragon was crusted with dried blood. William's blood? Or had it come from Nikolas?

An ember of rage grew in me as I imagined the horror of the death of the boy. My hatred for William had burned low for decades but when I pictured Nikolas in his final moments, the agony and fear he must have felt, that hatred began to burn once more.

Thomas groaned and I kneeled by his side again. "What is the message, Thomas?" He muttered, begging for water. "

Stephen pulled a blanket over Thomas' body. "What if this is the message?" he said. "Just this, returning him in this condition?"

"I do not have a mind to listen to your nonsense, Stephen."

"Your brother, he is devious, you said so. You said he once sent men to attack your manor, knowing they would be killed, simply to draw you to him. A manipulation of your actions, do you see? He wants you to give your blood to Thomas, to turn him immortal. What if that is what he wants to tell you?"

"I do not understand. How would my actions be a message? And why would he want that?" I said. "That would only serve to make me stronger."

Stephen opened his mouth to reply but closed it again.

I sighed. "I will feed him my blood."

Stephen nodded, placing a hand on Thomas' pale, glistening head. "He will not wish it. He thinks you are an abomination." He glanced up at Eva. "Both of you, and your brother."

"Perhaps he is right," I said. "He told you that?"

"Last night, when we returned to the ger. He urged me to stay away from you."

It annoyed me. Thomas was not wrong, not at all, and yet it annoyed me greatly.

Using the white dagger, I sliced into my wrist and pressed the wound to Thomas' lips. They were cold. He tried to turn his head away, tried to raise an arm and force mine away. But he was so weak.

And he drank. Slowly, at first, and then he sucked and gulped at my wrist.

"He will not like this," Stephen muttered, looking ill.

"It may not work at all," I said, quietly. "And if he lives and does not wish to, I will simply cut off his head."

While the others ate, drank and pondered the long journey ahead of us, I sat beside Thomas on the wagon, inside the little pool of yellow light given off by the lamp set down by his head. The small flame glowed within the waxed parchment sides, safe from the wind howling down the valley. Eva came to sit by my side, leaning her body against me for a time before she moved away to sleep. She draped me in furs and kissed my cheek before she left me.

Once in a while, I felt the skin of Thomas' chest, slipping my hand beneath the furs covering him to see if his heart was yet beating and if he still breathed. An intimate gesture that set me wondering about the old man's life, and whether he had ever had tender moments with a woman. At the start of the night, his skin was cold as ice and clammy. Later, he developed a fever that radiated from him like an iron pulled from the fire, and a sweat broke out to soak him right through.

"It is a strange life," I said, to Thomas, wondering if he would live to see the dawn. "We have seen much of the world. Seen many wonders. We have done many glorious deeds. But we have done ill, also. I have done murder. Killed men who have wronged us, or wronged others. Doing justice, as I see it, but the laws of England would say it was murder. And we have no home. That is to say, we have homes only for a while before we must move on. But you have been a Templar, sir. And you have served with honour, I have no doubt. You have fought in the Holy Land, and you have fought across Christendom. Perhaps ours would be a life that would suit you." I bowed my head and rubbed my tired eyes. "I shall have to feed you blood, as I do for Eva. You will not like that. No more than I will. But I hope that you will live, Thomas. The truth of it is, I could use a knight such as you at my side. A knight of your skill, and your experience, with the strength of one of the Immortals..." I leaned in closer to his ear. "Live, Thomas. Live."

The lamp ran dry of oil during the night and I fell asleep sitting by the man who was suspended between life and death.

As the sky grew light, before the sun rose, the old knight muttered through cracked lips and bestirred me from my fitful slumber.

"Thirst," he said. "Thirst."

"I know," I replied.

The old man seemed stunned by what had been done to him and sat subdued on the wagon rather than ride his horse, despite the way those carts bounced and juddered over the rough road. We were all of us well on the move as the sun dragged itself up above the horizon and I asked Thomas, finally, what William's message was.

Stressing that he could not recall the precise words, in between mouthfuls of wine he recited the message back to me.

"Tell him this, he said to me into my ear. I wished that you had forgotten me. He spoke it as if I were you, do you see? I wished that you had forgotten me and had decided to take a path of greatness for yourself." Thomas stared into nothing. "Brother, if you leave me be, so shall I leave you. But if you continue to oppose me..." Thomas squeezed wine into his mouth, so much that it spilled from his lips and he swiped it away. "Then he gutted me with a hooked dagger."

The words affected me deeply. There was so many barbs within it that I did not know which of them wounded me most deeply. Worst of all was the sense that, to me, William was my enemy, my sole purpose in life, my quest, my obsession. Yet to him, I was little more than an annoyance. If he spoke truly, it seemed as though he had forgotten me in the years since we had last clashed. All the while, I had dedicated every waking hour to finding him, reaching him. Killing him.

It cheapened it. Made my oath of vengeance seem small.

Thomas looked at me from under his hood with red-rimmed eyes.

"You have suffered terribly," I said to him. "And I ask forgiveness. If I had known that he would do this, I would have forced you to come with me."

"How can I forgive you? Why should I?" Thomas was silent for a while, shivering and white. "I listened to your stories about him but I did not believe. No, I did not understand. Not until I saw his madness with my own eyes. He killed Martin. A decent man, who deserved a good death, at the very least, not torture. Not mutilation. And little Nikolas, that poor lad. Do you know what they did to him?"

Terrorised, tortured and torn apart before he had even become a man. Another innocents' death on my conscience.

"He will die for what he has done," I said. "Call it what you will. Justice. Vengeance. I will kill my brother or die in the attempt."

"And the others?" Thomas said. "Hulegu, and the other Immortals that your brother has made?"

Hulegu was, to all intents and purposes, a king. Not just any king, but the most powerful man in the entire world save only, perhaps, for his brother Mongke, who was an alcoholic who had rarely strayed far from Karakorum. Whereas Hulegu was acting like a true conqueror like his grandfather, Genghis. His army was already the largest anywhere, it was the most well equipped, with the best artillery and the most professional system of organisation and logistics, and with the most experienced and talented officers of any force from the four corners of the Earth.

A man such as he, with the immortal blood of my brother in his veins, would be unstoppable.

"They will all die," I promised.

Part Four

Alamut

1256

I COULD BARELY CONCEIVE OF the distances we travelled. When we had first travelled from Constantinople, north almost to the lands of the Rus, it had taken months. Then, we went east. Day after day, month after month we had gone east all the way to Karakorum and through the entire journey, we had been official travellers. Taken from place to place, given fresh horses to ride, passed from stage to stage at an astonishing pace. Even then, I knew I had travelled further than I had believed possible.

For my entire life, all eighty-odd years of it, I had known the world as it was from England to Jerusalem. And that was right far. A pilgrimage by land and sea, so long that one would see many a man beside you die from disease or accident. Beyond Jerusalem, I knew, of course, was the land of Syria and beyond that, Persia. I had always imagined they were the size of England or France, and beyond that was a land of desert and barbarity and myth and legend. A land of fantastic monsters, dog-headed people, fabled kingdoms of Christians. But even then, I had not suspected that the land would stretch so far.

And returning, from that distant east to the known west, seemed to me to be farther still.

We travelled at a walking pace. Our horses had to be spared, for we could not find fresh ones except to purchase or trade for enormously disadvantageous terms. Provisions were our first priority, and though we all but starved ourselves, we had to seek all we could from people along the way.

Our route out had taken us north of the Black Sea, and north of the Caspian Sea and also the Aral Sea. The way back would take us to the south of those seas into the Iranian plateau, to Samarkand, Merv, Nishapur and then into the mountains of the Assassins.

I knew little of all that, though, during the journey. To me, it was relentless travel, along rivers, besides inhuman mountains that went on and on for weeks and months. Frozen highlands, bitter deserts, and the taste of dust blown by relentless winds that howled into your face, and through your clothing, day and night, steady or gusting and sounding in your ears like the groaning chants of a thousand monks singing from beyond the grave.

We were miserable. Eva suffered greatly, as did Thomas. Both were heart-sick with loss and resentment. But they had my blood to sustain them, take away some of their weariness every two or three days or so.

"I feel strong," Thomas said, on one of the first evenings before retiring. "Stronger than I have since I was a young man, and stronger even than that. I carried that casque of wine down from the wagon with such ease that I mistakenly believed for a moment that it was empty."

Eva nodded. "One of the more profound benefits."

He leaned in and lowered his voice. "The light of the day, even when the sky is grey, causes me to wince and hang my head due to the discomfort I feel behind my eyes. Is that the case with you, good lady?"

She nodded. "Wait until you experience summer in the Holy Land, Thomas. It is quite agonising. Any portion of exposed skin will almost immediately become red and blistered. Prolonged exposure will make it blister and crack before your eyes. Ever since I became an immortal, I have gone about shrouded and hooded whenever I am out of doors. Even in the shade of a hood, the light of a bright day is quite unpleasant."

"Dear God," Thomas muttered. "But then surely the Holy Land is the very worst place you could choose to be."

Eva glanced at me before responding. "You are not wrong, sir."

"I have often taken pleasure in the simple joy of the sun's warmth upon my skin. Do you mean to say this is something I shall never again feel?"

"You will welcome all cloudy days for the rest of your life," Eva said. "And have you noticed, Thomas, that your sight is very much improved in the darkness?"

"I thought it was perhaps some quality of the stars or the air here in these parts. So, there are indeed also benefits to this terrible affliction."

"The prime one, sir," I said with more of a growl than would have been courteous, "being that you are now alive when you would otherwise have been dead." You ungrateful old bastard.

I did not voice that final point because I was of course sympathetic with his situation.

The change in Thomas' demeanour was quite severe. He was morose and close to silent most of the time, his head hanging low as he rode. Though we did not discuss it overly much, I had vast stretches on which to dwell on how he must have been feeling.

He had dedicated his life to the Templars as a man of God and of the sword. Living by the principles of chastity, obedience and poverty from his youth to old age while travelling on the Order's business from Acre to Paris, and from Krakow to Cairo. This mission to Mongke

Khan had been a desperate hope but he had undertaken it because his master commanded it and because it was his duty to protect the Christians of the Holy Land. An alliance between the Mongols and the Franks would have had a critical effect on the balance of power in the Holy Land and Thomas had believed in the potential worth of his task, despite the enormity of it.

But the man was not all duty and honour. It was clear he held the Mongols in distaste, even disgust, and I would venture that in his heart he both feared and hated them for what they had done to the Christian armies of Poland and to his brothers and the subjects of the Order who had been slain by the barbarians.

These Tartars. They are masters of war. And we are children.

His words kept echoing in my ears. They were full of bitter admiration and also deep despair. And he had spoken them before his dutiful squire Martin had been murdered in cold blood before him.

As well as the Mongols as a people, Thomas certainly felt anger and resentment at Hulegu and his men, also at my brother William.

And he resented me.

The old Templar must have cursed the day he had ever approached me in the field outside Constantinople. But we all make poor choices in our lives and it is how we learn to live with them, and ourselves, that determines whether we face the future as slaves to our failures or as masters of our destiny.

Stephen had none of my blood and he was beaten into submission by the travelling, his cheerfulness eroded by the winds, and his parched tongue shrivelled into silences that lasted for days. I watched him age, as the hunger shaved the last softness from his features and his face became stretched over the bones beneath, the soft skin turning to flaking leather.

None of us spoke much. Weariness and hunger get into you deep. All we knew was taking the next step, and the next, and so on. Weeks, months. Were there seasons flying by in those places, or did we just pass from lands of winter into vales of summer and back again, over and over?

Excitement came rarely, and it was far between each visit. Cities were wonders compared to the landscape outside, though they were often sad places with mudbrick walls designed more to keep out the wind than any attacker. Lonely monasteries would welcome us in, despite them being idolaters, and give us shelter and, if we were lucky, hot broths. There were other travellers, and sometimes they would challenge us but the Mongol laws at least prevented outright banditry. Still, barbarians that they were, they would attempt to poke their greedy fingers into everything that we had and begged gifts with such forcefulness that oftentimes the Assassins acquiesced in order to avoid murderous consequences, first for them, and then later down the road, for us.

Time passed strangely. At times, I would be astonished that it had been only that morning that some event had occurred when it seemed as though it was many moons before. While other moments would feel as though they had happened the day before when it had in fact been months.

As we barely spoke, and only rarely even looked at one another, I did not grow to know Thomas very much better, nor Stephen. And as leader of the group of Assassins, Hassan was preoccupied with driving them on, returning them home. It was clear as day that each of them was loyal, dedicated, and obedient to him. Never did I see a bitter glance thrown at Hassan's back, nor did I ever overhear dissatisfied mumblings when he was out of his men's earshot.

There was rarely wine to drink, and never enough to become inebriated. And so, Abdullah ceased with his nights of loquaciousness and days in misery. Instead, he reached an equilibrium of nothingness. On occasion, I would even find him staring at a distant vista, or squatting to examine a blade of grass, twisting it in his fingers.

"He is finding himself again," Eva explained. I did not understand.

She always spent more time speaking to him, and all of them, than I ever did. I saw her place a hand on Stephen's shoulder, or arm, or hand, many times, to reassure him that his weariness would pass and that all would one day be well. Abdullah would stare at my wife with longing in his eyes, and yet it was clear he remained terrified of her.

The Mongol pair often seemed set to leave us. Her name, I discovered, was Khutulun. His name was Orus. They would on occasion argue in hushed voices, him full of passion and her cold as ice. Abdullah would come to me every now and then to speak for them.

"You swear you will kill Hulegu," Khutulun said.

"I have sworn it," I would say. "It will be done."

They found it difficult to believe but they stayed, for the time being. Where else could they go? Off from the road into the lands of the Mongols? They suggested they had potential allies here and there but they were hesitant to do so. No doubt any ally they could reach would be powerless should Hulegu turn his attention to them.

And, I soon discovered, they wanted something else.

"Will you give us your blood magic?" Orus, the man, asked. They both seemed hopeful.

"You do not want it," I said. "You would never father a child, young man. Nor could you bear one, young lady."

That silenced them for a while before the woman, Khutulun, responded. "I will take no husband. Ever."

Orus, on the other hand, continued to look disturbed by my words. However, he said nothing further about it.

"Why do we flee with the Assassins?" Khutulun asked. "The people of Christ are the enemies of these people, no?"

"These people are our best hope," I said. "Hulegu comes to conquer their homeland, and they are the only strong people between here and Syria who will stand against him."

"They will not be strong enough," Khutulun said.

Bit by bit, over the days and months, I picked up the history of Khutulun and Orus. The first surprise to me was that they were not lovers. They were siblings, sharing the same father and different mothers.

Their father was a chief of some tribe from an isolated and mountainous corner of the vast Mongol territories that had resisted the authority of Hulegu and his brothers for some time before being conquered and subjugated. The mother of Khutulun was herself a prize of conquest from a raid on the Tajiki tribes, who were a people closer in look to Persians, or even to Greeks or Rus, than Mongols. And it was from her mother that Khutulun got her astonishing beauty and also her wildness.

For she grew up with a love of fighting, riding, and hunting that was considered excessive for a girl but she did not care. Her father only encouraged her, because he loved her and her mother so much. Even when she reached the age where she should have been married, and she told her father and mother that she would never marry, they indulged her and believed that she would come around eventually, perhaps when she met the right suitor.

Then Hulegu had come. Their ordus was defeated and Khutulun was the greatest prize of all and he took her as one of his many wives.

Orus was a dutiful son, skilled in battle and destined to become a chief like his father. But he could not live knowing how his beloved sister would be suffering in the far-off ordus of Hulegu and so he said farewell to his home and dedicated himself to the impossible task of rescuing Khutulun.

Even though they had eventually been cornered and recaptured, I was astonished that he had managed it at all. I began to think that both of them could be even better assets than I had first imagined when it came to assaulting the ordus of Hulegu.

Little did I know quite how dangerous both young Mongols could be.

Despite what Orus and Khutulun said, the Assassins seemed to be a strong people. They travelled well, certainly better than I did through that land. I harboured a desire to learn their language, and to learn about them as a people, and to understand why they were heretics to other Saracens in Baghdad, Damascus and Cairo, and whether the rumours about them were true. But, though it was so long I walked and rode amongst them, I learned almost nothing until we finally reached their homelands in the mountains to the north of the Iranian plateau.

We ascended, on and off, for days. Sometimes rapidly and other times so gradually you did not notice until you turned and looked back on the way you had come. The mountains grew taller and more jagged as we reached the lands of the Assassins. They had over a hundred fortified settlements, possibly many more, but he would not give me the true figure, being that they were a secretive people. Abdullah whispered that it was most probably two hundred castles but some men desire to be givers of knowledge, even if their words are nonsense, and I waved him away. A hundred or two hundred castles, the Ismaili Assassins were certainly a powerful and well-protected people, but they were a small one.

All through that mountain range between northern Persia and the Caspian Sea, Hassan would point to peaks that we passed, and valleys that we could see, and say that there was an Assassin castle there. We stopped at a number of them, and Hassan and his people were welcomed as if they were dear family, though he assured me that they were not direct blood relatives but had great love for each other, for they all followed the true inheritor of

Mohammed.

We Christians and Mongols, who were of course heathens in their eyes, were treated with courtesy and respect. But that respect was for Hassan and was only extended to us through him. I have no doubt that without his protection, those generous people would have torn us limb from limb.

But we never stayed long in those castles, despite their protestations, and Hassan would move us along, with fresh horses and provisions, from place to place. He had a message for the Master of all Ismaili Assassins, and he had to give it to him.

"Hulegu is coming, finally," Hassan would say before we left each place. "Hulegu Khan is coming with vast armies and you must make ready."

The people of each castle were afraid by Hassan's warnings but they were committed to staying and holding their fortresses against the coming storm. I could not understand why they felt able to hold out against such overwhelming force in such small, isolated places with so few people in each place.

"What else can they do?" Hassan said when I asked him why they did not flee and gather in strength. "No other fortress is large enough to take them. Besides, this is their home."

"If the walls are stormed by thousands of Mongols, it will be home to no one."

Hassan could not find a way to explain it to me but he tried. "How could you call a place your home, if you were not willing to die to defend it?"

I had no answer to that. Wandering so far and so long, I had almost forgotten what it was to have a home.

We moved from mountain to mountain, through valleys and high passes by day, until, finally, after eight months of travelling, we reached our destination. The homeland of the Assassins.

"There it is," Hassan said to me as we crested a ridge and looked down into the plain beyond. "The Valley of Alamut."

All that time, all that way, listening to them talk about Alamut, I had expected a high and narrow gorge in the mountains. I heard talk of a river and lake and imagined it to be like valleys in Derbyshire, where one may stand upon the side of a vale and look across to the other, and see with perfect clarity the grazing sheep, and men and women moving about. Perhaps even a valley that, on a still day, a man might shout across from one side to the other and, though the meaning be lost, the call itself could be discerned and you might wave at each other.

Alamut was not like that.

It was vast. Wide, and flat along either side of the river, though surrounded by enormous and jagged peaks. We came in from the east and it curved away to the west until it faded into a haze of hills and peaks. In the lush lower valley were clusters of dark trees, scattered farmhouses, and well-ordered fields. Higher up on the sides, the vegetation was sparser, drier, lighter in colour. Steep pathways led up and along the uncounted jumble of slopes that undulated away along the complex valley, in between the giant, bleak peaks surrounding it all and in the far distance.

Hassan wore the expression of a man coming home. The others, too, stood and drank it in with reverence and solemnity.

I was jealous, and my heart ached for England.

Eva pressed herself against my side and slipped her hand into mine. I wondered if she felt the same sense of loss in that moment, or whether she was more apprehensive about what the end of our journey would entail. Whether we would face imprisonment, exploitation, violence.

I had dragged her all that way. And in my wake had come a Franciscan monk, a Syrian scholar, an immortal Templar, and two fugitive Mongols. Each of them looked wary of the sight before us. We were in no doubt we were all entering the heart of enemy territory.

"Will your lord truly let us stay?" I asked Hassan, for the thousandth and last time. "He will not have us all put to death for being unbelievers?"

He took a deep breath, sucking the air of his homeland into his lungs, and let it out with enormous satisfaction.

"We shall see."

* * *

While the valley of Alamut was lush and beautiful, bursting with orchards and livestock and green life, the castle of Alamut was perched atop a savage peak. As soon as I laid my eyes upon it, I understood why the Assassins yet had confidence that they could resist the might of the Mongol hordes.

The enormous defensive walls of the castle sat on colossal slabs of well-eroded rock. The narrow path up to the walls crossed back and forth up the side of the valley and the final sections of that path were within arrow range from the battlements and towers that bristled along the high lines of the defences. Spars and ropes jutted up here and there, silhouetted against the blisteringly blue sky, which I recognised as the arms of catapults mounted on the walls and the tops of the towers. The realisation caused a shiver to run down my spine, as I imagined the stones that they could throw from such a height. Projectiles that could surely reach halfway along the valley floor.

"How could an army of any size assault this place?" I asked Thomas when we had dragged ourselves all the way to the top and stood beneath the walls. The entrance was up even higher still, where the road curved up and around a corner of the rocks that the walls sat upon.

Thomas shook his head. "It would take an act of God."

"All of you should stay here," Hassan said. "Other than Richard."

Thomas stepped in front of me. "I do not like it, Richard. Once they have you up there, they can do as they wish with you."

Hassan understood his fear. "I have given my word that no harm will come to him, or to any of you."

"Your word?" Thomas said. "Your word? You are a people who survive through acts of murder. How can we ever trust your word?"

Hassan pressed his lips together and his men puffed themselves up, sensing that their lord was being insulted, or at least disrespected. Men had died for less.

I steered Thomas further to one side. Hot wind gusted up from the valley floor, bringing the smell of juniper and creosote. The sky was a searing ice blue above the castle walls and Thomas squinted beneath the hood of his light robe.

"Thomas, these men could kill all of us, right now."

He glanced around at the Assassins surrounding us. "We could make a fight of it, Richard."

I nodded. "You and I might even be the last ones standing. Eva, too. Then what? How far is it to Acre? A thousand miles?"

"So that is it? You just submit to them?"

"It is not submission," I said, urging him to understand. To see it my way. "We are negotiating. It is a trade. We cannot expect to be given shelter without giving something in return."

He sighed and glanced up, wincing at the sky. "You cannot give them that. These damned Saracens. Our enemies. Mohammedans. God's enemies. What they could do with this power."

"They will help us to kill Hulegu, William, and the others."

"Will they? And then who will they kill? The King of England?"

I hesitated. "We are a long way from such a thing, Thomas. In all likelihood, this Master of the Assassins will have us slaughtered to a man." I patted him on the shoulder and turned to Hassan. "Lead the way."

When I was finally led into the inner hall, deep within the castle, the Master of Assassins sat waiting for us on a low dais in an ornate but delicate throne. He was dressed in dark green robes of silk, with a sash about his waist. Over a dozen armed men stood at the ready, a handful behind the lord of Alamut, the rest arrayed about the hall. It smelled of incense and roasted spiced goat.

Still, he made us wait while he attended to some other business with clerks until, finally, Hassan was waved over. Silence fell over the hall while the leader of the Assassins glared at Hassan.

Rukn al-Din Khurshah had been the leader for a few months only. His father before him had lost his mind due to his great age, and so the respected lord, who was like a king and a pope to them all in one, was murdered. A murder committed from practical necessity, as the leadership has always passed from father to son upon the death of the elder.

Necessary and practical though it was, the new lord, Rukn al-Din Khurshah, had convicted the murderer and had him executed himself. It was likely that Rukn al-Din had ordered, or at the least encouraged, the regicide and everyone knew it. And yet the assassin still had to pay the price. It seemed strange to me, cold and improper, and yet it had secured for the Ismailis a secure succession during a time of great crisis.

Rukn al-Din was in the prime of his life, perhaps in his mid-thirties. His beard was thick and luxuriously oiled. He was not a tall man and his body looked soft; shoulders narrow and belly bulging.

Over the decades in the Holy Land, I had picked up fragments of Arabic, the language of the Saracens. Abdullah had grudgingly taught me a few phrases and the names for common items during our travel across the steppe and our stay in Karakorum. I had picked up a lot more during our return toward the west with the Assassins, listening to them work, joke, and argue when camp was made and struck.

Still, I struggled to make sense of the words that were traded by Hassan and Rukn al-Din. But with what little I did know, and by watching closely the gestures and expressions of the two men, it became clear that Hassan was angry. Furious, even. Yet, out of respect, he contained that fury.

Not only Hassan, but Rukn al-Din grew angry, too.

I was able to discern that much of it was directed at the foreigners Hassan had brought into their midst.

It was not long before Hassan turned to me.

"I have tried to explain to him," Hassan said. "What you are. What you can do. What you could do to us. He does not understand. And so he wishes to see your abilities demonstrated for himself."

I sighed and nodded. I had expected it and began to bare my arm so that I could cut myself, and so this Rukn al-Din could watch it heal.

"No, Richard," Hassan said. "Not those abilities."

Three of the bodyguards stepped forward from their positions by Rukn al-Din, and drew their swords before me, well out of striking distance.

"My weapons and armour are outside," I said. "Down with my companions."

Hassan drew his own sword and handed it to me, hilt first. "I have seen you admiring this blade. Now, you may try it for yourself."

I felt a need to protest. Explain to him, to all of them, that I had never trained with one of those long-curved blades, only played with them. That I always trained to fight in armour, with helm and shield. Always, I favoured thrusting with the point of my blade and yet there I was, expected to fight, unarmoured, with a strange weapon.

Against three men.

Three of the feared fedayin Assassins, men who trained to kill without thought to their own lives, and these three young men were considered skilful and steady enough to serve as bodyguard to their king.

It was not possible, for almost any man, to fight alone against even two competent opponents. The obvious strategy is to strike with speed at one man, to drive him away from the other and to finish him before the other can bring his blade to bear.

What good strategy there was for a man to fight three others, without armour, I could not imagine.

But I did not voice my protest. It would have achieved nothing.

And anyway, I had been more than a man for some time.

"What are the rules of this bout?" I asked Hassan while I looked along the blade to discern any sign of existing damage.

"If you die," he said, "you lose."

"Ah," I said, nodding while I flourished the blade to test the handling of it. "I have played this game before."

No signal, nor even any warning, was given.

They all three attacked at once.

Their blades slashed at me as I leapt back, swept my sword up and swatted away one of them with the flat of my blade. While Hassan fled to the edge of the hall, two circled quickly to either side of me while the third threatened to attack me head on.

The only sensible thing to do was to retreat back. Only, that would end with me cornered and attacked on three sides at once.

After feinting that retreat, I leapt forward, charging the man in front. Though I surely moved faster than any man he had ever faced before, he was not so surprised as I would have liked.

His blade slashed into my left shoulder. As he pulled the cut, he stepped back and to the side with well-practised footwork, and his blade sliced through the sleeves of my tunic, and my shirt, and deep into my flesh. Pain lanced through me, a sharp ache that took my breath away.

The clever move did not save him.

I sliced up and across his throat, pulling the edge across the front of his neck. He jerked back, so the cut was not as deep or as wide as I wanted but it was enough to cut into his windpipe and one of the great veins beside it. It would take him some time to die, and he was still dangerous. Using our momentum, I grabbed hold of his sword arm and twisted as I stepped by him, throwing him back at the men behind me.

Even as I did so, the tip of a blade sliced into the back of my skull, hitting bone but sheering off.

The swordsman was on me, following up with another blow. His cuts fast and precise, I parried with the strange curved sword in my hand and cursed my lack of a shield.

From the corner of my eye, I saw the other man leap over his falling comrade and come at me from the flank.

Both twirled their weapons, flashing and frightening by their display of mastery.

Why should I fear a blade?

Years of training had taught me how to defend. Any fool can learn to swing a sword, my old teachers had told us, but a great knight is one who can protect himself from harm. Any cut could be fatal, and often was, even if it was weeks later due to infection. Any blade thrust into gaps in your armour would very likely kill you quite quickly, assuming it severed an artery. Training that gets into you when you are young gets in deep. Old habits die hard.

And there was the fear of pain, of course. An animal fear, barely controllable, that says get away from harm, from injury, from some danger or other that you know, down to your bones, will be agonising. The pain from a sword cut will take your breath away, buckle your legs, cause you to weep and to shake in spite of your desire to be virtuous.

But I could heal my wounded flesh in mere moments. And I had already felt so much pain in my life that it was like an old friend.

I forced myself forward onto him and ground my teeth as his sword slashed me across the chest. Before he could retreat, I grabbed him by the upper arm, slashing at his groin while in close and butting his face. While he reeled, I stabbed my sword into his guts, twisting and tearing it out. The foul stench of hot shit filled the air as his intestines popped out through the gash.

Sometimes, your body takes an action before you realise it. And so it was as I turned, slid sideways and slashed behind me at the last man, whose own blade missed me by a hair's breadth. Mine caught him across the face, the impact from his skull jarring my arm. It was a poor cut, but it did the job and he retreated, wailing, his sword clattering on the tile floor. I had cut through one of his eyes and his nose was a bloody, flapping piece of gristle dangling from his face.

Someone in the hall shouted, perhaps a cry to let the man live.

But the smell of blood filled my head and I would not be denied.

I seized the man, though he flailed and attempted to flee, and slipped the curved point of my blade into his neck, slicing through the skin. While he still attempted to fight me off, I dropped my sword and grabbed him with both hands. I bent my head and placed my lips around the wound on his throat.

Oh, such sweet relief. That hot, rich blood pumped into my mouth and I gulped it down, mouthful after mouthful. It surged to fill my mouth, I swallowed, and another pulse flooded between my lips as I held him close, pressed to me like a lover. The man's black beard tickled my nose, and I could smell olive oil on his skin and garlic in his breath. His strong, young heart beat frantically, not yet knowing it was dead.

My belly felt good. Warm and heavy, the strength of it spreading through me. It was not long before I had my fill, and I dropped the dying man. He was as limp as a rag doll, and his ruined face hideous to see.

The other two men lay dead also. Under my feet, the white tiled floor was smeared with blood and dark pools of it continued to spread from beneath the bodies.

Around the edges of the hall, the other bodyguards stood with their own blades drawn, staring at me, some with disgust, others wore a look of horror. All would have liked to kill me, I have no doubt.

Rukn al-Din held a cloth over his mouth and nose. His eyes were narrowed above them, glaring at me with malice. He muttered something and the guards around me advanced.

This is it, I thought. This is the place where I die.

I took a quick step and scooped up my sword.

They all froze.

"Drop your sword," Hassan shouted. "They will not kill you."

"I do not believe you," I said, turning and turning to keep an eye on all of them. Yet they did not advance.

Rukn al-Din shouted at me but my Arabic was not good enough to understand.

"He says you will come to no harm," Hassan explained, walking forward into the blood with his hands spread apart. "He wishes to see if your wounds have healed, as I told him they would."

It seemed plausible. Anyway, even if I killed every man in the room, I would never escape from Alamut alive.

I dropped my sword and held out my arms as they seized me. Hands tore at my tunic and my undershirt, baring my shoulder and my chest to the Master of Assassins. Water was brought and they washed the dried blood away. My skin was marked with pink lines where the cuts had been. Even these seemed to fade while I watched. They turned me around and scrubbed the blood from my hair with their fingers.

Finally, they were waved away and I stood, naked from the waist up, wet and bloody. Rukn al-Din held the cloth over his mouth and nose while he stared at me, thinking. It felt as though I was being examined like livestock.

I decided that, should he order that I be led to the slaughter, I would be sure to kill him, Rukn al-Din, before they could do so.

But he muttered something to Hassan, leapt up and hurried from the stinking, filthy room, trailed by a handful of his men.

Hassan rushed forward, grabbed my elbow and dragged me from the room while the remaining men glared.

"What did he say?" I asked Hassan in the corridor. "What is happening now?"

When we reached the antechamber where his own men waited, Hassan paused and turned to me.

"I am allowed to hold you and your people at my castle, Firuzkuh. He orders me to use your blood to make thirty of my men into immortals. And with them, perhaps, he will allow us to infiltrate the Mongol army and kill Hulegu."

Hassan's Castle Firuzkuh was a journey of two days from Alamut. I was struck, time and again, by the beauty of the place. The lushness of the fields, the prosperity of the people who worked them.

"It will be very different in winter," Hassan explained when I spoke of it to him. "The snows will fill the passes. Travel will be impossible."

"Every winter?"

"It never fails. It is one of our greatest defences. Every settlement must be stocked with enough food and fuel every winter. We are well used to sieges here. God besieges us in our homes for months on end, every year."

"That is why you want the Mongols to make a concerted attack. You want the snow to kill them for you."

"The Mongols are hard people," Hassan said. "The hardest, perhaps. But if they are caught out in the mountains when the snows come, thousands of them will die while we sit content in our fortifications. It was always the plan of 'Alā' ad-Dīn Muḥammad, who was the lord of all Ismailis for my entire life, and who sent me on my embassy to Mongke Khan. He wished to delay and delay, to frustrate the Mongols for long enough that they would turn their attention elsewhere."

"Why would they do that?"

"Every time the Great Khan dies, a successor must be chosen. All campaigns are called off, all leaders return to their homeland to take part in the choosing. It has taken many years on previous choosings. It has saved Christendom when they turned back decades ago."

"And that was why your old king sent so many fedayin to kill Mongke. Not just for vengeance but because it could save your people. But you called them all off? So that you could leave with me and my companions. Why would you do that?"

"I swore that I would do it," Hassan said. "But it was not true. I could not call them off, even if I wished to. They are everywhere and I have no way to contact them all."

"You lied?"

He nodded. "Lying is a moral act if it leads to furthering the aims of our people."

Stephen was trailing close behind me, listening keenly as he often was. "This concept is known as taqiyya, is it not?"

Hassan turned to glance over his shoulder. "Where did you hear that word?"

Stephen nodded over to Abdullah, who was walking beside Khutulun, babbling away at her. "Abdullah told me about it. He said taqiyya means you can lie if there is a good reason for it, and by the law of the Mohammedans, it is no crime." Stephen smiled, as smug as always. He never discovered that the possession of knowledge was in itself worth very little.

"No," Hassan said, scowling. "It is much more complicated than that."

Thomas muttered in my ear. "These people have no honour."

Firuzkuh Castle and surrounding settlement supported a little over two hundred fighting men, and a little over five hundred people in total, including children. It was not on the highest peak, nor was it a massive fortification. But it was a remarkable place, with four towers. Two of them squat and square, and two taller and round. Like the other Ismaili castles I had seen, Firuzkuh was built expertly into the landscape. A steep and rather narrow approach from the front would confine an attacking force between a steep cliff and a jutting rock wall. To the rear, a bleak plateau that was only accessible via long and difficult paths across the jagged mountains.

Even though he had been away so long, and others had been in command of the place for years, the transition of power back to Hassan was seamless. More than that, it seemed to be a happy homecoming for the people and Hassan both. They loved him.

We were tolerated and welcomed with cold courtesy. Given fresh clothes, good food. They even had people move out of their rooms within the castle so that Eva and I could have private quarters within the walls. The others of our party shared rooms near ours.

"We are prisoners as much as guests," Thomas pointed out on our first night.

Stephen was simply amazed by the wonders that he saw. "What a place this is to be prisoners, though, is it not? Did you see the stores they have in place already to resist a siege? Rooms and rooms. That tank with the honey, it was big enough to swim in, I swear it was."

Eva rubbed her eyes. "Sometimes I wonder how you can know so much about the world and yet still be such a fool. But then I remember that you are very young."

Stephen did not like that. "In what way am I being foolish?"

"You do not seem to understand the danger that we are in," Eva said.

"Hassan loves Richard. He would not let anything happen to us."

Thomas scoffed. "He wishes to use Richard for his own purposes."

"Still then," Stephen said. "It is a fair trade. Sanctuary and support in exchange for... the Gift. Richard's Gift bestowed on thirty of the men here."

"And the Mongols," Eva said, smiling at him. "You are not concerned about the fact that a hundred thousand crazed barbarians are bearing down on us?"

"This castle is safe. Who could assault such a fortress?"

Thomas and I glanced at each other. He pinched the bridge of his nose. "This is a strong site. Sheer cliffs on two sides, steep approach from the front and a Godless wilderness to the rear. Good walls and sturdy towers. They have catapults. But do you think two hundred men could resist ten thousand, Stephen? We could kill five hundred, a thousand, five thousand. If they were determined, they could take us here."

Stephen shook his head. "They are marching into a trap, you heard what Hassan said. If they arrive soon, the winter snows will trap them in the mountains. If they arrive late, we will have months more to prepare. To make more men into Richard's immortals, if need be. More like you, Thomas. Make enough, perhaps, to defeat the Mongols?"

Thomas cleared his throat. It sounded as though he growled. "And that is what we wish to do, is it? These people are Saracens. Mohammedans. Do you wish for them to be made stronger? They are our enemy. Christ's enemy. We should do nothing to help them."

"But these Assassins are the enemy of all other Saracens. The kingdoms of Egypt, and of Syria especially. Mortal enemies. If we help to make the Assassins powerful, they could even help us defeat the Saracens in the Holy Land. With them attacking from the rear, with thousands of immortals, who knows, we could even take back Jerusalem."

We groaned and shouted him down.

"Your flights of fancy are of no help to us here," Thomas said to him.

We soon retired but I could not help but dwell on Stephen's words. It was the sheer ambition of it that struck me so powerfully. My brother seemed always to be putting into motion such grand plans, as evil as they were. He created for himself a religious sect in Palestine, preying on travellers and caravans to build his strength until he could do more, such as take over a town, then a city. Even the Holy Land itself.

And then he worked to crush the King of England, creating immortals from men like the Archbishop, and the sons of great lords. He poisoned King John and might have won control of the Crown, or at least a great part of the country for himself.

Now, he had made more immortals in the heart of the most barbaric and evil force the world had ever known. What is more, he had in some way turned them toward the Holy Land, and then meant to drive them on to conquer Christendom. If his plans succeeded, then William could end up as the King of France, or the Holy Roman Emperor, and he could rule and rule for centuries until the Second Coming of Christ.

The sheer audacity of it all. It was a sign of his madness, certainly, and his hubris.

And what was I doing? Wandering around from place to place, living the life of a mercenary, a freelancer, trying to shelter Eva from men who would do her harm.

I was ever afraid of being separated from her so that she would be forced to drink the blood of another and risk being caught and killed. A restless life. It was not a vain one, I had a purpose. But William always felt so far away.

The rage I had felt for him in my youth had faded. My pursuit of him had long ago turned to duty over emotion. No doubt someone like Thomas would say that was only proper but it had come to feel like an empty existence. Or, if not empty, then a small one.

What Stephen had suggested, in his naive way, was to use my gift to do something grand. To use the Assassins to bring down the Saracen armies of Syria and Egypt.

But Thomas was right. Say I did make a hundred, or a thousand, or ten thousand blood drinking immortals and they conquered the enemies of Christendom. What then? How could I ever hope to control them? To bind them to me?

William intended to set the Mongols loose on Christendom and even he would not be able to control them. And so he must simply not care about the consequences. He wanted to sow chaos, he wanted wanton and random destruction, for then he could take more power for himself from the rubble and dust of the kingdoms that had fallen.

Was that ultimately what separated me from my brother? Not a lack of imagination or ambition but a fear of chaos? A preference for law over anarchy?

Or was that simply another way of saying that I lacked imagination and ambition?

Was William committing the sins of greed and pride while I was consumed with envy, and mired in slothfulness?

Either way, I had sworn to Hassan that I would turn thirty of his men, and I was committed to that path for the time being.

We would begin in the morning.

And so it was that I began to turn a group of Hassan's fedayin into blood-drinking immortals, like Eva and Thomas. And like Hulegu and his men.

In the open interior courtyard, Hassan stood on the wall, looking down and explained it to all of them. I stood back and to one side, watching the sea of faces turned up to their lord.

That they would no longer be able to father children. That they would need to drink human blood, at least twice every week, to avoid turning raving mad. That bright sunlight would hurt their eyes and burn their skin more than it ever had before. But in return they would become faster, stronger, and, by drinking blood after battle, would be able to heal wounds rapidly.

The fedayin were men already committed to dying for their people and so Hassan had more volunteers than we needed.

"I am tempted to take more," Hassan said when the full count was made. "We will need men to father the children of the next generation so I cannot turn them all. And Rukn al-Din commanded that we make thirty but perhaps I shall make fifty, and report that we have made thirty."

"Is that taqiyya again?" I said. He did not like me using that word. "You and I agreed to thirty also. I swore to turn thirty, and that is what I shall do. Afterwards, perhaps I will make more. We shall see."

Now that Hassan was in his home again, he became ever more like the great lord he truly was. Already, he was unused to any resistance to his orders and while he looked calmly at me, his nostrils flared and I was sure he would argue.

But he nodded and we had our thirty men.

"Each man will need to be drained of blood, down to the point of unconsciousness," I explained. "But he shall need enough strength to swallow a pint of my blood."

"A pint?"

"An eighth of a gallon," I explained, though it did not make sense to him. "About this much," I said, making a shape with my hands to indicate the volume. "Roughly speaking, that seems to be what it takes."

"And it must happen at night?"

"I have only ever seen it done at night. I do not know if it will work during the day. Perhaps one of your men would like to take the risk, and then we may discover the truth of it?"

"We will do it at night. How many can you make in one night?"

"Losing blood weakens me. I would prefer to do no more than one, but I suppose I could do two. If you supply me with blood to drink in between."

"Of course," he said.

For he had also requested volunteers from the women and non-combatants of his lands. These folk would supply our company of immortals with blood from their veins. There were over a hundred of them all told, each one bleeding into a bowl every few days.

Eva and Thomas too would no longer be reliant on small volumes from my veins. And though Thomas liked to pretend moral outrage and claimed that it turned his stomach to think he was drinking the unholy blood from the veins of a Saracen woman, he guzzled the stuff down keenly enough. Between drinking from me or from them, he knew it was the lesser of two evils.

That night, I pierced a vein in my wrist and filled a jug with it while an Ismaili fedayin lay on a table nearby, drained of much of his own. Lamplight filled the room, along with the smell of blood. Unground seed corn filled the spaces between the floor slabs. We were down in the depths of the castle by the storerooms, away from where people lived and worked, which felt appropriate to what we were doing. To what I was creating.

The man was named Jalal. He was in his forties and a leader and warrior of some standing who would be in command of the thirty men. He had insisted on being the first.

Jalal was as pale as chalk when I lifted his head and commanded him to drink. He barely had strength enough to swallow.

Hassan hovered at my shoulder. "Is this correct?" he asked. "To be so weak? This is how it is done?"

I ignored him, and tipped the cup up, emptying the last of it into the man's mouth. Jalal coughed with his throat full of blood and it seemed for a few moments that he would drown in it until I turned him on his side and some of the blood was coughed out onto the floor. He breathed easy again and I pushed him onto his back.

"Will that lost blood cause the ritual to fail?" Hassan asked.

"The ritual?" I asked. "I do not know. I am sure that all will be well."

"What is the next step?" he asked.

"Now we wait," I said.

We looked down at Jalal, who—pale and cold as he was—seemed to be dead but for the occasional flickering of his eyes beneath the lids.

He lived. Before morning, he opened his eyes and said he was thirsty.

We gave him blood to drink.

For a month, I turned one fedayin every night, and on some nights, I turned two of them. Out of the first thirty, we lost eight men. The first of the eight stopped breathing before I could get enough of my blood into them, and so we bled others less. And yet those ones who were not taken to the very edge of death were more likely to die from violent convulsions. They would thrash about in spasms, their skin hot to the touch until they moved no more. One man opened his eyes in the morning but remained otherwise insensible for days, and neither blood nor fresh air nor anything else could elicit a response. And so, Hassan cut his throat.

Despite all this, finding replacements for the eight failures was no problem. The fedayin did not hesitate.

Thomas urged me to leave the eight dead men, and argued that it was within the letter of my agreement with the Assassins, and yet it allowed us to limit the number of immortals. But that seemed petty to me and would create bad blood between me and Hassan, which I strived to avoid.

I did not like being so beholden to him, or to the Assassins in general. For the first time in many years, I thought back to Ashbury Manor, and my time as lord there. It was no grand place, certainly nothing like a castle, but it was mine and I had servants, and I had knights and squires, all looking to me to command them. And I thought how that place was nothing compared to what I could have, should I so choose. What if I could find men who would serve me, as Hassan had his fedayin? With a fortified home, with immortal followers, I could become a great lord and I would be secure, finally. All I needed was an overlord who would protect me, who would help me to fend off rumours of my agelessness, and of the blood drinking that would no doubt leak out.

But what Christian lord would do such a thing? Unless he was an unchristian man. Perhaps I could offer the gift of my blood to a king from distant yet civilised lands. Somewhere like Armenia, or Georgia, I thought. Or even the semi-barbaric lands of the Rus.

And yet, an immortal king would have more power than I would have. And such a man could have me killed whenever he wished, so what kind of freedom was that?

I could make myself into a king.

The thought popped into my head, clear as a bell. The obvious end of such a line of reasoning.

"If you did that," Eva whispered to me, on the night that I spoke my thoughts to her, "then how would you be different to William?"

"No, no," I said. We sat on stools beside a table in the corner of our quarters. "I would do it, not from hubris or love of power over others, but only for our safety, Eva." I lowered my voice and took one of her hands in both of mine. "Imagine us, sitting on thrones, in the hall of some castle. In a Christian land, perhaps one in the East. Or in the Thracian kingdoms. We could make a kingdom in those hills and dark forests. The Hungarian mountains, surrounded by wolves and bears. No one could touch us."

"I think all your bloodletting has drained the wits from your head," she said, patting my hands with her free one. "Even if we could take power somewhere, a king rules with the consent of his people, whether he knows it or not. Do you think they would still support you after fifty years on that throne? A hundred? How long before they rose up to dethrone you, in your own castle? And those lands you just mentioned, you think they are defensible? They have all been crushed by the Mongols. Is that who you would like as your overlords?"

I sighed. "Are you not tired of all this? Running from place to place? With no home?"

She looked at me and spoke softly. "For a long time."

"So what do we do?" I asked her.

Taking a deep breath, she hesitated. "I do not know if you have ever asked me that before."

"Of course I have."

"I understand that you do not wish to be beholden to any man who is not worthy of your loyalty. You are an English knight. You want to serve a good king, and a king of England, too. But we are where we are. And we must do what we have set out to do," she said.

"I think," I said, then stopped myself. I did not speak for a long time but Eva simply sat and waited. How well she knew me. "I think, that my hatred for William has faded. It used to burn inside me. Oft times, I feared the sin of wrath would consume me, as I wanted nothing other than to kill him. And that wrath has driven me, driven me to murder and sin. But now..."

"William has done incalculable evil. Murdered your first wife, your brother's family. Who knows how many other woman and children. He murdered my father. He murdered King John. He must be killed. And who can do it other than you? You have said the Archbishop of Jerusalem told you that God made you this way so that you can put an end to William's evil. You do not need to feel wrath to do this. All passion fades. Richard, you are a sinful man, that is true. But since the time I first met you, to this moment now, I could always see that your heart is ruled by justice. You do not need passion, or wrath, to fulfil your oath and deliver justice to William. You will do it because it is your duty."

"What about my duty to Christendom?" I asked. "I have made thirty immortals for our enemies. Surely, I should turn only men such as Thomas. Knights, dedicated to preserving our lands, our people, against the Saracens and all other enemies. This is wrong, is it not?"

"Thomas has filled your heart with dread because he is a fearful old man who wants the world to stay the same as it ever was. And Stephen has filled your head with grand ambitions because he is young and wishes to remake the world with himself as some great part of it. They are both lesser men than you, and they will do as you say. They are followers of yours, Richard. Ignore their fretting and stay the course. We will use the Assassins to kill Hulegu and the other immortals. They cannot be allowed to live. Once that is done, and William is dead, we can find a place in this world."

"What would I do without you, Eva?" I asked.

I did not know it then but one day soon, I would find out.

The night air was cold but there was little wind. The waxing moon was half full and I could see across the rocks of the mountainside down to the faint shape of Firuzkuh Castle. Summer was all but over and winter was well on the way.

I could not see the men I was stalking but I could hear them, and I could smell their stink. They were down in the deep shadows under a steep cliff side. I could probably have climbed down it in the daylight, wearing light clothing. But at night, in my armour, I knew I would fall. So I began to work my way around, moving slowly and as quietly as I could.

My helm was back at the castle, as it would have blocked my hearing and sight too much. Instead, I wore my mail coif that covered my head and neck. My body was protected by my thick, padded linen gambeson and over that my mail hauberk. Over the mail, I had a cotton overcoat in the Persian style that fitted me perfectly, and I wore it to reduce the noise and cover any shine from my armour.

I had to move deliberately as I approached my prey, and yet still I kicked the occasional stone downhill or snagged myself on brittle bushes. No doubt the men below me could hear something of the noise, and I hoped that they would. If I made too much noise, surely they would think I was drawing them into a trap, and they would be wary. So I had to judge it right. They would expect a Christian knight to be a clumsy oaf, and so that was what I had to be.

In truth, it was not a difficult part to play. Put me in a damp woodland and I will slither through it like a wolf. I will slip from outcrop to boulder in the hills of Derbyshire but even after months of practice, in that stony land, with powdery sand underfoot I made for a poor Assassin.

And I knew that, in the dark, their eyesight would be better than mine.

They leapt out at me, striking fast and hard. Not with cries but with grunts of effort and hard breathing.

I fended them off as best I could, retreating back up the hill as they came at me. They were six, crowding themselves in an effort to be the one to strike the killing blow, and I backed myself against an outcrop of sandstone twice the height of a man. Cornered as I was, they attacked hesitantly, wary of my skill.

One rushed in and I cracked him on the head, just as the one behind lunged at me. I batted the weapon aside and stamped on his knee, breaking it. He cried out, the harsh throaty sound splitting the night.

They fell back a few steps to collect themselves, and the four that were uninjured took the lead, brandishing their clubs.

Finally, I heard a sound above on the rock, and Eva leapt from it. Her silhouette flitting above me like a bat. She landed behind the Assassins and smashed two of them before any could react. And Thomas rushed from the flank and crashed into another, bringing him down with the weight of himself and his armour. I jumped forward and brought my club down on the others.

We beat them down into submission, and they begged for us to stop. They lay whimpering in the shadows.

"You did well," I said to them in Arabic. "But you should not have left your position."

"We need blood, master," one of them said. "To heal."

"And this is why you must always win. Every fight, you can either get weaker or you can get stronger," I lectured. "When the Mongols surround us, you must drink the blood from those that you kill, and thus heal your wounds, and gain their strength. Do you understand?"

"Yes, master," they said, holding their heads and bodies.

"I think my leg is broken," one said.

"Well then," I said. "You should get yourself back to the castle and ask for blood, do you not think? Go, now."

After they scrambled to their feet, Thomas removed his helm. "What did you say to them?" he asked me.

"That they have a lot to learn before they can kill a thousand Mongols apiece."

Eva's shadow moved to my side. Her footsteps were as soft as a cat's. "Few of them are ready. And the Mongols are almost upon us. Perhaps you should turn more of Hassan's men."

Thomas scoffed. "Perhaps we should leave, while we still can."

"Come on," I said. "Let us go home."

Strange, to call it that. But that is what Firuzkuh Castle had become over those months. Gradually, the people had become less hostile and we had grown to see them, not as Saracens, or enemies, but as people. The men laughed and insulted each other as they worked and trained. The women laughed and gossiped as they did their work. Children ran and played, shouting always as if they were deaf, or they thought that all adults were.

Yet there was dread. The dread of the approach of the Mongol armies. Word came to us from the spies and scouts of the Assassins that Hulegu had brought the full might of his armies, over a hundred thousand Mongols, along with that many again of Turkomen and even Christian armies from the subject lands of Georgia and Armenia. Every day, the people talked of the snow that would come and save them, for another winter at least.

And there was something else. Some sense that I had, that many of us outsiders had, that the Assassins were hiding something from us. The feeling had grown over the weeks, and I saw less and less of Hassan. They often steered us away from the sacred parts of the castle, which was to be expected. None of us was a Mohammedan. But even Abdullah was barred from entry to the place of worship, and despite being from Syria, he was a Shiite, which I understood was a doctrine not so far from the teachings of the Ismailis. It even seemed to me like fear, that they were afraid of us going there. Thomas suggested that they had some Christian captives there that they were torturing, but that was pure speculation.

That night, we had just reached our quarters when Stephen rapped on our door and begged entry. It was so late by then that it was almost early, but then Stephen had spent years living as a monk, and they loved to wake in the dark of night, like soldiers.

Eva was removing her armour and he stared at her with his mouth open.

"What do you want, Stephen?" I said.

He tore his eyes away and shut the door behind him.

"I think he means to spend the night," Eva said over her shoulder.

Stephen gulped and came over to me. "Richard, I have discovered what Hassan is hiding."

Eva stopped and turned. "Keep your voice down." She came over, wearing only her undershirt, which was very thin, very loose and quite soaked with sweat.

Stephen cleared his throat, lowered his head and stared at Eva's chest while he spoke. "I do not know the full story, and it has taken days to discover this much. But Hassan has created living quarters for a group of fedayin. Quite separate from our thirty. They train in secret. And the servants are afraid of them. A woman was hurt a few days ago, and one of the old men who brought them water was killed yesterday, although no one will admit it fully. And these men, this new group, they have blood brought to them. Lots of blood."

"What is this?" I said, feeling anger building. "How can this be?"

Eva put a hand on Stephen's shoulder. "Are you certain of this? Be sure that you are because it makes little sense. How have more been created, if Richard did not turn them himself?"

"I am sorry, I do not know," Stephen said.

"Where is Hassan?" I asked him. "In his quarters, asleep?"

Stephen shook his head. "I believe he is with these men now, in the jamatkhana."

I pulled my coif back onto my head and grabbed my sword.

"Ricard," Eva hissed. "Think. Think before you act, here. Our position is precarious."

"I will act now," I said, strapping the sword around my waist.

"At least wait for me to put my armour back on," she said. "I will come with you."

"Put it on but wait here," I said to her. "Get Thomas and the others ready, we may have to flee. Stephen, help Eva and do precisely as she orders, do you understand?"

He wanted to argue, I could see it on his face, and he wanted to come with me.

Eva grabbed his arm. "Help me put my gambeson back on," she said and winked at me over his head.

I nodded to her and strode out, heading across the castle grounds to the jamatkhana. It was their communal hall, the place where they did worship and had other sacred events. It was a place closed to me, but I would force my way inside.

The castle was never quiet, not even at night, and I was seen by a number of people before I was halfway there. Someone or other must have run ahead to raise the alarm, and I was met in the hallway outside a doorway that led to the jamatkhana by Hassan and four of his fedayin.

They were all armed, and armoured.

The four men all had their swords drawn.

"Stop," Hassan shouted. "Halt, stop. Stop, Richard."

"What are you doing here?" I shouted as I came to a stop before Hassan. The men loomed behind him, blocking the way.

"You cannot enter here," Hassan said. "Come, let us return to—"

I was already angry at the deceit, and I was angry at myself for being so naive. For allowing myself to be deceived.

So I drew my sword.

The four fedayin stepped forward and pulled Hassan back behind them.

"I could kill you all," I said in their language. "And go and find out for myself. Is that what you want, Hassan?"

He called for them to lower their swords, and to stand aside. "Come, Richard. I will show you. I do not wish there to be secrets between us. And, if the truth is to be told, I must admit that I may need your help with a large problem... It is best that I show you."

Even though I knew he was not to be trusted, I still went with him. It is right and proper to be wary and to consider that almost any situation in life could be a trap, designed to capture and kill you. But you cannot avoid walking into risk, else you would never take any action worth taking.

Keeping my sword in hand, but the blade tip lowered, I followed Hassan into the jamatkhana. His men surrounded me at all times. As we got closer, the sound of voices and clashing wooden weapons grew louder.

"This is it," Hassan said as we entered the hall. He seemed nervous. "This is the secret I have been hiding from you."

The jamatkhana was like a church for them, and also something like a manor's hall, or a court. But they had turned over that space into what amounted to a bunkhouse. A few lamps in alcoves in the walls cast pools of dim light and left lots in shadow. Two long rows of beds ran down one side, and the other half was open space. A side for sleeping, and a side for training.

Most startling of all was the fact it was filled with raucous fedayin. It was the end of the night, not long before dawn, and they were shouting and fighting. Some men lay on the beds, awake and talking to each other. One man jumped up and down on a bed, laughing while another shouted encouragement. Groups of others stood fighting in the open space. Some wrestled, stripped to the waist or naked, while others sparred with practice swords made from wood.

It smelled strongly of blood. I saw jugs, cups, and bowls on tables or tossed to the floor, which had held the stuff, and some dried stains showed on the floor and even on the walls.

"What have you done, Hassan?" I asked, watching the scene before me. "How have you done this?"

"Please, Richard, you must understand what a dire situation we are in. I have asked you to turn more men. I have all but begged you. You would give me no more than thirty, and I had to have more."

"But how?" I asked him, as much curious as outraged.

He looked apologetic. "We used one of the men you had turned. It was Jalal. And we used his blood to turn these."

I could not believe it. It had never occurred to me that such a thing would be possible.

"And it worked?" I said, my anger turning to horror.

Hassan hesitated. "The blood is not as strong. Almost half the men we tried to turn died. And these immortals are also weaker. Slower than the first generation. But still much stronger than an ordinary man." He scratched his beard. "They are extremely sensitive to sunlight. Even more so than those turned by your blood directly. And they need to drink blood more frequently than the men you turned. They... they never seem to get enough."

"These are not your best men, I take it?" I asked, looking at them acting like fools and madmen.

He shook his head. "These are fine men. I mean... they were. They are themselves when their bellies are full of blood but is not long before they begin to lose their minds. It is like when the men you turn go without for many days, and they become angry, and they lose their control and seek conflict. The only way I am able to maintain discipline is through controlling the supplies of the blood."

"They sound dangerous," I said.

"To our enemies, I hope."

Hassan's betrayal of our agreement was considerable but I should have expected underhand tactics from such a deceitful people. The men slouched and grinned at each other and at me. The amused, smug expressions on their faces reminded me of children who had been caught breaking a petty rule.

They are themselves when their bellies are full of blood but is not long before they begin to lose their minds.

There were endless tales of strange peoples in those days, usually spoken of by ignorant common folk, soldiers, and gentlemen who were inebriated. One reoccurring notion was that the dead would rise from their graves to do harm to the living before returning to their tombs once more. It was said that these cursed people returned from the dead with barely any memory of their former selves, as they were in life. The word that these animated corpses were known by sprang at once into my mind.

Revenants.

Hassan's abominations brought to mind these revenants. Men who had died only to return as violent shadows of their former selves. The notion was so apt that it disturbed me quite profoundly.

I lowered my voice and grasped Hassan by the arm. "These men must be killed."

Hassan tried to pull away but I held him tight. He waved his own men back but they were at my back, ready to run me through. "I need to use every weapon that I have. Or we will all be killed anyway."

"We had an agreement. Thirty men, I said."

He lifted his bearded chin and looked me in the eye. "I must think of my people."

I nodded. "So, this is taqiyya, is it? You can break your oath with a man who has not broken his, and you may say to yourself that you have done it for the good of your people?" He began to reply but I spoke over him. "And how many people can you have left? You must have spent all of your men, now. What of their wives, and their children? Who will make more children in the years to come?"

"There are some men who remain mortal," Hassan said, though I could see it was weighing heavy on him. "But I fear that none of us will live to make more children anyway."

"You must take heart, Hassan. Your people look to you for their strength. Even if you do not feel it, you must show it so that they do not break when the time comes."

He shook his head. "You do not understand. Hulegu has come. The snows are late. Later than they have ever been, and nothing stands in his way. His armies have already besieged our castles to the east. His scouts are already in Alamut Valley."

"Why have you hidden this from me?" My fear made me angry.

He shook his head again, looking down. "We had a messenger from Alamut Castle before sundown." Hassan hesitated, drew me aside and lowered his voice even further. "Rukn al-Din has been summoned by Hulegu. The Mongols command our master to submit to Hulegu. And Rukn al-Din sent his son in his stead."

I was appalled. "He sent his son to the Mongols? Alone? What cowardice."

Hassan waved it away. "The messenger said that it was not truly his own son. I believe it was a bastard son of the last master, Rukn al-Din's father."

I laughed. "He sent a bastard brother of his to Hulegu, to pose as his son. Truly, you people have no honour."

That made Hassan angry. "It is simply a means to delay Hulegu." He took a deep, shaking breath. "As is the agreement that he made with him."

"Tell it, for God's sake."

"Rukn al-Din has agreed with Hulegu that he will submit to the Mongols, in exchange for the life of himself and the lives of his entire family. He has sent orders to all castles to dismantle the towers and battlements, as a symbol of our submission."

I stared, open-mouthed until I came to my senses. "That's more than a bloody symbol, Hassan. He has capitulated. It is over."

"No," he said, forcefully. "No, this is the true use of taqiyya, Richard. He lies to buy us time. There is still hope that the snows will come."

"So you will defy his order, and keep your towers and your battlements intact?"

"I will."

"How many other castles will do the same? And how many will follow his orders to the letter?"

"I do not know."

"So," I said. "The Assassins, feared throughout the world, have given up without a fight?"

"We will fight," Hassan said, raising his voice. "We will fight to the last man."

The men in the hall stopped to stare at us. Some grinned, others glared at me with murder in their eyes. Murder and madness.

"What good is that to me?" I asked. "We were here to kill Hulegu. Now you wish to go down fighting? Turn your men against Hulegu, now. Send away what women and children you can spare, save at least some of your people."

His lip curled, as if tasting bitterness. "Send them where? Every castle will be surrounded before long."

"Your people have castles in Syria."

"That is a thousand miles from here. It is too dangerous."

"More dangerous than being slaughtered by the Mongols when they take this place?"

The truth was, I cared very little for those Saracen women and children. At least, I would not allow myself to do so. But I wanted Hassan to focus on attack, not defence.

"They would never survive the journey. They could be taken by anyone before they reached Syria."

He was right. A group of women and children on foot would be snapped up by the first warband that came across them, whether Christian, Saracen or Mongol.

"But you must fight," I said. "Surely, you see that? If you submit, you are all dead anyway."

"Some of us would be made into slaves. We would survive."

"A few of your women, the youngest and prettiest perhaps, made into wives for those stinking barbarians? You call that survival?" I lowered my voice. "Send the first of the immortals with me and my people. We will make a break for Syria, fight our way through if we have to. We will come up with a way to get at Hulegu there."

He shook his head. "There is still hope. I believe that Master Rukn al-Din has a plan for our survival. He is playing for time. Why do such a thing unless there was a course of action that he has planned? No, none of us flee until there is no hope left."

I acquiesced. Likewise, I put aside my revulsion for his revenants for the time being and did not seek the conflict that would have arisen from slaughtering them, or for arguing further for their destruction. I chose the peaceful path for I would need guides to take me over the mountains when everything fell apart.

And I was increasingly certain that it would not be long before all hope for the Assassins was truly lost.

***

It was November 1256 when Hulegu finally lost patience with the delays and evasions from Rukn al-Din.

The Grand Master was given a final command to appear—in person, no proxies—, which he declined to do. And Hulegu's final message to Rukn al-Din stated that, despite the promises of submission, and the fact that towers and battlements at key castles were being dismantled, he did not believe that the master truly intended to submit.

The snows did not come. Even more than Rukn al-Din's pathetic and humiliating attempts at stalling for time did not dismay Hassan as much as the failure of the snows.

"God has forsaken us," he said, and many of his men said the same.

It was bitterly cold in the hills, despite the lack of heavy snows. Flurries would be whipped up by the biting winds and the icy flakes would slice into exposed skin from all angles, including from below. Mongol scouts roamed the hills, and we busied ourselves laying ambushes, day and night. Those few we captured alive we questioned thoroughly. Often, we encouraged them with the application of heated steel to delicate parts of their bodies, but they rarely knew very much that we could not discover through our own scouting, and through communication with other castles.

But one by one, those castles were cut off and surrounded.

The Assassin's castles were particularly well equipped to deal with sieges and most had at least one mangonel mounted upon a wall or tower so it could loose stones at attackers from a distance.

The biggest castles, at Alamut and the other regional centres, were equipped with the latest-style catapults, which were devices that Christendom called counterweight trebuchets. With such engines, we could throw massive boulders down onto the attackers to break up their assaults, harass their siege works and, ideally, smash their own trebuchets and engines, and break their assault towers.

By using those weapons, the Ismaili Assassins were employing the most powerful siege engines in the world. Even the siege masters of distant Cathay could not throw stones of such sizes as these were capable of. But the Mongols had something that no one else west of China had yet employed effectively in warfare.

Gunpowder.

From across the valley, well-hidden in the rocks, I watched the enemy mangonel throw something like a keg toward the castle of Nevizar. The small black shape tumbled slowly in the air as it hurtled up the hill from the Mongol siege lines. I lost sight of the object as it closed on the castle. Then, a flash of light and smoke and dust flew apart from the base of the wall. A few moments later, an almighty bang sounded, making us all jump in fright. The explosion echoed from the peaks. When the smoke cleared and the dust settled, the wall of the castle appeared unharmed.

"What in the name of God is that?" I said.

"I have heard of this," Stephen said beside me, for he had begged to journey with us to witness the Mongol forces that were pushing into Alamut Valley. "It is made with certain substances and creates an artificial fire that can be launched over long distances. A monk in Acre told me that by only using a very small quantity of this material, much light can be created, accompanied by that horrible fracas. He claimed it was possible with it to destroy a town or an army. But, see, it appears to do almost no damage to the walls. A simple stone launched from the same mangonel does more to wreak destruction upon the fortifications. I wonder why they use the artificial fire at all?"

Thomas scoffed. "Did you not hear the noise, young Stephen? Did it not stir your heart? Such a noise and us so far distant from the source of it. What do you think it would be like to be a man inside that castle? To be a man upon that wall?"

Eva's eyes shone as she stared down at the scene. "Imagine that fire, burning in that fashion, in the midst of us here. If one of those casks fell at our feet, how do you think we would fare, Richard?"

Over the decades, I had taken terrible wounds and healed them all. I feared decapitation, and I feared losing a limb. But such injuries were not very likely in the course of ordinary combat.

The sight of that Mongol bomb, however, awakened an old, mortal's fear of sudden death. More, it was a fear of the flesh and bone of my body being blown apart like the stones and twigs that weapon threw out across the mountainside with every detonation.

"I would prefer not to face such a thing, my dear, it is true. But we must attack all the same."

The detachment from the Mongol army was perhaps only five thousand strong, and yet that was a great many men more than we had. The most forward group encamped below us leading the attack numbered about a thousand and even that many would crush us easily.

Messages had flown back and forth across the free castles of the Alamut region and Hassan had urged his fellow leaders to make an attack on the Mongols while they could yet do so. As well as my own companions, I had brought the thirty immortals, who were steady men and Hassan had forced the thirty revenants on us also. Although they were dangerous, the immortal fedayin kept the revenants under control. And I kept my own people far away from them.

"Where are they?" Thomas muttered, looking up and down the valley. We were expecting a coordinated attack to begin but I was beginning to wonder whether any of the other castles had sent the detachments that they had promised.

"They should have been in position and ready to attack at first light," Eva said, looking up at the pale sun as a cloud passed across it. "If they are not here by now, why should we expect them to come at all?"

"Ever since I could remember," Thomas said, "the Assassins were spoken of in hushed tones. They were masters of death in the Holy Land. Men even feared their daggers in Rome and in Paris. And now I am witness to their complete lack of interest in fighting for their own survival."

"What can anyone do in the face of this?" Stephen said.

"Do you mean to say you would not fight to the death to protect England?" Thomas said, looking closely at him.

Stephen's eyes took on a faraway look. Above, clouds gathered quickly, as they often did in the mountains. Pale grey, swirling and thick, as though the sky was liquid lead.

"Well," I said, "if no one else shows then there is nothing we can do. Even with so many immortals, we would be too heavily outnumbered." Hard words to utter, for I was dying for a fight. I wanted to kill those Mongols and being abandoned by the other Assassins was infuriating.

"If there is no battle today," Eva said, and glanced over her shoulder, "then your immortals are going to be deeply disappointed."

"You too, no?" I said. "Thomas, also, I would wager you were looking forward to guzzling some Mongol blood." He ignored me, pretending that he was above such things. "But the immortals will accept it. It is the revenants, Hassan's mad blood drinkers, that we will have to contain. They will not listen to reason."

"When the blood hunger is upon you," Eva said, "reason is beyond your reach."

Thomas nodded to himself as she spoke.

And that hunger, that madness, meant they were almost as dangerous to our own side as to the enemy. It was as if they were no longer themselves, or not in their right minds, and the blood satiated them for so short a time. Whenever their bellies were not filled with blood, most of them delighted in petty violence and thrilled at the suffering of others. That was not so unusual in soldiers, but it was their lack of self-control that concerned me as their notional commander. In fact, the only thing that had kept them subdued and under the cover of the rocks and their cloaks was the sunlight, which they could not stand at all in midday and disliked intensely even on a grey winter morn.

It grew dark even as I pondered what to do about getting them all back to Hassan's castle without having to kill many of them. A light snow began to fall all across the valley.

"Oh, God," Eva said. "Richard."

The revenants had broken away and were descending the mountainside. Heading right toward the flank of the siege engines.

Down in the bottom of the valley, roaming Mongol patrols at the edge of the enemy formations spotted the approach of the group of Assassin fedayin. We watched from high on the side of the hill as Mongol horsemen moved to intercept. They did not move with haste. Why would they? They would have seen a group of around thirty men, on foot. And they were approaching a thousand.

"Should we flee?" Stephen asked. "When the Mongols are done with them, might they not search for others?"

"There is no rush," I said. "And I wish to see how long before they are slaughtered."

"At least we will be free from their madness now," Thomas said.

He hated the revenants more than anyone. I believe it was because he was unhappy with becoming a blood-drinking immortal. He had stayed as himself, but he feared the madness that he knew would come with the blood-starvation. Hassan's revenants, blood-mad and inhuman, reminded Thomas of what he could become, what he would certainly become, should he be deprived of blood. His resentment and fear were reflected onto the others. Also, their behaviour and conduct were objectively despicable.

The Assassin revenants advanced at a slow run, in three rough ranks, keeping a surprisingly disciplined spacing between each man, and the three ranks. A small group of nine horsemen drew near to them and loosed a volley of arrows.

A couple of the Assassins stumbled but their lines did not slow.

Two more volleys had no effect and the horsemen fell back at walking pace, where more of their comrades joined them. Quickly, a group of twenty, and then thirty or more horsemen milled across the line of attack. Most were the lightly-armoured kind, with the small horses, bows and light spears. But a handful were the Mongols in mail armour, steel helms, riding heavier horses and good swords and heavy lances.

The Mongols were in good spirits as they advanced to the charge. It would be little more than sport to them. A brief diversion from the boredom of a siege.

A moment before the first lines clashed, the revenants surged forward and swarmed the horsemen. They yanked the horsemen from their saddles and slashed at the horses, swords, and daggers flashing. Some tried to wheel about and ride away but the immortals chased them down on foot, accelerating faster than the horses, and pulled them to the ground.

"God's bones," Thomas muttered, standing up to get a better look over the rocks.

The revenants ran further toward the loose flank of the Mongol formation while the remaining horsemen scattered. It seemed as though few in the camp had yet noticed they were under attack, and they continued to mill about, busy with normal camp business. The artillery experts brought from distant Cathay continued to work their enormous devices, paying no attention. Even if they noticed, they would trust to their Mongol masters to keep them safe.

In fact, though, there were few soldiers between the revenants and the camp of the siege engineers.

"How far do you think they will get before they are surrounded and swamped?" Stephen asked.

I stood. "Stephen, you will stay here until we return."

"You are not going down there?" Stephen said, looking to Thomas to share his outrage.

Eva jumped up, grinning, and clambered across the rocks. She was already heading downhill when I turned to the leader of my immortals, squatting patiently in the shade behind the jagged boulders.

"Jalal," I said, speaking Arabic. "We will attempt to cut through to the Cathay engineers and kill them all. Then we will retreat."

He nodded and unfolded himself. The fedayin immortal was calm, and as icy as the sky above us, while he related the objective to the rest of his immortal men.

We hurried down the hill. The Assassins were ahead of us, spread out but staying together. Thomas was at my side. Eva in front, moving like a lioness. Orus and Khutulun moved by me and then pulled ahead as if they were racing each other. We slipped and stumbled and charged on.

"Are you," Thomas said, breathing heavily, "certain. About this?"

We both carried our helms in one hand, picking our way down the slope, sometimes using pathways that cut across our route, other times ploughing right through scrub and sliding down powdery scree. After so long feeling frozen, it was exhilarating to be moving.

Why had I ordered us to join an attack that was doomed to fail?

The most cunning course of action was certainly to allow the revenants to be surrounded and killed, as Thomas had earlier said.

There was an opportunity to kill some of the engineers, the experts from Cathay, but they would most likely flee before ever we reached them, and I was exposing myself and my people to great danger. We could kill five men apiece and still we could be swarmed.

Perhaps the only reason was that I was a killer. I loved nothing more than to fight and to kill, and I had been too long without. Far too long.

"We must keep watch on our route of flight," I said to Thomas. It was quite foolish to have such a climb back up a steep hill as our only direction to escape, but then an enemy in pursuit would have to contend with the climb, too.

I looked over my shoulder, to take note of the challenge, and there behind me I saw Stephen. He was a ways behind, stumbling and flailing his arms. Even as I watched he tripped and fell, rolling over in a cloud of dust.

Calling to Thomas, I ran back up to grab the young former monk.

"What in the name of God are you doing?" I said, shouting in his face as I yanked him to his feet.

He winced and cringed away from me.

"There were men up there," he said, breathing hard. "It was not safe to remain."

I looked up at the ridge. No movement.

"There is no one there, Stephen."

He was outraged. "There is. There was. I swear it."

"You saw them?"

He hesitated. "I heard them. Voices. Footsteps."

The hillside above was desolate and wild but nothing moved there.

I clipped Stephen on the head with my mailed hand and shoved my helm into his grasp. "Hold this and stay by me. You bloody fool."

The others had pulled far ahead, though Thomas and Eva had held back so they would not be so separated from me. A riderless horse ran by me. A few steps away, a Mongol warrior dragged himself across the ground. Where he thought he was headed, I had no idea, and I ran over, drew my dagger and dispatched him.

"One cannot be too careful," I said to Stephen, then dragged and prodded him on toward the others.

A thousand Mongols were camped nearby, mostly further down to the valley to my right, and the siege engines and specialists were directly ahead. We were at the head of the encampment and they had not bothered to build any defences.

Perhaps they thought the farmland would be protection enough. Just moments before, looking down from a height, the crisscrossing walls and ditches had seemed trivial, but now I was amongst them I could see how they would slow us down. But the walls would obstruct the Mongols too.

The truth was, they simply believed the Assassins to be fully cowed, and did not expect an attack.

Still, small groups of the enemy massed on our flanks but we pushed further in toward the trebuchets. Those engines continued to be worked. Another bomb arced into the air and exploded against the castle wall.

We leapt over a stone wall and stomped through the remains of a vast orchard. The Mongols had cut down every tree in Alamut Valley, for fuel, and for their siege engines, and also to ensure the Assassins' destruction, come what may. Even if you beat us, such an act said, you will starve next year. Farmhouses and outhouses had been demolished and the stones used as ammunition for the mangonels, and the timbers for the engines themselves.

A thought unbidden flashed into my mind. I pictured the Mongols thoughtlessly demolishing Ashbury manor house and tearing up our apple trees. My home no longer, all men that knew me surely dead, but the thought was pure horror.

"Come on, Stephen," I said, as we caught up to the others. He was panting, sucking air in and wincing. It was impossible to keep with the pace of us immortals. I felt pity for him, then annoyed that he had ignored my command to stay safe on the hillside.

"Richard," Thomas called. "The Assassins have gone ahead. Making a run for the engines."

I nodded. "Let us not become separated from them, we are vulnerable here."

The shouting grew louder as the raised voices of friend and foe swelled in the valley.

"Here they come," Eva shouted. "Cavalry east." She pointed with her sword.

Hooves drummed the hard earth. Arrows whipped through the air, thudded into the ground, clattered against the tree stumps. I covered Stephen with my body and cursed my lack of a shield. At least I thought to grab my helm and pull it down over my head. Horsemen rode toward us, loosing more arrows.

Shoving Stephen down behind a meagre tree stump, Eva and I charged the horsemen. There were eight of them, and they did not retreat. In fact, I was sure I could hear them laughing as they rode to meet us and surround us.

I slashed the face of the nearest horse, cutting a gouge into its face as it reared in pain and terror, and grabbed the shaft of the rider's spear and pulled him from his saddle. As I stabbed down into his guts, something smacked into the back of my helm, the sound enormous in my ears. Only an arrow, but the disorientation allowed another pair of riders to close on me. One, I smacked with the butt end of the spear I still held, but it was an awkward backhanded blow and he held on to his seat and swerved away. I kept moving, circled around the second rider and slashed at his thigh, cutting his leg and his horse's shoulder.

Thomas appeared on the other side of him, stabbing his sword up into the Mongol's body. Orus and Khutulun swarmed another rider and dragged him down. While Orus killed the man, Khutulun leapt onto the horse in a single bound, yanked the beast's head around and charged at another rider with her sword in hand, screaming some challenge or curse.

Eva shouted something from nearby and I ducked and swerved as I ran to her, heart pounding in my chest.

But she was not in distress. She was calling my attention to something.

"There," she said, breathing heavily inside her helm. She pointed at the castle.

The besieged Assassins were breaking out from inside their fortification, riding and running down the pathway toward us in their hundreds, or possibly thousands.

Eva slapped me on the shoulder and turned me around, and around again. I pulled my helm from my head and looked up at the hills on the north and the south, from where we had come.

Assassins. From every hillside, the free fedayin came to join the attack in groups of dozens or even hundreds. Each formation presumably from a different castle.

"They came after all," I said. "There must be two thousand of the bastards."

Eva laughed at me. "They were here the whole time. Too afraid to attack at first light or make themselves known to us. They must have just been watching. Waiting."

Stephen ran over with a stupid smile on his face. "I told you," he said to me, sounding very young indeed. "I told you there were men up there."

"And you still should have stayed. You could have been killed, you fool." I clipped him around the ear again but I was too exhilarated to even feign displeasure.

Orus rode over, leading another horse, and offered it to me. I climbed on its back and looked out over the Mongol camp. They were stirring themselves in the face of the onslaught and preparing for a battle.

What followed was a disorganised scrap. It was a rather shameful display of a complete lack of any coordination or cohesion on the part of the Ismailis but they got the job done. All those months, cooped up, inactive, and afraid of the Mongols. Finally, they could unleash their fury on a small number of them.

Hundreds of Mongols were slaughtered, and the rest driven out of the valley through the eastern pass. My immortal Assassins murdered most of the siege experts from Cathay. A handful were captured by Jalal so that their secrets could be winkled out of them later. The enemy's tents were burnt, horses and equipment taken as booty. We spent the night around a big campfire, and it was half of the next day before we managed to round up all of Hassan's blood-drunk immortals and headed back to Hassan's castle.

We lost two of Jalal's men, and one of those was murdered in an argument with one of the surviving revenants. Sixteen of them had lived through their suicidal attack, and those men were insanely pleased with themselves. They took credit for the success of the battle and seemed to think nothing at all of their fallen comrades. During the return journey, I entertained myself with imagining slaughtering those revenant survivors.

Instead, we returned home all together in good spirits, and all of them wanted to be the first to tell their lord the excellent news. Jalal felt proud that his men had performed so well in battle. They had killed a huge number of the enemy and had used their abilities to perform a tactical thrust into the enemy lines and deprive them of a key resource. Hassan and Jalal looked forward to using the immortals to punch through enemy formations on the battlefield in order to kill the enemy commanders.

Despite the enthusiasm of the Assassins, I felt a deep unease.

Two nights after our return, I gathered my people in a corner of the training hall. Some sat on the floor, others on benches against the wall. I stood in front of them and shared my concerns.

"The Assassins are not the force I had believed them to be," I said, keeping my voice low. "That much is clear now."

Abdullah was wound very tight, and he jumped in. "They have just won a great victory. Do you not believe they can defeat the Mongols?"

"It is the very fact they are claiming a minor skirmish as a great victory that has finally opened my eyes to what I have suspected for some time."

"They are effective at infiltration, and murders," Thomas said. "And their castles have no doubt served them well against their Saracen enemies in Persia and Syria. But they cannot fight."

Stephen spoke up. "They are too disparate. It is a strength of theirs, in some ways, but their military might is disbursed over too great a distance. An army of any size and competence can take each castle without facing the combined forces at any time."

I nodded, impressed that the young monk—or former monk—had the wisdom to see it.

"But the immortals," Abdullah said. "Can they not sway the balance?"

No one answered, and Abdullah slumped.

"The Mongols will be surrounding this place soon enough," I said. "These famous snows may never come. Either way, the Assassins can only slow the advance of the Mongols. They can never stop them."

"Can we take the immortals," Thomas said, "and cut through to Hulegu?"

"We should retreat," Stephen said.

I agreed. "But where can we go?"

"Is it not obvious?" Thomas said. "We return to Acre and prepare our people for the coming storm."

"That is a long journey," Eva said.

Thomas was not concerned. "It may take Hulegu another year to conquer all of these mountain lands. And then he must subdue Baghdad to the south of here so that his path and his supply lines are unchallenged. Surely that siege will last at least a year, perhaps even more. Then he will take Damascus and the rest of Syria before he comes for us. We have time."

Abdullah, who had been translating as usual for Orus and Khutulun had stopped at some point, and the Mongols were urging him to explain what we were speaking off. He stared at nothing. As if he was looking at something a thousand miles off. Khutulun turned to Stephen and asked him.

"We kill Hulegu," Stephen said in French, speaking slowly and using elaborate gestures. "We kill Hulegu in three years."

She jumped up, spoke to Orus, and both of them babbled at me.

"Yes, yes," I said, holding up my hands, "be silent, will you, you damned barbarians. You are quite right. That is too long to wait."

Stephen laughed. "But you will never die. You may live another century, at least. What is three years to you?"

"We will all die," I said. "We may not even survive this month if we do not flee before the Mongols encircle us. The longer we wait, the stronger Hulegu becomes. He is on the move with his army, he will be more vulnerable in such circumstances than if he is settled in a palace in Damascus."

"How, then?" Thomas asked. "How do we take him?"

No one had an answer.

"Armenia," Stephen said. "They have submitted to Mongol rule but they are good Christians and must chafe under the yoke. There must be men who would ally with us. Or Georgia, if not."

"I suppose that will have to do," I said. "Does anyone have any knowledge of those kingdoms? Or any possible allies there? Thomas? No? Do you expect us to walk from place to place, asking strangers if they would spare some food, shelter, and some blood for a group set on murdering their overlords?"

Judging by the despair on their faces, I had them where I wanted them. All I had to do was to persuade them that attacking Hulegu and William in the mountains, there and then, was the only possible course of action.

But fate decided otherwise.

"Baghdad."

We all turned to the voice who had spoken into the silence I had crafted.

Abdullah stood to one side, a cup in his hand. While we stared at him, he poured himself another cup of wine and drank it off. He turned and looked at me.

"Baghdad. We should go to Baghdad."

Thomas laughed. "Why would we do that?"

"It is the strongest city in the world," Abdullah said. "If any place can resist the Mongols, it is there."

Thomas turned to me. "We would not get within a hundred miles before being killed."

Abdullah responded. "I could guide us to the city. Through the city. Get us an audience with the Vizier."

More of us laughed. I smiled to myself. "You would get us an audience with the most powerful man in the city, other than the caliph?" I said. "And how would you manage that, Abdullah?"

"Well, you see..." He poured another cup of wine and drank it. "The Vizier is my uncle."

Two young rafiqs escorted me through Firuzkuh Castle but turned away from Hassan's quarters and brought me out into the freezing pre-dawn courtyard. An old man guarded the door and he handed me a thick blanket that I wrapped around my shoulders. I nodded my thanks but he only sneered, full of contempt.

The rafiqs led me across to the front of the castle and there on the wall stood Hassan, wrapped in a cloak, staring out at the darkness. A bitter wind whipped at the fabric. The old men surrounding him fell into silence and backed away along the wall as I approached, and the rafiq announced my presence. To the east, the peaks were silhouetted against the rising sun beyond the horizon.

"They tell me that you are preparing to flee," Hassan said without turning around.

I went and stood beside him. There was little to see out there but shadow and a cold that stung my eyes. The icy wind filled my ears, making them ache in moments.

"I was coming to tell you," I said, speaking over the wind.

"Tell me?" he said. "You mean, to ask my permission."

I pursed my lips. "I have fulfilled my part of the bargain. It is unfortunate that your people were not stronger. Not as strong as I believed."

I expected him to berate me for that, for it was a grave insult, despite also being the truth.

Instead, he sagged and leaned his hands upon the crenellation in front of us. In one hand, he grasped something, crumpled up.

"Not as strong as I believed, either," he said. His hood masked his face.

"Have you had another communication?" I asked, pointing to his hand

He took a deep breath and growled out a great cloud. "Betrayed. We are betrayed by our own master."

A ball of apprehension formed in my guts. "What has he done?"

"You know that Rukn al-Din was besieged? He has surrendered and delivered himself and his family into the hands of Hulegu. He has ordered that all castles, all of us, submit also."

I leant on the crenellation and turned to look at Hassan. His eyes glistened in the shadow. It was no wonder that he wept, for it was as deep a betrayal as I had ever heard.

"What are the terms of the surrender?" I asked. "For us, I mean?"

He scoffed. "The terms are that his family gets to live, and the rest of us will be killed and enslaved. Our women will be taken. Everything we have, everything we are, destroyed."

"Good God," I muttered. "But you will not surrender." It was not a question.

"We shall make them pay with their lives," Hassan said. I saw, then, that he wept from the anguish but also due to the depths of his rage. "But we will fall. All will be lost."

"So," I said. "We will flee at first light. You would not believe it, but Abdullah, our Abdullah, is the nephew of the vizier of Baghdad. He was banished, disowned, so it is certainly a risk returning with him. But we shall attempt to kill Hulegu there. When his armies surround Baghdad, it will take them months, perhaps years, to bring down those walls. While he is encamped, we shall slip through the lines and kill him, his men, and my brother." He did not respond. "What do you think, Hassan? It is the best course of action if we wish to avenge the dead, no? Who knows, perhaps Rukn al-Din will be with Hulegu in the camp and you can kill the man yourself."

"No," he said. "It is too late."

I could not believe what I was hearing. The defeatism had spread even to him.

"What do you mean, no? Come with us, Hassan. Bring Jalal and his men. Even your others, the savage immortals. Preserve your most powerful forces."

"Richard," he said, turning to look at me for the first time. "It is a fine plan. But you are too late."

He pointed out across the wall into the darkness beyond. Even as I looked, the first rays of morning light rose over a gap in the mountains, and I saw.

The other assassins on the walls gasped and exclaimed.

Men, horses. Mongols in their hundreds. I could even make out the beams and trusses of their great siege machines being assembled.

"But the southern gate," I said. "The route across the mountains. We must move, now."

Hassan stayed perfectly still. "My men have brought me reports all night. The Mongols are already in the hills. It is no use. All we can do is make them pay dearly."

I grasped his shoulder and turned him to face me. I sensed his men all around us come forward, ready to strike me down.

"You must act, now," I said. "So there are Mongols in the hills. We can cut through them,

Hassan. Think, man. Pull yourself together, for the love of God. Lead us out, Hassan."

He nodded, slowly. "The woman and children. I cannot abandon them to their fate."

"Their fate will be the same no matter where you chose to die," I said. "But you can still kill Hulegu. You can. But only if we take the best fighters and go. Now. Right now."

He stared at me. "Make your preparations. I must speak to my people."

While I ran back, he called everyone but the sentries to the jamatkhana. Standing ready by the southern gate, my people strained and fretted. Stephen suggested that I overpower the guards so that we could go before any more of the Mongols circled into our path.

Eventually, the assassins emerged, and Hassan himself came to us, along with Jalal.

"It has been decided. Jalal will lead the immortals and go with you to Baghdad. I will keep the others, my savages. I will turn them against the Mongols when the time comes."

"What will you do?" I asked him.

"They will send an envoy to negotiate terms," he said, his voice flat and his eyes distant. "I shall welcome them in and do everything in my power to prolong the negotiation. That should at least grant you a day, perhaps more."

Jalal could barely wait until his lord finished speaking. "All of us begged him to flee," he said to me. "We want him to leave. To avenge our families. It need not be you, why not allow—"

Hassan waved his hand. "Negotiation is a knife edge and—"

An almighty bang shook the castle around us. Dust fell down from the ceiling.

We ran through the corridors to the courtyard and up to the wall.

You have to give it to the Mongols. They were a horse people, from the steppe, from the endless grasslands. They had never built anything permanent, not even a timber hall, let alone a fortified settlement or a castle. And yet, in fifty years or so, they had become masters of siege warfare. Rather, they had kidnapped masters from Cathay and pressed them into service. But not only that, they had provided the necessary logistics so that these masters could ply their trade.

In less than half a day, they had dragged timbers the size of ship masts up the hillside, assembled the first of the massive engines, and launched the first missile. An A-frame crane perched over the second trebuchet and men covered the structure like ants. The first trebuchet was already being reset.

In front of the engines, dozens of Mongol troops stood in war gear, gesturing at the walls and towers of our castle.

Already planning their assault.

"They do not mean to assault us today?" Jalal asked.

While we watched, the trebuchet launched another stone projectile at us. The long arm moved in deliberate slowness through a vast curve, flinging the sling over at the top of its arc. The massive stone rose into the sky. It seemed to be coming right for me, though I could not quite believe it. The fact that, out of the entire length of the defensive wall, the murderous boulder would be coming directly at me seemed absurd. I almost laughed.

"Is that—" Hassan began.

I dived to my side, shoving Hassan and Jalal down before me with all my strength, sending them sprawling.

The impact was so loud, so close, that I felt it resounding through my body and for a long moment I thought I was hit. Debris and dust filled the air and my ears rang.

It had clipped the crenellation right where we had been standing. The boulder had then crashed into the courtyard and obliterated an unlucky rafiq. Other than a great smear of blood of his body was gone, but a weeping relative or friend clutched the dead man's tattered clothing. Someone else held aloft one of his severed arms in a corner fifty feet away. After bouncing once, the massive rock had crashed into the wall of a workshop and stopped.

After a moment where we checked ourselves for injury, Hassan and Jalal began shouting orders. The castle's mangonel crews were ordered to take out the enemy's trebuchets. Every able-bodied man was ordered to take up their weapons. The fedayin began to arrive, dressed in their full panoplies.

I hurried through the courtyard to my people at the gate.

"We are too late," Thomas shouted from the wall above. "They are in the hills."

I climbed to the wall and looked out at the jumble of rocks and hills. My heart sank. "Those devious savages."

Dozens, perhaps hundreds of Mongol soldiers were busy setting up positions all across the hillside, their true number and activities obscured by the rises in the jagged landscape.

"Are they there to keep us in?" Thomas asked. "Or are they preparing to assault the walls?"

There were bundles of arrows being stacked with each group of ten Mongols. I could see no ladders or ropes but that did not mean they were not there.

"Either way, we must attack them now," I said. "Break through and flee before we are trapped."

Thomas looked at me as if I was mad. "Break through? How, Richard?"

In truth, I had no idea. "We must break through, and so we shall do it." I clapped him on his back. We ran down to the others at the gate, as the castle walls boomed from the impact of further strikes. Would the walls crumble in a day? Would the Mongols even wait, or would they attempt to scale the walls directly?

"We have a fight on our hands," I said. "A rare fight. Listen, we will go through the gate and we will stay together. Do you all hear me? We will stay together. Not only do we have to cut our way through the men outside, we must fight off all pursuit, and avoid or slaughter any patrols we meet, for days on end. Our provisions will be only what we can carry, and what we can take from our enemies. The passes over the peaks cannot be traversed by horses, and so we will be footsore for a long while. Then when we reach the foothills, we shall take the horses of the Mongols, and ride for Syria."

They stared at me, apprehensive and unsure.

"Take heart. We get to show God what we are made of today, my friends. Are your swords sharp? Straps tightened? Make your final preparations, and I shall see what assistance we will receive."

They turned to go over their equipment. I was most concerned with Stephen and Abdullah, who were neither warriors nor immortals. If Stephen died, it would make no difference but I needed Abdullah to get into Baghdad. They each had a helm to protect their head but no one would provide mail for a useless scholar. I could protect Abdullah from anyone who attacked with swords and even spears but we were all at terrible risk from those wicked Mongol bows.

"We need shields," I said to the Assassins who were helping to equip me for the breakout. "Bring us shields, enough for each of us." Of course, their home was under attack and they were understandably distracted, so I went to find Hassan or anyone senior enough who could order their men to find shields for my people.

The castle was in subdued chaos. Men ran across the courtyards and along the walls, carrying bundles of javelins. Most wore their mail, and many already had their conical helms.

A group of captains stood around Hassan up on the wall by the northwest tower, protected from the trebuchet by the mass of the tower itself. I pushed through the mass of men and called for Hassan. Before I could reach him, Jalal appeared and cut me off.

"Richard, listen. This is what will now happen. My men will leave first by the south gate. We will engage the enemy. You will break through, and my lord Hassan will go with you."

I had questions that I wished to ask. What if we all joined together and routed the enemy on the south slope, perhaps we might lead a mass breakout from the castle and perhaps hundreds could escape into the hills. I wanted the immortals to come with me, to protect us on the road and to be used against Hulegu and William, so why not send the savage immortals, or even better, just the ordinary mortal fedayin?

"What about the immortals that you made with your blood, Jalal? Are they to stay?"

"They will replicate their success and charge the engineers. This may prolong our siege but either way should draw in the main forces to the front, hindering pursuit of you and Hassan, while my men tie down forces at the rear."

It was the best chance for me to escape, so I asked no more questions but one. "Can you find shields for my men?"

Time passes strangely in such moments. Did it take half a day to finish the preparations or was it almost an instant, as it seemed? Orders were shouted, advice and reminders passed along between us. My Arabic was very good but I found that I could understand not one word of the men around me, wound as tightly as they were. The stones kept pounding the wall on the other side of the castle and we stayed tight to the internal walls that we prayed would protect us from more overshooting stones or debris.

"What is taking so long?" I shouted to Jalal. "We must go, now."

"Not until my lord is here."

I threw down most of my gear and went hunting for the lord of the castle. I found him standing on the front wall, alone and exposed like a madman. Running to him, I saw what he looked at beyond the wall. The savage revenants that he had made using Jalal's blood, were charging the enemy. If the plan truly had been to attack the trebuchets then it was doomed to failure, as the machines were far back from the front lines. Hundreds of men blocked their path. The revenants were outnumbered ten to one, if not more.

Still, the revenants cut through the Mongols with ease. I was strangely proud, even though I had not contributed to their skills and had never wanted them created with my blood once removed. Yet the damned revenants did feel like my grandchildren, in a way, and I could at least appreciate their work. The first fifty Mongols were killed, and the enemy sent another fifty or a hundred forward. Arrows filled the air and some of the vampire assassins fell. The Mongols clustered around the twenty or so revenants who remained fighting.

"We must go," I said to Hassan. "Make their sacrifice meaningful."

He shook me off, turned, and shouted orders at his men inside the castle. Those orders were relayed, and the two mangonels on the walls slammed into action moments apart, and their projectiles hurtled out over the combat.

Bright fire erupted. Both objects smashed into the massed, disorganised group of Mongols and burst into flames. The roar of the fire reached me and I saw men dancing in the fire. The sound of screams came next.

"By God," I said. "Is that naphtha?"

He ignored me and shouted more orders down into the yard below. The front gates were opened and the fedayin marched out. Hassan was sending his troops out to take the fight to the Mongols rather than wait to be overrun.

The mangonels launched again, the fire bursting close to the immortals, surely engulfing and killing some of them, too.

"Hassan," I shouted. "I am leaving, now. You are coming with me."

He nodded, tearing his eyes away from the sight of his men dying in the flames. Bowstrings hummed as the assassin archers loosed a volley before advancing.

We fled back through the castle, his remaining men nodding to Hassan or offering a prayer or some other words. It was the end of their lives, their families, of their entire world. Their hopes for vengeance would be kept alive in Hassan, while they would achieve great holiness through their deaths, and spend eternity in Heaven with all the rewards that were due to them. Some were grim, others had the mad look that some men are filled with when they feel touched by God and have gone beyond the fear of death. I could only imagine what would happen to the women and children hiding deep within the castle. The best they could hope for would be a lifetime of slavery.

"Jalal," I shouted when we drew near. "He is here. Go, now."

Jalal's immortals were out of the gate like wolves after a deer. Sleek, swift despite their armour, they slipped through the gate and were gone.

"How long should we wait?" Thomas asked.

I pushed to the front, shoved Hassan at Thomas for him to take care of, and grabbed Abdullah. "You stay by my side at all times. Leave my side and die, understand?" He swallowed and nodded. The man shook all over like a newborn lamb.

Eva had Stephen by the upper arm, and he clutched his shield to his chest.

"We go now," I said to Thomas. "Orus, Khutulun. Go." I nodded out the gate and they slipped out. One by one I ordered my people out and counted them all to be sure no one was left behind.

Once clear of the protection of the castle, wind howled down from the peaks and icy dust whipped into my face. Ahead, Jalal and his men were cutting through the enemy and their shouts and clashing blades rang in the bitter air. I pulled on my helm, grabbed my shield and held it ready, placing Abdullah behind and on the flank opposite the enemy. Arrows flew but not toward us, yet. Ahead, my people stomped across the hilltop, heading across the enemy front at an oblique angle so we could get by them and off into the passes and secret ways through the mountains.

Hassan, Jalal, and his men knew them, and so I prayed to God that he would spare at least one of those Saracens so that we might find our way clear of the heathen Mongols.

We made good progress and the fighting was clear of us. A few arrows clattered on the stones around us but it seemed Jalal's men were keeping the enemy well occupied.

Then I heard—or rather, felt—the thing I dreaded most. A drumming on the hard ground, growing stronger.

"Cavalry!" I shouted, in French, English, Arabic. "Horsemen! Riders!"

I stopped to get a better look and saw a group of twenty horsemen charging into the flank of Jalal's men. They were lancers, on armoured horses. Madness that the Mongols had brought them up the mountainside for a castle assault. But the Mongols were nothing if not full of surprises. The Assassins were run over, speared, and broken up.

How I wished I had squires. Even one, who could pass me a spear or a polearm of some sort. Together with two squires, we could face a mounted attack with our flanks protected.

"Run to our people," I shouted at Abdullah and pushed him ahead while I followed, keeping an eye on the horsemen. "Come together," I shouted at the others. Stopping, I slung my shield and removed my helm. "Come together," I roared again.

Some of the horsemen turned to face our direction. One gestured at me with his bloodied lance.

Up ahead, my people were gathering in a group. The ones up ahead filing back, the ones nearest to me looking back for instruction.

"Keep moving," I shouted as I hurried to them. "Keep moving but stay together."

I reached them and Thomas turned his helmeted head to me. "By God, Richard. What I would not give for a horse."

I laughed, clapped him on the back and jammed my helm back on my head.

"On, on," I called, harrying them like a dog herding a flock. I searched in vain for a place where we could make a stand if we needed to.

The hillside curved away in all directions, and there were boulders and large stones, but nothing that would interrupt a cavalry charge.

"Richard!" Eva shouted from ahead. The ground thundered as the horsemen moved toward us.

I threw Abdullah at Hassan. "Keep him alive," I said.

Eva pushed Stephen at him too. "And look out for Stephen," she said. Eva was a warrior but she still had a woman's heart, filled with compassion for useless boys like Stephen, a weak English monk who was nothing more than a liability.

"Two lines," I shouted. "Thomas, Eva, you stay in front of Hassan. Work together. Orus, Khutulun, with me, understand? With me."

Orus looked wild, eyes bulging and filled with the madness for blood, and the lust for glory of combat, of death. Khutulun was calm as a mountain lake, holding a spear in one hand and her wicked curved blade in the other focused on the advancing cavalry.

Putting distance between my first and second lines, I edged forward, checking that my two Mongol rebels stayed with me. Six horsemen, their lances low, came on. Behind them, two more circled to my left so that they could take us in the flank. I would have to let Eva and Thomas take care of them.

The Mongols had no need to thunder at us in an almighty charge. Their horses were heavy, and horse and rider were weighed down with armour. So high in the mountains, the air was thin and the horses laboured mightily. I considered attempting to force them to chase me down and thus exhaust them. But I put that thought aside. They were too many, and even if I could out-pace the horses, it would take too long.

"Come on," I shouted. And I ran at the nearest rider. His armour was not mail but a kind of coat of plates, dozens or hundreds of small rectangular iron pieces covered his body and his legs to the knees. The horse had armour over its face and neck. He swerved to spear me but I was faster than he could have expected and I changed direction, ducked under his horse's nose and leapt up on the other side. My first thrust glanced off the armour covering his legs, jarring my arm. I swung my shield up and smacked it into him, hard, but he stayed in the saddle and swerved on, heading for Eva behind me.

Orus brought a horse down, somehow. Khutulun dragged a Mongol from his saddle.

I was letting myself down.

Another rider was almost on me. This one had no lance but held a single-edged curved sword raised in one hand while he shouted some barbarian scream at me. He was armoured like the others. Where were they weak? His helm had no protection over his face. His raised arm showed a very large gap in the armoured plates. His hands had no protection, not even gloves.

Charging at him, I twisted and cut across his front to his left side and swung a tight cut at the hand that held the reins, parried the blow that he aimed at my head and slipped the point of my sword up into a gap between his ribs. My blade caught, twisted between two ribs. I grabbed my sword with both hands and pulled. He screamed in anger and pain as he tumbled from his saddle and smacked hard into the ice-hard ground, his felt-booted left foot caught in the stirrup. Before I could finish him off, he was dragged away by his horse leaping ahead.

Eva and Thomas had brought down the rider I let through and Eva stabbed at him on the ground. Two riders circled Khutulun, shouting at her as they cut at her with their blades. I ran at the nearest one, crunching across the hilltop with my breathing loud inside my helmet. The Mongol faced away from me, all focus on Khutulun who darted and slipped from their attacks. From behind him, I slipped my blade between the saddle and the leg protection from his long coat of plates, slicing a vicious, deep gash along the back of his thigh. He kicked his horse away from me automatically, leaving Khutulun and I to kill the other.

So quickly, the tide had been turned. We outnumbered them now, and we killed them all but one, who rode away, bleeding heavily.

Jalal's immortals had been hit hard, and half of them had been killed.

But their attack had been so powerful that the Mongols had retreated. Pulled back down the hill.

I rallied everyone to me, and we continued on with our escape. Jalal's surviving men were almost all wounded in some way but I ordered them to cover our flanks and the rear, while Jalal and Hassan took the lead to guide us through the hidden ways.

We were free.

But we were far from safe.

It was hard, those first few days. Very hard. There were Mongols everywhere, and even with the masters of stealth guiding us through their homeland, we had to spend a lot of time hiding, huddled together, shivering and waiting for enemy scouts to pass by. We were spotted many times. Sometimes, they must have decided that a few fugitives far across a valley or gorge were simply not worth pursuing. Other times we had Mongols hunting us through the hills.

Jalal's immortals, hungry and damaged though they were, saved us through laying ambushes for our pursuers, and by leading them away down blind gorges while the fedayin climbed up and out and met back up with us. One time, three men waited behind to spring an ambush. We heard the fighting. Despite Eva cursing me for my foolishness and selfishness, I crept back close enough to see the remains of my immortals being hacked to pieces by the Mongol survivors.

After such heroic actions, the Jalal's immortal fedayin were down to two men. Black-eyed killers named Radi and Raka, dangerous and violent even before the disaster that had befallen them. Hassan, Jalal, Radi and Raka had lost their home and their families, including women and children, had been slaughtered or taken as prisoners while they fled in the faint hope of exacting future revenge on those responsible. It was a wonder that they did not break entirely but still I watched them all closely, lest they turn on us Christians.

My chief fear was that they would be seized by their lust and attempt to take Eva in the night but it was not long before I was disabused of that notion. Whatever their natural inclination may have been, the harshness of the journey turned each of us into hunched, shuffling old men who lusted only after warmth, bread, and blood.

Still, I endeavoured always to sleep with one eye open.

It was hundreds of miles to Baghdad, away to the southwest. Unimpeded and with enough supplies, we could have walked it in less than a month. But we could not walk straight there. Our route crisscrossed through the mountains and hills and later took us down from the highlands onto the vast Persian plateau before descending to the green plains of ancient Babylonia. First, we went northwest toward Armenia, driven away from Persia by the huge numbers of Mongols travelling in groups from place to place. They were everywhere. Soon, we discovered that they were many even in the north. We knew that Armenia and Georgia were in a state of formal submission but it was clear that the Mongols were a constant presence in those Christian lands, with horsemen carrying messages and even wagons carrying supplies through the winter. We spent many hours lying hidden on the bitter, hard ground in shallow depressions while we waited for groups of riders to pass.

If it had not been for the contacts that Hassan had in various small and scattered communities, we would certainly have perished. As it was, we barely made it. The journey was harder than any before, though it was far shorter in distance and in time than our previous crossings of central Asia.

It was not long before I had entirely forgotten what it was to be warm. My belly ached from hunger so severe that it was agony on occasion and many of us, myself included, woke ourselves in the darkness with involuntary wailing. We grew thin. The people who kept us for a night or more were themselves suffering in hunger. But even up on the plateau, it was not so cold as up in the mountains and so we could at least thaw ourselves a little.

One night, in a sheltered valley, we huddled in an outbuilding. The farmer and his extended family were asleep inside, the women and girls unseen by us. The trees of their orchard had been cut down and carted off by a band of Turkomen soldiers while the family hid in the hills. While the father was sympathetic and treated Hassan with respect, he could offer us nothing but a draughty roof where his sheep used to live. During the night, a hushed argument amongst Jalal's two surviving fedayin welled up and broke out. Hassan and Jalal subdued Radi and Raka, physically pinning them until they relented, but the bitterness between the Assassins remained for days. When we bartered for strips of dried goat two days later, Radi and Raka were not allowed to eat so much as a bite.

"They wanted to eat the family," Hassan admitted to me later.

"You did right to punish them," I said, although I could not judge them too harshly, for I had momentarily considered the very same thing. Still, it did nothing to allay my fear of the desperate killers.

"If it comes to it," I whispered one day to Eva while we walked, far back behind the others. "We will kill the Assassins, drink their blood and eat them."

She screwed up her face but nodded. "Thomas will not like it," she said.

Even without speaking their language, I knew that Orus and Khutulun would have committed any atrocity if it meant getting their revenge on Hulegu and William. I did not care what Abdullah thought.

"Stephen will be trouble, too," I said.

"No," Eva said. "He will be first in line."

It was true that the monk had dealt with the hardship well, far better than I had expected. When his shoes wore away to pieces, he silently cut strips from his clothes and bandaged up his bleeding feet and continued on without a word. In response to my gaze, he merely nodded once and set his eyes on the horizon once more. Yes, he did rather well. Especially as he remained a mortal, as did Abdullah. Still, Eva's certainty about him surprised me.

"Have you not noticed?" she asked, incredulous at my naivety. "Stephen is a wolf in sheep's clothing. He would kill us all if it gave him what he wanted."

"And what does he want?"

"I do not know," she said.

"He wants the Gift," I said. "He wants to become one of us."

"Obviously," Eva said, rolling her eyes. "But that is only a stepping stone toward the shores of his ambition."

I should have heeded her words, and the sense of foreboding that they aroused in me.

Other than Stephen and Abdullah, Hassan was the only other mortal amongst us. He was a remarkable man. A warrior, a leader, and a diplomat. Yet, the fall of his people, the loss of his castle, the deaths and unknown fate of the men, women, and children who he had sworn to protect, all weighed heavy on him. The first few days he was so dejected that I expected him to turn back or go mad. But, like Stephen, there was some ember deep within him that did not go out. And, despite the privations, he started to come back to himself.

Hatred can be a powerful motivation.

Stephen and Abdullah helped me to feed Eva, Thomas, Orus and Khutulun with our blood. While Hassan allowed Jalal and the fedayin to drink from him.

The mortal men resented it, for it was degrading and uncomfortably intimate, but they did it all the same. With familiarity, it became less unpleasant for them and even at times seemed to be an almost ritualistic undertaking. A ritual, if one could call it that, which was as disturbing as it was comforting. What is more, the immortals made sure to take good care of the mortal providers of their sustenance and usually offered them the first of the food and water.

So, stage by stage, over weeks that turned to months, we crisscrossed the highland plateau and finally descended to the fertile plains fed by the Tigris and the Euphrates. It was there where Abdullah, finally, began to show his worth. For all his faults, and for all he cowered in fear at the sight of physical danger, he could talk the hind legs off of a donkey. Local people would challenge us with scowls on their faces and after only a few moments listening to Abdullah jabbering away at them, they would be leading him into their homes for refreshments and begging his pardon for the state of the place.

The land around Baghdad, stretching for fifty miles or more from the city, was something like paradise on Earth. After so long in the pale, dusty, frozen hills and uplands, I had almost forgotten what deep green looked like. It was a land of superbly ordered canals and irrigation ditches, dividing the land into perfectly arranged parcels. It was a balm for the soul, I do not mind admitting so, despite it being the Saracen heartland. I felt like I could breathe again.

The people were wary but welcoming, and they were of a healthier stock than the desiccated folk just up over the hills in Persia.

They were aware that the Mongols were threatening the caliph and they were understandably concerned. And no matter what we said, they did not believe that the Mongols could come that very year to threaten their great city.

And finally, after months of walking, we were there. We were exhausted and dragging our feet along the road, looking like the desperate beggars that we were.

The city of Baghdad was on the horizon, her walls every bit as imposing as their legend had suggested even from a distance. Towers jutted up all along the lengths of the varied walls and behind them thrust the peaks of minarets, some glinting in the powerful sunlight. Coming as we were from the sparsely populated wilderness, running for cover at the sight of horsemen on the horizon and conversing with locals only rarely, the masses of people travelling to and fro along the roads into the city were quite overwhelming and we gathered close to each other like a clutch of newborn chicks.

"We cannot enter like this," I said, standing up straight and shaking Eva from my arm. Wincing in the sun, she pulled her robe tight over her face and muttered black curses at me. "Come, Abdullah, come to the front here. We must wash ourselves clean in the waters and comb our beards with sticks if we must."

On the city-side of the river, a wide sloping bank descended into the water on the inside of the lazy arc of a bend. There, hundreds of fishermen mended their nets while remarkably large coracles bobbed upon the sparkling, wide river. Strange vessels, circular with bowed sides coated in thick, black bitumen, large enough for a dozen men. Behind them were clustered a multitude of suburban houses on the outside of the grand walls that rose above it all and stretched away for miles to either side like the ramparts of fabled Troy. Our way across the river was a pontoon bridge with a sturdy roadway raised high over the anchored boats. Though the floating bridge was thronged with tramping feet, horses and camels, it hardly swayed at all.

"Abdullah," I said, dragging him by the arm as we crossed, "why are you dawdling so?"

His mouth gaped as he stared at the city and I believed first of all that he was overwhelmed by his homecoming.

In fact, he was staring in horror at the heavily armoured riders pushing their horses through the crowds.

They were coming right for us.

"Do not concern yourself," I said to my company as we clustered together once more, "they cannot possibly be coming for us."

We were promptly surrounded, seized, and thrown into gaol.

Part Five
Baghdad
1258

"YOU STILL WISH TO BECOME an immortal, Stephen?" I said into the darkness.

We were locked in a cell beneath the city. We Christians together in one cell, along with the two Mongols. Hassan, Jalal, and the two other fedayin were somewhere else. Whether they had been given better treatment as fellow Mohammedans or had been taken away and executed as Assassin heretics, I had no idea.

Abdullah had been taken away from us as soon as we were brought within the massive gateway through the grand outer walls. That wall was thicker even than the length of Ashbury manor house.

The riders from the city had surrounded us on the pontoon road as we crossed to the far side of the Tigris. Magnificently-attired men, all big, fine-looking fellows with shining armour and glistening beards.

"Someone we spoke to along the way," Abdullah had said, "must have run on ahead and sent word that Franks and Assassins were coming."

"Bloody shitting bastard Saracens," I had cursed.

But there had been no point in fighting. We had lost most of our equipment during the journey, through one means or another. I had dropped my shield not far from the mountains and sold my precious mail hauberk weeks after that for a pittance. Even my helm, which I had been determined to keep, had been sold for the price of six scrawny chickens. All I had left of note was my sword and white dagger, and the Saracens of Baghdad had taken those from me, too.

It was not quite the arrival into the city I had been hoping for. Not by any means. Still, it did not dampen my astonishment at the sight of the city itself. All my life, I had heard of how the place was a wonder, was enormous, was beautiful. Soldiers in Outremer had spoken of the impenetrable walls and myriad towers, of how it would take an army from all Christendom to take the city. The Franciscans had spoken of it as something akin to Rome, in that it was the spiritual home of the Saracens, as Rome was to us.

Seeing it with my own eyes, though, demonstrated the limits of my imagination. It was vast. Far bigger than any city I had ever seen. The waters around it were wide and beautiful. The towers and spires jutted over it all like the masts in the ports of Constantinople, only far larger, more numerous and almost as lovely.

Our captors did not treat us with any malice. Perhaps that was Abdullah's doing, for he had jabbered at them so rapidly that I could understand barely one word in ten, and he had spoken incessantly. The leader of the guards had hardly responded at all, and I could not tell if we were being escorted directly to the Vizier himself, or to our deaths.

In the end, we were dragged through busy guard quarters and pushed into a series of cells. The Mohammedans into one cell, and the rest of us into another. Before I was impolitely propelled inside, I saw Abdullah being escorted back up the steps into the light.

"Why would I not want to become an immortal?" Stephen replied. "Surely, that is better for me than being your blood slave, is it not? What shall my fate be now? To be drunk dry by Eva and Thomas and these two heathens, prolonging their lives while ending my own? Perhaps I would rather lose myself in the blood hunger and become a savage like those Ismaili revenants."

I considered turning him, there and then. Giving Thomas and Eva and the Mongols one last drink by draining Stephen, then make him one of them.

But he was right, in a way. What if I was taken, and could not provide Eva with my blood? I had to keep him human so that she might not be driven mad by the hunger.

"If you want me to turn you," I said to him in the darkness, "you must have something to offer. Can you fight for me?"

"So, I am unwise in war. But as I have shown you, I have my mind and my knowledge. I could advise you on the course of action you might take, for example, drawing on the writings of..." He trailed off, perhaps realising he sounded absurd. "I would do whatever I could," he said, quietly.

"Which is nothing," I said. "Nothing of value."

Eva, beside me in the dark, spoke. "Richard."

It was all she said. By her tone, I knew that she was warning me that I was being unnecessarily antagonistic and that I should stop bullying Stephen. She was always the more sensible one. The more rational one, less fuelled by rage, more aware of what was in men's hearts.

One day, not too long after, Eva would be at my side no more and I would miss her presence in every way.

"But why, Stephen?" I asked, softening my tone. "Why would you want this? You know the price. You renounced your vows, did you not? You could yet take a wife. Make some sons."

Thomas cleared his throat but said nothing, while Stephen shuffled around on the cold floor before answering. "I already feel the years slipping through my fingers. There is so much that I could accomplish, yet I am so far from where I need to be."

"And where is that?"

"You speak often of England, Richard," Stephen said. "And that is where my heart lies, also."

"I do?" I asked.

Thomas, Eva, and Stephen chorused that it was, in fact, the case. Eva reached out and patted my leg.

"You said before," Stephen continued, "that you feared what Hulegu could achieve as an immortal king. And rightly so. But what if there was a king who was good?"

Not bullying the man was all very well but I was exhausted, starving and fretting and so had little patience remaining. "You do understand that the blood could never make you into a king, do you not, Stephen?"

He sighed, almost growling in frustration. "You could advise a king. You could advise an entire dynasty, king after king, and shape a kingdom into what it needs to be. Make England into what it could be."

"And what is that?"

"A great kingdom. The greatest kingdom. A kingdom greater even than France."

I burst out laughing. "Your hunger has made you delirious, Stephen." He began to protest but I spoke over him. "It is a laudable fantasy, I am sure. But you are dreaming about something so far away from where we are, that it is meaningless. Stephen, we sit in a gaol, confined in darkness. Show me your worth by freeing us from this place. You do remember why we are all here? We have each sworn to kill William, Hulegu, and the immortal Mongols who serve him. We are here in the hope that we can somehow help the Caliph's army defeat the Mongol hordes and so complete our quest. Even if the Saracens cannot defeat them, we can use the chaos of the siege to creep into Lord Hulegu's tents and execute him there."

"And to save the Christians of Baghdad from slaughter," Thomas said.

I sighed. "If such a thing is possible."

Stephen was hurt, I could hear it in his voice. "I know why we are here."

"Good. Now, we all know what we need to do. But, ignorant and uninspired as I am, I do not know how we might accomplish these things. Can you show me your worth and tell me what we should do, Stephen?"

He was silent.

"Perhaps you could begin by drawing on the wisdom of ancient sages to get us out of this gaol?"

His only answer was a wet sniff.

Thomas cleared his throat, then spoke very softly. His voice gruff with age. "There is no need for you to turn your frustration at your own failures on the young man, Richard."

I was about to turn my anger on the Templar but Stephen finally answered.

"Perhaps we could pray," he said.

"I shall pray with you," Thomas said.

"Ha!" I scoffed. "Do what you wish. I am going to get some sleep."

I do not know how long I slept for. It seemed but a moment before the bolts on the door slammed back and it was thrown open, flooding us in the painful glare of lamplight.

We were escorted with relative civility by the soldiers who came for us. They wore magnificent armour, all polished and shining. All their cloth was shimmering silk. These men were the personal guard of someone important. I hoped that the Caliph of Baghdad had ten thousand such men in addition to his other troops, but I doubted it.

It was with some considerable relief that I saw Hassan, Jalal, Radi and Raka waiting for us in the antechamber of the gaol, blinking and dishevelled from their incarceration but no worse for wear than we were. A strange thing, to feel so connected to Saracens, to Assassins, men who would have happily seen me and my loved ones dead, had we been strangers to one another. I tried to tell myself that my relief was a result purely of their utility to me as soldiers but going through such an ordeal as our journey across Persia together had helped to strengthen the bond formed in Alamut. What is more, three of them had been changed forever by their ingestion of my blood and I felt a faint sense of responsibility for them. Not as one might feel for their own child but perhaps reminiscent of the accountability one feels when one of your trusty old hounds suddenly mauls the face of a little servant girl.

The Saracen soldiers guarded us closely as they led us through the corridors, beneath covered walkways and across courtyards that resounded with the sound of tinkling fountains. It slowly dawned on me that we were weaving our way deep into a magnificent palace via the routes used by servants rather than guests. The guards barked orders at servants and functionaries we crossed along the way, demanding they stand aside for us. We climbed flights of steps and were finally ordered in through a rather magnificently gilded doorway and into a large audience chamber.

One side was open with a view onto a beautiful courtyard, with bright green trees sculpted into perfect shapes surrounding a series of small pools. The high ceiling above was supported by slender pillars of pale red marble that arched together in scalloped carvings of intricate patterns. Beneath my filthy, half-rotten shoes, the floor was a gleaming cream and grey marble, polished so highly that it reflected everything above it with remarkable clarity.

A handful of men stood at the edges in small clusters. They had the demeanour of minor lords and senior functionaries but their clothing was very handsome indeed, and I felt utterly out of place in my tattered, Persian serf's robes. I was very aware of how we prisoners radiated a foul stench into that civilised beauty. Some of the Saracens glanced in our direction, disgust, and contempt on their faces.

In the centre, an angry Saracen lord was ruining the harmony of the space by ranting in a loud voice whilst pacing back and forth. His deep blue coat, worn over his patterned cream and white robes, flowed behind him and his huge sleeves flapped as he gesticulated. All of his clothing, including his red slippers, was trimmed in flashing gold. Over his neat, glistening beard and beneath his white and orange headdress, his dark eyes flashed and bulged.

The target of his ire was Abdullah.

Dressed as he was in fine robes, I hardly recognised him at first. And perhaps would not have done were it not for the way he bowed his head and curled his shoulders, withering under the verbal barrage from the older man.

"I assume that is Abdullah's uncle," I said under my breath to Eva. "The vizier."

The captain of the guard escort whipped around and snarled an order at me under his breath. I smiled and nodded, bobbing my head in what I hoped was a subservient manner. As I did so, I took note of how he wore his sword and where his dagger was beneath his sash. Probably I could snatch both of his weapons and cut his throat before he could raise a warning cry.

Our presence was noted by enough of the men in the room that the vizier must have sensed he was losing the attention of his audience and he broke off, turning to us.

The vizier pointed at us across the room and barked something I did not quite catch.

Nevertheless, I cleared my throat, preparing mentally for what arguments I would make when called upon to do so. During the journey to Baghdad, Abdullah, Hassan and I had thought up different points that might sway the vizier into taking immediate action to defend the city, such as describing the astonishing swiftness of the Mongol assaults on the Ismaili castles and stressing the expertise of the siege engines, and the vastness of the forces coming for his city. We had practised for months, refining our arguments with the most emotive examples we could think of, all for this one, vital meeting with the vizier.

So, I was quite astonished when one of the magnificently-attired Saracen lords strode across to Abdullah, seized him quite roughly, and dragged him through the audience chamber across where we stood. The vizier watched, hands on his hips, while his nephew was removed at his instruction, and then he gestured at us again.

This time, I did understand the orders he gave.

"Take them away. And kill them all."

The soldiers guarding us used their shields and weapons to herd us out of the audience chamber, following the lord who had taken Abdullah.

I knew that I would have to take the soldiers' weapons, kill them, and then flee. I thought it likely I could do that but escaping from the palace, and then from the centre of the biggest city in the world would be beyond me alone. If I could free Abdullah, then he could lead me and Eva out. Thomas, too, if possible. And perhaps even Stephen, seeing as he was an Englishman and all.

As a general rule, I have always found that it is better to take action immediately rather than to wait for potentially more favourable conditions. But in the circumstances, I wondered if we might be taken to the outer city, or even outside the outermost walls to some execution field. Eva could sense my tension, and she also began eyeing the soldier's weapons.

After a few turns through narrow and ornate corridors, our captors directed us into a walkway that had a dead end. They stopped behind us and propelled us forward. We were trapped. Cornered.

"Get ready," I said, in French and then in Arabic.

Thomas balled his fists and stepped in front of Eva as if she needed protecting. Hassan and his Assassins spread out along the wall at our backs.

"Wait."

It was the Saracen lord who spoke, in a powerful voice that echoed from the arched ceiling above. He pushed his way through the soldiers and stood between us and them.

"You will not be harmed," the lord said. "I am Feth-ud-Din. I will not kill you."

Thomas whispered. "What does he say?"

I ignored the old knight. My attention was wholly given over to the Saracen lord.

Most men that one meets in life are hiding behind layers of dishonesty. They lie to themselves about their abilities or what their station is in life and what they think it should be. Or they are confused about who they should be, what role in life they should fulfil the most fully. Many are deluded about how they are regarded by other men. Yet, once in a while, one will come into contact with a man who is totally self-possessed. A man who knows who he is, what his purpose in life is, what his true talents are and what he contributes to his society. These men may be a country priest, or the village blacksmith, secure in their position as shepherd for their flock, or father and contributor to their community.

As I laid eyes on the Saracen lord, I knew he was one of those. A man of robust build, with a rider's straight back and the shrewd eyes of a soldier. The stockiness of a strong man growing thicker in early middle age while yet radiating health. There was a stillness to him, a calm centre and a hard, steady gaze.

Though he was an enemy of mine due to his race and faith, and though he looked completely different, his presence brought to mind another man who I had known; William Marshal.

I think I understood the Saracen immediately. Understood who he was.

A moral man.

"You would disobey your master?" I asked.

He turned his eyes to me, took in my filth. If he was surprised by a Frank speaking Arabic, he gave no sign of it. Perhaps because I butchered his language so terribly.

"I serve Caliph Al-Musta'sim Billah," he said.

I fixed him with my gaze. "We have come to fight the Mongols. We have come to protect this city."

"Who do you serve?"

"I serve only my oath of vengeance," I said. "Against Hulegu Khan. And his keshig bodyguard and certain men of his court."

He glanced at the others. "And who do these others serve?"

"Me."

I caught Hassan whip his head in my direction but he had the sense not to argue. And anyway, it was not far from the truth, now.

"Why do you bring this one with you?" he pointed at Abdullah.

"He serves me, also," I said. "He served me in Karakorum, and he served me in Alamut. He wants only to save his city from the Mongols. We had word of them during our journey, as their riders ranged about all across these lands. One day, soon, sooner than any of you think, Hulegu Khan will bring his vast army down on you."

He looked at me. "We had word today. Hulegu has left Hamadan. They approach."

I asked Abdullah. "How far is that from here?"

The Saracen lord, this Feth-ud-Din, answered instead. "With so many men, with their wagons and siege weapons? We expect three or four months."

Hassan laughed without mirth. "Whatever you expect, you will be wrong. They will come sooner than that."

"Perhaps," Feth-ud-Din said, revealing only a little distaste at addressing a heretic. "There is another Mongol and allied army coming from the north. I believe they will seek to cut off armies coming to our aid from the west."

"You are expecting help?" I asked. "From the Mamluks in Egypt? From Damascus?"

"The Caliph has requested aid," Feth-ud-Din said.

"Will they come?"

His face alone told the story.

"Is that why you want us?" I asked him and glanced at Hassan. "You seek allies. Any allies, even heretics like the remaining Assassins in Syria." I almost laughed. "You are even willing to consider asking the Kingdom of Jerusalem for aid, through us?" I gestured at Thomas, who could not understand what we were saying.

"I will do anything, explore every path, pay any price, to save the City of Peace," Feth-ud-Din said.

"We will help you," I said at once. "If you swear to help us to kill Hulegu."

He looked at us, one after the other. He must have seen a strange group of people. Franks, heretics, Mongols, all thin and filthy.

Feth-ud-Din snapped his fingers at one of his men and commanded something too rapidly for me to catch. The man handed over a dagger and Feth-ud-Din held it up balanced on the fingers of one hand.

"Your weapons were taken. My men recovered this from a guardsman who was already attempting to sell it for a considerable price. It is fine work. Armenian, is it not?"

"It is mine," I said.

He pursed his lips at my impudence and his men stirred beside him but after a moment he inclined his head and held it out to me. "Indeed."

I took it, bowed, and thanked him, for it was truly a noble gesture. "If you return our weapons also, we shall all fight for this city, and we will cut off the head of the snake."

"I will keep you safe in my home," he said, shaking his head. "And you will begin drafting letters asking for aid."

He was desperate indeed.

Thomas and I knew that all Christian states would rejoice at the destruction of Baghdad and would find the notion of helping them in any way to be laughable. Indeed, the Christian kingdoms of Georgia and Armenia formed a large contingent of the army approaching from the north.

But we went through the motions while we regained our strength and health in the enormous, opulent home of the powerful general Feth-ud-Din, hidden away from Vizier Ibn al-Alqami. We wrote letters that were passed to messengers who were to rush to Acre, Antioch, Tripoli, and even Constantinople. Thomas was sincere in his pleas to the Templars, writing on behalf of the Christian population of Baghdad even though they were Syrians and other peoples.

"Will your brothers and the Master not be confused," I said to him, "when they read both your letters and reports of your death?"

Thomas waved it away. "Like as not William of Rubruck is still in Karakorum. And if he has returned, I doubt his first concerns will be writing to the Master of the Order of my fate. Even if he has done so, it is likely his report of my death will be disbelieved when they read my letters."

More likely they will consider the letters a Saracen or Assassin trick and so ignore them.

But I said nothing and he sent off his letters to Castle Pilgrim, the White Castle, Tortosa, and further afield to Cyprus and beyond.

And in the end, it was all too late.

The great military minds of the caliphate confidently predicted that the Mongols would take four months to surround the city so that the siege would begin in early spring. In fact, it took less than six weeks. By late January 1258, the Mongol vanguard approached from the east.

Living in that great lord's home had chafed on me. The Saracens, even the soldiers and servants, considered themselves to be above me and all of us, because we were Christians, heathens or heretics, and their continued condescension for those six weeks had driven me into a tightly-woven ball of frustration. Thomas also had been driven close to mad by the continued proximity of his lifelong mortal enemies.

So it was with some excitement that I urged our host for news of the recent expedition of his forces. For Feth-ud-Din had returned from a few days away from the city and then summoned me to his private quarters even before he had washed or changed his clothes. There had been a steady, light rain for two days and his robes were spattered in mud thrown up by the hooves of galloping horses. He first wanted to know if any of us had received word from the messengers we had sent off just six weeks earlier. It was absurd to hope for such a thing and revealed the desperation of the man. I ignored his question and asked my own.

"You rode out to meet them?" I asked Feth-ud-Din. "What happened?"

"We were forbidden to take forces from the city," Feth-ud-Din said, in response to my question. He looked exhausted. His eyes wide and staring, rimmed with red and his household guards could not hide their concern for their master.

"Was that an order from the Caliph?" I asked. "Or the Vizier?"

He chose not to answer, which was confirmation in itself. The word in the household was that Feth-ud-Din and some other commanders had defied the order and taken a huge force out to stop the Mongols before they even reached the massive walls of Baghdad. I wondered if the man who sheltered us would now fall to internal politics before the battle itself began.

"You have done as I asked and written to your lords in Dar al-Harb," he said while his servants hovered around him. "Before the siege begins, you may take your people and go."

He turned away as if expecting me to hitch up my robes and run from the room.

"We do not wish to go," I said. "We want to fight. Why do your people not?"

He turned on me, full of rage. I was sure he would draw his sword. "We did fight. At Ba'qubah. Two days ago. Our men won a victory against the Mongol vanguard. Twenty thousand of our men smashed them, drove them back."

I resisted scoffing at his supposed victory. I could well imagine it. The Mongols feigning retreat or simply withdrawing and the foolish Saracens calling it a triumph.

But it was far worse.

"Then why do you look as if you suffered a defeat, my lord?" I asked.

He did not turn away. "We took the position that they had held and fortified our camp for the night. Ba'qubah is low ground. Somehow, in the darkness, they destroyed the levees and dams. They massed their forces on the high ground and cut off our retreat. Most drowned in the flood waters."

I was astonished. The Mongols had somehow baited the Saracens into a trap set on their own home ground. I had never heard the like of it.

"How many men did you lose?"

Finally, his strength of will failed and he turned away. "Fifteen thousand. Perhaps more. Mostly cavalry. Some of our strongest forces. Survivors are yet trailing back but they are so few."

A true disaster. There was nothing to be said about it.

"What will now be the plan to defend the city?" I said.

"The Caliph has given orders that citizens be armed and trained. Also, that the walls be repaired where they have been neglected."

I could barely believe it. The Mongols were a day or two away and there was no time for these orders to be enacted. It was farcical.

There was perhaps still time to flee but Hulegu and William were close, and I could not in good conscience run away from my oath yet again.

A city under siege was a dangerous place and that danger was not only from the enemy beyond the walls. The populous would be in the highest state of anxiety, full of well-founded fear and to be an obvious foreigner at such a time would invite attack. I knew from experience that a mob of angry citizens could be almost as deadly as a horde of Mongols.

"If my people leave your home," I said, "we will be set upon by the people of this city. Let my people fight for you. Equip us, as you would your own men, let us fight by their side when the assault comes."

General Feth-ud-Din agreed, ordered his secretary to organise our equipment, and then dismissed me. His servants led him away so that he could bathe, and he seemed already like he was broken. Every time the Mongols fought, their enemies were left stunned in this way. Disbelief, their world shattered by a foe that seemed centuries ahead of them.

I recalled something that Thomas had said to me, a long time before, on the steppe.

These Tartars. They are masters of war. And we are children.

* * *

Four columns of Mongols and their allies converged on Baghdad. In every direction to the horizon, enemy forces filled the fields and villages. The city of Baghdad may have been the largest in the world, but it had been surrounded by the largest armies on Earth.

One army occupied what had been a commercial quarter, on the west bank of the Tigris. Hulegu's force established itself in the Shiite suburbs beyond the eastern walls, and the Sunnis inside the city spoke in bitterness of their easy capitulation.

The rattling of their innumerable carts, the bellowing of camels and cattle, the neighing of horses, and the wild battle-cry, were so overwhelming as to render inaudible the conversation of the people inside the city. It was a sound like the continuous crashing of a vast wave against a rocky shore.

In less than two days, the enemy dug a ditch and rampart to protect their siege engines from attack by the Saracens within the walls. No such attack was forthcoming.

On 30th January 1258, the bombardment of the city began.

I gathered my people together on a section of the inner eastern walls just before it all started. There was a pause, a lull from both sides as if they were both taking a deep breath before plunging onward to death.

Thomas was remarkably unhappy. I know that he was cursing the day that he ever met me, that he ever asked me to accompany him on his quest to Batu.

"All that is left for us is to protect the Christians of this city," he said.

Hassan and his men, Abdulla, Orus and Khutulun all looked at me and I felt the pull between them and us. Eva and Stephen were aware of the gulf within our company, even as Thomas remained oblivious, staring out at the mass of forces.

"Our agreement," I said to Thomas, "between all of us here, was to work together to bring about the death of Hulegu, William my brother, and the immortals that they have made."

Thomas dragged his attention away from the cacophony beyond the walls. "I mean no offence when I say this. But how can we hope to carry that out, now? In the face of this." He gestured unnecessarily at the Mongols. "There is no chance of us reaching him."

Stephen, keen as ever to find a solution despite his fear, spoke up. "Perhaps Hulegu will enter the city when it falls?"

I looked to Khutulun. Her understanding of French had come on leaps and bounds. Still, she furrowed her brow as I rephrased the question.

"Hulegu never come here," she said, shaking her head. "Inside here? No, no."

Orus agreed with her, and I did, too.

"It will be madness when it happens," I said to Stephen. "A city of this size would take weeks to subdue." He stared at me, nodding slowly. "Do you understand what I mean when I say subdue, Stephen? I mean that they will kill every living soul."

"I know that," Stephen said, bristling.

"The only people who may just live through it," Thomas said, "is the Christians. We all know this. Does anyone deny it? Well, then, perhaps we should help to protect them in order to help bring that about. And, they may then even shelter our friends here who are not Christian."

Hassan rolled his eyes. "I will not hide amongst the Christians. Nor will my men. And neither would they protect us."

"I do not believe," Abdullah said, "that the Mongols will spare the Christians."

Thomas was about to argue but I had heard it from both sides a dozen times already for weeks, so I cut him off before they all started again.

"William may come into the city," I said.

They all looked at me.

"He loves death. He loves chaos. He creates it, and he is drawn to it. It is no accident that he is here." I nodded out at the masses of enemy. "He helped to make this happen, did he not? He would not be able to control himself while the blood flows within. Perhaps he will bring some of the immortals with him."

For the first time in months, Hassan smiled. "We can lay an ambush for them. These buildings all around are ideal. We can lay in wait upon the roofs, inside upper windows. Come at them from the front and rear, and from above."

His grin spread between all of us as we imagined catching our enemies in an enclosed space.

"This city has how many gates?" Eva said. "And how many breaches will they make with their stone throwers? There are hundreds of thousands of people within these walls, and a hundred thousand or even more outside. Richard, you know that I want to kill him as much as you do, but we will never find him amongst the chaos."

I growled and clenched my fists, and my teeth. Frustrated at every turn, for weeks and months and years now. "There must be a way."

"What about..." Stephen started, staring out at the Mongols. "No... never mind."

"Do not be so bloody coy, Stephen. Out with it."

"I was wondering if you could make a banner," he said. "Something that William might recognise. Something that would draw him to you. Or to where you wanted him to go. But I recall that you do not have any personal emblem that would be known to him, and any other possible symbol such as a cross would only serve to bring the soldiers of both sides down upon us in a rage."

His mind worked in ways that mine never could. So many times now, his suggestions had helped me, from Karakorum to Alamut and in a thousand ways ever since. It annoyed me that a man such as he had a wit so superior to my own but I could deny it to myself no longer. He was useful to have around.

And we were about to face an assault more terrible and more massive than anything I had ever known. Perhaps more than the world had ever known, for when before had such a force ever been assembled? We had done what we could to teach him the sword and how to use a shield but it was not his forte and in the face of even the most useless Mongol, Stephen would be instantly slaughtered.

There remained one way to grant him the speed, strength and heartiness that might just give him the chance to survive. It would also bind him to me, or so I believed, in a way that would allow me access to the wisdom and knowledge that I sorely lacked.

"Stephen," I said, placing my hand heavily on his shoulder. "Do you still wish to become an immortal?"

His mouth smiled but his eyes were filled with hunger. I wonder if it was the first flush of what he would become, or if I had simply seen his mask slip. He had told me his ambitions for England, for the English people, to make us into a great nation that would rival or exceed France. Such an ambition might be suitable for a king but for a lowly jumped up villain like Stephen it was gross pridefulness and certainly sinful in the extreme. Eva had told me Stephen was a wolf, that he would enthusiastically partake in cannibalism for the sake of ambition. All the warnings were there but out of selfishness, I ignored the unease that I felt.

Hassan stepped forward. "It is time for me, also."

I nodded. He had done well to last so long while maintaining his authority, being as he was so much weaker in body than Jalal, Radi and Raka, the men who he commanded. But then, the Assassins were a highly disciplined people who obeyed their superiors without question. An admirable trait in general but one which had helped enable their destruction.

As much as I did not wish to bring more blood-drinkers into the world, promising it to each of them came easy after I had already granted the Gift to so many. Not only that, as I looked out over the uncountable multitude of savages covering the plains all around, I did not expect all of us to survive the coming assault.

And so it was on that night that I turned Stephen and Hassan.

I made Stephen swear an oath to serve me for the rest of his life but even as he dutifully repeated my words, I recalled how easily he had thrown off his life as a brother of the Order of Saint Francis.

As for Hassan, I asked him only to follow my orders until Hulegu and the immortal Mongols were dead. He also agreed, and I remembered how he would draw on taqiyya, and promise me one thing while intending another. What a sad thing it was, I reflected, that I had ended up surrounded by such men so far from my homeland, a place where oaths were binding and held a sacred power.

For half the night, I sat watching their bodies fight the blood within them. For a time, Stephen appeared so pale and still and cold I thought he would not make it. But their hearts were strong and at sunrise they were welcomed into the strange brotherhood of the blood that I had created. The Assassins knelt before their lord, while Stephen was clapped on the back by all of us. Khutulun kissed him hard on the mouth and he blushed like a maid.

And the next day, the siege continued apace.

The Mongols demolished homes, farms, commercial buildings in the suburbs beyond the walls and used the stones as ammunition. They even uprooted the massive plantations of palm trees and flung entire tree trunks at the walls, and over them. The trebuchets were enormous. The largest machines I had ever seen, indeed, that any of us had ever seen.

The Saracen military response was appalling. The thousands of soldiers and militia inside the city were struck with inactivity or carried out ineffective training that only served to demonstrate their poor morale. We urged anyone who would listen to ride out and make assaults on the enemy positions. Burning the enemy equipment would slow them down, and we knew that the Saracens had naphtha and incendiary weapons. And many captains and soldiers would agree with us to our faces. Yet they would do nothing. Indeed, it seemed that the soldiers grew ever less visible on the walls and I suspected that they were either hiding in their quarters or even deserting within the city. That is, throwing off their armour and slipping away back to their families in the vain hope of avoiding violence.

It was a failure of leadership, of course. The Saracen soldiers were perfectly capable of mounting a sustained defence, if only they could be directed to do so. They claimed that there had been fifty thousand soldiers in the city, and the place was so vast that it was certainly possible that had been the case before up to twenty thousand of them were drowned north of the city. But the thirty thousand remaining could have formed a core, and with citizens armed and organised, they could have put up stout resistance even in the face of such a multitude of savages outside.

But there was not the will to do it.

For instance, for many days while under bombardment, the Mongol mounted archers rode in their hundreds to the walls and shot arrows over the tops of them into the streets.

Tied to these arrows were tightly rolled pieces of paper, upon which messages had been written in good Arabic. These messages promised safety to the people of the city if only they would surrender.

In response, the Saracens loosed a few half-hearted volleys back at the horsemen each time but that was all. No one organised a force to seize these messages before they could be read.

"Give me a horse and I will ride out and fight them," I said, to the captains at the gates, not because I would actually do it but in the hope of shaming them into taking action. Of course, I was ignored, or driven off. I could see in their eyes that they had already lost the battle in their minds.

The city was battered, uninterrupted, day after day, for an entire week. A bombardment of stones, and explosives that shook the walls and the people to their roots. Those outer walls and buildings slowly crumbled, and so did the remnants of the people's will.

Escape from the city was impossible. The wide Tigris, flowing as it did through the outskirts of the city, appeared to present the best hope of slipping away. But everyone could see how the river was blocked upstream by the pontoons that the Mongols had built so their troops could flow between both sides of the city. Downstream, it was plain that the shores were patrolled by masses of horsemen who certainly watched closely for people to try to float away by one means or another.

Every day, the caliph or someone serving him sent messengers out from the gate. The rumour was that the caliph was now begging to be allowed to surrender the city. But every day, the messengers returned and the bombardment continued without let up. The caliph had left it too long. Hulegu, I was sure, would never now be turned from the blood-letting that awaited him once the machines of his enslaved Cathay engineers broke through the walls.

The focus of the bombardment was on the eastern wall.

That eastern portion of the city was quite distinct and separated from the rest of Baghdad by the River Tigris that snaked in between in a pronounced curve. Although the walls were said to be over a hundred years old, they were three miles in length, massively built and studded with strong towers. It was not a weak point in the defences. For all their faults as a people, the Saracen builders had designed it well. Joining the eastern section of the city and the rest was three bridges. So even if the Mongols took the east, they would still have to fight across the river. No easy feat.

And the eastern part of the city would surely be fought for. It was newer than the core of the city and contained a beautiful royal palace, and their law college known as a madrassa, as well as the ubiquitous canals and holy buildings.

Masses of Mongol forces converged on that eastern side behind their massive counterweight trebuchets. The troops camped in good order, waiting, and waiting for the walls to crumble, for the towers to fall.

***

"What if all this focus on the eastern wall is merely to divert our attention away from the real direction of the assault?" Stephen suggested as we planned our ambush in the shade of a row of ornate low palms by a narrow canal.

It was a cold day for the lands of Babylon but perfectly comfortable for an Englishman. Indeed, it was warm enough to be comfortable sitting on the paved floor in no more than long Saracen tunics. It would have been a peaceful place, but for the garrison troops sitting and standing in groups all around, just as we were, many in a state of high agitation.

There was also the regular resounding boom of projectiles smacking into the massive, thick walls out of sight to the northeast about a mile away from us.

"Why break a wall," Hassan said, "only to ignore the breach?"

"To concentrate the Saracen defences here, so the walls elsewhere can be scaled at will before the defenders can cross the city." Stephen was rightly suspicious of Mongol trickery. "Diversionary assaults are a common tactic, are they not?"

"That is true," I said, well aware that tens of thousands of men surrounded each side of the city. Any one of the enemy armies would be enough to overwhelm the Saracens within, if they did it correctly. "Let us take a look at it again, shall we?"

Abdullah unrolled the map of the city that he had procured for us and spread it on the floor between us. It was by no means a highly refined document and was seventy years old but it served its purpose well enough. The Tigris snaked and arched through the map, dividing the eastern quarter from the ancient Round City beyond the western bank of the river.

The Round City had three concentric walls, cut through by four roadways leading out from the centre, with gates in the walls. The gates and roads divided the city into quarters, and each gate pointed in the direction of the lands for which it was named. There was the Syrian Gate on the northwest, which led to Damascus. The Basra Gate opposite would lead a man along the route of the Tigris. Southwest was the Kufa Gate, named after the great city on the banks of the Euphrates. And northeast, closest to the river and the eastern quarter beyond, was the Khurasan Gate that led to Persia.

A man travelling into the Round City would proceed along a plumb-straight roadway, walled upon either side, all the way into the open centre. Along the road, he would pass through three gatehouses, in order to pass through the three concentric walls. These gates were like small forts in themselves. Like squat towers. Passing through them was like entering a cool, dark tunnel. There were doors at either ends of the tunnel, with an iron portcullis in the middle. An attacking army would have to fight through that corridor, while defenders above could shoot arrows and throw God-knows what else down on the poor bastards fighting their way along it, step-by-step.

No doubt the Mongols would do it, though. They might force their prisoners through first, then send their Turkomen and Georgians in. Hulegu had enough men to spend a thousand on each gatehouse.

The Round City was a marvel of a design, truly. A work of mathematical precision. Easy for an engineer to draw upon parchment, I suppose, but the Saracens had actually made the thing from stone. And the Round City was vast, filled with homes, mosques, palaces, gardens, pools.

"Where are we now?" I asked.

Abdullah tapped a point across the river in the eastern quarters. "Here. You see, this is the road to the bridge. On the other side is the Palace of Khuld, then the Round City via the Khurasan Gate."

"Stephen? Did you survey the bridges?"

"As they are pontoon bridges, they can be easily cut if the Mongols attempt to cross by them from the east and so we would find ourselves cut off. We should remain on the western side of the Tigris when the attack proper comes."

"The eastern city will almost certainly be attacked first," I said. "William will come. I believe it. Like a feral dog to a carcass, he will be drawn inward and then we shall draw him to us. They will breach the walls in one place or many on the east." I jabbed my finger into the eastern quarter, where we sat. "Where is the square where we lay our ambush?"

"It is here," Abdullah said, placing his finger between the outer and middle wall of the Round City.

Hassan let out a long sigh. "It is a wonderful place to lay an ambush, Richard. But getting away from there will surely be almost impossible."

"I am certain you have it right, Hassan," I said. "But how likely is it any of us can escape from this city with our lives?"

It was not something we had spoken of overly much, but we all knew it was the truth. Eva caught my eye for a moment with a look that was full of meaning. Fear, sadness. Perhaps even hope, or relief that we would at least die together.

Hassan coughed and stroked his beard. "As long as Hulegu Khan is dead, I shall die with peace in my heart."

"Fine, fine," I said. "Is the square close enough to the road that William or Hulegu could be drawn into it? Could they see a banner that we might hold aloft?"

Eva nodded. "A banner could be seen from there if the riders can see over the walls that run beside the road. We could make it more certain if the main road was blocked by something between the outer gatehouse and the middle one, then our square by the madrassa and the palace would be the most obvious route to ride through to go around the blockage."

"Why not go the other way around a barrier?" I asked, tracing it with my finger on the map.

She had thought of that, of course. "A man can get through on foot but the archways in the wall on that side of the road are too low for riders. And Hulegu and William would be mounted, would they not?"

Of course.

"We draw his company into the square between the palace and the madrasa, yes?" I asked. "Thomas, Abdullah, did you find a way to the roof of the palace?"

The Templar nodded, a smile forming on his lips. "You would not believe it but there are no great lords within, now. Just Saracen soldiers lounging about. A few captains challenged us but Abdullah shouted them down, saying we served Feth-ud-Din and he would have them castrated if they obstructed us."

"Good man," I said. "And it overlooks the courtyard?"

"A section of the wall, perhaps twelve or fifteen feet high. As high as that tree over there with the dead palm leaf. But with clear view down into the square, yes, good for archers and perfect for javelins."

"Could you jump down from that height?" I asked.

"I would rather not," he said.

"I could," Khutulun said. "So could Orus." She muttered a translation to her brother, who nodded in confirmation.

"And it is possible to block the exits from the square?" I asked Eva.

"There are five ways in at ground level. Three pathways from the streets, and one leading into the madrasa."

"That makes four," I said.

She nodded. "A corner of the square overlooks a pool. There is a fence that I doubt any horse could jump."

I looked at Hassan as I spoke because he had described how his fedayin would carry out such a murder. "We let his first soldiers through, then block the exits behind them, trapping Hulegu, William, and the others within. We attack from all sides."

"Assuming Hulegu comes into the city," Thomas said. "Which he will likely not."

"Assuming William comes at all," Stephen said.

"And the other immortals of Hulegu's court," Eva pointed out.

"Indeed, all of it is based on the assumption that William and Hulegu's immortals will enter the Round City at all," Stephen said. "And if they do, that they will use the Khurasan Gate."

I snatched the map from the ground and rolled it up, growling at them. "We have thought it through as well as can be. Do not lose faith, you doubting fools. All will be well. Trust me, I have done such things many times. This plan will work perfectly."

In fact, it would be a disaster.

The trebuchets slammed ton after ton of rock into the high, thick eastern wall. Stones in the wall shook with the impacts, then cracks between them began to form. Chunks of mortar and sandstone were chipped away, piece by piece, and the base at points along the long wall began to accumulate piles of rubble.

Enemy formations continued to ride close to the city and rain their arrows down onto the defenders up on the walls.

The Abbasid soldiers fought back from the wall, shooting arrows and throwing javelins. But the Mongol's Turkomen infantry were sent forward to collect the massive piles of rubble and bring them back out beyond the suburbs to the irrigated fields where the trebuchets sat. Even though hundreds were killed in the process, the Turkomens were so numerous, and they worked so tirelessly, that they constructed a number of stone platforms out in the wet fields.

In less than a day, the trebuchets were brought forward onto these platforms. Hassan and Abdullah said it was to provide a solid base to spread the weight of the machines and stop them from sinking in the friable, fertile earth. Stephen suggested the extra height to which they were raised would increase the range and elevation of the projectiles the machines threw. I pretended to be unimpressed.

"Have you ever seen a siege progress this rapidly?" Thomas asked me on the third day.

"I have never seen anything like any of this," I admitted.

I had ordered that my people stick together at all times. The common inhabitants of the city were suffering incredible fear, and although we were all dressed as Abbasid soldiers and Baghdad housed people from all over the world, some of us were quite obviously foreigners. That was not a safe thing to be in such a situation and we had to deal with everything from angry glances to arguments that had to be diffused, to being cornered by garrison troops and forcing our way free. Eva and Khutulun kept their faces and bodies hidden but still they were subjected to hungry looks every time we were on the streets. While we could not be all together all the time, I felt safest when I had Abdullah with us, because giving the plebeians an aristocratic tongue-lashing turned out to be one of his greatest talents.

Beyond the wall, the barbarians swarmed amongst the partially ruined suburbs that lined the crisscrossing canals and channels. The conurbations thinned and became the homes of the agricultural people in the distance, where the thousands upon thousands of barbarians had dug their camps.

"The benighted bastards are in a rare hurry," Thomas said, shaking his head in wonder.

Enemy forces swarmed forward, under attack from the walls. A group of dozens and then hundreds began to form about half a mile along the wall from us. We could not see clearly, because of the towers and the buildings of the suburbs blocking the view. But we pointed out to each other the sight of ladders and ropes being brought forward.

"They're making an attempt at the walls," I said.

"Don't think much of the Saracens, do they," Eva muttered.

I knew what she meant. Chances of storming a well-manned wall were very low unless the defenders were to break and give up the position.

"They are used to their enemies running in terror," I said. "The bloody bastards."

"We should rejoice," Thomas muttered very softly. "We should praise God that this, the greatest city of the Saracens, is destroyed."

I glanced along the wall to where Abdullah stood, watching the attack with a face full of anguish. He still had family within the city, and although they had disowned him, he must surely have felt the terror that we all feel when our loved ones are in danger. His mother was old and useless to the Mongols. His brothers were minor functionaries and would surely be slaughtered. His sisters' husbands would also be killed, and the women would be taken as slaves and forcibly married to some filthy barbarian, treated horribly and would be expected to bear him children until she died. If she was lucky.

"It is good that the city falls," I said to Thomas. "And we are thankful to God. But where will these demons be stopped? Do you believe that Damascus will stand where Baghdad falls? Will Acre withstand this army?" I gestured at the uncountable horde that camped in companies as far as eyes could see. "Or even a quarter of it?"

"God will not allow Christendom to fall," he said.

I nodded. "As He did not allow Jerusalem to fall? As He protected Spain?"

The Templar grew uncomfortable. "We must be worthy of His protection."

I sighed. Theology was beyond me. "I hope He can see we're doing our bloody best."

One of the towers far to the north along the wall flung a smoking projectile at the massed companies near the base of the wall. It slammed in amongst them and a great belch of flame bloomed to engulf dozens of men. It roared, like some demon. I imagined the agony, the screams. The survivors streamed away in panic, horses bolting. The Saracens on the wall cheered and Abdullah pounded a fist on the stonework.

"Can we not find a way to fight?" Abdullah asked, turning to me with tears in his eyes. "We could help fend them off, could we not?"

I felt a momentary urge to do just that. There was the smell of blood in the wind and then smoke with the mouth-watering scent of burning flesh. It would feel good to kill a few Mongols or their allies. Or Saracens, for that matter. But that was all a distraction.

"We have discussed this many a time," I said to Abdullah. "We must stay the course. Our revenge is close at hand. Come. Watching this does nothing for us. There is still much to prepare. Come, Abdullah, come away."

After less than a week, three breaches were created in the eastern walls and multiple towers fell.

The Mongols attacked the eastern walls by climbing up the rubble piles at the base of the breaches and the Abbasid garrison defended as best they could. Using their poorest troops first, the enemy sent hundreds at a time with ladders and ropes to scale the slopes and the standing walls at the sides of them, even while the trebuchets continued to send their stones crashing into the walls and towers. Most assaults were turned back with relative ease, with thousands of arrows pouring down on the Turkomens and Uyghurs. There were Saracens employed, also, many of them formerly of the Khwarazmian lands centred on Samarkand but also former allies from closer to Baghdad were employed. The Atabeg of Mosul and the Atabeg of Shiraz sent armies from their cities against the wall. Khorasani and Turanian troops threw themselves up the ladders, determined to break into the greatest city in the world and loot the caliph three ways from Sunday.

I never understood the enmity that the Sunnites and Shiites had for each other. At least, not until hundreds of years later when Christendom was engulfed in decades of warfare between the Catholic and Protestant nations. But it seemed Shiite cities in the province like Basra, Kufa, and Najaf had thrown open their gates to the Mongols and then sent detachments to join in the destruction of their overlord, the Caliph. This made it even more dangerous within Baghdad for Shiites like Abdullah and we kept off the streets as much as possible. Fights broke out all over the city, and looting had already begun, especially between the different sects and tribes. It had always been somewhat rare to see women in public but now we began to hear them, wailing in despair from behind the walls of their homes.

Thomas urged us to take shelter with the Christians, which we did after the fifth day of the bombardment. We made the move into the Christian quarter under the cover of darkness so that we would be less likely to be seen and challenged by a mob. Still, it was a tense night crossing the city with our belongings which we had begged and stolen from our former hosts.

Jews and Christians lived in the city as dhimmis, that is as second-class citizens who paid an excessive tax to demonstrate their utter subjugation to the Mohammedans. I found the very fact that they lived in such a state to be contemptible but my companions had great pity for the Christians. They were not proper Christians, following the Roman law. They were mostly Syriacs, supposedly subject to the Patriarch of Antioch, but there were also Coptics from Egypt and even some who followed the laws of the Church of Armenia.

Within the homes and churches of the Christians, the people were feeling quietly optimistic. Of the many thousands of messages shot over the walls of the city had been messages swearing the archons—that is, the priests—should feel comforted as they were not fighting against Hulegu and so would not be harmed when the city fell, nor would their families be harmed or their property damaged.

"You cannot believe his lies," I said to them when I heard this. "Hulegu would say and do anything in order to win."

"Do not frighten them, Richard," Thomas hissed at me. "They must have hope."

"A false hope is no hope at all, but self-deception," I said, grandly and loudly so that the priests who had welcomed us would hear me well.

"Who are you to say whether this hope or that is false?" Thomas pointed out.

He was right but I did not wish to concede the point in front of those people, who chose to live so utterly at the mercy of the Saracens. Mohammedans who wished to see all of Christ's children dead, converted, or subjugated. Perhaps I was angry because I had put myself in precisely that very same condition.

"We shall see," I said.

Only a day later, a rumour spread that the Vizier had ordered the garrison to cease resisting, to cease their defence of the eastern wall and to return to their homes. Some said, no, the order was only that they should cease throwing stones down on the attackers because they would only be launched back up again.

Whether the order was real or not—and it certainly sounded like hysterical nonsense to me—it was believed by those men who wished to believe it. And so many hundreds or thousands abandoned their posts along the eastern wall.

"It will surely happen quickly now," I said, as we watched the troops file back across the pontoon bridges over the Tigris and into the Round City and to other parts.

There was so much more they could have done. So many more tactics they could have employed. But every soul in the city, and for a hundred miles all around, must surely have felt the inevitability of it all. Any civilian east of the Tigris with any sense in their head fled across the river, away from the coming danger.

And then, one morning, the bombardment ended. The Mongols had captured the entire eastern wall and the eastern quarter, filling it with their shouts of victory. We were miles away across the city by that point but I could imagine them pouring down the stairs of the wall, and over the piles of rubble where they had crumbled the tops of the walls, and into that beautiful quarter.

They sat there, poised to take the rest of Baghdad.

Across the river, the garrison manned the barricades between the beautiful buildings and waited for the hammer blow to fall. Waited for the thousands of barbarians to come streaming across the river to murder them all and seize their families.

And we waited, my people and I. Waited to lay our ambush and to spring our trap.

But there the Mongols and their allies waited, also, occupying the eastern quarter of the city as if their work was already done. And gradually, the city surrendered itself. The garrison, the nobility, and the scholars. They lost their backbones and their minds.

"The rest of the city is ready to fall, why do they not attack?" Stephen said, angry at what he saw as the savages' lack of reason. But it was just that Stephen did not understand. Brutal savages they may have been, but they were still men. No one wants to fight if he does not have to.

Almost no one.

"There is no doubt now," I said. "The city cannot resist. There is no hope left for the Saracens. The Mongols hope to draw them out without losing any more of their own men, which they certainly would if they forced a crossing of the river."

"So," Stephen said, with hope twinkling in his eyes, "so, the city may now fall peacefully?"

I laughed in his face. "No."

Hulegu sent messages to the commanders of the garrison troops in the city. The messages said to lay down their arms and abandon their posts. The captains could not believe their luck, and they pretended to be saddened to be leaving their home, and their families.

But I could see the relief on their faces.

"Do not go," I said to the soldiers near to the quarters that my company had taken over.

Hassan and the others urged them, too. Abdullah begged them, that they did not understand the Mongols. That they had no honour like civilised men had honour. That their promises meant nothing, that they had massacred entire cities before, many times.

It did no good. No man would listen to us. Why would they? We were all foreigners, and Abdullah was an exiled Shiite academician.

Besides, they did not want to believe it.

It was a false hope, I knew it. But it was all they had.

"God is punishing the Saracens," Stephen said. "It is the only reason they would march to their deaths like this."

"Praise God," Thomas said.

I suppose it was a good thing that the Mohammedans were going to be slaughtered but it did not feel like it. Their idiocy made me feel nauseated.

And so we watched from the eastern end of the southern wall, at the Tigris, as they marched out, unarmed, in their thousands. Perhaps thirty thousand men, a great army of men, taking hours to pass through the gates. They marched smartly in their companies and were escorted away from the city by the Mongols out to the fields in the west. Each company was divided up from the others and forced into tight groups by the Mongol forces.

"They handle groups of men with such ease," I muttered, realising it for the first time as I looked out at the formations in the distance beyond the city.

"This is how it is when they fight on the field of battle," Thomas said.

Hassan nodded. "They are herders by profession, by nature. On the steppe, they manage animals from a very young age. There are many more animals than people out there in the grasslands. They round up sheep or horses. And they hunt, all together, riding out beyond the sight of each other before turning and driving all the game in an area into an ever-tighter circle. Like a noose tightening, do you see? And so they gather up a great multitude of beasts all together and there they slaughter them."

I felt sick as he said it, for that described how the Saracens were being herded, into small groups of a few hundred or a thousand. Surrounded on all sides by horsemen, and dismounted infantry with spears.

And then the killing started. Arrows first, in their many thousands, rising and falling in clouds. Then the survivors were speared and any remaining men were cut down with sword and dagger. Their screams and the jeering of the Mongols was like the crashing of some hellish ocean.

They made short work of it. Thirty thousand men killed in a single afternoon.

It was butchery, not war.

Thomas was quite right, and it was true that the Saracens were my enemy, and that they would have slaughtered a Christian city in just such a manner, given the opportunity. Still, it was difficult not to feel a great pity for their ignominious, pathetic end.

The groaning and wailing from inside the city was as loud as a hurricane, and people tore at their hair and clothing and they howled in despair. There was yet half a million men, women and children inside Baghdad, and the Mongols were still outside or perched high upon the eastern wall.

After another two days of negotiation, the Caliph was persuaded to come out himself, along with his three sons and three thousand courtiers. Along with them, thousands beyond counting of citizens attempted to surrender also.

The Caliph was taken prisoner by Hulegu, as they had agreed. As were his sons, and the members of the court, those great nobles and their families who stood shivering in their finery, subjugated before their new masters.

As for the ordinary citizens who had hoped and expected to receive the same mercy, they were rounded up just as the soldiers had been, and then they were slaughtered. Some of the women and girls were dragged away from the mass slaughter, but most were savagely murdered. The Mongol method for mass extermination was like some unholy device, an infernal machine that churned through people with all the relentless efficiency of a millstone grinding corn.

So much death.

And then, finally, on 13th February, the order was given to sack the city.

It was a risk. Staying inside the city as it was sacked. There would be thousands of Mongol and allied savages losing their minds in an orgy of destruction.

We staked out our territory inside the Round City, using for our fort the former home of a senior scholar of Mohammedan jurisprudence, located between the palace and the madrasa, and we fought to defend it. The scholar had fled weeks before and his home had already been quietly looted before the Mongols even attacked the walls. But we repaired the building, cleaning away the damage and fixing most of the doors and windows shut. Over a few days, we brought in what provisions we could barter and steal. I did not know how long we would have to wait to attract Hulegu or William but I knew that roaming the streets during the height of the destruction would be akin to murdering oneself.

The building had a narrow tower in one corner, as many of the prestigious buildings did. Inside, a steep stair around the inside edge of the tower led to a top floor with large arched windows. Abdullah claimed such structures, called minarets, were utilised for allowing hot air inside the home to rise up with the tower and escape, while Hassan said they served to allow cool winds to flow down from the sky. It hardly seemed to work in either capacity, but we used it as a watchtower and as the point to fix my banner.

No single symbol any of us could conceive of would be unique to me. We discussed variations of crosses, or perhaps the lion of King Richard.

Instead, we wrote a single, short word. Painted in black letters, on both sides of the white cotton fabric.

ASHBURY.

"It is hardly legible," I complained, looking up from a hundred yards away across the square when it was first erected. "And it can hardly be seen. There are so many towers and domes and bloody great buildings in this God-forsaken, pestilent heathen bastard city."

Eva punched me in the shoulder, a glint in her eye. "This was the best idea we could come up with."

I shook my head. "That is the worst aspect of this situation. I can feel that this will not work to attract our enemies. How could it? A man could spend a month walking back and forth across this city and never see that pathetic little banner. If William is not with them, even if Hulegu's men see it, they will not know its meaning."

"Then you should pray," she said.

If there is one thing I have learned over the centuries, it is that when someone suggests that prayer is your best chance, then you know that you have made a grave error.

"God help us," I said, praying all the same. "Come, let us get out of sight before the savages get here. I can hear them. They are close."

Hulegu wanted the people remaining in the city rooted out and killed. He wanted the food, wine, and other supplies dragged out from stores and from homes and consumed by his men. He wanted the wealth of the city plundered, for his men to take for themselves and so grow rich and be happy with him as their lord, and fight for him all the harder for the next city, and the next. But he did not throw all the gates open and send in a hundred thousand men. He knew, I am sure, that sending so many would only result in his men murdering each other in the orgy of violence, for there would not be enough of the populous to go around and so they would turn on each other. Still, there were many thousands in the city, moving in companies from quarter to quarter.

I have seen more cities sacked than I can remember, and they follow a similar pattern. The men who loved wealth most made first for the palaces and mosques and madrasas and any building that looked as though wealth may lay within. Other, lustful, hateful men, loved rape and murder, and they would swarm into the homes of the city folk, smashing through ceilings and floors to find the pathetic hiding places of the terrified people who had stayed, hoping for a better fate. Some men are gluttons first of all, and they sought wine with which to render themselves insensible. Most of these men, their most pressing passions sated, then seek other sins to surrender themselves to, over and over, for days on end until their energies are spent or their lords send in sober men to round them up and drag them out.

"They are like animals," Stephen muttered, aghast, as we looked down at the violence in the streets from our vantage point atop the minaret of our commandeered house. The screams of the victims could barely be heard over the roars of triumph and savagery.

Abdullah was also keeping watch from the upstairs rooms of the house somewhere below us, peering through peepholes in the shutters.

"No," Eva said. "No animal is capable of such depravity, Stephen. Only man can be filled with evil."

"No Christian man," Stephen said, his eyes wide.

Eva and I exchanged a look, both thinking of the things we had seen Christian men do.

And thinking of the things we had done ourselves.

"You have read more texts than I have ever seen, Stephen," I said. "But you have a lot to learn about the world."

"Well then," he bristled. "No true Christian."

A banging sounded far below.

"Is that our door?" Eva asked.

I nodded. "They are trying us again. We should go down."

"Should I stay, perhaps?" Stephan asked, innocently. "Someone should be responsible for keeping watch, no?"

"What a generous fellow you are, Stephen," I said as I descended the stairs behind Eva, who flowed down them like a cat.

We had cleared the entrance hall of any furniture that might hinder us and had reinforced the heavy doors with two mismatched table tops, held in place with boards pulled up from one of the floors. Still, the doors shook with the impacts from those men trying to get inside our temporary home. The looters clearly assumed that a building of such size, in such proximity to a palace and other grand structures, would contain riches of one kind or another. They could not have known the home had been emptied of riches and the fact that the door was barred would have seemed like a sign that breaking through it would be well worth the effort.

The floor of the entrance hall was already stained with blood from previous, brief incursions by unwanted guests.

"Is it them?" Thomas asked as Eva and I came down.

"Not that we could see," I replied. "Perhaps we should open the door and find out?"

"Same as before?" Orus asked, grinning like the maniac he was.

"As my old steward used to say, if your pail is not broken, then one repairs it not," I said. Orus stared blankly at me while the doors shook and men shouted outside. "Never mind. Just open the bloody doors, will you."

Orus and Hassan unbarred the doors and ran back to us as the doors were thrown inward. Eva and I hid from view in the doorway to the dining area, while Khutulun and Jalal hid around the other. Orus and Hassan ran straight ahead toward the inner courtyard with its lovely fountain and pool, and so they could be seen escaping by the Mongols who strode in through the front door behind them.

I could hear how they were full of madness and fury. One of them shouted and their footsteps stopped, while their voices immediately rose in argument as they clustered inside the entrance.

"Six?" Eva whispered.

I nodded. "Smells like six hundred. But yes, six or so. And they know it is a trap." I raised my sword and looked across the hall to the opposite doorway where Jalal and Khutulun crouched. The Mongol woman grinned from ear to ear. A savage's smile on an angel's face.

Even though they were wary, they were still not ready for my attack. Coming out of hiding at a run, I caught them unawares. It was not six, but nine men crammed into the entrance hall just inside the door. Not the finest Mongol troops, as they were clad in filthy coats and not mail or other armour. A few wore iron helms rather than leather caps or hats. Beyond, the courtyard was bathed in sunlight, the men somewhat silhouetted.

Two men were arguing, and the others were glaring or grinning. At a glance, I knew they were drunk. Most did not have a weapon drawn, and only two held their swords ready. Others gripped daggers. One man had a remarkably ornate mace with a steel shaft that he had no doubt looted from somewhere in the city.

My sword sliced him across the neck before he had time to flinch and I slashed at two more, roaring at them as I shouldered my way through. I was fast, and loud in the enclosed space, and they leapt back to let me through.

While they stood momentarily dumbfounded, I heaved one of the front doors shut.

That snapped them into action and they came at me, suddenly understanding I wanted to trap them inside with me.

I slashed wildly, back and forth, connecting with an arm, a helm. A thrown dagger bounced off the door beside my head and clanged on the paved, bloody floor.

And then my own followers crashed into the Mongols from behind. Eva's first cut took a man's head from his shoulders in a single blow. Khutulun, screaming in joy, sliced a man's face open from ear to ear, then shoved his falling body towards her brother to finish off while she leapt into the next enemy.

We made short work of them, and they were soon lying dead or dying in the darkness of the entrance hall.

"Do not finish that one," I said to Thomas, as he stalked over to a man crawling away. I called out to my people. "Drink what blood you need, then throw the bodies with the others into the storeroom."

"Bodies give bad smell," Orus said. "We throw from roof into alley, yes?"

He was a truly gifted fighter but, unlike his sister, he was not the sharpest tool in the box. "That would attract attention, Orus. The storeroom, please."

Orus shrugged, slung one filthy dead Mongol onto his shoulder with graceful ease, and strode off.

"Should we save the blood?" Thomas asked.

"No need. We will be seeing plenty more soon, I am certain."

"What do you want with him?" Hassan asked, coming up and pointing with his dagger at the prisoner.

"Get him to tell us where Hulegu is," I ordered Hassan.

The Assassin was sceptical. "This one is a nothing. He will not know where his lord is."

"Get him to tell you everything he has heard. How long were they given to sack the city? Tear it out of him."

Hassan's eyes were cold when he nodded and stalked toward the dazed Mongol.

A cry echoed from above.

"Richard!"

It was Stephen, shouting so loudly that his voice cracked. I took the steps up the inside of the minaret three at a time.

"What is it?" I called as I ran. "Is it Hulegu?"

Stephen had his face pressed against the ornate stonework carving in the corner, staring out at something, his hands planted on the stone either side.

"He is gone," Stephen said as I came up behind him.

"Who has gone?" I asked, dragging Stephen away from the window and pushing my face where his had just been. The city beyond thronged with Mongol troops. "Who, Stephen?"

"Well, I do not know for certain," he began. "I thought that I saw a knight—"

"Where?" I said. "Was it William? Did he look like me? What did he look like? Where, Stephen? Where?"

"Down by the path to the palace. I may well be wrong… in fact, it is quite likely that I am mistaken. It may be that I have been looking down for so long that my mind's eye has deceived me—"

I turned, grabbed him by the shoulders and jammed him against the wall. "Who did you see?" I snarled in his face.

He swallowed. "Sir Bertrand. Possibly. That is, Bertrand de Cardaillac, and possibly also Hughues, his squire. But, surely, that cannot be—"

I leapt away from him back down those damned steps. "Come on, you fool," I shouted over my shoulder. "Everyone, to me," I repeated my call to my men to assemble in the entrance hall.

The bodies of the Mongol troops and their weapons littered the floor.

Hassan looked up from where his prisoner was propped against the wall. "What is it?"

"Kill that one and take his coat," I said. "Get the coats from all of them, and their helms and the hats." My people filed in from all over the house, asking each other what was happening. "Everyone, clothe yourself in the enemy's garb. We are going to leave this place, seize one or two men, and bring them back here. Stephen, Abdullah, you close the doors behind us and guard the building."

Stephen was appalled. "What if the enemy break in again? If it is only Abdullah and I—"

"You are an immortal now, Stephen," I snapped. "Take up a weapon, use your strength, remember your training. Defend this place until we return."

"Why go and take another one?" Thomas asked, pointing at Hassan's now-dead prisoner. "We had a perfectly good one already."

They busied themselves stripping the bodies and trying on the stinking, blood-soaked clothes of the Mongol men.

"Stephen saw Bertrand de Cardaillac heading for the palace," I said.

He stammered. "I am not certain what I saw. It may be that—"

Thomas froze, his arm halfway into a Mongol coat. "Why in the name of God would he be here?"

"It makes perfect sense," I said. "My brother William has brought him. Him and his squire. He had him prisoner in Karakorum, did he not? The night he killed Nikolas and stabbed you, Thomas."

"I remember," Thomas said, his jaw set. "Hulegu promised to let the monks go free, and Bertrand was their escort."

I shook my head. "William would never let a man like Bertrand go free. He would use him, make him a follower."

Eva spoke up. "He would turn him."

"By God," I said. "You are right. He would have turned him into an immortal. Given him the Gift. Hughues, too. Two more knights to follow him."

"It is too dangerous out there," Hassan said, stepping forward. He held a Mongol's hat and coat but made no move to clothe himself with them. "These disguises will never pass any inspection."

"We will not stop for any inspection, Hassan," I said, feeling the red anger burning. "We will go quickly, heads down. Ignore all who speak to us. Orus? If anyone seeks to obstruct us, shout that we are on important business for Hulegu or some other great lord whose name is feared, understand?"

"Bertrand may be a mile away by now," Thomas said. "We may never find him."

"We bloody well better find him," I said, letting my anger show. "Or else all this, everything we have done, will be in vain. He will lead me to William, do you not see it? And William will lead us to Hulegu. And all of them will die. You are all coming with me, and we will all have our vengeance. Agreed?" I stared at each of them in turn. "Agreed? Agreed?"

One by one, they acquiesced.

"We will stay together. We will keep moving. We will not allow ourselves to be cornered. And we will not allow ourselves to be distracted. Understand?"

When we were all cloaked in bloody, stinking Mongol clothing, I led them at a run from the house and into the square where we had hoped to lay our ambush. No enemies in sight but their shouts and the screams of their victims echoed from the walls. The sun was bright and my immortals flinched from it, shielding their eyes.

I sensed that my terrible plan was already falling to pieces but, despite what Thomas believed, God cares nothing for a man's intentions and hopes, and so we must accept disasters and respond swiftly to overcome them. We followed the wall of the house and crossed to the huge madrasa on the other side, heading for the path that led to the entrance of the palace. It would have been quicker to cross directly but I wanted to avoid detection from anyone for as long as was possible.

At the edge of the building, I peered around the corner at the pathway, lined with ornamental trees. A large band of soldiers filled the grand entrance, many lounging on the steps or against the walls. Others carried loot from inside the palace. A group carried piles of clothes and other silks to a row of carts in the open forecourt. A trail of dry blood stained the stones of the path and continued into the light dust of the courtyard. It led to a pile of bodies tossed against the wall of the palace. The building rose up three or four storeys high above, with window after window reaching up to the roof above, each one with intricately patterned stonework jutting over the arches.

Could Bertrand truly be within? Even if he was now one of William's men, how could he walk freely through a company of drunken, looting Mongols?

If he was within, he was certainly my best hope of finding William himself, for surely Bertrand would know where he was. But how could I storm such a place with so few men of my own? How many were inside? Twenty? Fifty?

Although there were dozens of palaces in Baghdad, and this was a small one, it was perhaps a madness that drove me to head into the palace, an enclosed space full of looting Mongol soldiers. Taking all my followers down that path and into the palace was likely to end in disaster, surely.

"Wait here," I said to my people. After all my talk of staying together at all costs, they stared at me in surprise. "I will draw Bertrand and Hughues out, and lead them here where we will take them. Disburse yourself about here and fall on them from all sides."

Eva moved in front of me. "We stay together. Do you recall the last time you went into an enemy force alone?"

"No," I admitted.

She punched me in the chest. "Forty years ago, you went into that village alone in Nottingham to rescue me. And you were captured, and I had my throat slit."

"But that was a trap, laid to lure me in."

She tilted her head. "What makes you think this is not?"

I froze, astonished that the thought had not even occurred to me.

Reaching my hand out, I stroked her cheek. "Truly, my love, I would be dead a dozen times over, if you were not at my side. What would I do without you?"

She did not smile at the compliment, as any other woman would have done. Instead, she slapped my hand away. "You are a bloody fool, Richard."

I laughed, because the battle thirst was upon me, and she could tell that was so.

"Orus?" I called. "You will come with me. We will lure the enemy into the square. And the rest of you will cut them down, do you hear me? Kill them all. We want Bertrand or Hughues, and we want them to tell us where to find William, and Hulegu. Come, Orus."

We strode toward the Mongols, who had not yet noticed us.

"Kill them?" Orus asked, with a hand on his sword.

"Tell them that a gaggle of Saracen princesses are fleeing across the city and that you need help killing their guards. Do you understand? Tell them a dozen Saracen maidens are making a run for it, across the square, and they have their wealth with them. Do you see, Orus?"

A cunning smile stretched across his handsome face.

After a moment to compose himself, he ran forward raising his arms out at his side and began shouting at the men in an agitated voice. He jabbered and roared at them. The sharpest few came to him with their swords drawn but Orus did not respond to their threats, other than to beg and plead in the barbarian tongue for them to help him to take this great prize which was getting away, just out of sight, so close, so close.

I watched the hunger light up their eyes, and more and more jumped to their feet and dropped what they were carrying. A handful more came out from within the entranceway. I kept my head lowered so that my Mongol hat would shield my face from them. Some were wary, but they were overcome by the greed filled amongst them, who dragged them forward. Orus kept on at the stragglers, no doubt urging that they needed every man. The first moved by me and I backed away, making myself smaller and meeker. A few barked words at me and I bobbed my head and mimicked the gestures that I observed the Mongols making in my time at Karakorum and on the steppe. No one troubled me, for they were hurrying to seize their prize before it escaped.

I slid by them, sidling to the palace entrance where those too drunk or too lazy remained. Orus tried to rouse them but I clapped him on the back and told him to cease. The bulk of them were moving away and would soon feel the blades of my people cutting them down. But some would no doubt escape, and there were many more nearby and within, so we had to move quickly now.

Orus followed me and we ducked inside the decorated archway into the entrance hall. It was bright and airy and open, with clear lines and geometric designs in the stonework. The polished floor was littered with detritus and spattered with blood. Rooms led off through high arches in front and to either side. Above, two levels of balconies looked down on us. Two doorways led to stairways that wound up to other storeys above. Banging and crashing noises echoed through the building.

"It is too big," I said to Orus. "How will we find them??"

He nodded, cupped his hands around his mouth and mimed shouting.

"You bloody heathen madman," I said. "Why in the name of God would Bertrand come to me if I—" I paused, thinking.

He would not come to me.

I cupped my hands around my mouth and roared. "Bertrand!" My voice echoed from the walls. Did I sound enough like my brother to fool him? I had to hope so. "Bertrand! Hughues!"

Taking a breath, I was about to hurl insults at the man, as I imagined my brother might have done when I stopped myself. Thinking back on Palestine and Sherwood, it seemed as though his men worshipped him. He commanded depths of loyalty and devotion I had seen only in the followers of Richard the Lionheart. It was unseemly and quite profoundly un-English, but there it was. William treated his men with courtesy and addressed them with respect.

"Come down, brothers!" I roared. "I require your presence!"

Orus stared at me with a lopsided grin on his face, and I shoved him across the hall into the archway so that we would be hidden from view. The banging subsided somewhat but three Mongols wandered in from outside and stood together in a group, watching us. Orus raised a friendly hand at them and babbled something. Whatever it was he said, they appeared to be unconvinced and their hands remained on their weapons.

I sighed. "Nothing in this world ever goes according to plan, Orus. I suppose we can at least take comfort in that."

He smiled, nodding, not understanding me at all.

I pointed at the three Mongols, and then dragged my finger across my throat.

He grinned, drew his sword and charged at the Mongol soldiers. They scattered, but he caught the first one with a thrust to the unarmoured soldier's lower back, driving him to the steps. It would have been visible to any others outside the palace.

Footsteps resounded on the stone floor behind me, echoing out of the stairway nearest to me. I slipped across the room to place my back against the wall beside the archway and drew my sword, ready to strike down the two or three armoured men who clattered down the steps.

The first man stepped out into the hall. A man dressed in the garb of a Frankish man-at-arms, with his straight-bladed sword at his side, and his helm tucked under his arm. His surcoat was faded, dirty and much-repaired but it was a familiar one.

In fact, I recognised him at once.

Hughues. Bertrand's squire and cousin.

The second man, which was surely Bertrand himself, stopped within the stairwell, out of my sight.

I willed him to step out also so that I could take them both.

But he did not.

I watched as Hughues peered through the archway and out into the entrance hall where Orus fought with the Mongol soldiers.

Hughues turned back to the stairwell and began to call out in French. "There are merely—"

His eyes widened when he saw me, and I am sure the sight confused him for a moment. Brandishing a curved sword, I wore a Saracen soldier's armour and clothing, from head to toe, and over the top wore the massive coat of a Mongol rider, with a fur-lined conical hat pulled over my Saracen helm. An ill-fitting ensemble, with my grimacing face staring out of it. No wonder, then, that the young man was struck by a momentary bafflement.

I leapt into his confusion, charging him with great speed and shouldering him in the chest. He was a big lump of a man and it hurt me, but it would have knocked the wind from him and he flew back off his feet toward the entrance, his helm clanging away. His skull smacked into the floor with a wet thud, like an apple being crushed, and he bounced into motionlessness. I had not intended to murder the man.

Footsteps behind me.

I ducked and twisted away from the blow that was surely coming, turning to face my attacker as I retreated away further into the palace.

Bertrand.

I had forgotten how big he was. His helm obscured his face but I could imagine the look upon it. His sword point danced in the air as he feinted his way closer to me. Neither of us had a shield but his armour was certainly better than mine, and I had a rather light blade with which to attack his. It would have to be my dagger, slipping it beneath his helm or through his eye slits, or up into his groin beneath his hauberk.

Then again, I needed the bastard alive.

He lunged at me to drive me back, then launched a series of rapid cuts at my unprotected face.

So fast.

Any doubt that he had been granted the Gift was now gone. He was certainly one of William's immortals.

And now that our strength and speed was closer to equal, I could truly appreciate his skill as a swordsman. Bertrand was an emotional, prideful man but he did not fight with emotion. Instead, he attacked with controlled, precise cuts and thrusts, the point of his sword searching for gaps in my defence. My sword blade was shorter and was not designed for the thrust, and I parried and retreated. Even if I had been armed and armoured in my native style, I would likely still have been outmatched by his skill.

His point glanced off the top of my helm as I mistimed a lunging thrust at his lead knee and I shifted away as he followed up to keep me off-balance. Another cut struck me on the shoulder and I changed direction again to avoid being cornered. Frustration and fear began to surge inside me. A terror and anger that I would die an ignominious death at the hands of an arrogant Frenchman. That rage gave me strength to turn his sword and slip inside his guard to thrust my sword into the mail at his stomach. The force of it at least caused him to wince and grunt and suddenly he was on the backfoot. To get through his armour, I would have to grapple him to the floor and employ my dagger in a way that would disable but not kill him outright.

Across the hall, far behind Bertrand's back, I noted that Hughues climbed gingerly to his feet with one hand on the back of his head but the other hand already gripping his sword. His face was covered with blood that must have leaked from a wound on his skull, unseen beneath his aventail. The tough little bastard had surely also been turned by William and I would have to now deal with both of them, just as soon as Hughues could shake the wits back into his head. The younger man staggered toward us while we fought, before lurching over to lean one hand on the wall.

"Bertrand!" Hughues shouted. "I cannot see. Is that you?"

The knight attempted to break off from me but instead, I pressed my advantage while he was distracted by his cousin's wailing.

Behind Hughues, a dark shape darted and loomed up.

"No!" I shouted.

But it was too late.

Orus gabbed Hughues from behind and jabbed a dagger into his face and dragged him off his feet. Hughues screamed as he died.

While Bertrand was momentarily frozen in indecision, I hammered my sword into his helm, grabbed his arm and wrestled him off his feet. We crashed into the floor, and I struck him with powerful blows about his chest and body. Orus joined me, yanked Bertrand's helm from his head and bashed his face into a bloody mess. Together we subdued the massive knight, lashing his hands together behind his back.

"You have murdered him," Bertrand said, his lips split and oozing blood. His eyes fixed upon his young cousin's body.

"It was not my intention," I said, as I dragged him to his feet and propelled him rapidly from the palace and onto the path and into the orange sunlight. Dead Mongols lay on the steps, slain by Orus. The sun had moved far across the sky and was sinking low. It would not be long before evening came.

"There," Orus said, nodding at the approaching group.

It was my own people, coming from their ambush in the square to escort us quickly back to our safehouse. Quickly, I found Eva amongst them and saw that she was unhurt. All of my company had survived the ambush they had sprung.

"We all live," Eva said, falling in beside me with barely a glance at Bertrand. "A few injured. No Mongol escaped. But surely our combat was noted by others. We cannot remain long in this place before more come for us."

I nodded my thanks to my wife and then threw Bertrand down against the entrance hall wall just inside the doors to our home on the edge of the square.

"Where is William?" I asked him, while the others shut the doors and checked themselves and their equipment after their ambush of the Mongols.

"You murdered him," Bertrand said. "Your savage killed my dear Hughues. Killed him dead."

He was a knight and a lord but our survival in that place was precarious and would not suffer delay. I dragged the aventail from his head and punched him in the temple. "Where is William?"

Bertrand's eyes glazed over and he screwed up his face. "How did it come to this?" he said, almost in a wail. "You and your brother, you are an evil pair. You bastard. True evil."

I sighed and crouched in front of him.

"What happened in Karakorum?" I asked, lowering my voice. "You were free to return with the monks. Instead, you chose to follow my brother. Why?"

He laughed until his throat gargled and he spat a mouthful of clotted blood onto his surcoat. "I believed his lies."

"What lies were those?"

When Bertrand hesitated, I grabbed my dagger and reached down to hold the top of his head still. "I am going to cut off pieces of your face now, Bertrand. I will cease only when you speak to me of my brother."

"For the love of God," he said, eyes wide and staring at the blade point hovering an inch away from the tip of his nose. "I will speak, Richard, I will speak." When I did not withdraw the dagger, he quickly continued, swallowing hard. "William promised me a dukedom. In France."

"And how would he accomplish such a thing for you?"

"The Mongols would invade France, he said. He had urged them to do so for years now. And after the kingdom falls to Hulegu, it will be rebuilt and new lords chosen to rule. I would be one of them."

It was just as we had feared. After the Saracens were crushed, the Mongols would be turned against Christendom and the same horrors inflicted upon the people there.

Driven by fear, many questions leapt immediately to fill my mind. When would this happen? How many years would it take? What could we do to stop it?

But then I recalled what Bertrand had earlier said. "But now you believe his promises were lies? Why? What has happened since between you?"

"Between William and I? Nothing. But William and Hulegu?" Bertrand hesitated, glancing at my dagger.

"Come on, out with it," I said. "My brother is nothing if he is not a braggart. I have never known him to keep his grandiose plans from his men. Speak."

Bertrand licked his bloodied, cracked lips and looked away.

I sighed. The prideful ones always have to make it difficult. "My hope, sir," I said, "is that once this unpleasant business is concluded, and you give me your word to do me and my people no harm, I will free you to do as you will. And I would rather you did so as a whole man, and not one lacking his ears or one of his eyes. Or some other part."

It was sad, how the hope filled his eyes when he turned them to me. He must surely have expected that I was lying about sparing his life, yet the hope that he could survive the encounter overcame his sense of reason. Such as it was.

"Hulegu and his men, they grow tired of William urging them to conquer Christendom. All in good time, they say. First, the Mohammedans and then, later they will finish their conquest of the remaining peoples of the Earth. The Khan and his retinue, those changed by William's blood, they speak now in terms of twenty years, or forty years, or even longer. They know that they will live forever, and are in no hurry."

"And William is impatient?" I asked. "Why?"

Bertrand glanced at my dagger again. "There are men like us. In France and throughout Christendom. William has given the Gift of his blood to many great lords and I believe he fears that these men will grow powerful in his absence and that they will challenge him when the time comes. Possibly, I do not know for certain, he does not speak clearly of such things." He trailed off, no doubt seeking to obscure the truth through vagaries. But I did not care about him, as my heart was gripped by a cold sense of dread.

I glanced around at Eva, who stood watching beside Thomas, Stephen, Hassan, and some of the others.

"William has made many Christian lords into immortals?" I said. "When? How many?

Who are they?"

"I do not know, I swear it. He did not tell me. That is to say, he said he granted the Gift to many after he last fled England, and he journeyed through Christendom on his way east. It was many years, so he said, and he chose which men he could count on to do what he needed them to do."

"And what was that?"

Bertrand attempted to shrug. "Some he wished to accumulate power and wealth, so that he could take it from them when he returned. Others, he said were good only for sowing chaos and disorder. Criminals and outlaws, by law or by nature. Their deeds would weaken the kingdoms that William would then conquer."

"How many?" I asked.

"I do not know, I swear it."

Pushing the back of his head hard against the wall, I took the dagger and pressed the point against his cheek beneath his left eye. "I sincerely beg your pardon, Bertrand, but I am going to take your eye now."

"Wait!" Bertrand squirmed. "It was perhaps a dozen. A dozen."

I hesitated. "So few? That cannot be true, Bertrand."

"Forty, perhaps," Bertrand said. "Yes, a great many, perhaps. Or less."

"For God's sake," I said. "You truly have no idea of how many, do you."

He let out a shaky sigh. "No. He would not say. And I do not know."

"Where is William right now? Is he in the city?"

"Yes," Bertrand nodded. "We came in together, along with Hulegu's courtiers. The damned savages."

"Where are they now? Where is William, Bertrand, right at this moment?"

He breathed heavily, for he was betraying the lord he had sworn himself to, and it weighed on him. "William went to the house of learning near to here. He wished to find texts and maps on Cathay and the lands of the East."

"He is in the madrasa?" I said. I could feel Eva shifting behind me. "How many men with him?"

"Six of the Gifted, and a hundred or so royal troops loyal to Hulegu."

"And Hulegu wants maps of Cathay? Why?"

Bertrand shook his head. "No, no. It is William who wants such things. He told me in secret." Despite everything, there was pride in his voice that William had taken him into his confidence.

"Why does William want them?" I asked.

"I am sure he has his reasons," Bertrand said, grudgingly admitting his knowledge of my brother's plans went only so far.

"If all this is true, why were you and Hughues in that palace instead of by William's side?"

"It was the residence of the lord of the madrasa," Bertrand said. "We were to find him or his family, or his belongings and writings, and bring them back to William."

Abdullah came striding in behind me and mumbled something to Thomas before hurrying away again.

Thomas stepped close and bent to speak into my ear. "The enemy are concentrating nearby. We must flee, immediately. Else we shall be surrounded and crushed."

I nodded my thanks as he retreated and turned my attention back to Bertrand.

He licked his lips again. His face was already healing.

"If I gave you fresh blood to drink," I said. "which would heal your wounds, and put a sword in your hand, would you serve me?"

I saw how the idea of it outraged him. He, a great lord, serving me, a landless, rootless knight. But he must have known that he could never go back to how he was and he marshalled his civility and nodded.

"You would take no revenge against Orus, the man who killed your cousin Hughues?"

Hatred crossed his face but again he nodded.

Thomas bent down beside me. "We will be hurrying across the city for a long time, avoiding patrols. One shout from him would condemn us all."

Bertrand glared at the old Templar before fixing me with what I am sure he believed was a sincere expression. "I would serve you faithfully." He swallowed. "My lord."

Outside, shouting filled the air, and my people gathered together in the hall behind me, ready to leave.

"You should pray now," I said.

"I swear, Richard, you can—"

I stabbed my knife into his head. He went down, bucking like a landed fish. He was an immortal and would have died hard from such a wound. For all that he had to die, I did not want him to suffer unduly. I pulled the blade from his skull and sawed it across his throat, worked it through the gristle and hacked through his spine.

Thomas was white as a ghost when I turned around. Stephen mumbled a prayer over the body.

"What do you think?" I said to them. "What is William doing here?"

"We must go," Stephen said. I ignored him.

Thomas growled. "It sounded to me as though William has fallen out with Hulegu and is attempting to flee from him. No?"

"Yes," I said. "Why send that damned fool and his squire into the palace at all?"

"That is it," Eva said. "William was sending him on a fool's errand. While Bertrand and Hughues were occupied elsewhere, William was going to flee."

"Leave by himself?" I said. "Yes, that is what he does. When his plans fail, he flees. Like a rat. He has lost control of Hulegu and he has fled."

"What was all that about immortal lords that William has made in France?" Thomas said.

"If we survive this city," I said. "We can think on it then. So, where is William? In the madrasa?"

"We believe William is fleeing, yes?" Stephen said. "So where is he fleeing to?"

"Anywhere," I said. "Away from Hulegu first, then he can go where he pleases. He has done so before."

"Abdullah?" Hassan said. "If you wished to flee to the west from the madrasa, which route would you take?"

The Saracen scholar needed no time to ponder it. "The Syrian Gate leads northwest, and the Kufa Gate to the southwest."

"Word is that Kufa surrendered to Hulegu's armies," Hassan said.

I nodded. "And the Syria Gate road leads to Damascus. And from there, he could travel to Acre and back to Christendom." Looking around at my men, I was struck for a moment by the uniqueness of each of them. They were powerful, grave, reliable. Almost all of them wanted revenge on Hulegu and not William. "Are we agreed that we shall travel across the city and cut William off before he flees through the Syria Gate? If he has already left through it, we shall pursue. Once William is dead, we shall withdraw." I held up my hands at their protests. "We shall withdraw from this Hell and prepare for an assault on Hulegu when he moves against Damascus. It is too dangerous here, we have pushed our luck far enough already and now we must push it further, travelling across the city. If we stay and wait for Hulegu we shall be caught for sure. This way is best, is it not?"

Some were unhappy but they acquiesced.

Quickly, we collected everything we needed, wrapped our Mongol clothing tighter about us, and set out once more into the boiling chaos.

In spite of the thousands of men rampaging through the streets, we made it all the way across the city and were closing on the Syria Gate when we met with disaster.

It was growing late in the day and I prayed for the night to envelop us. We kept together as we moved through the smaller streets, heading north, then west, then south, and west again. The city was scarred and bloodied. The frenzied first days of the sacking was fading into exhaustion, as the easiest pickings had been plucked and countless thousands of the residents of the city had already been slaughtered. Most doors were thrown open and the rooms within dark and covered in debris and blood. We cut through the side streets and alleys until we came to the main road.

That roadway, leading from the centre of the round city to the edge through the three concentric walls, led right the way through all three gatehouses. The road was itself bordered by walls with open arches every few yards, leading to the streets to either side. Beside one of those arched entrances, we paused and my company gathered in a loose group, looking outward along the main road.

"We are now between the outer gatehouse and the centre gatehouse," Abdullah said, peeking out.

"Orus," I said, pointing up. "Climb the wall. Look for a Frankish man. Any man who looks like me."

The Mongol nodded, and Khutulun—always at his side—scrambled up beside him. After only a moment, Eva followed, pulling herself up the ornate stonework of the wall all the way to the flat top.

"We cannot go this way, Richard," Hassan said, pointing to the enclosed roadway. "We could be surrounded and trapped."

I did not bother to disguise my contempt. "That is why it is the perfect place to ambush William." He began to argue but I stepped up to him and lowered my voice. "Flee, then, if you are so afraid."

He was gravely insulted but he did not have time to voice his protestations for a shout came from above my head.

"By God, Richard," Eva said from up on the wall. "He is there!" She pointed toward the outer gatehouse. "Dressed in Mongol attire."

My heart hammered in my chest and my people stirred all around me.

"You are certain?" I asked.

She glanced down at me and her eyes were cold as the winter winds of the steppe. Eva had been his prisoner. William had held her and he had cut her throat, bleeding her to the point of death. It had been decades but I could picture it in my mind's eye. Of course she was certain.

"How far?" I said as she and my two Mongols jumped down.

She grabbed me. "He is right there. Close enough to spit on. A hundred yards. He stood out as he is alone, on foot, walking swiftly."

I grinned. My quarry was about to be under my blade. "Come," I ordered my people.

"But if he is dressed as a Mongol and not even mounted," Stephen said, "how can we be sure it is William and not some—"

I shoved him aside and ran out into the roadway. It was wide enough for two wagons to pass each other and as straight as an arrow. Far ahead was the massive, squat, outer gatehouse with its shining cupola on top. Close behind me was another gatehouse. These structures turned the roadway into a tunnel, and I knew I had to reach William before he reached the outer one.

For there he was. A solitary man up ahead, dressed as a rich Mongol warrior—in mail armour and steel helm—but his tall frame, upright posture, and loping gait marked him out as an Englishman in a barbarian's clothing. At the pace he was making, he would be through the gatehouse and outside the round city walls in little time.

There were other men about. A group of three riders ambled in my direction. Behind, in the centre gatehouse, a dozen or more men joked and shouted, drunk and belligerent.

But William was alone. Without followers.

Without protection.

My feet pounded on the paved surface as I ran headlong at my brother. There was no thought of honour in my head, simply the urge to slay him. I would draw my sword and assault him without challenge, and then my companions would assist me in cutting him into pieces. There were so many of us, and so few of him.

It was so close that I felt that my task was already done. I could taste the victory on my lips.

But God is cruel.

He had given me that taste, had brought me and William together on that road from across a city of a million people as though it was fated that I would finally fulfil the destiny that He had set out for me.

Only to snatch it away.

Just behind William, a group of Mongol warriors streamed out of a row of archways in the side of the road on their horses. They came out quickly, a half dozen, then quickly more followed behind. They spilled out to fill the road from one wall to the other. They were not looting, they were a zuut of close to a hundred sober soldiers, mounted and armoured, clutching their lances and bows.

William was lost from view beyond them.

I wanted to push my way through but there was a wall of horse and metal in my way. Behind me, my companions drew to a stop and looked to me.

Eva, Thomas, Hassan, Orus, Khutulun, Jalal. Stephen and Abdullah.

We were outnumbered more than ten to one.

"Are they here for us?" Thomas said, his voice tight and anguished.

The enemy were indeed taking an interest in us, and many rode toward our position. We must have looked incredibly suspicious. A few of them already had their hands on their weapons.

Every moment we delayed, William was getting further from my grasp.

"It does not matter," I said, drawing my sword. "I am cutting my way through."

Would my people follow me? Eva would, and Thomas too. Would Stephen flee for his life? Would the Saracens and my Mongols turn tail and decide that Hulegu was their only target after all?

There was no time to discuss it or to force them into obedience.

One of the dozens of Mongols just ahead saw me for what I was. A foreign enemy with a drawn sword. He pointed with his spear and raised his voice to his fellows riding at his side and they were not the sort to hesitate.

Then again, neither was I.

So I charged them first.

The sturdy horses were mostly unarmoured and so I slashed my blade into the animals' faces and eyes and sent many reeling. I moved into the mass of enemies, laying about me at man or beast who ventured near. Some riders fought to hold on to their injured animals, but a few slid off their horses and came at me on foot. Spear thrusts and sword blades flashed, clanged against me. Something smacked into my helm, and I was struck hard on the shoulder.

My armour held but my anger built. I cut at whatever flesh I could see, and punched and shoved, always moving forward.

Sounds of battle grew behind me, and I knew that at least some of my men were fighting.

But the enemy were too many. The horses were like mountains of flesh and the air grew close and the shouting loud. I could not find my way through and clear. Their number appeared endless. It was difficult to see in any direction but for a moment I had a glimpse through the chaos.

Behind me, my company was surrounded and attacked on all sides. Eva was swarmed by furious Mongols, their lances thrusting at her all from all directions as she twisted and danced in an ever-smaller space. Thomas thrashed at the spears that jabbed down at him. A blade flashed at Abdullah, who screamed as he fell, blood gushing from his neck, before an axe crashed into the top of his head.

My people needed me. And yet, with every moment, William's escape grew ever more certain.

Marshalling my strength, I threw down the men around me and climbed up onto a horse. It tried to throw me but the others were crowded so tight around it that the beast could not even turn. There was a half dozen mounted between me and the nearest wall. I struck down the men in my path, avoiding or turning their blows. A weak spear thrust from an overextended Mongol hit me on the chest, checking my progress. I seized the weapon and heaved. The foolish man attempted to hold on to the shaft of his spear and he fell from his horse amongst the stamping hooves. As he fell, I jumped over him to the back of the next horse. Those Mongols had never faced an enemy as strong and fast as me and as brave as they were, they were also afraid. I powered through them all the way to the wall and leapt up to the jutting stonework over the archway. My sword blade scraped against the plaster but I dragged myself up onto the top of the wall. It was flat and level and wider than shoulder width. On the other side, the street leading into the city was also packed with Mongol horsemen. I was wrong about it being a single zuut of a hundred men. It was two zuut at least, crowding the streets and ready to kill us when they got clear.

Glancing behind me, I saw my company engaged with the Mongols down on the road, making little headway. They were surrounded. Orus and Khutulun fought back to back. Thomas stabbed into the horses with a fury I had never seen in him before. Stephen crouched behind Eva, who ducked and slipped from the blows while striking back at the Mongols who tried to kill her. Hassan, Jalal, Radi and Raka fought together and cut a swathe into the enemy at an oblique angle away from the others. But all four Assassins looked wounded already, Radi with a great gash across his crown, and Raka being supported by Jalal. The air reeked of blood. Writhing Mongol bodies littered the path and more fell with every moment. The shouts and screams echoed between the walls as they died. But there were so many. How long could my people survive against such odds?

Glancing the other way, I saw William still hurrying away, now almost at the massive gatehouse. Almost free. He seemed to half turn at that moment but I did not know if he saw me or not.

I had to kill him. It was my last chance.

But it meant sacrificing my people.

Losing Eva.

An arrow struck the wall at my feet and snapped, just as another slashed the air by my head.

I ran.

Along the wall, heading for William.

My leather shoes slapped on the stones that capped the top of the wall, and I raced along it faster than any mortal man. A Mongol archer can hit a bird on the wing but none of the arrows shot at me brought me down. In no time at all, I left the roaring mass of men behind me and the gatehouse loomed ahead. It was the size of a squat castle keep but was a simple structure. I considered climbing from the wall up onto the top of the gatehouse, running across the roof and then dropping down the other side to cut him off.

If only I had made that choice. I may have ended William's life there and then and so saved the people of the world from centuries of his evil.

However, I saw men up there on the top of the gatehouse. Mongols or their allies had seized the building and I would have to avoid them or fight them. I was afraid that any delay on the roof would mean William escaping beneath me and so decided on the direct approach. Nearing the gatehouse entrance, I stepped down the stonework over the last archway in the sidewall and then dropped to the road, landing heavily in my Saracen armour. Ahead of me, the road became a dark tunnel. Inside the gatehouse, William fled.

Shouts behind me. It was the Mongol zuut. Of course, they were chasing me. Of course, they would never have simply watched me run away in full view and done nothing to follow. There were at least a dozen riders, perhaps many more.

I felt dread descending. A sense that, on that day and in all the years since I left Constantinople, I had always been making the worst choice in every moment.

But what could I do? I had to fight on along the path before me.

So I ran for William, ran into the chill darkness beneath the mass of the gatehouse.

"William!" I roared, in my battlefield voice. His name echoed from the black walls and the low ceiling above.

Ahead, halfway along and silhouetted against the square of light at the end of the tunnel, he stopped. He turned.

Despite the darkness, and his Mongol garb, I could see it was certainly my brother. His build, his stance and the outline of his features in the gloom. And he would have been in no doubt who it was that challenged him. Finally, after so many years in pursuit, we would face each other in combat, one man against the other, with God alone as our judge.

And William ran.

The coward turned back and ran away from me toward the outer city and freedom.

Even though I should have known, I was outraged by his cowardice. My anger gave my feet wings and I gained on him while I outpaced my mounted pursuers. William grew so close that I could hear his shoes slapping on the stone, could hear his breath heaving. He was in front of me, so close that I could almost reach him with the point of my sword.

And then there was a sound. At first, I thought it was the thundering of hooves closing on me. But it was instead a great clanging sound that came from all around and especially from above me. Instinct slowed me as I searched for the source of the danger. A metallic clashing of chains running and a rumbling sound that grew in volume and pitch as if some mighty armoured monster descended from the sky.

It came from above.

At the last moment, I looked up and saw something massive rushing toward me and so I checked my run and fell backwards. I scrambled away, terrified and confused by what it could be.

The huge portcullis crashed down with an almighty bang, closing off the tunnel. It had missed my outstretched feet by a few inches. For a long moment, the only sound was my panting breath and the blood pounding in my ears. Then, behind me, dozens of hooves echoed and I rolled and jumped to my feet.

On the other side, William rose and turned. He looked up at the thick timber and iron portcullis that divided us.

He laughed.

William looked through one of the square gaps at me and he laughed.

"Do you doubt that God is with me, brother?" he asked, smiling like the devil.

I was struck dumb. Stood there, breathing heavily, shaking with rage. After a moment, I dropped my sword, grabbed the portcullis and heaved upward. I was ready to jump back from him in case he attacked me through the square spaces but William simply watched me, an amused expression on his face.

Of course, I could not move it. Not even an inch. Not even with my great strength. I may as well have tried to lift a castle wall.

"Are they friends of yours, Richard?" he asked, pointing behind me. "Or should you be concerned?"

I snatched up my sword.

Mongol soldiers from the zuut filled the entrance of the tunnel from wall to wall. Gathering in a mass of horses and men and approaching slowly, cautiously. No doubt unsure about what was happening, and frozen in indecision by their race's unwillingness to be trapped in an enclosed space. Yet they still approached, and when they decided to attack, they would have me cornered and outnumbered at least twenty to one.

"Friends of mine?" I said. "Friends of yours, you heathen bastard."

He made a sound like a snort. "I do not know those barbarian filth. And they do not know me."

A mad, faint hope that he would be able to call them off died into nothing.

I looked back at him, keeping an eye on the Mongols. "Ah yes. You have fallen into conflict with Hulegu, your lord and master."

His grin fell from his face. "I have no master. Lords and princes serve me."

It was my turn to laugh. "You are a damned fool. You gave the gift of your blood to these barbarians and you expected them to stay subservient. You were always mad but now you have betrayed your people."

He scoffed. "My people are whoever I chose them to be. You cannot understand, Richard. You lack the wits to see it. You lack the courage of thought. My plans are beyond you."

"Your plans?" I said. "Like granting your gift to certain lords in France? Who are they, William? Who did you turn into an immortal?"

The Mongols argued with each other behind me.

William tilted his head, a frown creasing his forehead. "You have been speaking to Bertrand, I take it? How is our friend? Is he with you?"

"I cut off his head. As I will do to you."

He sighed, pinching the bridge of his nose. "Richard, that is the difference between us. You had him in your power. A knight, a lord. Immensely rich. Known to the King of France. You could have turned him into a follower, an acolyte, and strengthened yourself immensely. Instead, you destroyed him. You are a fool."

"Is that what you were doing in France, then?" I said. "Who there did you turn into a follower?"

His eyes flicked to the Mongols and back to me. "Are you not concerned that you are about to be murdered, Richard? I hope you have a plan to escape? I would hate to witness your death."

"Save your jests. And do not tell me, then. It matters not. I will undo your plans, wherever you have laid them in France."

He waved a hand, casually. "I gave the Gift to many people, great and small, and not only in France but all over." William grinned at my shock. "But you should not be concerned about them. If you do return to Christendom, you should seek our grandfather. The Ancient One."

The Mongols edged closer. A small group dismounted and strutted toward me, spreading out as they approached. At least two clutched bows but they did not shoot at me.

"What are you blathering about?" I said over my shoulder. I assumed he meant our father's father. "The old lord de Ferrers was long dead when we were sired."

"The old Lord de Ferrers was not our father's true father." William laughed. "Our true grandfather lives, and he is thousands of years old, Richard. Thousands! The things he has seen. The power that he has. You would learn a lot from him, brother, if you would but go to him."

Before I could respond, eight of the Mongols moved quickly to surround and then attack me. Spear thrusts to keep me pinned against the portcullis, while others darted in with their swords.

I was too angry to fight intelligently. I cut down two of them and wounded three more before they retreated. But I took a hard blow on the helm, which hurt terribly and I had irrevocably bent my sword blade so I picked up one dropped by an attacker. The Mongols did not retreat far, and many more of them pushed their way closer inside the tunnel. Behind them, more still seemed to come from the road to block out the light and fill the tunnel with their stench. I wondered whether any of my company had survived. I wondered if I had sacrificed the life of Eva for nothing. William was so close but he may as well have been on the other side of the Earth for all the good it did me.

And I was growing ever more certain that I could not fight my way clear of so many. Dozens of Mongols now, many mounted, many with bows, spread themselves around me and prepared to attack once again.

I was going to die in that tunnel, and I would die alone, and without honour. Dishonoured and unremembered.

"Here they come again, brother," William said.

"Waiting to see me die?" I said over my shoulder, bitterly.

"I would prefer it if you lived," he said.

The Mongols rushed me again, coming in a group of ten. A full arban, ten men who lived and fought together as one. They fought well, but they had never trained to fight just one man all at the same time, and they had never faced any man like me. When one grappled me, I threw him into another. I grabbed a spear swung at my head, ripped it from the wielder's grasp, flipped it and stabbed it through the bones of his face before he had time to flinch. Again, they fled from me before I could bring them all down.

"You are rather good, Richard," William said, pointing at his own cheek. "Though, you took a wound there."

I felt my face and my fingers slipped into a gash beneath my left eye. As is often the way with wounds, I could not recall any specific blow that might have caused it.

"It is nothing," I said, as the hot blood welled down to my neck.

"Perhaps you might try drinking the blood of these next fellows?" William said. "You may find it helps, you know?"

And more came at me. I pushed out into them and kept moving along the portcullis, keeping my back to it so that they could not fully surround me.

I was tired. My arms seemed to move slowly and I missed a spear strike and it punched me high on the chest, causing me to miss a cut aimed at a Mongol neck. The interruption of my timing caused my defence to fall apart and I was struck on the head and arms and then a rain of blows knocked me hard against the portcullis. Mongol soldiers fought mostly in silence but they were now shouting and the roar of voices filled the tunnel, filled my head as the pain of their attacks thundered in my head. With horror, I realised I had fallen to one knee, and the fear drove me up to my feet again and I threw them off from me, lying about me with a sword in one hand and a broken spear in the other.

When they retreated, I fell against the portcullis, sucking air into my lungs and shaking all over.

Blood ran into my eyes and I felt the sharp-cold pain of a cut on my forehead somewhere.

I dropped the spear and raised my left hand to my face but there was something wrong with my trembling arm. A gash on my wrist pumped blood over my hand and down to the floor in a thick stream. The mail at my left shoulder was torn open and a wound beneath gaped, shining black in the darkness.

A fallen Mongol at my feet groaned and crawled away. I took a step to him and stamped down on his neck to immobilise him, then stabbed my blade through the side of his neck. I had to be quick while the others argued about who would attack me next. No doubt they were enjoying the fight, otherwise they would have finished me with a storm of arrows. The injured man groaned as I dropped my sword and pulled the man up by his filthy coat with one hand and held him while I sunk my teeth into the wound on his neck where his blood spurted.

The warm blood filled my mouth and my belly

It made me strong, and my wounds felt hot as they began to heal.

A hail of arrows crashed into me.

The Mongols had perhaps been horrified by blood drinking, or they were simply done with testing themselves against me and repeatedly failing. All I knew was the storm of a score of arrows, and then a dozen more, hitting my helm, my leg, the portcullis behind me, and many hit the body of the dying man in my hands. I retreated to the portcullis and used the body as a shield, ducked behind it. Arrows stuck in his clothing, others hit his flesh with a wet smack. The force of the arrows pushed me back into the portcullis while I held on to the body, though it shook with the impacts. An arrow stuck in my lower leg, and another hit me in the shoulder, slipping deep into the wound beneath the ripped mail. The pain was exquisite and I wailed and hugged the body to me as my legs failed and I went down. The archers had spread out to either side and peppered me from angles that my meat shield could not defend. My helm was hit again and my skull rang with the pain, my vision clouded with silver-white snow.

Perhaps I blacked out. Lost my senses, at least. A voice roared at me to get up. The smell of fresh blood filled my nose.

A mass of Mongols picked their way toward me in a wide arc, swords, and daggers drawn.

Something was by my head, demanding attention.

William had pushed his bared forearm through a square gap in the portcullis. He had cut his wrist and blood welled and gushed out of it, covering his hand with glistening, dark blood.

"Drink!" he roared at me.

I did not hesitate. I grabbed his arm, sank my teeth into his wrist and sucked the hot blood down.

It had been sixty years since I had last drunk my brother's blood. I remembered how it had given me greater strength than any mortal blood. And once again, it was like drinking lightning, like consuming the whirlwind. Shards of ice and fire ran like lightning through my veins, to the tips of my fingers and filled my head with clarity of vision, clarity of thought.

Every sense burned and the world became hard-edged and bright like the midday desert sun. Every muscle felt as if it would burst, as if I had grown to twice my size. I felt like a giant, though I knew I was not. A great passion for murder filled every part of me, and I had to kill, had to tear down every man and every building in the city.

I stood and threw the arrow-filled Mongol body at a man in front of me as if it was no heavier than a stone, knocking the man down and the one behind him. Most of the others froze in shock and I ran into the men, a red mist descending and my sense of self fading. I was all passion and no thought. It seemed as though God or the Devil was in my bones, and I grabbed the men and smashed them with my hands. I drove their heads into the portcullis, into the walls. I threw them up into the ceiling and snapped their necks and crushed their skulls. My fists broke their faces into bloody pulp and I stamped their throats and chests, crushing them underfoot. Though they fled from me, I was faster than the fleetest of them and killed a dozen, and then two dozen, even before they could flee into the light beyond. It was so bright out there that the glare hurt my eyeballs and I shielded my eyes, looking for more men to murder.

Beyond the escaping Mongols, the sounds of battle filled the air. They were being killed from the rear also, and the great mass of them scattered away from where I stood, cringing against the walls of the tunnel. They were brave men, but they were right to be afraid of me and I chased them down also, dashing their brains out against the blood-smeared walls while they wailed and screamed and prayed to their barbarian gods.

The stench of blood was glorious. I drank from the tattered neck of a head that I had ripped from its body, the last of the blood within streaming into my mouth and over my face. But soon there were no more men to kill and, though it yet raged, I felt the bloodlust of William's blood diminishing.

Someone was calling my name, a distant sound that echoed through the groans of the men who were dead but did not yet know it.

A man strode toward me and I turned and seized him, lifting him so that I might bite his throat out and fill myself once more.

"Richard, stop!"

A woman.

Eva cried out and then she was at my side, holding my arm.

"It is Thomas, Richard," she cried. "You hold Thomas. He is a friend, Richard. You must let him go."

His grimacing face came into focus and I dropped him, pushing him away so that he fell. Eva backed away from me and the fear in her eyes shook me further out of my rage.

Looking about me, I saw a slaughterhouse. Bodies everywhere, walls and ceiling sprayed with blood and the floor underfoot splashed with it from the disembowelled and dismembered men and horses that filled the tunnel. Someone finished off a dying horse, cutting off the horrendous sound of its suffering.

My surviving companions, bloodied and battered, stood about the entrance in the light of an orange sunset. Beyond them, Mongols rode hard away from us down the roadway toward the distant middle gatehouse, fleeing the bloody horror. Orus supported a wounded Khutulun. Stephen had somehow survived but was covered in blood and had the mad, blank post-battle stare. Hassan leaned on a spear, without helm and with tattered armour hanging from him. There was no Jalal, Radi or Raka. I remembered that I had seen Abdullah fall and indeed, he was also absent. No doubt lying dead back there on the road with the three Assassins.

I had abandoned my companions for William.

Recalling my brother, I turned and ran to the portcullis. William was still on the other side, grinning at me, at the carnage that I waded through. Behind him, small groups of other men drifted toward the portcullis, Mongols or Turkomens, staring at the blood and gore and smashed bodies. Their voices were raised in protest but they stood and did nothing, for now.

"Why?" I shouted at William. "Why give me your blood?" I grabbed the portcullis and glared through it at him.

"You are my brother," he said as if that explained it.

"I will still kill you," I said. "I will still hunt you to the ends of the Earth."

He took a deep breath. "I wish you would not. For it is to the ends of the Earth that I am going, and I do not believe you will fare well there. Look at what a mess you have made in this city. Go home, Richard."

"The ends of the Earth?" I asked. "Where is that? You are fleeing Hulegu, no?"

"Hulegu and Mongke have other brothers. One of them is Kublai, and he controls the East. He means to conquer all Cathay and he can do it, with my help. There are a hundred cities there the size of Baghdad, and a thousand grander than Paris. If Mongke should fall, Kublai will become the Great Khan, again, with my help."

"You will not be able to control him," I said. "No more than you could Hulegu, nor any of these others who you have given the Gift."

He smiled. "I do not wish to control him. I will make myself a prince and do my work in peace. All I need is wealth, I see that now. Wealth, and land. You should return to Christendom, brother, you are not capable of surviving in foreign lands, amongst foreign people. You have too much hatred in your heart."

"I will never stop coming for you," I said. "God desires you dead, and I am His instrument."

William sighed. He looked around at the Turkomen who gathered closer to him. No doubt they were wondering who he was and why we were conversing.

"Is there any chance you would return the favour and let me drink your blood, brother? I would greatly love to feel that power. I would make short work of these men, would I not?"

"My only regret in seeing you cut down before my eyes," I said, "will be that it was not my own sword that ended you."

He sighed again and spoke rapidly. "A deal, perhaps?" He held up a hand as I began to protest. "I gave my blood and turned at least thirty, serfs and lords, between Nottingham and

Acre. Do you want to know who they are, where they are, so that you can hunt them?"

I hesitated. How could I deal with a devil such as he? I was a fool to even consider it, I knew that much. But how much destruction could thirty immortals do to my homeland? To Christendom as a whole? What deviousness were they working on my people even as we spoke?

"You can never turn me away from my pursuit of you," I said.

"Perhaps I could postpone it?" William said. "All I need is two hundred years, brother." I laughed with scorn but he continued. "What is such a span to the likes of us?"

"You could turn a thousand men into immortals in such time," I said.

"But no Christians," he said.

"You would turn your Cathay armies against Christendom," I said.

"Never," he said. "I swear it."

I laughed at his lies.

"I will tell you where our grandfather lives," he said.

That gave me pause. "You are filled with lies."

"Never to you, brother." He tilted his head. "Have you ever known me to tell a lie?"

A clanking noise echoed around the tunnel and William glared at me.

"Quickly, Richard. Swear you will not follow me to Cathay and I will tell you where to find our ancient grandfather. And I will tell you where my Gifted are."

I punched my fist into the portcullis so hard that the entire thing shook and my skin split, leaving blood on the wood. "Agreed. I swear it. But I shall kill you the moment you return to Christendom."

He grinned. "Our grandfather is in Swabia. In a forest, living in a cave. The locals live in terror of him."

The portcullis shook and shifted up as the chains took the strain. William began backing away.

"Who did you make immortal?" I shouted.

"A French lord named Simon de Montfort," William said, raising his voice and still retreating. "An English knight named Hugh le Despenser. Both of them men after my own heart, you will find."

"Who else?" I roared.

But he turned and ran. He ran through the massing crowd of Turkomen and they made only half-hearted attempts to stop him. He struck down a man or two and sent them flying as he ran. The portcullis shook and began to rise, slowly. So slowly.

"Richard," Eva said, at my shoulder. "We must go." She stared at the massed soldiers on the other side.

"We can kill them all," I said, unwilling to let William go without more names.

"Perhaps," she said. "But your men are hurt. Exhausted. They need you."

I looked at her. She was injured. She had no sword. The others behind me were in a similar poor condition. And there was the stark absence of the men who had already fallen.

The portcullis shook and rose further, winched up from some mechanism beyond the ceiling. I slammed my hands against it, sensing that I had somehow been bested by my brother once more.

"We need horses," I said to my men. "Supplies."

"And quickly," Thomas said. "Before he gets too far."

"Quickly, yes," I said, as we moved away from the tunnel. "But we are not pursuing him."

They stared at me.

"We must retreat from this place," I said. "Eventually, we shall return to the Kingdom of Jerusalem. We must gather our strength and take our time doing so, waiting until our moment is right. And then we must kill Hulegu at a place of our choosing."

"What about your vile, murdering brother?" Thomas said, raising a shaking finger to point down the tunnel of the gatehouse.

"He has gone to the East," I said. "And I will kill him when he returns."

"When will that be?" Stephen asked.

"One day," I said. They were outraged. Furious, even, and they had every right to be. "We will slaughter the Khan and his men, first."

Orus smiled and looked at Khutulun. She nodded. "Hulegu now."

None of my people were happy with our failure. My failure. And yet I am certain they were relieved to be leaving that horror of a city.

Moving as a group, we slipped further through Baghdad toward the gate, avoiding contact with enemies where we could. As night fell, we rounded up a horse for each of us, and a few spares, killing the men guarding them. We wrapped ourselves in Mongol coats and followed Orus and Khutulun through the final gate into the mass of the surrounding army and rode in the moonlight as if we were an arban about an official task. We were challenged only a few times, and Orus shouted responses that satisfied our enemies. It was in our favour that the armies were so disparate, from so many nations and cities, and all expected to see strangers amongst them. Still, I was shocked by the size of the forces that stretched here and there for miles. All come to share in picking clean the monstrous great carcass of the greatest city in the world.

Then we were free, riding on or parallel to the Damascus road until we turned off to hide out in a village a hundred miles away. There we drank blood from the Saracen villagers and took over their meagre homes while keeping them prisoner. Hassan pointed out that it would be better to kill them outright in case they alerted roving Mongol patrols to our presence but I had seen quite enough murder for the time being. Instead, we ate their goats, mended our gear.

And we waited.

Following my abandonment of my companions on the road in Baghdad, I found that the relationship between me and each of them—other than perhaps Orus and Khutulun, who had a barbarian's immorality—, had changed. There was no denying I had committed a great sin by fleeing from them when they needed me to fight to save them and they would all trust me even less than they had before. The only one I truly cared about was Eva and she did not wish to discuss it, assuring me that it was not important. I knew she was lying but I was happy to accept the falsehood.

Stephen was shaken by the whole terrible event and had faced certain death by the screaming Mongols all around him. It was indeed remarkable that he had survived but he did not forgive me for putting him in that situation nor, of course, for leaving him to die. I think that he also mourned Abdullah.

The Saracen had taken a Mongol axe in the top of his head, splitting his skull in two. I had never much liked the man, despite finding a grudging respect for him in time, yet I felt particularly guilty for his death. Despite being banished for a social impropriety, he had cared enough about his homeland, his city, his people, to stay and fight when he could have done anything else and many thousands of his countrymen had given up. After all his snivelling and complaining, the man had discovered an admirable moral core to his soul but thanks to my actions, he would never be able to develop further. At least he did not have to witness the complete annihilation of his city.

There was no doubt that the esteem in which Thomas held me had declined. The man was always reserved but his demeanour became rather cooler for quite some time. On the other hand, he was a man who well understood the importance of duty and the conflicts that could arise between one duty that clashed with another.

Hassan was deeply angered because he had lost Jalal, Radi, and Raka and all three had died in order to protect him, their master. Even so, Hassan had almost himself been cut down. I could well imagine that he cursed me and chastised himself for ever trusting a Frank like me but he silently seethed instead. It seemed likely that any night he would cut my throat in my sleep but Eva thought otherwise.

"He will very likely do it," she said. "But not until we have killed Hulegu."

Later, I found out what had happened in Baghdad after we escaped it.

The Christians who assembled in the Nestorian church and some of the foreign visitors were spared, but the Mohammedan population was subjected to almost complete extermination. The Christian soldiers from Georgia and Armenia took great joy in it, for killing Saracens was what God wanted. And no civilised man could contend otherwise.

When all in the city were dead, and all the wealth plundered, then the palaces and the mosques, the university and libraries, the homes and the markets, were set on fire. The contents of the Caliph's treasure house were loaded into two vast wagon trains, with one sent to Mongke Khan in far-off Karakorum, and the other sent to a city called Maragha in the north of Persia where Hulegu would make his capital.

During the week of slaughter, Hulegu held a banquet with the Caliph in the palace itself. Hulegu pretended that the Caliph was the host and that Hulegu was the guest. He mocked the caliph for not using his treasure to pay soldiers to protect his city. For what was treasure worth if you could not keep it?

When the city was finally in ruins, the Caliph and his sons were sewn up in beautiful carpets and trampled to death beneath the hooves of the horses of Hulegu's immortal retinue.

The Vizier, Abdullah's uncle, was retained in his office and served the Mongols. He faced the impossible task of rebuilding the city. He began immediately and worked to the best of his ability for three months.

He attempted this task for three months only because then the Vizier died.

The Shiites said he died of a broken heart because his city had been destroyed. The Sunnites said it was due to the guilt and shame he felt at betraying his caliph, and that he could not live with that decision.

The truth is that I killed him myself.

Although my companions and I argued over the risks involved, ultimately, I believed it would be worth it. We crept back to the city after most of the armies had moved off to new pastures and slipped through the few Mongols that remained. After three months of plundering, there was nothing left to protect, so no one was guarding anything with any great dedication. The Mongol garrison troops within the city were spread out and living in half-demolished and burned palaces, carousing and drunk as lords all night and lying insensible in their own piss through the day. It was remarkably simple to avoid any trouble.

While the others guarded the approaches and held our horses ready for the escape, Hassan and I walked almost right up to the Vizier's bedchambers before cutting down the armed servants who attempted to thwart us. Hassan had been angry for three months, since the deaths of his men. Angry at me for the failure of my Baghdad strategy, for my tactical errors and abandonment of them during the sacking, and he was angry at the world and at himself. He rejoiced in the killing of the Vizier's men and I was glad that he was taking it out on them rather than me.

Letting ourselves into the enormous, marble room, the most powerful man in Baghdad fell to his knees before us, weeping and begging for his life.

"We are here for your treasury," I told him and he told us all we needed to know about how to take it.

"God is greatest," he said, praying through his tears.

"Was it worth it?" I asked him.

The Vizier seemed almost relieved when my dagger pierced his neck.

I drank a little from him and passed him to Hassan, who savagely sucked down the blood before tossing his body across an ornate couch. We were already long gone by the time anyone raised an alarm. Perhaps no one ever did.

The wealth that had been left to the vizier by the Mongols was in the form of gold, silver, and gem stones locked in the much-reduced treasure room to be used for rebuilding the city. All that treasure, we stole, packing it into bags shared between two dozen horses that we rode and led out from the ruins of Baghdad without being challenged once, nor even pursued.

A mercenary act on the face of it, perhaps, but I needed a large amount to buy horses and equipment, to find places for us to live, and to pay for slaves to serve us and to provide blood for my people. And I had to pay vast sums for information on the whereabouts and activities of Hulegu while we planned our assault on his palace and the final assassination of him and his men.

It took us seven years.

But then, in early AD 1265, we were ready for the final assault on Hulegu Khan and his immortals.

Part Six
Maragha
1265

I WAS THE FIRST ONE TO CLIMB the border wall of Hulegu's palace compound, my fingers clinging to the cracks between the dark stone in the black moonless night. The compound was within a city, and there were thousands of people in homes and in the streets all around us, and guards and servants within the palace walls. My weapons were wrapped tight so they could not make a sound, and I wore no armour. Dressed in a close-fitting tunic in the Persian style, with a rider's trousers beneath and a Mongol hood and coat over it all, I was able to move swiftly in relative silence. Beneath me, hanging suspended from my belt, was a heavy sack and the sound that it made brushing against the stone as I climbed seemed loud enough to wake the dead. I prayed that it would alert no one, as the rest of my company scaled the wall behind me or waited their turn to mount the wall in the shadows below.

Years of planning and preparation had preceded my scaling of that wall, and I was just about as nervous as I had ever been in my life. It seemed to me that anyone within fifty feet would be able to hear the thumping of my heart and I had to remember to breathe in and out or else I would have suffocated myself from apprehension. I felt like a weak-kneed squire riding toward my first battle.

A chunk of mortar broke off beneath my fingers and I crashed against the wall, cursing under my breath. The sack I was carrying bounced off the wall and the contents jostled inside. From somewhere below, I heard the nervous hissing of my comrades.

Stealthiness had never been my forte. Always, I had been made for the direct approach and the intricacies and timings of our infiltration had me rattled. If the slightest thing went wrong, we would be assaulted on all sides by numbers that we could never hope to overcome.

Gathering myself, I climbed on.

On the other hand, if everything went according to plan, then it would end in an orgy of tremendous violence all the same.

And that was something I was familiar with.

As my hands reached the top of the wall, I pulled myself up and peeked over into the cluster of service buildings with yellow lamplight glowing from windows and doors, and the marble mass of the grand palace itself.

It was quiet below and so I whistled faintly and listened as my companions began their climbs. Sliding over the top, dragging the sack carefully behind me, I slithered down into the shadows and waited for the others to join me.

How we came to be scaling that wall on a cold night in early 1265 involves an assassination, the Mongol Empire's first great defeat, and a massive civil war.

So much had happened since Baghdad fell. So much had changed.

After sacking Baghdad and massacring its people, Hulegu Khan intended to go on and conquer the rest of the Mohammedan lands and then to subdue Anatolia and destroy Constantinople. Once that great bastion of civilisation on the edge of Europe was gone, there would be nothing stopping them pouring across Christendom all the way to the Atlantic coast. The knowledge of those plans, won through interrogation of captured soldiers and bribed merchants and diplomats, instilled in me both a terrible fear and a determination to stop the khan at all costs, even if it meant my own life. But I knew that I must be patient, for I would get only one chance to put an end to him and his men.

Hulegu left three thousand Mongols in Baghdad to rebuild it but without the Vizier in charge, they accomplished nothing. I had seen their greatest city, and Karakorum was a pathetic, barbarian place. For all the wealth they had plundered, for all the multitudes of engineers and artisans from civilised peoples that they had pressed into slavery for them, the Mongols remained incapable of building anything of note, let alone rebuilding the greatness and beauty of Baghdad. In fact, even a hundred years later it remained mostly a ruin. And the people living around the city could no longer even be supported, as the Mongols had destroyed the intricate irrigation systems around the city and they were never rebuilt. Armies bring diseases and eat up the land like locusts, and vile plagues and famine remained after the Mongols left.

Other Mohammedan princes witnessed this destruction of Baghdad from afar, and it certainly appeared as though they felt any resistance to the Mongols to be hopeless. After Baghdad, Hulegu led his armies north to Tabriz to regroup and the remaining princes of Syria and Anatolia came one by one to offer their submission. For a time, we intended to assault him there but he remained on a war footing, with hundreds of thousands of men surrounding him and so instead we watched and waited.

After a period of consolidation lasting almost a year, Hulegu resumed his advance, this time towards the coast and Aleppo. His immortal second in command, a Mongol lord named Kitbuqa, commanded the vanguard and Hulegu himself commanded the centre of three grand armies. On his way to the coast, Hulegu finally subdued upper Iraq, where there were still holdouts. The Mongols reached Aleppo in January 1260 and took the city in mere days, although the town's citadel held out for another month. In that campaign, Hulegu was assisted by the King of Lesser Armenia and Crusader Bohemond VI of Antioch and Tripoli. The Mongols extended their power south into Palestine and it appeared to everyone that the entire Mediterranean coast would fall to them.

Watching it all happen from afar made me feel sick to my stomach. Most appalling of all was the relative weakness of those who attempted to stand against him and the ease with which Hulegu's forces overran them. I wondered with dread whether even the Kingdom of France and her allies could resist such a relentless onslaught. How long would Paris stand? Would Rome even take up arms?

But in truth, the Mongols were a long way yet from Europe and not all the Saracens had fallen. The great Sultan of Syria and the Mamluks of Egypt represented the only remaining chance for the Mohammedans. Hassan, even though they would have considered him as a dangerous heretic, wanted us to help the Mamluks just as we had hoped to help the Abbasids.

I said no.

We were done with that. Done with attempting to ally with the enemies of Christ and done with relying on anyone other than each other. Thanks to the Vizier's treasury, we had wealth enough to survive and to bide our time, and I told Hassan in no uncertain terms that is what we would do. Hassan grumbled but came to agree. Though his thirst for vengeance was as powerful as any of ours, the Assassins were well-versed in patience.

And then, across the world in the East, the Great Khan Mongke died.

It was many months before all Mongols heard and none of them knew that this death would signal the beginning of the end of a unified Mongol Empire.

The Great Khan had taken up the assault on the great nation of Cathay. News took a long time to travel, of course, but I heard eventually that he had died assaulting some Cathay fortress. There were a dozen whispered stories about how he had come to his end. We paid merchants for news and some told me that Mongke died of cholera during the siege. Another said he had shit himself to death in an endless bloody flux. Another told us that Mongke had drowned in a warship in the high seas while his armies besieged an island fortress. Another story said he was crossing a river, another swore he was being transported across a lake in a barge, and the vessel was destroyed by enemy fire, or it was a simple accident. A Hungarian silversmith fleeing his Mongol masters swore that Mongke had been killed by an arrow shot by an archer during an attack on an eastern castle, and then later the Hungarian's wife said the Great Khan had been incinerated by an explosive bomb launched from a trebuchet.

But I knew the truth.

William had killed him.

The timing was too perfect for it to be otherwise. By my calculations, it would have taken about a year and a half for William to travel from Baghdad all the way to the Mongol assault on China. There, he had somehow managed to poison Mongke. Poison was a method of murder familiar to him and no doubt the Great Khan's lifelong abuse of wine had thoroughly weakened his constitution. And surely the number and sheer variety of stories indicated that the Mongols spread misinformation to cover up what they must have known to be a shameful assassination that demonstrated a terrible failure in state security. Or perhaps they believed Mongke had simply drunk himself to death. Thousands of other Mongols had gone the same way before.

But I was sure. It was a remarkable assassination, and one perhaps greater than any Ismaili Assassin had ever achieved, though Hassan insisted that it had to have been one of his own four hundred fedayin who had finally succeeded in their mission.

Why, Hassan had challenged me, would William have done this thing?

"Chaos," I said.

Following the death of the Great Khan, once again the worldwide campaigns of the Mongols came to quite a sudden halt. Chaos ensued.

And chaos was what William thrived on. Mongke's death in 1259 led to a four-year civil war between two of his brothers, Kublai and Ariq Boke. William had told me in Baghdad that he meant to throw in with Kublai, and with William's support, Kublai eventually won the succession war.

Although he never sought the position of Great Khan for himself, the struggle for the succession took Hulegu away from Syria and Persia, and he left his subordinates in charge. I was sure that Hulegu now knew that he and his core group of bodyguards and lords were immortal and he could afford to take his time. It was clear that he meant to become lord of all lands from Persia to France, and so he left the Middle East and headed home with most of his armies.

One of his immortals was named Kitbuqa. This man was left in command of a single tumen of about ten thousand men and, with this small force, he made the fatal mistake of attacking the Mamluks.

The Mamluks were newly in power in Egypt and were the vanquishers of the King of France in his dismal failure of Louis' crusade eight years earlier. Those Mamluks were not like the other Mohammedans the Mongols had faced. In fact, they were a slave army taken mostly from the steppe people of the north, especially the Kipchaks. These former steppe people understood Mongol tactics, and even employed them against the Mongols. Not only that, the Mamluks had the advantage of being equipped with the highest quality Egyptian armour and weapons and had much finer and more powerful horses than the Mongols did.

The Mamluks were led by a man named Baibars, under the Sultan Qutuz. Baibars would be remembered as a great leader of the Egyptians, though he was, in fact, a tall, fair-skinned and light-haired former slave stolen from his Kipchak people near the Black Sea when only a boy. Baibars knew that the great Hulegu and his officer corps had gone to the East and so they baited the Mongols into attacking by doing the one thing that was guaranteed to draw them in. They beheaded the Mongol envoys, which as any horse nomad could tell you, is how you categorically declare war on the steppe.

In September 1260, the two forces clashed in what came to be known as the Battle of Ain Jalut. The site was known as the Spring of Goliath, and it was the very place that King David flung his stone at the Philistine champion.

It was an appropriate coincidence.

Strangely enough, although my companions took no part in it, we were not very far away when it happened, as the battle took place in Galilee and we were only thirty miles from there, on an estate near Acre. When the armies met, the first to advance were the Mongols, supported by men from the Kingdoms of Georgia and the Armenian Kingdom of Cilicia, both of which had submitted to Mongol authority. The two armies fought for many hours, with Baibars provoking the Mongols with repeated attack and retreat, without committing and losing too many of his men. It was said that Baibars had laid out the overall strategy of the battle since he had spent much time in that region as a fugitive earlier in his life. When the Mongols carried out another heavy assault, Baibars and his men feigned a final retreat, drawing the Mongols into the highlands to be ambushed by the rest of the Mamluk forces concealed among the trees.

The Mongol leader Kitbuqa, already provoked by the constant fleeing of Baibars and his troops, committed a grave mistake. Instead of suspecting a trick, the foolish Kitbuqa decided to march forwards with all his troops on the trail of the fleeing Mamluks. I believe that Kitbuqa's immortality had gone to his head and it led him to make rash decisions. Whatever the reason for his foolishness, when the Mongols reached the highlands, the hidden Mamluks charged into the fray and the Mongols then found themselves surrounded on all sides.

The Mongol army fought very fiercely to break out but it was too little and too late. Kitbuqa and almost the entire Mongol army perished.

"One of our immortal enemies, Hulegu's right hand, Kitbuqa, has fallen," I said to my companions when we heard the news.

"I do not understand," Khutulun kept saying, for it was the first time that the Mongols had lost a battle. "I do not understand." Orus likewise scratched his head. All they had ever known their whole lives was Mongol victory, from one end of the Earth to the other.

"They can be beaten, then," Thomas said to me later. "It is possible." For all his hatred of them, he seemed almost disappointed. I think that, in his mind, he had made them into something like demons and now he found that they were men after all.

But Hulegu would soon return and we all expected him to crush the Mamluks. In the Mongol civil war, Hulegu supported his brother Kublai and then returned through Persia to take up his war against the Mohammedans.

Knowing this, my companions and I prepared to kill Hulegu as he approached through the lands of Palestine. I spent considerable wealth in exploring a number of potential ambush sites in the hills, and even hired a few desperate mercenaries to help us scout likely areas. It was a dangerous place to be roaming around, with bands of Mamluks, Mongols, and brigands clashing on the borders.

But Berke, brother of the deceased Batu and the leader of the Golden Horde of Mongols on the steppes of Russia, had recently converted and now called himself a Mohammedan. After Baghdad fell, Berke was angry at the insult to his new faith and he moved to attack Hulegu, who had to make his way up to Azerbaijan to defend against this new enemy.

Which took Hulegu far away from us once more.

The presence of a serious threat from fellow-Mongols on his northern flank boxed Hulegu in, and he settled down once more and decided to wait out his cousin Berke, who was already old and who Hulegu, being immortal, would easily outlive. In the cities he had won along the Tigris and Euphrates, Hulegu put his viceroys into power, and rewarded some of the helpful Shiites. Thus establishing his vast dominion, Hulegu declared himself to be the Ilkhan, and his empire as the Ilkhanate. This word il-khan meant subordinate khan. The term had been agreed to by Hulegu, in exchange for in practice having complete autonomy from Kublai. It was said by those we bribed that, behind closed doors, Hulegu laughed that Kublai was concerned with appearances where Hulegu cared only for real power. And Hulegu ruled his vast Ilkhanate not from Iraq but from western Persia and the city of Maragha.

Maragha was up north, near the Caspian Sea. Northeast of Mosul, northwest of the ruined Alamut and south of Armenia and close to the enormous saltwater Lake Urmia. The lake had a number of large islands, the largest of which was about six miles long. An island that I would later visit.

The city of Maragha was situated in a narrow, north-south valley at the eastern extremity of a fertile plain between the valley and Lake Urmia just twenty miles to the west. The land all around in fact was rich with vineyards and orchards, all well-watered by canals led from the river, and producing great quantities of fruit.

It was no wonder that Hulegu was content to wait out the Mongol civil wars and the Mamluk power grab in such surroundings. It was not only the great abundance of the land but the strategic location of the city that allowed him to cover any attacks from the Golden Horde to the north, as well as govern his Persian subjects to the southeast and control his newly-conquered peoples to the southwest in Iraq and Syria.

We knew that the time for us to kill the Ilkhan was approaching. He was ruling from one city and most of his armies were disbursed hundreds or thousands of miles away.

And yet the Hulegu was very careful with his security. Such a conqueror had made thousands of enemies, even millions. And it was not only the Ismailis who were capable of poisoning their enemies or murdering them in their beds. And so we watched from afar as he ruled and, under Hassan's guidance, we slowly and carefully built a network of spies. Slave traders, merchants, musicians. The jugglers and acrobats. Physicians and masons. Anyone who would travel through the region, first of all. Then we found people who could approach or even enter the city and provide information on the layout of the streets, the important people, and so on. Eventually, we bought off a man named Enrico of Candia who provided a steady stream of slaves to the rulers of Maragha and so could provide a wealth of insider information.

Enrico was a Venetian by birth, though he claimed to have left as a boy, never to return. He had grown rich transporting slaves across the Black Sea in all directions and had grown fat and enormously wealthy ever since coming under the protection of Batu Khan. Since Batu's death, he had come over to Hulegu's side following a falling out with Batu's brother Berke. Hassan and Stephen, both devious men by nature and in practice, believed that Enrico had feigned this conflict with Berke and was, in fact, spying for him. We were therefore concerned about trusting him in any way.

"What if he serves Hulegu and yet only pretends to Berke that he serves him?" Stephen said to Hassan, one evening as we ate together in our home in the Kingdom of Georgia.

It was easy enough in those times and in that part of the world for me to pose as a wealthy French mercenary, especially with such a mixture of foreign peoples in my entourage. Especially, also, as the opposing armies of the Golden Horde to the north and Hulegu's Ilkhanate to the south were at risk of coming to blows in the lands that lay between them, like Georgia. With a fabricated reputation for martial brilliance and reliability that we had sent ahead of us, the local lord had provided me with a perfectly acceptable residence so that I and other soldiers of fortune like me would be on hand should hostilities break out.

"Perhaps our man Enrico serves both masters?" Hassan said. "Giving information to both Hulegu and Berke, and so serves only himself?"

"Might it be that he trades information to anyone who can pay?" Eva suggested. "The Latin magnates of Constantinople, his fellow Venetian traders, and the Saracen lords. It would seem that Enrico of Candia knows everyone. Surely, we may expect to find him accommodating. We should pay him well, not ask too much of him in return, and grudgingly provide him with a plausible story about why we wish to know about the palace. Something that he would not feel honour bound to sell us out for."

"What might such a thing possibly be?" Thomas asked.

"Horse thieves," Eva said. "We will steal the Ilkhan's most valuable horses right out of his stable, for breeding in Acre, where good horses are a fortune."

Hassan sighed, and pinched his nose, for he had little regard for the wisdom of women, especially when it was sound. "And if we make contact and he sells us to Hulegu, what then of our entire undertaking? We must be cautious."

"For God's sake," I said to the group, and banged my hand on the table, causing them to turn to me all at once as the plates and cups rattled. "Stephen, go to his people and buy us some blood slaves for ourselves, will you? The usual type. Mutes or morons, if possible. Foreign savages if not. We shall continue to move cautiously but we must act, and not sit around talking about the matter."

Two years later, I still did not know whether the Venetian Enrico of Candia was loyal to Hulegu or not. Whether he had sold us out, and whether we were walking into a trap. And that thought, along with a thousand other worries about our assassination plan, played on my mind as I scaled the wall of Hulegu's palace on a cold night in February 1265.

Maragha was not a large capital but it had a high city wall and four sturdy gates. The outer wall to the north had a small postern gate big enough only for men and not horses, and we had promised a fortune to a certain Kipchak guard if he would but open it to us on that night. Praise God, the young fellow held up his end of the bargain. Orus seized him, and whispered threats should we find he had sold us out to his masters. When the terrified Kipchak swore to Christ—for he was a Nestorian—, that he had done precisely as we had required, Orus expertly cut the young man's throat.

I have killed uncounted thousands in my life and been witness to many times more deaths, but it is the dishonourable ones such as that squalid murder which have plagued my dreams down the centuries. An inauspicious start to our infiltration, and it unsettled me all the more as it felt as though our venture was tainted with the underhanded act. But it was an act of necessity for, once he had let us in, we could not let him go lest he be captured and give us up, nor could we tie him up lest he be discovered and do the same. And so, a treacherous blade to the gullet it was, and his body we shoved into a dark doorway.

I told myself that the incidental deaths of the innocent were necessary in order to save Christendom from Hulegu's horde. We would kill hundreds to save millions.

Slipping into the city through the postern was straightforward. Making our way through the streets was likewise a relatively simple matter and we did so swiftly and without challenge. Alas, there was but a single gate into the walled palace compound and so over the wall we went, climbing like lizards up the stones with our gear hanging from sacks behind some of us. We had a lot of men to kill, and we needed the means to do it. For they were not ordinary men, but Hulegu and his immortals, and they would die hard.

The others followed me, dropping as quietly as shadows down the inside of the wall into the dark soil and ornamental bushes near to the base of the wall.

I counted down Eva, Thomas, Stephen, Hassan, Orus, and Khutulun. We were all there, and all ready.

One of the Mongols that William had turned had been killed by the Mamluks and our information suggested Hulegu had twelve immortals left alive to serve him.

Every one of them was in the palace with him that night. Eight of them were Hulegu's personal bodyguards, collectively known as the keshig, and they were with him or near to him almost all the time and had been for years. By all accounts, they were battle-scarred brutes who terrified the courtiers. But the other four immortal lords had been recalled from their regions of Hulegu's Ilkhanate. It was the Mongol new year celebration, and they would feast together and discuss the Ilkhan's strategic priorities for the following year.

It was the first time Hulegu's immortals had all been together for many months and we knew we may never have a better opportunity.

There were seven of us and thirteen of them, so already we were at a numerical disadvantage as far as immortals of the blood went. Another disadvantage was that one of my men was Stephen, who I had trained to fight with basic competence in the intervening years but who would never be anything like a true warrior, even with his immortal's strength. And I had two women on my side. Deadly and skilful though they were, neither Eva nor Khutulun had the strength to match an immortal man of similar skill. And Hulegu's keshig bodyguards and lords were all seasoned soldiers.

Not only that, there would be mortal men in Hulegu's hall. Retainers, servants, supplicants, family members, soldiers, bodyguards, and slaves. Every Mongol court was a jumbled web of alliances and relationships and anyone we found in that hall would have to be killed, too. At worst they would fight us, and at least they would get in our way. For all I knew, I was leading my six companions against two hundred men or more.

Waving at them to follow, I led my company along the inside of the wall, between it and the lines of heavily-pruned fruit bushes that bordered the Persian style palace gardens. It was an absurd indulgence for a Mongol prince but Hulegu had settled into a luxury that would no doubt have been beyond the imagining of his barbarian fathers out on the savage steppe. An indulgence that displayed the confidence he had in his position, far enough from his enemies than no army could surprise him, and security in his own immortality. He would not be the only Mongol seduced by the degenerate wealth of the people he had conquered with such contempt.

I crept along beside the rows of ornate bushes, bent double and listening carefully for any signs that we had been seen by the patrolling night guards. If the alarm was raised before our attack was begun, then our chance of success would be gone, and the chance that any of us would escape would be close to nought, for we would be cornered and assaulted by hundreds of soldiers.

But we had our advantages. Assuming that none in our network of spies had been compromised or had been an enemy all along, then we would have surprise on our side.

Also, many Mongols would become fall-down drunk on an ordinary night in the ordus and we had timed our assassination to coincide with the celebration of the new year. Orus and Khutulun swore that everyone at court would have feasted all day on milk, cheese, mutton, roast horse, rice and curds and especially endless mountains of buuz, which were steamed dumplings stuffed with meat and were the only halfway edible food in the vile Mongol diet. They would certainly be stuffed to the guts and guzzling down gallons of fermented horse milk and rice wine. Our informants had told us that Hulegu's men mixed blood into their drinks to make an intoxicating potion they revelled in, to the confusion and repulsion of all who were not immortals. The gluttonous brutes had been hunting and banqueting for several days already and so they would surely be suffering from their excesses.

Whereas we had been practising. At Hassan's urging, we had rehearsed our roles in the assault on the palace many times. We had discussed it at table, we had even staked the ground in estimated dimensions of Hulegu's hall and acted out our parts as if we were revels or guisers performing for each other so that we could coordinate the timing of our attacks. We practised fighting in confined spaces. We all practised throwing. Eva and Khutulun became expert at tossing fist-sized stones into distant baskets.

Alert to every sound, I heard the cooks in the kitchens behind the palace shouting at their servants while they roasted meats, the smell of which filled the air and made my guts churn. Figures hurried here and there. A muttering boy dragged a basket of firewood along the ground toward the servants' entrances at the rear of the palace. Two men carried a freshly-slaughtered goat from one building to another, laughing about something as they went.

When we reached the centre of the north wall, we paused and unwrapped our weapons from the strips of wool or sheepskin that had kept them from clanging or rattling during our incursion. After all of us were ready, I nodded to Stephen.

For just a moment, Stephen's features in the gloom reminded me of when he had been a bookish English monk too afraid to even approach me on the ship in the Black Sea. He nodded back at me and hurried past us, all alone in the shadows, toward the palace stables with his heavy sack clutched to his chest. Whether he buckled under the pressure of his mission remained to be seen.

Looming above us in the darkness, Hulegu's palace seemed rather bigger than it had when we had staked out the dimensions on the ground.

After Stephen vanished into the gloom, the rest of us headed straight toward a specific servants' entrance at the rear of the palace, listening hard for any sign of the guards or anyone else who might discover our intrusion and raise the alarm. The kitchens were close by now, just across a courtyard, and the fires within were casting light from under the door and smoke from above the roof. A door in the kitchens opened, throwing a shard of yellow light slanting across the ground, and a young man came out. I waved my people down and we ducked low on the path. The lad carried a heavy jar in his arms, no doubt filled with wine for the celebrating lords within the palace. Tensing, I prepared to run him down and destroy him before he could raise the alarm. But he continued on across the courtyard, kicked open a door into the palace, and headed inside.

I let out the breath I was holding and waved my people to follow me. My nervousness only increased as I went. Killing enemy soldiers had rarely bothered me, even when I was young but I knew innocent people would die in our attack and I could not shake the feeling of guilt. I kept telling myself that they would be victims of war and their incidental deaths would help to avoid a great many more deaths in the future and so the sin would be mitigated. Besides, they would only be Saracens, Persians, Mongols, mostly, and Armenians and I would be saving all Christendom west of Jerusalem from the irresistible invasion of the Mongol lords of war.

Assuming, of course, that our attack worked.

We moved swiftly and slipped up to the palace itself. All but Thomas and Hassan, who continued on around the building, heading for a side entrance to the other side of Hulegu's hall. My steadiest man, the old Templar was a great comfort to me and watching him disappear alone into the darkness stirred my heart greatly. He and Hassan were heading further into the palace than the rest of us and their task was immensely dangerous. I felt certain that I would never see them again, and I wished I had spoken to Thomas of my high regard for him. Then again, what was the point of such things? We all die, and either we will see each other again or we will not. And either way, God knows the truth and surely that is all that matters.

What a foolish old man I had become, feeling so emotional and apprehensive. An indulgence I could not afford.

Inside the servants' entrance was a large chamber where food and wine was prepared for the hall upstairs. The room was lined with shelves, and dried meats and herbs were hanging from the beams. Lamps hung from chains gave off a good light. Already, I could hear the cacophony of raised voices talking further within the building and above our heads, muffled by the stones and timbers of the building.

The boy who had carried the jug of wine across the courtyard was at a bench along the wall, ladling the contents into smaller serving jugs. I saw and smelled at once that it was not, in fact, wine but fresh blood he was transferring. Two old women in servants clothing turned from preparing a huge platter of roasted meat on a workbench and stared at me with confusion written on their faces. The fact that they appeared to be innocent Armenian servants doing their duty caused me to hesitate to do what was necessary.

My companions pushed into the room after me while I stood staring at the three servants, wondering if I might not have them bound and gagged instead of dispatched. One of the old women dropped to her knees with her hands raised in supplication as our intentions dawned on her. The other screwed up her face in anger and took a deep breath.

She did not have time to utter a cry, for Khutulun pushed past me and cracked the woman's head open with the hammer side of her axe, and then buried the blade into the skull of the other one. Through it all, the boy stood stock still, arms by his sides and his eyes screwed shut. Khutulun whipped her axe blade from the old woman's skull and hacked into the lad's face, dropping him like the women. Wiping her blade on her coat, she turned and sneered at me, her expression mocking my weakness. I had a foolish urge to protest that I would have killed them had she not intervened but Eva grabbed the sack from my hand and shoved me into motion.

Without further idiotic delay, I headed into the servants' stairwell and ran up the timber stairs, the others right behind me. It was dark and narrow and the boards creaked underfoot and though we attempted to be quiet, we sounded like an invading army as we ascended.

A man's voice growled something above and I ran up the last few steps, drawing my dagger.

It was a Mongol soldier, dressed for war. A kezik, a guard protecting his lords within the nearby hall. And though he was there to stop unauthorised entry and to fight intruders, he was not truly expecting to have to do so. Since the dawn of time, almost every guard who ever stood on duty has served an unremarkable watch where the greatest danger to him is being found dozing by his commanding officer. There are a few moments where his expectations conflict with reality and he must adjust to the fact that he will have to shake himself for sudden violence.

Those few moments were all I needed.

I leapt up the steps and slammed my dagger up under his chin and forced him clear from the landing area into the antechamber, bearing him down beneath me with my hand over his mouth. His dark eyes were wide in shock that he was being killed.

Orus jumped over me and brought down the second kezik with a terrific blow from his mace. The crash the man made as he hit the wall and bounced onto the floor was sure to bring more men from within the hall to investigate. The kezik's dented helm rolled across the floor until Orus stamped on it.

The kezik beneath me stopped struggling and I savoured the smell of his blood and watched as his eyes faded and he breathed his last breath into my face. It reeked of sour wine and onions.

Khutulun and Eva continued on up the stairs to the gallery above, their feet making a terrible din.

The revelry within the hall continued unabated but I could not feel relief. At any moment, they could discover us. Thomas and Hassan, or Stephen, could already have been killed or—even worse—captured.

Our dead keziks had been guarding the rear door into the hall where Hulegu and the other lords celebrated the new year. A small, sturdy door of dark wood was all that separated me from my enemies. Orus stood before it, a mace in one hand and a bulging sack in the other.

"Bar the door," I hissed at him.

He turned with a confused expression. "How?"

Certain that he was being foolish, I stepped beside him, cursing his stupidity.

Yet he was correct.

Our paid informants had sworn that the doors at either end of the hall could be barred and yet there was nothing to suggest that had ever been possible. Merely an ornate iron latch.

I took a deep breath and clapped Orus on the shoulder. "Do not let even a single man through," I said and relieved him of his sack, for I would need the contents in short order.

Before I ascended the next stair to the gallery, I glanced back at the young Mongol warrior. He stood with a mace in his left hand, and his sword now drawn in his right. A single man to hold that small antechamber against a horde who would be desperate to escape.

He turned and looked at me over his shoulder. For once, he did not grin. Instead, he nodded once, slowly and in response, I bowed my head.

I took the final stairway in a few leaps to find Eva and Khutulun crouched at the top of the steps. Another servant lay dead, face down against the wall with blood pooling beneath him.

I had reached the gallery, which ran along one side of the building just beneath the edge of the vaulted ceiling, with a beautifully carved balustrade at waist height, that looked down onto the hall below. At the far end of the gallery I knew was a stairway leading to some other part of the palace beyond the hall but I had to trust that Hassan and Thomas would do what they could to block or distract any reinforcements from that end once the assault began. In its normal function, such a gallery could house musicians, at other times it was where lords could look down on those inside the hall without having to mix with them.

It would also, I hoped, provide the perfect platform for committing a massacre.

The voices down in the hall were loud and the stink of the men and their vile food filled my nose. Laughter and arguments suggested that they were all steaming drunk and I prayed that we had timed it correctly so that their inebriation would inhibit their strength and coordination. Judging from the sound alone, there could have been fifty or a hundred men below me. Perhaps more.

With any luck, we could launch our attack without them ever knowing what hit them.

"Quickly, now," I whispered to Eva and Khutulun.

We yanked open the sacks and began to unpack the contents. Inside, we had ceramic pots twice the size of a man's fist, each one wrapped in its own pouch of soft sheepskin of the highest quality. The soft coats protected the thinly-walled pots from breaking prematurely, and also prevented them from clanking together and giving us away. We shoved the pouches back into the leather bags and tossed them aside while lining up the pots on their flat bases. Each pot had a tube of waxed paper jutting from the top. The tube of waxed paper was filled with black powder that fizzed and burned like the devil when it was lit.

From inside my coat, I took the length of slowmatch I had lit before we made our final approach on the city. It was a short length of twisted hemp impregnated with some alchemical substance that allowed it to retain an ember within for many hours which could then swiftly be utilised to light a fuse. I had been repeatedly assured of their impeccable reliability.

Mine was cold.

I blew on it but it was completely out.

"Bloody useless Saracen bastard," I said, meaning Hassan, who had procured the devices from the surviving Syrian Assassins. "How do yours fare?" I asked Eva and Khutulun.

But then there was a shout from the far end of the gallery.

A Mongol guard stood staring at us, open-mouthed and outraged at our presence. No doubt the dead servant next to me also helped to give the game away. Another kezik came up beside him and there were more armed men behind filling the space.

Ripping my sword from the scabbard, I ran at them. I knew I would be in full view of anyone in the hall who looked up but there was nothing else I could do.

I felt the plan crumbling into pieces. So close to success, it had instead fallen to failure.

All I could do was fight on, fight through. It was all I knew. It was my profession. My passion.

The first Mongol drew his sword but I slashed my own blade across his face and he went wheeling back into the men crowding behind him. By God, I thought, there are so many of them. Too many to kill before the alarm was raised, if it was not too late already.

I kicked the next man's legs out from under him and stomped on him as I lunged at the men behind. The floored man rolled away and I half fell, raising my blade to defend against the dagger swung at my head. I kicked out with such fear and anger that the man was sent tumbling over the balustrade and down into the hall below with a crash.

The revelry stopped all at once, like the last candle being snuffed out.

I slashed at the remaining men, catching one and the rest jumped back from the gallery onto the landing beyond.

Behind me, Eva and Khutulun squatted, hunched over the rows of pots.

A cry went up from the hall, jeering and angry at the fallen man and I peered over the balustrade, leaning on the pillar of an arch.

The great hall was packed with Mongols. At a glance, it was well over two hundred men, plus almost as many servants or slaves, most young girls. The revellers lined the hall on either side of the centre, most sitting on benches or on rugs and furs on the floor. It was laid out like a ger, only there was no women's side. What women there were mixed in amongst the men, and I saw none being treated with anything close to respect. There were no honoured wives, no domestic side to proceedings. Just slave girls.

I searched quickly for the lords amongst them. The ones who William had turned into immortals. There were many men dressed in silk finery, surrounded by clusters of followers and which of them were my targets, I could not easily tell.

Then again, it hardly mattered.

Most of them were staring at the body of the man who had fallen onto a group carousing below the gallery. Almost as one, however, every face in the hall was turned upward in search of the point from which the unfortunate fellow had tumbled. Of course, they all saw me.

At the top end—the end we had entered, and the one with the door guarded by Orus—sat Hulegu, surrounded on all sides by his keshig bodyguards who were dressed for war.

The Ilkhan, the most powerful man on Earth, other than, perhaps, his brother Kublai.

His eyes met mine and grew wide.

Holding my arms out by my side, I leaned over the balustrade and raised my voice to a powerful roar that echoed in the now-quiet hall. "Hulegu Khan! I am Richard of Ashbury. Your crimes are legion. And now your death is at hand!"

I doubt anyone understood my words precisely but Hulegu certainly caught the crux of my declaration. He jumped to his feet and jabbed a finger up at me, scowling in pure hatred and barked out orders.

All about the hall, men bestirred themselves to attack.

Our key inside man, the slaver Enrico, had assured me that the only men with weapons would be Hulegu's immortal keshig but it was not just those eight soldiers who leapt to their feet and rushed across the hall toward the gallery. It seemed as though fully half of the drunken savages in the hall staggered across the benches, trampling slaves and servants as they charged my position. The first of them jumped up to grasp enormous painted fabrics hung on the wall and clambered up hand over hand.

A sword stabbed toward me from the side and I jerked away from it, bringing my blade up to defend the vicious attacks from the Mongols beside me up on the gallery. I could not defend the balcony from the men swarming up the wall hangings, as well as the men already up on the same level as me. Forgetting the hall for a moment, I rushed into the Mongols clustered near me in order to cause disorder amongst them and so destroy them rapidly. Cutting as fast as I could, slashing across their hands, their faces and shouting some wordless cries of fury. I stabbed one through the throat and he ran, blood gushing through his fingers, into the men behind him. While they threw him down, I killed them, too. Blood gushed out on the timbers underfoot amongst the writhing bodies.

"Richard!" Eva shouted from behind me.

The first men from the hall were climbing over the balustrade and I ran back along the gallery to cut them down. It was loud with shouts and jeering from the drunken merrymakers down below who were confident that they were themselves under no threat, that they would witness a short hunt followed by the violent execution of a Frankish interloper. They had no idea that it was their own horrifying deaths that were coming.

All along the balustrade, Mongols were dragging themselves up and over the railing. I cut the first man on the back of his exposed neck and his head came clean off, the body falling away. I cut off the hand of another man and crashed my blade into the skull of the next. On I ran to the next and smote him, and the next. They were drunk and slow and I was an immortal knight, faster than anything they could have imagined. I kicked a very fat man in the face and then the whole teeming bunch of them fell as one, as if by God's own hand.

The rope suspending the wall hangings had snapped and the row of fabrics all collapsed under the weight of dozens of climbing men, and they fell tumbling into a pile at the base of the wall. Many of the spectators cheered and laughed at their comrades.

Not all were unaware of their danger. A group of men hammered on the main hall door but it seemed they could not force it open from the inside.

Well done, Thomas. God save you.

But the rear door that Orus guarded, behind Hulegu's dais, was being advanced on by a group of men determined to rush out, climb the stairs and attack me from that side. Worse still, the Mongol bodyguards, armed and armoured though most without helms, now stood in a line below me, looking up.

Seeing me once more looking down, Hulegu roared and his eight keshig jumped into action, throwing themselves against the bare wall and scrambling up against the stonework. One climbed the remnant of the wall hangings rope at the far corner.

I knew then that it was over. I could not fight eight immortal warriors, not all at once in a confined space. They would surround me and overwhelm me and I prayed that they would kill me outright so that I would be spared the sight of Hulegu's face, smug in his victory.

Nevertheless, I prepared to kill as many as I could before I fell and hoped to give Eva and Khutulun the time that they clearly needed.

A pot sailed through the air from the end of the gallery in a great arc trailing smoke and a fizzing, smoking fire.

It smashed on the wall just above the rear door and the evil liquid inside gushed out and down for a moment before it was ignited by the waxed paper fuse. The sound was like a demon being thrust out from Hell, and the explosive ball of flame engulfed the men beneath in a shroud of boiling flame. Their screams filled the hall from floor to the timber roof high above. Safe from assault, the door was guarded by a raging fire. Flames leapt and bounced close to Hulegu's dais and he skipped away from it.

While the Mongols were frozen in horror or shrieking in fear at the sight of their fellows writhing in agony, another incendiary pot flew, angling right across the hall from end to end. This time it smashed beside the main door and tossed out fire like a beast searching for men to consume. The fire drove the men there back from their efforts to break out and as the people within saw that both exits were aflame, every man and woman, lord and slave, panicked. Screams of terror echoed from the rafters.

Two more fire pots flew and both doorways were further engulfed in explosive flame. Eva and Khutulun were throwing them as rapidly as they could get the fuses lit and so more and more followed quickly, smashing into the floor or into people or benches everywhere in the hall. Each fire pot belched out so much fire that every one of them immolated a half dozen people or more. The screaming crowd gathered in groups, clutching each other. What tempting targets they made. When these groups were hit, they all died.

The roaring of the fire grew, as did the screams and cries of agony and pure terror. Smoke billowed up in plumes and built steadily, quickly filling the hall with thicker and thicker smoke and the flames danced higher and licked the walls and the roof beams above.

All the while, the strongest and bravest Mongols clambered up the wall to the gallery, and I fought to keep them from overwhelming us. I cut and shoved and kicked like a demon. Some made it up over the balustrade momentarily and I killed them or threw them back into the ocean of fire below.

An armoured, immortal keshig leapt up and threw himself over onto the gallery close to Eva and Khutulun. He paused, looking between them and me, as I ran at him from the other end. He wisely chose me but had foolishly turned his back on Eva, who stood up behind him and swung her dagger into his neck and punched out his throat in a shower of blood and gristle. Without missing a beat, she snatched up a fire pot and tossed it down the wall into the other immortals climbing up.

But not all of them. Another keshig lunged from where he clutched to the rail and I thrust my sword into his open mouth and pushed it hard into him, my blade getting caught in his teeth and skull.

I was getting tired, and sucking in lungfuls of filthy, hot smoke and the sweat and tears running into my eyes stung and partially blinded me. My strikes were growing sloppy as my arms grew tired and the fear of the flames grew rapidly toward panic. Simply put, I was getting carried away and I paid for my carelessness when the keshig I had run through the mouth flung himself away and ripped my sword from my hand.

Two others clambered over the balustrade onto the gallery either side of me and I ran to one in order to throw him down. Before I could grab him, he slashed my arm open near the shoulder. Grasping his sword arm, I drew my dagger but he clamped onto my wrist and held on so hard I could not shake him off. I let go of his arm and punched him square in the face hard enough to crush his nose and spread the split flesh halfway across his face but still he clasped me. The other immortal stomped toward us. His braids and long moustache were singed and his skin burned but still the mad bastard grinned as he reached us. All I could do was retreat and use the body of the man entwined with me as a shield.

Dread filled me when, behind the grinning savage, half a dozen men at once climbed over onto the gallery.

The Mongol I grappled with butted me hard in the face with his helm, breaking my nose as I had done his. As only a man who has experienced such a thing will know, the pain of a broken nose is quite exquisite and uniquely disorienting. My eyes filled with tears and I was blinded. In panic at my sudden vulnerably, I seized him by the head with both hands and sank my teeth into his face and ripped off his cheek, upper lip and a good portion of his crushed nose. His screams filled my mouth, as did his blood and I drank it down for a moment, then heaved the writhing, faceless bastard at the keshig behind, just to slow him down as I backed away and wiped blood from my eyes.

When my vision cleared, I saw that he was no longer grinning. In fact, his face was contorted in fury and, sword held ready, he strode forward to cut me down.

A fire pot smashed into him. The blistering heat of the flame rolled over me and the keshig became a screaming torch, while the blaze covered the gallery from side to side in a wall of fire. I backed up to Eva and Khutulun, who were almost out of fire pots. Four sacks of the evil things and they had gone through them with admirable rapidity. Both were drenched in sweat and coughing from the smoke, eyes running, and their hands were burned.

"We did it," I shouted at them.

The entire hall was engulfed. The heat was incredible and most of the people within were already long dead.

Eva clapped me on the back and pointed into the hall, shaking her head.

I looked down through the shimmering, boiling air to see Hulegu drinking blood from a dying woman's neck before pausing to shout orders. The Ilkhan was blackened with oily soot and his clothes were tatters where they had burned on him, showing bright pink skin beneath. He directed a group of loyal men who attacked the rear door with their fists and feet. With horror, I realised they were all but through the timbers. The fire had burned the door, weakening it and though it was all aflame and the fire licked and burned the men who tried to break through, they did it for their lord, for their Khan. They killed themselves, died in agony, so that he might live.

"He will get away," I shouted at Eva.

Lighting the fuse, she hurled her very last fire pot at him. Her aim was perfect and it was certain that he would be drenched in flame and killed.

Hulegu raised up the dying woman and ducked behind her. The pot exploded on the woman and a ball of fire engulfed him. Yet he stood and tossed the screaming, flaming woman aside before jumping into a group of servants cowering at the food of his dais. He seized another girl to use as a shield, holding her aloft as easily as a wineskin. His boots and one trouser leg had caught alight but one of his surviving men threw his own body around his lord's limbs to smother the flames.

"Come on," I said to Eva, as Khutulun threw her last pot down into the screaming masses. The heat and smoke were almost unbearable and we needed to retreat down the stairs, join Orus and go into the hall to kill Hulegu by the sword. I raised my voice to shout over the roar of the flames and the screams. "We have to go down and—"

A group of shrieking Mongols rushed through the wall of flames on the gallery and brought me down beneath the weight of them.

They brought the fire with them. The men were all burning as they fought me and their burning clothes and hair licked my skin and the pain seared through me. A blade cut into my head, glancing off my skull.

A dagger was punched into my lower back and I arched and bucked, throwing the men off of me. Eva killed them and dragged me out from under them while Khutulun put out the fires on me with her hands and then yanked the dagger from my kidney.

I screamed and shivered with the agony of it as they pulled me to my feet. The burns were excruciating.

"Blood," I said, or tried to. Eva was already dragging a burned, bloody, dying man up to me and I drank a few mouthfuls from the puncture wound in his eye, enough to give me the strength to move.

As we fled from the gallery, I peered into the hall one last time. The masses of flames and smoke obscured the details but surely everyone was now dead. Nothing could have survived such an inferno. The flames had caught the beams and joists of the ceiling alight and flames jutted up at the roof. It would soon all collapse in and bury any survivors in masses of burning timbers.

We stumbled down the stairs and Khutulun cried out. A wail from the depths of her soul.

Orus was dead.

Lying against the wall of the antechamber amongst a pile of dead Mongols, his head almost severed under his chin and his eyes staring wide, mouth hanging open. His clothes smouldered. Thick, black blood from wounds on his chest welled out.

The door into the hall was a burning ruin, the charred remnants hanging on the hinges, with fire pouring out of it at the top and rolling upward along with billowing black smoke. The hall beyond was a mad wall of bright orange flame.

I paused by Orus but a moment, for I was filled with a rage that made the fire in the hall pale in comparison.

Hulegu had escaped me.

Throwing myself down the stairway into the storage area, I kicked through the door and ran out into the black night. After the cacophony and incandescence within, I was hit with the bitter darkness and it was like plunging into a winter lake. My eyes were filled with the glare and I could see almost nothing and the stench of smoke was everywhere around me.

A bell was ringing, clanging frantically, and people shouted all around the palace and in the city beyond. Unseen hooves and feet drummed in panic on the paving as people fled the massive conflagration.

But I staggered on toward other sounds. Fainter sounds. Footsteps, laboured breathing. The sounds of men hurrying away. As I followed, my vision cleared and I discerned the outlines of three men I was pursuing, cutting across the servants' courtyard toward the royal stables. All three limped or shuffled as they hurried away, wounded and burned.

Two immortal keshig turned when they heard me coming after them. Hulegu glanced back and snarled an order before continuing on.

It was only as they attacked that I recalled I had no sword. No proper weapon at all, and no armour either.

One hulking bodyguard was silent and armed with an axe, and the other big sod roared some Mongol insult and swung his sword wildly as he rushed in.

It would have been prudent to retreat and procure a weapon but I was very far from rationality by then and in my madness, I believed that I could fight through them with my bare hands.

I dodged the blow from the axe and shifted away from the wielder but was forced to block the sword of the other man with my forearm. It was that or lose my head. The blade hit the bones of my wrist and, as we both moved, it ripped downward along my forearm and tore off a great flap of muscle and skin before biting deep into the bone. While his sword was bound in my arm, I grabbed his wide-open mouth with my other hand and yanked with all my might, ripping down in fury. His jawbone came off in my hand along with the stretched, tattered skin from his temples, cheeks and neck. I tossed it away and he fell, making a horrendous, gargling scream and clawing at the ruin of his throat.

The axeman winged his weapon at my face and I jumped back, yanking the first man's sword from my arm. I tried not to think about the sight of the flesh from half of my forearm flopping back and wet, like I had been peeled.

With a sword finally in my hand, I rushed the keshig, grappled with him and slid the point of my blade up into his groin and wriggled it in, cutting the great vein there, as well as gelding and, eventually, disembowelling him also.

Astonishingly, the man with no lower face climbed back to his feet and came at me making a gurgling, keening sound from his chest. His eyes were screwed up in desperate rage as he threw a pathetic punch at my face. I stabbed him in the chest. As repulsive as it was, I needed blood and so I drank from his ruin of a neck while he struggled with the last strength of his life, drowning in his own blood. After spitting out an enormous, slimy clot or a length of vein, I tossed him to the ground and looked for Hulegu.

"He went in there, Richard!" Eva shouted, running up behind me. She pointed across the courtyard to one of the nearby kitchen buildings.

Without wasting time on thanks, I chased after Hulegu and kicked my way inside. I saw right away what it was. The low-ceilinged, one-room building was for housing a group of blood slaves. It was dark, lit by only a couple of smoky lamps. There must have been forty or so men and women chained to the two long walls, with piles of straw for beds.

At the far end, Hulegu Khan limped alone through the filthy room and barged his way out of the door.

He was still heading for the royal stables. Hulegu meant to take his swiftest horses and to ride off into the night, to find his armies out in the country where he would be safe from me.

Following at a full sprint, I kicked open the door and rushed back outside. I found myself at the edge of a large, paved courtyard.

Where I stopped.

Ahead, the palace stables were ablaze. Great red-orange flames jetted up and lit up the night, throwing manic shadows and lights all around. Horses bolted away from the roaring fire toward the front of the palace complex, directed by brave stable hands but many other servants fled in panic.

God love you, Stephen. You did it.

Silhouetted against the flames, stood Hulegu.

He had his back to me and I stalked toward him.

Rapid footsteps sounded behind me. I could tell at once that it was not Eva's familiar gait, so I jumped to the side and whipped around with my blade up and ready.

Khutulun ran past me and struck Hulegu in the base of the spine with her sword, thrusting him forward off his feet. He landed on his face and she was on him, flipping him over onto his back and pulling her sword back while spitting a furious stream of insults in the Mongol tongue, while he snarled up at her like an animal and writhed in pain from his wound.

I seized Khutulun by the shoulder and dragged her away before she killed him. She turned on me, mad vengeance in her eyes, and shook her sword in my face while she raged.

But I was too gripped by my passion for the death of that man, and I would not be denied. My own anger was very great, and though she had lost far more to him that I had, I was the lord and would make her submit to my will. I struck her in the face, kicked her legs out and stole her sword. She screamed and tried to attack me but Eva jumped in and restrained her while I turned on Hulegu.

His wild, barbarian features, twisted in rage, were cast in mad shadows by the slanting, dancing red light of the flames. His arms flailed and grasped at the ground but his legs were motionless due to the wound to his spine. A pool of blood spread through his silk coat low on his body, and a shining shadow of blood leaking from his body grew and spread beneath him.

"My brother made you," I said. "And now I will unmake you."

He growled in his own language and spat a mouthful of blood onto his chest. Hulegu's contempt turned to bitter laughter. I sensed that he was mocking my judgemental tone. And he was right. I had just murdered hundreds myself, including innocent slaves.

But I already knew I was not a righteous man. Just as I knew that he was an evil one. All of a sudden, I was filled with a powerful loathing, for him, for his entire people. For William.

I slashed my dagger across his throat and dragged him upright while his fists hammered ineffectually against my head. My rage consumed me and I sank my mouth into the gushing wound and sucked down the hot blood, which spilled over my face and soaked my chest. His blows grew weaker and I stopped to look him in the eye. Hulegu's mouth opened and closed and his eyes glared at me even as the light began to go out from them. I tossed him to the ground, snatched up my dagger again and planted one foot on his chest while I sawed through his neck with my blade. I was shouting at him, but I do not know what I said. When I ripped his head from his body, I held it aloft and sucked the last remnants of blood from the tattered neck. Finally, I tossed it to the ground and spat on his corpse.

I let out a huge sigh and looked up at the smoke billowing into the night sky.

It was done.

When I turned, Eva and Khutulun were holding on to each other and their eyes glinted red with the light from the inferno of the palace stables. Behind them, the palace itself was being swiftly consumed by the vast conflagration and the roofs were already collapsing, throwing sparks and flame into the black night.

"Richard?" Eva said. "We must flee."

I nodded. "You go." I pushed past her, snatching up my stolen sword and heading back to the outbuilding near us. "I will see you at the meeting place."

She stared at me, aghast, as I strode back into the hall of the blood slaves. Those inside cowered away from me on their filthy piles of straw. Of course, I was drenched in blood and no doubt looked like a horror. While they wailed, terrified of me and the fires all around their prison, I moved to pull their chains from the iron rings affixed to the timber walls. A young man shivered in terror as I used my blade to prise the ring out. The Mongol sword bent and I tossed it aside and gripped the ring and pulled.

"What in the name of God are you doing?" Eva said from the doorway.

"Go," I said, through gritted teeth. "Please, go."

She came closer, incredulous. "Leave them, for the love of God, Richard. We must flee in the great rush of the people or we shall be isolated and captured. You know this. Leave these slaves."

"I will not," I said, growling as the ring wriggled loose and came free. The idiot blood slave stayed where he was, eyes wide and shivering. I tossed the ring into his lap so that he could carry the chain with him. "Go, you damned fool." I said it in Arabic and when he still did not move, I grabbed him and threw him to the door and moved to the next slave. She was a hideously ugly young woman but her eyes said she understood her freedom was at hand. I grabbed the ring by her with both hands, planted my feet and heaved backwards.

"You are a bloody fool, Richard!" Eva shouted as she pulled out her dagger and stomped to the next slave.

Instead of killing him, she used her dagger to hack at the iron fixture next to his head.

Khutulun had no compassion in her, no Christian conscience or moral consideration for the weak. And yet she also came back to help. Working together, we freed the blood slaves from their chains very swiftly and followed the last of them out.

The palace complex was in chaos, and we joined the flow of fleeing people without being challenged. Our agents in the city had started small fires in various quarters when they saw the flames in the palace. They had the effect that Hassan had sworn they would. The danger of fire panicked the residents and soldiers in the city. When we made it beyond the palace gate we fell into the crush of people pushing and shoving their way out. We were covered in blood and burns and blackened by smoke and I assumed we would have to fight our way clear at some point. Yet, the people were Armenian Christians and Persians and Mongols and people from all over the region and the lands that Hulegu had dominated and thus everyone was a stranger to everyone else. So, although some people around us gave us suspicious looks, we escaped unchallenged into the suburbs and then into the rural farmland just as the sun began to lighten the sky.

Hulegu and his men were dead and Eva and Khutulun had made it out with me.

Whether Thomas, Stephen and Hassan had survived, we had no idea.

* * *

Our meeting point was an isolated fisherman's house many miles to the west on the shores of Lake Urmia that we had taken over days before. We chased down an escaped horse and, later, another one, and the three of us made it to the house before midday.

Stephen was already there. The shrewd young man had used his fire pots to thoroughly burn the stables and had ridden one of Hulegu's magnificent Saracen mares all the way to the shore before dawn. He was wide-eyed and shaken by it all and filled with the disbelieving giddiness that men experience after surviving battle.

Inside the house was a large table stained with fish blood, a few stools and benches and the supplies we had stashed there. Chief amongst them was the wine, which I drank with great enthusiasm.

Khutulun spent the day alone, on the shores of the lake, deeply affected by the death of her brother. I wondered whether she regretted trading Hulegu's life for his. Those in mourning contemplate past moments shared with the fallen but they also lament facing the future without them. If she was considering the future, perhaps she already regretted her immortality and the bareness that came with it.

"She should come inside," Eva muttered. "She will draw attention to us."

"Leave her be," I said.

None of us truly expected to see Thomas or Hassan but late in the day the old Templar appeared on the horizon. I rode out and brought him in. He trudged all the way across the plain wounded and thirsty and cold and he collapsed once inside the door. After I gave him my own blood, he recovered rather quickly.

"Hassan sacrificed himself so that I might escape the palace," Thomas explained while he drank some wine. "We defended the hall door against more men than I could count. They all wanted to free their khan. We abandoned the position when the door turned to flame and yet we were pursued by a great number as we fled. Hassan pushed me through and closed a door, defending it from the other side so that I might make my escape without him." Thomas shook his head. "A Saracen. Sacrificed himself for me. A Templar."

Stephen nodded as if he understood. "The Assassins are obsessed with death. All they want is to enter Heaven."

"No," I said. "His home was destroyed. His family. Everyone he knew was dead. All he had left to do with his life was to end it."

"And what is left for us?" Thomas asked. "Half of our task is done. It has taken so long. And now we must find William."

"No," I said.

They looked at me.

"William has gone to the East. He swore that he will be gone for decades, at least. Centuries, perhaps. If he returns at all."

"So that is it?" Thomas said, growing angry. "He saved your life with his blood in that Baghdad gatehouse and you just forgive his crimes?"

"I forgive nothing," I said, keeping calm. "William will certainly die. And yet, he will wreak his evil on a distant people. His mischief will be directed amongst the Mongols and their enemies in the East. When he returns, I will kill him."

None of them wanted to face that journey eastwards again.

"So," Stephen began. "What do we do until then?"

I looked at them. Stephen, Thomas, Eva and pursed my lips, considering whether I should speak what had long been on my mind.

"Do you mean to slay us, now?" Thomas asked. He spoke softly, with no challenge in his voice. It sounded as though he would have almost welcomed it. "To be rid of all those given the Gift of the blood?"

The truth was, I had considered it. I had ruminated upon it, on and off, for years. By my hand as well as William's, there had been a great proliferation of immortals walking the Earth, and I felt that it was my duty to put an end to all of them, including the ones from my own blood. Other than Eva, of course.

Spreading my open hands, I spoke softly. "It never crossed my mind," I said. "However, we know from Bertrand and from William himself that my brother left dozens of immortals in Christendom. Knights and lords and God only knows who else. They must be stopped. No one will stop them if I do not."

"If you do not?" Eva asked. "You alone?"

I held her gaze for a moment. "Stephen, my good fellow, would you be so kind as to ask Khutulun to come inside now. There is something I would like to propose to you all."

All but Khutulun sat on the benches on the other side of the table from me. They were all exhausted and should have been resting. But I needed to speak and I think they needed to hear it.

"You were each thrust into this existence, in one way or another, through the actions of my brother." That was true for Eva and also for Thomas. I looked at Stephen and Khutulun, who had joined me voluntarily and then begged me to grant them the Gift, each for their own reasons. "Some more than others, perhaps. And yet we have remained bound together for years. You have followed me for thousands of miles, through horrors and hardships. You men renounced sworn oaths because you knew you had a higher calling. A greater moral duty, to destroy a particular form of evil that no one else could. You swore to defeat that evil. And now you have." I cleared my throat, hesitant to continue in case they refused what I was about to offer. "But perhaps it is time to exchange new oaths. Perhaps, I would swear to you that I would protect you from all who would do you harm and provide for you wealth and the blood you need to survive. And perhaps you would swear to serve me and do as I command, where it serves the cause of our Order."

"Our Order?" Thomas said, frowning.

"An Order, yes. An Order dedicated to a single purpose. We would make oaths to dedicate our lives to destroying all immortals that William de Ferrers has made. First in Christendom, and then wherever else we may find them. And we swear to kill William himself when he returns from the East."

Stephen was nodding enthusiastically. The others did not immediately protest, at least.

"And if he does not return?" Thomas said. "What then?"

"Then we will swear to pursue him to the ends of the Earth and cut off his head wherever we find him."

I wanted to say more. I knew I had said it all rather badly, and I wished to explain how it would give us a common purpose, and it would mean that we continued to rely on each other but I fell silent.

"I will swear it," Stephen said, eagerly. "I will swear the oath. We can do great things together, I know we can. Yes, I will swear it."

Thomas pursed his lips. "It would be an honourable duty." He inclined his head.

"You want me to live in your land?" Khutulun asked. Even filthy and unkempt, and in a dark hovel, her beauty shone like the moon and the stars. "I will not do this. I will return to my people."

Eva's head snapped sharply to me and I knew what she was thinking. That I could not let her go. She was a blood drinker. She would never age, so far as we knew, and she was a killer besides. Clever, dangerous. To let her go would immediately undermine everything I wanted to establish. It was easy to read Eva's thoughts in that fleeting glance.

Khutulun should be the first immortal executed by our new Order.

"Very well," I said, instead. "Go home. Be with your people." I leaned forward and pointed a finger at her. "But if you make any trouble. If you become another Hulegu, I will kill you, too."

Khutulun laughed in my face, her expression utterly contemptuous. "I will wait until the Ilkhan's funeral. Only then will I go." She held my gaze, daring me to challenge her even though she surely knew I would best her.

How she had gotten wind of my plans, I could not comprehend, for I had been careful not to tell her. Then I looked at Stephen, who was studiously inspecting a point on the ceiling.

"Stephen, you great blabbering fool," I muttered. "Are your virtues so easily overturned by the handsomeness of a woman's face?"

Eva barked out a bitter laugh. "Why do you look at the speck of sawdust in your brother's eye and pay no attention to the plank in your own?"

I smiled. "A fair question."

"Khutulun," I said to her, "it is important that you understand. If you make any other immortals with your own blood, or if you use your strength against Christian kingdoms, or if you speak of me or our Order to anyone, I shall not hesitate to slaughter you. Do you believe you could stand against me?"

She tossed her braids and scoffed but she lowered her head in submission. "I understand. I have no further interest in you or your Order."

After living together with her, fighting beside her, teaching her our languages and training her to fight more effectively, she could throw us off so easily. Perhaps it was because her heart was broken from her loss. Perhaps it was the unassailable gulf that existed between our two peoples. Or perhaps it was that she was only ever a black-hearted Tartar with a beautiful countenance.

"By what name should our Order be known?" Stephen said, suddenly.

"It will not be known," I said to him and to all of them. "It will be a secret known only by the members of the order. But its name amongst us will be the Order of the White Dagger."

Eva's head snapped up at that, her eyes shining. Thomas looked to the heavens, perhaps recalling that it was as he was being sliced open by my brother in the Khan's palace that little Nikolas had used my dagger to attack William.

"You have named it this," Stephen said, "because your fine dagger has upon it the image of Saint George and we will be dedicated to protecting Christendom from the dragon that is William's men. Perhaps we should call the Order after the saint?"

I shook my head before he had even finished speaking. "No, Stephen. We will protect Christendom from the dragon, that is true, and we will seek to uphold knightly ideals. But we, too, are the dragons."

We waited near to Maragha for the dust to settle. Without Hassan to help organise the network of informants, it was difficult but we watched and waited and saw how the Ilkhan's great funeral was planned. It took place on the huge island in Lake Urmia. Only the inner circle of the Ilkhanate's Mongols was in attendance, including Hulegu's sons, all sired prior to William's Gift, of course. The eldest, Abaqa, became the ruler of the Ilkhanate. Following his death after seventeen years, another of Hulegu's sons became the ruler, Tekuder, who was also at the funeral.

The ceremony also featured the sacrifice of twenty-seven beautiful virgin girls. Their blood was poured across the burial site and then entombed with Hulegu.

Entombed along with vast amounts of treasure.

We did not want all of it. Indeed, we could not have transported so much as half of it without buying masses of slaves and horses and wagons to carry it and then we would have required an army to protect it.

But we crossed the lake at night, hopping from island to island in our two small boats. I was tired by the time we got there but I had energy enough left to kill all of the honour guards and slay the barbarian priests chanting and praying for the soul of their departed lord.

Of all the gold and silver and fine furniture and cloth that was buried, we took only the precious coins and the gemstones, and the finest jewellery.

It was a fortune, and we would need it.

I allowed Khutulun to take more than I should have because Eva was right and I was always a fool for women.

But there was enough left over to pay for passage across the Black Sea, and even to pay for comfortable cabins on a ship to Venice. We could afford to pay for plenty of healthy slaves for the journey who we bled every other day or so. That was how, after many days at sea, we came back to Christendom. Back to the lands where we all belonged, amongst people like us, where we could begin once again to track down and slaughter the spawn of William de Ferrers.

And that was when my dear Eva left me.

Part Seven

Venice

1266

THOUGH WE HAD CALLED at numerous ports on the journey home, disembarking from the ship at Venice felt like I had finally returned to civilisation. Though the Venetians were a haughty, arrogant people and were interested only in trade, and power over the Genoese, with whom they had been at war, their remarkable city was a fine sight to see after so many years in foreign lands. The urchins surrounded us the moment I set foot on the dockside, asking where we had come from and touting their wares. A few of the more desperate tugged on my sleeves until I clouted them about the ears.

"Best wine in the city, sir," they would say. "Come, follow me and you will see."

"Our rooms are clean. How many beds do you need, lord?"

"Such food we have, sir, you will never leave Venice."

"Are you looking for a woman's company, my lord? My master's house has all that you could desire."

The cleverer ones spoke French, and one or two even had a stab at English. And yet for all the familiarity I felt for the place and for the people, it was not England. It was not even France.

My companions and I had a task to complete and oaths, made to one another, to fulfil. There were two lords that we knew of, in France or in England, who we had to hunt down.

Stephen had been talking to me for months about his grand ideas for how to maintain the efforts of the Order of the White Dagger over many decades or even centuries, should we need to do so. A day after arriving in Venice, we sat all together while we ate at a busy tavern overlooking the lagoon. It was time to make a final decision about where we went after Venice.

"We should most certainly establish ourselves as merchants," Stephen said, gesticulating with a chunk of bread. "And we should absolutely do so in London. Use some of our wealth to purchase an appropriate sturdy dwelling, perhaps buy a ship, buy and sell goods. And then we have an explanation for the wealth that we have and for our presence in society."

"You are always so keen for us to be merchants, Stephen," I said. "What do you even know of it?"

He waved his bread around. "It cannot be a difficult thing. Look at the fools we have met who are as rich as princes. But surely you see that we can have public wealth and means in this way without the responsibilities that come with obtaining land in fief from some baron who we would have to answer to?"

"Do you think that the merchants of London, or anywhere, will simply allow us to join them?" I pointed out. "Do you know how closely these merchants guard their trade? They do not know us."

Again, he was unconcerned. "We can convince them."

"How?" Eva asked, peering at him over her cup.

He grinned and shrugged. "Every man wants something. We will have to find out what each man wants and then give it to him. And so we will become established in London."

"Why not Paris?" Thomas asked.

I nodded. "London is the worst place on all the Earth," I said, and then remembered Karakorum. "Almost."

"We are English," Stephen said, then coughed. "Other than you, Thomas. We would do better with London as our home."

"We have not needed a home these last years," I said. "We can continue to move from place to place, as we need."

Eva sighed. "Always, we have needed somewhere, have we not? Why continue to live like steppe nomads when we do not have to."

I tried to get them to understand. "I had a home," I said, thinking wistfully of distant Ashbury. "It is all very fine for a while but your servants, your friends, your lord, will all begin to notice that you do not age. And that is not something you can easily explain away. Why make a home at all? Why become established in a place when we would be run out of it within a few years? Perhaps even earlier than then. After all, it is likely that our blood slaves would speak to the servants of other masters in the city of our regular bloodletting. Gossip can be deadly in a town of meddlers like London."

He nodded, excited to tell me what he had evidently been thinking for some time. "The blood slaves have never been a problem so far, Richard. A little bloodletting is good for everyone, is it not? The gossip might say we are overly concerned for our servants' health but no more. Anyway, my thinking is that we operate two homes, in different parts of the kingdom. And I could live alone in London while you all continue to search for William's immortals wherever the scent leads. After some years living in London, when my eternal youth begins to be remarked upon, I would move to the second house across the country and call myself by a different name, leaving the London house in the hands of a capable steward. And then, after a few years when most of the existing merchants have died, I can return to the first home in London and continue to support your ongoing searches with the necessary funds. When I so return, I could claim to be the son of myself, do you see? As you yourself have done, Richard. And so we may inherit by legal means that which we would already own." He dipped his bread in his wine and sat back to chew on it.

"Sounds complicated," I said. "Complicated plans fail."

"Not always," he said, trying and failing to charm me with a grin. "Not in Maragha."

I shook my head, still feeling uneasy with his ideas but unsure precisely why. His blind confidence, perhaps, which was certain to come crashing down when it met with the complexity of reality.

"So," Thomas said. "You wish to be an idler in London while the rest of us trawl the Kingdom of France and the rest of Christendom for William's spawn, is that it?"

I laughed but Stephen made a show of being greatly wounded by the suggestion. "Indeed, no, sir," Stephen said. "I would apply what I have learnt from our dear departed lord of Assassins. We all saw the value of the knowledge we gained through speaking to merchants, troubadours, doctors, and any itinerant traveller, did we not? Imagine the very same thing, only for Christendom."

"Men's tongues wag only for coin," I said. "And thus, you would burn through our fortune in a matter of years. Already, Stephen, you have purchased two homes for yourself in your mind's eye. And you imagine that our order's wealth would survive such expenditure?"

He sat back, satisfied with himself. "And that is why I must also become a successful merchant."

Eva stared at Stephen thoughtfully. At the time, I believed that she was as grudgingly impressed as I was by the cunning young fellow's creativity. And yet, my wife was having quite different thoughts.

Before leaving Venice, we spent time depositing and withdrawing wealth from the Templars and banking houses. We had those names to pursue, and we agreed first to head overland into France to track down Simon de Montfort, the French lord who William claimed to have turned. We decided that Stephen was to travel on alone by ship to England and there set himself up in the manner which he had been envisioning for many years.

That is to say, the decision was made for Stephen to travel alone but that is not what happened in fact.

And there was another thought on my mind I had not been able to truly ignore for years, no matter how often I attempted to dismiss it. When I came close to catching my brother in that gatehouse in Baghdad, he had made a claim so preposterous that it could not possibly have been the truth.

William had spoken to me of what he called the Ancient One. A man he claimed was our grandfather. A man who could be found in Swabia, perhaps three hundred miles north of Venice. Across difficult terrain but not a long journey, certainly not compared to the distances I had travelled before.

I was sorely tempted to head north.

"I recall quite clearly what William said," I muttered to Eva, speaking softly. "He said that our true grandfather lives, and he is thousands of years old. Thousands of years. The things he has seen. The power that he has. You would learn a lot from him, brother, if you would but go to him. That is what William said to me in the gatehouse in Baghdad."

"And what do you think he meant by that?" Eva asked me, stretching her long, naked body beside me.

We lay in bed with the morning sun streaming in through the open window. In the street below, Venetian voices shouted and the tangy scent of the waters mixed with the smell of fish being cooked on the dockside.

It would be one of the last times we shared such a moment together.

"I have been thinking of it often," I said. "All these years, I believed that God had made me as I am. I believed that either God or the Devil made William immortal after the Battle of Hattin, and He made me the same so that I had the strength to put a stop to William's evil. A long time ago, the Archbishop of Jerusalem told me that very thing. I swore an oath to my brother's wife, Isabella to avenge her and her children, and I swore revenge for William's murder of my first wife. But the notion that my blood was changed, was given this power by God... well, that is a notion I have accepted ever since and so my purpose is not simply a moral good but a God-given duty. The Lord changed my blood so as to create balance with William's evil. And so the evil that I have done, the slaughter that I have done, that was ultimately just. But what if none of that is true? What if I was never gifted this power but was born with it, through this man who is the father of our father? What does that mean for my soul?"

I fell silent, irritated at my intellectual deficiencies. I had half a mind to ask Thomas what he thought or even, God forbid, Stephen. But these were questions, or vulnerabilities, that I could express only to my wife.

Eva waited until she was sure I had stopped speaking. "You are losing your wits by using them so much. Twisting yourself into knots for no more than a few mad words by a twisted man."

"William has a way of making me dance to his tune, does he not?"

She sighed, thinking. "Perhaps you imagine his abilities to be greater than they are."

"How so?"

"What is the likelihood that you have some secret ancestor still living in Swabia? It is an absurd notion. So why would he say such a thing? Perhaps he was speaking whatever words formed in his mouth, without thought, and he never even dreamed up the notion before he spoke it. Perhaps he does believe it because he is mad. Which clearly he is. And it could be that he was deceived himself by some decrepit old trickster. You imagine that he has some grand plan that he is unleashing on you and so you give his mad words credence when you should simply forget them."

I listened to an argument break out on the dockside beneath the window. It was rather heated, especially for so early in the morning. But that was the normal manner of social interaction for Venetians.

"It is indeed a bizarre claim," I said. "Our true grandfather is thousands of years old, and he lives still. The outlandishness of it alone makes me believe there is something to it. If he was going to lie, would he not have made it credible?"

"You may be right about him manipulating you," she said. "His words always get their claws under your skin. Could it not be that some of his spawn are in Swabia? He is sending you to them so that they can kill you."

I sat upright. "That is it. By God, that is it. It is so obvious, why did I not see it? I am a fool. Of course he has laid a trap. We should go there, immediately, find these immortals and slay them."

Eva rolled over and faced away from me. "Why do what William wants? If it is a trap, by going to Swabia you may very well be charging headlong to your death."

I could not understand her reticence. "This is why I founded the Order. We must go to Swabia and kill these immortals."

"Immortals who may not even be there. You are giving his words credence when the truth is unknown. His other admissions are far more credible. He turned knights in France and England and we have their names, do we not? This is far more credible, as it mirrors his previous actions. You should focus on those men first, and then see what they have to say about the immortals of Swabia."

I nodded, though she was not looking at me. "That is a reasonable course to follow. One immortal thoroughly questioned will lead to more. We should do precisely that." I clapped her slender flank and grinned, banishing thoughts of William's cunning. "What would I do without you, my love?"

She climbed out of the bed and pulled on her undershirt.

"We should go out and find some food," she said over her shoulder. "And some strong wine."

My smile fell from my face. "A little early for strong wine, is it not?"

She did not look at me. "We shall both want wine."

Her words and demeanour filled me with dread.

All through the journey, Eva had been wistful, and distant. She had never been an overly-affectionate woman but it seemed as though she spoke her thoughts less and less. We would not make love for weeks or months, even when we had the chance, and then she would suddenly seize me in a great lust and cling to me with a desperate passion. Other times, she would weep and then deny it. Although she also often seemed her old self—sturdy, confident, wise—I believed her changed from how she was before we set off into the steppe years before. I clearly recalled the Eva I had grown to love as we travelled from England to Spain, Italy, and Outremer, fighting in local wars and making our way in the world. She had been different when we ranged deep into Mongol lands, and those of the Assassins and the Saracens. And then there was the Eva who I had now. Aloof and gloomy.

Being a mere ninety-seven years old at that time, I had not yet begun to understand the mind of a woman and so I did not know what to make of it all.

I suspected that the toll of spending so much time amongst Godless peoples had worn her down. It certainly had me. And I was apprehensive about the world we were going back to yet I could not wait to see the French countryside and travel amongst my own people, or people almost the same as mine. Why Eva did not feel the same, I could not say.

Whenever I attempted to ask her about it, I would find myself angering her.

"You should be happy," I recall informing her in our cabin on the way home. "French taverns serve proper food. Think on that. Think on riding all day in the rain before drying our boots on the hearth while we eat roast mutton and drink good wine from Bordeaux."

"Think on what you like," she said, not looking at me. "Do not direct my thoughts, so."

"You are only bitter that we have not lain together for such a long time," I said, grinning and reaching for her. "Come here to me."

She slapped my hands away. "Come to yourself instead. And keep your tongue behind your lips so I can get some bloody sleep."

There was a strong chance that it was the murder we had done in Maragha. Such a sin weighed heavy on me and on Thomas and it was not either of us but Eva and Khutulun who had lobbed the fire pots and so delivered the inferno to the Mongols and their innocent slaves. Women are not created for war, and despite all her skills with the blade and her unfailing, uncomplaining toughness, Eva was certainly a woman.

Yet, when I broached the notion of penance, she cursed me and said that our quest for William's monsters, our very continued existence was our penance. And although I did not quite understand what she felt, I agreed to let the matter lie.

There was another great sin that I had committed. One which I pretended to myself and to God that I had not done. And yet I had carried with me, for years, the guilt and the shame of my abandonment of her in Baghdad. I had looked at her, my wife, surrounded and assaulted on all sides, and I had left her to die. No matter that I justified my actions post hoc by telling myself her strength and skill would always have saved her from the horde. I left her to die.

It was my greatest sin, though it already had such mighty competition. What is more, the abandonment had accomplished nothing. William had eluded me anyway.

That decision that I made must surely have demonstrated to Eva, beyond all words that I could ever utter, that my quest for vengeance against William would also come before her, my wife.

Ours had never been a proper marriage. Looking back with the power of hindsight, I saw how I had treated her in many ways just like the squire that she often pretended to be and indeed served as. I had neglected to provide her with what she needed. A wife is subordinate to a husband, of course, but while the male domain is the world, the married woman's realm is the home. A marriage is for producing and raising children, but even for those who are barren, a woman, a wife, rules her home, she commands the servants and directs the meals and company, creates income from the assets, manages the economy of the household. She has that power. She serves that role, as the man serves his in turn as provider and protector.

But Eva had never had her own place, her own realm. Her own life. Never had anyone to command, anywhere to grow, and had been at my side like a servant more than a wife.

I was such a fool. A fool for women, people liked to say of me, ever since I was a boy. It was meant to imply that beauty made me stupid, and that has been true from my first decade to my last century. But in truth, it was more than that. I was foolish in all ways, where women were concerned.

And I had not seen any of that at the time.

Which is why it hit me with such terrible force and brought me so low when it happened. We sat opposite each other across a small table in the morning sun outside the tavern near to our rooms. It overlooked a quiet, narrow inlet and though there were people all about, they were going about their daily business and paid us no mind. The wine was good, and Eva drank off three full cups before she had the courage to say what she had to say.

"I will not travel with you into France," Eva said, looking me in the eye. "I am going to England, and there I will establish one of the two houses that we will run for our order."

A thousand thoughts ran through my head. Mostly, I was simply confused. "Why have you not spoken of this to me before now?"

"Cowardice. I feared saying all that I must say. And I feared your reaction."

My heart began racing as I struggled to comprehend what she was getting at. "You have not yet said all you must say?"

Her courage faltered and she looked away for a moment. "When William killed me, and your blood brought me back, you saved me. We were together. We have been together ever since." She sighed. Eva had never been gifted with speech. "I am tired, Richard. Tired of always travelling. Tired of dressing this way. Pretending to be a man, to be your squire. You will not stop your quest. The thought of trailing from town to town in the search. I cannot do it. I will go to London, and make a house there, or I shall go to some other town. My oath to the Order stands. I am committed to our purpose. My life will be dedicated to finding and ending all of William's spawn. But I will live my own life."

"Your own life?" I said, stuttering like a boy. "And not a wife to me?"

She looked at me again. "Not a wife, no. I shall pose as a widow, in order to have the appropriate station. I will take no husband."

Suspicion crept into my thoughts. "Is this some scheme to marry Stephen?"

Eva stared in astonishment, then laughed in my face. "He is a boy. I want nothing of love from him. But, in truth, yes, I also wish to learn more from him."

"Learn?" I said. "What could you learn from him? He is a boy, as you say. You could never learn from him what you have from me."

"He is a boy in his heart. But his mind is devious and he burns with ambition. He is clever."

"And you wish to be around him, rather than me?" I could not believe my ears.

"It is not him that I want," she said, growing irritated. "I will live my own life but will correspond with him, visit with him, coordinate our efforts. You see, it is his cunning I wish to cultivate. Cunning that can be turned into power."

I struggled still to understand. "You want power?"

She waved her hand and shook her head, growing impatient. "You have listened to Stephen, but you do not take him seriously, so you do not take his ideas seriously. Imagine it. Look at us. We still have not aged. How long will we live? Decades more, certainly. Centuries, perhaps many centuries. Imagine what we can build in that time. We would have to be careful, pretending to be small people while hiding our wealth and our connections, but with the knowledge to find all of William's spawn. And then, when they are all dead and our oaths are complete, God willing we will still be here. What else might we achieve with what we have been given? With this Gift?"

Stephen's ambition had infected her. I should have seen it earlier but perhaps I could have done nothing even if I had known where it would lead. Although, I could always have cut off Stephen's head and thrown him into the sea before we ever reached Venice. Perhaps that would have kept Eva by my side over the centuries.

But it may also have condemned England to a tawdry existence on the edge of the world, rather than becoming the greatest empire that ever would bestride it. Stephen and Eva made that empire. With my help, of course.

In Venice, sitting before my wife under a pale blue sky, the stench of the lagoon and with a cloud of flies determined to die in my cup of wine, I had more selfish concerns. "We took oaths," I pointed out. "To be undone only by our deaths."

"We have lived together for fifty years, Richard." Her eyes grew damp. "A lifetime of marriage for mortal men and women. We have been faithful to each other, in all ways. I think God will forgive us."

Eva had decided. She was not asking permission, as a woman should, which was typical of her forthrightness. Quite rightly, she had not considered our marriage to be an ordinary one. It struck me suddenly as quite astonishing that she had lasted as long as she had. Even before I had met her she had received some simulacrum of a knight's training and had served as a bodyguard for her perverse father. But no other woman in all the world would have entertained for a moment's thought what she had embraced with me as we fought and killed across the world.

"You will need blood," I said. "Every few days. You must be prepared. I will not be there to give you mine and you must not be without for too long."

I do not know why but at that she burst into womanly tears. The first time I had ever seen her weep.

***

In the face of the rampant Mamluks under Baibars and his successors, the Crusader kingdoms in the Holy Land would not survive for very much longer.

The remaining Syrian Assassins were initially overjoyed by the Mamluk defeat of the Mongol armies. Of course they were. Hulegu had destroyed hundreds of their castles in Persia and had slaughtered everyone who had lived in them. For a time, the Mamluks were an avenging force, delivering a righteous blow against the Mongols.

But when the Mamluks had subdued the Mohammedan peoples of Syria, Baibars turned his attention to wiping out the heretic Assassins between 1265 and 1273. Even with their fine castles, the Ismailis of Syria could not resist the might of Egypt and their new allies, and they ceased to be an independent military or political force. Baibars did not exterminate them as Hulegu had done to the Persian Assassins, and so the Ismaili Assassins struggled on in Syria, keeping their faith but lacking any power in the world. Indeed, they survived only by being subjected to the authority of Baibars and the Mamluks and agreeing to carry out the political murders that the sultan ordered.

Saracens turning on each other should have been a good thing for Christendom. But the Assassins were so easily subdued that it barely slowed down the Mamluk assault on the Crusader Kingdoms.

The Mamluks raided Antioch in 1261. Nazareth fell in 1263 and Acre was encircled, only surviving due to ongoing supply from the sea. Caesarea and Haifa fell in 1265 and then all our remaining inland Crusader castles could not survive. In 1271, it was the White Castle of the Templars and the magnificent Krak des Chevaliers, Beaufort and Gibelcar that fell. Without reinforcing Christian armies to save them, the greatest fortifications could not survive the Mamluk siege engines.

The Mamluks even employed a Syrian Assassin to murder the chief baron of Acre, Philip of Montfort in 1270. Unholy savages that they were, the fedayin struck down poor Philip while he prayed in his chapel.

From being the terror of the Holy Land, feared by the Abbasids, Persians, Mongols and Crusaders alike, the Assassins ended up becoming nothing more than hitmen for the sultan. A truth demonstrated by their attempt on the life of my future king, Edward I of England.

Prince Edward, as he was then, joined the Crusade that was to undo the conquests of Baibars.

And who was the great saviour of Christendom come to save the Crusader Kingdoms? The great King Louis IX launched a new Crusade to smash the Mamluks and was even seeking to coordinate with the Mongols of Persia who had inherited Hulegu's empire.

And yet, the great fool messed it up once again. Louis diverted the Crusade to Tunis with the intention of converting the sultan there to Christianity. No doubt they convinced themselves it was for good and noble reasons, and not due to their fear of facing the ferocity and ability of the Mamluks. Either way, they paid for their cowardice when the army was struck with the bloody flux. The pestilence tore through the men on the North African shore and even took Louis himself. Good riddance. An ignominious end to an incompetent crusader.

Prince Edward of England, son of Henry III, and a man destined to become a truly great king arrived in the Holy Land in June 1271. He led a force on Louis' Crusade to Tunis but was not willing to accept that failure and so sailed on to Acre. His army was small but the Mamluks rightly feared the might of Christian knights and so Baibars decided to have this English prince killed.

Edward struck into the Plain of Sharon, near Mount Carmel and coordinated with the Mongols, who sent a tumen of ten thousand to Syria to support him. But without the leadership of Hulegu, the Mongols quickly withdrew in the face of the Mamluk counterattack, leaving Edward to negotiate a peace with Baibars.

The Mamluk peace was negotiated to last ten years, ten months, ten days and ten hours. This is the timeframe allowed for hudna, the truce that is allowed to interrupt jihad if there is a justified tactical advantage for the Mohammedans to temporarily halt their duty to annihilate the infidel. Such practices show very well their fundamental deceptiveness and cunning. As does their continued love of political murder.

Not satisfied with the peace, Baibars sent a Syrian Ismaili fedayin to assassinate Prince Edward of England. The Mamluk governor of Ramla pretended to be willing to betray Baibars and sent a messenger with gifts for Edward. With a cunning and patience that Hassan would have been proud of, the messenger was admitted many times into the prince's presence while the false negotiations were undertaken. Even though he was searched for weapons, the fedayin's patience had caused Edward and his men to let their guard down. A knight who claimed to be there later told me how it happened.

Edward was unused to the climate and reclined on a couch in no more than a cotton tunic. The fedayin, posing as a messenger, approached in order to pass the prince a document, a false letter supposedly from this traitor Mamluk lord. Edward took the letter and asked the messenger a question regarding its content. The messenger bent over the reclining prince, directing Edward's attention to a line in the letter with one hand, and with the other, he drew a concealed blade, cunningly hidden on the inside of his belt.

He thrust this blade at Edward's chest.

But the future King of England was no ordinary man. He had a lifetime of martial training honing his instinct and he was a big, powerful fellow.

With remarkable speed, Edward twisted so that the blade caught him on his arm instead of his chest. Quickly, the prince struck the treacherous Saracen to the ground while tearing the man's dagger from his hand. Edward, showing a decisiveness that was fundamental to his character, immediately used the enemy's weapon to stab the fedayin. Before Edward could restrain them, his servants smashed the Assassin's brains in with the prince's footstool.

Though he was furious, Edward considered himself to be unscathed. But he was thinking like an upstanding Christian, and not a treacherous Mohammedan.

For the Assassin's dagger had been poisoned.

Edward became seriously ill.

His flesh around the wound on his arm began to fester and oozed a steady stream of thick, stinking pus. No supposed antidote worked and his condition deteriorated. Finally, his surgeon simply cut away all the rotten flesh from around the original wound and his robust constitution enabled him to overcome the poison in his system.

The very moment he was well enough to travel, he left the Holy Land forever and returned to the civilised people of England.

What if the fedayin's poison had taken Edward's life? What then for England? His younger brother, Edmund, was also on the Crusade. Presumably, he would have become King of England. Edmund was a good man. Solid, dependable. A dutiful second son all his life. But he was no Edward, and I doubt he would have conquered the unruly Welsh and hammered the mad Scots into submission.

Thanks to God, and to the Plantagenet robustness, Edward survived and returned home. In time, I served in many of his campaigns and did more than my fair share of the work.

The monks William of Rubruck and his elderly companion Bartholomew left Karakorum in the summer we had, back in 1254. Both of them somehow managed to make it to Tripoli little over a year later and eventually to Rome and finally home to Paris, although the shrivelled-up Bartholomew died immediately after. At some point, Rubruck wrote an absurdly long and detailed letter to King Louis about everything that had occurred. Years later, Stephen claimed to have read a copy of the letter that had belonged to another Franciscan named Roger Bacon and said it mentioned nothing at all about an English knight and the trouble he caused. Poor Thomas as leader of the expedition was also excised entirely, as was Bertrand. Even Stephen was barely mentioned in the rambling narrative. Considering how we had abandoned him, in one way or another, such hurt feelings were to be expected. Amusingly, King Louis seems to have taken no actions based on the content of Rubruck's letter, and no other lord, priest or monk read it either. Rubruck returned to obscurity as a monk for the rest of his days. One might say his great efforts were entirely wasted other than the fact that his mission provided cover for mine and so ultimately helped to rid the world of Hulegu.

Tragically, our great city of Acre fell to the Mamluks in 1291. After so long stemming the tide of Saracen expansion, the Crusader kingdoms were finally no more.

Failure.

Our people could no longer resist the ferocity of the Mohammedans and the kingdoms of Christendom turned against each other rather than uniting to drive out the invaders from the Holy Land. Even though I had seen their fanaticism first hand, and for so long, I did not imagine that they would eventually take Constantinople and threaten to overrun Europe itself.

One of the most severe consequences of the loss of the fall of the Crusader states would be the fall of the Templars. Their collapse in the face of the Mamluks and the Mongols brought them into disgrace and the order was much criticised by those who wanted someone to blame. Pressure on the Templars grew from many sources until Philip IV of France arrested every Templar in France in 1307. The vile French king seized the order's assets, tortured and tried the men and eventually burned the final master to death in 1314. Thomas took it hard, of course, for he remained a Templar at heart even after decades serving the Order of the White Dagger. For a time, he was convinced that Philip IV was one of William's immortals and I was willing to believe that the cruel bastard was a vampire. But it turned out not to be the case, as far as I know. In time, the hurt of it faded but Thomas never got over the betrayal. Without the Templar's presence linking different kingdoms together in resistance to the Saracen expansion, successive states would be isolated, overwhelmed and conquered in turn. We needed the Templars. May Philip IV burn in the hottest fires of Hell for eternity.

It would be two hundred years before I returned to the East but I would again fight to protect Christendom from the rampaging Turk.

It was many years before I heard what happened to Khutulun. She returned to her people as she had intended, and found a great Mongol named Kaidu who was an enemy of Kublai, who William was supporting. Kaidu was the leader of the House of Ogedei and Khan of the Chagatai Khanate. Khutulun must have chosen him because of his opposition to Kublai, and William, and also because he was a war-loving steppe warrior at heart, just like she was. No doubt when she presented herself to Kaidu, he would have wanted her for his wife but she certainly refused because she became famous as the daughter of Kaidu. When I heard that, I laughed, for I can well imagine this Khan's confusion and ultimate compliance to her demand. The lie could have been made quite easily. I imagine her riding alone across the step and claiming that her mother was some woman that Kaidu had taken years before. Whether that was the way of it, or whether he believed her or not, he certainly claimed her as his own.

In return for this dishonourable act of deceit, she offered him her brilliance as a warrior, a tactician, and political strategist.

With her help, by 1280 Kaidu was the most powerful ruler of Central Asia, reigning from western Mongolia to Oxus, and from the Central Siberian Plateau to India.

In time, stories of her ability made their way to Christendom.

There was a lowly Venetian merchant and conman named Marco Polo who claimed to have visited the court of Kublai Khan. I know for a fact that he never travelled further than the shores of the Black Sea, and his accounts of the East were stolen from hundreds of braver men, who themselves had only heard the tales second or third hand, while he plied them with cheap wine in the Venetian trading colonies. This Marco Polo was a man who wished to be a great traveller but he also lacked the courage to venture from safety. As a collector of stories, he made a great impression, however, it was not he but another man who wrote down those collected stories which were presented as the experiences of the fraudster Polo himself.

Whatever his personal lies and deceit, he at least got some things correct. He described Khutulun as a superb warrior, one who could ride into enemy ranks and snatch a captive as easily as a hawk snatches a chicken. She fought with Kaidu in many battles, particularly those against Kublai and William. The story goes that Khutulun insisted that any man who wished to marry her must defeat her in wrestling but if he failed she would win his horses. That certainly sounds like her as she knew that no man on Earth could ever defeat her. Well, I supposed I could have done but whether she would have married me is another matter. But through this cunning challenge, she spent years winning horses from those competitions and the wagers of hopeful suitors and it is said that she gathered a herd numbering ten thousand.

There are a half-dozen stories of who was her eventual husband. Some chronicles say her husband was a handsome man who failed to assassinate her father and was taken prisoner. Others refer to him as Kaidu's companion from another clan. A Persian chronicler wrote that Khutulun fell in love with Ghazan, a Mongol ruler in Persia.

So many contradictory tales surely mean one thing. She had no husband. No doubt many eminent men professed their certainty that they would be the one to claim her, and thus these stories spread. But she had no interest in such things and wanted only to fight and kill and be a great warrior.

Kaidu had fourteen sons but Khutulun was the one from whom he most sought advice and political support. Indeed, he named her as his successor to the khanate before he died in 1301. When Kaidu died, Khutulun guarded his tomb. But his sons hated her brilliance, hated her ageless beauty and strength and they feared whatever dark magic prolonged her youth. Above all, perhaps, they knew she was not of their blood, so the sons of Kaidu banded together all their men and they killed her, though she is said to have killed a hundred of them before she fell.

If she had stayed with me, fought with us in our order, she would likely have lived longer. But she would not have lived the life of a Mongol warrior and that was all she wanted. Her death at the ungrateful hands of men she had made great caused me to feel a terrible surge of hatred and a thirst for revenge on them. But by the time I heard, it had already long come to pass. Besides, I am sure her death was also glorious and I smiled to imagine the ferocity and virtuosity with which she would have fought to her last.

What of her enemies, Kublai Khan and William de Ferrers? The Great Khan slowly and relentlessly conquered all China and established the Yuan dynasty and became Emperor of China as well as the Great Khan of the Mongols. That conquest was perhaps the most remarkable of all the achievements of the Mongols, for the Chinese were the most advanced, the most numerous and the most well-defended people the world had ever known. Indeed, their cities were so well defended, by walls so high, wide and strongly-built that William advised Kublai to send word to the Ilkhanate for the great trebuchets used by Hulegu to smash the walls of Baghdad. With those weapons, the Great Khan was finally able to break through city and after city and complete the conquest.

Kublai was astonishingly successful, and yet he also experienced great failure. His attempted conquests of lands that would become Vietnam and Japan ended in disaster. His favourite wife died and that broke his heart and his spirit. A few years later, his son and heir also died and this calamity broke what remained. The most powerful man on Earth indulged his gluttony and grew disgustingly fat and riddled with gout and God only knows what else. He died in 1294, aged 78.

William, it seems, had learned his lesson. He had not made Kublai into an immortal and had instead served in a quieter role, advising and steering. Manipulating and assassinating.

After Kublai came his grandson. And after him, a series of young successors who each ruled for only a short time. Some were more capable than others but all were severely lacking in the glory and ability of their forefathers, becoming no more than administrators of their enormous empire. Like all Chinese dynasties, the Mongol Yuan dynasty turned inward and became obsessed with the machinations of the court. While they called themselves Khan as well as Emperor, they soon became nothing like steppe nomads and lost that which made them unique. Still, the Chinese always knew they were ruled by northern barbarians, no matter how sinicised they became, and after only a hundred years they were overthrown.

So many Yuan Emperors died young and died early into their reigns. What was William hoping to accomplish by his machinations? Always, he tried to remake the world, and remake the people of the world, into what he wanted them to be. William wanted naked power. He wanted to be worshipped. But he dressed it up in grand notions of religiosity or civic glories for ordinary men. I do believe that somewhere in his black heart he wanted to build great things, to change the world for the sake of some confused, empty notions of change and progress. That is why he always told men precisely what they wanted to hear. And yet because of his evil nature, all he ever truly did was destroy. Just as his efforts to shape the Yuan dynasty ended in their overthrow and destruction.

William would return to the West and begin to wreak his evil on the people of Christendom once more but it would not be for some time.

But in his prolonged absence, we still had many immortals scattered throughout the kingdoms of Europe to find and to kill.

William's immortals had to die. We had two names only from William but I knew well what I would do. The plan was a good one. I had been repeating it for months, even years.

Take either man alive, or even both of them, and torture them for the names of all the others that they knew. Then I would behead them and chase down the next one. Thusly, I would clean the corrupt filth from all of Christendom.

I knew of Simon de Montfort. He was a French lord and also Earl of Leicester in England. He was one of the men who joined Innocent's Crusade and took part in the shameful sacking and conquering Constantinople decades before.

The other was an English knight named Sir Hugh le Despenser. I half-remembered some fellow named Despenser but it had been a long time since I had been in England.

When Thomas and I rode into France and asked after de Montfort, we eventually discovered that the man I knew of had died fighting the Cathar heretics, almost fifty years earlier.

"Then our work is done for us," Thomas said. "Fifty years ago, or nearly."

"Perhaps," I said, partially relieved and also enormously disappointed. "Yet, these immortals can be tricky. William would have chosen the most cunning of men."

The old de Montfort's son, also the Earl of Leicester, had lately been stirring up trouble against King Henry III. No matter how often I had heard it, I was still astonished that the little boy I had known before my self-imposed exile was still the King of England, now an old man. This new Simon de Montfort had risen in rebellion.

"He is the true ruler of England," said a giggling, fat, Burgundian townsman in Dijon. "Henry is nothing."

The story was confirmed a number of times before it dawned on me.

"The son is the father," I said to a bewildered Thomas. "Do you not see? They have done the very same thing that we have proposed to do in order to pass our wealth down from generation to generation. The very same thing, or something similar. This new Simon de Montfort is the same man as the father. William must have granted him the gift, he lived for some time and then decided to pretend to die." With sudden inspiration, I could imagine how it could be done. "You or I could do the same thing, Thomas. On the battlefield, you are run through and fall dead. A trusted man takes your body away, perhaps gives you blood to drink. And much later you return, claiming to be your own son, now grown. I am sure it could be done."

"This is all a fancy," Thomas said, for he always lacked imagination. "You believe this only because Stephen suggested it for us."

"William said that they were men after his own heart," I replied. "And this Earl of Leicester has seized England for himself. Does that not sound like something William would do? Our duty is to slay this de Montfort, and to thus save the King and his kingdom."

Thomas remained sceptical until we discovered that de Montfort's right-hand man in the rebellion was none other than Hugh le Despenser.

Our joy at discovering both our quarries were already flushed into the open was short lived. When we neared Paris, we found out that the rebellion had been crushed in battle, and both de Montfort and le Despenser were slain.

"Perhaps they are feigning death once more," I suggested. "We should observe the men who claim to be their sons. Perhaps they have simply pulled the same trick once more."

As I would eventually discover, I was wrong about that and the vampires de Montfort and

Despenser were truly dead. Our best chance for smashing William's immortals was snuffed out.

But we continued on to England in order to investigate.

Whenever I had imagined coming home, I had pictured myself walking through damp woodlands and colourful meadows, with the hills of Derbyshire as my horizons.

In fact, our ship crossed the channel and hugged around the coast of Kent and then up the Thames into London. It was a truly vile place, and only ever became worse as the centuries rolled by. It was a city for the grasping, the ambitious, and the perverse. Seekers of power and pleasure. Desperate men and women living in filth, breathing in the smoke and stench of rotting shit while dreaming of one day winning great wealth and marrying their son to an impoverished lady. A city of pimps, jesters, smooth-skinned lads, flatterers, pretty boys, effeminates, paederasts, singing girls, quacks, sorceresses, extortioners, night wanderers, magicians, mimes, beggars, and buffoons.

Stephen was right at home.

Stepping off the boat was just like it was in every other port between Calais and Acre. A swarm of skinny boys shouting questions and saying welcome back, sir, or welcome home, as if they recognised you.

And yet…

It was different. The stench was more powerful than anywhere but Paris, nevertheless there was a familiarity to everything that confused me at first. The sounds of so many English voices raised in cries as men laboured on the dockside or shouted their wares from the public cookshops just up the way along the waterfront. I found myself drawn to the smell of hot pastry and the savoury aroma of boiled beef.

"What can I get you, squire?" the cheery man in front of his shop said as I drew to a stop in front of him. He was plump and ruddy cheeked, as was appropriate for an English vendor. "Fresh game and fowl, the best in London, as I'm sure you know, squire."

I could smell suet, onions, eggs, and butter, and I wiped the drool from the corners of my mouth. The roasted birds looked wonderful but I pointed to a dark, glazed pie big enough to feed a dozen. "What is in that?"

"Beef and kidney, squire. The finest cuts, by God's hooks, they are. Onion stewed for half a day until it—"

"I shall take it."

I fished coins from my purse while the fellow scratched his head. "You'll be sending your servant to pick it up, will you, squire?"

"Hand it over."

He was uncomfortable and unsure but he took my coin readily enough and handed the thing over like he was passing me a child and I tucked it into my arm. The smell was glorious and I could not resist a moment longer. Punching through the thick, inedible crust, I pulled out the rich, savoury filling within and shoved a fistful into my mouth.

"Steady on, squire," the shopkeeper said.

The taste of it was remarkable. Salty, tender meat, slippery with the rich juices.

Fifty years. I have not been home in fifty years. Half my life.

In my mind's eye, I saw the hall of Ashbury Manor filled with smiling faces. I recalled sneaking into the kitchens of Duffield Castle to snatch some of the stewed beef before it was spooned onto the platters and being caught by the cook. He cracked me on the skull with an enormous wooden spoon. Standing there on the busy waterfront I laughed out loud, like a madman. I was filled with emotion. So much so that I almost wept.

Fifty years.

"Here, Thomas," I said. "You must share this with me. This is the taste of England."

He wrinkled his nose. "Then perhaps we should have stayed in France."

England had been in turmoil for decades but the rebellious barons had finally been crushed and the remaining rebels cornered and destroyed by King Henry's son, Prince Edward. The prince was already in his late twenties and a man in the prime of his life. A man who had been campaigning against the rebels for years, and who had fought in half a dozen pitched battles. Once the rebellion was over, and the country was finally at peace, Edward left on his crusade which would end in his attempted assassination at the hands of the subjugated Ismaili fedayin.

King Henry grew ill and died when his son was on the way back to England. When I had left, fifty years before, Henry had been a young boy under the regency of William Marshal. While I had remained ageless in my absence, he had ruled for decades and died a decrepit old man. I was pleased that he had lived and ruled for so long but I felt very guilty for abandoning him when he had clearly needed me. If I had stayed in England, or returned sooner, I would have been on hand to kill the vampires de Montfort and Despenser and end their rebellions.

That guilt was one reason why I perhaps lost a little fervour for the aims of the Order of the White Dagger. When Edward became king, I found myself fighting for him against the Welsh and later against the Scots. It was simple to find the employment of a lord to keep me funded and occupied, and at other times I was paid as a mercenary directly by the Crown. Always, I said to my peers and lords that I had grown up in the Holy Land, the grandson of an English knight named Richard of Ashbury.

No man had heard of him.

Once Acre fell, in 1291, I knew I would have to come up with a new story to tell. But as long as you fought well and did not seek to climb above a low station, few men cared where you came from. Everyone always assumed the worst. Why else would a wandering Englishman be cagey about his origins if he was not some form of criminal? But a man-at-arms' trade is the murder of the king's enemies, and so sinners were always welcome.

In all the fighting, I pushed my knowledge and experience onto the men I fought with. I had learned from the Mongols that mobility was vitally important in war. Likewise, I championed the use of the small horses called hobelars as the best means for moving men rapidly in a campaign. At first, they told me I was mad but over the years I saw the changes happening until men treated it as so obvious a thing it was not worth so much as commenting on. Likewise, thanks to my experience with the Wealden archers against the French and witnessing and hearing accounts of the Mongol arrow storms, I pushed always for bringing more and more archers with us. Again, at the start of Edward's reign, I was mocked for wasting resources on such men but, in just a few decades' time, we could not recruit enough of them.

In between campaigns, we searched for the immortals of Christendom that William had created.

Stephen wormed his way into London and began to quietly establish himself as a man of standing, though he had to be warned repeatedly to stop bringing so much attention to himself. My dear Eva set herself up first in Exeter, possibly because it was so far away from London, and then in Bristol. When we crossed paths, we both pretended that we were happy. Both of them inconspicuously cultivated contacts with the itinerant folks who returned regularly to the cities. Through the words passed between them, Thomas and I tracked down reports of bloody crimes and suspicious outlaws. For some years, Stephen and Eva would swap houses and trade lives, each pretending to be the relative or descendent of the other. For a few years between wars, I myself ruled the townhouse in London that we had taken for our order. It only confirmed what I had already known; that I was not well suited to city life.

Finding the spawn of William was hard work. Most leads led nowhere and it would be some years before we found a true vampire once again. It would be in the reign of Edward's grandson, Edward III, and during his wars against the Kingdom of France. After the elder Edward died, the crown passed to Edward II who was rather a disappointment, to say the least. He very nearly undid all of his father's gains.

But, just as the soft Henry had produced the iron-hard Edward, so his weakling son produced a lion in his turn.

Ever since he was a young man, and before any of his famous deeds were done, I had great affection for Edward III. Despite the protestations from Thomas, Stephen, and Eva that I was abandoning my oaths to the Order of the White Dagger, I had thrown my lot in with him early on and I was at his side when we seized the would-be usurper, Roger Mortimer.

And I would fight for him when we campaigned against the French, defeating them time and again thanks to our mobility, our unity of action, and the power of our archers.

It would be at our great victory at Crecy that I discovered a foul vampire on the battlefield and the Order of the White Dagger would bend our will to capturing and killing the monstrous bastard. Our quest would be interrupted by the disaster of the Black Death and for the sake of the Order I would have to journey through unprecedented death and horror in the hopes of finding salvation.

But that is a story for another time.

I had not known how much I had missed England until I had returned there. From the savages of the east to the madness of the Greeks, and the volatility of the Italians, I had been amongst strangers for half my life. Returning to my own country, campaigning alongside men who were just like me, it made me never want to leave ever again. In fact, I would be ready to venture forth again after a mere couple of centuries but for the time being, all I knew was that it was my land. I was an Englishman. And the English were my people.

Finally, I was home.

VAMPIRE TEMPLAR

The Immortal Knight Chronicles

This short story takes place between books 3 and 4 in the series.

Richard of Ashbury
and the Destruction of the Templars
1311

DAN DAVIS

Chinon, France

AD 1311

Thomas and I stole through the darkness of the ancient crypts beneath the Château de Chinon. With only the faint glow of our lantern to see by, it was slow going and Thomas fretted and hurried me all the way.

"Quiet, sir," I hissed at him for the umpteenth time while pulling a spiderweb away from my face. "Lest you give us away."

"Only the dead can hear us down here," he replied, his voice echoing in the gloom.

"We shall be dead men ourselves if you do not slow your pace."

Thomas stopped, his shoes scraping on the bone-dry floor, and spoke through gritted teeth. "There is no time to waste, Richard. If we do not reach them and escape by dawn then all this has been for naught!"

That was true enough.

Our quest that night was to free the leaders of the Templars before they could be further questioned, convicted, and ultimately executed.

"Come, then," I whispered. "Yet do not give such full voice to your fears. We must be close to the gaol now and surely the gaolers themselves shall be within earshot. If they raise the alarm—"

"I will be silent," Thomas hissed, "if you will but hurry."

We pushed on deeper through the tunnels.

The seeds of the fall of the Poor Fellow-Soldiers of Christ and of the Temple of Solomon, commonly called the Knights Templar, or simply the Templars, were many but the most fruitful were sown when Acre was lost. In 1291, the last Crusader city fell to the Saracens and our presence in the Holy Land was finally ended. The Jews and the Saracens mocked us, worse, they mocked Christ for failing to defend us. It was a terrible blow and the Templars received much of the blame.

It was true that they and the Hospitallers had grown increasingly embittered against each other and their conflict had weakened the Christian presence. Following the tragic loss of Acre, both Orders were rightly criticised by lord and commoner alike but the Templars had the worst of it.

And yet, it was not only the fault of the military orders. I had seen over the decades a loss of fervour as far as the Holy Land was concerned. In my youth, men had burned with the desire to take back what the Saracens had stolen from us. We had felt in our bones the wanton aggression from the Moors in their assaults on Spain and Sicily and the devastation caused when the wild Saracens had long ago smashed the Christian Roman cities and forced those good people into subjugation. Protecting the pilgrims who were so abused by the Mohammedans was inspiring, as was the chance for winning glory for ourselves.

But our lords and knights grew ever more concerned with fighting each other rather than uniting against the common enemy. We knew, or thought we knew, that the Saracens could never conquer our homelands and so they were not considered to be a true threat. Our Christian neighbours, on the other hand, often were a danger and smaller kingdoms and counties were swallowed up by the greater kingdoms until those emerging empires threatened each other. And so Christendom turned inward.

Still, the Templars played their part in the transformation. They had become ever more comfortable as facilitators and bankers rather than carrying out a spirited armed defence of the people of the Holy Land. Their attention had turned to the rest of Christendom and their squabbles with kings, dukes, and the other military orders had morally weakened them. Supposedly subordinate to the Pope, the Templars had become a force unto themselves, almost independent of the Church and certainly free from control by even the most powerful kings. When Acre fell, there was considerable criticism and many a man spoke the thought that the Templars and their rivals the Hospitallers should be merged into a single order and brought to heel.

Indeed, that was one way in which we could win back what had been lost in the Holy Land, so our lords said, and it was urged in all quarters. Leading royal and spiritual voices formed a consensus that conquering small castles and cities at the borders of Saracen territory and slowly working our way in to the heart of the Holy Land was the best way forward to retake Jerusalem.

The Templars alone resisted. Led by Grand Master James of Molay, an honourable but ageing and old-fashioned knight from Lorraine, they urged the Pope and the Kings of Europe to launch a large-scale invasion of Egypt with a combined force of ten thousand knights, transported by the Venetians and Genoese, to smash the enemy swiftly in grand battles. This proposal was met with an embarrassed silence by the kings. As far as they were concerned, their fathers and grandfathers had attempted this method and had failed time and again.

What is more, Grand Master Molay was illiterate, unimaginative and stubborn and powerful forces sensed weakness in this inflexibility. His contemporaries recognised that he was a man made from an outdated mould, no longer fit for a more complicated and cynical world.

Of course, I could well sympathise.

Illiteracy was ever rarer in the heartlands of Christendom as the new century came and the lower classes began to take advantage of the opportunities that widespread learning enabled. Lawyers were on the rise. Jumped-up, clever second sons of the middling orders of society, the lawyers began to wield power far above their station. Nowhere was this truer than in France, where the power of law grew along with the cunning of King Philip IV. With the French Pope and a mass of French Cardinals in his pocket, he felt secure enough to go after the Templars.

A group of iniquitous knights had recently been expelled from the Order for their degenerate behaviour, and they in turn made accusations of impropriety which the Grand Master James of Molay, knowing them to be false, had begged the Pope to investigate. He was a straightforward man who naively believed that the law would discover the truth, not realising that the law may be used by the powerful as a tool to destroy their enemies.

There were five charges lodged against the Templars.

The first was the renouncement of and spitting on the cross during initiation into the Order. The second was the stripping of the man so initiated and the thrice kissing of that man by the preceptor on the navel, posterior and the mouth. The third was telling the neophyte, that is the novice, that sodomy and other unnatural lusts were lawful and indulged in commonly by knights, sergeants, squires, and priests. The fourth was that the cord worn by the neophyte was consecrated by wrapping it around an idol in the form of a human head with a great beard and that the idol was adored in all Templar chapters. The fifth, and perhaps greatest charge of all, was that the Templar priests did not consecrate the host when celebrating Mass.

On these obviously false pretexts, Philip IV seized James of Molay on Friday 13th October 1307, at the Templar compound outside Paris.

And it was not the Grand Master Molay alone. Far from it.

Three weeks before, King Philip had sent secret orders throughout France commanding his bailiffs and seneschals to detain all Templars for undefined but terrible crimes. I was astonished when I discovered that fifteen thousand Templar knights, sergeants, chaplains and servants were rounded up and detained in a single day. As far as I could recall, nothing the like of it had ever been done before.

Thomas was incandescent with outrage.

He had spent his adult life as a devoted Templar knight, before he had his guts ripped open by my brother in far-off Karakorum, and it was only at Thomas' urging that we had gone to Chinon at all.

"We must do something, Richard!" he had said when news of the arrests spread like fire across Christendom. Thomas and I were in the hall of our Order's house in London in the middle of the day, with the sun streaking through gaps in the closed shutters.

"What can we do?" I asked.

"Save them."

I scoffed. "We could never save even a fraction of them. There are thousands of Templars, Thomas. Thousands, from Scotland to Cyprus, and most of them are in France."

"A few of them, we may save a few. Some will be better than none."

"I do not disagree," I allowed. "And yet it is not for us to do anything. Our Order exists to uncover William's immortals and this assault on the Templars is not of our—"

"For the love of God, Richard! My brothers will be destroyed. And for what? Because this damned king wishes to remove a rival power? To seize the Order's wealth? We cannot stand by and do nothing. We must act, not as members of the Order of the White Dagger but as good Christians. As knights. It is our duty. None other than us could do it and so it must be us."

"By God, you lay it on thick, sir. But how could it be done?"

"With our strength and speed and skill. With Stephen's connections and the wealth he has cultivated. We can have boats ready on the coast of France which will bring the Templars to England. The most senior of the lords, at the least. They will be safe here."

I was tempted to action by the very impossibility of it but I was not so enamoured by the Templars as was Thomas.

"What if they truly are guilty of these crimes?"

"How can you say such a thing?" Thomas asked, affronted.

I cleared my throat, wary of offending him too greatly but it had to be said. "Some of the charges… I do not know, Thomas, they sound… plausible."

"The causes of this could not be more apparent. It is no more than a disgraceful attempt to seize the Templar's wealth. To do away with a potential challenge to Philip's authority."

"Yes, yes, I am sure that is true." I eyed him. "Is there no chance that your former brethren were perhaps engaged in some nefarious practices?"

"No, of course not. Never." He hesitated. "That is to say, we always had a certain affinity for elaborate initiation rituals but there was nothing heretical about them or our beliefs. We are entirely orthodox, I assure you."

"As far as you know, perhaps. But you were initiated long ago."

"They could not change so much as to worship idols and spit on the cross. It pains me even to utter such nonsense."

I pursed my lips. "And what about the unnatural lusts? We both know what young monks get up to in the darkness. Squires, too, the filthy little brutes."

He looked away. "Not ours. Not the Templars. They are good men. Dutiful men."

"I suppose you are right enough about that. But whatever the truth of it, we cannot interfere. We must not risk the lives and the resources of the Order of the White Dagger for these leaders of the Templars. We have other sworn responsibilities. For the love of God, Thomas, we could be killed in such an attempt."

On and on we went. I denied him for days but in the end, I agreed. For all his grand arguments, ultimately it was because Thomas was my friend, a brother in arms, and I could not deny him. Also, I thought I might have a chance to kill Frenchmen, which is an opportunity never to be passed up.

And that was how we found ourselves creeping through the tunnels beneath the massive Castle Chinon that night, already four years after the Templars initial arrests. Many of the lesser men had been swiftly released while others had been held in various secure places from Paris to Avignon until at last the most senior leaders had been diverted to Chinon for their final questioning by the Inquisition before their trial.

The town of Chinon nestled on the bank of the River Vienne just a few miles from where it joined the Loire. Above the town was a vast outcrop of stone and atop that was the castle itself. It was an ancient place. The Romans had a fort there and before them, no doubt, the pagans would have done the same, for it commanded views over a rich and fertile land, full of vineyards and orchards with trees heaving under the weight of their fruit. After the Romans, an order of monks built a monastery and then later a series of local lords built the castle and added to it over generations until it covered the plateau. The stone for all that building had come from the vast rock itself and the tunnels the quarrying left behind had been used for storage and as a mausoleum for monks' bones. The secret ways had been used in Henry II's day, when that great king of England had held the castle and greatly added to the fortifications. I had heard of the tunnels' existence in my youth by old men who had seen them and walked them. Those ways had been forgotten by all but a handful of smugglers and prostitutes in the town and one desperate sergeant. Luckily, these were precisely the sorts of people willing to give up their secrets in exchange for money.

"This is the stairway," Thomas said, pointing into the shadows. "The one the sergeant told us about."

"Is it, indeed," I muttered, for I had my doubts that the supposedly sympathetic sergeant was telling us the truth about any of it. I was more than happy to pay him for his revelations about the secret way inside but something about him had seemed off. "How can you know that this is the stair he told us about?"

"How many other stairways are down here, Richard?"

I shrugged and pulled out a long dagger before making my way up to the trapdoor above. "Shield the light."

The sudden darkness was complete, shrouding us like a blanket. Mercifully, the door was unlocked, just as the sergeant had promised, and I pushed it up as slowly as I could, straining to hear and to see in the silent blackness above. The stench of sour wine hit me.

We came up in the corner of a storage cellar. All was quiet.

Thomas pushed by me. "Come, we must make haste."

I grabbed him and whispered close to his face. "If we do not take care, we shall be discovered and then we will have to start killing your countrymen. You claimed to wish to avoid such a thing."

"We may accomplish this feat without harming a single man," Thomas muttered, pulling away. "As long as we hurry."

The cellars were more extensive than we had expected and we made our way through, looking for the door out. We had descended into the catacombs from the edge of the town at sunset and it felt as though half the night had passed already, so Thomas was right to hurry. And yet we bumped into so many barrels and scared out so many scurrying rats that anyone listening in the chambers above our heads would surely have heard our approach.

Finally, the door into the bowels of the gaol was up ahead. Thomas, almost overcome by pity for the plight of his Templar brothers, did not wait for me, nor did he shroud or extinguish his lamp as he yanked the heavy door open.

Quite frankly, I was astonished that it had been unlocked. It seemed that the old sergeant had done as he had sworn to do and so we were into the castle.

Beyond was a low corridor lined with squat doors on one side and at the far end sat a table with a single candle, an empty wooden plate and an upturned cup.

Sitting at the table was an ugly young soldier who peered at us, shielding the light of his candle with one hand.

"Ah!" I called out. "How wonderful to see you, my dear fellow. Might we trouble you for directions to the privy?"

He jumped to his feet and shouted over his shoulder at the stairwell behind him. "Intruders! Sergeant!"

I was already running before the first word was out of his mouth and I covered the distance so rapidly that he was incapable of responding before my shoulder collided with his chest. He flew clean off his feet, travelled eight or nine feet through the air and hit the wall behind him with a wet crunch. He bounced off and fell into a heap by the base of the stairwell.

"You killed him," Thomas said, coming up behind me.

"I believe I did," I replied. "Poor lad. Let us have his keys, shall we? Quickly, now."

Thomas went back and began unlocking the squat doors behind us while I waited at the bottom of the spiral stairs with my dagger drawn. Sure enough, two pairs of feet came running down the steps along with heavy breathing and the clatter of arms.

The first man to appear held a spear outstretched before him, which I grasped and pulled on while slipping behind it and stabbing my dagger up into his throat. The man behind swung his spear down at my head. I darted to the side and leapt up the stairs at him. He wavered then turned to flee before I caught him by the ankle and dragged him down to the bottom. He was right dazed from the fall and I gave him a quick punch on the nose to keep him that way while I disarmed him.

"Where are the other prisoners?" I asked him.

"Dear God," he mumbled, despairing. "Dear God."

Behind me, Thomas called out. "Richard? Help us."

Keeping hold of the guard, I peered into the dim light as Thomas led a stream of broken men out of their gaol cells.

The French Inquisition had tortured the Templars.

Barred from spilling blood during their interrogations, the Inquisitors favoured using the rack to stretch limbs into dislocation at the joints. They also enjoyed using the strappado, where the victim's wrists were bound behind his back before being raised by them over a beam so that the pressure put an incredible strain on the limbs but primarily caused slow suffocation through the pressure on the chest. The Inquisitors also used fire. Applying fat to the soles of the feet before placing those feet in the fire where they would be slowly cooked and the skin of the feet turned into thick, crispy crackling like roast pigskin.

The broken men emerging from the darkness were like the living dead. Shuffling and groaning as they came, supporting each other and leaning on the walls while dragging their weak limbs on shattered feet. Many blinked and covered their eyes as if the single tallow candle at the end of the corridor burned with the power of the noonday sun.

"Thomas," I hissed, dragging him to me. "We cannot escape with these men."

He nodded, eyes wild. "And yet we must."

"Use your eyes, man," I said. "None of them will so much as make it through the cellar before dawn. What is more, look at their bearing and their features. Surely, these are the servants and blacksmiths and other worthless men of the Order. We must leave them and find Grand Master Molay and the other commanders while we yet can."

A man's voice intruded. "What is that you say?"

He made his way toward us. A fine-looking young fellow, he was. Tall and fair and big boned but much weakened by his confinement and hobbling on injured feet. Even so, a fire burned in his eyes and I knew that he was a man of good breeding.

I stepped forward. "I said that you may make your way through that door into the cellar. At the far end is a stairway down into the tombs. Follow them until you find your way into the narrow, secret tunnels and then go out into the town. From there your life is your own. God be with you."

He shook his head and jerked a thumb over his shoulder. "Tell them, instead. Who are you?"

"Friends of the Templars, here to free Grand Master Molay and others. Who are you?"

"I am John D'Arcy. A knight. And I know where the Grand Master, the Treasurer and Preceptor and others are being held. I will show you. This way."

"You are English?" I said, noting his accented French.

He paused. "No. My father served John FitzGerald, the Earl of Kildare."

"Close enough," I said, recalling that the Earl had been subject to King Edward I and no doubt to Edward II also. "Very well, lead the way, sir."

John made his way up the first few stairs with barely a glance at the dead guards on the floor. He was hurting, that much was clear, but he moved well enough all things considered.

"Just a moment," Thomas said. "While I direct these poor brothers."

We pointed the broken men down into the cellar and told them where to go. We threw our dazed French prisoner into one of the stinking cells.

I grabbed him. "If you make any noise, I shall come back here and silence you for good, do you understand?"

Just for good measure, I knocked him on the head and he fell down in a jumble of limbs.

"Another needless murder, Richard," Thomas said, darkly.

"I barely tapped him," I protested. "And cease your scolding."

We locked him in just in case he ever woke up and went up after the Templar knight called John D'Arcy.

"You could flee, sir," I said to him as we paused at the doorway out into the chambers above. "Tell me where to find the Grand Master and flee with your brothers."

"I shall help." He glanced at me and then behind at Thomas. "What are your names? Why do you help us?"

"We are friends, that is all," I said, before Thomas could confuse things with claims of being a knight of the Templars, which he had not been for half a century. "And we must hurry if we are to get Grand Master Molay and the others away from here before sunrise and the changing of the guard."

John raised his eyebrows. "You have guards in your pay?"

"They have played their part already. Now, the chambers of the Grand Master are one floor above this one, are they not?" Our paid-off sergeant had informed us of the location.

John shook his head. "No longer. They were moved and I saw their new chambers on this level, not upstairs."

Thomas growled from behind us. "Not what we were told, and our man has proved trustworthy so far."

"I saw them, I tell you. They are near to the chamber where the Inquisitors put us to the question. It was only yesterday." He frowned. "Or the day before."

"Do you even know what day it is today?" I asked John. "What hour?"

John hesitated, and Thomas growled in frustration. "We must hurry."

"Come, then," I said, deciding. "Let us go to this new chamber, as John advises. We would trust his word over a sergeant of Philip, would we not?"

We made our way out across the dark hall, following John. In spite of his keenness, it was clear he was suffering. He let out small whimpers as he walked, flinching with every other step. A light burned in an alcove by the door ahead and I saw that John's feet were wrapped in bloody bandages, blackened by filth. I realised we would likely have to abandon him if we were hotly pursued.

"That is their chamber," John said, pointing it out.

Thomas reached the door first, lifted the latch and heaved the heavy door open.

Other than the furniture, the chamber was empty.

"They were here!" John cried. "In this very room. I swear it."

"Well they are bloody well not here now," I said. "Let us away to the floor above this one, before it is—"

A cry pierced the silence.

I turned to John. "The Inquisition perform the questioning during the night?"

His face was taut. "At all hours."

"Where?"

We followed through the chamber and into another, down a short flight of steps and then we rounded a corner.

A grey-robed monk stood conversing by an open door, with a bored soldier leaning on a polearm. Light spilled from the doorway, along with pained cries and the aroma of roasted flesh.

They froze, just as we did.

The monk recovered his wits first, turning to shout through the open door behind him. "They are here!"

Words to chill one's blood.

They.

We were expected.

My dagger already in my left hand, I immediately drew my sword and shouted to Thomas. "We are betrayed!"

It must have been that sergeant from the town. Either he had been caught helping us or he had been a stooge the entire time, feeding us enough rope with which to hang ourselves.

"Stay where you are."

The soldier levelled his wicked-looking polearm at us while behind him came the sound of men rushing toward us from the chamber. I edged away, thinking we could flee, until I heard an even louder clamouring of feet above us.

"Dozens of them," I said over my shoulder while keeping my eyes on the wary soldier before me. "Waiting for us upstairs."

"Coming here, now, by the sound of it," Thomas noted.

"A trap? Is this rescue become failure, sirs?" John asked, his voice faint. He recovered from his shock almost immediately. "I need a weapon."

I lunged forward without warning and ran the soldier through his face before he could react with his polearm. The Dominican friar hitched up his robes and ran from me into the chamber.

"Here," I said, tossing the dying man's polearm to John. "Come on."

In the chamber beyond, five soldiers drew to a stop before me, clustered together in confusion as I sauntered toward them. I was dimly aware of the ropes, chains and other men in the background. The soldiers were not sure whether I was friend or foe until, grinning, I held up my bloodied sword and charged into them. I cut them down, moving swiftly to one after the other. They were not battle-hardened veterans, but men used to the tedium of guard duty which was not real soldiering at all. The last one I killed appeared unable to fully draw his sword before my blade sliced open the inside of his thigh, spilling hot blood to soak his loins. He fell to his knees, weeping and I finished him through the heart.

"Who did you say you were?" John asked, staring with his eyes wide.

"Close the door," I ordered.

Now that the soldiers were lying dead on the floor, the room held only three grey-robed

Dominicans and half a dozen servants.

And four prisoners who were the subjects of the torture. One strung up awkwardly with his hands behind his back, another tied to a post with a cold brazier at his feet and the third and fourth men lying bound on the floor, no doubt awaiting their next bouts with the torturer.

"Free them," I ordered the Inquisitors.

Not one of them made a move.

I strode to the nearest one, the fellow who had raised the alarm, and he backed away frantically with his hands up. "No, no, no. It is a sin to do harm to a—"

My sword point entered his throat and I pulled it across him as he fell, tearing a great gash through his neck and spilling hot, sweet blood before he clasped at the wound, gargling and thrashing on the floor.

Everyone stared, shocked. I had startled myself but the sight of the tortured men had caused my blood to run very hot indeed.

"Free them, I say," I snarled, pointing with my bloody sword while the monk died behind me.

A number of the servants rushed to undo the bonds holding the men. Thomas gaped at me while the other monks gathered their wits enough to begin to hurl outraged protests and curses down upon me.

"You cannot kill monks, Richard," Thomas cried. "Even if they are Inquisitors. We are not here for such things."

John marched past us both, straight toward an older, fat Dominican. "You may not be here for such things, sir." The Templar held his polearm before him. "And so I shall be the instrument of justice on the Inquisitor."

"How dare you!" the old Dominican cried. "By the power of God, I command you to cease. God Himself commands you to halt at once."

John thrust the spear point of his stolen polearm into the man's chest and bore him to the ground. The Inquisitor was still praying when John expertly dispatched him with a twist to the weapon that destroyed his victim's heart.

A commotion at the door, followed by sustained hammering of fists upon it, brought me back to the bigger priority. There were no windows. No obvious doors other than the single one by which we had entered.

"Is there another door out of this chamber?" I asked the servants. They shook their heads and pointed at the door.

"Only... it is only...." He spluttered, with tears in his eyes. "Only that one way there, my lord."

I grabbed the man but he wailed and cried. "I swear it to Holy Christ!"

I threw him down.

Thomas was busy untying the wounded prisoners and John had crossed to them and knelt by one. The old fellow who had been strung up by the wrists. He was pale and gaunt, with a haunted look in his red, unfocused eyes as he sank to his knees with a sigh.

"By God, Grand Master. What have they done to you, my lord?" John looked up at my approach. "It is Grand Master Molay, sir. The leader of our Order."

"My name is Richard of Ashbury, my lord. We came to rescue you and your men but it seems we were sold a duck and now we are all trapped."

"Escape?" Molay said, his voice barely a dry croak.

John hung his head. "There can be no escape, now, my lord."

"Oh, I do not know about that," I said, brightly. "There cannot be more than a score of men outside. I shall fight my way clear through the lot of them and you men will follow if you can but walk."

They both looked at me as though I were mad, and the other wounded old men muttered. I assumed they were the Treasurer and the Preceptor and if anything they were in worse shape even than the Grand Master.

"We can do it, my lords," Thomas said, turning from his place by the door. "Richard and I will fight our way through those men, I swear it."

"Ashbury?" Molay said, blinking up at me. His broken mind was working but slowly. "Richard of Ashbury? I believe I heard of that man. A long time ago. Your grandfather, perhaps?"

"If you like," I said. "Come, now, sirs. Let us help you up. We must away before they bring more men and bar our escape."

Molay shook his head. "I shall not flee."

Thomas and I shared a look.

"I fear they have taken your wits, my lord," I said. "You are much weakened, yet—"

"No, no!" He grasped my arm. "I shall not flee. I must see this through."

One of the other prisoners stirred, dragging himself to his feet. He had the appearance of a man already dead and the smell of one, too. "We shall all remain. I am sorry that your bravery and daring has been in vain but to flee would be to admit wrongdoing to all Christendom."

The third man spoke from where he sat on the cold floor. "And that is something we shall not do."

Molay nodded. "It is our duty."

The fourth man, a youngster, simply stared at the old men, aghast that his chance for escape was being quashed.

"Your duty to die?" I asked, aghast. "How can you be so—"

The door shook, and the hinges creaked. A few more such blows and they would be ripped from the frame and the soldiers would be upon us.

"We understand," Thomas said, solemnly.

I glared at him. "No, we do not bloody understand. How about I truss you up like a prize hog, Grand Master Molay, and carry you to freedom, whether you like it or not?"

"Richard," Thomas said, in his scolding tone. "We must honour his wishes."

"He is not in his right mind," I argued, pointing at him.

John, a man I had only just met, placed his hand on my arm. "Sir, I know the Grand Master. I would do as he commands. We stay."

"No," Molay said, his eyes wide, and his voice was stronger than before. "No, John, you must flee. And take Hugh there with you."

The fourth man looked up. Hugh had the kind of delicate boyish looks that young maidens find terribly appealing and real men find contemptible.

Molay continued. "You two need not die nor face further agonies. Take word of this to those who would listen. Care for the men who escape death. John, Hugh, you must both do your duty. We may yet come through these horrors in the end."

The fact that he thought he would survive his torment made me sick to my stomach. How could he not see that the King of France meant to wipe him and his Order from the Earth?

As the door cracked and splintered, it was clear that there was no time to argue further.

I stood.

"Are you fighting, sir?" I asked John. "Or staying?"

He looked at the squire, Hugh, and then to the Grand Master of the Templars, who nodded.

"Do your duty," Molay said.

John stood on his burnt feet and grasped his polearm, holding it close to the point so that he could manoeuvre in the close confines.

He reached down to the younger man named Hugh and hauled him upright beside him. They grasped each other's arms for a moment, steeling themselves for the fight.

"What say you, Thomas?" I said. "Shall we make our way home?"

"God be with us," he said, kissing his sword.

"We will move quickly and both of you men will stay with me or be lost," I said to John and Hugh. The older man nodded. The younger one swallowed and shook from exhaustion and from the injuries sustained during his questioning.

"Your name is Hugh?" I asked him and he nodded. "Can you fight?"

"I am a squire," he said.

"Hugh fights well," John said. "Do you not, brother?"

"In truth, I have seen better days," Hugh said. "But I will fight with everything I have left."

"That is well," I said.

I did not expect either man to survive. They were more than half dead already.

Thomas lifted the iron bar and yanked the door aside, causing a half dozen armed soldiers to tumble over themselves as they spilled through the doorway. An oak bench fell beneath them. Two iron helms rolled across the floor.

A laugh escaped me as I pounced on them before they could recover and jabbed my sword point into necks and armpits, killing or wounding four then six men before those behind leapt back from me.

I roared a wordless cry as I stomped over the dying men and slashed at the others to keep them away from me as I crossed the bridge of writhing, bloody flesh. The soldiers retreated as far as they were able, and Thomas, John, and Hugh followed on my heels, shouting the motto of their Order.

"Beau-Séant!"

Together, we forced our way through into the open hall behind and I rushed for the far corner, intending to use the cellar to get to the catacombs. Before I got halfway there, a mass of armoured men emerged from the stairway and stood together, holding their spears at the ready. These new men all wore iron helms and sturdy coats reinforced with strips of plate.

Real soldiers.

Unarmoured as we were, I doubted we could force our way through such a wall of steel without being cut to ribbons. Yet, there was another route of escape we had prepared. One that I had hoped to avoid. Still, beggars cannot afford to be overly particular. Changing direction, I raced toward a dark stairway in the opposite corner only to find there were no steps leading down.

Only up.

There was no time to hesitate, as the soldiers advanced at our rear and I was aware that John and Thomas were fending off the keenest of our pursuers and the squire, Hugh, came after me bent over and weak from his recent torture.

"Up!" I cried at them and raced up the steps taking two in each stride.

Appalled, I discovered that it went up beyond a single storey, and then surely another, before there was a door out of the stairwell. I saw the light of lamps and rushed into a room, startling two young servants carrying piles of folded linen.

"Out of my way!" I roared at them. In their intense surprise they turned and promptly ran into each other and so I bowled them both over, sending white linen sheets flying into the air.

On we ran, through a bedchamber and into another, all the while the shouts of the men pursuing echoed through the rooms.

Our rescued knight John fell behind and with him the smaller squire. Both men were exhausted and close to collapse and it dawned on me that our rescue attempt had been doomed to failure right from the start for just that reason. Even had we remained undiscovered and attempted to flee through the tunnels, the weakened prisoners would have been unable to make it out before sunrise. We would have been seen making our way through the town to the river and someone would have raised the alarm. I had been swayed by Thomas' endless words of duty and honour and I had allowed myself to be carried away by the potential gloriousness and bloody violence of the venture.

Watching John and Hugh clinging to each other a full chamber length behind us, both breathing hard and ashen-faced, I was angry at my foolishness and Thomas' naivety.

"Leave them," I said to Thomas.

My friend was appalled. "I shall not."

"Yes, go," John replied, hearing us as they came closer. "Take young Hugh with you and I will hold them off here while you make your escape."

The squire looked at the knight, aghast at the notion.

"Oh, for the love of God," I replied. "Not another honourable man. Go, you chivalrous fools. All three of you, go. I will hold them here."

Thomas grasped my arm. "Go where?"

"You know the only other route."

He gaped. "But we are only ever going up and up, Richard."

The first of the pursuing soldiers burst through the doorway in a clattering of feet and hard breathing and there they froze, shocked to see us standing in conversation as if it were market day and we were debating the value of a ham.

I slapped my brother knight on the shoulder and pushed him away. "And what goes up, Thomas, must certainly come down. Go!"

While the three Templars, two young and one ancient, fled further, I turned to give the cluster of wary soldiers my full attention.

"My dear fellows," I cried. "My name is Richard of Ashbury and I came to Château de Chinon to free Templars and to murder Frenchmen. How kind of you to deliver yourselves to my bloody sword."

A huge sergeant at the back shoved his men forward and roared at them. "Have at him, you damned fools. He is one man. He is unarmoured. Take him, now!"

I laughed. Partly to unnerve them further, and so slow them down, but also because the battle madness had descended on me and I knew that in the next moments I would walk the knife edge between life and death. And there is no greater joy on this Earth.

The bravest ones came and at me and the bravest ones fell. The cunning among them circled to my flanks, attempting to get behind me, so I retreated as far as I could to the doorway behind to ensure I would not be cut off. The dead and the wounded littered the floor and the wails of the dying frightened the living, who could not understand what was happening. No one man should have been able to kill so many others. It was not possible. And yet they fell.

Without warning, the huge sergeant threw himself forward in a rage, determined to do the job himself.

I stamped my leg forward and thrust my sword toward him, knocking the blade of his polearm away. He was momentarily stunned by my strength and I smashed his nose with my pommel and cut his throat as he fell. I turned and fled as fast as my legs would carry me.

It was a good while before the surviving soldiers gathered their wits enough to take up their pursuit and I gained a lead on them. One chamber led to another, they became increasingly well appointed, until I raced by a very fine bedchamber where an old gentleman, his wife and their servants stood in the corner, the servants brandishing their knives.

"Good morning!" I shouted as I ducked into the already-open door that led straight onto another stairwell. Dragging their door closed behind me, I took a step or two down before I heard fighting echoing between the dark, curving stone walls. Blades clashing and men shouting.

The sound came from above me.

I turned and ran toward the fighting, up and up, round and round the steps.

Thomas, John, and Hugh were defending against almost a dozen soldiers who jabbed and thrust at them with their polearms while the three Templars backed across the room away from me.

This time, I was silent as I began killing those at the rear, cutting throats with my dagger and breaking skulls apart with my sword. When they noticed they were being attacked, they scattered and I shouted at my men to follow me. Thomas grabbed John and Hugh, who were both slumped and weakened beyond their bodily limits, and shoved them through the retreating, horrified soldiers and those writhing in agony on the floor.

As they reached me, I again made to flee down the stairs but the pursuing men were already coming. Instead, I ran up once more, going around the winding stairs passing by a slit window that fleetingly showed the sky beyond lightening with the dawn, and then I came to a dead end.

The single door at the top was locked.

"No!" I shouted and slammed my shoulder against it. The door shook but it was solid. "Help me, Thomas. We must break it down."

"The key!" Thomas shouted, pointing at the wall. "The key!"

"Praise God," I said, as I grabbed the door key, hanging by a ring, from an iron nail on the frame. I had overlooked it in the darkness and in my panic at the sound of pursuit so close behind. And Thomas, through some strange effect of my blood, had eyes that could see far better in the darkness than could mine.

I turned the lock and shoved the weakening John and Hugh through the door after Thomas, then jumped after them and slammed the door closed as the hands on the other side grasped at it. Someone screamed as his finger bones snapped when the door crushed them against the frame. I turned the key while the men on the other side hammered on the timber and shouted at us and each other.

"To where now?" Thomas asked, his head swivelling one way and another.

We were atop the curtain wall of the castle. Nothing was higher than we were, other than a handful of the towers that dotted the wall at intervals stretching away around the enormous perimeter.

The weather was clear and the air cool and dry. The sun had not yet risen but I could see the grey-purple roofs and walls of homes of the town down around the castle, with small trees and compact kitchen gardens in the shadows between them all. The curtain walls, towers and battlements of the fortifications all around led only from one to another, of course, as well as down into the dark interior of the great castle.

The soldiers behind the door fell silent for a moment before their banging took up a coordinated rhythm. It shook with each impact.

I looked over the edge of the wall. The River Vienne flowed along the base far below. Small, dark boats bobbed all over on the surface and barges and larger vessels were tied up along both banks. I could make out the bridge downstream.

"Perfect!" I said. "God does love us, after all, Thomas."

He stared at me, aghast, his eyes white in the gloom.

"I cannot swim, sir," Thomas reminded me, hissing the words. "And Sir John here would not even survive the fall."

"It is a long drop for a mortal," I allowed. "Why do you worry only for the knight and not the squire?"

John whimpered and I looked closer at the young man, slumped in shadow against the wall with his head lolling, clutching his guts. The bandages once covering his feet were gone and the blackened skin was cracked and bleeding freely. Only then did I notice that the front of his shirt was soaked with blood where he clutched at it. I had missed the wound he had received during combat and no doubt the mad flight had only opened him up further.

"Go," he said, his voice barely above a whisper. "This wound is mortal."

"No," Hugh said, grasping him. "You must have faith, brother."

"You pray for me, Hugh," John said. "For all of us. After you get free."

"Wheresoever you go, sir," the squire whispered, "there go I."

The soldiers hammered on the door with steady, powerful blows. "Axes," I said, recognising the sound. "They will be through soon enough."

"More men are coming," Thomas said, pointing into the gloomy courtyard below us.

"Do you swim, John?" I asked him.

He nodded but Hugh spoke for him. "We learned together to swim in the Cher, five summers past."

"You may think me mad, sir," I said to John, "but I can heal you, if you do exactly as I say. Heal you so that you will survive the fall, or perhaps bring you back to life if you die from it."

In fact, I knew I would have to drag Thomas through the water to safety and would have little chance to save John if the fall did him in.

"Madness," John muttered, confused and weak. "Yes, yes. What is this madness?"

Thomas strode to the young knight and seized him quite roughly. "It seems to be madness yet it is truth. There is a magic in Richard. In his blood. A magic you must imbibe now, or you shall die on this wall or in your goal."

John's eyes flicked around. "What magic?"

I sliced my wrist. "The magic is in my blood. Drink, and live."

He was confused and disgusted and Hugh crossed himself.

"Who are you men?" Hugh asked. "Sorcerers? Heretics?"

"There is no time for reason," I snapped, watching the soldiers coming through the shadows towards us. "Will you live on or will you die?"

"There can be no magic without faith," Hugh said, though his eyes betrayed his concern for his brother Templar.

"I doubted once," Thomas said. "When I was a Templar and had my guts ripped open. This blood healed me fully. I swear it by Jesus Christ and all His saints."

John shook his head but did not resist when I held my bloody wrist to his mouth. Deciding all at once, he grasped my arm and sunk his lips onto my flesh and sucked the blood into his mouth like a hungry child on the breast.

The door behind us splintered and the soldiers within shouted like baying hounds as they threw it open. Below, the men from the courtyard clattered up the wooden stairs and reached the wall walk at the top, mere yards from us.

"Come now!" I shouted and jumped up onto the wall, dragging John up behind me.

Far below, the river was black like an abyss.

"The blood takes time to work," Thomas shouted as he clambered up beside us with an arm around Hugh. "It is too soon!"

He was not wrong, of course, and I expected that John would die from his wound before the blood could do its magic. And I thought Hugh would be knocked senseless by the impact and drowned. But what choice did we have?

Soldiers were atop the wall, running from both sides with their spears up, shouting and cursing us.

"Keep your feet together!" I cried and then shoved John hard. He fell, tumbling slowly like a sack of turnips. As if he was already dead.

Muttering a prayer, Hugh leapt out into the emptiness after his brother Templar.

"Thomas, jump, you damned fool!" I shouted but he stood shaking as he looked down at the distant black surface.

A thrown dagger clattered off the battlements beside me and I ducked as a spear swished above my head and disappeared into the cold dawn air.

I whipped my sword at the nearest soldier to drive him back into his fellows before wrapping an arm around Thomas.

I jumped, dragging Thomas down with me.

The sun came up at that moment, peaking over the horizon and bathing us for an instant in glorious yellow light. Our fall into the shadows seemed to last forever and I was close to a kind of momentary ecstasy at the terrifying thrill of it before the violent impact of the hard, black, icy cold river slammed into my feet and body, knocking the wind from me.

I fought and clawed my way up, struggling to keep my breath in my body. I still had no idea if drowning would truly kill me but it certainly felt as though it would. For a moment, I was aghast with the certainty that I had been swimming down the entire time toward the riverbed, only for my head to break the surface. As I took a rasping gulp of cold air, I pulled Thomas up spluttering and clawing at me like a cat tossed into a water butt.

"Calm yourself, sir," I managed to say. "All is well."

The men atop the wall threw weapons and God only knows what else down on us but the current was already taking us away down river. I held Thomas with one hand and sculled away with the current.

"John?" Thomas asked, spluttering and gasping. "Hugh?"

"Cannot see them," I replied. "I am sorry."

I knew that our pursuers would not give up and that they would already be racing to get ahead of us. But we had already planned for such an eventuality and, tied up by the stone bridge downstream, we had a boat ready and waiting for us.

"Swim with me, Thomas. Kick your legs slowly. That is the way. By God, she is there, Thomas. She is bloody well there, and all."

For it was true that Eva, our dear companion and fellow member of the Order of the White Dagger, was precisely where she was supposed to be.

"You said you would be coming by the road," she said, after she dragged us into the boat. We lay there, gasping like landed fish. "No Templars?"

"We had a pair of the bastards," I said, breathing hard. "They died."

Thomas dragged himself to the stern and peered out into the darkness. "Hugh!" he shouted. "John!"

"Be silent, you fool!" I hissed. "We must away. They are lost."

"No, no," Thomas said. "They are there! Look, will you. There!"

"Good God Almighty," I muttered. "They will dash their brains out. Get after them, Eva."

Hugh and John's heads went bobbing past us in the current and they were swept through the breakwaters of the bridge at a remarkable pace where the waters rushed, loud and white.

Without delay, Eva rowed us out into the current toward the bridge. Thomas and I took an oar each while Eva moved to the prow and we rowed so hard I feared the oars would snap.

"Slower, slower. Stop!" Eva cried. And then, "I have them."

With her immortal strength, she pulled them in one after the other and dumped them, soaked and shivering and weak as new-born babes, into the bottom of our boat.

We rowed on with our immortal strength, away from our pursuers downstream toward the Loire in the north and from there downstream again toward the distant coast. We would be out of the water soon enough, just before Saumur where the Loire split around an island and where, on the eastern bank, Stephen would be waiting with a dozen fresh horses for our escape.

"You could find only two?" Eva asked, not hiding her disappointment.

"We freed a few commoners," I replied. "But they were like as not recaptured before they could flee from the town, for we were betrayed. They were waiting for us. Even so, we managed to reach Grand Master Molay and some other senior men but they refused to flee with us."

Eva scoffed. "No wonder the fools have been defeated. I mean no offence, Thomas. But honourable men are always the first to die."

Because she was a woman, she did not fully appreciate the necessity for a man to sometimes choose honour over life and I wanted to argue with her. But I was tired and I suspected that I would lose that argument and so I held my tongue.

John lay on his back for a while, breathing deeply with his hands on his belly as the sun rose high and warm enough to dry him. His eyes closed and I watched closely as Hugh prayed over his Templar brother in a fervour. Before we reached the Loire, John opened his eyes and sat up, pulling his filthy, blood-stained shirt up and feeling where it had been pierced.

"My wound is healed," he said to Hugh, a smile on his face. "That is, my wound is gone. It is gone, I tell you."

Hugh ran his hands over John's belly, shaking his head as he did so.

"It is a miracle," Hugh said.

"Not a miracle," I replied.

"It is magic," Thomas said.

In fact, I had no idea what made my blood do what it did, and so I supposed that magic was as good a word as any to describe it.

"Examine your feet also," I suggested as I pulled my oar.

"The magic is true," John muttered, as Thomas nodded.

"Sir John. Squire Hugh," Thomas said. "Your Order is almost extinguished. But you have heart and guts, sirs."

"And balls," I said. Eva laughed.

Thomas gave me a long look, full of meaning. In his eyes was a question.

I thought about it, watching the two men we had rescued. They had suffered for a long time and had fought to survive their tortures, they had fought the soldiers that tried to stop them fleeing, they had fought the cold dark of the river. They were fighters.

I nodded at Thomas.

"You men have honour and you both understand duty," Thomas said to them. "I would like you to consider joining an Order that fights a great evil. A great evil worth dedicating your life to. Many lifetimes. Greater even than the evil of the Saracens."

"What evil can be greater than that?" John asked, wide-eyed.

"Well sir," I replied, watching the sun rise above the trees and hills and bathe the river in a million sparkles, "it all began one morning in the year eleven ninety, at the old manor house in Ashbury, in the finest land that God ever made, that is to say Derbyshire in England."

Grand Master James of Molay was burnt at the stake in Paris on 18th March 1314. The poor old fool had confessed under torture that he had denied Christ and had spat on Christ's image when he was inducted into the Order. Many of the Templars confessed to such a blasphemy but Thomas, John, and Hugh swore blind that it was all from the twisted minds of the Inquisitors. Other leading Templars had confessed that sodomy was rife amongst the brothers of the Order and, what was more, that the leadership had not only allowed but actively encouraged it.

When the Grand Master met with three cardinals sent by the Pope, he at once recanted his confession and ripped open his shirt to show the scars upon his body that he received in the torture chambers of the Inquisition. The Pope formally absolved all those men but it did no good against the power of King Philip, who turned all his legal and financial power against the Papacy and eventually won, for his power was earthly rather than divine and that is ultimately what counts upon the Earth.

On a scaffold in front of Notre Dame, the Templar Grand Master and three more of the most powerful other Templar lords were brought from the gaol to receive the sentence—that of perpetual imprisonment. The affair was supposed to be concluded when, to the dismay of the prelates and wonderment of the assembled crowd, the Templars arose. They had been guilty, they said, not of the crimes imputed to them, but of basely betraying their Order to save their own lives. They stated that the Order of the Knights Templar was pure and holy and the charges were fictitious and the confessions false.

King Philip was furious.

A short consultation with his council was all that was required for his wishes to be agreed. The canons pronounced that a relapsed heretic was to be burned without a hearing. They said that the facts were notorious and no formal judgement by the papal commission need be waited for. That same day, by sunset, a pyre was erected on a small island in the Seine, the Ile des Juifs, near the palace gardens. There the Templar lords were slowly burned to death, refusing all offers of pardon for retraction, and bearing their torment with a composure which won for them the reputation of martyrs among the people, who reverently collected their ashes as relics.

Before he was burned, Molay was stripped to his underclothes and bound to the stake. After he prayed, he raised his voice and despite his advanced age and years of imprisonment, his voice was powerful and filled with righteousness so that all the assembled heard his words and trembled.

"God knows who is in the wrong and has sinned. Soon, misfortune will come to those who have wrongly condemned us. God will avenge our death."

All he and his brothers had needed to do was to hold their tongues and they would have lived. Instead, they chose honour over life.

But out of all the death and horror, we had won the freedom of the knight Sir John D'Arcy and the squire Hugh de Tours.

On the boat that morning with the sun warming us as we rowed downriver away from our pursuers in Chinon toward Stephen, waiting with fresh horses by the town of Saumur.

"This is all so incredible," John said, after we had related most of our story and the purpose of the Order of the White Dagger. "And the change has already taken place in me? I am immortal now? With strength and swiftness that will be the envy of mortal men. And yet I am required to drink human blood." He sighed, looking at the banks as they flowed past.

"You may drink my blood," Hugh said, eagerly.

"Actually," Thomas said. "We have servants who will provide you with blood. Both of you."

"Me?" Hugh said.

"We have need of dutiful men," Thomas said. "Do we not, Richard?"

"I suppose so," I allowed, smiling.

"If you would be willing to join us," Thomas continued, "it would mean giving up the chance of fathering a child. Of making a family."

"I gave up that chance when I joined the Templars," Hugh replied without hesitation.

"Well, then, young man," Thomas said. "Will you renounce your oath to one Order, which is dying, and join another which has a greater purpose?"

John smiled at Hugh's astonished expression. "We would be brothers in arms for eternity, my friend."

"Yes," Hugh whispered. "Yes, I will do it gladly."

John and Hugh embraced with great passion and fervently kissed each other upon the mouth, their eyes shining.

"Oh, for God's sake," I said, looking at Thomas, who stared studiously away at the distant bank, pretending to be oblivious. No doubt, he had employed the very same tactic during his decades in the sleeping quarters and dark corners of the commandries and castles of the Knights Templar.

After we escaped, Hugh allowed his blood to be emptied from his body before he drank of mine and rose to become the newest member of the Order of the White Dagger beside his dear friend and close companion John.

Both men would serve us faithfully for decades and help our cause greatly as the enormous conflict between the kingdoms of England and France began. It was a conflict that history would come to call the Hundred Years War and it was then that our Order encountered a new and brutal immortal enemy on the battlefield by a village named Crecy.

A cunning and monstrous enemy that we would come to know as the knight of the black banner.

AUTHOR'S NOTE

Richard's story continues in *Vampire Knight: the Immortal Knight Chronicles Book 4*

You can find out more and get in touch with me at dandavisauthor.com

BOOKS BY DAN DAVIS

The GALACTIC ARENA Series

Science fiction

Inhuman Contact
Onca's Duty
Orb Station Zero
Earth Colony Sentinel
Outpost Omega

The IMMORTAL KNIGHT Chronicles

Historical Fantasy

Vampire Crusader
Vampire Outlaw
Vampire Khan
Vampire Knight
Vampire Heretic
Vampire Impaler
Vampire Armada

For a complete and up-to-date list of Dan's available books, visit:
http://dandavisauthor.com/books/

Printed in Great Britain
by Amazon